HIDDEN MOON

The Stoneridge Pack Book 4

CJ COOKE

Hidden Moon

Stoneridge Pack: Book Four

By

CJ Cooke

Version 1.0: April 2022

Published by CJ Cooke

Copyright © 2022 by CJ Cooke

Discover other titles by CJ Cooke at **https://cjcookeauthor.wixsite.com/home**

All rights reserved, including the right of production in whole or in part in any form without prior permission of the author, except in cases of a reviewer quoting brief passages in review.
This book is a work of fiction. Names, characters, places and incidents either are products of the author's imagination or are used fictitiously. Any resemblance to actual events or locales or persons, either living or dead, is entirely coincidental.

Formatting: © 2022 Incognito Scribe Productions LLC
Cover Design: © 2021 MiblArt

❀ Created with Vellum

ALSO BY CJ COOKE

OTHER BOOKS IN THE SERIES

THE STONERIDGE PACK

Wolf Hunts

Shadow Wars

Blood Feud

Hidden Moon

OTHER BOOKS BY THE AUTHOR:

DESTINY SERIES

Destiny Awakened

Destiny Rising

Destiny Realised

(Completed Chapter)

Revelations

Retaliation (Coming Soon)

THE ARCANE (COMING IN 2022)

The Arcane: Part One

The Arcane: Part Two

READER NOTICE

This book contains themes which some readers may find triggering, including but not limited to, violence, references to sexual assault and references to child abuse.

This is a reverse harem romance novel. The main character has multiple partners and does not have to choose between the two. If this is something which you offends you, please do not continue reading.

1
GREY

Staring down at Calli, entwined in the arms of Tanner and Lachlan, did nothing to calm the raging alpha inside of me. She'd been hurt, and there'd been nothing I could do to prevent it. Again.

Stone had gone too far this time. Surely this wasn't something the Council could sweep under the rug, if they were even aware it was happening in the first place? Lachlan was right, though. Stone couldn't pull off something as big as this by himself.

The funds alone to set up that lab should've been more than he had access to. Not to mention the people. Someone had to have snatched those shifters from their packs. Was that something Stone could coordinate alone? I doubted it.

I'd thought I knew the man, and we'd already seen just how despicable he was. But seeing that place, seeing those people who'd been kept in cages; the tubes housing his less fortunate victims… just how deep did his depravity run? But, more importantly, what the hell was he up to?

"You need to sleep," River's tired voice mumbled in the darkness behind me.

River, Maverick, and I'd been camped out on the floor. None of us had wanted to leave Calli so soon after what we'd seen, and there wasn't a bed big enough in the house for all of us to pile into. So we'd dragged a couple of mattresses with some blankets and pillows, attempting to sleep on the floor.

Maverick had been asleep in seconds, and I suspected River wasn't far behind him. It just seemed to be me who was stuck staring at the ceiling even though exhaustion weighed me down. Now, I'd resorted to prowling around the room in the darkness, my agitation making it impossible to rest.

"I can't sleep. My wolf is still spiralling," I told him. "I might go for a run. Try and appease him by scouting the pack borders."

"Do you want me to come with you?" River asked, his voice breaking into a yawn.

"No, it's okay—sleep, River. I know you're as tired as I should be right now. Anyway, Davion and his clan are out keeping an eye on things. So I'll have plenty of backup in the unlikely event I need it."

River mumbled something about being careful, but then his soft snores filled the room. It had been a gruelling past 24 hours, and I should have been exhausted, but I knew my wolf needed to make sure everyone was safe, and there'd be no sleeping for me until I'd checked the borders and appeased his worry.

Quietly pulling on some clothes, I slipped out of the room and headed down the darkened corridor. We'd never had this many people in the packhouse before, and as the alpha, it was my job to make sure they were all safe, which probably contributed to why my wolf was restless.

Before heading downstairs, I cracked open the kids' door and peered inside to make sure they were asleep. Little eyes peering back at me in the darkness were a sure-fire indication they weren't.

"Can't sleep?" I asked, moving into the room and dropping to my knees at the side of the bed.

"Kai had a bad dream," Coby told me quietly.

"He misses his mummy," Jacob said, sniffling as he did.

These four kids had all lost their parents and somehow found their way here to each other. Abby, Coby, and Jacob knew exactly how Kai was feeling right now, and I was sure his pain was probably reminding them of their own.

Abby and Kai slept soundly on the bed, clinging to each other. Even though the two of them were snoring softly, I could see the faint trails on Abby's cheeks from where her tears had fallen. As I watched, Kai whimpered softly, and she snuggled closer to him, making him cling to her with that fierce desperation children had when they were sad.

"How about we do something fun tomorrow?" I suggested to the two boys who were awake.

"Can we make cookies?" Jacob gasped.

"Well, I mean, yeah, but you might have to do that with Calli. How about we do something that doesn't involve putting something in your belly?" I suggested instead, giving him a poke in the stomach that made Jacob snort out a laugh.

"Maybe we could go shopping for Kai's bedroom?" Coby suggested. Even in the room's dim light, I could see the shine of excitement in his eyes.

Internally, I cursed myself for not having this conversation with the kids earlier. Of course, they'd automatically assume Kai coming here meant he was joining our family.

"Kai might not want to stay with us, bud. He might want to go and live with another family in the underground," I told them softly.

I didn't want to make life any harder by separating them,

but this had to be Kai's decision. He might be young, but he was old enough to have a say in this. Besides, it would probably be safer for him to be as far away from us as he could get.

"He has to stay," Coby whispered, gripping the shirt of the sleeping boy a little tighter.

A flow of calming alpha energy seeped out of me and started to fill the room. It was an unconscious gesture now. A few months ago, the realisation would've filled me with panic at thinking I was losing control, but now, it was the most natural feeling I'd ever had. This was what I was meant to be —a true alpha. I could feel it deep in my soul that whatever changes were taking place had always been there, waiting for the right time.

As Coby's shoulders drooped, I felt my wolf's anxiety ease along with the little boy's panic.

"He can make that decision for himself tomorrow. And if he decides he wants to stay for a little bit, that's alright too."

Coby nodded sadly but seemed to accept what I said, so I was happy to leave it there for the night.

"You guys snuggle down and try and get some more sleep, okay? It's still nighttime."

Both boys relaxed back on the bed again. I could tell from their breathing that it wouldn't be long until they were asleep, so I quietly left the room, content to leave them to it for now.

We'd have to look at the bedroom situation tomorrow. We couldn't carry on like this. Not to mention that Calli still didn't have a room to call her own. It had worked for us up until now because she seemed to go to whoever needed her. But it shouldn't be all about our needs, and she needed a space to call her own. Even the library had been taken over by everyone else at this point.

If these shifters agreed to stay with the pack, Nash would

need to follow up with the timber suppliers for the cabin kits we'd ordered. If we could move up the timeframe of their delivery, it would ease at least some of the pressure.

We also needed to get the top floor of the house finished. It would give Calli the space she needed, and be somewhere we could all be together.

But the reality was both construction projects were far more than we could handle, at least not in the timescale we needed.

Tanner was right that it would solve a bunch of our problems if the shifters agreed to stay. But we didn't have the means to give these people a comfortable home they deserved, at least not yet. Then there was the problem of whether we could in good conscience expect these people to fight? Hadn't they been through enough already?

With my mind lost in plans of how we could house everyone comfortably, I crept down the stairs. It was one of those situations where I tried to make as little noise as possible, but the impossibly quiet house seemed to amplify every creak of the floorboards into a sonic boom. The last thing our newest collection of housemates needed was to wake up to a shadowy figure creeping around in the night.

I could feel my wolf growing agitated again as my mind started to spiral around the nightmares of what Stone had been doing to them, so I quickly made my way outside before my alpha powers started to leak out.

The sound of a hushed voice talking quickly on the porch had me stopping in my tracks as I closed the door behind me.

Wasn't *anyone* in this house asleep?

Peering around the corner and along the wraparound porch, I found Blake sitting in a chair as he put his phone back in his pocket. His eyes flared wide in surprise as he caught sight of me.

"Everything okay?"

"Yeah, just catching up with Jean. Feeling a bit out of sorts with everything that happened and wanted to talk to my little man."

"You do realise he's literally days old." I laughed, slightly confused.

"He knows his daddy's voice," Blake said smugly, leaning back in his chair and crossing his arms with a smirk on his face.

It spoke to something inside of me, and it must've been written all over my face.

"Awwww, alpha. You're thinking about babies, aren't you?" he joked.

I shrugged, trying to play it off casually, even though my wolf was practically baying in my mind in agreement. Dropping down into the seat next to him, I cast an assessing gaze over Blake.

"Today, or rather yesterday by now, was hard. No one would blame you if you wanted to meet up with Jean and Tucker in the underground, Blake. You don't have to stay here with us. You don't owe us anything."

Blake turned away from me to look out into the trees, but I caught the gleam of tears in his eyes before he did.

"I miss them—a lot. But I need to see this through. I have to make sure they're safe. I need to know… that we did something. That Stone isn't going to walk away from this like all those people didn't matter."

I completely agreed with him, but for some reason, the fact that Blake felt so strongly about this surprised me.

"I can't tell you what's going to happen, Blake, but I can promise you this. That man doesn't get to walk away from this. Even if I have to go to every single pack and tell them what we saw, everyone is going to know."

"That's not enough," Blake burst out. "He's... he's fucking evil, Grey. He needs to be stopped."

"I know. But we can't exactly walk up to a Council member and kill him. No matter how much we might want to. It would be certain death for the entire pack when the Council retaliated. So we need to do this right. We need proof, and we need to make sure whatever moves we make, we have the support of our people when it finally comes to light."

"You've been thinking about it, then." He almost seemed to deflate as he spoke. Like the fight he'd geared himself up for had bled out of him when he realised I wasn't planning on letting Stone breath for a second longer than necessary.

"Yeah, of course. You didn't see it all, Blake. You didn't see the worst of it. I don't know how we're going to get this done. I was just a small-town mechanic, and then our whole world imploded in a matter of days. Fuck, I'm just making all this up as I go along and failing at it."

The pressure of what needed to be done was overwhelming. I could feel my wolf starting to spiral again as I finally admitted what I'd been thinking for weeks. I wasn't trained to do anything like this. We didn't have the resources, and we didn't have the necessary knowledge. A few lessons on fighting from an ex-council guard wasn't enough. We needed an army, not a collection of broken and traumatised shifters with a score to settle.

"We'll find a way," I decided aloud, feeling a sense of certainty settle in around me. "We have to."

These people were counting on me, and I wouldn't let them down.

Blake didn't say anything. He was still staring off into the trees, his mind no doubt filled with thoughts of his family.

"I'm going to run the borders. You're welcome to join me if you need to," I told Blake in concern.

Tomorrow I'd have to find a way to reunite him with Jean. His wolf must be losing it, being so far away from his newborn cub.

"I think I'm going to head to bed. Try and get a few hours sleep," Blake murmured, still not seeming entirely with me. "I'm bunking in River's room if you need me for anything."

I'd forgotten that we'd given his cabin over to the vampires. Fuck. The housing situation really was fast becoming a problem.

"I'll be fine. Get some rest, Blake. We'll get everything sorted in the morning." I clasped his shoulder as I stood and went to leave. Part of me wanted to wait and make sure he went to bed, but I'd be coming back this way at some point, and I'd check on him then. Blake had gone above and beyond for the pack over the last few days, and it had to be costing him dearly.

Quickly shifting, I trotted down the front steps of the house and raised my nose in the air, inhaling all the scents of the packlands deeply. I caught the faint scent of Davion's clan out in the woods and the shifters in the house behind me. But apart from that, there was nothing out of place.

Taking off at a slow lope, I headed into the trees. I'd already decided to head for the border closest to the packhouse and then travel the perimeter until I looped back around. It wasn't too far, and my wolf could travel it in a few hours, assuming we didn't run into any problems.

The soft ground of the forest flew passed quickly beneath my paws as I wound my way around the trees, following the border where Calli's wards lay. There was something comforting in following the wards. I suppose it came from the brush of Calli's magic against my fur, even though she wasn't here with me. Except that wasn't entirely true. I could feel her with me even when she wasn't physically present. The bond between us had grown so strong it felt like an almost physical presence, and at the end of it, always within reach, was Calli.

It was hard to remember what life had been like before she'd come here. The life we had now was perfect, even with the lingering threat on the horizon. It was having Calli with us that made it perfect. I could see it in the others as well. I could see the way River was finally allowing himself to believe he was enough, how the darkness in Tanner's eyes he tried so desperately to hide receded in the light she shone. Maverick was learning how to trust, and even Lachlan, who'd only been with us for a short amount of time, was starting to grow in confidence.

Calli shone that light of hers on every dark corner of our minds, showing us that what we perceived as flaws were nothing in the bright light of day. She proved we were not only enough, but that we meant everything to her. Calli's love for all of us blazed through our bond, burrowing into our core, and it was changing us.

The pack bond was changing in ways we'd never even known possible. But it was also changing the pack itself. Lachlan and Cassia, pure-blood witches, had shifted. It made sense now how Hunter's wolf had been able to recognise his mate in her, but how had he known it was even possible? Was there a primal part in all of us that the wolf could see, or was there something else going on here? Everything we'd ever been told was either a lie or a distortion of the truth. I had a feeling we were closing in on finding out something that was going to rock our society to the very foundations.

The question was, though, would it rock us hard enough to unseat the Council or were we going to have to physically remove them? Because if there was one thing I knew for sure, even if Stone was acting alone, the rest of the Council were still guilty of crimes against our people, and it needed to be stopped.

The snap of a tree branch pulled me from my thoughts, and I started to pay closer attention to my surroundings. When my eyes landed on Davion standing in my path, the broken branch in his hands, I nearly rolled my eyes at his antics.

I shifted back to my human form, still running the last few steps, and stopped in front of him.

"I thought some advanced warning would be a good idea. I didn't fancy meeting the pointy end of your wolf in some kind of mistaken identity scenario." Davion laughed, throwing the broken pieces over his shoulders. "Besides, I like this suit," he told me, brushing what I could only imagine was imaginary dirt from his perfectly pressed suit.

"I don't think it's my pointy end we should be worrying about," I deadpanned.

"Why, alpha, are you flirting with me?" Davion laughed, purposefully mistaking my meaning. "And here I was thinking you were happy with your beautiful mate."

A soft growl flowed through my lips, but a chuckle soon followed. The vampire was slightly amusing, I supposed.

"How is the clan?" I asked, opting for a safer subject instead.

"Fine, a little blood and mayhem every so often does them good," Davion told me as he turned and started to walk along the ward with me.

I didn't doubt that Davion was fully aware of what I was doing, and the fact he was content to accompany me on my task spoke of the person he was. At a different time, he and I could have been friends. Fuck, I think we might already be friends, even after everything that had happened. However, I could also recognise he was the pack's strongest ally. He had the knowledge and experience we needed to get through this.

"This might seem like an insurmountable task, but I have every faith in you, you know," Davion murmured after we'd been walking in silence for a while.

"I hope so," I mumbled. It would have been easy to keep walking in silence, and Davion would have probably let me if I'd wanted. But I decided to take this opportunity he was giving me. "We're going to need help. Contacts. Fuck! I don't even know what else."

"Are you asking me for assistance?" Davion asked, still looking ahead, strolling along like we were discussing something entirely different and not the start of what would definitely be a war. "Making a stand against the Shifter Council could make life exceedingly difficult for me with the other clan heads."

"Is that a problem?" I asked with a grin because by now, I was reasonably sure I knew the type of person Davion was.

He finally turned and looked at me with a broad grin on his face. "Of course not. As I said, a little blood and mayhem does you the world of good."

2
TANNER

I'd slipped out of bed to use the bathroom and returned to see my younger brother had stolen my spot beside our mate. Even though I desperately wanted to kick him out to curl up to Calli again, I also knew there was a room full of pups who'd want breakfast soon. Not to mention a house full of traumatised shifters. Of course, it helped that being the one to bring Calli a cup of tea in the morning would win me massive amounts of brownie points.

Fucking hell, that still threw me through a loop. My brother. It wasn't something I thought I'd ever say in the literal sense. But, as he clung to Calli in his sleep, his soft brown hair mussed on the pillow, I felt a fierce need to protect him. He looked so vulnerable when he was asleep. I'd only just found him, and I'd nearly lost him once. I wouldn't risk him again. I would be the brother he needed me to be.

Pulling on some clothes, I slipped out of the room and made my way to the kitchen. The sun was starting to rise, meaning it was still pretty early. The packhouse was blissfully quiet, but it wouldn't stay that way. Not with so many people here.

I was surprised to find I wasn't the first one to make it down to the kitchen. Even more so when it was Nash who was standing at the counter making a list. It made a bit more sense when Holly appeared out of the pantry, though.

"Hey," she whispered quietly, nodding over to the table where Grey was sitting, face down fast asleep at the table. "We thought we'd run out to Walmart and grab a load of essentials for people. Try and make the morning a bit easier. Not to mention, we don't have enough food to feed all of them."

Fuck, we hadn't thought of that.

"This one was up moving around and keeping me awake, so I decided to put him to work," Holly supplied happily, making Nash look down at his list guiltily.

As was my nature, I had a joke at the tip of my tongue about Nash bugging his mate in the mornings, but it stalled at the awkward downcast look on his face. It wasn't like Nash to act like this. He was usually the laid back one of us, too concerned with the logistics of running the pack to care about much else. Yesterday had been so out of the norm for all of us. It was bound to affect us differently.

"Let's see what you've got so far," I said instead, pulling the paper to me, mostly just to try and get Nash to talk to me because he was acting so weird.

"I'll pull the truck around while you finish here," Nash hastily said instead, quickly kissing Holly on the cheek and then disappearing out the door.

Holly and I both watched him go, and when I turned back to her, she had a frown on her face.

"Is he okay? Yesterday was… difficult for everyone."

Holly stared at the empty doorway he'd just left through, her concern written all over her face.

"I don't know," she finally said. "He's been acting weird ever since I woke up. I don't think he even slept."

Sliding the list back across the counter, I tried to reassure her. "We'll keep an eye on him. It's going to be okay, Hols." Even though I had no idea if it would be. From the look she gave me, Holly wasn't entirely convinced either.

"I should go and catch up with Nash before he decides to go and do something stupid. We probably won't be back for a few hours. There are protein bars and some other stuff in the pantry if they start to wake up before we get back. You know you're going to have to feed the kids before then, right?"

"I know how to look after the pups!" I scoffed.

From the look Holly gave me, she wasn't convinced, but she at least didn't voice her doubts before she left.

Suddenly, I found myself practically alone in the kitchen. Even though it was what I'd intended, I still found myself feeling bereft. Grey was softly snoring at the table, so at least we hadn't woken him. But it also meant I couldn't bug him about the growing list in my mind of everything that needed to be done.

There was so much happening in the pack right now, and it was my job to make sure everyone was working through it. I wouldn't exactly say I was failing at that right now because I could recognise it was an impossible task, but there had to be something I could do.

The packhouse was blissfully quiet with everyone else asleep, but it wasn't going to last long. Once the rescued shifters started to wake up, we'd need to be prepared to make sure they were settled and reassured. Then, they needed to decide what they wanted to do. If that meant staying with us, so many plans needed to be made.

My eyes moved to where Grey was slumped at the kitchen table. After only an hour or so of tossing and turning, he'd left the bedroom. As much as I wanted to go through our next steps with him, he needed some sleep, and I didn't have the heart to wake him. The same went for Calli. She was still healing, and we needed her back on her feet as quickly as possible. I hated it, but she was the biggest gun we had right now, and we couldn't afford for her to be out of the fight. It was going to be hard enough convincing her to take it easy. Waking her up early wasn't going to help the situation, even if I was doing it to give her the one thing that seemed to set her world right—tea.

Quickly checking in on the rest of the people in the house, I stuck my head through the door for the dining room and then the lounge. Most of the shifters were laid out on the floor or huddled together in small groups. One group, in particular, seemed to be concerned with one guy, but from the looks of distrust I got from them, I knew my intrusion wouldn't be welcome. Even so, if he was hurt and needed attention, leaving it for later could cause a greater problem.

I was just about to step further into the room when one of the group looked up and locked eyes with me. It was the first time any of them had been able to meet my eye. He wasn't very strong, but I could feel the glimmer of an alpha in him. It called out to my beta nature, but it was more of a whisper, whereas Grey was a storm of power.

He took a moment, seemingly weighing me up, and then shook his head. It was clearly a dismissal, and even though I was happy to leave them alone, I was slightly insulted at the move as well. I knew I shouldn't be. These guys had been through a lot, and it was understandable that they'd be distrustful.

Instead of letting my hurt feelings push me to do something stupid, I nodded in acknowledgement and slowly backed out of the room. I had to trust that they'd seek out the help they needed if things were bad enough.

Looking around myself at a loss now for what to do, I decided to retreat to the one other place in the house that settled my nerves—the library. Calli spent so much time in there now that her scent lingered on almost every inch of the room. It calmed my wolf just being in there. So, I quickly made a cup of coffee in the kitchen before slipping down the corridor, heading to what I was hoping was the one remaining refuge in the house.

Unfortunately, I was wrong.

Even before I opened the library door, I realised it was occupied. Reaching for the handle, I suddenly realised that what this room held was beyond precious to Calli, but also vitally important to the pack. Having people we didn't know at the packhouse and leaving this door unlocked had been foolish.

Creeping inside, I was relieved to find it was only Aidan stretched out on one of the couches and no one else.

As I closed the door behind me, he cracked open one eye and peered across the room at me.

"Does anyone sleep in this place? I'd have thought everyone would be exhausted after yesterday," I grumbled, partly because I'd hoped to have some time to myself before the pups woke up.

"I wanted to make sure Calli's books were safe, so I camped out in here until we could get a read on the new people." Aidan sat up and stretched his arms above his head as he let out an enormous yawn.

"You concerned about the witches we brought back?" I had no idea where the idea came from, perhaps because the shifters wouldn't know what to do with most of the books here.

"Nah, they've been huddled in the alcove under the stairs since they got here. You must have walked past them before coming down here."

"I was too lost in thoughts of coffee," I admitted, saluting him with my mug. "They're not having problems with the shifters, are they?"

"Some sideways looks we'll probably need to keep an eye on, but nothing so far." Aidan frowned as he spoke, and I could practically see the gears turning in his mind. He'd never once looked at Calli and the others differently for being a witch. It genuinely never seemed to bother him. "You think they might be a problem for Calli?" he asked.

It was nice to see Aidan taking on the brother role so easily. It could have become an awkward situation between them, especially putting Jacob in the mix. If anything, they'd all been overjoyed by their bond. Calli needed to feel those bonds around her. She'd lost so much before she came here that she deserved to find something for a change.

"Did you manage to get any sleep at all?" I asked, changing the subject, even though I could see the answer written in the dark circles under his eyes.

"On and off. But every time I fell asleep, I kept seeing that place." His voice sounded haunted, and it made me want to reach out for him. There would be so many people in the house feeling this way right now.

Aidan pushed himself up to sit with his elbows braced on his knees as he stared down at the ground as he spoke. He was clearly uncomfortable talking about this, but the fact that he was pushing against those feelings to talk to me meant something.

"Do you think we did the right thing?" he asked quietly. "Part of me thinks we should have called in the human police. All of those people, Tanner. Even if they knew of our world, the women had to be humans. So many families must be sitting at home right now wondering if their loved ones will walk through the door ever again. We took away their peace of knowing what happened to the people they loved by destroying that place."

None of us had thought of that. At the time, all we were consumed by was the need to give those people the final rest they deserved. To pull down Stone's chamber of macabre and put an end to the ghoulish display.

"We may have our issues with the Council right now, but bringing in the humans would have far-reaching effects for our whole society. It would change people's lives, and there'd be no going back. We don't know how the humans would react to the knowledge of our existence, but we have a fairly good idea. I'm tired of living with the current target on my back. I don't need to add another one in its place."

Aidan nodded thoughtfully, but I could tell he wasn't convinced.

"What do you think the Council will do now?" he asked.

"I suppose it depends on how many of them are involved in this. All we can do is help these people and then sit back and wait. Prepare for the worst and hope for the best." I shrugged as I answered. This wasn't really a shrugging situation, but what could we do?

Stone was going to be beyond pissed. He wouldn't have proof it had been us, but he'd no doubt suspect. Although, if he came here and found the people we'd freed, that would be all the proof he'd need.

We needed information. We needed to know how he'd managed to take all of these people, and why no one was asking questions about where they'd gone. The only way to get that was to ask the traumatised people we were currently sheltering to tell us their stories.

With a sigh, I turned to leave the library. As much as I might want to hide out in here, there was too much happening for me to bury my head in the sand right now.

"Where are you going?" Aidan asked in a small voice that pulled at my heartstrings.

I paused at the doorway and looked back at him, nodding my head toward the stairs. "Come on, we need to intercept the pups and get some food in them before they wake Calli."

If there was one thing in this house that could soothe our wounded souls, it was spending time with the pups. Besides, we needed to speak with Kai. That kid had to be hurting right now, and we were all familiar with that type of pain. Our whole pack was filled with people who'd experienced it.

Aidan jumped up from the couch with more energy than I possessed, and I'd at least had a couple of hours of sleep. I'd known the mention of the pups would motivate him. Aidan would take any excuse to spend time with Jacob, his new half-brother. It was good to see the two of them bonding, even if I was pretty sure he was trying to steal my spot as the favourite.

As we approached the stairs, I noticed that some of the shifters in the downstairs were starting to move around. While it was tempting to slip away upstairs, I couldn't abandon them when their frightened eyes met mine.

"You head up and intercept the kids. If Kai looks scared, go and wake Maverick, he seems to have bonded with him already."

Aidan nodded and moved away as I turned back to the living room.

Just to be sure to secure my spot, I quickly pulled out my phone and sent a message to Holly asking her to grab a couple of boxes of donuts. I'd slip one to the kids, and the sugar rush would definitely buy me another day as the favourite. Ah, bribery! Worked every time.

I made sure to move slowly as I walked into the living room, where most of the shifters had crashed. I sensed some of them drifted out of the dining room, interested to hear what I had to say.

"Hey."

Wow, that was lame, even for me.

"Okay, I don't know what to do here, so forgive me as I make this up as I go along," I joked, getting a few smiles and chuckles of amusement from them. That was encouraging. "I'm not going to stand here and insult you by saying I know you've just been through something traumatic. It goes without saying, and you don't need me droning on about it now. We're going to have to speak with some of you at some point today to get a better picture of what we're up against. But trust me when I tell you, our pack has been through some shit recently too, and anything you've got to tell us, no matter how unbelievable it may seem, we will believe you. But let's set that aside for now. Let's make this morning about regrouping. Some of the pack has headed out to get food and clothing and any basic supplies you might need. If anyone needs anything specific, come and see me, and I'll make sure that it's arranged. We showed you where all the bathrooms and such were last night. Get clean, get settled. Food will be here soon. We'll scrounge up some basics to tide you over until they get back. We're going to make sure you're safe here. You don't have to think about the future yet, but just know you're not alone."

I saw a few watery eyes in front of me, but we all chose not to acknowledge it, being the manly men we were. Turning around, I was glad to see Grey standing at my back in support, happy to let me take the lead. It was part of what made him a great alpha.

Clearing his throat, Grey added, "If you have people you want to get back to, we can arrange that for you. If you want to stay here with our pack, you're more than welcome. Otherwise, we know someone who can make arrangements to take you someplace safe. But Tanner is right, try not to worry about that right now. Let's just take this one step at a time. Everything moved so fast last night, and I know no one wanted to take us up on any medical attention, but come and see me if your situation has changed overnight. Asking for help is not a weakness. We're all in this together."

My wolf's hackles raised at the mention of medical attention, and Grey put a calming hand on my shoulder. Calli was too injured to help these people right now, and even though we'd taken them in, we still needed to be careful with them around her. These were pureblood shifters, and we didn't know what prejudices they'd brought here with them. I wouldn't tolerate another Wallace-sized issue when it came to Calli. She'd been through too much to put up with that shit again.

Grey's alpha power leaked out into the room, sending a calming wave around everyone. Most relaxed at the feeling, but a few eyed him curiously, and I made sure to commit their faces to memory. We had a lot of secrets in this pack, and there would be no hiding them from these people. We needed to remember that just because they'd been locked inside that torture house didn't mean they were on our side.

Grey's hand tightened on my shoulder as he steered me over to the doorway. "Keep an eye on them," he murmured. "We need to make sure we didn't inadvertently rescue one of Stone's spies."

I nodded in agreement. It was exactly where my thoughts

had been taking me as well. I wouldn't put it past my father to have a man on the inside, picking up information from these poor people as they sat in their cages.

The fact that he was my father turned my stomach. I hated him so much that it pushed me toward madness. Knowing Maverick now only made me hate him even more for what he'd done to my poor brother. There was something inherently wrong with him. He was so evil, it almost seemed impossible that he'd been able to create someone as pure as Maverick, even if he'd tried his best to pollute him.

I could still remember my mother. She'd been kind and gentle. As a child, being in her arms had brought me a sense of peace and security as only a mother could. I'd never understood how someone as pure as her could have been with my father. I had so few memories of him as a child because he was always consumed by his alpha duties. Sometimes, I wondered if he was always a completely evil bastard or if it was losing her that pushed him over the edge. At the end of the day, it didn't really matter, though. He was the monster we were dealing with. It didn't matter how he'd become like that. All that mattered was how we were going to put him down.

"One of my pack needs medical attention," a voice said from behind me, pulling me out of my thoughts.

Turning around, I found one of the shifters glaring down at us. He had that touch of distrust in his eyes that none of us would take personally. It was the alpha I'd seen this morning who didn't want me to approach them.

"Okay, let's move him somewhere quiet and see what we can do," Grey suggested, stepping forward.

The guy in front of us bristled at the move, and I could see the apprehension in his eyes.

"You can all come with him. We won't separate you," I told him quietly, so no one would overhear.

His eyes moved between mine as he seemed to weigh up the options. Then he gave us a nod and turned away, moving over to the corner where some shifters were huddled together, shielding one of their packmates from view.

"The only place we've got to move them to is the library," I pointed out.

Never had I regretted not getting all the rooms finished in this place more than I did right then. I'd even admit that when Grey talked about adding extra cabins on the land, I thought it was wishful thinking. Now, I was kicking myself that we hadn't been quicker about it.

Grey seemed to take a second to think about it before he nodded in agreement. So much for guarding our secrets.

The shifters huddled tighter together as we approached until their alpha raised a hand to calm them. Including the guy on the ground, there were five of them. I couldn't help but wonder how big their pack had been before they were taken. Then, I quickly tried to push the thought from my mind.

Reluctantly, they parted to allow us to see the person behind them, and he didn't look like he was in great shape. Even from where I was standing, I could see a large, festering wound on his chest. His wolf should've been able to heal something like that before an infection could set in, though.

"Why isn't his wolf healing him?" I asked without thinking.

They all bristled at the comment, and even I realised it had been a bit tactless.

Grey squatted down to look at the shifter, who was slumped against the wall. From his face alone, he looked like he was clinging to consciousness out of sheer determination.

Grey frowned, placing a hand on his shoulder, his head tilting to the side.

"Your wolf is blocked from you," he said quietly. "You should have told us about this yesterday."

It sounded like a criticism, but it wasn't. We'd have done the same thing if we'd been in their position. We'd have hoped his wolf would emerge, and none of us would have allowed them to expose our weakness until we had no other option.

One of the pack started a low growl, taking a step toward Grey. We might have been here to help these people, but not at the expense of ourselves. Two steps took me to Grey as I sheltered him behind me, facing down the frightened shifter.

"We're not here to hurt you," I snapped.

"How do we know? How do we know this isn't just some fucked up test?"

"You don't," I shrugged. "There is absolutely nothing I can tell you that will convince you otherwise. All you can do is trust us until we prove ourselves."

"It's easy to talk of trust when it isn't the lives of the people you care about on the line," he challenged.

"Isn't it? We've welcomed you into our pack, into our home. We have pups and mates here. You far outnumber us. But even though we don't know who you are or what your intentions could be, we've provided you with aid and shelter because we know the man who was holding you, and we know exactly what *he's* capable of."

"Don't give me that 'your enemy is my enemy' bullshit. You have no idea what we've been through," he snapped.

I could see the fear in his startling blue eyes, and I knew his anger might have been aimed at me right now, but I wasn't the person he wanted to be fighting.

"Enough!" snapped Calli's voice from the doorway. "You

can stand there and argue all day while your friend dies at your feet, or you can bring him to the library and let us help him. Decide now because I'm aiming to pass out very soon, and then you're shit out of luck."

I noticed River hovering at her side and frowned at how she seemed to lean so heavily against the doorway. She shouldn't be out of bed, let alone even considering healing someone. This was a bad fucking idea.

"It's you," the alpha stated, paying far too much attention to my mate.

"Yeah, me again," she shrugged before turning away and leaving in the direction of the library.

The alpha watched her leave, his eyes staying on the empty doorframe for far longer than I liked.

"You heard what *my* mate said, let's get him moved." I tried to act like a grown-up, but I couldn't help stressing that Calli was mine.

The alpha turned back to me with a smirk, clearly finding amusement in my tone. Perhaps it was because he had the boyish good looks you expected to find in a boy band, but either way, I'd decided I didn't like him.

I sullenly followed everyone to the library, where we found Calli slumped in one of the armchairs.

"You should be in bed," Grey chastised her, being the braver man than I was.

"I'll be fine," Calli panted.

She really wasn't okay, but there'd be no holding her back from this if she already had her mindset on it.

"Is he the only one?" she asked, watching as the shifters laid their now unconscious friend on the couch. "Or are there more wounded?"

"Not to the extent that their wolves can't sort it out. Something is different about him. It's like his wolf is out of reach," Grey said, casting a curious look at the unconscious man on the couch.

"This is something that happened at the facility?" Calli asked the alpha, and he nodded grimly.

"There won't be anything we can do about that right now. I'm not strong enough. But we can try and fix it in a few days when I've recovered my strength," she explained to the pack who were worriedly watching their friend.

"What are you?" the alpha asked, stepping between Calli and his packmate.

I'd wondered how long it would be before this happened.

"Does it matter?" Calli sighed. "Right now, all you need to know is that I'm the person who's going to save your friend's life. Everything else can come later."

"Trust goes both ways," the shifter who'd snapped at me before said. "You can't expect us to trust you with someone we care about when you won't even answer our questions."

"Very well," Calli sighed as she climbed out of the armchair with a groan. Her arm came to her stomach as she wrapped it around herself in her first outward sign of pain. "Tanner, can you help me back upstairs?" she asked, wavering on the spot from the exhaustion of just standing.

I didn't need asking twice, and I scooped her up into my arms, ready to take her out of there.

"Wait!" the alpha called out. "Please. I know we're being unfair to you right now. But if you knew the things that happened in that place… it's hard to step outside and pretend everything is right in the world. If you can help him, please try."

It probably didn't make me a good person, but his desperate plea had me clutching Calli tighter to my chest.

"I don't think you're strong enough for this, sweetheart," I told her.

"I know, but there's no other way, and the last thing we need right now is the attention of a wraith on packlands."

Grey and I both cringed at the mention of the monsters, but the alpha in front of us seemed more and more intrigued with every passing moment.

With a reluctant sigh, I set Calli on her feet beside the unconscious shifter, and she reached out, setting her hands on his arm. As she closed her eyes, a serene look fell over her face.

"Tanner…"

"I know, sweetheart. I'll catch you when you fall," I said grimly.

Calli nodded briefly, but she was already wholly centred on the task at hand. It didn't take long for the soft glow to cover her body as she accessed her magic and filtered it into the shifter in front of her. It wasn't as bright as it usually was, and it seemed to flicker like a lightbulb that was reaching the end of its life.

My fists clenched at my side, and I watched every single bead of sweat break out onto her forehead as Calli pushed herself too far. We knew what it meant for her to be drawing this much when she was so weak. Calli was dipping into her own essence to save the man in front of her.

I wanted to reach out and tear her away from him. I wanted to drop to my knees and beg her to stop. But that wasn't the person Calli was. She'd never stand by while someone else was suffering, especially if it was within her power to help.

We all watched with bated breath. At one point, Grey had to tear himself away and pace to the window where he stared outside, every muscle in his body tense to the point of it looking painful.

After what felt like an age, Calli sighed and fell forward. I caught her before she fell on top of the shifter in front of her. Even the alpha, who had stood anxiously by, darted forward to help her, but she was in my arms before he could reach her.

Pulling Calli away from the couch, I cradled her against my body as I pressed my face into the curve of her neck. I took a moment to listen to her breathe, inhaling her scent, to try and calm the waves of grief that flooded my system at watching her hurting yet again.

A gasp of breath from the sofa signalled the shifter jolting awake.

"What… what happened?" he stuttered out, his hands roaming across his chest, searching for an injury that was no longer there.

"Danny! Thank fuck!" the alpha sighed as he dropped to his knees in front of his pack brother. "Wait, just, just fucking wait. Take it easy. We came far too close to losing you."

"I'm fine," Danny said, a note of disbelief in his voice. "How am I fine?"

"My mate just nearly sacrificed herself to save you," Grey said through gritted teeth from where he was still leaning against the window. At least he was able to look at us now.

"What is she?" the alpha asked again.

"She's the reason why your friend here is still alive, and the fact that you aren't even concerned about her wellbeing right now speaks fucking volumes," Grey snapped.

The war of emotions that crossed this alpha's face drew my attention away from Calli momentarily. He seemed to swing from anger at the challenge from Grey to shame for his shitty behaviour.

As much as I hated to admit it, I understood. And if Grey really thought about it for a second, he'd understand too. He'd be acting exactly the same way if he was in this guy's shoes. Alphas were hardwired to care unwaveringly about their pack. Their whole purpose in life was to keep them safe, and to watch one of them slipping closer and closer to death would have been torturous for him.

Deciding I didn't have the energy to defend this stranger in front of me, I got up from the floor, cradling Calli against my chest.

"Wait!" Danny called out from the couch, where he'd been staring at his hands in disbelief. "Is she okay? What did she do? How did she… fuck, I know it doesn't matter right now. I'm just, my brain doesn't seem to be able to move in a straight line at the minute. Is there anything I can do to help her?"

"She healed you," Grey filled in, even though the question had been directed at me. "Hopefully, she'll be fine after she rests. It's not the first time she's had to push herself past her limits."

The sadness in Grey's voice as he spoke echoed the ache in my own heart. How did this keep happening? What had we done to piss fate off so much that she'd be putting us through these constant challenges?

The small pack we'd rescued stared at Calli, almost like they were only just coming to terms with what had happened. It was pretty incredible if you were coming from a background where stuff like this didn't happen. I'd felt exactly the same way the first time I'd seen Calli heal someone.

"Thank you," the alpha whispered, his eyes locked on Calli's unconscious form. "My pack and I owe you a great debt. My name is Colt. This is Danny, Bast, Ridley and Asher. If there is anything we can do to help, we would gratefully do it." Colt held his hand out to Grey, and it felt like the tension in the room deflated instantaneously.

"Let's get you all cleaned up and fed," Grey sighed, shaking Colt's offered hand. "We can talk about this later."

Striding forward, Grey held out one arm, showing the gobsmacked shifters the door. It was smart to get them out of the library before they realised what they were standing in the middle of.

Something about what had happened was screaming at me that we couldn't trust them, despite what Colt had said. It was probably only because Calli was hurt yet again, but, yeah, I was still going to hold it against them, even if it was unfair.

I didn't wait to see if they left. Grey could handle them. Instead, I slipped out of the room and up the stairs until I was back in my room.

I went to shoulder the door open and was surprised when it opened of its own accord. Of course, seeing Lachlan standing in the doorway made more sense than the house taking on its own consciousness, but right now, I wouldn't be surprised if it did. That just seemed to be the way our lives were going at the moment.

It was kind of surprising to see Lachlan still in here, though.

"River and Maverick are making breakfast with the kids," Lachlan filled in, answering my unspoken question. "I felt Calli pull on her magic, so I decided to wait here in case you needed any help."

"What happened to Aidan? I sent him up here to intercept the kids?" I asked.

Lachlan shrugged, not having an answer for me. He probably got pulled into something else just like I had. A lot was going on around here at the minute.

Lachlan pulled back the covers on the bed, and I gently lowered Calli to the mattress.

"I hate this," I whispered as we stared down at our mate unconscious in my bed.

"What happened?" Lachlan asked gently.

"One of the shifters was injured, and she healed him."

"It couldn't have waited?"

"No. I doubt he would have made it through the day. He seemed in pretty bad shape. But... something seemed different with Calli's magic." I could feel the frown on my face as I brought her image in the library to mind.

"How do you mean different?" Lachlan asked, sitting on the edge of the bed and gently placing his hand on Calli's forehead, brushing her long blonde hair away from her face.

"She started to do the glow again, but it was different. It was faded and flickering in and out."

"I wouldn't worry. It's probably just because she's so drained. I can still feel her magic and her wolf. I can't sense anything wrong with her."

Now that was a surprise to me.

"Have you always been able to do that?" I asked.

"No. It started yesterday," Lachlan answered, his eyes firmly on Calli.

"Does that mean your magic has been unblocked or whatever?" I asked.

That got his attention as Lachlan looked up at me in surprise.

"Nothing really stays a secret in a pack, or rather, it shouldn't." I couldn't help but think of Coby and the terrible secrets Wallace had been able to hide from us.

Thankfully, the thought of us knowing about his issue had Lachlan shaking his head as he laughed in amusement.

"Not being constantly ignored is definitely going to take some getting used to," he murmured and then flushed in embarrassment at the admission. "And no, I'm pretty sure it's still there. I think the difference has more to do with being joined with Calli in whatever the coven bond has turned into."

"Things have gotten pretty crazy over the last twenty-four hours, haven't they?"

It was an understatement of epic proportions, but also, even though things were changing between us all, it didn't feel like it was changing for the bad. Instead, it felt more like this was how we were always supposed to be.

"I'm going to take a nap for a bit. You can stay if you want," I told Lachlan as I shucked off my jeans and climbed into bed at Calli's side.

None of us had really slept last night, and I doubted we would get many opportunities in the coming days either. Best to collect a few hours here and there while we had the chance.

Lachlan stretched out on the top of the covers on Calli's other side and stared up at the ceiling. At first, I thought he was uncomfortable about me being here as well, but then he said, "You realise the kids will be in here as soon as they've finished eating, right?"

"Noooooo," I groaned, snuggling my face into Calli's hair again.

I didn't mean it. I never would. Spending time with the pups was my favourite thing to do. Besides, Nash and Holly would be back with donuts soon, and I couldn't let someone else steal my thunder.

3
RIVER

As we'd stood in the living room doorway, listening to Tanner and Grey speak to the others, I could see how exhausted Calli was. But I heard the kids stampeding towards the stairs, and the last thing Calli needed to be dealing with was trying to herd them all under control.

So, as Calli moved towards the library to help heal someone, I stopped at the bottom of the stairs, waiting for the herd of pups to appear.

Walking away from Calli when she was in that condition had been something I'd never have imagined myself doing. But Tanner and Grey would make sure she didn't push herself too far, as much as they could anyway. Once Calli got something in her mind, it was hard to deter her from her chosen path, especially if it was to help someone else.

Surprisingly, Maverick brought up the group's rear, even if it was at a slightly more subdued pace. The soft smile on his face was good to see. It was hard to not find yourself shedding your worries for a moment when the kids were roping you into their mischief.

"Aidan's on the phone with Nash putting in an order for

some more things we need," Maverick said, his eyes flicking to Kai, indicating it was stuff for him. "If you need anything, you'll want to text them. It sounded like they were nearly done at the store."

I nodded in acknowledgement, but nothing came to mind at that second. Instead, I ran an assessing gaze over the procession of kids to ensure they were all their usual happy selves.

Kai was following the kids down the stairs, but he seemed to be keeping an anxious eye on Maverick to make sure he was staying with them.

We'd need to speak to him today about what had happened and what he wanted to do. He didn't need to come to any decisions today, but he needed to know we were here to support him, and he wasn't alone.

We were probably going to have to talk to all of the kids to make sure they understood what was happening. But then, I wasn't sure I really understood what was happening, or rather what was about to happen.

Fuck, we needed to have a pack meeting, but how were we going to do that with all of these people here expecting us to have all of the answers. We were so woefully under-prepared for this that it was almost laughable.

"Hey guys, how do pancakes sound for breakfast?" I asked, putting on the happiest face I could muster.

Jacob eyed me suspiciously. "How much experience do you have in making pancakes?"

"Hey, I can make pancakes!" I protested.

Or at least I was hoping I could.

Maverick found the whole thing hilarious as he laughed at my expense.

Abby stepped forward, threading her hand in mine. "It's okay, Daddy River. We can help you."

And then the four-year-old child had to pull me across the hallway toward the kitchen because those two little words had not only floored me but brought tears to my eyes.

Shaking my head to clear the bewilderment, I scooped Abby up in my arms and swung her around to my back, where she clung with a giggle as we headed toward what I was hoping was a successful pancake cooking session.

They did mixes for these things, right? Because I had no idea what was in a pancake. Flour? And like, butter, maybe?

As the kids ran into the kitchen, followed by Maverick, my eye caught on a small group of men huddled in the alcove beneath the stairs. The three looked exhausted, and it seemed like while one of them slept, the other two were keeping watch.

I knew they were the witches we'd brought back from Neressa's chambers from how they were dressed. We'd given them shirts and joggers last night to cover up the ridiculous pool boy type clothes she'd had them parading around in.

Putting Abby carefully back down, I ushered her toward the kitchen. "Why don't you make sure the boys aren't up to no good? I'll be there in a second," I told her, and she skipped away without question.

"Is there anything I can get for you?" I asked, turning to the one glaring at me from out of the shadows. "There were blankets and pillows in the living room. Wasn't there enough for everyone?"

Before Calli had come along, that would definitely have been the case. But I knew for a fact that when she'd sorted out the kids' rooms, Calli had also located a linen cupboard none of us had really known about and filled it to the brim.

"The rest of them weren't exactly in a sharing mood," he spat, nodding toward the living room.

Now that had me seeing red.

Spinning on the spot, I marched back into the living room. Sure enough, not only did the remaining men in there have plenty to make themselves comfortable, but there was a stack of blankets and pillows thrown in the far corner.

"We invited you into our home as guests," I snarled, gathering up the blankets and other items. "You do not run this pack, and you do not decide who is worthy to be here. I'd think long and hard before you try and pull something like this again."

I could see the hateful looks in their eyes as I left the room, but I didn't give a crap. Yes, they'd been through a lot, but they should appreciate that the others we'd brought back had too. One person's pain did not outweigh someone else's. It wasn't a competition. If they couldn't accept the pack we had, they wouldn't be welcome here. It was as simple as that.

I tried to calm down as I walked back to where the three witches were huddled. We should've made sure something like this didn't happen before leaving them last night. It was on us to make sure they were safe here.

Passing them over to the one who'd spoken to me before, I waited while he passed a blanket to his quiet friend and then turned and covered the other who was sleeping behind him.

"You didn't have to do that," he finally said when he was done. "We'll be out of your hair as soon as we've had something to eat. A pack isn't a place for our kind."

"You're wrong," I told him gently. "This pack has three members who are witches. We don't discriminate, and we protect what is ours. If the others aren't on board with that, they will be asked to leave. I won't risk my mate around people who can't be trusted."

I could see I had his interest now.

"The woman who killed Neressa. She's your mate?"

"Yes. Calli."

"She's not a witch. I don't know what she is, but I saw her using magic."

"She's something we can talk about later. You're welcome here if you want to stay. At least until you've had a chance to recuperate and come up with a plan of where you want to go… I'm sorry I don't know your name," I admitted. I hadn't found out anyone's names yet.

"It's Brendan. This is Lucas, and that's Elliot," he said, nodding to the sleeping man behind them.

"I'm River," I held out my hand to shake, and he reluctantly did. It would be hard to convince these three that they could be safe here with the pack. "If there's anything else you need, just ask. Some of the pack members have gone out for supplies, and they should be back soon."

"Like I said, we're leaving once we've rested."

I nodded in agreement and then left them in peace. Arguing with Brendan wasn't going to change his mind. Perhaps once they saw what the pack was really like, they'd come to a different conclusion.

The kitchen was pretty quiet. Most of the shifters had stuck to the living room and the dining room. I think Cassia and Hunter had taken a couple to their cabin when we'd realised we had nowhere to put all the people we'd suddenly accumulated.

The kids were already excited, bouncing around the kitchen as I randomly opened a cabinet. I was pretty sure we kept flour in this one and, hopefully, pancake mixes. But, judging by the giggles that followed, I'd either picked the wrong cabinet, or it was obvious even to the kids that I had no idea what I was doing.

By the time I closed the cabinet, having come to the embarrassing conclusion that it only held Tupperware, I was presented with the sight of a grinning Coby standing next to the freezer, holding a bag of frozen pancakes Calli had batch cooked.

My eyes raised to the ceiling in thanks for the amazing mate I'd been provided with before I sheepishly took the bag from the seven-year-old who had better kitchen knowledge than I did.

"Okay, even I can reheat pancakes." I laughed. "Coby, Jacob, why don't you see what we've got in the fridge that we can use for toppings? And I'm talking about fruit! I don't fancy facing the wrath of Calli for letting you guys have whipped cream and chocolate for breakfast."

"Awwwww," the boys protested.

"Okay, you can have whipped cream and chocolate, but there has to be fruit on there as well."

Both boys dived for the fridge, and Abby actually rolled her eyes at me for giving in so easily.

"Abby, why don't you show Kai where the plates are, and you guys can set the table," I suggested as I helped her down from the counter surface.

It hadn't escaped my attention that Kai was standing awkwardly off to the side. It was understandable, though. The kid had no idea where he fitted in here. It was up to us as the grown-ups to make sure that whatever transition he was about to go through, he went through as smoothly and painlessly as possible. The kid had already been through far too much in his short life.

Maverick clapped a hand down on Kai's shoulder before moving to the fridge and reaching over the boys' heads to grab the orange juice and milk.

"Who wants juice, and who wants milk?" he asked, moving over to the counter.

By the time he put the bottles down and turned to get the glasses, we were all looking at him in surprise.

"What? I can be all domesticated and fuck!" he protested.

"Ommm, Daddy Mav said a bad word," Abby chastised as Jacob and Coby giggled conspiratorily.

The slapped with shock look Maverick had at what Abby just said to him was probably the same one I'd had moments before. In contrast to my own frozen in shock moment, though, Maverick dropped down to his knees, so he was at eye level with the little girl in front of him. A single tear ran down his cheek, and Abby reached out with her little hand to wipe it away before she leapt and wrapped her arms around him.

Maverick clung to her, burying his face in her hair, completely broken by the simple act of being accepted by a little girl.

When he pulled away, Abby wiped the tears from his shocked face.

"Don't cry, Daddy Mav. We're going to look after you now."

How this little girl could always see right to the heart of things constantly shocked me.

"I'm sorry, firecracker," Maverick muttered. "I didn't know you felt that way about me."

"Of course I do, silly. I had all the bad, but then I got a mummy and my new daddys. We're a family."

This was the first time Abby had ever mentioned anything close to what had happened to her. None of us wanted to push her to talk about it. Especially not while she was so young and seemed to be dealing with everything in her stride. In time, she'd need to see a proper therapist, but we didn't have the luxury of that right now. I swore to myself that I was going to make sure I did. I, of all people, knew how easy it was to hide behind a happy mask when you were actually breaking apart on the inside.

"Yeah, we're a family," Maverick muttered as he held her close again for a minute before trying to brush it all off as he stood again. "Now, who wants juice and who wants milk?" Maverick asked, clearing his throat and turning back to the kitchen counter.

The kids happily placed their orders, and Jacob and Coby piled up what they could find in the fridge on the counter. It became shockingly evident that we really had needed to go to the store.

Abby marched over to Kai and grabbed his hand, pulling him closer to us as we sorted through who was having what for breakfast.

It wasn't until we were sitting down to eat that I decided to try and broach a conversation with Kai. For some reason, I was weirdly nervous about the whole thing.

"So, Kai, how are you feeling this morning?" I asked, and then cringed at the hundreds of different ways you could take that one question the wrong way.

"Okay," he muttered, his eyes firmly fixed on his plate as he moved his food around, not really eating much. He must be hungry, though, because we knew he hadn't eaten for at least 12 hours.

"I can make you something else if you like," I offered, trying not to be too pushy but also getting concerned.

"His tummy feels funny," Abby offered innocently, utterly oblivious to the glare Kai just shot her.

"Yeah, well, sometimes that happens because you're worried or sad," I explained to Abby, watching Kai out of the corner of my eye. "It happens to everyone. It even happens to me. What can help is finding someone you trust to talk to about it."

Abby nodded thoughtfully, taking in what I was saying before she cast a nervous glance at Kai. I wondered if he'd voiced his worries to the other kids yet or even Maverick, but I had a feeling that he was keeping it all to himself.

The rest of breakfast was pretty quiet. Even the kids didn't want to push Kai too far. By the time the food was all gone, and it became obvious Kai wasn't going to eat anything, an awkward silence descended around us.

"Can we go for a run today?" Coby blurted out, trying to find something to ease the situation.

Kai peered up at us through his frown, finally breaking the death glare he had on his breakfast. "What do you mean?"

Okay, if this was going to help him out of his shell, it would definitely be worthwhile. The rest of us could do with cutting loose and going for a run too.

"I can shift," Coby bragged, puffing up his chest proudly. "We all can."

Kai looked around the three young ones, his eyes wide in wonder, before he squinted suspiciously. "No, you can't. You're only babies."

"I'm not a baby!" Coby scoffed like he'd never been more insulted in his life. "I'm six."

Kai grinned, clearly thinking that still made Coby a baby.

"You're only eleven," Abby added while she was sipping on the last of her milk.

Kai's eyes widened in alarm as he looked between Maverick and I, worried at being caught out in his earlier lie.

"Don't panic, kid. None of us bought you being fifteen for a second," Maverick told him casually.

"I'm sorry I lied," Kai said sulkily as he slumped down in his chair. "I didn't think you'd take me with you if you knew I was just a kid."

"I wouldn't worry. This place seems to collect kids." Maverick laughed, tickling Abby's ribs as he did.

This side of Maverick was so wholly alien to me, I

couldn't help but stare at him like we had a body swap in our midst.

"Don't make me say a bad word again," Maverick warned, squinting at me in annoyance.

Holding my hands up in surrender, I laughed. "I didn't say a word."

Maverick just humphed in return before looking around at the empty plates on the table, well, all except Kai's.

"Let's get these dishes in the dishwasher and make some space for the stuff Holly and Nash are bringing back. There's going to be a lot to go through. Kai, they're grabbing you a few bits, but I know Calli wanted to take you shopping tomorrow if she's up for it. Is that okay with you?" I explained as I started to gather the dishes.

The kids happily jumped off their chairs and carried their dishes through to the kitchen. It wasn't until we were in there that I realised Kai hadn't followed us. Looking up, I saw him still sitting at the table and Maverick moving into the chair next to him. He caught my eye as he did, and I raised an eyebrow in question in case he wanted some support. Maverick shook his head, so I decided the best thing to do would be to distract the rest of the kids so Kai and Maverick could talk. It wasn't exactly difficult. I only had to mention the switch and cookies, and they were running for the stairs. Before she left, Abby looked over at Kai in question. I was about to explain to her that he'd be along soon when she just nodded at the sight of Kai talking to Maverick and then ran after the others.

What I wouldn't give to be able to look inside that girl's mind.

4
MAVERICK

I'd seen the shocked expression on Kai's face when River casually mentioned they would provide him with things. I also saw the sheen in his eyes. As the other kids scrambled away from the table to take their dishes into the kitchen, Kai stayed frozen to his seat.

It was easier for me to understand how he felt. I knew what it was like to assume you were a burden to those around you. To not expect anything from anyone, and then to search for how much it would cost you when it did appear. I'd been this kid. I knew exactly how he was feeling right now.

I also understood just how lost the poor kid felt. Kai's entire world had crumbled around him, and now he was sitting in a house full of strangers and worrying about where he fit into the world.

Sliding out of my seat, I moved to the chair next to him, ready to try and ease some of his fears. Now, that was something I never saw myself thinking a few short months ago!

"You're probably wondering what's going to happen now, but daren't ask in case someone asks you to leave," I said as casually as I could.

Kai's shoulders hunched up as if I'd lashed out at him with the words, and I had a sudden overwhelming need to bail out of this conversation and make River do it instead.

"What happens next is completely up to you, kid," I told him softly. "You can have a home here with us if that's something you'd like. If it isn't, that's okay too. We can make sure you find your way to somewhere safe, where you want to be. The ball's in your court, but just know we'd really like you to be here with us."

Kai turned to me with watery eyes, and I slowly put an arm around his shoulders and drew him into my side. He didn't resist, but he sort of just leaned into me, almost like he wasn't quite ready to let go of the tension yet.

"I knew she was gone. When they wouldn't let me visit her. I knew if she was really in there, she wouldn't let them keep me away," he admitted. "When my wolf came out, he was so sad. He already knew, even if I wasn't ready to admit it to myself."

His shoulders didn't shake, and his voice didn't waver. I wouldn't have known he was crying if I hadn't been able to see the glint of tears on his cheeks.

"My mum died when I was born, so I can't pretend to know what you're going through. But the other kids here, hell, even most of the adults, they all know what it's like to lose a parent. Everyone here will help you get through this," I reassured him.

"That lady in the truck, that was Calli, right?" he asked.

"Yeah. She's our mate." I didn't know why I felt the need to fill him in on that piece of information. It wasn't really important, but for some reason, it felt like one of those reassuring things you told people.

"She was hurt," he said quietly. "Is she going to be okay?"

"She's going to be fine, bud. Calli is strong, like super strong. She's different to us, and we're still figuring out what that means. She just needs some time to rest, is all."

Kai nodded slowly, and it was like I could see the gears moving in his mind as he weighed up his options.

"I think I'd like to see what it would be like to stay here," he said slowly.

"Ha! It's pretty crazy most of the time, and there's definitely some trouble on the way, but I'm glad you want to give us a chance. There's no pressure about staying, though, okay. If you get two months down the line and decide you can't stand us, there'll be no hard feelings." He seemed reassured by that as he straightened up and then looked forlornly down at the cold, mushed up pancakes on his plate. Now that he wasn't so worried about what would happen next, it seemed like the kid was getting his appetite back. "I have it on good assurance that donuts are coming soon," I whispered conspiratorially to him.

That got a small smile out of him.

"I don't think you guys should spend a lot of money on me until I know I'm going to stay."

"Yeah, I doubt that's going to hold us back. But you can always try and persuade Calli if you want to."

This was a kid who needed a bit of spoiling. He'd been on his own for a long time while Stone's pack lied to him about his mum. He needed to be shown he was cared about, and there were people in the world who gave a shit about him. It hadn't escaped me that his clothes didn't look like they'd been cleaned for a while and were starting to wear thin in places. He was skinnier than he should have been, and he looked more than just the gangly nature of some boys as they were approaching their teenage years. I'd always thought the bigger packs looked after all of their members, but from the state of the boy in front of me, I realised just how naive I was to the world I lived in.

"We're back!" Holly's voice shouted through the house, followed by the sounds of banging and swearing as she struggled with the bags she was carrying.

"Let's go give them a hand with the bags, and then we can get first dibs on the donuts," I suggested to Kai, giving him a grin.

When he gave me a small smile back, I knew he'd be okay. He was shaken, grieving and scared. But he was with a group of people who'd throw their arms around him and make sure he knew everything would be okay. I should know, they'd done exactly that for me, and I couldn't thank them enough. Not only had it given me Calli, but for possibly the first time in my life, I had a family and a home.

5
GREY

Davion and I were about to run through some plans when Nash and Holly pulled up in the truck, piled high with supplies. It was a good job the pack finances were healthy for once or this whole rescue mission would've ruined us otherwise.

Holly grabbed an armful of bags and practically fell through the front door of the house, shouting her arrival. That probably wouldn't do the survivors' nerves much good. Still, I supposed you could argue it was a kind of trial by fire situation.

Nash rolled his eyes as he gathered up more bags in his arms. "You should have seen how excited she was at the store. We spent an absolute fortune," he cringed.

I couldn't help but shrug. "It was necessary. Given the whole housing situation, the least we can do is make sure they have the basic necessities."

"Hmmm," Nash hummed thoughtfully, looking off to the side of the house. "The lumber for the new cabins should be here tomorrow. We could probably get them up in a couple of weeks. Maybe it would be quicker to try and get Calli's house back into some kind of order?"

I grabbed a couple of the bags from the truck and was surprised when Davion did the same.

"My clan can work on the house," he offered. When he saw our surprised looks, he added, "We're probably better suited to the task given the amount of blood we left behind."

I cringed at the thought. Calli's old house hadn't exactly been at the top of our priorities list, and after we'd boarded the place up, we'd just about left it as was. It wasn't going to be pleasant opening it up again. In fact, a part of me wondered if it would be better to tear the thing down and start over, but that wouldn't exactly lend us a solution to our current dilemma.

"If you want to get the place cleaned up, we can order the new windows and have them fitted fairly quickly if we all muck in together. Then, you could move the clan back in there if you want. Otherwise, there's a pack here that could probably take the house for a while," I offered.

"Don't take this the wrong way," Davion purred as we started to walk toward the house. "But it would be nice to move slightly further away from the pack. Whilst we have no issue with you or anyone here, we aren't used to so much... company."

I nodded, even though I had no idea what he was talking about.

With a sigh, Davion explained. "It's not impossible for us to drink shifter blood, and James is still very newly turned. It might be prudent to remove the temptation of feasting on your new friends."

"Oooohhh."

Now that, I hadn't considered.

"Of course. Let's get it opened up today and get the

measurements we need. Then, we can get a rough timescale on the glass. Do you want me to ask the pack to stick to the house and the woods at the back of the property to try and make it easier for him?" I offered.

There was a time when I would have just shrugged and chalked this up to a vampire problem. But Davion and his clan had been there for us throughout this whole mess, without question. They'd lost far more than we had, and the least we could do was make sure they were comfortable.

"That sounds agreeable. We can discuss it further when we talk about our immediate situation and try to figure out what calamity might be coming for us next."

I nodded in agreement, placing the bags I'd carried on the kitchen counter once we'd finally made it inside.

"There's a lot we need to organise and go through. I'm going to help Holly and Nash get this stuff distributed and speak with the shifters we brought back from the facility. We should meet in the office and go through our options. Shall we say, an hour from now?" I suggested, already starting a mental checklist of what needed to be done.

"Perfect, I'll run back to the house and retrieve the laptop."

"Laptop?"

"The one we recovered from the facility," Davion explained, peering inside the bags he'd just carried, pulling out a loofah and looking at it like it was the most foreign object he'd ever seen.

"What? I... Fuck! Yes!" I babbled.

Davion looked at me in amusement and then, with a nod of his head, disappeared out of the house. Not one for good-byes, that guy.

As I watched him leave, I tuned in to the house and the sounds around me. I could hear the kids banging about upstairs and hoped it wasn't disturbing Calli. I knew she wouldn't be alone right now, but that didn't stop me from wanting to go to her. Sometimes I hated being the alpha. Putting everyone else first meant you always came last. Most days, I didn't mind it. But when my mate was lying injured in bed, I wanted the reassurance of curling up at her side to make sure no one could get anywhere near her.

"Grey!" Holly snapped.

Turning back to where she was standing at the counter with her hands on her hips, I realised she must have been talking to me while I was zoned out worrying about Calli.

"I said, I think we should organise these into basic kits and hand them out to everyone. There are a few specific items we grabbed for people and other things we picked up that I thought they might need, but we can always set up a station somewhere for people to collect them. I also made sure to put together some things for the women. Has anyone seen them today?"

I wanted to say no, but the reality was I had no fucking idea.

"Has anyone been to check on them?" Holly asked incredulously.

"I've been running the borders, making sure we're safe," I protested.

"I thought Davion's clan were doing that."

A soft growl rumbled out of me at the sense of the challenge in her tone. Nash wisely stepped in front of Holly, moving her out of view as he tried to defuse the situation. My wolf was on edge, and the slightest thing was all it would take for him to snap.

"Holly isn't issuing you a challenge, alpha," he told me respectfully. "She's just concerned for them."

I had to remind myself that Holly hadn't been raised as a

shifter, nor had she been part of a pack before. This was all new to her, but Nash needed to make sure she was better appraised of our way of life if she was going to avoid any misunderstandings that could end up with her getting hurt. We might not have lived by the old ways, but some rules still applied—namely, you didn't challenge an alpha unless you planned on backing it up with violence.

I could hear Holly grumbling behind Nash, not liking the way he'd stepped in between us.

"Perhaps you could both check on them while you take the supplies you obtained. It would also be wise of you to explain to your mate what she just did." I didn't want there to be a harsh snap to my tone, but it was there nonetheless.

I couldn't be the easy, laid back alpha anymore. I'd realised that when I was out for my run. There were so many vulnerable people here relying on me, and I wouldn't let them down the same way their alphas before had done. It was almost like fate had turned up the power inside me, knowing what I was going to face. Knowing how many people would be coming to us needing our help.

Over the last couple of months, I'd changed. I was embracing my role more than I ever had before. It wasn't like I hadn't been a decent alpha before. I was the alpha my pack needed back then. But they needed someone different now. They needed someone to lead them into a fight and get them through it alive. I wasn't going to fail at this. I couldn't afford to.

"Holly, I love you, babe, but right now, I need you to shut the fuck up," Nash snapped.

I heard her gasp of outrage before she fell silent. Nash would be paying for that later, no doubt.

Holly spun around and started to very noisily unload the bags on the counter. By the cringe on Nash's face, he knew what he'd done, but I wasn't about to get in the middle of it. In fact, the smartest thing to do was to slip away, and that was precisely what I did.

Moving through the downstairs, I noted all of the new shifters, cataloguing their faces and looking out for anyone who needed any extra attention. Apart from the fact they were all run down and in shock from what had happened, there were very few serious injuries. In fact, the shifter Calli had healed seemed to be the only one suffering from anything that serious. The rest all seemed to be suffering the effects of malnutrition and neglect, which was bad enough, but at least now that they were here, it wouldn't be life-threatening.

We'd brought twenty shifters back to the pack, not including Kai. Six had gone to Cassia and Hunter's cabin, and fourteen had remained here. The two women had taken one of the rooms upstairs, and the twelve others were adult males. They seemed to have split evenly between the lounge and the dining room, and whilst it wasn't the best situation, we'd coped for the night.

The three witches who'd come back with us had stayed huddled together in the alcove beneath the stairs. They seemed to want to stay clear of the shifters, and I couldn't blame them. I'd seen the sideways glances they'd been getting, and they had to be feeling pretty vulnerable right now.

If we could get the clan out to Calli's house, that would free up one of the cabins. The shifter Calli had healed, Danny, seemed to be part of a pack of five. If we placed them in the cabin, that would leave… fuck, where was a pen when you needed one.

As I was fishing my phone out of my pocket to start making some preliminary notes, Holly stormed up the stairs with a backpack thrown over each shoulder.

Nash stood at the bottom of the steps, watching forlornly as she walked away. When he turned and saw me watching him, he shrugged. "We agreed that I'd do the packs down here while she went to talk to the women."

"Agreed on that, did you?"

"Well, Holly expressed what would happen, and I didn't argue. It was kind of a silent agreement." He grinned. "Anyway, you realise this is your fault?"

"Not exactly. She needs to know what life in a pack is going to be like, Nash. We should have dealt with this earlier."

"We should have dealt with a lot of stuff earlier," he said quietly as we both turned back to the kitchen to distribute the supplies.

When I stepped into the kitchen, I was actually surprised by what Holly had achieved. I wasn't even going to pretend that Nash had done more than drive and push the cart because I'd known him for far too long for that.

They'd bought plain backpacks and filled them with the basic toiletries and some sets of clothes for each person. There was even a pair of tennis shoes beside each pack.

"Holly got all their sizes before we left," Nash explained.

I nodded in acknowledgement because I didn't know what to say. We should have stuff like this on hand, and I made a mental note to talk to Holly about setting up an area of the basement where we could start pooling basic supplies like this. If the pack was going to grow in size, we would need to start bulk shopping anyway. Store prices would be killing us soon enough with the amount we were buying at their inflated prices.

A brown tag hung from the handle of each bag, clearly marked with a name. Of course, she'd asked them for their names when none of the rest of us had even bothered.

"It will probably be easier to get everyone to collect their own bag unless you know all the faces that go with these names," I pointed out.

Nash cringed, and I at least had the comfort of knowing I wasn't the only one.

"I'll go and speak with them all. Do you want to wait here in case anyone has any questions?" Nash offered.

"Sure."

The kitchen table was filled with pastries, fruit, cereal and drinks, and I helped myself to a danish and a bottle of water while I waited.

Every person who walked through the kitchen door looked like they were looking for where the axe would fall next. They were almost reluctant to take the food, and it wasn't until Nash, and I had both reassured them numerous times, that they dived in. It wasn't much, and they needed a proper meal, which I was going to make sure would be coming to them soon.

One more thing for the list.

The hour I had before meeting with Davion flew by. The witches had grabbed what they needed and retreated back to their corner, and I decided to get Cassia to speak with them as soon as possible. The shifters were already pretty well acquainted, having been held in the same room for so long. There were a few questions about the women we'd recovered, but they all seemed to be out of concern. Once we explained that they'd taken a room upstairs, they seemed pleased they were at least being taken care of.

The alpha from earlier, Colt, was the only one who seemed confrontational at all, but it was only in terms of the safety of his pack. We needed to get them into a separate house as soon as possible. Tension would grow quickly, having another alpha under the same roof as me, and I wasn't about to let him try to call the shots. While they were here, I was squarely in charge. He could look after his people if that was what he wanted, but at the end of the day, my word was law on these packlands.

"Colt, I'm going to speak with Davion and some of the other pack members about future arrangements in the office. It would be a good idea for you to join us." I didn't phrase it as a question as such, but he could back out if that was what he wanted.

Colt eyed me suspiciously before agreeing, and I showed him the way to the office. Davion was already there when we arrived, lounging on the couch, and Tanner was seated at Lachlan's desk.

"Maverick and River are with the kids," Tanner explained. "And Lachlan is staying with Calli."

The mention of her name had my wolf's hackles rising in annoyance at being kept away from her. Right there with you, buddy.

Cassia and Hunter silently slipped into the room next and made themselves comfortable. Hunter leaned back against the wall and pulled Cassia in front of him, so she was leaning back against his chest. It was nice to see that she was starting to feel more comfortable around the pack. There was a time when she would never have let her walls down this far around us.

"And Aidan?" I asked Tanner, trying not to make the couple uncomfortable by staring.

"I asked him to make a note of what we have in terms of food and head out to Sam's Club to get loaded up. We've got a lot of people to feed."

Making myself comfortable behind Nash's desk, I pulled out one of the iPads and opened up Notion, which Nash had started to set up as a collection of information for the pack.

"Right, first things first, we're facing a crisis because we need to make sure that the basic needs of these people are met, and we don't currently have the facilities to do that. So, what do we need, and how do we get it quickly?"

The next hour was spent going over the logistics of how we were going to house and care for twenty extra people, even if that was only temporary. Nash joined us after a while. With some negotiation, meaning, of course, more money, we now had four cabins worth of timber kits being delivered tomorrow.

Colt had been fairly quiet through most of it, interjecting here and there when he had an idea about how to improve something we were discussing. He'd kept an assessing eye on me throughout, though, and I could tell he was gearing up to say something.

"Why are you doing this?" he suddenly blurted out.

"Doing what?" Tanner asked, looking confused. I knew exactly what Colt was referring to.

"Why are you helping us? Helping them?" he asked, nodding his head to the door.

"Would you prefer we cast you all out and let you fend for yourselves? I suppose we could have just left you there when we set fire to the building," I said in amusement.

"Obviously not. I'm just wondering what the benefit here is for you. This is costing more money than I knew any one pack had. Why would you do that when there's no return in it for you?"

"Perhaps because it's the right thing to do," Calli's exhausted voice said from the doorway.

My head snapped in her direction, where she was leaning against the doorframe. Lachlan stood behind her with a slightly annoyed, exasperated look on his face.

"She should be in bed," I told him.

"Yeah, well, you try and tell her that." Lachlan sighed, even though the corner of his mouth ticked up in amusement.

I could only imagine the wrath he would have faced from our feisty mate, trying to get her to stay in bed when there was so much to do.

Colt went to stand from where he was sitting on the couch, no doubt to offer Calli his seat. It warmed me toward him slightly, knowing that he was the type of person to do that.

Calli, not realising he was about to do it, though, walked over to me and sat herself down on my lap. My wolf purred in relief as she snuggled against my chest, making herself comfortable.

"She can think for herself. And I can rest just as well here as I can in bed."

"I can't say I'm disappointed by this turn of events," I told her, kissing her lightly on the top of the head.

A piece inside of me suddenly seemed to settle. I hadn't even realised it had been raging until the calm settled around me. This woman in my arms was my absolute everything. Her soul spoke to mine in a way that no other could.

Tanner left his seat, vacating the spot, so Lachlan could sit at his desk. He pulled out an iPad, similar to the one I had, and started tapping away as the conversation slowly filtered back in about the food situation.

"Has anyone had the chance to ask them if they want to stay or be relocated?" Calli asked. "I was going to give Sean a call in a couple of hours, and it would be helpful to give him an idea on numbers."

"We haven't had much chance to speak with most of the shifters. However, the witches seem pretty adamant that they'll be leaving. I don't think they're feeling too safe being in the midst of a pack," River supplied.

"They should be cast out," Colt snapped. "And that's being generous."

"Why?" Calli asked him curiously.

If he couldn't see the shitstorm he was about to walk into, then perhaps this was a lesson he needed to learn. Davion, who had been sitting beside him on the couch, looked like he was about to clap his hands in glee as he turned in his seat to get a better view of the show that was about to go down.

"They're witches," Colt spat. "They're responsible for the hunts. For all of the pain and suffering we've been through. I only had a small pack, and we lost over half of our members when the witches blazed through our packlands. Those of us that are left were herded together and thrown into that cage. You have no idea what we've been through."

"You're right. I don't. And I hope to be able to sit down with you and speak to you about it if that's something you'd be comfortable with. But you need to understand that not all witches are the same. Just as not all shifters are. That facility you were in was on packlands. It was organised and run by a shifter. One of our Council members, no less. Of all the things I've been through recently, they've been done by both sides. We all have responsibility for what is happening, and we're all just as guilty for spilling blood. If you can't be in a pack that shelters witches, you need to leave. Those three men aren't the only witches here. I'm half-witch, and you didn't seem to have a problem with that when I was healing your friend."

Calli didn't raise her voice. Instead, she spoke calmly and politely, and I'd never been more proud of her. Davion almost looked disappointed.

Colt sat staring at her for a moment, his mouth opening and then closing as he tried to organise his thoughts. In the end, he just said, "Okay." And leaned back in his seat, his brow furrowed in thought.

Whether that okay meant they were leaving or okay, he'd accept that and was going to stay was something I guess we would find out later.

"Cassia, can you speak with the three witches to see what they want to do? They'll probably be more comfortable speaking with you," Calli asked.

Cassia nodded in thought, eying Colt suspiciously and staying silent on the matter.

"I think it would do them good to stay. I think I can help one of them improve his healing skills. It would be nice to teach someone the same things my mother taught me," Calli said, more to herself than anyone else.

I clung to her a little tighter because I knew how much it hurt Calli to think about her parents sometimes. Since Sean's revelation that they'd been murdered, she'd been pretty quiet on the subject of her parents. Especially once Jessa had told her she could only see the future and not the past. I had no idea how we would get answers for Calli on what had happened to her parents, but we had to find a way. With everything she did for those around her, Calli deserved to have some peace herself. But I was worried about what we'd potentially uncover. Not knowing the truth could be haunting, but sometimes reality could be so much worse. There were some things that we were better off not knowing. We could only hope this wasn't one of those.

"If you trust them, I think they'd be more comfortable if we relocated them to the library," I told Calli as the thought struck me. "It would give them space to be alone, rather than huddled in that corner of the hallway, and it's not like they can read the books anyway."

I watched the twitch in Colt's eye as we discussed making

the three witches more comfortable. Really, we should have sent them to stay with Cassia. I was sure they would have been far more comfortable with just Hunter there than the number of shifters in the packhouse. The problem was with the lack of space we currently had. We needed to put more bodies in Cassia's house than just the three of them. When you started to add other shifters into the mix, it negated the whole reason for sending them there.

"How long do you think it will take before the cabins are up and habitable?" Colt finally asked, deciding not to address what was actually bothering him.

"I suppose it depends if anyone has the strength and the knowledge to assist us in putting them together. If not, it's going to be at least a month."

And that was the problem. We had an immediate need with these people and no immediate solutions.

"Before we get ahead of ourselves, why don't we talk to everyone and see what kind of numbers we're looking at," Nash suggested. "We might be panicking over nothing. They may all want to leave, and if that's the case, we only have to house them until Sean can make alternative arrangements."

"Who is this Sean you keep talking about?" Colt asked. "And why will he be able to help the people who want to leave?"

I looked to Calli to answer that question. She was better suited to gauging how much information was supposed to be shared with others. The rest of us were still relatively new to the idea that the underground even existed.

"Sean and a group of people run a… well, an underground railroad. They help people escape when they're in danger of being persecuted," Calli told him.

Colt sat up in interest, his focus solely back on my mate again.

"I've heard rumours," he said slowly. "I can't believe it's actually real."

Colt looked around the room and seemed to see us all with fresh eyes. Perhaps now he understood why we were helping them. We might not have much to do with the underground, but we were like-minded people, and we'd do whatever needed to be done to help them in their mission, especially after everything we'd seen and been through.

"If the rest of my pack agree, I'd like to stay," Colt said slowly, his eyes turning back to me as he seemed to assess the problem he no doubt realised would come from them being here. "If you can provide us with the supplies, we have the skills to put together our own cabin and assist with the others."

"That would help," Nash said absent-mindedly, not seeing the bigger issue yet. "If the five of you can help, that would effectively half the timescale on erecting the buildings."

Tanner, being the good beta he was, saw the issue straight away. "This pack already has an alpha," he pointed out.

"Yeah. I'm more than aware of that. And, if my pack wishes to stay here, I'll step down as their alpha if you'll have us."

The sadness that lined his voice made me feel bad for him, but the reality of the situation was that there couldn't be two alphas in one pack.

"That doesn't seem right," Calli said with a frown.

"It is what it is." Colt shrugged like it didn't matter, but we could all see how much it was tearing him up inside.

"I know how hard this decision is, and if they want to stay with us, you're more than welcome. When you've had a chance to speak to them, come to me, and we can talk more," I offered. This would be hard for him, and if there was anything I could do to help him with the transition, I would.

The reality was we needed to expand the pack, and Colt and his pack were ideal candidates for that if they could get on board with the situation here. I wouldn't accept them if they were going to make Calli or Lachlan's life difficult, though. Although, watching Hunter take them down a peg or two if they decided to look at Cassia wrong could be fun.

"Okay, well, we have an idea on housing. We should have the food and clothing situation sorted for at least the next few days in a couple of hours. All we can do now is speak with everyone to see what they want to do and then work from there," I told the group.

"Nash, why don't you go with Colt to speak with the shifters? See if you can get an idea on numbers," I suggested.

Colt eyed me suspiciously, realising I was trying to get rid of him. I couldn't get a firm read on the guy yet. In any event, he didn't need to be part of the next conversation until he'd had more time to heal. The best thing he could do for now was being there for his packmates.

Nash left the office without a word of argument, as I'd known he would. We probably could have done with keeping him with us for what we were going to talk about, but he was also the best person for the job at speaking with the shifters.

Once the door was firmly closed behind Colt, I turned to look at Davion. "Have you tried to access the laptop?" I asked, getting straight to the point.

Everyone else in the room seemed confused, so Davion filled them in. "I was able to recover a laptop from the lab on the way out, as Calli suggested. And no, there hasn't really been time to investigate the contents yet. I'd be surprised if it wasn't password-protected, though, it's fairly commonplace nowadays, and I don't have the necessary skills to hack through any password, even the standard minor ones."

Davion shrugged like it was no big deal, but the reality

was I doubted many of us would be able to do it either. We were a pack of small-town shifters. Before all this started to happen around us, the most we had to deal with was a supplier trying to overcharge on parts. Hell, I was a damn mechanic by trade, not a general.

Lachlan looked across at Davion, or more specifically, the laptop pushed down between him and the couch.

"Can I have a look at it?" Lachlan asked, holding out his hand.

Davion shrugged, and the laptop was passed around the room until it ended up in Lachlan's hand.

"I may not be able to get through the password myself, but I have some minor skills in opening up the minimum security requirements. If Nash can't do it either, I may know someone."

Colour me impressed. Did that mean Lachlan had hacker friends? Either way, it was the best bet we had right now.

Lachlan opened up the laptop and nodded when the password screen appeared. "It's encrypted, and it looks to be a secondary program rather than the standard screen you'd get when booting up. I'll look at it, but I can put some feelers out for decryption software in the meantime."

It was then that Lachlan seemed to zone out as he randomly started pressing keys, doing whatever it was that someone trying to hack into a laptop would do.

"Does anyone else find it strange that they'd have a computer with encryption software?" Tanner asked.

He'd sat down in one of the spare office chairs that had been shoved in the corner of the room when we'd refurbished, and was currently spinning around in it while he stared up at the ceiling.

"Think about it. Daddy dearest decides, I think today I'm going to start experimenting on my people and set up a super-secret torture facility," he said in a voice that was actually pretty accurate for Councilman Stone. "So he goes to Bad Guys R Us and gets his torture equipment to set up his lab, finds like-minded evil people with a similar interest in torture and gets about the business of whatever they were doing. But at the end of the day, he's still just a normal, yet mostly evil, person. Why would he then seek out encryption software for his computer equipment? As far as he's concerned, he's untouchable, and no one knows about the torture kingdom anyway. Why bother?"

It was a good question, I supposed. I could see that as a private person and not some government body, you might not consider encrypting a computer. But Stone was also paranoid as fuck. That was probably how he'd gotten as far as he had in life.

"Perhaps the laptop belongs to one of these lackeys he hired?" Davion posed, seeming rather disinterested. "It could have already been encrypted before they went to work with Stone."

Another good point, and at this stage. I wasn't really sure it was something we needed to be worrying about.

"No point worrying until we can find out what's in the laptop," Calli pointed out, mirroring my thoughts. "The bigger concern is what we're going to do if we face any blowback from burning down the facility. Even if Stone doesn't outright attack us, he could still call us before the Council. It's been some time since he used the excuse of needing to see me for research purposes."

I'd been thinking the exact same thing when I was out on my run earlier. The easiest way for Stone to get rid of us would be to call us to the Council for another of those fucking meetings, and then never let us leave again. It would be easy enough, and I suspected all of the missing prisoners who made their way through the cells at the Council headquarters ended up at his facility. Once we were out of the way, it would be easy for him to send his pet witches here to pick up the rest. Or at least it would have been if we were still alone. Now that we had Davion on our side and Sean supporting us, sporadically at least, I had a feeling it would be harder than Stone would anticipate.

Regardless, that didn't help if we were issued with a summons.

There was only one thing I could think of that could potentially help us if it came to that, and I had no desire to be further in Wells' pocket.

6
CALLI

I was so tired, my bones ached. My entire body felt like it had been drained of blood, and it had been replaced with fire ants, which were currently making some kind of conga line journey through me.

In other words, I felt like shit.

After the doom and gloom meeting in the office, we'd left Lachlan pouring over the laptop. Tanner and Grey had gone outside to map out where the cabins would go, muttering about plumbing and stuff. To be honest, I'd zoned out during that conversation because it was insanely boring.

All I wanted to do was crawl back into bed and sleep for a week, but there was stuff I needed to do, and first things first, I wanted to see the kids. I was starting to crave time with the little troublemakers, especially with the way they seemed to be able to make you forget about all the other crap going on.

It wasn't hard to find them. I could hear the racket as I started to drag myself up the stairs. Needless to say, I located them in Coby's bedroom playing a game with Maverick. Abby was sitting on Maverick's knee, and Jacob was next to them, apparently they were a team, and Coby and Kai were playing as the other team.

I took a moment to watch their light-hearted fun as they threw down their cards, smack-talking each other in a way that only kids could. Then, Abby drew a card, and a crestfallen look fell on her face as everyone else cheered 'exploding kittens' and threw their cards down.

"What on Earth are you playing?" I laughed, loving the happy vibe in the room.

"Exploding kittens!" Jacob cheered excitedly before he launched into an explanation of how to play.

"Well, I'm glad you're all having fun. How's your day been?"

I was anxious to talk to Kai to make sure he was settling in alright, but I didn't know what, if anything, the guys would have spoken to him about yet, and I didn't want to push him too much. Remembering how I'd been when Tanner had tried to insert himself into our lives—what seemed like so long ago—I didn't want Kai to swing to the extreme of pushing us away out of fear.

"Great!" Jacob cheered. "We've been hanging out."

"Well, that does sound fun." I laughed.

Coby and Kai looked at each other and rolled their eyes, and I nearly burst out laughing at the way they'd bonded so quickly. Hopefully, Jacob and Abby wouldn't get pushed out of the big boys' group. Although, Coby wasn't exactly that much older than the other two kids.

Maverick leaned back on his hands, and his eyes roamed across my body. I knew he was assessing how I was feeling, but I still felt that stare like a caress across my skin.

"You should be in bed," he finally told me.

"Don't you start with me," I all but growled at him.

In all seriousness, I could feel the exhaustion setting in,

and it wouldn't be long before I did retreat back to bed. In the meantime, though, I wanted to actually do something that didn't make me feel like an old lady.

"Can we go and get Kai his bedroom furniture tomorrow?" Abby asked me, excitedly jumping up and running toward me. Clinging to the hem of my shirt with her two little fists, she looked up at me with her big manipulative kid eyes —you know the look. "I've done it twice now, and I'm super good at it."

She wasn't wrong there.

"Well, I'm not sure where Kai's bedroom will be," I realised as I considered her question. "He might have to share with one of you guys until we have fewer people in the house."

"He can share my room!" Coby suddenly shouted, and I actually did laugh that time.

Lord, these kids were adorable.

"I was going to suggest he take my room," Maverick said sheepishly. "It's just across the hall from the kids, and then he can have his own space."

"But then, where will you sleep?" Abby asked.

Maverick flushed a deep red at the obvious answer to the question that her child brain couldn't reach.

"Well, we've been talking about finishing off the rooms on the top floor, which will make some more room," I added to save him.

Maverick gave me a grateful look, and then a slow grin stretched across his face as a wave of heat seemed to wash over me. Now really was not the time or the place for this. Maybe I *should* take a nap…

"That means we can go shopping!" Abby suddenly realised doing a happy little jig where she stood.

Kai seemed a bit reluctant about the idea and nervously

shifted on the spot. He was old enough to make his own decision, with the help of a grown-up, and we were kind of talking over him right now.

"We can go shopping if Kai is comfortable with that," I settled with. "And we can get as much or as little as he's going to need. There will be plenty of time for shopping in the future if he doesn't want to do it all in one go."

Kai seemed to sigh in relief, and I decided it was a good call to take some of the pressure off him.

"Okay, but we can still get ice cream on the way home, right?" Abby asked.

"Oh, and pie!" Coby added.

"Do you guys ever get full?" Maverick laughed.

Only to have Abby protest, "I'm not a guy, Daddy Mav!" like the mere insinuation was an insult.

"I'm sure he didn't mean it like that," I said, trying to placate her, even if the pout she currently had was cute as hell.

As the exhaustion started to settle in around me more, I leaned heavily against the doorframe. Maverick's keen eyes seemed to notice the movement, and he stood up from the floor in one fluid movement and prowled toward me.

"Come and lie down with me for a bit?" he asked, leaning in to whisper in my ear, so the kids wouldn't hear.

I knew he was just trying to make me go and lie down and was using himself to sweeten the deal. I wasn't stupid, though, and I would definitely take him up on the offer.

"I'm going to take a nap," I told the kids, and Jacob looked up at me with his eyes full of worry. "Don't worry, bud. I just need some sleep to get my energy back up."

He nodded seriously. "You've used too much again," he accused.

"And what would you know about that, little man." I

laughed. He looked so much like our mother at that moment that it hurt my heart. She'd get the same pinched look between her eyebrows whenever she chastised me for wanting to use my magic.

"More than you, apparently," he snarked back at me, making Maverick guffaw in laughter.

"Oh, is that right? Maybe we should get you back in those magic lessons then, little man," I challenged.

Jacob puffed up in that way only men could, even when they were still little boys, ready to take on the challenge.

"You can do magic?" Kai asked, his eyes wide in wonder as he stared at Jacob.

Perhaps he would make it into the cool guys club after all.

"So you can all do magic, and you can shift?" Kai asked carefully, almost like he was sensing there was a trap in there somewhere.

As if to prove a point, Jacob quickly shifted into a wolf pup and got the zoomies around the bedroom.

The shocked look on Kai's face soon turned to laughter at his antics.

"Yes, the kids can shift," I explained to Kai. "But Abby and Jacob are the only ones who can do magic. Coby is a full blood shifter. Although I suppose there is the possibility that he will get some form of magic through the pack bond, we don't really fully understand that situation just yet."

Kai's laughter stalled, and his eyes widened in surprise again. "So if I stay in the pack, I'll get magic?" he asked excitedly.

"Let's not get ahead of ourselves, squirt." Maverick laughed as he tried to scoop up the unruly wolf pup tearing around him. "You should decide if you want to join the pack based on if you like us and not because you might get magic.

But, like Calli said, we don't really know what will happen with all that yet. It might not happen."

The words of caution were too late, and I could see the excitement starting to set into Coby as well. I shouldn't have brought it up, and I was kicking myself for mentioning it. What kid wouldn't want magic? Especially at their age.

"River said we could go for a pack run," Coby suddenly blurted out. "Can we, can we, can weeeeeee? Pleeeeeease?"

"Okay." I laughed as his eyes turned comically big to accompany his pleading. "If Grey says it's okay too, then I'm on board. I won't be coming with you, though, I need to rest. If you go out, you have to make sure you stick with the pack and do as you're told. No wandering off alone. We still don't know how safe it is out there."

"Awwww, you're not coming," Coby sulked.

"I can't, sweetheart. I promise I would if I could." It was nice to know the kids wanted me there, but I wasn't stupid. At this rate, I'd barely make it to the bedroom. As much as I wanted to bound through the forest with this bunch of troublemakers, it was not on the cards for me today.

"We can wait," Abby said sweetly. "We want you to come too."

I could see the disappointment on Coby's face at my not going now. When you were a kid, it was all or nothing and waiting was something the devil invented to torture you. Oh, to be young.

"I won't be upset if you want to go without me. We can always go again later," I placated them.

I could feel the weariness starting to pull me down. I'd pushed too far past my limits today, and it was a miracle I was still up and about.

"Come on," Maverick said gently, pulling me to his side. "You need to rest."

"Can we come visit later?" Jacob asked as he shifted back into the precocious little boy he was.

"Of course, buddy. You can always come to visit."

"Let's leave Calli to get a bit of sleep first," Maverick added, looking at me worriedly.

"Behave yourselves," I called out as Maverick started to lead me out of the room, having given up on waiting for me to go by myself.

If I could, I would have stayed with the kids all day. Hiding away in that room and playing games was definitely something I'd rather do than be facing the reality of our current situation. But sleep was calling to me, and I was powerless to resist, especially when I had a snuggle buddy lined up already.

"You need to look after yourself better," Maverick chided as he led me back into Tanner's room, closing the door behind me.

I didn't argue. He was right, and I knew he was. Maverick slipped out of his jeans before starting to help me undress. It was a testament to how tired I was that it wasn't getting me all hot and bothered.

As he tucked me into bed, Maverick gently kissed my forehead. "Sleep, sweetheart. We've got everything from here."

I knew it didn't all have to rest on my shoulders, and sometimes I wondered what it said about me that I acted like it did at times. But hearing Maverick say those words soothed me enough that when I closed my eyes, I fell into a deep, peaceful sleep rather than the fitful stressed-out dreams that usually plagued me.

7
TANNER

After the meeting in the office, I headed out with Grey to measure where we could put the new cabins. We didn't have a lack of land, but we weren't prepared for this many buildings to go up so soon.

We had two clear plots and one we could potentially work with if we rotated the frame in the other direction. We'd probably have to take one of the trees out nearby for safety reasons, but I'd already convinced myself that turning it away from the other cabins would at least give the occupants the illusion of privacy.

"These three will be a lot closer together than I'd wanted them to be," Grey said in concern as we stood back and looked over the marked out areas.

It wasn't ideal, but we were also in a beggars-can't-be-choosers type situation. There was nowhere else suitable to put the bases down. As it was, we'd have to clear some land to get the footprint down for the fourth cabin.

"How long until we can get the Bobcat in here to dig out the foundations?" Grey asked.

"Nash has a connection with someone who apparently

owes him a favour. They've got one we can borrow. We can pick it up first thing tomorrow."

I hadn't asked what that favour was. None of us would. But I had a strange feeling this favour he was owed had to do with something illegal, and before all this happened, I'd never have thought Nash had it in him.

"Okay, first thing in the morning, we get the digger in and get these areas cleared and prepped. We should be able to order the cement to have the foundations poured next week if we work in shifts," Grey told me, staring down at the iPad he'd brought out with him as we walked back to the front of the house. "Check in with Nash and River to see how many takers we have to stay on. If we only had to put two cabins down in that area, it would be a lot better for the future."

"I'll check in with them after I force you to take a break to eat something," I said, eyeing Grey to see what he would say.

Grey had thrown himself into this situation head-on and was blazing through, trying to get everything organised as quickly as possible. It was admirable, but I wasn't going to sit back and let him do it at the expense of himself.

We needed him more than ever now that the pack was expanding, and we still had the threat of the Council sitting on the horizon. The pack couldn't afford for Grey to work himself to the point of exhaustion.

With a sigh, he actually looked up from the screen and made eye contact with me. "We can eat and talk at the same time," he said with a grin on his face.

I'd take it. At least he wasn't going to try and fight me on it.

"And while we're at it, I want an update on the two women upstairs," Grey said, striding towards the front door in full business mode again. "I'm worried about how they're dealing with this whole thing and how we can get them the help they need. I don't want them to feel like they're not welcome here, but Sean's contacts probably have more experience dealing with trauma like this than we do."

I knew what he meant. What had happened to the two of them was something that needed specialised care. Care none of us were qualified to give them.

We didn't have time to discuss it any further. As we approached the front door, the unpleasant sensation of tingles running down my spine alerted us that someone had just crossed over the wards.

"For fuck's sake," Grey muttered. "If this is Stone or any other fucker from the Council, I'm just killing them and facing the consequences."

"Wow, someone got out of bed on the wrong side this morning," I joked, knowing full well that Grey had laid on the floor until giving up on sleep and running the perimeters. The kitchen table hadn't looked like a comfortable place to nap when I'd found him this morning.

I'd have gone for the run with him, but I had prime mate side real estate at the time. I'd already missed out on taking the credit for donuts this morning. It was every man for himself in this pack now. Well, not really, but it seemed like it at times.

We stood shoulder to shoulder, waiting for whoever was approaching the house. When a dark SUV rolled down the driveway, it was hard to tell who it was. Why did everyone buy the same type of fucking car?

The SUV pulled to a stop a few metres away from us after it turned to face back the way it had come. That had me thinking. This was someone planning ahead for a quick exit, and I couldn't decide if that was good or bad for us.

When a woman I didn't recognise stepped out of the vehicle, I was more than a little surprised. When I scented that she was human, I was downright shocked.

"Something we can help you with?" Grey growled. "This is private property, you know?"

We weren't exactly the friendliest bunch when it came to strangers coming onto packlands. We could just about tolerate locals coming by when they needed something, but they weren't complete strangers. And this woman screamed out-of-towner.

Reaching into her jacket pocket, she pulled out a wallet. I immediately recognised it for what it was as she flipped it open and passed it across to Grey. FBI. As if this whole thing wasn't just getting curiouser and curiouser.

"My name is Special Agent Milner. Mind if I come inside to have a word?"

"Yes, I absolutely do mind," Grey said flatly.

Antagonising the human law enforcement was just what we needed when we had the Shifter Council breathing down our necks.

The Agent in front of us squinted in annoyance, but there wasn't much she could do about it. We knew our rights, and she couldn't make us take her inside the house.

"Very well, I suppose we can do this out here."

"Actually, we don't have to do this at all. Unless you have a warrant, I'm under no obligation to talk to you," Grey pointed out.

"Okay, I think we've got off on the wrong foot," she smiled, raising her hands in the air and cocking her head to the side in an attempt at an innocent look. "I'm in the area investigating a number of missing people. A lot of people have disappeared in the surrounding area, including one James Gallagher from this town. I'm just asking around to see if anyone has seen anything suspicious," she told us with a shrug.

"We haven't seen anything."

Grey was going for the brief and to the point approach. Ordinarily, I would have agreed with him, but I wasn't sure antagonising this woman was the best way forward. We were hiding a lot right now. The last thing we needed was the human law enforcement agencies paying attention to us.

"We don't get into town much," I said with a friendly smile, drawing her attention to me and away from the bristling alpha next to me. "We tend to pretty much keep to ourselves. You'd be best asking the folks at the diner. They tend to hear all the gossip about what's happening around here."

"Yeah, I checked in there earlier this morning," she told me, actually leaning to the side to look around me. Okay, now I was getting annoyed too. "They told me you guys used to run a profitable business in town. The local garage, right? They also told me that you've not been working for a while. Seemed to shut up shop out of the blue. They thought it was a bit strange. You folks having a get-together or something?" she asked, suddenly changing the subject, her keen eyes watching the movement inside the house through the windows.

"Family reunion. There have been some problems in the family. Everyone's pulling together to help out. The business will still be there in the spring when we come back to it," I shrugged, stepping in the direction of her vehicle.

Thankfully, she took the hint and walked with me back to the driver's side door.

"Big family you've got here," she commented casually, but I was on to her by now, so was Grey, it would seem.

"Family can mean a lot to people like us," he said gruffly.

"Hmm, people like you. Yeah, I had heard that too."

I nearly stumbled forward at the insinuation in her comment. Did this woman know we were shifters? A few people in town knew, but I'd bet my life on it that none of them would have told her. No, it couldn't be possible. The Council would never have let information like this leak out. They had safeguards in place to ensure that it didn't. There was no way this would've made it up to the fucking FBI. No, she had to mean something else.

"Well, this is my card. If anything happens that you think could assist me, I'd be grateful to get a call," she said, climbing into the car. Before she shut the door, she added, "Folk around here seem to come from all walks of life, but these missing people will have something that links them together. Things like this can't just disappear into a file somewhere."

"I'm sure you'll get to the bottom of it," I told her, not knowing what I was supposed to say.

It was almost like she was trying to give me a hidden message, but the only one I could see was one she couldn't possibly know herself.

We watched her drive away, making sure to wait until that tingle down our spine signified she'd left our lands and hadn't doubled back around.

"This is a problem," Grey grumbled.

"Oh goody, we haven't had a new one of those for a whole twenty minutes. I was worried it was about to get boring around here."

8
LACHLAN

After twenty minutes of looking at it, I wanted to pick the laptop up and throw it across the office. The encryption software was way past anything I'd ever dealt with. In fact, the only thing I'd ever dealt with was a general windows password when someone had forgotten their login details. I had no idea what possessed me to think I could do this alone. Everyone else seemed so prepared to help, and here I was, sitting in the corner with no practical skills to offer the pack.

Shortly after coming to that realisation, I'd fled the office and retreated to the library, where there was at least a small amount of quiet for now. This would soon be offered to the three witches if they decided to stay with us, and then there wouldn't be any refuge in this place.

What I wouldn't give to be able to take off for a run like the shifters could. The freedom to get a moment's peace would be highly appreciated right now. Except, I did have that ability, didn't I? Or I assumed I still did. The shift I'd gone through hadn't exactly been something I'd done on purpose, and I had no idea if it was something I could replicate. At the time, it had been the panic of realising we were about to lose. Seeing Neressa closing in on Calli had made something inside of me snap, and it just sort of happened on its own.

I had no idea how to replicate what had occurred, and I wasn't sure I even wanted to. It wasn't exactly painful, but I'd never experienced fear like that before, and I had no desire to do so again.

Slumping down into what was now my favourite armchair, I sighed in annoyance. There was so much about myself I felt like I didn't know. My magic had never been strong, but at least it was a familiar presence, and now I didn't even understand that any more.

Looking inside myself, I sank into my well of magic, examining the changes that had started to occur inside me. They'd been slow at first. Barely noticeable. But the closer I'd come to Calli, the more I'd sensed that something was different.

The coven bond was there, wrapping around my magic, but not in a restrictive way. It was almost like I'd become linked to a river of magic that flowed through each coven member. That river fed into me, giving me access to things I'd never realised I was missing before. And in turn, it flowed out of me to the others.

It was a far more intimate connection than I'd ever anticipated a coven bond would be. And I was even more grateful now that I'd never had one with the coven I was with before I came here. They'd never seen me as worthy of such a bond. But now, knowing everything I did, I could recognise that it was them that hadn't been worthy. Just one more thing Calli had given me—the start of some confidence in myself.

But as I examined the magic inside, I could also feel the binding around it. It was like an itch. I'd gone a whole lifetime without noticing it, but now that I'd acknowledged it, there was a buzz, like an incessant reminder it was there.

It was hard to believe I'd never felt it before, but maybe the way my magic was changing had something to do with it. Either way, I could feel it now, and I could also feel the binding weakening. It felt thin in places, almost like an elastic band that had been stretched too far. It was only a matter of time before it broke, and something about that terrified me as much as it intrigued me.

My magic had to have been bound for a reason. What if that reason was that it was dangerous? I wouldn't be able to live with myself if I hurt any of the pack. Fuck, if it was one of the kids, I didn't know what I'd do.

I made a decision to talk with Cassia and Calli about it tomorrow. We needed to try and break it ourselves in controlled circumstances. Perhaps then we'd be able to contain any backlash to make sure no one was hurt. If that wasn't an option, then the only thing to do would be to reinforce the binding and keep everything contained.

A commotion started further inside the house, probably somewhere around the kitchen. But I didn't get up to see what was happening. I'd been too used to being alone, and the pack had potentially tripled in size overnight. That was a few too many people for me right now.

Perhaps I could see if Calli had finally given in to her exhaustion and gone back to sleep. Crawling into bed beside her seemed like the perfect way to pass a few hours. And it wouldn't exactly be a hardship to hold her while she slept.

I could feel the bond between us crying out to be completed, and I wanted her so fucking much. But, every time we'd gotten close to completing the mate bond, something had interrupted us. I didn't know how much longer I could hold off before I exploded. And now she was hurt, again!

Maybe my unrestrained magic would allow me to study healing magic like Calli had. That would definitely come in handy if things around here continued like they had been, and I had a terrible feeling they would.

Deciding to seize the moment, I quietly left the library and slipped upstairs, avoiding whatever was happening in the kitchen. I hadn't spotted Calli downstairs in my brief glance, so I hoped I'd find her upstairs instead.

When I reached the top of the stairs, I could hear the laughter coming from the kids inside one of the rooms. At least all of the upheaval below wasn't affecting them. This was their home, and it seemed to be in a constant state of flux at the moment. There had been a plan to get the homeschool started up, but it seemed to have been placed on the back-burner with everything the pack was dealing with.

Maybe that was something I could do to help out. The duties I'd picked up in the office helping Nash had occupied me, but now that we were moving into the construction projects, it was fairly outside my expertise. I had enough work to keep me busy for a few hours a day, setting up some other minor things, but I could take this on to help out everyone else.

It would do the kids good to get back into a routine, not that they'd probably thank me for making school that routine.

Most of the doors on this level were closed, so I decided to start in Tanner's room, where we'd all ended up last night. Before I came here, I never thought I'd be comfortable sleeping in a room full of other men, let alone men with whom I shared a mate. But last night had been exactly what I'd needed after everything we'd been through.

No one had slept well, but there was a comfort in knowing you weren't alone. That someone who completely understood the chaos running through your mind was right there, and you only needed to reach out to them.

I shouldn't have been surprised that she wasn't alone. Calli had a lot of mates, and we had people in the house we didn't truly know. None of us would trust her to be alone while she was still vulnerable and weakened. But seeing her laying on the bed wrapped in Maverick's arms, I had the sudden sense that I was intruding.

Thankfully, Calli was asleep, getting some much-needed rest. A part of me settled, seeing her taking some time to recover. Calli thought too much of others to the detriment of herself. She might not know it, but she truly was the centre of this pack.

I was about to quietly back out of the room and leave them alone when I saw Maverick's eyes were open, and he was watching me carefully.

Before I could move from my spot by the door, he reached out and pulled the covers down on the other side of Calli, nodding me toward it in a quiet invitation.

Toeing off my shoes, I carefully climbed in beside them. Calli had rolled onto her side, and Maverick was wrapped around her back, holding her while she slept. Turning on my side to face her, I moved her hair from her face, tucking it behind her ear as I ran my fingers through the silky golden strands. She sighed happily in her sleep and continued sleeping.

"You were going to leave," Maverick whispered from behind her.

Leaning up on one elbow, Maverick peered over the top of Calli, so he could see me.

"I didn't want to disturb you," I said with a shrug.

"You wouldn't be disturbing us," Maverick said with a frown. "You belong by her side. By our side."

For some reason, those few words meant so much to me. I didn't feel like I was part of the pack. I had the coven bond with Calli, but there were times when I wondered if the shifters here just tolerated me. After all, none of them had good experiences with witches, and I was starting to realise the reality of the world outside of the coven was a lot different to what witches were led to believe.

The shifters were subjected to hunts, and whilst it may not have been every witch that partook, or even every coven, it was enough that they all lived in fear of it. Every shifter had a story of someone they knew who'd been affected by the hunts, whether it was someone they shared a pack with or someone in a nearby pack. The fear of the hunt was an everyday reality for them.

Witches were raised to believe that it was only Neressa's rogue coven who undertook the hunts. That they were isolated incidents, few and far between. We believed the shifters unfairly blamed us all, tarnishing us with their hatred when we had done nothing wrong. But Calli was right. If that had been true, and it had been the actions of one coven, we'd collectively had the power to stop what they were doing. Instead, we were so concerned with the wrongly placed blame, we did nothing to solve the problem.

Now, seeing how these people lived, seeing that they weren't the vicious monsters we were all told they were, I felt a sense of shame about my own lack of action, but also my lack of concern. How could I have heard about the hunts and not be absolutely horrified by the facts? How was it possible I'd lived in a world which had numbed me to the horror of what was happening without even realising it?

Seeing the faces of the people we pulled out of that facility, the sheer number of women displayed in those tanks, there was absolutely no doubt in my mind that this couldn't be the actions of just a few witches in one rogue coven.

Now that the clouds had been cleared from my eyes, I couldn't believe I'd thought logistically that it was even possible. The hunts were too far-reaching to be instigated by one single coven.

To be capable of pulling off what Stone had, to take so many without anyone really realising what was happening, it would've taken a massive amount of organisation.

So, I suppose the question was, whether Stone could pull something like that off, or was there something else going on here that we weren't seeing? Neressa couldn't have been involved in the planning or the continuation of the hunts because she'd been in the sarcophagus. Whilst her coven could have stepped in on her behalf, something about that didn't feel right. They'd been so consumed by their need to get her back, it seemed unlikely they'd even have the manpower to pull off the raids that would have been necessary to supply Stone's facility as well.

"You've gone very quiet," Maverick pointed out, drawing my attention back to him.

I flushed in embarrassment as I realised I'd zoned out and totally ignored his attempt to help me.

"I'm sorry. My brain just ran away with me for a bit," I told him.

To give him his due, Maverick didn't smirk or laugh at me. Instead, he just nodded in understanding. "I'm not used to the whole pack thing either," he finally said. "I mean, not to the extent that it's like here. Obviously, I grew up in my father's pack, and I saw what happened there on a daily basis, but it was nothing like this. These people actually care about each other. All of the pack members are bonded together, and there isn't even a question in their minds about whether they belong. When I first came here, I thought Grey's idea of a pack without a hierarchy was madness. But after spending time here and seeing them together, it's hard to understand why pack life would be any other way. We aren't animals. We may have an animal side or an extra soul, whatever you want to call it, but we're still people. The old beliefs don't work, and they never should have. This is what every pack should be like."

"It is strange to suddenly find myself in a place where people actually see me," I said sadly, thinking back to how I'd lived my life before I was sent here.

"Yeah, I can relate to that." Maverick fell silent for a moment, and I could see he carefully considered his words before he spoke. "At that… place… you shifted. Do you, I mean, since you got here, have you felt like there's something extra inside of you…"

"Broke free?" I asked, suddenly realising that was how I felt. I hadn't been able to put my finger on the changes before, but that's how it felt. Not like changes as such, but something that had always been there but lay just out of reach before.

Maverick nodded before looking down at Calli, who still slept soundly between us. "I feel like she freed me in every sense of the word."

I'd heard about how life had been for Maverick before he came here, and I couldn't help but feel for him. I knew what it was like to live with barely veiled hatred in the guise of tolerance. It was hard as a child to know you weren't wanted and have the evidence of it presented to you every day.

"I can still feel it," he confessed in a whisper, his eyes never moving from Calli's face. "I can still feel the moonlight and the fire that blazed through me when I was changed."

"You reunited with your wolf. You didn't change him in the process. I suppose it's likely that whatever magic he absorbed in the ritual is still there."

"It's more than that, though. It doesn't feel like something foreign. It feels more like a natural part of what I am. It's hard to explain."

"We can look into it if you want. There have to be case studies of people who have absorbed foreign magic during a ritual and the changes they went through."

"That's the thing, though. It feels like it's mine. Do you think… could it be part of the animage thing?"

"You're asking the wrong person," I told him regretfully. "I don't have any knowledge about the animages. But if you want, we can look into them together."

Maverick finally met my eye, and I could see how grateful he was from the look on his face. We needed to stay on top of the animage revelation anyway. It was something that was going to affect the whole pack. If we could try and understand what was about to happen, maybe we could get ahead of this thing. Make it work in our favour for once.

"You've got that look on your face again," Maverick said with a chuckle.

I huffed in amusement. He'd soon come to learn it was nearly a permanent look for me.

Taking off my glasses, I rubbed my eyes as a tension headache started to form from all the thoughts tumbling through my mind at once.

"Get some sleep," Maverick told me, settling back down behind Calli and snuggling closer to her. "You didn't have much last night. Catch a few more hours now, and I'll wake you up in time for food tonight."

"Thanks," I muttered, placing my glasses down on the bedside table and turning to look at Calli again.

Hoping that Maverick wouldn't be annoyed with me, I shuffled a bit closer, linking my hand with Calli's.

I was nearly fully asleep when I heard Maverick whisper. "You will always be part of our pack, you know." And I drifted off to sleep with the knowledge that I finally had a place in the world.

※

It felt like I'd only closed my eyes mere seconds ago when soft fingers ran down my cheek, rousing me from my sleep.

Smiling from the simple act of a touch from my mate, I kept my eyes closed as she trailed a fingertip across my lips before sealing hers to mine in a soft kiss.

"I didn't mean to wake you," Calli told me quietly.

"Don't apologise," I whispered, moving forward and capturing her lips again as I wrapped her in my arms.

Calli's leg came up over my hip as she kissed me back greedily, and I grabbed her thigh, hauling her closer. She lined up perfectly with me as I trailed my hand up her side, slipping my fingers under her shirt.

I felt my magic reach out to her through the bond, and the glimmer of her magic reaching back in turn. It wasn't as strong as it had been, but she was still recovering. I could sense it nevertheless as both tendrils twinned together.

Calli was my anchor. In all the chaos of the current events, all of the questions about what I was, what my magic was and the implications of everything combined, there she was. Standing calm and strong against the storm. We may not have completed our bond yet, but she'd captured every corner of my heart.

The groan she gave as she pushed me to my back, straddling my hips in the process, spoke of how frustrated she was about our lack of bond as well. At least I had the comfort of not being the only one getting annoyed about our constant interruptions.

Pushing her shirt further up her body, I cupped her breasts in both hands, pinching her nipples between my fingers as Calli ground her hips down onto my hard cock.

But fate apparently hated us, and as if I'd tempted them with my thoughts, sudden shouting echoed up the stairs, followed by the sound of people rushing around.

Calli suddenly sat up straighter, pulling away from me with a gasp, and I felt the faint tingle of something run through her magic.

"Someone just crossed the wards." Calli groaned with regret as my hands fell away from her.

I flopped back down on the bed. The heat of the moment still radiated through my body, along with a deep sense of regret. At this rate, I was just going to steal this woman away and hide out in a cabin somewhere until I'd thoroughly satisfied her.

"We should go and see what's happening," I sighed.

Calli nodded, but she was already moving away from me before I'd even spoken. We both knew we had other priorities, no matter how much it pained us.

Grabbing hold of Calli's hips, I hauled her back to me, flipping us and pinning her to the mattress as I ground my hard cock against her core. Her mouth opened on a moan, and I took my chance, slipping my tongue into her mouth and stroking along her tongue with mine before I pulled away.

"This is just a pause, Calli. I can't stay away from you much longer. I need you more than I need to breathe. My soul reaches out for you, for my missing piece." The emotions I was feeling started to overwhelm me. A part of me was begging her to accept me, to accept the bond, even though I knew she wanted it just as much as I did. But not having her, not breaking that final thing holding us apart, was tearing me up so much that I was starting to doubt even my own feelings at times.

Calli leaned forward and touched her forehead to mine, her face scrunching in pain. "Walking out of this room will be one of the hardest things I've ever done. You are everything to me, Lachlan. I don't want you to ever doubt that."

"But we have bigger things happening around us, bigger responsibilities," I finished for her.

Even though I hated it, I understood. A tiny part of me resented every single person outside of this room, but that wasn't fair. They were as helpless to the tide of these events as we were. None of us had a choice. We were all just along for the ride and hoping to not get pulled under. The only thing keeping us afloat at the moment was the fact that we had each other, and as frustrated as I was, I needed to remember that.

9
CALLI

Lachlan and I both reluctantly made our way downstairs. Neither of us wanted to pull away from the other, but there were so many things in motion now that we were helpless to stop them.

The shouting got louder as we got downstairs, and the panicked undertone to it drew me quicker down the steps.

"What's happening?" I asked loudly as the rescued shifters started to rush past me, retreating further into the house.

I could see the back door hanging open and some of them shifting and disappearing into the trees. Whether we'd see them again would have to be something we waited to see. We couldn't afford to leave the pack vulnerable if we were under attack, so there wouldn't be anyone to go after them. It would be their choice if they wanted to spend the rest of their lives running or if they were willing to stand with us.

When it became clear that no one was going to answer, I grabbed hold of the next person to try and rush past me. When his alarmed eyes met mine, I did feel slightly guilty for manhandling the man, mainly because it was one of the shifters we'd only just rescued from Stone's facility.

"The Council is here," the shifter I grabbed hold of said, his wide, panic-filled eyes starting to water as he wrenched his arm free of my grip. "I'm not going back to that place. I won't do it. I won't survive again. I knew this was a trick. I knew we couldn't trust you," he spat.

I saw the moment his panic turned to rage, and I knew he was about to lash out at me. I could see his need for retribution, and as far as he was concerned, I was just the same as the people who'd caged him. He thought I was part of the whole thing. In his shoes, I probably would have done the same thing.

The problem was, I wasn't about to stand there and take it. I'd been through shit too, and I wasn't taking it out on him. We'd all risked our lives going there, and I nearly didn't make it out.

It was as the memory of the knife plunging into my stomach filled my mind, together with the familiar rage of the way Neressa planned to so callously use my mates, that my fist whipped out, and I punched him straight in the throat.

Okay, maybe I was slightly taking it out on him.

As the shifter fell to his knees, wheezing for breath and clutching his throat, I stepped around him, heading to the door where I could see Grey and River standing.

Tanner was in the doorway, having been about to intercede with the shifter, and he gave me a cheeky wink when our eyes met. For some reason, it was that one gesture that had regret flooding through me with the need to turn around and apologise.

I had to be strong, though, so I stepped through the doorway and took my place with my mates, waiting to see what would come next.

None of us expected the battered SUV that rolled down the driveway. One side was caved in, and the back windows were peppered with holes that looked suspiciously like bullet holes, not that I knew what bullet holes actually looked like in real life.

The engine stuttered, and one of the front tires was dangerously close to being flat as it suddenly stopped in front of the house.

And then nothing.

The darkened windows gave the hint of a figure inside, slumping over the steering wheel, but that was about it. It was too hard to see if there was anyone else inside. The mud and dust covering the windshield, not to mention the darkened interior, shrouded the vehicle in even more mystery.

"Tanner, River, stand by to shift if something comes out of that vehicle we don't like. I'm going to open the door. Calli, Lachlan, be ready to fight," Grey growled out between gritted teeth as he flexed his fists, opened and closed at his sides.

I appreciated that he wasn't trying to make me hide inside, even if he had essentially given me a job behind them all. Baby steps were giant strides for the alpha.

Huffing the air out through his nose, Grey strode forward with purpose, moving to the driver's side door and throwing it open as he stepped to the side. It was anticlimactic when nothing happened, and River sighed in relief.

"It's Wells," Grey called out, moving to reach inside the car. "And he's hurt."

Tanner and River rushed forward, and Lachlan moved forward to help them pull Wells out of the car.

"Lachlan, there's someone in the back, and he doesn't look good," Grey called out to him as he reached over Wells and unclipped his seatbelt, giving him a better view of the back seat.

Tanner moved to the back door with Lachlan as Grey pulled Wells out of the car, River grabbing his feet as they moved him, and together they rushed him up the steps of the porch. I caught sight of Tanner and Lachlan pulling a similar move with another man I didn't recognise before I turned and rushed into the house after Grey and River.

"Clear the dining table," Grey shouted to Blake, who was emerging from the back of the house somewhere.

Blake rushed ahead of them into the dining room. There was a clatter of dishes as he literally swept the tabletop clear, giving Grey and River room to lay Wells on one end and the unknown man on the other.

It was strange seeing the usually overconfident Councilman without his trademark smirk.

I moved Grey out of the way and immediately took over. Wells had a slight gash over his forehead, which had bled a lot but seemed to have stopped some time ago. Judging from the bruising to his face, he'd been in a fight. A slow trickle of blood started to pool on the tabletop beneath him, but his shoulder and stomach injuries caused me the greatest concern.

I gently placed my hands on his torso and had started to reach for him with my magic when consciousness suddenly flooded through him. Wells' hand whipped up and pulled me away from him as his eyes snapped open.

"No," he croaked out. "Heal Ethan first."

Wells tried to sit up, but he didn't have the energy to do much of anything. Instead, he groaned in pain as the slight attempt at movement no doubt had it ricocheting through his body.

"You've been shot in the shoulder, and you have a knife wound to your stomach which is still bleeding," I told him firmly. "You've lost too much blood, and if you don't allow me to heal you, you will continue to do so until you pass out. At which time I will heal you in any event. You may as well just let me do it now."

"No," he ground out through gritted teeth. "Ethan first. He was leaving the Council compound when they ran him off the road. He's more hurt than I am. I couldn't get to him straight away, and he'd collapsed in the forest. He'd been there for at least a day before I found him."

"It isn't as simple as who goes first," I told him. "I have very little energy. I can only do the minimum to keep you alive. If I heal him first, I will have nothing left for you. There is every chance you could die from these injuries."

Wells' eyes met mine, and even though he didn't give me his usual smirk, I could see the glimmer of it in the look he gave me. "I never realised you'd miss me that much," he joked.

"There was nothing about what I said that even implied I would."

He was always a ridiculous flirt, and it seemed he couldn't lose the attitude even now.

"Ethan is important. He was working for us on the inside, keeping eyes on Stone. We need the information he has," he whispered.

Wells' energy was fast leaving him, and I could tell he was about to pass out.

Grey, who had been standing quietly beside me, finally spoke. "Who is 'us'?"

I hadn't missed it either, and I suspected I already knew. Secrets on top of secrets. When would they ever trust us to bring us in on what was happening?

Wells was fortunate enough to pass out at that point to save him from answering. It did, however, leave me with the unfortunate job of having to decide what to do. For a moment, I just stood there, indecision warring inside me. I wasn't the type of person who could stand by and let someone else die, not when I had the power to stop it.

"Lachlan, will you lend me your magic," I asked, holding my hand out to him.

Lachlan didn't hesitate as he placed his hand in mine with a smile. "You never even need to ask, love," he told me.

"This is going to hurt," I warned him. "I've only ever done it once before, and I don't think Cassia found it all that pleasant. Hopefully, our bond should help, though."

The mention of a bond had Lachlan flinching, and I immediately regretted the word as it left my mouth. I was starting to worry that he'd think I was pulling away on purpose.

Lachlan's eyes met mine, and he gave me a firm nod. There was no time to waste worrying about our failed attempts for time alone, so I turned back to Wells and gritted my teeth. This really wasn't going to be pleasant.

"We heal the bare minimum and then move on to the other man," I said aloud to no one in particular. "Tanner, can you assess him and see if you can determine what's wrong. River monitor his pulse. The moment it seems like we might lose him, you need to tell me, so we can switch out."

Both men moved to do as I'd asked without comment, but I wasn't going to be able to split my focus to pay attention to what they were doing. Instead, I closed my eyes and sought out the coven bond between Lachlan and me. As soon as I located it, I dived into the connection, wrapping it tightly around me, as I hoped I could work out how to make it do what I needed. I could still remember how Cassia's magic had tried to cling to me when I'd done this last time, and the wrongness of it all. I wasn't exactly looking forward to trying this again.

Placing one hand on Wells' chest, I was about to attempt to wrestle the magic to do what I wanted it to do when it suddenly surged out of me and into his body. It was unlike anything I'd ever done before. There was no need to try and pull the magic from Lachlan. It was like a dam suddenly burst open. The amount of magic surging through my body pulled my mind and consciousness away from the reality of what was happening around me.

My awareness plunged into the magic like I'd dropped into an ocean of starlight. It wrapped around me, moving through every cell in my body. This wasn't just my magic, though. It wasn't even just the magic from our coven bond. There were elements of all of us here. I could sense Grey's strong alpha power and his protective nature wrapping around me like a promise to keep me safe. I could sense the fun-loving warmth of Tanner and the giving purity that was River. Underlying it all was the cool light of Maverick, as gentle as the moonlight but with the potential to move oceans.

I thought I could sense the pack for a moment, there was something that felt like Aidan, but it slipped away from me before I could examine it further.

The magic swirled around me, picking up pace. It was almost as if it was trying to coax me into doing something, but I had no idea what. The more I wasn't doing whatever task it had in mind, the more agitated it became.

Through the chaos of the tangled stream of links I held with the pack and my coven, I glimpsed a dark patch. A well of sadness and regret. I knew it was someone in our pack, and the fact that I had no idea one of us was hurting like this had the magic crashing against me in response to the overwhelming sense of shame that surged through me.

The crashing waves of magic blotted out whoever it was,

and no matter how much I fought to try and reach them, it was like the magic thickened more around me to prevent me.

It needed me to do something. It was like the sensation of having something there on the tip of your tongue and not quite being able to grasp it.

As quickly as it started, it suddenly finished, and I was thrown out of the chaos, repelled by my lack of action as the magic rejected me.

I came back into myself with a gasp, my lungs aching for air as the sound of Grey's shouting reached me.

It took a second for my eyes to start working, and I fluttered my eyelids to try and focus when the bright light of reality blinded me momentarily.

Once my vision cleared, I realised I was on my knees on the hard floor of the dining room. Grey was kneeling in front of me, and my mind almost couldn't work out why his hands were raised in the air until I realised he was leaning against a barrier.

Panic rose inside me as I looked around and realised that I was somehow encased in a dome of glittering magic. It looked exactly like the moonlight magic that had glowed from Maverick when he was in his moonlight form. Reaching one hand out to the barrier, I'd only touched it with the tip of a single finger when it seemed to disappear, dropping the shimmering curtain from around me.

"Fucking hell, woman," Grey swore, diving forward and wrapping me in his arms. "If you continue to scare the shit out of me at every available opportunity, I swear I will take you over my knee and tan your ass red until you can't sit for a straight week," he threatened in a whisper.

Hot lust flowed through me at his words, and Grey's arms tightened a fraction more around me as a soft growl flowed from his lips.

"Curious," Wells' voice said from above us, shattering the moment.

Looking up, I saw him peering over the table with the same easy smile he usually wore. Now that he wasn't on death's door, I remembered how infuriating it was.

"Did you know you glow when you do magic?" Wells asked.

"So I've been told," I deadpanned, not really wanting to enter into a conversation about it.

"You're terrible at following instructions, you know," Wells pointed out. "I wholeheartedly support Grey's suggestion."

And then I felt my face heat as I realised Grey's whisper hadn't been as quiet as I'd assumed it had been. Talk about a literal cold shower. I could have pouted at how that fantasy was definitely ruined for me now.

"As fun as it is to traumatise your young brain, my friend is still dying," Wells pointed out, and I leapt to my feet.

The sudden movement had my head swimming, and Grey's strong arms wrapped around me once more as he stood to be by my side.

"Steady," he warned.

"Lachlan!" I gasped, realising he wasn't beside me still.

I was the worst! I couldn't really blame Lachlan for believing I felt less about him than the rest of my mates, if that was indeed what he was thinking.

"I'm here," a weak sounding Lachlan said, and I found him slumped against the wall to the side.

"Oh my god," I gasped, about to rush to his side.

But then River broke into my panic as he barked across the room, "Calli, his pulse is getting really weak."

I looked at Lachlan, then over to River, then back to Lachlan and found myself suddenly torn. I didn't want

Lachlan to think I would ever walk away from him, but this man was seriously hurt, and he needed help.

"Go," Grey told me, moving to Lachlan's side. "I've got him."

When he saw me hesitate, Grey added, "You have to trust us to have each other's back."

It should have been reassuring, but something about it wasn't. There was no implication that I didn't think they trusted each other. This was all about the fact that I felt like I was pushing Lachlan away at every available opportunity. He was just as important to me as the rest of my mates, yet he was the only one I hadn't been able to complete the bond with.

I moved over to Wells' companion, even though my mind was screaming at me not to. Why had my life devolved into something where I had to keep making these crappy decisions? I shouldn't have to choose between Lachlan and this man. None of us should be in this position, and a small angry voice in the back of my mind raged at my parents for the unfairness of all this. They should have done more. Sitting back and moving people through the shadows wasn't what they'd taught us to do. They'd taught Jacob and I to stand up to the unfairness of things, to fight for what we thought was right, yet the more I found out about what was happening in our world, the more I came to realise they hadn't lived by the same standards.

By the time I came to a stop beside Tanner and River, even though it was in reality just a few steps away, I was so done with our entire world I wanted to pack up my mates, the kids and all our friends and just leave. Then the clarity of my parents' situation struck home, and I realised that was precisely what they'd done.

My hands hovered in front of me as I tried to help the

man in front of me, but I found myself suddenly afraid to reach for the magic. I didn't have the connection with Lachlan now, so there was little chance the same thing would happen again, but there was still a lingering fear in the back of my mind that it would.

"I've looked him over, he's got severe bruising over nearly all his torso, but most of it is located to his abdomen. I'd take a guess that he's got some pretty severe internal bleeding," Tanner told me, thinking my reluctance was me assessing the damage in front of me.

They'd already cut the shirt from him and dark heavy bruising covered nearly his entire abdomen. If he wasn't a shifter, he would have died from these injuries already. No doubt, it was only his enhanced healing abilities that kept him hovering on the brink of death.

In the end, my eyes moved to this man's impassive face. He was bruised, cut and unconscious. He hadn't stirred since we'd brought him inside, and I doubted he'd wake again without treatment. His blond hair hung dirtily around his face, and I took a moment to take him in. He looked about my age. He had his whole life ahead of him, and the only way he would get to live was if I could get my head right and do what needed to be done. There was no time to hesitate and second guess myself.

With a sigh, I gently laid my hands on his torso, about to close my eyes and do whatever I had the energy to do.

"Do you need any help?" a familiar voice asked.

Looking up, I saw the three witches standing near the doorway. At the front of them was the nervous one who'd healed me at the facility. He looked terrified, almost like he couldn't believe he'd actually offered to help, but then his eyes glanced to the man on the table, and I saw in him the same need I had. He didn't like to see this man hurting when he might be able to do something to help him.

"I have very little magic left. If I start, will you be able to join the process and finish what I'm doing?" I asked him. "I can guide you through what to do," I offered, and then flinched slightly.

I didn't want to insult him, but the memory of the agony I'd felt as he healed me came to the front of my mind, but I knew with some instruction he'd be able to heal as effortlessly as I did. He clearly had an affinity for healing; it just needed some nurturing. In fact, I was surprised no one had done that before. Healing magic was pretty rare, and this was something that should have been coveted by his coven, not sold into slavery to some sadistic bitch.

Meeting my eyes, he nodded and came to stand on the other side of the unconscious shifter before looking at me nervously.

"Okay. Place your hands over mine, close your eyes and feel for my magic. I'll warn you, it's pretty weak right now. You might have to look closely. Once you have it, let me know, and I'll start. First, feel the flow of what I'm doing and see if you can move your magic to flow alongside mine."

I could see all the questions running through his mind, but he did as instructed and moved his hands beside mine before closing his eyes. I wasn't sure what had sparked him to question what I'd said. This was exactly how my mother had taught me when I was a child.

I watched his face as his forehead scrunched in concentration. I could already feel the tingle of his magic reaching for me, so it shouldn't be long before he felt the sensation of my magic. It occurred to me then that I didn't even know his name. I didn't know any of their names.

Suddenly he gasped, and a smile lit across his face. "I can feel it. I can actually feel your magic."

Closing my eyes, I took a deep, cleansing breath as I reached for my magic. I could feel the foreign presence of his in the background, but for now, I tried to put it to the back of my mind and only think about what I needed to do.

Gathering my magic, I filtered that soft presence to the man in front of me, sinking into the feeling of what needed to be done. This time, there was no rush of strange magic pulling me under. It was the way it had always been, and I felt the tension drain out of my shoulders as I went through the familiar motions of feeling for what was wrong and coaxing my magic to repair the damage.

After a much shorter time than I was happy with, I could feel that I was reaching my limit, so I started to pull back. Then, the magic that had been lingering in the background slowly seeped forward to replace what I'd withdrawn. Using the last of my power, I helped guide him, nudging him back on the right path when the magic felt like it wanted to reach for everything all at once. The trick was to ease through it and go with the body's natural flow.

By the time we were finished, I was back to virtually nothing, but I at least didn't feel like I was on the verge of collapse. If anything, I was almost energised at the rush of showing someone else how to do something I'd always taken for granted. Healing had been a complex skill to learn, but once I'd grasped it, it had come so naturally to me that I barely had to think about what I was doing now.

"That was incredible," the witch in front of me gasped. "The way your magic responds to you is unlike anything I've ever seen before."

I couldn't help but get caught up in his enthusiasm. "I'd love to show you more if that's something you'd like. You have a natural affinity for healing. With some nurturing, you could improve how fast you can work and the types of things you can do."

The witch in front of me opened his mouth to excitedly agree, but then he shut down, and his eyes cast to his friends who'd stood in the doorway watching the entire time.

"I… erm… I'm sorry, but we'll be leaving soon," he told me sadly, taking a step back from the man between us like he needed to withdraw himself from the situation.

Looking at his friends, he suddenly rushed from the room, pushing his way past them, and the sound of the front door slamming sounded through the house at his exit.

"I'm sorry, I didn't mean…" I started, looking at his friends, who'd stood and watched him leave.

"It's fine. You didn't do anything wrong," one of them told me. "I'll go after him."

And with that, they both left to look for their friend, as I stood and silently watched them leave.

"What the fuck just happened?" a voice sounded from below me, and I looked down to see the man now awake and looking down at his bare torso in surprise, before his eyes cast up to me. "You!"

Now that he was awake, I recognised who he was.

"You! What the fuck, Wells?" I shouted, whipping around to glare at the Councilman sitting cross-legged on the dining table watching us in amusement.

"What did I do?" he laughed.

"Why would you bring him here? Are you working with Stone?" I shouted, taking a step closer to him.

I could feel the urge to shift taking over, and I knew my hands were about to transform into claws. I'd never had the urge to undertake a half shift without consciously trying to push it forward before. But, right now, I could feel an itch at the end of the fingertips like my talons were begging to be released.

"What?" Grey growled, standing in one fluid motion as he started to prowl towards the Councilman. "Explain, now!"

Grey was fully focused on Wells, and his alpha power started to seep out of him, trailing around the room, filling it with a sense of danger. Now was not the time to get flustered by the show of power he was putting on, but damn, it was always so hot to see!

"Calm down, alpha," Wells said slowly as he slid off the table surface, so he was facing Grey on his feet. "Your beautiful mate just recognised my companion. And no, in answer to your question Calli, I am not working with Stone, and neither is Ethan. He works for me."

Grey's eyes flicked to me before they returned to Wells. I knew it would be difficult for him to take his eyes off what he deemed to be the threat in the room.

"Calli, I need you to explain," Grey said, taking a slow step closer to Wells.

I could practically see Grey's muscles bunching, as if he was preparing to leap for Wells at a second's notice. A low, steady growl started to emanate from his chest. For a second, I thought I could actually see the alpha power as it started to thicken in the air.

"This man is the doctor from the compound. He's the one that used to draw pints of my blood for them," I clarified.

He'd always been kind to me, but he'd always taken too much. I knew there was something off about him.

"He's also the man who prevented them from harvesting anything apart from your blood," Wells pointed out, like it should make a difference.

It actually did, but I wasn't about to give him the satisfaction of admitting that. I still remembered that extra vile he took and put in a different container. There was something we still hadn't been told about this whole thing.

Wells pulled himself taller as he stared Grey down. It didn't seem like a smart move if you asked me, but then the alpha in him wasn't exactly going to take Grey's challenge lying down.

"It's good to see that you've gotten stronger, Grey. You're going to need it with what's coming," Wells told him, sounding weirdly proud.

"Is that a threat?" Grey snarled, taking a step closer as Tanner and River came to stand at his back.

Blake, who'd been quiet up until now, came to my side, and I could see the indecision in his eyes as he tried to assess if he should stay with me or stand beside his alpha.

"Aren't you even going to pretend to support me," Wells laughed, making light of the situation as he took his eye off Grey and looked at the man I'd come to hate.

I could see his attempt at humour for what it was. This was Wells standing down from Grey. By leaning to the side and looking around Grey, he was showing the other alpha his neck without technically submitting to him. This was why he was in politics. However, it could also hugely backfire if Grey was too far into his rage to realise what was happening.

"I've got banged about enough for you," the compound doctor laughed, still laying at the end of the table and moving his hands behind his head as he relaxed. "I deserve a vacation from this bullshit. Besides, I don't want this one to hate me any more now I've had a glimpse of what she can do," he said, nodding towards me. Ethan, that's what Wells had called him.

"What do you mean?" I asked in confusion, letting my thoughts distract me from the potential danger around me. "I only healed you."

"You sent your magic inside my body to make changes," Ethan pointed out. "Yeah, you did it to heal me, but what's stopping you from making those changes to create the damage in the first place?"

Huh, I'd never actually thought of that before. Was that even possible? Why would I even want to do something like that?

I must have been projecting my confusion across from my face because he laughed and sat up with a grin.

"You've never even considered the potential of your magic before, have you?" he asked.

"I'm a healer. My magic heals," I told him. It was the only way I could think to tell him what my magic and my mind had always known.

No, I hadn't considered it because that wasn't who I was. I wasn't someone who searched out ways to hurt other people.

"I told you she was one of the good ones," Wells said smugly.

Hearing his voice reminded me of what had happened, and I looked over at Grey to see that he wasn't exactly relaxed, but he was definitely coming down from the need to hurt Wells to protect us.

"As enlightening as this all is," Tanner broke in. "How about getting off the place where we eat, so we can clean up the mess you've made."

"Oh, apologies," Wells laughed as he slid off the table. "I didn't mean to almost die in your dining area. Although I will point out, I was put here without any say in the matter."

Tanner shrugged and instructed Blake to get something to try and clean the blood off the table, while the rest of us reached the awkward position of standing around, not really knowing what to do next.

"You still need to explain what is happening," Grey

pointed out. The echo of his wolf lingered in his voice, betraying how annoyed he still was about the whole situation.

"You're right, I think it's time that you were all…" and then his phone rang.

Everyone in the room froze as Wells pulled the phone from his pocket, and with a glance at the screen, he answered the call like he didn't have a care in the world.

Maybe that wasn't the right way to look at it. Maybe the man just had a death wish because the slight annoyance Grey had managed to simmer down, ratcheted up to full-blown fury again.

Seeing what was about to happen, and like the good beta he was, Tanner distracted Grey by pulling him off to a corner, where they started to murmur.

River moved to my side, not entirely comfortable leaving me with Ethan, who had seemed to remain standing beside me instead of going to Wells when he slid off his end of the table.

"Well, this is all slightly awkward," Ethan laughed, looking around the room at the others. "I'm Ethan, by the way. No hard feelings about the whole blood thing, I hope. I was only doing what I needed to keep my cover."

"And the extra vial you kept for yourself?" I asked, my eyes not leaving Grey and Tanner as I tried to figure out what they were talking about.

"Who said it was for me?" he joked, but not exactly answering the question either. "I think you might have taken a friend of mine into your pack," he randomly added on the end.

At that moment, I tuned back into Wells as he was finishing up his conversation, missing whatever it was that Ethan was about to say.

"Yeah, I'm already there. It's time. They deserve answers. You can't keep avoiding this. She's almost ready." Who was Wells talking to?

I wished like hell I could hear the other side of this conversation, but something about what he said had an itch in the back of my mind like I should know who it was.

Wells locked eyes with me, and a wicked grin lit across his face.

"Yeah, I'll give her your love, you big growly bastard. See you see soon." And then he hung up the phone.

"That was Sean." I realised.

Grey and Tanner's attention was immediately back on us at the mention of Sean's name.

Wells' grin just got wider. There wasn't a question in the statement I'd made. It all made sense. There had been times when it seemed like Sean and Wells knew each other. They were both clearly up to something, and they knew a lot more than they were telling us. It made sense that they'd be working together. The problem was, that either meant we could trust Wells, or we couldn't trust Sean, and at that moment, I had absolutely no idea which it was.

10
GREY

I'd known something was going on with Wells, but working with Sean? That I hadn't seen coming, even if he hadn't outright admitted it to us yet.

After Calli's comment, Wells had made some excuse about not being able to talk with us until everyone had arrived. He needed to check in with his pack to ensure everything was secure there. He assured me he'd fill me in on what had happened that resulted in him and Ethan becoming injured, but he wanted to check in with his pack first.

The only reason I let him go and didn't demand he give me answers was because I knew how he'd feel as an alpha if he thought his pack was in danger.

As he stepped outside to make his calls, Hunter came through into the house, looking his usual gruff self.

"I heard we had company," he said evasively, smartly not advertising that we had the wards in place with so many strangers close by and capable of listening.

"Yeah, Wells just turned up half dead with…"

"Hunter?"

Hunter's head whipped to the voice behind me, and his

mouth fell open in dumbstruck surprise. I didn't think I'd ever seen the man blush before as he stared at Ethan, who'd just walked out of the dining room in a new shirt someone must have gotten him.

"Fuck!" Hunter suddenly sighed before he strode forward and wrapped the man in his arms. "I didn't think I'd ever see you again," he finally said as he pulled away.

Some days I marvelled at the strangeness of my life, but then others I felt like I just waited to see what insanity happened next. I almost turned to the door to wait and see who else would turn up. It kind of felt like one of those days.

"Ethan, this is Grey. My alpha," Hunter said proudly as he turned to me with a beaming smile. "Do you remember when you asked me if there were any guards at the compound who might be able to help us, and I said no, but there could be someone? This is the guy," he told me proudly, slapping Ethan on the back. "What the hell are you doing here?" he asked, turning back to Ethan.

Ethan kept his eyes firmly on Hunter as he spoke about him. Even if Hunter was completely oblivious to that look, I knew it well. It was on my own face every time I looked at Calli. That was the look of someone in love, which raised an interesting question. If he had those kinds of feelings for Hunter, could this guy be another one of Cassia's mates?

"I've… well, I've been working with Wells on the whole 'the Council is trying to kill us' problem," Ethan admitted, blushing as he did.

"Hmmm, and he nearly got himself killed in the process," Calli added as she came out of the dining room to join us.

Hunter turned back to Ethan in concern, and I could see his eyes roaming over his form as he assessed him for injuries.

"Please, as if I'd leave anything you'd be able to see. You know me better than that," Calli joked.

"Well, technically, it was that other guy," Ethan added with a cheeky smile.

Calli made a pfft of denial and wandered off further into the house, leaving us standing in the hallway.

As much as I wanted to hate the guy, I had to admit he did seem alright. And if Hunter was vouching for him, that went a long way, given my respect for the ex-guard.

"Ethan, you need to come and meet my mate," Hunter suddenly said before turning back to his friend. "Cassia is back at our cabin. You don't mind if I borrow him for a while, right?" Hunter asked me.

"Why the hell not?" I sighed.

Ethan gave me a cautious side-eye as he trailed out the packhouse behind Hunter. The fact that he was wary of me gave my wolf at least the satisfaction of knowing he knew his place. I wasn't quite over the fact of what he'd been party to at the Council headquarters, even if Wells was trying to argue it had been in Calli's best interests.

At least I was starting to get a hold of my emotions more now. Or rather, I felt like I was. Hopefully, everyone else didn't think I was still acting like a sullen teenager. It almost felt like whatever changes were going on with me were finally starting to settle. The power levels I could churn out were still off the chart, and they still caught me unaware at times, but it felt like whatever was causing the increase and my wolf was in sync now.

As Hunter and Ethan left the house chatting quietly in a way only friends could, I looked around and, for once, found myself in blissful quiet. It didn't feel right. The packhouse had become a place that was alive, filled with people and noisy chaos. That was how it was supposed to be, and I couldn't go back to those days of coming home from work late at night to a silent house. A silent pack wasn't a pack. It was a prison where we smothered everything it was to be a wolf.

I knew the kids were upstairs. We had the two female survivors upstairs as well, who had latched onto Holly, and she was caring for them as well as she could. I could sense the wolves in them, but it didn't feel right. It felt wrong, forced somehow. As much as I wanted to see to their well-being, I knew a man wouldn't be the person they needed around them right now. But, I was still the alpha here, and I needed to be in the loop on what had happened and what they needed. So, if it couldn't be me, it would be the next best thing, so I went in search of Calli.

After drawing a blank outside, I found her where I always found her, well, one of the two places. Sure enough, as soon as I walked through the door, I found her pouring hot water from the electric kettle into a mug, making tea.

I took a moment to take in her posture as she went through the motions of making herself tea. I'd already realised that the act of doing so was something Calli turned to when she needed the calm.

Walking up behind her, I made sure she heard my approach before I wrapped my arms around her and pulled her back to lean against my front.

"I can almost hear the chaos running through your mind," I murmured, running my cheek against her hair as I inhaled her scent deeply. I was so addicted to this woman, I didn't think I could go an entire day without feeling her in my arms. "Want to talk about it?" I asked.

Calli brought one hand up to entwine her fingers with mine, and then reached back with the other arm to wrap a hand around my neck as she pulled me impossibly closer. I knew she was doing it because she needed the comfort of me closer to her body. Still, my rock hard cock currently pressing against her ass decided it was for entirely other reasons.

"Something is going on with my magic," she sighed almost reluctantly.

It surprised me. I'd assumed it was the whole Sean situation that was bothering her. Removing her hand from the back of my neck, I spun her around and lifted her to sit on the countertop as I moved between her legs, so I could wrap my arms around her waist. I'd intended it to ease the need to bend her over the counter and take her there and now, but this new position wasn't helping either. Christ, get your mind out of the gutter Grey, so you can take a moment to ease your mate's worries.

"Tell me," I basically ordered and then wanted to roll my eyes at myself. I couldn't help the dominant part of me pushing forward whenever I found myself getting turned on around Calli. From the subtle tick of a smile on her lips, she knew it.

Calli shuffled closer to the edge of the counter and wrapped her legs around my hips, pulling me closer to her before she began to speak. It took every ounce of self-restraint I had to listen to her, and the minx knew exactly what she was doing.

"When I joined with Lachlan, it wasn't like it usually is when I used my magic. It felt like, well, it's hard to describe," she sighed with a frown on her face. "It was like my consciousness got pulled into the magic, and I wasn't aware of what was happening around me or what I was doing."

"So you didn't know you were healing Wells?" I asked in surprise.

We'd all watched as Calli had closed her eyes and sunk into the healing process, as she always did. Yes, she'd had that subtle glow that she'd started to get when she used her magic. In fact, it was less than subtle now and seemed to be getting brighter, but that wasn't the point. We'd known something different was happening when the strange barrier seemed to form around Calli, keeping us away from her.

"No. I felt like I was fully submerged in the magic. It was like it wanted me to do something, and when I didn't, because I had no idea what it was, I was thrown out."

"But when you healed Ethan, you didn't have any problem accessing your magic?" I asked in concern.

The last thing we needed when we had a fight for our lives on the horizon was Calli losing her magic. Not just because we'd grown so used to having her around to heal us, but because it was one of her greatest weapons.

"It was the same as it always was when I used it the second time," she clarified.

"Perhaps it was joining with Lachlan that caused it? Or the coven bond?" I suggested. In reality, I knew almost nothing about magic. That would change over time, with Calli being my mate. We just hadn't had enough time when we weren't fighting for our life to learn the everyday things like that.

Calli shrugged, and I could see the disappointment on her face at not knowing the answer to something about herself. I knew it was bothering her, and I'd sensed the growing resentment she was starting to feel toward her mother for not having taught her all the things she was going to need to know. It wasn't really her fault, though. No one likes to face their own mortality, and we all assume we have all the time in the world to achieve the things we want.

"I wish I knew," Calli sighed. "I'm going to see if I can get hold of Jessa or Marie, basically anyone who potentially knows more about this than us. We need answers, and I'm fed up with people hiding information. It's time we started getting some honesty and accepting that the people who won't give it to us aren't standing at our side."

A fierce determination came over her face, and even though I was proud of her, a small part of me was sad as well. This was changing her. Yes, Calli was becoming stronger, but I didn't want her to look back at this time in years to come and feel like she'd lost a part of herself.

"Okay, whatever I can do to get you answers, I will," I reassured her. "But first, we need to know what's happening here. We need to know what these people have been through and who wants to move on. I won't force anyone to stay in this fight if they don't want to. Hell, some of them might want to, but aren't able to. We need a read on everyone, and so far, we barely even know most of their names."

That fact stung a bit. We'd had such a chaotic start where we focused so much on getting them here and then rested, I hadn't had time to speak with most of them. It didn't feel right, and it was one thing I definitely needed to rectify.

"Can you go and speak with the women upstairs for me?" I asked. "I don't think I'm the person they'll respond well to, and we need to know the best step forward for them. I think it would be best to ask Sean to find a place for them in the underground. We can't ask them to join this fight. They've been through so much already," I said sadly.

None of us had much information from the two women who had come back with us, but judging from the fact that Calli and the others had found them naked and in a cage, it didn't take a genius to work out some of what they'd been through. It had me thinking about the men who had come back with us in a different light. If they'd participated in what had been done to them, even if it had been unwillingly, then sharing a house with these men was the last thing these women would need.

Fuck, we needed information, and we needed it now. We'd invited a lot of people into our home, and we had no idea if we could trust any of them. At least I knew I had the pack at my back. None of them would betray me. We'd always stood by each other, and we always would. We were pack brothers, and nothing could ever come between that.

11
CALLI

I hadn't wanted to leave Grey. As soon as he wrapped his arms around me, there was only one thing on my mind, and the fact I wasn't about to get it had me pouting as I slunk up the stairs.

It had been a hard few days, and I needed the closeness of my mates. The fact that I kept having a non-starter with Lachlan wasn't helping. But after everything, I wanted those blissful moments in one of their arms when the rest of the world fell away. We all deserved it, and we all needed it. The problem was there was only one of me and apparently an entire world against us.

We'd placed the two women in Coby's room, and I gently knocked on the door, waiting for someone to say I could enter. I didn't want to barge into their space. They needed to have the security of a safe place to call their own, and the least any of us could do was wait for them to invite us inside.

It didn't take long for the door to open, and I was surprised to see Holly's face staring back at me through the gap in the door. When she saw it was me, she sighed in relief and opened the door wider, inviting me inside.

The room inside was empty, and I was more confused than anything. I knew they hadn't left, but it all made sense when Holly pointed sadly at the closet door. I should have come here first this morning, and I felt like the worst person in the world for not doing so.

Moving across the room, I sat down on the floor outside the closet, bracing my back against the door frame. I might need to speak with them, but I wouldn't force them to do that if they weren't ready yet.

The sight of the two of them huddled together in the back corner broke my heart. The woman who'd shown that glimpse of strength back at the facility met my eyes as she cradled the other woman against her chest. Silent tears tracked down her cheeks, but that fire still lingered in her eyes. She might be hurt, she might be traumatised, but she hadn't let them break her.

"Did you kill her?" was the first thing she said to me.

"Yes, Neressa is dead, and we burned down the facility," I told her.

"And the other one? The one in the white coat." From the look on her face, I could tell that she already knew, but she needed me to say it anyway.

"There wasn't anyone else inside the building. She must have left by the time we reached Neressa."

I knew who she was talking about. We'd seen the woman in the white coat arguing with Stone before storming the building. None of us had seen anyone else inside, though. We should have left someone outside watching the exits, but there hadn't really been enough of us to do that. The fact that we made it out with minimal injuries was miracle enough.

The woman she cradled to her chest started to weep again, and I hated that I didn't have better news for her.

"My name is Calli," I told them both. "You're at my pack.

No one will get anywhere near you here. We have friends who operate an underground, and we're going to get you somewhere safe," I reassured them.

I saw the hope in her eyes, but it was also accompanied by determination.

"You're going to stop them, aren't you?" she asked. "You'll go after her?"

I nodded, hoping she could see the sincerity in my eyes.

"Then I need to tell you everything," she answered with determination. "You need to know what they're doing so you can fight them."

I was proud of her. She'd clearly been through something traumatic, but she was going to help us anyway. Going through what had happened to her wasn't going to be easy, and I could tell from the look on her face that she was dreading it. But, she was pushing through that to help us anyway, and it told me everything I needed to know. She was going to be okay. She would get through this.

"My name is Lea," she told me. "And this is Jess."

"It's nice to meet you both," I automatically replied and then cringed at the words.

She gave me a wry smile, knowing where my thoughts had taken me, but not holding it against me. I supposed it was something they'd probably have to get used to. At least with a fresh start in the underground, people wouldn't know what they'd been through unless they wanted them to know. They wouldn't have to live with people gently stepping around them. It would be a chance to try and build a normal life if that's what they wanted.

"Let's talk about this out there," Lea suggested. "Jess doesn't need to go through all of this again."

She turned back to Jess and started to pull the bed covers

and blankets up around her, cocooning her inside, before pulling away.

"Just wait here," Lea whispered. "I'll be right back, but I need to speak with Calli about some things first."

Jess blankly nodded. I didn't think she really understood what she was agreeing to. She'd seemed so lost in that cage when we'd found them, and she had the same look on her face now. Perhaps she hadn't even realised she'd been rescued. She looked like her mind was still back there, locked in the cage. She'd given up, and no one could fault her for it.

"I'll stay with her," Holly said, moving into the back of the closet and shuffling closer to Jess. She didn't move at first. It almost seemed like she was lost in a blur of what was happening around her. In the end, Holly moved across to her and gently laid her down, so Jess' head was on her lap while she stroked her hair.

I backed away from the closet like a coward. I didn't want to watch the broken woman anymore. It was too painful to see how much she was hurting and not have a way to heal it for her.

Lea moved slowly out of the closet, squinting at the bright light coming in through the curtains as she walked out into the room.

"She's been like that for weeks," she told me as she sat down on the edge of the bed. "I tried to keep her going. I told her someone would come for us, but I think she gave up hope long ago. She was there before I got there. I think she'd been there a long time. She survived all that just to keep living in a cage in her mind now we're free."

I could hear the anger in her voice. And even though it appeared to be directed at Jess, I knew it wasn't. She had every right to be angry. They both did. Sometimes, holding on to your anger was the only thing that kept you from collapsing under the weight of the pain you were feeling.

"It will take time, but we'll make sure she gets help," I told Lea, even though I had no idea if that was actually the case. In reality, once they went with Sean, I'd probably never see them again.

I sat down on the edge of the bed beside her, not knowing how to start the conversation. I wasn't a therapist or a counsellor. I didn't know how to talk to people about this sort of thing.

"I met him in a bar," Lea said quietly after a beat of silence. "I don't even know what his name was. He was just some guy in a bar. We had some drinks. He invited me back to his place. I thought I was being sensible when I suggested we go to a nearby hotel instead. I didn't think it was safe going to his, and I didn't want him knowing where I lived."

She laughed at that point. It was self-deprecating, and it hurt me, knowing how much this was going to affect the rest of her life.

"He must have slipped something in my drink. I don't even remember passing out. I woke up in that cage, and I never saw him again. I guess he took me there?"

"He was probably one of Stone's pack or one of the witches working there," I told her. I don't know why I felt like I needed to explain it. I suppose I didn't want her worrying about this guy catching up with her again, but it's not like we were going to kill the entire pack.

Lea shrugged like it didn't matter, and then she continued with her story. "When I woke up in the cage, Jess was already in the one beside me. They'd taken my clothes and left me a single bottle of water. I was afraid to drink it at first, but then Jess told me it would be the only one I'd be getting for a while. In the end, I couldn't stop myself. I was so fucking thirsty. I could taste the drugs in it. They didn't even try to hide them."

Reaching out slowly, I held her hand, and she clung to me as she continued with her story.

"It started out slow at first. I was so out of it that I didn't even know what was happening. They took me into a lab and did a whole bunch of tests on me. That woman in the white coat was always there. I don't even know what most of the tests were, but they were like normal doctor stuff. That went on for about a week until they deemed me fit to proceed. After that, it became a constant cycle. They'd inject me with stuff. The pain would be so bad, I started to hope I'd die. Eventually, I'd just pass out when I couldn't take it anymore. When I woke up, I'd either be sick, back in my cage or… in one of the other cages."

She paused for a bit as her face blanked, and her grip tightened on my hand. I could tell she wasn't in the room with me. She was back in the cage, seeing all the things that had happened to her.

I held her hand as firmly as I could to let her know I was there with her, to keep her grounded in the present.

"You don't have to tell me anymore if you don't want to," I told her, even though we both knew that she did. There had to be an easier way than this, though. There had to be a way to do this without her going through the whole thing again.

"No, it's okay. I need to say it out loud, I think. I need to know I'm not there anymore, that it's in my past."

I nodded as if I understood, but in reality, how could I? No one would understand what she'd been through except the woman who was catatonic and huddled in the back of the closet. Jess was the only other person alive who'd been through it too.

"The cage… there was always at least one shifter in there.

I didn't know that's what they were at first. I thought they were just men. People who'd got caught up in this mess like I had." I tried not to be insulted by her words. After all, she was brand new to this world, and she hadn't exactly seen the best of it. "They tried to stay away from me, but it was too hard. They'd done something to us, and they… they couldn't stop themselves. It's not their fault," she whispered at the end.

"None of you were there because you wanted to be," I told her. "You're all victims to what these people did, and we will find justice for you."

I didn't make her say out loud that she'd been raped. It wasn't necessary. I wasn't going to make her declare it like that. She should be able to do that when she was ready, on her own timescale.

"Do you know what they were trying to achieve? Why they were doing this to you?" I asked quietly.

"They always talked in the lab like I wasn't there, but I didn't really understand what they were talking about. They were talking about magic and shifters. Something about a Queen. She was talking about a breeding program at first, but then it wasn't working. I don't really know. I'm sorry."

She didn't have to explain. I thought I already knew, even if I didn't understand the reasoning behind it. The problem was, it was something I hadn't exactly shared with everyone else yet. Not because I was keeping it from them, though. I'd been trying to understand my own feelings about being an animage Queen. With everything that happened, I hadn't had the chance to talk to the others about it.

"It's okay. You did really good." I sighed as the tension settled around me. I had no idea what I was supposed to do with all of this. We needed a plan. But how was our small pack supposed to stop everything that was already in motion? This was so much bigger than us.

But now I needed to figure out if she realised there would be long-lasting effects to all of this, and I didn't want to be the one to break it to her if she didn't.

"Lea, how do you feel now? Is there… can you feel something different?" God, I was shit at this.

"I feel like… I'm not me. Except that's not right, it's like I'm not *all* me." Then, with a sigh, she added, "Basically, I think I've gone crazy, and there's someone else in my head. It's like I can feel them. See! I told you I'd gone crazy," she rambled.

"I think they were trying, and possibly succeeded, in turning you into a shifter," I told her calmly, my eyes darting between hers as I waited to see if she'd freak out. When she didn't react at all, I continued. "I have my own type of magic, and I can feel something similar to shifter magic in you."

"Similar? Not the same?"

She was taking this a lot better than I thought she would.

"Yes. I don't have any answers for you about what it is. I've never felt it before. But I promise you that I will try to find the answers for you."

It was a promise I fully intended to keep for her. We had the laptop. If that didn't hold any answers, I'd find another way. She deserved that, at least.

Lea nodded, her eyes straying to the closet door. "I can live with that," she finally said before falling quiet.

I wished I could look at the laptop now, but we couldn't get past the password yet. The only thing I could do for Lea and Jess now was to try and help them with their immediate needs.

"Have you eaten? Is there anything you need?" I asked

Lea, trying to take my mind away from the lingering doom that seemed to forever hover over us.

"Holly brought us some breakfast up, but I could definitely eat again. I don't think Jess really had much either. We tried to get her to have as much as we could, but she's… yeah. Calli, don't take this the wrong way, but we really need to get out of here. Knowing that all the men who raped her are sitting downstairs isn't doing her much good."

I winced at the matter of fact way she'd put it. There was no escaping the reality of it, though. She had been assaulted by those men. Even if they had been made to do it and their control had been taken away from them, it didn't stop the violation she'd suffered. They would always be the face associated with her trauma. Keeping them all together wouldn't do any of them any good.

"I'll speak with our contact and see if I can get a time frame on getting you out of here. In the meantime, I can ask one of our pack to stay by your door if it would make you both feel safer. No one will come in here while you're here."

"If Holly doesn't mind staying with us, I think that would be enough. Jess won't settle if a man is lingering outside the door."

"I'll make sure the men are kept downstairs away from you. What do you think Jess would be up to eating? You both need some proper food in you if you think you can stomach it."

"Honestly? I don't think she will eat whatever we put in front of her, but anything hot sounds amazing to me," Lea told me with a soft smile.

"Okay, I'll get something sorted out and be right back."

The kitchen was quiet, with only Lachlan standing at the counter, dicing some vegetables.

"Where is everyone?" I asked, looking around at the

empty house and almost getting an eerie feeling at its suddenly vacant interior.

"When the chaos kicked off with Wells' arrival, most of the rescued shifters fled into the woods. Most of the pack have shifted and gone to find the ones they can. Nash and Aidan are with Colt's pack out back, looking over the area where the cabins are being put up."

"They're staying then?" I asked, settling beside him and picking up a carrot and the peeler.

"Seems that way," he said, staring down at me with a soft smile as I started to peel. "This is nice," he added, dropping a kiss to the top of my head before returning to his task.

"It almost feels like something normal," I joked. "What are you making anyway? I need to sort some food for the ladies upstairs."

"I just thought I'd throw a beef casserole together. I found some meat in the fridge, and it seemed like something most people like," Lachlan said with a shrug. "Will the kids eat this?" he asked, then looked down at the potato he had in his hand in sudden concern.

"Probably. Jacob will pretty much eat anything as long as it comes with a Yorkshire pudding. I suspect Abby and Coby will give it a go because he's eating it. I don't know about Kai yet. I should really try and talk with him today," I added with a sigh.

"Hey, what's up?" Lachlan asked, dropping what he was doing and turning towards me as he leaned against the counter.

"Do you ever feel like you're failing at what you're supposed to be doing? Like you have all these balls in the air, and they're constantly raining down around you because you can't keep up?"

"All the time," Lachlan said with a laugh. Then, hooking

an arm around my waist, he pulled me closer to him. "The trick is to get someone else to help you," he whispered before pressing his lips to mine.

Rather than a kiss, it was more of a brush of his lips against mine, but it was exactly what I'd needed. A promise. A reminder. We had each other, all of us did.

"So, which balls can I help with?" he asked, returning to cutting up the vegetables.

"Whose balls are we playing with?" Tanner's cheeky voice asked from the back door when he came striding inside. "Mine, I hope?"

Lachlan guffawed in laughter at my side, and I rolled my eyes at the pair of them. This was the problem with living with a bunch of men. Sometimes you got sucked into the boy talk.

"Calli said that she felt a bit overwhelmed, and I was offering to help her," Lachlan explained once his laughter was under control.

"Ah," Tanner said. The way his eyes lit with mischief as he spoke had my panties flooding and the heat pooling between my legs. As he prowled closer towards me, Tanner's voice dropped to a husky level, "The trick with not feeling overwhelmed is to completely let go and not feel anything at all," he murmured.

As he reached me, Tanner pressed himself against my back, taking the peeler out of my hand as he entwined his fingers with mine and pressed our hands onto the countertop. Then, running his nose up the length of my neck, Tanner inhaled deeply before he told me, "Did you know that the house is virtually empty now? The kids are with Cassia and Hunter. The others are either out by the new cabins or chasing the shifters through the woods."

My eyes moved to Lachlan as Tanner pressed harder against my back, essentially bending me over the island countertop as he did.

"Do you remember the last time we were here?" Tanner asked me, letting go of my hands and trailing his fingers up my arms. "Does Lachlan know about how I bent you over this island and feasted on your delicious pussy?"

I watched as the pupils of Lachlan's eyes blew. His breaths were coming in sharp pants as his tongue darted out to wet his bottom lip.

"Mmmmm, have you tasted her yet, Lachlan? Our mate is delicious, not to mention naughty. She came so hard when I asked her how she'd feel if Grey came and joined us."

I whimpered at his words. The lust in my body was reaching an all-time high. I'd been craving the touch of my mates since this morning, and if I didn't get it soon, I felt like I would combust.

"I haven't had the pleasure yet," Lachlan growled, the hint of his wolf coming through into his voice for the first time. "But I'm dying for the chance."

I felt Tanner shift for a moment, his voice becoming more sincere as he tried to rain his desire in. "If you need me to step away and give you both time alone, I will."

It sounded like it physically hurt him to suggest it, but it proved how good a man he was that he was offering. If I ever had any doubts over whether my mates would be able to share, it would have been erased at that moment.

"No need," Lachlan purred as he stepped closer to us. "I know how to play well with others."

And my jaw just about hit the counter from the shock of those words coming out of my usually reserved mate's lips.

Tanner seemed to find the whole thing amusing, but

before I could ask if he was sure, I found myself airborne and suddenly draped over Tanner's shoulder.

"Then I know just the game I want to play," Tanner purred cheekily as he strode out of the kitchen towards the stairs.

"But we were…" I protested as I pressed my hands against Tanner's lower back and peered up, only to find Lachlan hastily shoving the meat back in the fridge and turning off the burners on the stove. "And the women need something to eat."

"Holly!" Tanner bellowed as he jogged up the stairs with me draped over his shoulder. "Order some pizza!" And then he turned in the opposite direction to the room the women were staying in and strode into River's bedroom at the far end of the corridor.

"Will River mind…" and then I squealed as I was launched across the room toward the bed.

The whole thing was not only ridiculous, but it also made me hot as hell because whilst I wanted to protest that my need wasn't urgent enough to physically throw me at the nearest surface to fuck me on… it actually probably was.

Lachlan stepped into the room, closing the door firmly behind him and taking off his glasses, dropping them on the dresser next to the door.

Sweeping his blond hair back from his face, he looked down at me, licking his lips like the predator he was now.

"Calli," Tanner growled. "If you want one of us to leave, you need to say, sweetheart." Then he pulled off his shirt before moving his hands to the button on his pants.

"Don't either of you fucking dare," I growled as I started to pull my clothes off as quickly as possible.

I needed this more than I needed to breathe right now. I

needed to feel them fill me. Tanner was right. The only way I would let go of everything that felt like it was crashing down on top of me was to let them take me to that blissful nothingness that came after screaming out your release.

"Hmmm," Tanner sighed, "I can smell how turned on you are, little mate. If I ran my fingers across your pussy, how wet would you be?" he asked.

"Why don't you come here and find out," I purred, lying back on the bed now I was completely free of my clothes.

My eyes wandered to where Lachlan was tossing his shirt to the ground, and I ran my gaze across his torso, taking in the perfect dips and swells of his muscles. His physique was unlike any witch I'd come across before. He already had the body of a shifter. It almost seemed ridiculous that we hadn't seen it in him before.

Tanner stole my attention as he moved between my legs, getting a much closer look than I'd suggested as he ran his tongue up my slit.

"Mmmmm," he moaned, licking across my pussy again as he teased my opening with a finger. "Delicious," he purred.

My eyes rolled back at the sensation of Tanner's tongue finally finding my clit as he gently flicked it across my bud.

I sank into the sensation, feeling that teasing finger slide across my opening before dipping inside my pussy and slowly sinking inside of me.

When I came back to my senses, I saw Lachlan prowling toward the bed, completely naked, his hard cock pressing against his abs.

"Lachlan, I need you in my mouth," I all but begged him.

I did need him. I wanted to feel his silky length push down my throat as he helped me completely forget about everything that had been stressing my mind.

As Lachlan climbed onto the bed, moving toward my head, I looked down my body and saw Tanner's grinning face hovering just above my pussy as he watched.

"I love seeing you please your mates, sweetheart," he purred.

It shouldn't have surprised me. I'd had a particularly memorable time in bed with River and Tanner before, and he'd whispered the dirty suggestion of Grey joining us the last time we'd been in the kitchen. It seemed that Tanner had a particular interest in others joining in our fun, and I was definitely there for it.

Opening my lips, I ran my tongue over the head of Lachlan's cock, keeping my gaze locked with Tanner. He mirrored the movement of my tongue as he dipped his head and rewarded me with a teasing lick against my clit.

Opening my mouth wider, I swallowed Lachlan down deep, my eyes looking up at my mate kneeling above me. Lachlan's hand moved my hair away from my face, giving both him and Tanner a better view of how his cock disappeared between my lips.

"Fuck," Tanner swore softly as Lachlan's hips slowly started to move, pushing himself against the back of my throat.

I hummed in content before relaxing my throat and letting Lachlan slowly push himself down further. I loved the stretch and the sting of his cock filling me. The burn as my lungs begged for air.

When Lachlan pulled back, I almost chased after his cock, not wanting it to end, but his grip tightened in my hair, keeping me where I was.

"Hold still, Calli, and let Tanner watch me fuck your mouth."

I felt my pussy spasm around Tanner's fingers at the sound of Lachlan's words.

"I think she's on board with that idea," Tanner chuckled, pumping his fingers inside me before adding another to add to the stretch.

Lachlan's grip tightened on my hair, and before I could say a word, his cock sank back between my lips. He started at a slow pace, pushing himself into the back of my throat and holding himself there before starting the slow drag out again. It was like he was trying to give me time to adjust to the size of him, and ordinarily, I would have been grateful for it because Lachlan wasn't exactly small in that department.

But right then, I was impatient. I knew what I wanted, and as Tanner's tongue returned to tease at my clit, I didn't want to wait.

Slowly running my fingers up Lachlan's thigh, I grasped his hip and pulled him toward me, helping him thrust harder into my mouth. That self-assured masculine chuckle dripped from his lips as he took my hint and started to move his hips with purpose, pushing deeper into my throat with every thrust.

It was exactly what I needed, and as Tanner's tongue lashed against my clit, working me into a frenzy, I knew I wasn't going to last long.

At that moment, Tanner pulled his fingers from my pussy and started to tease the tip of one finger against my asshole instead. It was something we'd only briefly done up until then, but I found myself pushing down against him, needing more, needing everything.

Tanner groaned in encouragement as he pushed that finger into my rosette up to his first knuckle, slowly pumping it inside me as he lashed at my clit, drinking down my juices.

All the sensations coming at once accumulated into one pulsing need inside me. I could feel the bonds between us glowing with magic as my orgasm drew near. The mating bite at my neck seemed to pulse in time with my heartbeat, and then white lights burst across my eyes as my orgasm crashed into me.

I screamed around Lachlan's length as he pushed deep into my throat at the moment my orgasm hit. Tanner sucked my clit into his mouth as he pumped his finger deeper into my ass, and I ground down against his face, loving every dirty second.

I felt like I blacked out for a second, as I came back to my senses to find that Lachlan had pulled his cock out of my mouth. Tanner was staring up my body from where his head was resting against my thigh with a cheeky look on his face.

"I think it's time to swap," Tanner grinned, looking at Lachlan.

A burst of nerves flooded through me at the insinuation.

"I don't know if I can do that again," I said nervously as Tanner stood and moved to my other side.

His hard cock bobbed as he walked, and I felt my mouth water at the sight.

"You're looking at me like a starving woman," Tanner laughed. "Something tells me you can definitely do that again."

Lachlan chuckled as he moved his delicious cock away from me before grabbing my hips and flipping me onto my stomach.

"Hands and knees, Calli," Lachlan instructed.

If I'd have had to guess before then, I would never have pegged Lachlan as being dominant in the bedroom. I guess it was right what they said, it was *always* the quiet ones.

With a grin on my face, I climbed up on my hands and

knees, bringing my face level with Tanner's cock as he knelt on the edge of the bed and moved closer.

Lachlan's fingers swiped through my wet pussy, moving up to my ass as his fingers circled my hole.

"The next time we do this, I'm going to fuck your ass while Tanner takes your pussy," Lachlan growled, pushing one finger slowly back into my ass. "So we'd better get you used to taking something here."

My arms shook as I felt the head of Lachlan's cock brush against my pussy as his finger pumped inside my ass.

"Fucking hell, that's even hotter than watching you take her mouth," Tanner swore.

Then my mouth fell open as Lachlan slowly pushed his cock into my pussy. I felt my walls quiver around him as he forced himself into my body. His finger never relented from fucking my ass as his cock took possession of my pussy.

My mouth dropped open, and Tanner's cock brushed against my lips.

"You are so fucking beautiful right now," he told me, not giving me a chance to respond before his cock filled my mouth.

Lachlan paused as he finally had his cock fully sheathed inside me, his finger relentlessly pushing in and out of my ass.

"We need to get you a plug," he growled. "Your ass is so tight, sweetheart."

I groaned at the sound of his words. With his fingers in my ass now, I'd agree to just about anything. I was fairly new to all of this, but I wanted more, so much more.

Tanner's hips snapped forward in response to Lachlan's words, and he swore softly.

They quickly fell into a rhythm, both of them pushing inside me at the same time. Words of praise dripped from their lips as we all chased the release that was promised at the end. For the first time in days, my mind completely cleared. The worries and stress fled me as my two mates occupied my body and thoughts.

Tanner came first, spilling down my throat with a shout as I hungrily drank him. He didn't move away. Instead, he flopped back on the bed, watching the way Lachlan drove himself inside of me like we were his own personal show.

Lachlan pulled me up from the bed, holding me close against his chest as his hips snapped forward hard, thrusting his cock relentlessly inside of me. His hand reached my throat as the other cupped my breast, teasing my nipples between his fingers.

It was so many sensations all at once, and my head fell back onto his shoulder without thought.

I could feel the orgasm building inside of me like a storm brewing on the horizon. My magic joined the turmoil, and I recognised it as the mate bond pushing to be made. My mouth watered at the thought of placing the mating bite on Lachlan's body, and I felt Lachlan's lips graze against the soft skin of my neck and my shoulder.

"Don't fight it," Tanner mumbled from in front of us. "What you're feeling is completely natural for your wolf. It won't hurt her."

Lachlan seemed to hesitate, and his pace slowed. I could tell without seeing him that he was struggling with the urge that was filling him.

Taking his hands, I stopped his movements, moving away from him, so his cock slipped free of my body. I couldn't help the whine of distress that fell from my lips at losing his touch, even though I had been the one to move.

It wouldn't be for long, though.

Turning around, I pushed Lachlan back on the bed, and he

fell backward onto his butt with a look of surprise on his face. It quickly turned into one of masculine approval, though, as I straddled his lap and sank myself back down on his cock, my head falling back as I sighed in contentment.

At first, I set a slow pace, locking eyes with Lachlan as I rode his cock. I could see the hesitation and the indecision brewing in his look. I could also kick myself for not seeing this coming before. It was like Lachlan's human brain was at war with the natural instincts of his wolf. He hadn't been raised in our world, and he'd only just gotten his wolf. This was bound to be confusing for him.

"I feel it too," I reassured him. Then, craning my head to the side, I drew his attention to the faint mark Tanner had left on my neck. "This is how we complete the bond, Lachlan. I promise you, it's going to feel incredible, and you aren't going to hurt me. But if you aren't ready for this step, we can always…"

And then he bit down on my shoulder, and my orgasm flared to life at the feeling as my pussy clamped down around him, and I shouted out as wave after wave of sensation flowed through my body.

I didn't remember making a move to place my own bite, but my teeth sank into Lachlan's shoulder as he leaned up on his knees, grabbing my hips and thrusting hard inside of me as he shouted out his release.

The magic between us soared and crashed down around us. The bond was complete, but it was different this time. I could tell this was my last mate, the final bond I'd had to make, and the contentment coming off my magic felt so right. It was like a warm hug as it wrapped around us, and a surge of emotions came through the bond that I knew came from each of my mates.

"That was so fucking hot," Tanner's amused voice said,

breaking through the moment as Lachlan and I sank down to the mattress, sweaty and satisfied.

"You are so fucking kinky." I laughed, patting Tanner's hip as he shuffled closer to spoon me from behind. "I absolutely adore it."

"Why, thank you." I could hear the smirk in his voice. "Is she going to let me do this again? Is it weird that I want to watch her with the others?"

"It's not weird," Lachlan said sleepily as he nuzzled against my front. "It was hot watching you with her."

"And we are absolutely doing this again," I added, just to make sure everyone knew this was definitely becoming a thing because I could totally get used to this.

"What the fuck?" Tanner gasped, sitting up suddenly; and I pouted as a rush of cold air ran down my back from his absence.

"Nooooo," I complained, flailing one hand around behind me, trying to grab hold of Tanner and pull him back against me.

Tanner gripped my hand with a chuckle and squeezed it gently. "Resist the sex coma for a minute. We need to talk," he joked.

"No, I like the sex coma," I groaned. "You were the one to suggest it. We only agreed with you. It's okay if you don't really want to do this again." I'd definitely be disappointed, but I wasn't about to make him do anything he wasn't comfortable with.

"What? No, of course, we're doing this again. I fucking love watching one of the others make you come," Tanner told me seriously, and I felt him shuffle on the bed behind me, knowing that just the thought was turning him on again. "What I'm talking about is that I didn't say that out loud."

"I distinctly heard you say something about would I let

you do it again, and you asked if it was weird that you liked to watch. You just did that talking without realising thing. It's nothing to be embarrassed about."

Now that I had hold of his hand, I tugged Tanner's arm across my body, attempting to get him back where I wanted so we could have a cheeky nap.

The sudden tug on his arm had him losing his balance and falling across my body instead. His face came dangerously close to Lachlan's crotch.

"Now, this is a place I've never been before," he laughed before flailing about as he tried to straighten himself up. "But we need to be serious. I didn't say that out loud," Tanner persisted.

Lachlan sat up, starting to take Tanner seriously, and I was going into full-on pout mode now that I'd lost them both. There went my nap. Maybe I could pretend I needed sleep to recover. No, that was a bit of a dick move. I couldn't lie about something like that.

"We heard your thoughts?" Lachlan asked Tanner, his brow dipping in thought.

"It's not far from the realm of possibility. We can do it in wolf form. It's another of those weird things that happen around me," I said with a shrug.

Lachlan looked down at me, his eyes wide in surprise as his mouth opened. "Can all wolves do that?" he asked.

"No, when Calli joined, the pack bond was changed. I've never heard of another pack having a bond like that before," Tanner told him.

"I wonder if that's part of the animage thing?" Lachlan wondered aloud, and I could see that he was seconds away from getting out of bed.

"Gah, we're getting up, aren't we?" I sulked. But now

that they'd brought it up, I had to admit I was curious about the whole thing myself.

"We should gather everyone in the mate bond and discuss this between ourselves," Lachlan decided, swinging his legs off the bed. "We shouldn't advertise this to the others until we know more about what is happening."

It was sensible. Especially when we had Wells and that squirrelly doctor here. Well, he wasn't exactly squirrelly. I just didn't like him.

"Nah, he's definitely squirrelly," Tanner agreed, even though I hadn't said the words aloud.

Looking at him in alarm, I realised how problematic this could be if we could all hear every thought the others in our bond had.

"Yeah, we should probably go and find out how we control this thing," I decided, quickly getting out of bed and looking around for my clothes that were scattered on the ground.

"What's the rush?" Tanner laughed, lounging on the bed, completely naked with his hands behind his head.

My eyes roamed across his naked body, and I could feel myself heating up just from the sight of him. All I could think about was trailing my tongue up his body and riding his now hardening cock.

"Mmmmm. I, for one, am loving having access to every thought you have," Tanner smirked, his eyes flaring wide with lust.

Lachlan loudly clapped his hands together, startling me out of my lust-filled brain.

"I'm going to be the killjoy that stops this getting out of hand before we get carried away," he said almost reluctantly. When I looked up and saw the evidence of him getting aroused again, I understood the tone.

Quickly pulling on my clothes, I picked up Tanner's clothes and threw them at him.

"Please, for the love of God, put some clothes on. Otherwise, I'm going to start thinking about all the things I want to do to you, and we're never going to make it out of this room." I laughed. At least I wasn't the only one pouting now.

12
RIVER

I was so busy trying to stop Grey from attacking Wells that the wave of lust suddenly flooding my body took me completely by surprise. Especially when I realised it wasn't my own.

"What the fuck was that?" Grey groaned, his voice mirroring exactly how I felt.

"I…I think it was the bond," I said, my brow furrowing in confusion.

I caught the way Wells looked at us in interest, and even though the need to discuss this at length was grating at me, I tried my hardest to hold it in.

Grey turned and looked toward the stairs. When we'd come back to the house and found the kitchen with a half-prepared meal on the counter and the downstairs strangely empty. It didn't take a genius to figure out where the others had gone. What surprised me, though, was that Tanner seemed to have joined Lachlan and Calli.

I was certain this would be their first time together. Even knowing about Tanner's newfound love of watching, I didn't expect Lachlan to be into that sort of thing.

"What!" Grey spluttered. "I don't really think that's something we should be talking about in front of Wells, River!"

"I didn't say anything!" I protested, not liking the accusation, even though I had no idea what he was talking about.

"Look, River…" Grey started, only to be interrupted by Wells.

"He actually didn't say anything," Wells said in my defence, looking between Grey and I like he'd never been happier in his life. "But you heard him nevertheless."

The satisfied look on Wells' face confused the fuck out of me, but it also pissed me off. It was more and more evident he knew a lot more about what was happening than we did, and while he still felt like an outsider to us, it felt like a massive violation.

Clearly, he was more entangled with whatever events were unfolding than we were aware of, since we'd continued to be kept on the outside. So the fact that Wells had become one of the super special flowers that actually got to know what was happening felt a bit insulting.

Wells sat back in his seat, steepling his hands together in front of his face.

"They will be here in a few hours," he finally said. "We can discuss it at length once they arrive."

"This is bullshit!" Grey spat. "This is my pack and my lands. If you expect to stay here, you'll start showing me some respect and spit it the fuck out."

At his outburst, the lash of alpha power that filled the room had me gasping for breath. Not only was it stronger than I'd ever felt before, but I was pretty sure the enraged growl I could hear in my mind didn't belong to my wolf.

"Grey," I spoke calmly, gently putting a hand on my brother's shoulder as I turned him to look at me instead of the smirking wolf in front of us. "Challenging him isn't going to get us answers any quicker. The only thing you can do now is help the newcomers to the pack. Make sure they're settling. We still need to speak with the witches," I pointed out.

I'd soon learned that the quickest way to pull Grey out of a surge of alpha emotions was to redirect him toward something that would speak to the alpha in him. Right now, we had that in bucketfuls. There were constant fires around here that needed putting out, and it was probably contributing to his volatile mood right now.

"Fine," he snarled through gritted teeth, striding out of the kitchen without looking back at Wells.

"You'd do well not to aggravate him," I warned Wells. "He's balancing on a very thin ledge right now, and I'm not sure you have enough friends here to stop him if he suddenly falls."

"Well, that's just hurtful," Wells said with a faux pout. "When you know how much I've done to help you all, you're going to regret that."

It wasn't a threat, it was a playful warning, but it was also a fucking annoying reminder that he knew so much more about what was happening right now than we did.

Not wanting to engage with Wells any further, I decided the best course of action would be to follow Grey and make sure he didn't get into any more trouble.

We'd managed to find a small group of the survivors on our search, but in reality, there was just too much ground to cover and from the scent trails we'd picked up, they'd all scattered when they left the house. We'd brought a group of four shifters back, and they were adamant that they wanted to leave now. Not trusting us in the slightest since a council member had turned up.

We'd offered to find them a place with the underground,

but they wouldn't listen. They didn't want anything from us, not trusting that we weren't sending them back to another facility. Finally, we'd persuaded them to wait until the morning when we could get them a vehicle, so they wouldn't be on foot. They'd at least agreed to that much. Perhaps between now and then, we'd be able to change their minds about the underground. On their own, they'd be easy targets to get picked up again by whoever was responsible for all this.

I found Grey with Aidan and Colt's pack, standing next to the foundations they'd dug out for the first cabin. They'd gotten a lot done this morning, and it was impressive progress.

Aidan explained the layout to Grey, and whilst I could see him trying to take it all in, I could also see that he was still pissed as hell.

"What's going on inside?" Colt snapped, breaking into the conversation.

It wasn't helping with the mood Grey was in.

"Don't we wish we knew!" Grey snapped back.

"It would appear that Councilman Wells is more involved with certain events than we have been led to believe, and he won't explain himself until certain other parties have arrived," I explained, feeling pretty proud of my diplomatic wording.

I caught Grey's eyes rolling. Dick.

Grey's head whipped in my direction, and his eyes squinted in annoyance. Okay, maybe I needed to be careful with what I thought until we had a hold on what was going on.

"You think?" Grey snarked.

The others looked between us, clearly confused about what was happening.

"Is he on our side, or are we standing here with our thumbs up our asses waiting for him to close a trap around us?" Colt asked, looking toward his other pack members in concern.

Grey sighed, and I saw a bit of the tension leak out of him. He was dealing with the changes he was going through better than anyone I knew would be able to. If it was me, I'd be a quivering wreck by now. But, he'd always possessed an inner strength I'd never been capable of.

Grey's hand clasped my shoulder, acknowledging that he'd heard what I'd been thinking, but he didn't say anything to further confuse the people standing around us.

"Wells may be an annoying asshole, but he's helped us in the past, and as much as I hate to admit it, he's a pretty good guy. I don't doubt he has his own agenda, but I don't think he'd do anything that would put us at risk."

I nodded in agreement with Grey's words, and the others seemed to settle a little.

Aidan looked back at the house in concern.

"Perhaps we should keep the pups out of the house more until we know what's happening," he suggested. He was just as attached to the kids as everyone else, especially since he'd discovered Jacob was his half-brother.

"That's a good idea," Grey agreed. "Can you ask them to go and bug Davion for a bit? I'd prefer them somewhere safe, and there's no one I trust more outside of our pack."

Aidan nodded in agreement and then jogged off in the direction of the other cabins where the kids were currently, no doubt, causing chaos with Cassia and Hunter. But, unfortunately, they had other house visitors as well.

Colt pursed his lips as he turned back to the foundations. "I suppose we can keep ourselves busy digging out the next foundations. That way we're outside to keep an eye on things from here."

It surprised me how much Colt seemed to be settling in with our pack. I'd expected some blowback having another alpha here, especially when Grey was so unpredictable at times.

"Thanks. That would be really helpful. Where's Nash? I thought he was out here helping you guys," Grey asked, looking around like he expected Nash to pop out a foundation trench or something.

"He said something about making a call to arrange for the concrete, but that was over an hour ago. I don't know where he went," Colt said with a shrug as he picked up some spray paint to start marking out the next area to dig.

I looked around suspiciously, Nash wasn't one to wander off, and it wasn't wise for him to be on his own or away from the pack. I couldn't think of anything that would draw him away from the house. Holly was upstairs, and the garage was closed. There was nothing we couldn't do from here. Unless he'd gone on a supply run. But he and Holly had brought enough stuff to get us through the day, and there were already plans in place for Aidan to go to the wholesalers later.

"Perhaps he got caught up with some stuff in the office?" I suggested.

Something didn't feel right, and it was then that I realised a large amount of the anxiety I was feeling wasn't actually mine. It was coming from Grey.

"Come on, let's go check out the office," I told Grey, trying to prevent another spiral of emotion from him.

Colt wandered off to talk with another of his pack as they organised where the next set of foundations would be dug. He seemed pretty confident with what he was doing, so why not leave him to it?

Grey and I started back toward the house, "I thought I had this shit under control," he sighed when we were far enough away that Colt couldn't hear us.

"You're doing a lot better than I would be," I reassured him. "I think once we have our answers, it will be easier. But something has definitely changed with the bond again, and I suspect it's because Calli finalised her final mate bond."

I resisted the urge to think of all her soft curves and the things I'd like to do to her. It was weird knowing my brother would be privy to those thoughts as well, and Grey chuckled, clearly hearing what I was thinking.

"I don't want to disturb them, but we need to know what's going on. All of the not knowing is driving me crazy," Grey sighed, looking up the stairs as we walked into the house.

As if she'd been summoned by his words, Calli appeared at the top of the stairs. She was fully dressed, but she had a thoroughly fucked look about her hair that had me reciting multiplication tables in my head so I wouldn't think about anything else, especially if there was a chance Calli would be able to hear my thoughts as well.

"Ahhh, so I see you've realised what's happening." Tanner laughed, coming up behind Calli and skipping happily down the stairs, the lucky fuck. "I'm kind of disappointed. We could have had so much fun with this. So we were…."

"Wells, we'll be in the office," Grey announced loudly in the direction of the kitchen, giving Tanner a pointed look, who nodded in understanding.

"I'll go and grab Maverick," Tanner said, moving toward the doorway. "He still with the kids?"

"Yeah, he was trying to stick with Kai and see if he could help him feel more settled," I told him as he disappeared out the door.

The rest of us trailed toward the office. I caught Calli

staring longingly at the library door, it was a lot more comfortable in there, but we'd told the witches they could take the room, so they had a bit more privacy. They weren't in there now. I was pretty sure they hadn't come back to the house after Elliot helped heal Ethan.

There was no sign of Nash, and Grey immediately grew anxious again.

"See if Blake can have a look for him," I suggested.

Grey nodded, pulled his phone out of his pocket, and typed out a message.

"What's going on?" Calli asked in concern.

Sitting down on the couch, I pulled her down onto my lap.

"We're not 100% sure where Nash is," I said, trying to make it sound casual to not alarm her.

"And by 'not 100% sure', you mean you have absolutely no idea. Some people would call that the definition of missing," she snarked back, raising an eyebrow as she spoke.

Yeah, it wasn't easy to try and get one over on Calli. But the thought had a grin pulling at my lips.

"Flattery will get you everywhere," she murmured, dropping a soft kiss on my lips before she turned to look at Grey.

Curiously, I couldn't hear what he was thinking, but I could feel his anxiety. It was uncomfortable feeling someone else's distress rub against your own. All it did was bank my own anxiety higher.

Maverick and Tanner came through the door then. Tanner looked around the room and then frowned in disappointment.

"He wasn't with the kids or Davion," Tanner informed us.

"We've got Blake out looking for him. So let's not panic just yet. Let's wait until we hear back, and then we can form a plan. We've got enough on our plate without adding things to it prematurely," I reasoned.

"Has anyone tried calling him?" Lachlan asked from where he'd been quietly sitting at his desk, shuffling through some paperwork.

Grey looked down at the phone in his hand like it was some kind of foreign object, and then with a laugh and a roll of his eyes, he called Nash.

We felt the relief through the bond before Grey even spoke, and the rest of us relaxed.

"We were worried," Grey told Nash gruffly. "Come back to the house. We can't have people wandering the woods alone. We're in the office talking through some issues. We're expecting some more visitors soon. Keep an eye on Wells, and we'll be done before the newcomers get here."

Nash must have said something in response because Grey went quiet for a moment, listening to the call.

"Okay." And then he hung up the phone.

"He was running around the woods on his own?" Tanner deadpanned, clearly unimpressed with this information.

"Apparently, he thought he saw someone moving through the trees and went to go and investigate," Grey responded, but the look on his face seemed to imply he wasn't sure if that was the truth. Which was crazy. Why would Nash lie about something like that?

"Because he's hiding something," Grey said in a low tone, responding to the thought I'd just had.

"Okay, well, that's creepy because now I'm here with you all, and I just heard what River was thinking. I'm starting to believe Tanner, which is weird in itself," Maverick told us, giving his brother the side-eye followed by a grin.

It was good to see the two brothers starting to bond with

each other. They deserved this bit of happiness after everything they'd been through.

"Awww, I didn't know you cared so much, Riv," Tanner laughed.

"Yeah, we need to get a lid on this or something because it's going to drive us all crazy," I laughed.

At least I hadn't been thinking…nooooooo, think of flowers, trees, and the bluest sky you'd ever seen.

Everyone started to laugh at my expense, and I couldn't help but join them. But, yeah, this was going to get awkward real quick.

"You said you didn't believe Tanner," Calli pointed out to Maverick. "That means you couldn't hear us when you weren't close by."

"Nope, I didn't get a thing when I was over at Cassia's. I felt a surge of something through the bond, and I was coming to find out what was going on, but I didn't get anything as clear as thoughts. It was more of a feeling," he said with a shrug.

"Well, we can't exactly spend the rest of our lives keeping a 100-yard distance between us at all times," Tanner told us, and then a flash of an image of Calli completely naked on a bed came through the bond.

"Tanner!" Calli screeched over the sound of every male in the room growling in approval.

"I can't help it!" Tanner protested.

"Okay, okay, I think we all need to calm down a bit," Lachlan told us, standing from his seat, which unfortunately was followed by an image of Calli bent over in front of him, taking Tanner's cock into her mouth.

"Lachlan!" Calli screeched even louder.

"Gah, brain bleach! I need brain bleach now!" Maverick screeched louder still.

"I'm sorry, I'm sorry," Lachlan blurted out, his laughter completely ruining the apology.

"Well, let's see how you like it," Calli huffed, but thankfully everyone's shouted protests and begging stopped anything coming through.

"We really need to get a handle on this," Grey chuckled, looking around us. "Ideas?"

Calli sighed, settling back against me. "This is different from when we're wolves. When we're in that form, you have to purposefully project your thoughts out to the group. Maybe the reverse will work?"

"And why can't we hear Grey?" I pointed out in case no one else had realised it too.

"You can't?" Grey seemed pretty surprised, and his face scrunched up in thought, but still, nothing came through the bond.

"I can feel your emotions, but I'm not getting a voice in my head like I do with the others."

Grey locked eyes with me, and then his voice came through as clear as day. "Can you hear me now?"

"Yeah, I fucking can." Shit, it was kinda freaky when he did it like that.

"So Grey has to purposefully project his thoughts. Perhaps it's something to do with him being an alpha," Calli theorised.

Calli didn't sound like she was entirely sure. While her idea of consciously trying not to project sounded exhausting, it also wouldn't hurt to try.

"Perhaps this is all just because the bond is new. Maybe it will change again once the bond has had time to settle," Tanner suggested.

"And then when it changes again, it will all go crazy again," Calli's thoughts came through to us all.

"If the bonds are finalised now, I don't think that will be a problem," Lachlan told her, trying to soothe her worry.

"Don't think, don't think, DON'T THINK," Calli thought, clearly panicking.

"Calli!" Grey warned, the rumble of his wolf lining his voice.

I felt the shiver run through her body at the sound. I'd never got to experience the sensation of lust flooding through her before, though. My cock hardened instantly, but then the confusing thought of wondering if it was my brother's voice that had given me a hard-on instantly had me deflating.

Tanner burst out into hysterical laughter, and it was impossible not to join in with him. Life was going to get very amusing until we had this under control.

When we'd managed to settle down, I realised that Grey had Calli pinned with his stare, and she looked like a child about to be chastised.

"What's going on?" I asked, wrapping my arms tightly around my mate. It was impossible not to reach for her when I thought she could be hurting in some way.

"What are you hiding, Calli?" Grey growled.

"I…I didn't mean to hide it. I'd just found out, and then everything happened all at once with Stone and the facility and I kind of, sort of, forgot to talk to everyone about it." Calli visibly deflated the more she spoke, and I started to worry.

"Spill it," Grey barked, his alpha power seeping out into the room.

At that moment, the tingle of the wards being crossed ran down my spine, and it was hard not to understand how Calli could have gotten sidetracked into forgetting to tell us something. We were constantly moving from one fight to the next around here.

"This isn't over," Grey said softly as he stood from his seat and strode over to us. Then, looking down at Calli with a disapproving look, he added, "We don't hide things from each other. There's nothing you couldn't tell us."

Calli nodded and looked around the room at all of us. "I promise you, it wasn't intentional," she told us. "As soon as we deal with this, let's go upstairs and talk."

Everyone nodded, and we all started to move to see who was approaching and what would happen next.

One thing was certain: life would never be boring around here.

13
MAVERICK

Calli looked so deep in thought as we moved to the door, clearly beating herself up for something that wasn't her fault, when I realised I couldn't hear her.

"I can't hear what you're thinking," I blurted out, looking at Calli in alarm. I could feel the faint glimmer of panic running through me at the thought that I'd lost the bond.

"Neither can I," Lachlan said with a frown. At least I wasn't the only one, but that wasn't exactly a pleasant thought.

"I just did what we suggested. I made sure I wasn't projecting my thoughts," Calli said with a shrug.

"How did you do it?" I asked quickly. I'd pretty much try anything if it was going to prevent the view of my brother's balls from being blasted into my mind.

Tanner chuckled softly behind me, and I already knew I'd thought that out loud, if that even made sense.

"There's no need to be intimidated, little brother," Tanner laughed, slinging an arm around my shoulders. "Not everyone can be as lucky as I am in that department."

Calli rolled her eyes at his antics. "I imagined a barrier around me, kind of like a ward," she said with a shrug. "Think of it as pulling on a coat," she suggested.

Everyone fell quiet as we tried to do what she'd suggested. There was no way it would be as easy as that, though. Calli had years of experience with magic, so she would probably find this easier than we would.

"Can you see my dick yet?" Tanner asked, making me jump away from him like he'd just declared he had cooties. "Not my actual dick," he laughed like it hadn't been obvious.

"No, thank god!" I declared with a shudder.

"As entertaining as this is," Grey said, reaching for the door handle. "We don't have time for this. We can talk about it later when Calli confesses all her secrets."

Grey gave Calli a cheeky grin as he pulled open the door, but I caught the edge of worry coming through the bond from her. The others must have felt it too because River pulled her tighter to his side, and Lachlan grazed his fingers against her hand as he passed her.

Maybe this new bond development wasn't as bad as we'd initially thought. There was something about knowing none of us would be able to hide anything from the others that felt comforting.

I knew it was coming from the fucked up way I'd been brought up, but I was working on those feelings. And there was no better place for me to do that than here with this pack —my family.

We all moved as a group to the front of the house and walked through the front door just in time to see some people climbing out of a car. I recognised two of them, Calli's uncle, Sean, and the witch, Jessa, who was her newly discovered Aunt.

I felt the spike of pain Calli felt at seeing her Aunt, the

twin of her mother, and I reached between us to hold her hand in support.

The second woman, who'd gotten out of the other side of the car, was a complete mystery to me. I'd never seen her before, and even though she scented as a human, I had a feeling she wasn't.

"Marie!" Calli gasped, dropping mine and River's hands and jogging down the steps to the woman. "Comment vas-tu, que fais-tu ici?" she asked, throwing her arms around the woman who held her tight, laughter lighting her face.

"Ma belle fille. Oh, comme tu m'as manqué "

Fucking Christ! Calli speaking French was possibly the sexiest thing I'd ever heard, and I was pulling that barrier around me as tight as I could as my entire body responded to her.

"Sean," Grey said, nodding toward him as he extended his hand in greeting. "Wells is inside. He's promised us an explanation. I trust it's actually coming this time."

Grey had his big dick alpha power on display. He was obviously displeased with being kept in the dark. But he was handling it better than any other alpha I'd met before. My father would have killed someone in a tantrum by now.

Sean, however, seemed more amused than anything. Something about the man always came across as not quite right, and it seemed like everyone else was starting to think the same thing.

The two women stood and watched the interaction with interest, Marie with her arm wrapped around Calli's waist. They'd clearly been close at some point in time, and I hoped that whatever was about to come out wouldn't change that for them.

"I'm pretty sure men do this when they're about to kiss,"

Jessa whispered cheekily, which had Sean spluttering in denial as he pulled his hand out of Grey's.

"It took you long enough," Wells sighed from behind us. "Can we get down to the whole explanation part now? I'm hungry, and I feel like I'm not going to be fed until they're satisfied. I nearly died today, you know, not that any of you are apparently concerned about my well-being," he sulked.

Jessa laughed at his dramatics before she jogged up the steps and surprised us all as she wrapped her arms around the Councilman, laying her lips on his.

"I'll kiss it better later," she whispered, which had Calli recoiling in horror.

"Oh my god, I am not calling you Uncle Wells," she gasped dramatically.

It was a bit creepy given how much of a flirt Wells always seemed to be.

"Let's get this over with," Sean sighed, moving toward the steps to the house. Then, with a second thought, he paused and looked back at Calli. "Everything we've done has been for you. I know you don't trust me anymore, Calli, but I hope that once you see that, you'll learn how to again."

We all heard the sorrow in his voice, and Calli looked away from him, unable to hold his gaze. Sean had a long way to go if he was going to gain her trust again, and it broke my heart on Calli's behalf. She'd lost so much already. It wasn't fair that she should have to lose Sean as well.

This whole situation was so fucked up, and I had a terrible feeling that once we learned the truth, it would get so much worse.

We moved inside the house as a group. Grey led us to the library, which was thankfully vacant. Someone was going to need to try and find the witches soon. They might not have been shifters, but it still wasn't sensible to wander alone right now.

Everyone settled around the room, Calli between River and me on one of the couches. Grey was standing by the fireplace, and I could practically see the restless energy vibrating from him. Something was bothering him. Something more than what was happening right now. It wasn't like him to keep things to himself, not when he'd just been telling Calli she needed to spill her secrets.

Maybe it wasn't such a good idea to figure out how to block each other.

14
CALLI

Sean started to pace by the window, and I could see he was getting ready to explain everything.

It hurt to see him here with Wells. I was dreading what he was about to tell us. It wasn't about how much he'd been hiding from us. It was because I didn't want to push him any further away than he already was. Sean was an important part of my life, and I didn't want that to change.

Wells had taken one of the armchairs, and Jessa was inexplicably sitting on his knee. The more I looked at them out of the corner of my eye, the more I started to suspect that she was his mate, and that was raising all kinds of weird and complicated questions.

Sean finally came to a stop and turned to look at me. The regret and pain in his eyes was beginning to make me feel like I was going to throw up.

"I'm not sure I know where to start," he said sadly, looking at Jessa and Marie to ask for help. It was the only time I'd seen the dragon shifter look even remotely vulnerable.

"I shall start then," Marie said in her thick French accent.

"Your mother came to me when we were both young witches and told me all about a vision she and her sister had seen. A vision of a terrible, terrible future. I have never been so scared in my life. I knew the power of our seers, and I knew what she was telling me would be unavoidable. But then she told me they had a plan to prevent it from happening. They had seen a different future for us, but it would come with great sacrifice."

She stood as her eyes welled with tears, and we all waited for her to compose herself before she could speak again. Marie had been close with my mother. I'd always thought they should have been sisters. She'd taken the loss of my mother as badly as I had. Everyone who knew her had loved her. It was impossible not to be devastated by her loss.

"Calli, your parents knew that there was a specific path you had to follow. A dangerous and terrible path. But it would only be by letting you follow it that you would be able to reach a place where you found all of your mates. We couldn't risk interfering with any of the events that would bring them to you because it's only when you have them by your side that you can ascend to the position of Pack Queen."

All of my mates turned to look at me in surprise. This was the information I hadn't told them yet. The animage Queen.

Jessa looked around us in surprise, clearly seeing that my guys had no idea what Marie was talking about. "I'm confused. I gave you the means to read the book. Have you not done that yet?" she asked.

"I have," I sighed before pulling that block of magic from around me so my mates could feel how much I meant the words I was about to say. "I didn't know how to deal with everything I read, and I wanted some time to think and try and wrap my mind around it all. But then everything started to spiral out of control, and we haven't had the time to sit down and talk about it."

Grey looked pissed, but when he walked over to me, he dropped to his knees in front of me.

"I'm sorry that we haven't been able to support you through this. You shouldn't feel like you can't come to one of us when you need help with something. We're here for you, Calli. Completely and wholly yours. There is nothing in this world more important than you. Never doubt us, you only need to reach out, and one of us will be there. At any time, in any situation. There is nothing that could keep us from you."

I saw Marie swipe a tear from her eye, but I was so centred on Grey, I didn't have it in me to pay any attention to the others in the room. Slipping off the edge of the couch, I straddled his lap and wrapped my arms around him.

Grey wrapped me in his arms, clinging to me, and a feeling of safety and love flowed from me through the bond to the others. I felt the wave of love that came back from them. It wrapped around me, blanketing me in love and security. Maybe this bond wasn't so bad after all.

Looking back up, I glanced around the room to see our visitors staring down at us in happiness. I had a feeling they'd been through a lot to get us to this point. I shouldn't be angry with them. I should be grateful they were willing to make such a sacrifice for me.

Grey gripped my hips and lifted me back to the couch before saying, "It's time, Calli. Tell us what you read."

So I did. I told them everything I'd read in the book and everything I'd come to realise during our encounter with Neressa. I told them about how a Queen was born from animage and witch bloodlines when they were combined. Explaining that when an alpha took a Queen as his mate, and she had bonded with all of her mates, her magic would change the pack and those inside it. Gifting them with magic they'd never had before. As much as I didn't want to, I even told them that the strength of a Pack Queen was determined by the number of her mates, and before me, the most on record was three.

The guys fell silent as they started to digest the information I'd given them. It was a lot to take in. But as I sat there and waited, even if in reality it was only for a few seconds, my stomach felt like it was about to plummet to the ground.

"I suspect this is why Neressa always called herself the Witch Queen," Jessa filled in. "She wanted what the animages had so badly that she decided to take the title for herself."

"As soon as your bonds are completed, you'll start to see changes throughout the pack. Everyone will start the final process of returning to their animage heritage. Because of your strength, Calli, we believe that you'll be able to return the pack to what we always should have been," Wells told me.

Hearing him talking about completing bonds was creeping me out, especially while he still had Jessa sitting on his lap.

"This is incredible," Lachlan said, leaning back in his seat. I could practically see his mind spinning as he went over the information in his mind. "We knew the bond between us was different, and we've already seen the evidence of the changes we've been going through. Yet it still all feels kind of unbelievable."

"Yeah, it takes some time to wrap your head around," Wells agreed wryly. "Try finding your mate and then having to let her walk away for ten years," he grumbled.

"You're jumping ahead," Jessa chastised, playfully pushing his shoulder.

"Tell us about the future we're trying to prevent," Grey demanded, turning towards Marie. "We need to understand what we're fighting for."

"For our lives," Marie said simply. "Your mother and Jessa saw a future where the wolves and the witches break out into an all-out war. The wolves were able to harness a form of magic and turn it on the witches. They retaliated, and thousands died. It was impossible to keep what was happening from the humans, and our world was exposed. Eventually, the humans found a way to detect those that were different and a cull began. The witches were wiped out within a matter of weeks. Shifters were on the verge of extinction. Small pockets had escaped to less populated areas, but it was only a matter of time."

"So we're trying to stop a war between both sides," Lachlan said slowly, working it through in his mind. "But both sides are still trading blows and have been for years. They're never going to find peace. It's impossible."

"Taking Neressa out of the picture is a big win. Without her stoking the flames of hate, the witches are unlikely to keep hitting out at the shifters," Sean started.

"It won't stop the hunts," Jessa cut in. This was clearly an argument they'd been having, time and time again. "Those who have a taste for it aren't going to stop."

"But they don't have Neressa and her coven to cover their tracks now. So they will have to stand up and admit what they're doing," Sean sighed. "None of the witches will accept the shame of admitting something like that. It would jeopardise their positions in the covens."

"Not if their leaders are doing it as well," I added, already seeing how this would happen. And if I was right, it would be impossible to stop. "The Triquetra gave three male witches to Neressa as a gift. They're clearly working with her in some capacity. They came to us asking for help to get rid of her. There's no way they would have done that without exhausting every possible avenue first. That would include partaking in the hunts themselves for the power boost."

"How do they mask their scent, though?" Maverick asked. "It's easy to scent corrupted magic. Witches must be able to tell the difference too."

"Marie masked my scent. It's difficult, but it's not impossible. If we could do it, there's no saying someone else couldn't," I pointed out.

"But for the hunts to be as widespread as you're suggesting, it would have to be an easy enough process that virtually anyone could do it," Tanner argued.

He was right. From what I'd learned, it had taken Marie and one of her friends years to come up with the spell. It wasn't something just anybody could do. Marie was one of the best spell casting witches there were.

"We don't know how they're doing it, but they are," Marie said with a shrug.

"So the only way to stop this is to stop the wolves from acquiring this form of magic you're talking about. You want us to stand against our own people." Grey didn't look happy by his realisation, and I have to say, I wasn't all that impressed with the idea either. It might stop the war, but it would also mean the wolves would stay vulnerable enough for the hunts to continue. With their own magic, they'd finally have a weapon to fight back against the witches.

"Not exactly," Sean told us, giving us a glimmer of hope. "I think you can already guess that Stone is the one we're up against. From what we can gather, he's been doing something at the facility to try and access some kind of power."

"Neressa knew I was an animage. She called me 'Little Queen'," I said aloud as I started to put the pieces together.

"The women we rescued, something was done to them to turn them into shifters, but it's almost like it wasn't done right, or they changed them into something else."

"You think they're trying to create animages," Sean realised.

"They had access to Neressa and presumably her coven. They were imprisoning shifters and experimenting on them. It's not entirely out of the realm of possibility that they were trying to combine the two sets of DNA to make an animage," I said with a shrug. I was so out of my depth that I didn't even know if what I was suggesting was possible.

"But then what? Once they have an animage, what would their next step be?" Wells asked, looking concerned.

"Lea said that after they worked on them in the lab, they'd wake up in one of the cages with the men. She said they did something to them, so they weren't able to…resist. I think they were trying to force a mating," I told them, feeling sick to my stomach.

"If they could somehow manufacture a Queen and find a way to force her to take a mate, Stone could presumably mate with the Queen and obtain access to her magic that way," Jessa pointed out. "The bond, if successful, would have the impact of changing his entire pack if they accepted her as their Queen."

"I don't see Stone ever accepting anyone to be Queen over his pack," Wells scoffed.

"He's right," Maverick agreed, "My father would never allow someone to come into the pack and take that much power, even if they were just his puppet. He'd never lose face like that."

"There's something else I don't understand," River cut in. "Why would the witches even work with Stone? What do they have to gain from it?"

"The Triquetra hated the amount of magic the animages could wield. But, if they could get their hands on that amount of power and have the ability to gift it to those in their coven, there would be no one that could stand against them. They'd essentially rule over our race, and no one would be able to stop them," Jessa explained.

"So they're hoping for a cut of the action," Tanner nodded like we were suddenly in some kind of mafia movie.

"But how would Stone creating a Queen for himself do that?" I asked.

None of this made sense. We were obviously missing something. The problem was, what were the chances of us ever finding it out, and would we be able to fight Stone without that missing piece of information?

"We might get some more information when we get into the laptop," Lachlan pointed out.

I'd forgotten about the laptop!

"What laptop?" Sean and Wells both asked simultaneously, both of them looking intently at Lachlan.

"Davion recovered one from the facility before we set it alight. But, unfortunately, it's password-protected, and we don't have the skills to get into it," Lachlan told them. "I have someone I trust working on it."

"This could actually help," Sean said, a gleam of hope in his eyes.

The room fell quiet, almost as if we were waiting for something to go wrong. Wins came so rarely now, it almost seemed too good to be true.

But as we all took a moment to absorb the fact that we potentially had answers at our fingertips, I couldn't help but start to grow anxious about what it was they hadn't been telling us. What could be making Sean so nervous that he was worried about me hating him once it was said?

"So, now we know the why," Grey said slowly.

He'd moved from in front of me to stand behind the couch, and I felt his hand come to my shoulder as he spoke. He knew the next bit would be hard, and he was here for me. River and Maverick gripped my hands a little harder, and I saw Lachlan and Tanner look across the room to me. They were all here. They always would be.

Sean sat down on the window sill, his elbows coming to his knees as he threaded his fingers through his hair, tugging at the lengths.

"It's about your parents. I didn't know Calli. I swear I didn't," Sean said slowly, not lifting his eyes from the carpet at his feet. "Your mother knew that none of this would start until they were gone. They always knew there was an end date for them, that they wouldn't be around to help you get through this. It broke their hearts, Calli. Knowing they'd be leaving you tore at them every day." Sean looked up to meet my eyes, and I could see tears already coursing down his cheeks.

I'd never seen this man cry before, and seeing it now absolutely terrified me.

"The rogue coven was stepping up the hunts, and more and more shifters were going missing. We were worried that we were running out of time. She...she was desperate," Sean stuttered.

"What did she do?" I asked, dread forming in my stomach.

I could feel myself withdrawing. I was opening up that dark place in the back of my mind, getting ready to shove whatever he was about to say inside. We didn't have time for this. I couldn't crawl beneath the blankets and hide away from the world. The world wasn't going to let me. I apparently had people to save, whether I wanted to or not.

The tears were coming fast down his face now, and Sean just shook his head, unable to speak.

Marie reached out and placed a hand on his knee, turning to look at me. I could see her gathering the strength to tell me the news herself.

"Your mother was driving home that night. She knew what needed to happen to start the chain of events, and she took matters into her own hands," Marie whispered quietly.

"Are you trying to tell me that my mother murdered my father and killed herself at the same time?" The cold, emotionless voice I spoke in didn't even sound like my own.

"She loved your father more than anything else in this world," Jessa protested. "It wasn't like that."

"She drove their car off the road, Calli," Sean told me sadly.

"You told me they were murdered," I screamed at him, leaping out of my seat. "You let me think that someone had killed them, when it was her all along."

"I didn't know then. I promise you, Calli. I would never have told you that if I didn't truly believe it. There weren't any signs of another vehicle at the site. I never considered that your mother would…everything pointed to foul play."

Sean stood from the windowsill, taking a step toward me, almost like he was begging me just to listen, to understand.

"How do you know now?" I asked, part of me hoping that maybe he was wrong again.

"I called in a favour from someone I knew a very long time ago. Dragons aren't the only things our world has forgotten about," Sean said evasively. I could admit that my curiosity had peaked, but now wasn't really the time. There was only so much I could deal with in one sitting.

Images flashed before my eyes. All of the happy times we'd spent together as a family. I looked at every interaction I had with my mother with different eyes. Should we have seen it? Was she suicidal? Should we have known she was going to do something crazy?

My father had loved her unconditionally, and she'd taken his life. I'd always thought they were perfect together. I'd placed her on a pedestal my entire life. How could you ever say you loved someone and then hurt them so much? How could she do this to Jacob?

"How am I ever going to tell Jacob this?" I realised out loud.

At that moment, I'd never hated a single person more than I did my mother. The tears that flowed down my cheeks weren't from grief. They weren't from the sadness at the unfairness of it all, at the perfect childhood I'd perceived being crushed in front of me. No, they were from hate, from shattered illusions and the loss of respect.

No one answered my question. What was there to say? My only choices were to tell Jacob the truth and inflict on him the pain I was currently in, or let him live a lie, believing our mother had been a good person.

"What else are you keeping from us?" I asked, completely detached from the moment.

I couldn't take much more of this, but I wanted it all done now. Everything needed to be out in the open. I didn't want to come back to this room and go through all of this again. It was time to rip off the band-aid.

"The underground isn't what you think it is. Well, some of it is. We do have locations to hide vulnerable people. Everyone else is given a chance to join Wells' pack. We've been training an army."

My mouth dropped open in surprise.

"If you have an army, why do you need us?" I asked in astonishment.

Why were they playing with our lives if they were already prepared for the worst?

"Because an army is just going to lead to the downward spiral of exposure. We need to make one direct catastrophic hit on Stone, and we can't do that without a Pack Queen," Wells said, his eyes fixed seriously on me.

Grey rounded the couch quicker than I'd ever seen him move, and his alpha power lashed out in Wells' direction as he hunched down, ready to fight. Tanner was at his side before I'd even realised he'd moved, and surprisingly Lachlan was crouched, ready with magic sparking at his fingertips, ready to fight.

"You will have to go through us before you lay a hand on her," Grey growled.

Wells stood from his seat, and in one fluid movement, he had Jessa protectively behind him as his lip raised in a responding snarl.

At that moment, Sean let loose his own power, flooding the room and most likely the house with a rattling dragon growl. The two alpha wolves staggered to the side as the power lashed out at them.

"Enough," Sean roared. "We are not here to take Calli away from you," he barked at Grey, staring him down.

It wasn't the smartest move. Grey was enraged at the implication of his mate being separated from him. But we also had the new bond glimmering between us all, and his rage and need for violence flowed out to the rest of us. I felt my adrenalin spike in response, and the fingertips itched as my talons pushed through in a partial shift.

This whole situation was about to break down, and it would only end in blood.

Grey snarled, taking a step closer to Sean. A dark smokey cloud seeped out of him as he did, flowing around him, almost like the alpha power that leaked out of him had become visible.

Marie gasped, and a massive smile broke out across her face. "It has started. They have already started to go through the change," she cried happily.

Sean and Wells seemed to deflate on the spot as they watched the smokey magic roll and tumble as if it was floating on a breeze, playfully entwining around Grey's form.

"What other changes have you had already?" Sean asked as if the last few minutes hadn't just happened.

"What are you talking about?" I shouted in a fairly high-pitched, annoyed voice. I couldn't cope with the roller coaster of emotions I was being put through anymore.

"If Grey is exhibiting signs of magic, you are closer to the final change than we realised. You're nearly ready to take your place in the pack," Sean said in excitement.

"She's not going anywhere with you," Grey snarled, taking a step closer.

I watched in fascination as talons burst through from the ends of his fingertips and was stunned for a moment. A half shift was a rare talent, and not one I'd known Grey had. In fact, apart from myself, I'd never heard of any other shifter who could do it.

"You misunderstand," Jessa said calmly, pushing Wells to the side and straightening her clothes, annoyed by his sudden manhandling. "You will all be going to the pack. The intention is for you to take over the pack, and Calli will be able to gift the pack with animage powers when they accept her, their new alphas mate, as their Queen."

Words completely escaped me. They wanted Grey to take Wells' pack from him?

"Are you insane?" the normally calm River roared.

It was a crazy plan. There was only one way for an alpha to take a pack from another, and it was through violence and blood. Grey would have to challenge Wells and fight him in a dominance challenge. We didn't have them in our pack, but they were commonplace amongst the others. Wells would have to be either dead or nearly dead for Grey to be declared the winner.

Surely Wells wasn't willing to lay down his life for this. Not when he had his mate to think about as well.

"Not afraid you can't take me, are you pup?" Wells goaded.

Grey's head whipped in Wells' direction with a snarl. He was too close to the edge of losing control. We could all feel it through the bond. It wasn't wise to push him now. He was hanging by a thread, and I could feel the bloodlust pumping through him.

"I'm just not sure why you would volunteer to lie down and die," Grey snarled. His wolf was completely in control now. He didn't even sound like the man I knew.

Wells laughed, but smartly sat back down in his chair. It was as much as he'd no doubt do in terms of submitting to Grey, but it was enough to show that he wasn't a threat. He hadn't bared his neck as such, but he'd put himself in a position where he'd stand no chance if Grey decided to attack.

Grey took a step back, but I could still feel the heightened need to protect running through him.

"I think we've gone through enough for today," Marie suggested keeping the peace. "Why don't we take a step back and take the night to think through what's been said. Then, when everyone is calmer, you can come back and talk more tomorrow."

"We have others at the packhouse that we need to discuss

first," I pointed out almost reluctantly. To be honest, their leaving was the sanest thing they'd said since they got here.

Sean raised his hands and stepped back to sit on the windowsill, showing Grey that he wasn't a threat to any of us. After that, everyone seemed to retreat back to their previous positions except for Maverick, who smartly suggested Grey take his seat as he moved to stand behind the couch instead.

Grey sat down heavily on the couch and pulled me into his lap, banding his arms tightly around me as he glared around the room. He wasn't taking any chances, and if this was what he needed to calm down a bit, then it was the least I could do.

"What can we do?" Sean asked simply.

"We have three witches who want to leave, the two women we rescued, and we did have about 15 other shifters, but most of them got spooked when the Fed turned up and then ran when they saw Wells," Tanner said, filling him in.

Grey wasn't at a point where he could communicate in anything but growls and snarls.

"Wait, what cop?" Sean asked in surprise.

"Some human cop is looking into the disappearances. It's not gone unnoticed. And, if I had to put money on it, she knew what we were as well," Tanner said.

This was the first I'd heard of it, and to say it was alarming was an understatement.

"There is a section of law enforcement who are aware of our existence," Wells explained calmly. "It's not like we'd be able to keep a lid on our entire world. The logistics alone! There are some humans in power who are in the know. It filters down through to relevant people who deal with any shifter related crimes."

"But I thought humans finding out was the beginning of the end," I said in alarm.

"They've always known. Those in power don't especially care. They have their trade-offs, and it works in their favour to assist us. It's when the normal everyday folk find out that we're screwed," he explained.

"Right, normal people," I muttered, not quite sure I'd ever met one.

What was normal anyway?

"I wouldn't worry about the cop. What I am worried about, though, are the traumatised shifters you've got running around here," Wells sighed.

There was an implication of blame in the way he said it, and I wasn't the only one who bristled at the comment. Personally, I thought we were doing pretty fucking well, considering that everything that had happened until now we'd done alone.

"Four of them came back to the packhouse, and eleven remain unaccounted for. There's still a chance some of the others might come back. Let them watch us and assess if it's safe on their own. Going after them will only make them feel like they've something to run from," River sensibly argued.

"Fine, we wait until the morning then," Wells said with a shrug like it didn't matter.

The man was confusing as fuck, and I didn't envy Jessa for being stuck with him.

"I'll need time to make arrangements anyway. I have a place in mind where the witches will be safe, and the women probably won't want to come to the pack either," Sean said, pulling out his phone as he started to tap away. "Felix has connections with a coven in Italy which could be a good fit for them."

"Felix!" I suddenly blurted out, startling everyone in the room. "I forgot that Felix is on his way here."

Christ, I needed a vacation or something. I really needed

to find my iPad and get my life in order. This was starting to get ridiculous now. Maybe I could get a PA?

"How far out is he?" Sean asked, glancing up from his phone.

"I dunno." I shrugged. I couldn't keep track of myself. I didn't know how he expected me to keep track of anyone else.

Sean huffed a laugh and shook his head before returning to his phone. It grated on my nerves, and I was so done with this day.

"Oh, I'm sorry, is my entire life collapsing around me causing you an inconvenience? The next time I'm getting stabbed by a psychotic witch, I'll ask for a pause so I can update my notes app for you," I scoffed, slouching back against Grey and crossing my arms.

Marie snorted and then coughed to try and cover up the fact that me snarking at Sean was clearly hilarious. There weren't many people who ever stood up to the dragon, but he'd always just been Uncle Sean to me. At least he was when I was growing up. I wasn't too sure what he was anymore.

"My apologies," Sean drawled, and I swore he rolled his eyes. "I know you've all been through a lot. Look, get some rest, regroup. We've got some rooms booked at a hotel in the next town. We'll drop by tomorrow at breakfast and make more solid plans. It will give everyone time to update their notes app," he added cheekily.

It might have been funny, but it also made me want to launch myself at the infuriating man.

Everyone leaving was the most awkward event I'd ever witnessed. Marie and Jessa gave me hugs, which I tried to return with some enthusiasm, but I just didn't have it in me. My head was all over the place, and I couldn't decide how I felt about them. They'd hidden just as much from me as Sean had. But in truth, there was only one person I was angry at right now, and she wasn't around anymore for me to scream at her.

Sean awkwardly moved over to the car after giving me a small wave. I knew he wanted to reach out to me, but I wasn't ready for that yet. It wasn't fair of me. Even now, I knew it was unfair to be placing all the blame on him. I think it was because he'd been the only one I'd trusted out of all of them. It felt like such a bigger betrayal because of it.

They stopped at Cassia's cabin to pick up Ethan and take him back to the hotel with them. It was only when I realised Wells hadn't told us how or why they'd gotten hurt and turned up here in the condition they did. I supposed it could wait until tomorrow. If it wasn't urgent enough that we desperately needed to hear it, then I didn't have it in me to listen at that moment.

All I wanted to do was drink an entire bottle of wine and curl up with my mates in front of a movie which I'd inevitably pass out in front of. Was that too much to ask?

15
TANNER

Everyone was exhausted, and it was barely early evening. We still had a house full of people to feed, not to mention a gaggle of pups to locate. As entertaining as it would be to leave them with Davion for an entire night, I wasn't sure I could do it to the slightly annoying vampire. I might like him too much for that, which was a strange enough thought on its own.

Thankfully, in the end, Cassia, Hunter and Ethan appeared with the kids in tow.

"I thought you were heading back with Sean and the others?" I asked Ethan, confused.

"Ah, yeah, I decided to stay awhile longer." His eyes flickered to Cassia, and it didn't take a genius to read the blush on her face. "There's some more stuff we wanted to talk about. Anyway, how could I possibly leave these munchkins when we've been having so much fun."

"Hunter was teaching us how to whittle!" Jacob cried, jumping up and down in excitement.

"I'm sorry, I thought you just said that Hunter was letting

you play with knives," Calli deadpanned, scowling at the guy in question.

"No! Even I'm not that stupid. I showed them how to do it, but I was the only one holding the knife. They were just watching," Hunter protested.

Calli's scowl deepened, and I could tell she didn't think that was any better, but she didn't argue with him anymore.

Calli was exhausted, and we could all feel it through our bond. She wasn't doing as well at getting that ward around her, and we kept getting hints of her grief and anger raging through the bond to us.

It was so fucked up what Sean had said about her mom in a room full of people. Yes, it was a room full of people who loved her, but there were some things you needed to approach more gently. And telling someone their mother had killed their father, and then themselves, was one of them.

Calli had called it murder, but was it? They'd both known they were going to die when they set this whole thing up, and it seemed they were both prepared to do it if that was what it would take to protect their kids. It seemed hard to believe that Calli's father wouldn't have been fully aware of what was happening. I wasn't sure I'd have made a different decision if I was in their shoes, and it was our pups on the line.

One of them should have left some kind of explanation, though. Anything to try and ease what Calli would go through when she found out. It was like she'd lost her mother all over again, only this time she didn't even have the happy memories to comfort her.

None of us knew what to say. Calli was powering through like nothing had happened. She was trying to be strong, at least in front of the kids.

The early spring sun was warm and gentle, and we moved to the yard at the side of the house. The pups were running around, causing their usual chaos. Everyone else took the opportunity to sit back and just be. It was nice to spend time together, especially now that we had some new members to the pack we all wanted to get to know.

The four shifters who were adamant they were leaving didn't want to join us at first. Instead, they chose to stick to the house, not wanting to get caught up in pack life. I think they still thought this whole situation was some kind of trick.

When it came time to eat, we pulled out the grill, and the kids sat down with burgers and hot dogs while we grilled food for the growing number of adults we had in the house. It was the easiest way to feed this amount of people all in one go, and I had a feeling it was going to be a go-to method over the next couple of days. At least it wasn't pizza.

The missing shifters didn't return. I had a feeling they were a long way from here by now, and it was the last we'd be seeing of them.

Hopefully, they found somewhere they could call home and were at least sticking together. Running off alone not only presented the possibility of being captured, but there was something unfair about surviving that whole ordeal just to go insane from the loss of pack.

Colt and his pack were starting to settle in with us, and from the small amount of time I'd spent with them, they all seemed like good guys. I'd even nearly forgiven him for his dickish behaviour in the library.

Danny was fanboying constantly over Calli to the point where it was starting to get annoying. I got that he was grateful she'd healed him, but she was my mate, and he needed to step the fuck back.

"I'll grab you a drink, Calli," Danny gushed, springing up from his seat and running into the house before she could even say anything.

The growl that rumbled out of Grey as he watched him go would have been funny if I wasn't feeling exactly the same way.

Colt, however, was starting to find the whole thing highly amusing.

"He's just grateful to be alive," Colt told us, trying to make excuses for his friend's overly friendly behaviour. "I'll tell him tonight to calm the fuck down."

"See that you do," Grey grumbled, making Calli snicker in amusement.

From the raised eyebrow Grey gave her, she was going to pay for that later, and by the way that she shifted in her seat, I wished I could be there to see it happen.

Fuck, I needed to get this under control. The others might not like me intruding on their time alone with her, even if Calli did seem to enjoy the extra attention. There was something about watching one of the others make her fall apart that was so fucking hot.

My eyes drifted to Lachlan, who happily talked to Nash about something. Lachlan certainly hadn't objected to having me there, and he was forming his mate bond at the time.

I suppose it did take the pressure off for him. It must be weird to suddenly find yourself in a bonding situation if it wasn't something you'd grown up knowing about.

Everything Lachlan was going through must feel kind of strange to him. I should probably check in with him to make sure he was settling in okay. He seemed to be, but we were all guilty of putting on a happy face to try and work through stuff on our own.

The rescued witches shyly emerged from the house. I'd had the chance to talk to them today, and of the three of them, Brendan seemed to be taking more of a leadership role, protectively making sure that no one fucked with his friends.

Elliot, who had healed Calli, was definitely not happy about leaving, but then he'd look at Lucas, his friend. It was apparent the guy was finding it difficult being with the pack. Every time Elliot recognised that Lucas was struggling, he always looked torn up about it. As the day wore on, Lucas seemed to be shutting down more and more, and I was starting to get concerned about it. As much as we might want them to stay, it clearly wasn't in his best interest.

I'd spoken with Grey earlier about putting them into Cassia's house and seeing if maybe Hunter would mind bunking with us for a day or two until Sean could get them out of here.

As Elliot and his friends strayed closer to the group of us, they settled down on one of the blankets Calli had scattered around for everyone. Chairs were another thing we really needed to get more of.

As if the witches being braver was putting them to shame, the four other shifters emerged from the house, not wanting to appear weak. I observed them closely as the witches tried to merge with the group. They didn't feel welcome here, and whilst our pack had no problems with them, the side-eyes they were getting from the four shifters was proving hard for them to bear.

Now that we'd had the majority of the rescued shifters take off, though, the atmosphere outside was definitely more relaxed.

Talk about dropping the ball. Of course, they would be anxious about people turning up at the pack, and a council member was just about the worst person for it to be. We should have pre-empted it somehow. There was no way we could have anticipated Wells turning up like he did, half dead and with a torn apart shifter. Still, maybe we should have given them a heads-up on our association with him.

"The books…" Elliot started, but a glare from Brendan silenced him pretty quickly.

Calli assessed the three of them carefully before turning in her seat to face them. Her friendly smile was completely non-threatening, but Brendan still bristled at the attention.

"It's my mother's collection," Calli told them, not paying any attention to Brendan's need to withdraw but still speaking softly and making no moves to approach any closer. "She left them at the house for me. They've definitely come in handy over the last few months."

Now that was an understatement. We'd have been completely fucked if we didn't have half the information she'd left for us.

Elliot glanced at Brendan out of the corner of his eye. Taking in the death glare he was currently receiving, that fire I'd witnessed earlier stoked in him again as he took a breath and decided to ignore his friend.

"I've never seen a collection like it before. I…I may have tried to look at one, but…."

"Yeah, there seems to be some kind of spell on them. Cassia wasn't able to read them when she first came here either. But, once we established a coven bond between us, that seemed to end. I don't know how she managed to enchant them, or I'd remove the spell for you. I'm still learning a lot of stuff myself."

Elliot nodded slowly, digesting what she was saying. I could see the squint of annoyance on Brendan's face and found myself completely invested in it. He obviously wanted to know as well, and I couldn't help but wonder how long it would take for him to snap and ask his questions. I suppose an amount of trust would be needed, and he seemed too stubborn to give in to something like that.

Elliot's eyes moved to Cassia, and unlike Brendan, he

seemed done with holding back, much to his friend's annoyance.

"You didn't always live here then?" he asked.

"No, I was sent here to kidnap Jacob and kill a couple of the pack if I got the chance," she told him like it wasn't even a thing. I suppose it wasn't now. In fact, looking back at it, it had obviously been terrible at the time, but it was sort of funny in a macabre sort of way.

"And now you just live here?" Elliot asked incredulously.

All three of the witches seemed beyond confused. It probably didn't help that Cassia was perched on Hunter's lap. The big shifter was wrapping a strand of her hair around his finger, utterly oblivious to the conversation around him.

Ethan had also taken up the chair next to them, and I couldn't help but notice how he had one hand that kept creeping to Cassia's leg as his fingers played along her thigh. It would seem that Cassia had a new mate about to join her group.

"I wasn't in a good situation with my last coven," Cassia said slowly, almost like she carefully chose her words. "My magic is unusual, and it makes me an outcast. Calli saw that I needed a way out, and she gave me one, even though her brother had been taken and one of the pack got hurt in the process, this pack took me in. They gave me a chance to have a life free of the torment I was living in. There's nothing I can do to repay them for what they've done for me, but I will make it my mission in life to try."

I hadn't known Cassia felt that way, and from the way Hunter clung to her, it seemed the big guy was finally paying attention to what was going on.

"The Council sent me here under the guise of a guard for Calli, but in reality, I was expected to spy on them. They wanted me to find their weakness and exploit it, so they could come in and take her. Even though Grey and the others knew what was happening, they still took me in. I realised Cassia was my mate and asked them if I could join their pack. They accepted me without question, even though it could have caused them further problems with the Council," he explained.

The gruffness in his voice held all the emotion he seemed able to hide from his face.

I'd never really thought much about the circumstances of the two of them coming to be with us. They were pack now, and that was all that mattered. Any other pack would have killed them both on sight, we were different, and we'd always known that, but I guess you never really see the differences until someone makes you look at them. This was just us. It was how we'd always been, traditional pack life wasn't for us, and we were building something better here. Something to be proud of.

"Why?" Brendan suddenly blurted out. "Are you so insane that you would welcome any obvious threat into your home without considering the circumstances?"

Grey shifted in his seat to lean back in a relaxed manner that was completely at odds with the snap of annoyance I'd felt come through our bond from him. The alpha wouldn't like being questioned, but the way he was holding it in made me proud. The overwhelming power surging through him now must be difficult to handle, but he made it look easy most days.

"Sometimes what you see as a threat is someone who actually needs help. We aren't the type to turn away someone in need. But don't get me wrong. The last true threat to our pack was tied to a post and left inside that building we set on fire. There will be no holding back if you intend to do my pack harm. But if you want our help, if you need a new start or a refuge to regroup in, we will help you in any way we can." A sliver of Grey's power seeped out of him as he spoke, wrapping around us all in that comforting way it did. Even the three witches sitting amongst us seemed to relax a fraction, which was more curious than anything. Could they feel it too?

"We could have a chance for something here," Elliot spoke softly, and it was obvious he wasn't addressing the rest of us, but rather the two men at his side. Listening now felt intrusive, but we hadn't really been given a choice.

"They're shifters. They will never accept us," Brendan sighed, glaring suspiciously at us.

"There are two witches here, and Calli may only be half-witch, but you accepted she was the strongest we'd ever felt. You can't honestly believe they would hold the fact that we're witches against us."

"They're all mated to shifters," Brendan pointed out. "I've had enough of being traded as a commodity. I won't sell myself just to fit in here."

"Hey, whoa there. I think there's some kind of misunderstanding," I blurted out when I realised what he implied. "We don't expect anything from you if you want to stay here. We certainly don't expect you to hand over your bodies to anyone. Cassia is Hunter's mate. It was fated to be. As were Lachlan and Calli. I don't know what you're thinking right now, but I can one hundred percent tell you that you're wrong."

Brendan looked around at everyone, and I followed his gaze with my own. He took in the way Cassia was sitting on Hunter's knee with Ethan seemingly unable to take his hands off her. Even Calli was snuggled up close to River with Maverick on her other side.

"Okay, I might get that you would think there's some kind of sex thing going on," I realised and found myself blushing as I did for some reason.

Brendan's eyes moved to me, and it was like the atmosphere around us suddenly cracked when he burst out laughing. "Sex thing?" he wheezed out. "The look on your face."

Everyone watched incredulously as the previously antagonistic witch broke out in what could only be described as a fit of giggles. When those giggles turned to sobs, Elliot and their silent friend wrapped him in their arms to comfort him.

Lucas whispered softly into Brendan's ear, his words too quiet for us to hear. I probably could have made them out if I'd tried, but it wasn't a conversation for the rest of us. This was one friend comforting another.

Brendan nodded his head, hearing what his friends were saying as he slowly pulled himself away from the edge of hysteria. None of us had heard their story yet of how they'd ended up in that place. Not truly. We knew the Triquetra had traded them to Neressa, and I could only imagine what she'd expected from them, especially considering the outfits she had them dressed in.

"I don't know if I can promise you trust, but I will try," Brendan finally said, unable to meet our eyes.

It wasn't clear if it was an acceptance to stay, and no one would push him on that tonight. But, from the gleam in Elliot's eyes, I could tell he hoped it was. Lucas didn't appear to be quite as confident, and it made me more determined to find a better place for them here where they'd be more comfortable. If they'd been through what I suspected they had, these men deserved some sense of peace now, and we should've made sure they'd had it.

The rest of the evening was pretty reserved. Everyone

spoke amongst themselves, but the overbearing sense of weariness hung heavy around us. It wasn't long until people started to make excuses about heading in for some sleep.

Davion and his clan hadn't shown up, but after he revealed the difficulties James was having around the pack, I supposed it was to be expected.

"Before everyone leaves," Grey started, and a few of the people around us tensed like this was the catch they'd all been waiting for, "I need to ask that you all stick to either the house or the woods out the back here. As you know, Davion and his clan have taken residence in one of the cabins, and they've been absolutely vital in our survival to this point. In truth, we wouldn't still be alive if they hadn't allied with us. One of the clan is newly turned, and he's finding it difficult to be around so many people. I can assure you he isn't a danger to you. Davion will keep him firmly under control. But until we can move them back to Calli's old house, it only seems fair that we try and make life a bit easier on him if we can."

There were muttered agreements through the small crowd of people we'd taken in. No one seemed upset about the presence of the vampires, and yet a few of them still glared at the witches like their mere existence was an insult. I made sure to make a note of their faces, so I could speak with them tomorrow. We were offering them a place to stay, but if they couldn't accept everyone here, that offer would be withdrawn. We weren't going to invite people into the pack if they were only going to cause discontent, not when Sean could offer them a place of safety in the underground.

"I'm going to get the kids into bed," Calli said, easing herself out from between Maverick and River.

The words to offer to help were on the tip of my tongue, but I held them back. I'd been monopolising Calli's time today, and I could see my brother's eyes as he watched her stand. He needed her just as much as I did. We all did.

Calli held out her hand to Maverick, and he gratefully took it, a look of relief crossing his face at not being left behind. He'd changed so much since he first came to us, and even though I'd only known about my brother for a short amount of time, I was starting to become fiercely protective of him.

I was his older brother and his beta. So it was up to me to make sure he knew he wouldn't be left behind ever again. Not by the pack, not by me and certainly never by Calli.

16
MAVERICK

As my hand met Calli's, I felt my wolf's emotions soar before he settled at the forefront of my mind, observing his mate in contentment.

It had been too long since my last shift, and the overwhelming new urge to shift and run had been starting to fill me. In all honesty, it terrified me. The thought of shifting and losing myself again was always at the back of my mind. Even though I knew my wolf would never willingly leave Calli's side, especially not now we had completed our bond, I felt like it was a constant risk.

At first, I'd been terrified that she'd leave me, but then after absorbing the moonlight, that fear turned around and squarely became focused on myself.

It wasn't until I saw her injured in the fight at my father's facility that I realised Calli would always fight for us, no matter what the cost was to herself.

But even after seeing that, the doubt still lingered, itching at the back of my mind as it taunted me. The fact that the taunting sounded like my father's voice spoke volumes of just how screwed up I really was.

I followed behind my mate, watching the sway of her ass as she made her way to the back door. This woman was so completely captivating, I'd follow her anywhere. If my wolf was the moonlight, Calli was the sun that made me shine.

She turned to say something as she reached the doorway, catching me staring at her unashamedly. It wasn't like I was the only one wholly entranced by her. I was just the closest at this very second.

The sultry smile she gave me in response had me nearly dropping to my knees in want. It might not have been that long since I'd held her in my arms, but that smile had elicited a need for other things.

Walking into the house only to be hit with a wall of noise from the kids, was like someone had dropped a bucket of ice over me. Right, we were there for the kids and not the filthy sexscapades I had in mind.

"It's time to head up, kiddos," Calli sang as we walked in to find Coby and Jacob chasing each other around the table while Abby looked on in shock. Kai was holding back a smile of amusement, but I could see how his eyes followed their movements, almost like he longed to join in.

Kai needed to learn how to be a kid again. My father's pack had basically stolen his childhood from him. They had an uncanny knack for being able to do that. I might have lost mine, but I'd be damned if I was going to let the same thing happen to him.

"What on Earth is going on here?" Calli sighed as the two younger boys seemed to screech to a halt only to start a strange, subtle shoving match like we couldn't see them doing it despite them standing directly in front of us.

"Coby stole my seat!" Jacob sighed like the other child had committed the worst crime of the century.

"You sat next to Abby all night. It was my turn," Coby

snapped, looking seconds away from stamping his feet on the ground.

My mind went blank suddenly. This was the closest I'd come to parenting, and I was starting to realise I was way, way, way out of my depth—wait, that might not be enough ways. I could do the friendly, almost brotherly stuff, and I could admit that being called Daddy gave me an overwhelming need to pull out a credit card and buy Abby the world. But this was something utterly alien to me, especially considering I hadn't exactly had a parent that had interacted with me.

The horror must have been etched across my face because Kai seemed to be finding the whole thing even more amusing. Abby did that thing where she rolled her eyes, and the one simple gesture aged her about ten years.

That had me falling down the rabbit hole of the subject of boys. Followed by the screaming realisation that she had three right here, two of which seemed completely devoted to her, and one was far too old to be considered appropriate, even if he was just looking at her like the little sister he'd never had.

I was on the verge of a panic attack, and all it had taken was two small children having an argument in front of me.

"Is Daddy Mav alright?" Abby asked, looking at me suspiciously.

"He totally looks like he's going to be sick," Coby sniggered.

Calli looked at me in amusement, and I knew she could tell where my mind had gone and not because I'd probably been screaming it through the connection between all of us.

"I think he's just over-excited about the prospect of reading you a bedtime story," Calli cheered.

Both boys and Abby cheered at the idea, and then before I knew it, all three of them were charging up the stairs.

While it wasn't helping the overwhelming feeling of panic that was starting to claw at my mind, a glimmer of pride was also starting to shine through that they were so happy it was me they were about to spend time with.

"Little kids can be tough to deal with," Kai told me as he jumped out of his chair to follow them.

"You're not that old yourself, you know," I pointed out. Latching onto the interaction with him because it seemed to be pulling me back from the overwhelming need to find a paper bag to breathe into.

"Well, not compared to you, old man." He laughed, eyeing me closely before he charged off in the direction of the stairs after the others.

Calli burst out laughing, the sound of her joy ringing through the house. While the need to chase the kid down was strong, I couldn't help but pull her into my arms, sealing my lips to hers in a bruising kiss.

The way she wrapped her arms around me, pulling me close to her as she pressed her body against mine, had me never wanting to let her go. She fit against me so perfectly that it seemed like proof we'd been made for each other.

"We should make sure the boys aren't trying to smother each other," Calli whispered against my lips as I continued dropping kisses against her mouth.

She tasted like summer mornings, and the kids were the last thing on my mind right then.

"They'll be fine. It will help them sleep."

Calli laughed again, and it just made me want her more. Her life should be filled with laughter. She deserved so much more than how life was for us now.

"I think that's actually death as opposed to sleep," she

pointed out, moving away from me as she grabbed my hand again and started to pull me in the direction of the stairs.

My first reaction was to resist, pull her back toward me and refuse to let her leave. But then I realised where we were heading was upstairs, where all the beds and the semi-privacy was. As soon as that thought registered, I was striding toward the stairs, pulling Calli behind me, who giggled as she realised what was happening.

Damn, kids went to sleep quick, right? You just made sure they were in bed, said goodnight, and that was it. Please, god, let that be all it took!

※

An hour later, Calli and I slipped out of the kids' bedroom, a hint of exhaustion pulling at my mind. Four stories! Four! I was adamant it would only be one, and I still had no idea how it had turned into four. Those kids were sneaky! And damn if that didn't make me proud.

We paused at the door, listening to the telltale noise of the kids all getting out of bed and crawling into the same one.

"Do they ever not do that?" I whispered to Calli as I watched her soft smile as she listened to them getting settled.

"I don't think they've slept apart since they found each other." There was a hint of sadness in her voice, mainly because we all knew what these kids had been through to make their way to each other.

Some days it felt like they clung to each other because they knew the pain they all felt. Because there was comfort in having someone close to you. But then, other times, I saw the way Jacob and Coby fought for Abby's attention, and I couldn't help but wonder if it ran deeper than that. I wouldn't be surprised if they all realised there was a mate bond between them. Hopefully, that sort of realisation wouldn't come until they were older because if I'd felt close to a panic attack before, that was nothing compared to thinking about dealing with this lot going through puberty and realising there was something more between them all.

"Just try not to think about it." Calli chuckled as she turned me away from the door and gave me a gentle push in the direction of Tanner's room, which seemed to be where we'd all taken up residence.

It would be interesting to see if we ended up with all of the others in here tonight. Whilst I was hoping for some alone time with Calli right now, I found myself not hating the idea of all of us sleeping in the same room. Maybe the kids were onto something with these puppy piles they ended up in every night.

When the door closed behind us, I had a strange sense of discomfort, which I'd never had with Calli before. It wasn't that I didn't want to be here or doing something with her. Fuck, I wanted her so badly, my mouth was practically watering. I supposed with everything we had going on around us, it felt selfish to take a moment to find happiness when there were so many in the house that were hurting right now.

Calli moved toward the adjoining bathroom before looking back at me over her shoulder.

"It's okay to need something for yourself, Maverick. The world doesn't stop because we're happy or sad, and it also doesn't explode because you took a moment for yourself."

I could feel my anxiety radiating down the bond toward the others, but I could also feel the reassurance coming back from not just Calli, but also the guys. Nothing about it felt weird. It should've been strange to have such an open connection with other people who'd become so in tune with your emotions they could feel them when you weren't even in the room.

It felt like we were moving to a place where we were more than a pack, more than brothers. Still, for someone who had been completely starved of affection throughout their life, I lacked the ability to put it into words.

"Come and take a shower with me," Calli offered, holding her hand out to me. "Nothing has to happen. Let's just wash off the day and sleep. I may be slightly more exhausted than I've been letting on," she finally admitted with a cheeky grin.

We'd all known how much she was struggling. We could feel it after all. And we'd all watched her with a careful eye. But Calli was the type of person who, whilst she liked to care for those around her, didn't want the same concern for herself. If anything, she just pushed back harder against it.

"You don't say." It was hard to get out without laughing, especially when she rolled her eyes in exasperation at me. Perhaps we hadn't been all that subtle in our concern for her today.

Following her into the bathroom, I quickly stripped off my clothes as Calli set the shower running, holding her hand under the water to test the temperature. When she turned around, her lips parted almost like she'd been about to say something, but the words stalled as she found me standing, watching her in awe.

I had no idea what it was about her that made every act seem sensual, but every time I found myself alone with her, my mind only ever went to one place.

Reaching forward, I grasped the hemline of her shirt, pulling it up over her head. Calli lifted her arms without a word, letting me free her of her clothing. When she reached for the button on her jeans, I pushed her hands away. Snapping it open myself as I moved closer to her.

The sound of me pulling down the zipper on her jeans almost seemed to echo around the room in the near silence that surrounded us. The only sound was the gasp of breath that came from Calli as I hooked my fingers into the top of the jeans and pulled them down her legs, dropping to my knees in front of her as I did so.

Calli delicately stepped out of her pants, and I tossed them to the side as I stared up the length of her body. This was how the world should look at my beautiful mate, on their knees in front of her, ready to take up worship.

My hands seemed to move of their own free will as they glided up the soft skin of her thighs to the simple white lace underwear she was wearing. There was something so innocent and yet sexy about white lace. Like it wasn't made to be seen, but when you got a glimpse, you knew it was only being used to hide a treasure beneath.

Calli's hands moved to her back as she unclasped her bra and let the straps fall from her shoulders. A growl of indignation fell from my lips at her removing it herself. I wanted to be the one to strip every piece of clothing from her body. But I had to admit that now that I found myself on my knees before her, I didn't want to stand and do so when I was already exactly where I wanted to be.

Hooking my hands behind her thighs, I jerked Calli forward, closing the small distance between us. The sweet scent of her pussy filled my senses, and I hauled her to me, licking the length of her as her head fell back with a gasp.

Before Calli, I never would have dropped to my knees in front of a woman, believing it beneath me. Women were only good for one night, and once I'd found my own pleasure, I didn't give a shit about them. I hadn't been a good man before she came into my life, before she showed me how life was supposed to be.

Reaching up, I pressed Calli's back against the cold glass of the shower as I hooked one of her legs over my shoulder. Gazing up the length of her body as her breathy moans started to fill the room had my cock throbbing to be inside of her. Then, when she cupped her own breasts, pinching her hardened nipples between her fingers, I was ready to explode.

I didn't want to rush. I didn't want this to ever end, but I needed to watch her shatter, moaning my name, before I finally gave in to letting myself be inside her.

Pushing two fingers into her soaking wet core, I toyed with her clit with my tongue. Rolling the bud around before sucking it between my lips.

Calli's hips rolled as she rode my face, trying to impale herself further onto my thrusting fingers.

I could already feel her pussy starting to quiver around me, and I knew she was getting close to the prize I was holding out for myself.

Her thigh muscles clenched as she pulled me in closer with the leg I'd put over my shoulder.

"Maverick!" Calli gasped.

I fucking loved it when she moaned my name like that.

Starting to pump my fingers faster inside her, I increased my assault on her clit, sucking it between my lips before circling it quickly with my tongue.

I wanted to hear her cries of ecstasy, and the more she ground her pussy against my face, the more I loved being on my knees at her feet. If I could spend the rest of my life worshipping this woman, showing her every conceivable way to bring her pleasure, I'd be the luckiest man alive. Well, one of five of them, at least.

As Calli's moans started to increase, I knew she was close. "That's right, sweetheart. Just let go," I encouraged, working her clit with my thumb as I watched, completely entranced by the look on her face.

Calli was the most beautiful woman I'd ever seen. But the look she had on her face as she finally soared with her release was something that needed to be worshipped.

I watched her in complete rapture as Calli thrashed against the glass, my thumb teasing her clit, pushing her higher and higher until her moans became pleas to stop. I didn't want to. I wanted to watch her come again and again. She was the most delicious addiction I'd ever formed, and I never wanted to quit.

Surging to my feet, I slammed my lips to Calli's, pushing my tongue into her mouth as she sucked the taste of herself from me.

I couldn't wait any longer. I needed to be inside her, and Calli seemed to be feeling exactly the same way as I picked her up, and she eagerly wrapped her legs around me.

It was easy to lift her up and push my cock through her slick folds, spearing into the heat of her pussy as her head threw back with a throaty moan.

I could feel the dissipating quivers of the earlier orgasm still spasming through her pussy as I lifted her higher before dropping her back down onto my cock.

Fuck! The sounds this woman made were nearly enough to undo me.

Ignoring the shower completely, I sat Calli down on the edge of the vanity, tipping her back, so her shoulders pressed against the mirror. Hooking my hands under her knees, I unwrapped her from around my hips so I could spread her legs wide. I wanted to see every inch of her. I wanted to watch as my cock moved into her delicious heat, coating myself with her come.

Slamming my hips forward, I pushed deep inside of her. Calli bit her lip, whimpering at the sensation.

"Don't hold back from me, Calli," I warned before surging into her again. "I want to hear every moan that slips from your mouth. I want to hear how it feels when my cock completely owns your pussy."

Calli's pussy clenched around me at the words, and it only spurred me on. This wasn't about claiming her as mine and mine alone. This was a promise—we'd make it through this mess, and we'd do it standing at each other's side. I'd never leave her, and I'd never let anyone take her from me. Let them try. Because our pack was changing, growing stronger with every day, and we would crush anyone who tried to hurt our family.

"Maverick! Yes, don't stop!" Calli gasped as my thrusts became harder and harder, rocking her back against the mirror's glass with every one.

I could feel the release I was chasing teasing at the edges of my mind, and as Calli's moans grew louder, I knew she was reaching her peak.

My pace grew choppy as the orgasm seized hold of my mind. I tried to hold out longer, but as Calli's pussy clamped down around my cock, and she screamed as she came hard and fast, I was a complete goner. I emptied myself inside her with a groan of disappointment, not wanting it to end.

Panting for breath, Calli sat up with my cock still sheathed inside her and wrapped her arms around me, pulling me against her chest.

"There's no need to sound so disappointed," she whispered. "Who says I'm done with you yet?"

I couldn't help but chuckle at her words. Even with five mates, she still wanted me. There was always something that surprised me about that, even now when I held her in my arms.

Picking her up off the vanity, I carried her into the shower.

"What's wrong?" Calli asked as I gently set her on her feet. "I feel like something just happened to change your mood."

I shook my head, not really wanting to admit my insecurities to her. Not after we'd just had sex. I couldn't be that lame!

"Maverick, please," Calli pleaded, looking at me with her pleading emerald eyes.

Damn! I could never deny her when she looked at me like that.

Grabbing a wash cloth and her shower gel, I dropped down to my knees and ran the soapy cloth up her legs, unable to look at her as I admitted my feelings.

"Sometimes, I…it's hard to believe that you would want me." I shrugged, trying to play it off as inconsequential, but Calli wouldn't let me off that easily.

Calli fell to her knees in front of me, cradling my face in her hands as she gently tipped my head up, so I had to look her in the eye.

"I'm not going to tell you that your feelings are wrong or that they don't matter. I know you had a hard life before you came here to be with us. Just know that I love you, Maverick. I will always want you, and there is nothing in this world that could take me away from you."

I could see the fierce, shining love in her eyes that she had for everyone around her, and knowing that it was directed at me at that moment was humbling indeed. Did she even realise how important she was to us? It made so much sense to know that she was meant to be our Pack Queen. There was no other way to describe Calli. She was everything to us. It wasn't a case of whether we would accept her as our Queen. We were just waiting for Calli to accept it herself.

Kissing her softly, I almost felt my soul settle just from the touch of her lips against mine.

"Let's get clean and into bed," Calli said, climbing to her feet and pulling me up with her. "I, for one, am in desperate need of some snuggles."

"How could I ever say no to that?" I couldn't help but laugh with her. I never would have thought of myself as a snuggler before now, but it did sound like an excellent idea.

We rushed through our shower before climbing into bed together. The mood had changed between us. I could tell Calli was in her head, falling back into the thoughts of everything that we were constantly being pulled into. But, at least we'd been able to find a few moments of peace together. I supposed that was all we could hope for at the moment. Soon, though, we'd find our way through to the other side of this chaos. We had to.

Gathering Calli into my arms, I pulled her against me, and she laid her head on my chest, tickling her fingers across the muscles on my stomach. Never had I been more glad of all the hours I'd previously felt like I'd wasted in the gym trying to escape the boredom of my previous life.

I could tell that something was troubling Calli now, but I could wait. I knew her well enough to know that sometimes Calli needed time to work through her thoughts before she was ready to talk about them. I could give her time to do that now, but she would have to spill it before I'd let her get out of this bed. In the end, I didn't have to wait long.

"Some days, I wish we could just pick up everything we care about and walk away from this whole thing. And in those moments, I don't care that the whole world could set on fire or that our entire species could end. Does that make me a bad person?" she asked me quietly.

"No." I held her a fraction tighter as she made her quiet confession. "I'm pretty sure it makes you a normal person."

"My mother's a murderer," she whispered. "What if I'm like her?"

I felt a dampness on my chest, and I knew it was her tears. We all knew that this had been weighing heavily on Calli. The relief that she was finally in a place where she was ready to talk about it far outweighed my nervousness about whether I'd be able to say the right thing.

"Calli, you could never be someone that didn't cherish the lives of others. Your heart is too pure to ever let you do it. And I know you might not want to hear this right now, sweetheart, but you might be judging your mother too harshly here. We don't really know what happened yet, and it seems like your mother and father both knew they wouldn't be here to see you through this. But, they seemed to have accepted their fate if it meant you and your brother would be safe."

Part of me was kicking myself for saying it out loud, but it was something she needed to hear.

"This situation is so screwed up, and no one should ever have to go through this. I can't help but think they were just like us. Trying to make the most of the terrible situation they found themselves in," I added when Calli didn't say anything.

Calli stayed silent, and I hated myself for ruining what had turned out to be an amazing evening and pushing her back into her silence on this subject when she was just getting ready to talk about her feelings.

"She never drives," she finally said. Then, at my confused silence, she added. "My dad always drove. If they were together, he was always the one to drive. If she was driving when he was in the car, then she knew what she was going to do. If they'd both decided, if he knew what was going to happen, and he'd agreed, why wasn't he driving?"

My heart broke for her for what she had to be feeling right now. It wasn't a far stretch for me to believe my father was a murderer and an overall shit person. I'd experienced it my whole life. But to have had two loving parents, people who actually cared about you and openly showed it, only to have that called into question? I could see how that could turn your world completely upside down.

The only thing I could do right now was listen to her talk and hold her through it. I didn't have any answers, and it was absolutely killing me.

I held her as she broke down, as Calli finally let out all the pain and the heartbreak she'd been holding inside, trying to put a brave face on for the rest of the world.

As her tears subsided and her breathing evened out, I assumed she'd fallen asleep until I heard her whispered words.

"Why does it have to be like this? Why do we have to be the ones to fix all this? There has to be someone better suited. Someone who knows what they're doing? Someone with training?"

"Because I think the Council has carefully manipulated our world, so there isn't anyone who could stand up to them." It was something I'd been thinking about more and more when I'd had the same feelings Calli was going through. "They isolated the packs, making them insular and, at the same time, encouraged them to revert back to the old ways. To a time when position inside the pack meant everything. Everyone turned away from what was happening on the outside and became so involved in what was happening in their own corner of the world that the Council had free rein to do whatever they wanted. We trusted them to protect us, and they became the only ones that trained a force of guards. Anyone within the packs who showed any strength was pulled into the Council guard. We never stood a chance."

"Except now we do because your parents saw it coming, and they started to gather people. Some that could lead the cause, some that just needed help. And even though you don't feel like you're prepared for this, you are. They raised you to be the woman you are, sweetheart. They taught you how to care for others. They showed you how to recognise what was right and what was wrong. They instilled in you the bravery to stand up for those who couldn't stand up for themselves. And then, when they knew they wouldn't be able to stand at your side, they found a way to bring you here to your mates who would do it in their stead."

Calli finally raised her head to look at me. Her tears had dried, and the determination I saw in them gave me the hope she'd get through this.

"They sacrificed, sweetheart. Because we somehow ended up in a world that couldn't be fixed without it. I never had the chance to get to know them, and I know that my life is worse because of it, but I'll always be grateful for their sacrifice. Because it brought you to me, Calli. You saved me from a life I didn't know how to tolerate, and you saved me from the person I was slowly turning into."

It was like the dam had burst, and now that I was acknowledging the feelings inside of me, they were all rushing to the surface. Did I just tell the woman I loved that I was glad her parents were dead because it was starting to feel like it?

Calli's hand cradled my cheek as she searched my face, almost like she was trying to measure the truth in what I'd said. I wanted to reach out and take the words back, except I did mean them. It wasn't my place to judge her parents for what they'd done. I wasn't in their position, and I had no idea what I'd do if I was. In fact, I was pretty sure I'd have done the exact same thing, but now didn't seem like the time to be pointing that out.

"I...I know you're right," Calli started and then seemed to lose her words along the way.

"It's okay to be angry, sweetheart. And it's okay to question, but don't lose sight of the people you grew up with. It's okay to still love them, too."

Calli's shoulders slumped as the tension leaked out of her. "I think deep down I feel worse because I should be angry. I feel like I'm supposed to be declaring that she isn't my mother, that I'm supposed to hate her," she confessed. "But I keep seeing the same woman who sat at my bedside and read to me well into the night because I had a fever and couldn't sleep. I see the mother who always made sure to have my favourite cookie dough in the freezer just in case I wanted it. The woman who must have travelled the world to collect the books down in the library because they contained all the lessons she'd never be able to teach me herself."

"Then just hold onto the image of that woman, Calli. No one is expecting you to have all the answers."

"Aren't they? Sometimes it feels like they do."

"We may need answers to some questions, but that doesn't rest solely on your shoulders. We're all working toward the same goal. We can share the burden." There was a part of me that needed her to say yes. Watching her try to shoulder everything herself was physically painful. And I was starting to worry that if Calli couldn't learn to lean on her mates when she was feeling the pressure, eventually, she was going to break.

Calli nodded slowly before finally promising, "I'll try.

But I need you to promise that when you see me not doing it, remind me that I don't need to do it alone."

"That, I can definitely promise."

I meant it, too. As long as I lived, Calli would never need to do anything alone again.

17
CALLI

When I woke up the next morning, wrapped in Maverick's arms, it was to a sense of calm like I hadn't felt in days.

Crying it out did wonders for the emotional build-up, but it was always embarrassing the morning after.

The dishevelled bedding around the room indicated that the others had slept in here again last night, even if there wasn't any other trace of them this morning.

"What time is it?" Maverick asked me groggily.

Rolling to the side, I grabbed my phone off the bedside table. I hadn't picked the thing up in days, and I was surprised it was plugged into a charger, because I definitely hadn't remembered to do it myself.

"Eleven twenty!" I gasped, the time distracting me from the messages waiting for me. "How? Why didn't anyone wake us up?"

"Probably because you drained your magic until the point you collapsed and then refused to rest like a sane person," Maverick mumbled.

"Excuse me?"

"Hmmm? I said we should definitely blame Tanner. It was probably his idea," Maverick told me, beaming up at me with a smile that only made him look guiltier.

Well, at least if there was one thing I could take from this, it was that Maverick was getting worse at hiding his emotions from us.

"We should get up and shower," I mumbled, going to get out of bed only to find myself trapped inside Maverick's arms instead.

"As much fun as a repeat of last night sounds, I find myself preferring to stay in the soft, warm bed," he mumbled as he trailed kisses up the back of my neck.

Staying in bed was definitely what I'd prefer to do. However, the pack was still trying to accommodate more people than we had beds for, and someone needed to make sure the kids were fed and entertained. Not to mention the two women we'd brought back from the facility had been left solely to Holly's care, and someone needed to give her a break.

"You're doing it right now, aren't you?" Maverick mumbled, and pulled away from where he was nuzzling against the side of my neck.

I didn't know what he was talking about for a second, but then our conversation from last night came back to me.

"Erm, yeah, maybe a little bit," I confessed.

"What specifically is worrying you?" Maverick asked, sitting up in the bed next to me. The fact that he was taking this so seriously and not trying to push me into what he clearly had wanted to do a few seconds ago meant a lot.

"The people we rescued."

"The guys will be on it. Tanner and Aidan said they'd be working with Colt and his pack on the new cabins today, and the others asked if they could help out."

"The kids."

"Are not screaming or running around, so someone is already making sure they're cared for."

"The women we rescued."

"Are only comfortable with Holly at the minute and want to be left alone until they can move away from all the male shifters we have around here."

Damn, I really didn't need to try and shoulder the responsibility for everything. Was it weird that I was disappointed they didn't seem to need me?

"Do you know why everyone else has banded together to deal with any issues and let you sleep the day away?" Maverick asked me with a cheeky grin, no doubt because he knew the wording of his question would annoy me slightly.

"No," I said with a pout. It wasn't strictly true. I could guess why they'd do that.

"It's not because they don't need you," Maverick pointed out. "It's because they care about you. You were very recently hurt and need to rest to heal, not just because we want you healthy, but because trouble always seems to be just on the horizon for us. And if you aren't strong enough, you're in danger of getting hurt again."

He did have a point. Even if I hated to admit it.

Needing something to do so I at least felt useful, and maybe also because I was starting to think I might be a massive control freak, I checked the messages that had been waiting for me on my phone.

Felix had checked in to say he'd dealt with his issue and was on his way again. He didn't give any other details, so I figured it wasn't something we needed to know about. He was hoping to arrive in the next day or so.

The only other message had been from Sean saying he and Wells would be coming back to the house this morning, and he'd like to talk. Given that it was nearly lunchtime already, I was guessing they were already here, and the thought of having a heart-to-heart with my uncle had me groaning and flopping back on the bed.

"Wow, I really hope that was about your phone and not because of me." Maverick laughed, his head cocking to the side as he hit me with his best boyish grin.

I couldn't help but smile in response, even if my mood had plummeted at the thought of facing Sean.

"Sean wants to talk, and I'm pretty sure he's downstairs."

"Ah, not up to apologising this early in the day?" Maverick asked, flopping down on the mattress beside me and putting his hands behind his head as he settled in to talk me down from my next freak out.

I never would have thought Maverick would be the one to become my confidant, not after the way he'd been introduced into our world.

"Why would *I* be apologising?" I scoffed in outrage.

"Maybe because he's dedicated a large portion of his life creating an elaborate underground network and rebel army just to help you survive some fight your mother saw in your future?" he suggested with a nonchalant shrug of one shoulder as he stared up at the ceiling.

My words stalled in my throat, threatening to choke me as every ounce of outrage I'd felt over the last few days crossed my mind. The way I'd treated Sean, the heated words that had been said. With that one sentence, Maverick had shown me the situation from a completely different perspective. Now I felt like a massive ungrateful bitch.

"Am I in the wrong here?" I sighed, realising that I was, but needing to hear it from someone else. I trusted Maverick to tell me how it was. Maybe that's why I found myself confessing my feelings to him first.

"Not wrong exactly. Maybe just jumping the gun until you had time to properly think the whole thing through?"

"I think you're giving me more credit there than I deserve."

Maverick turned to look at me, the corner of his mouth ticking up in a smile. "I'm here whenever you need the boost."

It was sweet, really, but also slightly annoying that it felt like he might be agreeing with me.

"Why don't you go and have that shower, and I'll make you a cup of tea to help you power through what needs to be done," he offered.

Even the thought of tea didn't make me want to get out of bed and face the music, and it was only when Maverick laughed and gave me a gentle shove to get moving that I relented.

"Fine!" I sighed.

The scorching water of the shower did little to relieve the dread that started to form as soon as I climbed out of bed. By the time I was walking down the stairs, I was sick to my stomach, and I had no idea why. The thought of apologising to Sean wasn't something that upset me. I could accept that through the ups and downs of the last few months, emotions had run high, and perhaps I hadn't thought through the other side of the story; what it had taken to step up and sacrifice on blind faith that what my parents were saying was true.

And he had sacrificed.

Sean was alone. As much as we called him uncle, he had no family of his own. No close friends outside of those in the underground. Although, I suppose I'd had no idea of the existence of Wells, so what did I know about his life?

Either way, Sean had no family outside of Jacob and me. He'd never taken a mate, and he'd never started a clan. He was alone. But he was alone because I'd let him be. Because he'd taken my wrath and allowed me to force the full brunt of my anger on him when he knew he didn't deserve it. And he'd done all that because he'd cared enough to let me.

Wealth, position, and power were never things to take the measure of a man from. It was the lengths he'd go to, not just for the people he loved, but those he'd never even met.

Our world would never know the sacrifices Sean had made for them. As I walked into the kitchen and saw him standing by the counter speaking softly to Wells, every childhood memory of the man flowed through me with a sense of shame.

He'd always been there for us, and I'd repaid him by pushing him away.

Lachlan and Maverick were both at the counter, busy preparing food, and didn't immediately notice my entrance into the room.

Wells saw me first, and the smirk on his face screamed an inappropriate incoming comment, except he didn't have a chance to say anything.

Striding across the room, I walked straight into Sean's arms. The 'ouff' that came out of him was evidence of his surprise, but his arms automatically wrapped around me with a crushing grip.

It was like coming home; it was that familial comfort that could only come from someone you knew would always be there for you, and it was the thing that had the sobs surging out of my body.

Sean held me closely, stroking my hair like he had when I was a child, and I clung to him, wishing he'd never let me go. There was something about clinging to someone you had as a child that made you feel safe. Sean was the dragon who would keep the monsters away.

Except this time, it was my job. And I'd never been so unprepared for something.

Pulling back, I looked up at Sean, and the dampness in his eyes was the thing that strengthened the resolve inside me.

I wouldn't be the one to continually ask him to sacrifice for me. It wasn't fair that the burden had been laid on him.

My mother had seen this future, but she'd also seen a way for me to prevent it. It was my turn to shoulder the load.

"I'm ready," I told him firmly, conviction lining my voice.

It was possibly the first time I'd thought it *and* actually meant it.

Pride shone in his eyes as Sean cupped my cheek in one hand and then pulled me close again.

"I know you are, kid. And you're not in this alone," he said gruffly. The emotion in his voice gave away the tears he was holding back.

"I could almost cry. This is so fucking touching," Wells croaked, completely ruining the moment.

"Why do you always have to do shit like that?" Sean laughed, actually sounding lighter as he broke away from our hug.

"Maybe I've got emotional trauma, and I find other people's open displays of emotion painful to watch," Wells sniffed haughtily.

"Or maybe you're just a dick." Sean laughed back, lightly shoving his friend's shoulder.

It was so strange to see them acting like old friends. Mainly because we'd had no idea they were friends, and because they'd both been these authority figures in our lives. Now it was like we were finally getting a glimpse behind the curtain.

"It's like seeing monkeys use tools," Tanner whispered as he sneaked up behind me.

The light-hearted laughter that flowed out of me was definitely needed. Everything felt so heavy these days. It was like we were losing ourselves to the events around us. We needed these moments to remember who we were and what we were fighting for.

Maverick came over and passed me a mug of tea, which I gratefully wrapped my hands around. I wasn't particularly cold, especially not with Tanner pressed against my back, his hands on my hips as he pulled me tight against him. There was just something comforting about cradling a hot drink in your hands.

"Just like your mother," Sean mused, "Tea always made the world seem brighter for her as well."

The room fell quiet at the mere mention of my mother. Apart from Maverick, who'd taken the time to point out some truths to me that I hadn't been ready to see, everyone else still thought we were at the point of tiptoeing around the subject of my mother.

"I think that's where my obsession came from," I said, smiling fondly at the memory of my mother making tea in the kitchen.

The kettle had never been cold at our house. Whenever the slightest thing had upset me, the kettle would go on, and we'd sit at the kitchen table drinking tea and eating biscuits while I confessed my childhood dramas to her. Considering the life we'd had then, it was never anything significant. In fact, at one point, I was pretty sure I started to complain about the smallest things just because I'd wanted to eat an entire plate of biscuits with her.

Knowing my mother, she'd known, but she sat and

listened to me anyway, playing along as if she was none the wiser.

Those were the types of memories of her that I wanted to keep and cherish. Not the suspicions or the way she'd had to manipulate the course of my life to ensure I came to this place, at this time, to walk a path she'd carefully laid out for me.

It was hard to resent that I'd had so little say in this future when it had brought me to my mates. Even if I'd had the choice, I wouldn't have changed a thing. There was nothing in this world that I would have traded them for. I supposed the issue was, I just didn't like that my choice had been taken away from me. Even if I hadn't been aware of it at the time.

"We should take this into the living room where we can be more comfortable whilst we discuss the upcoming life-altering events for you all," Wells joked. "It's pretty convenient that you managed to lose all those people you rescued. At least the sofas are free now."

"Firstly, we didn't lose them. You charged in here with your smashed up car and unconscious friend and scared them away," Tanner pointed out. "And secondly, those people are in danger out there on their own, and it's not really something to joke about."

Seeing Tanner snap at someone was so unlike him that it made me turn and wrap an arm around him in comfort. I should have known how difficult it would be for him to feel like he'd failed those who'd run in fear.

My eyes cast around the room, looking for Grey, but he was nowhere to be seen. He must be going through something similar.

"Where's Grey and River?" I asked, not following the trail of people out of the room.

For some reason, I needed to know before I was willing to

walk into the next conversation.

"Grey is out with Colt and his pack, doing something to do with the cabins, and last I saw River, he was with Cassia talking with Brendan, Lucas and Elliot," Lachlan filled me in. "I've already sent messages to them to let them know you're awake, and we're ready to start talking through some things."

Of course, he had. Lachlan might have been quiet and unsure about his place here, but he was always so in tune with everyone else's needs. He probably would've been a beta if he'd been born a shifter.

Accepting that they were on the way, I followed everyone else into the living room, and Maverick and Lachlan packed away whatever they'd been doing so they could join us. I'd barely made it to the door when I heard the front door open and close, indicating that one of the others had already arrived.

"What else have I missed this morning?" I asked as I took in the empty living room.

There was something depressing about finding the living room empty of the survivors. Had we failed them by not keeping them safe enough? There wasn't really anything else we could have done in the circumstances, but that wasn't exactly making me feel better.

I needed to start accepting that I wasn't responsible for everyone. Then, maybe the weight on my shoulders wouldn't feel quite so oppressive.

"Marie headed out with Lea and Jess this morning. She knows a group nearby who can help them with their recovery, and while they wait for them to arrive, Lea thought it best they do so at the hotel," Sean filled me in.

"What? I should have been there," I sighed, already knowing that it was all already handled, and the last thing the two of them needed was an audience as they left the pack.

"Lea left a note for you," Lachlan told me, passing me a sheet of paper he'd pulled out of his pocket. "This was how they wanted it to be. Staying here was hurting Jess, and there was nothing we'd have been able to do to prevent it."

I knew he was right, but a part of me still felt like I'd let them down. I felt like I should've been there for them more. Even though they only seemed comfortable around Holly, I still felt I'd somehow failed them. Maybe I *was* a massive control freak?

Putting the note in my pocket, I decided to read it later when I wasn't about to enter into a conversation that would determine our future. Perhaps I'd message Marie to make sure that Jess and Lea knew we'd be there for them if they ever needed anything. It felt like the least we could do.

Everyone else settled in around the room, preparing themselves for the talk that was about to happen. I was dreading it, but also, there was a sense of significance here. This was a turning point for us. Yes, we'd made plans before to keep ourselves safe. But this was different, now was the time to start talking beyond just our pack and look to the future of our people as a whole. To look destiny in the face and tell it to bend to our will for a change instead of constantly fucking with our lives.

For what felt like the first time in a long time, I sat alone in one of the armchairs, crossing my legs and sitting tall, ready to take on the challenge I'd been constantly in denial of.

It sometimes felt like I was always sitting in the lap of one of my mates when shit started to get real. Even though it was comforting, there was a sense of hiding in it too. That I was sheltered in their embrace rather than standing tall on my own two feet.

I'd never been one to hide from a challenge before, and

just because the challenges were starting to get bigger didn't mean I needed to start changing who I was at the core.

My parents had raised me to know the difference between right and wrong, and to want to stand up and fight for those who couldn't do it themselves. I hadn't by any means been hiding from that part of myself. But I could see now that I'd been doing the bare minimum and not looking at the bigger picture, the picture outside of our own little world as a pack.

Maverick and Lachlan took one of the sofas, and I saw Tanner glance at me in question before he reluctantly took a seat with them. The hint of a pout on his face betrayed his frustration at not being able to squeeze onto the chair with me.

Wells dropped down into one of the other chairs, pulling out his phone and tapping away on the screen while we waited for the others to join us.

It was strange watching Sean anxiously pace the room. He'd never been a pacer, or I'd never noticed that he was. But now, preparing to fill us in on exactly what was expected of us seemed to have him more nervous than I'd ever seen him. It was grating against my anxiety about exactly what I was getting us into. There was no doubt in my mind that there would be no turning back now. Hopefully, the others wouldn't resent me for wading into this without discussing it with them first.

Grey and River both strolled into the living room together, and, surprisingly, Jessa trailed in behind them. I hadn't even been aware that she was here, and now I was curious about what exactly she'd been up to.

"Calli, my dear," Jessa greeted me, and I rose from my seat to give her a hug and a kiss on the cheek. Things between us were strange, and I could tell she was shocked by the gesture. But Jessa was family, and I knew she was hurting too. I didn't want to be yet another source of pain for her.

"I meant to ask you yesterday, but where is your pendant?" she asked, pointing to my neck as she cocked her head to the side in question.

"I think it's upstairs," I told her with a frown. "I never really put it back on after using it in a ritual. It all felt pointless once the cat was out of the bag on what I was."

Where the hell was it actually? It hadn't felt right putting it back on for some reason. The spell wouldn't work to mask my scent now, but even if it had, I wasn't sure I'd want it to. Being here with my guys was the first time I hadn't had to hide what I was. And now, I had embraced the freedom of being myself, I didn't think I'd ever be able to let it go.

"The amethyst is an important stone for you. You must find it and put it back on," she told me earnestly.

Jessa pointed me back to my seat, and I sat down with a frown.

"Crystals have the ability to retain the signature of a person's magic, and they are a potent tool for powerful magic users when they need to focus their energy," Jessa told me before sitting on the arm of the chair and giving me one of those motherly shoulder pats that make you equal part relaxed and nervous before feeling the need to throw up. "Your mother gave you the amethyst for your amulet so that it would have time to adjust to your signature. It's time to put it back on again."

The magnitude of what this was all about finally hit home. This wasn't some plan that had been thrown together on a whim. They'd spent all of my life, possibly even longer, working toward this. Finely tuning the outcome of every event to give us the greatest chance of success.

"This is…how long have you been working toward this?"

I stuttered, making no sense, but the overwhelming realisation that the people in this room had sacrificed so much for me was about to render me speechless.

"It doesn't matter," Sean said with a shrug. His eyes met mine, and I saw nothing but love there. He didn't regret anything he'd done or sacrificed to be here. He was part of our family, and he'd always treated Jacob and I like we were his own kids. He might have given up a chance at a normal life for us, but he'd also gained a family from it.

Jessa nodded in agreement before she slipped off the arm of my chair and made her way across the room to sit with Wells. She had that graceful sway of movement that made every woman in the vicinity jealous. It was like she oozed what society told you a woman should be, and the result made every person in the room want to drop to their knees and worship her.

I glanced around at my mates. Not a single one of them was paying her the slightest bit of attention. Now that she had moved away from my side, it might as well have been like she'd left the room. Every single one of them was entirely focused on me. Concern, love and understanding shone in their eyes. I could feel it radiating through the bond to me.

Could we actually do this?

Could the handful of people in this room sway the course of events? It would mean that potentially thousands of people could go on living their lives without ever realising the danger lying steps from their doors.

Part of me wanted to scream out to the packs and tell them what was happening. To demand they stand with us, fight with us. To just open their fucking eyes and see what our world had turned into when none of us thought to watch.

But deep down, I knew it wouldn't do any good. Fuck, from what we'd heard of the scary as fuck future waiting for us, it was exactly what we were trying to prevent. But how were we supposed to prevent it? Every possible avenue seemed to have only one end—a fight for our lives. But wasn't it precisely what would place the targets on our backs?

"I think it's time you filled us in on the plan," Grey said gravely, nodding at me in support.

I wasn't sure I was ready to hear it, but if we were going to do this, we needed to know how to get it right.

Talk about pressure!

"The underground we have masked by Wells' pack isn't big enough to take this fight head-on," Sean started, and the urge to vomit slammed into me. "We suspect Stone has the allegiance of the witches, although we don't know how or why. He also seems to have a third party benefactor we haven't been able to reveal. We know from Ethan's efforts that he's been taking calls in his office reporting to someone we haven't been able to identify."

"Reporting to them as in Stone isn't in charge?" I asked curiously.

For some reason, I felt better thinking that Stone wasn't the one calling the shots. Maybe it was because he was Tanner and Maverick's father? Even if they hated him, they didn't deserve to live through the knowledge that he was some kind of evil mastermind hell-bent on destroying our entire species.

"I'd say it sounds more like they're partners, but whoever it is definitely seems to have some kind of hold over him," Wells theorised.

"Maybe just that they could reveal his betrayal to the Council. Without his position and access to the things that gives him, pulling off something like this wouldn't be nearly as easy as it apparently has been," River thought out loud.

It made sense, I suppose, but I had that nagging sense in the back of my mind that we were missing something. The whole motive of Stone's involvement in this didn't make sense unless he wasn't aware of the end goal. Unless his end goal was completely at odds with what everyone else seemed to be working toward.

"You must tell them everything," Jessa muttered before heaving a heavy sigh at the look of annoyance on Sean's face.

"We don't know the accuracy of our information," Sean objected. "It would have been prudent to investigate further once we had them safely at the pack, rather than raise their suspicions. Tempers will flare, and fingers will be pointed. Just know that it could have been prevented had you not jumped the gun on this." The look Sean shot at Jessa as he spoke to her screamed how much he didn't want to talk about this.

I'd never seen Sean annoyed at someone close to the family before. I'd seen him annoyed at the people who made his job a necessity, but I'd never seen him close to snapping at someone we all cared about.

"What information?" Grey asked carefully, his muscles already bunching as if ready for a fight.

The increase in his alpha energy had Grey constantly on edge. He'd been managing it better than I think any of us gave him credit for. The half information and attempts to keep us in the dark were starting to wear thin for him. And I was right there with him. When I told Sean I was ready, I'd meant it. I didn't need him to try and take control and baby us. If they wanted me to step up and take on this fight, then he needed to get the fuck out of my way.

"Sean, I appreciate that you want to protect us as much as possible, but you can't expect us to step into this fight if we don't even know what we're fighting against. I'm not a child anymore. I don't need you to fight the monsters under my bed for me. I need you to point them out to me and then pat me on the head for a job well done after you watch me tear them apart. This is my family, my pack, and I will do whatever is necessary to save them from this."

Sean raised a single eyebrow at me, and a slow smile spread across his face. It was nice to see the appreciation growing, but it was starting to get old. It constantly felt like one step forward and two steps back with these people. They'd spent too long fighting in the shadows and had no idea how to let go of the reins, even when they insisted we take them.

"Stone told his partner that he has a man inside your pack," Wells told us nonchalantly like it wasn't a massive bomb he'd just dropped.

"A member of our pack or one of the shifters we brought back from the facility?" Tanner blurted out.

We'd all been thinking about it even before now. We'd been watching the people we'd saved, wondering if one of them was a well-placed spy by Stone. It made me feel like shit to suspect them after everything they'd been through, but I wouldn't put it past Stone to have someone in those cages reporting on the rest. In fact, in terms of evil plans, it would have been an excellent idea.

"We don't know. That's why I didn't want to tell you right away," Sean gritted out, turning a withering gaze to Wells, who just seemed to be amused by it.

When I was a kid, I was fairly sure I'd seen a man piss his pants when Sean had turned that look on him. Wells had some balls on him to not let it bother him. Either that, or he was a few brain cells short of an ounce of commonsense. Maybe all the subterfuge had finally gotten to him.

"It has to be one of the others. None of our pack would betray us like that," River said resolutely.

"I'm surprised you don't think it's me," Maverick laughed, even if there was a hint of nervousness about it.

I didn't for a second doubt him. Maverick had no love for his father, just like Tanner didn't. He'd suffered through his abuse his whole life, and there was no way he'd go back to that. Not to mention the fact that he was my mate. No, he'd never betray us. Maverick wasn't that type of man. He'd been willing to sacrifice himself to save me, and I was hoping he was starting to realise that every one of our pack would do the same for him.

"We already ruled you out," Wells said with a shrug.

Thankfully, Maverick didn't seem to take it too personally. Still, any other person would have probably been upset at the lack of confidence someone had in them.

"Given that most of the others have left, our suspects have at least decreased," Tanner pointed out.

Lachlan was sitting quietly, watching the conversation with concern on his face. I knew exactly how he felt. It didn't seem right to start treating these people with suspicion after everything they'd been through.

"How do we know he wasn't just trying to make excuses to whoever he was talking to?" Lachlan added quietly, almost like he was nervous about interceding. "We've interacted with all of these people and started to listen to their stories. I really don't think any of them would side with Stone. They all seem to hate him. I'm not sure of anything he could have offered them to make them willing to take up his cause."

He had a point there. None of the shifters who had come back had been in any state to be considered as receiving favourable treatment.

"What about the witches?" Wells suggested. "They're a

variable none of us considered before. We don't know what their role was at the facility. It could all have been a ruse to get you to trust them."

Lachlan, Jessa and I all bristled at the comment.

We were used to shifters always pointing the finger at witches, but I'd never had to experience it here. At least not after Wallace had left.

"You cannot accuse them just because they are a witch," Jessa snapped, and I could already see that the conversation was about to devolve into an argument any second.

"I'm not suggesting it because of that, and you know I would never," Wells grated, sitting straight in his seat as his eyes flashed with anger. "You're my mate, Jessa. I would have thought you'd realise by now that I don't hold the same prejudices as most of my kind does."

Jessa rolled her eyes, and I could see the alpha's anger starting to grow at the way that she didn't back down from him.

"Wait, are you an animage?" I asked, suddenly realising something I hadn't considered before. "Is Cassia? They're both witches and mated to shifters," I pointed out.

"No, there's no shifter blood in mine or Cassia's lines. From what we can gather, it is only when the old animage lines in shifters today merge with witch genetics that an animage Queen can be born," Jessa explained, looking grateful for the sudden subject change.

The tension in the air was at the point where an argument was about to break out. So it seemed sensible to turn the subject of the conversation away from the spy for now until people had a chance to settle down.

"Do we know of any others? Anyone else who has the potential? Surely it would help if there were others we could persuade to our side," I asked.

It was the beginnings of a plan, and perhaps a naive one. But if we could find other packs where a Queen had found mates, perhaps joining forces would make us strong enough to face whatever was coming.

Stone's pack was one of the biggest. With the inclusion of the witches and whoever he had the support of, he could easily overwhelm us with numbers. The only way we could ever beat him in a fight would be to have the stronger side.

"I suspect there may be one other, but she is far too young to be able to take any mates," Sean told us.

Well, there went that idea.

"We don't have the numbers for this," Grey murmured, his frown creasing as he started to follow the same train of thought I'd had. "Even if we're able to bring Calli to her full power and the pack develops whatever magic it will develop. We'd still be facing a huge fighting force on Stone's side. It won't matter how powerful we are if he outnumbers us hundreds to one. That's even assuming we have time for the pack to understand how to use whatever magic you think we'll get."

Grey hadn't even touched on the fact that an outright fight to the death with the numbers we talked about would play straight into the prophecy we were trying to prevent. No, the goal of this whole thing had to be to end it quickly and quietly. There had to be another way that didn't involve two armies facing each other and fighting to the death.

"You will have the numbers when you take over my position as alpha of my pack." The look on Wells's face as he spoke only confirmed that he was being deadly serious, but no matter how many times I heard it, I couldn't take him seriously. Even Grey seemed to be fed up with hearing him talk about it.

"I told you before that isn't happening. I'm not abandoning my own packlands, and we sure as shit are not fighting to the death. I may not particularly like or trust you, but that doesn't mean I want to see you dead," Grey snapped.

"It's the only way. We've been planning this for years. If there was a way to have stopped this earlier, to have prevented you from ever needing to have this future, don't you think we would have found it by now?" Sean sighed.

The problem we seemed to be having was discussing this with a group of people who'd been living through the problem we'd only just realised we had. And possibly for longer than any of us had even been alive.

Though they might have had experience, they were also weary from fighting this battle from the shadows for too long.

Sean and the others needed to accept that we might have ideas they hadn't considered or had written off as impossible because they didn't have the knowledge or the skills we did. If they couldn't accept that we had something fresh to bring to the table, even if that was just perspective, we wouldn't get anywhere in this.

"There's no point discussing this with them. We're just going round in circles because they aren't going to listen to anything we have to say. The best option we have is to obtain as much information as possible and then discuss it alone. Maybe if we come up with an actual viable plan, they'll listen to us then," I said through the packlink.

A hum of approval came down the link to me. It was strange not even needing to speak to someone because you could sense how they were feeling, but it was also comforting. These men were so in tune with me that there was nothing we couldn't face together.

"I'm not saying I'll do it. I want to hear what the plan is before we commit to anything," Grey told the others gruffly.

Even though I could feel his intrigue through the link, he certainly wasn't showing it on his face.

"The only way to stop this all from escalating to an outright war that draws the humans' attention is to make a decisive strike and end it once and for all. Stone's packlands are far enough away from the humans that if we move in and take them by surprise, we can take out Stone and contain the problem," Sean told us sternly.

I got that they'd been at this for a long time, but surely they'd come up with something better than this?

"Contain the problem?" Grey murmured. The air around him started to thicken as the alpha energy seeped out of him. "You're talking about slaughtering an entire pack. There are hundreds of shifters on those packlands. Not all of them will deserve such a fate. There are fucking children there! And what? You expect us to go in there and wipe them all fucking out. Are you out of your minds?"

"You didn't have a problem killing his pack members when you took down the facility there," Wells pointed out. His mouth twitched with a barely suppressed smirk. I was starting to think it was some kind of nervous habit because surely he couldn't be finding our outrage at this idea amusing?

"That was different," Grey snapped. "Those guards knew what they were part of. They knew about the members of their own pack that were being taken to that place and tortured."

"Did they? Or were they just guarding the door like good little dogs? Did you stop and check before you ripped out their throats?" Wells wasn't even bothering to hide the smirk on his face now, but I was starting to realise what it was. This was him goading Grey. Wells was trying to make it easier for him to challenge him to a fight.

Grey suddenly stood. The air around him thickened with his power and almost obscured his features. I'd never seen it react so strongly before. I could feel his rage vibrating through the link, even though he was trying to hold it back from us. Underneath it ran a glimmer of shame. He was worried we'd killed those people unnecessarily. Grey wasn't the type of person that would be able to take that fact lying down. He'd be ashamed of hurting anyone innocent. Even if Wells was doing this to try and make the next steps easier for him, he didn't have to destroy him in the process.

Grey was an honourable man. He knew the difference between right and wrong, and he wasn't afraid to stand for those that needed someone to protect them. He was a far cry from what alphas had become in our age. And he shouldn't be made to feel ashamed of that. He shouldn't be made to doubt his actions, not when he'd saved so many.

The rest of my mates tensed, waiting to see what Grey would do. I didn't like our chances if this was about to break into a fight. After all, we'd be against an alpha wolf, a dragon and a powerful witch. To say we'd be fucked would be an understatement. But then, that seemed to be our go-to level at the moment, and we'd made it this far. Clearly, someone was looking down on us.

Without saying another word, Grey stormed out of the room. The sound of the front door slamming had us all cringing, especially when the crack of glass accompanied it. I guess that was one more order we'd be putting into the building suppliers then.

I went to stand to go after him, but Tanner stopped me. "Give him some time to blow off some steam. When he gets like this, he needs to run it out before he can talk to anyone."

Tanner was a good beta, and he knew Grey better than

anyone here, but it hurt to think of Grey as in pain and not go to him.

"I know this is difficult," Jessa told us quietly, making sure to look at each one of us. "We've had to live with the knowledge of what needs to happen for a long time, and it hasn't been easy. But this is what needs to be done for the good of us all."

I found myself nodding in agreement, even though my entire body revolted at the idea of what they were suggesting. Wouldn't this just be giving the Triquetra what they and Neressa had wanted all along? It didn't feel like this was a solution that would benefit anyone.

"Look, this is all new to us, and it's a lot to consider. How about we all just take a moment and calm down. We can discuss it more this afternoon. Let's grab something to eat and wait until Grey feels ready to come back," Tanner suggested, already standing ready to walk out of the room. "I'm going to check on the pack. I want to make sure that someone from the pack is with the others until we have any further information on the possibility of one of them being a spy for Stone," Tanner said through the link to the rest of us.

I had no idea why he felt the need to keep that information to himself, but Tanner strode out of the door before any of us could respond to him. It wasn't like we couldn't talk to him through the link. We'd be able to speak with him for a short while until he'd moved far enough out of our range. It was more like he didn't want Sean and Wells to know what he was doing. Why? I had no idea.

We would have a lot to talk through tonight when we'd finally be alone.

"Come on, kid. Let's make some tea, and you can talk to Jessa and me about how your magic is coming on?" Sean suggested getting out of his chair with a sigh.

I had no idea how old Sean was. Old. That much was for sure. Looking at him, he looked like he was maybe moving toward his fifties in human terms. His once dark hair had started to grey around the edges, but in a way that looked like he dyed it in. Hell, for all I knew, he did dye it in to try and fit in more. He was still in shape like most shifters were, but there were the odd times, like now, when you'd get a glimpse of a weariness in him that only comes with having lived through too many years. If anyone needed a break, it was definitely Sean.

I'd asked my parents once when I was younger, and the sad look on their faces made me never ask again. They'd told me that Sean was older than anyone I'd ever meet, but that it wasn't polite to ask him about it. My mother had explained that when you lived longer than those around you, you lost far more than anyone could ever imagine. I'd wanted to ask why he didn't have a mate, but I'd lost my nerve when she said that. I had a feeling I didn't want to know the answer.

We all trailed through to the kitchen, much like we'd all trailed into the living room before. We must look like a strange procession to anyone outside watching us walking around with the weight of our world on our shoulders.

"I'm going to check in with Nash in the office and make sure there's nothing he needs help with," Lachlan told me as he strode up to me and kissed me on top of the head. "Call out to me if you need me," he told me through the link.

I had no idea why we kept so many things from the people who were here to fight with us, and it felt like I was missing something important.

As we made our way into the kitchen, Sean started to make tea for Jessa and me, and I heard Wells try to draw Maverick into a conversation.

"Have you seen any more signs of the human police who

came by?" he asked, moving to stand next to River, who'd taken up a spot by the windows, watching out into the trees for Grey, no doubt.

"No, which is worrying. Tanner and Grey both felt that she knew more than she was saying. Judging by your assertion that some are aware of our existence, I'd guess she must be one of them. She could be a useful asset to bring onto our side if this thing gets messy."

Wells nodded in agreement but said nothing. He looked kind of sad, staring out into the trees. How did he feel about this whole thing? He seemed so adamant about what needed to be done and strangely okay about not only losing his pack to Grey but having to fight him for it.

He must know there was a very high chance he'd die in a dominance challenge, and I couldn't figure out how he was so okay with that for the life of me. Especially considering he had a mate. Jessa was my aunt, and I might not have had the opportunity to know her throughout my life, but she had the same face as my mother, and whether it was that, or the strange sense of kinship I felt toward her, I still felt protective of her. The thought of him sacrificing himself so easily and not considering the fallout for her was pissing me off. If she'd been a shifter, she wouldn't survive the loss of her only mate. Would it be the same for her as a witch? Was he sentencing one of the few surviving relatives I had to die at his side?

I fucking hated everything about this plan, and Grey was right to refuse to go along with it. Everything about this felt so wrong. It almost felt like we weren't fighting on the right side. Not to say that Stone was in the right. That man hadn't known right from the moment he was born. But there could be more than two sides in this fight, and the more I thought about what they expected us to do, the less I wanted to join forces with them.

Sean passed me a cup of tea, pulling me away from the ranting in my head, and the strange look he gave me made me realise he knew exactly what I was doing.

"Your mother got the same look when she was pissed off about something too," he told me with a smile as he swallowed down his scorching hot drink like it was nothing but tap water. "I'm almost afraid to ask because I'm fairly certain it's about me."

It was hard not to want to confess all my secrets to Sean. I'd known him my whole life, and I had a feeling he knew exactly how to play me by this point.

"This whole thing just feels, I don't know," I ended with a shrug.

"I know, kid. We all feel exactly the same way. We've just had a lot longer to get used to the idea."

I sipped at my tea, enjoying the burning feeling as I swallowed it. My mother always used to laugh at how hot I drank it, but if it didn't burn a bit, it was too cold for me. Maybe I'd spent too much time with the dragon at my side.

I was just about to ask everyone what they wanted to eat when that familiar sensation tickled down my spine.

Tanner's head snapped in the direction of the driveway, but that didn't seem right. The breach wasn't coming from that direction.

A soft growl flowed from Maverick, and Lachlan rushed back into the room.

"What was that?" Jessa asked, gently placing her cup down on the kitchen counter. I could see her starting to draw her magic to the surface as she reacted to our own tension.

"Someone just breached the wards," I mumbled as I moved towards the front door.

"I need the entire pack at Calli's old house," Grey yelled through our link. "We're under attack."

18
GREY

I had to leave, or I was going to rip into Wells and then his pack would become mine whether I liked it or not.

How fucking dare he question what we'd gone through? He hadn't been there. He hadn't seen that place. He didn't have to stand by while they came after his mate, time and time again.

But in the back of my mind, there was that voice, that one whispered question of what if he was right?

Fuck!

This whole situation had gone from bad to a fucking shit storm in the blink of an eye.

Calli was right. This whole thing felt off. Storming in there and killing everyone in sight couldn't be the answer. Even if it was, I wasn't sure I'd be able to do it.

There was a big difference between fighting for your life and killing people in their beds.

I barely knew Sean, but he didn't seem the sort of man to accept this. What if this was another one of their situations where they were only telling us what we needed to know?

There had to be more to this. And the fact that I didn't know what it was, was likely to drive me crazy.

I heard the glass in the front door crack with the force I'd slammed it shut, but I didn't have it in me to care right now. So instead, I shifted and sprinted toward the trees. A run around the borders should help calm my mind, and it needed to be done anyway.

We relied on the vampires too heavily to keep our pack border safe. While I had no doubt that we could trust them, we should at least be shouldering the load. Yes, we had a lot to do to make the place comfortable for everyone to co-exist, but we needed to make sure everyone was sharing the tasks equally.

Tonight I'd go through everything we had on our plate with Lachlan and see if we could put a schedule in place. We might have lost a lot of the rescued shifters, but, as callous as it sounded, it did take a lot of the problems we currently had off our plates.

There were more than enough people able and willing to work around the pack, and maybe not treating those we'd rescued with kid gloves would better help them adjust to life outside of a cage.

Tuning back into my surroundings, I realised where I was and veered off to the side. When the clearing came into sight, I found my wolf sprinting ahead even faster than usual.

The soft grass between my toes when I came to a stop actually helped my rapidly spinning mind. Sitting down, I cocked my head to the side and listened.

There was nothing but the sound of birds and the creak of the trees moving with the wind.

I moved over to the side of the clearing, trailing my nose along the ground to see if I could catch any lingering scent.

This was where I'd first seen Calli's wolf all those months

ago. It was crazy to even think that a trace of that night would still linger here after all that time, but I still wanted to try.

Looking at the patch of grass where I'd laid dying, you almost wouldn't know anything had happened there. There was no trace of the incident now.

When I'd seen Calli's white wolf dive headfirst into the fight, I'd thought she was some kind of spirit that came to save me. Never before had I seen a wolf with a pure white coat, and the scent of her being a female was nearly enough to throw my mind out of the fight at hand.

Watching her protect my back, I'd known she was special. My wolf knew exactly what she was to us, and I'd been so overjoyed I nearly didn't feel the knife ripping into me. Instead, it was the pain of realising I'd never get to be with her that had me crying out.

Laying on the ground and staring into her beautiful eyes, I'd nearly missed the amethyst hanging around her neck. Of course, the impossibly beautiful girl we'd all been so obsessed with would be the incredible she-wolf in front of me.

Even though I'd never known it was possible at the time, it all made sense.

Calli was too special a person to be ordinary. She had to be an incredible impossibility, there was no other explanation.

I almost missed the subtle shuffle of someone moving through the trees close by, so absorbed in the daydreams of my beautiful mate. Moving silently out of the clearing, I kept close to the ground as I went to investigate.

Considering their numbers, it was impressive how quietly they were moving. If they hadn't been clumsy enough to make that one slight noise, they probably would have passed by without me even noticing them.

From my count, twelve shifters were moving along the edge of our territory. They weren't any of the people we'd pulled out of the facility, which meant they had no reason to be here.

My guess was they were Stone's pack, and they were here to deliver a message.

It was surprising we'd made it this far without him lashing out in retaliation for us burning down his facility, in all honesty.

I trailed behind them at a safe distance downwind. It wouldn't do me any good to alert them to my presence. Even with the power boost I'd had over the last few months, I couldn't take on twelve shifters alone, even if I did have the element of surprise on my side.

For now, I was more curious about what they were intending. Plus, they'd yet to cross into our territory. Attacking them before they did would be all the evidence Stone would need to drag us before the Council. He might not have reported us for taking out the facility, but then doing that would have meant he'd need to admit to its existence in the first place.

It was at least a glimmer of hope that not all of the Council were in on what he was doing.

Being pulled before them would be a one way trip into whatever new facility Stone could throw together. No matter how much I'd relish getting to take a chunk out of him, I wouldn't risk Calli to one of those places, especially not after what we'd seen there.

One of the group ahead of me raised a hand, and they all stopped, hunkering down close to the ground while they waited for further instructions. Finally, the group leader pulled a phone out of his pocket and checked the screen before passing it to the man next to him to read whatever was on it. Then, with a nod to each other, the leader waved the group on again, and they set off, still skimming the edge of the border and not setting off the wardings.

I couldn't for the life of me figure out if they were purposefully able to avoid them, or if it was all just luck. They seemed to have a particular destination in mind. Still, the fact that they hadn't even triggered the wardings accidentally would seem to indicate they knew where they were.

Even if the wardings were keeping them out, it didn't help that our enemy potentially had them mapped out and could be moving around just outside of them without us knowing about it.

It was something we'd need to think about more closely, especially with the pups still on the packlands.

It soon became clear where they were heading because there was only one thing in this direction that could be of any interest to them, and they were heading straight to it—Calli's old house.

As they approached the place where the wardings branched out to run around Calli's land, the group stopped again, and the leader checked his device. When he pocketed it, he looked ahead of him with steely determination.

Something about this guy was familiar to me, but I couldn't for the life of me figure out what it was.

He wasn't from my father's pack, and outside of them, I hadn't really had any dealings with any of the other packs. Yet, this guy was nudging a memory to the forefront of my mind, but I couldn't quite grasp hold of it yet.

Turning back to the group, the familiar shifter nodded in resolution at them. They all tensed, looking ready to spring into action. One of them even cracked his neck from side to side in some ridiculously over-dramatic way.

Trying to hold the laughter in at that was nearly harder

than holding back the waves of alpha power that wanted to lash out at them for daring to even consider breaching my lands.

Suddenly they were up and running, passing through the warding and moving through the trees. I felt the tingle run down my spine, alerting me to their presence, and I knew the pack would have felt it.

Reaching for the others in my mind, I yelled instructions as I started to sprint after the group of interlopers, keeping them in view.

"I need the entire pack at Calli's old house. We're under attack."

It took less than a second for Calli to respond, "Don't you dare confront them alone," she snapped, no doubt still thinking I was in a rage from earlier.

Strangely enough, I was oddly calm. They might be invading my lands for a purpose I had yet to know, but they also had no idea I was so close behind them or that my pack was on their way here. Whatever they thought they were about to get away with, would cost them dearly, and my wolf was practically salivating at the idea.

Stone wouldn't be able to bring us before the Council for attacking these people who had trespassed on our lands. And by striking out at us in anger, he'd put the ball firmly in our court because the Council would hear about his encroachment on our lands.

As I reached the last of the trees before they faded away to the grass at the back of Calli's house, I slowed down to a stop.

The shifters were circling Calli's house, looking confused about it being all boarded up. Surely Stone knew what had gone down here when the coven had resurrected Neressa? If they were working together, she would have told him of the losses they took when they came for the last ingredient in their spell.

I felt a crackle of magic whisper across my fur, and then Cassia stepped out of the shadows of the tree and crouched low to the ground next to me.

"The pack is on the way, and I came on ahead. Davion and his clan are moments away from you and are approaching the house from the opposite direction. He asked what your instructions are," she said, speaking low so as not to alert the shifters to our presence.

I shifted back into my human form, so I could speak with her. Cassia was yet to join our pack link, and we really needed to find a way to rectify that. She was one of our major advantages in a fight, and it would make life a lot easier if we didn't have to keep shifting forms to communicate with her.

"Tell Davion to move in when we do, and we can pin them between us. If they react peacefully, we let them leave. If they're here for a fight, then that's what they'll get. Don't take any chances. If they fight, put them down hard. They came here to do damage, and I won't risk anyone for their sake," I told her.

Cassia nodded and then stepped back, disappearing into the shadows. What I wouldn't give to be able to do that. While we had enemies coming at us from every angle these days, it would be a handy skill to have.

I shifted back into my wolf form, preferring to be in this form if I was about to go into a fight. It wasn't that I couldn't hold my own as a human, but if multiple wolves were coming at you, teeth bared, it helped to have a set of your own available for use.

I could feel my alpha power pushing to the surface with a need to be unleashed, even more than usual. It wasn't easy to hold back, but I could have sworn it actually listened and eased up a bit when I told it to wait just a little while longer.

I didn't have to wait long before the others arrived. They'd made it to Calli's house far quicker than they should have been able to, and they weren't even panting from the run. Looking at them now, I could see the subtle differences in their wolves. River had an almost blue hue to his light grey fur, and I could swear there was a red shine coming into Tanner's eyes.

I shouldn't have been surprised by the sight of Lachlan's wolf, but I was. He'd shifted before, but we hadn't discussed whether it was something he would need assistance in doing. I felt oddly proud that he'd worked his way through it without my assistance.

Blake, Aidan, Hunter, Nash and even Holly were standing behind Calli and the rest of her mates. The sight of an unfamiliar wolf had my hackles rising at first until I recognised his scent as Ethan.

I looked around my pack with pride. This wasn't the first fight we'd gone into together, but this time it felt easier. Maybe this life was changing us more than we'd realised.

"I told Colt and his pack to stay by the house. I wasn't sure if we were trusting them with this," Tanner instructed me as he moved to my side.

"Until we know for sure, that's just the way it will have to be." It pained me to admit it, but that was just the reality of how life was for us now. "We move in fast. Keep in groups of at least three. With Davion and his clan moving in from the front, we far outnumber them. My count has them at twelve. But I don't want anyone to take any risks by separating out on their own. For all we know, more of them are approaching. Go in hard. Take them down fast. We give them one chance to back down, then we put them down for good. I'm fed up with this shit," I told the pack.

A soft round of growls of agreement flowed from them, and a subtle shine of magic started to fill the air. This was going to be the first time we went into a fight with this untested magic. It wasn't wise, but we didn't exactly have control over these circumstances.

Turning back to Calli's house, the smashing and splintering of wood heralded that Stone's shifters were making their move. It enraged my wolf that they'd even dare to try and enter the den of our mate.

I didn't call out to the pack. They were just as on edge as I was. As I sprinted out of the trees, they were hot on my heels. Maybe we were all pissed, maybe we were all on edge, or maybe this life had changed us to the point where we were starting to enjoy the fight.

Shouts of alarm started to flow from the group who had invaded our lands. They were already prepared for a fight, half of them having shifted and been stationed at the rear of the others breaking into the house.

It fed into my suspicions that they were aware of the wardings' existence, even if not the placement. They'd known we were coming.

The shifted wolves dashed forward, meeting us head-on in a clash of fangs and claws. There was no need to give them the opportunity to leave peacefully, they were here for a fight, and I wouldn't risk any of my pack by having them shift to try and reason with them.

The alpha power in me surged to the surface, and for the first time, I let it flow. I didn't try to hold it back, I just embraced the havoc it wanted to cause.

Black tendrils of smoke skated out across the ground and wrapped around the legs of a shifter who was trying to creep up behind Maverick. He yelped in surprise at the contact and tried to spin around to free himself. But once the power had a hold of him, it tightened its hold.

I felt the bones in his leg shatter under the pressure, and with my ears down and teeth bared, I crept towards him, letting him see exactly what he'd brought upon himself.

The shifter tried to flail in my grip, but the pain coming from his broken leg had him whimpering and cowering instead.

I could see out of the corner of my eye as lightning flared out of Lachlan, hitting another wolf square in the chest before he dropped to the ground dead. All of the pack had the gleam of magic, but it seemed dimmer in some. In fact, only those of us who were mated to Calli seemed to have any active signs of magic.

River and Tanner both crept in toward their own target, who was backing away in alarm. The tendrils of blue and red magic snaking out of them seemed to have made this shifter realise he was well out of his depth in this fight. His eyes widened further in fear as the pair leapt for him. In the end, he didn't even have the sense to try and fight back.

The noise of the attacking wolves dropped to nothing. Those who hadn't already fallen under our response to their initial attack were now cowering on the ground. A smell of smoke started to drift along on the breeze, and it became blatantly obvious what they'd come here to do.

I suppose it was fitting that Stone's response to what we'd done would be to start a fire of his own.

The black smoke held firm to the wolf in front of me and started to slowly drag him along the ground toward me as he yelped and cried, clawing at the ground to try and get away.

I could only imagine what it must look like to him to be

dragged toward some kind of wolf that no doubt looked like it had just stepped out of hell.

One of the few remaining shifters in the group in front of us shifted back into his human form, and I realised it was the one who had led them here.

"Wait, wait, please," he begged, raising his hands in the air in surrender as he looked at me with pleading eyes.

I didn't want to wait. I wanted to drag this terrified man into my jaws and end him before turning on the rest of them.

I could see the flames starting to lick at the windows of Calli's old home, and it was already obvious that there would be no saving the building.

Even though the power inside of me was practically salivating for blood, I paused. Maybe it would be prudent to send at least one of them back to Stone with a message of how this had not been the easy fight he'd assumed.

Shifting back into my human form, I glared at the men kneeling on the ground as my pack circled around them. Three were still alive, six were dead on the ground, and the ones who'd gone into the house had never re-emerged, no doubt having come across Davion and his clan instead.

"Wait? You came here to attack my pack, and now you ask for mercy?" I growled.

The alpha in me relished the look of fear in his eyes. He should be afraid. These were my lands and my people. This was what anyone who tried to hurt them would receive.

"We…we…" He didn't say anything else. What else was there to say? He couldn't exactly deny what they'd come to do when the house was steadily burning beside us.

"Tell me. What was the next step in your plan after you set ablaze to my mate's property?"

His eyes widened in shock as he realised the implications of what I was saying. Not only was he attacking my pack, but it was an act of violence against my mate. A look of almost resignation crossed his face when he admitted the rest.

"We were told to take the she-wolf if she crossed our path and to take down any wolf we saw while we were here. This was supposed to be a warning of the consequences of your actions."

I felt the grin pull at my lips as I looked around at their so-called warning. It would be inconvenient to lose the house because Davion was convinced it could be restored enough for the clan to live in again. I hadn't been wholly convinced it could be done without first ripping out the interior walls and flooring. They were probably doing us a favour by burning it down. We could at least rebuild now.

The only other thing their warning had achieved was the death of the men who'd accompanied him. None of my pack had sustained even a scratch. It was more of an exercise in what we could do now, even if none of us had been aware of it.

The smoke that represented my alpha power started to curl up the body of the whimpering man that now lay at my feet as I stared at his leader.

"You realise that you were all sent here to die?" I pointed out. "Stone knows what my mate is. He knows that the pack is changing. After all, it's what he's been trying to get his hands on. There was no way he thought you were all going to walk away from this," I pointed out.

I wanted to know what these men thought of Stone when the reality of their situation was presented to them. It would be a deciding factor in whether we would ultimately go along with Sean and Wells' plan.

From the look of horror on his face, none of them had been clued in on what we were now.

"What are you?" he asked quietly, tapping into his last

reserves of bravery. "I'm obviously about to die. It would be nice to meet the end of this life with at least a drop of the truth available to me."

It was the best thing he could have said. And it was potentially the only thing that saved his life.

"We are animages. We are what shifters were before our heritage was ripped away by people like Stone." It was strange saying it out loud. I didn't think I'd ever considered myself as different from shifters until this moment. But we were. Because we would no longer blindly follow those in power.

I could see the curiosity in his eyes pushing against the resignation of what was going to be his fate. Yet, this was a man who wanted to know more. He wasn't ready to die yet.

"You can ask your questions," I told him, only to be rewarded by a squint of suspicion on his part.

"Why bother spending time explaining it to me? You're only going to kill me."

"I never said that."

"It's hard to believe that when you're strangling my friend at your feet."

Looking down, I realised that the black smoke had indeed crept around the shifter's neck and was slowly squeezing the air from his lungs. I pulled back on the power, pulling it back inside me where it was contained from apparently acting out of its own volition. I should have realised something was wrong when he'd stopped whimpering in pain.

"Hmmm, apologies. I'm pretty new to this whole thing," I told his friend with a shrug.

The shifter in charge took half a step closer to me, but the flash of red in Tanner's eyes with his accompanying growl had him halting in his tracks.

"If you spare the others, I will willingly give my life," he told me, straightening his back in defiance as he took advantage of his moment of bravery.

Tanner and River shifted back to their human forms and came to my side. Then, the pack shifted, even though they stayed close by, but the whole while, he stood determined in front of me. When Calli's beautiful white wolf strode to my side and nuzzled my hand, he finally looked away from me.

Holly shifted at the same time as Calli did, and his jaw just about hit the ground.

"You…you have *two* she-wolves!"

He looked between the two of them, his eyes wide in surprise. Stone obviously hadn't gotten this much information from his spy yet, if there was one here.

At that moment, Cassia trotted around the corner in her wolf form, bounding toward Hunter until she shifted at his side. As Hunter wrapped his arm around her, drawing her close and dropping a kiss on the top of her head, I thought we were going to have to pick this guy up off the floor. Ethan protectively moved in front of the pair, staring down the man who dared to look at them.

"Well, I guess the cat is out of the bag now," Calli laughed.

"This is because of what you said? Because you're animages?" he asked.

"Partly. It's too complicated to get into right now."

He nodded silently, his eyes skimming all three women until Hunter pulled Cassia behind him with a growl. He couldn't have announced it any more clearly if he'd tried.

"She's your mate?" he asked, seemingly losing all sense of self-preservation.

Hunter growled again, but a look from me silenced him. We couldn't have him killing this shifter. I had plans for him.

"I'm going to let you live," I announced, and he actually

didn't look surprised by the announcement, given how much shock he was in. "I want you to go back to your pack and really look at what you see there. Shifters were not made to be dominated. To be kept under the control of an alpha who retains everything for himself while the rest of you survive on scraps. There will be a change coming, and I'm going to give you the opportunity to decide what side of the fight you want to be on."

"Don't trust them," one of the others snapped. "As soon as our backs are turned, they'll kill us!"

"Does it matter?" Calli purred with a menacing grin. "Whether we kill you now or kill you as you walk away, you won't have lost anything. But if we actually let you live, let you go home and realise what we've been fighting for, you could have so much more to gain than just your lives here, in this moment."

The one in charge turned his gaze to my mate, and even though every part of me wanted to pull her away from his view, I waited to see what he was going to do. In the end, he nodded and moved to pick up his wounded friend, who still lay at his feet.

"We're leaving," he said resolutely, slinging his friend's arm over his shoulder as he hauled him up to his feet.

Calli cocked her head to the side as she regarded the two men in front of her. These people wouldn't have been our enemies in a different time, and they shouldn't be now. It was Stone and the people like him who'd made us unnecessary enemies. We should have looked at each other as kin. Packs should band together, not fight tooth and claw for dominance.

Holding out her hand, Calli offered, "I can heal your leg if you want me to."

Both men froze, unsure of what to do.

"It won't hurt, and all you need to do is take my hand. I promise I won't do anything else. I'll just heal the breaks so you can make your way home."

The injured shifter reluctantly held his hand out to Calli. From the dots of perspiration on his face, he was clearly in pain. It was impressive that he hadn't passed out by now.

Calli closed her eyes and then, on a second thought, opened one to look at him again, "I might start glowing when I do this, but don't be alarmed. Apparently, it's just something I do now."

I could see the panic flash in his eyes, but before he could consider whether he wanted to pull his hand out of Calli's grip, she started to glow softly in the telltale sign of her magic, and he sighed at the sudden relief of the pain withdrawing. Sagging against his friend in relief, he held still while she slowly mended the breaks in his leg, everyone else watched tensely to make sure these three men didn't show us why letting them live was potentially a massive mistake.

By the time Calli was finished, he stood on his own two feet and looked at her in awe. That slither of annoyance ran through me again, but I ignored it for a second time. What we were doing here could be enough to turn the tide in our favour. If these men went back to Stone's pack and turned to our side, word could spread inside the pack of what we were trying to do.

We silently watched them walk away as Davion and his clan stepped out of the tree line behind us.

"Are you sure that was wise?" Davion asked, clearly having been watching for some time. I just shrugged in response.

"No one speaks of this when we return to the pack," I instructed. "If we do have a spy amongst us, we can't afford for Stone to find out that these men may move to our side."

Everyone nodded in silence before silently moving back to the treeline to head back to the packhouse. In the end, it was just Calli, Tanner and I watching as the fire truly took hold of the house in front of us.

Wrapping an arm around Calli, I held her tightly as we watched the house that was to be her home burn to the ground. This was too close for comfort. We weren't sheltered enough here on our lands to weather a larger force if Stone decided to send a second attack our way.

"We're going to have to relocate to Wells' pack, at least temporarily," I finally admitted as the sound of sirens started in the distance.

Looking around, I realised the other bodies were gone. Finding Davion leaning against a tree off to the side and licking his fingers wasn't exactly a comforting sight. Still, at least he'd had the forethought to clean up after us before the humans showed up. It would have been hard to explain the burning building, let alone the six dead men at our feet.

"We should leave before they arrive," Davion said when he noticed me looking in his direction. "It will be easier to explain this as an act of vandalism if we aren't found standing here watching it burn."

Calli nodded and turned around as she started to walk toward the trees without a word. When Tanner looked at me in question, I nodded for him to follow her. He jogged to her side and then wrapped an arm around her shoulders as they disappeared into the trees.

Davion moved to my side as I took a last look at the place.

"I'm sorry you won't have the house to move into," I told him, actually meaning it.

Davion was the only ally we had that I trusted one hundred per cent, which was a strange thing for me to admit.

I'd wanted to make sure that life at the pack would be easier for them, so they'd agree to stay.

"It is what it is," he said with a shrug before we both started to walk away. "So you're taking them up on their offer then?" he asked, trying to sound casual.

"I will take the pack there until the threat of Stone is dealt with. Today has shown me that we don't have the resources, or the know-how, to adequately protect our lands when we have people coming at us from every possible direction. We didn't build this pack anticipating that we'd need to survive a war. But I'm still not willing to challenge Wells for control of his pack."

"Is it possible you've actually come to like the obnoxious alpha?" Davion asked with a laugh.

"More like I think he's trying to lumber me with some kind of epic problem. Why else would he be so willing to die?"

It was strange, and I couldn't wrap my mind around what his motives could possibly be.

"Hmmm, it is a strange turn of events," Davion agreed.

"Will you come with us?" I asked, needing to know if we'd still have them to count on.

We had no idea what we were walking into. But, for some reason, doing it with the force of the clan at our side made me feel a bit easier about the whole thing.

"I'm not entirely sure the invitation extends to the clan." Davion laughed, but I could see the pinch at the corner of his eyes that spoke of his true feelings. "Besides, I've heard of some rumblings in the vampire world, which may need my attention."

"Anything I can help you with?" I meant it, too. In fact, at this point, I felt more inclined to help Davion than to wade further into this mess with Stone.

"Don't you have enough on your plate? I would have thought pack problems should come first?"

"You're pack now."

I didn't realise it until I said it, but it was true. Somewhere along the way, Davion had moved from ally to friend to pack. We wouldn't be alive if it wasn't for him, and he'd more than proved himself. The whole clan had.

Davion's hand clasped my shoulder as we wound our way through the trees. "I feel the same way, friend."

"This is getting eerily close to us having feelings," I joked, trying to break the heaviness of the moment.

"You're right! Quick, punch me, so no one suspects anything when we get back."

I couldn't help but laugh. Davion was the lightness we needed in these dark times, which was a strange thing to think, given his race.

I felt the rush of tingles down my spine, heralding the arrival of the fire engine at Calli's house. It was followed by two other short bursts. Assuming it was more help arriving on the scene, I was actually surprised when we emerged from the treeline to see an old truck driving down the driveway toward the packhouse.

"For fuck's sake! What the fuck now?" I sighed, done with this day already.

"Always so eloquent," Davion laughed. "Let's go and see who else needs to die today. I feel like I could do with some dessert."

19
LACHLAN

It was strange walking back to the packhouse like nothing had happened. Or rather, that was how it felt. But there was a strange buzz in the air coming from all of us.

The rest of the pack was clearly excited about their first glimpse of what power they could hold, even if they were trying to contain it. Because, let's face it, we'd just killed six people, and it was hardly an appropriate moment.

If I was honest with myself, I could also feel that slight buzz of excitement.

I'd shifted. Again.

It had been more difficult than I'd thought it would be. But, this time, it had been more of a conscious decision. When the pack had shifted, I hadn't wanted to be left behind. At first, I didn't know where to start, but when Maverick had shifted beside me, it was like I was able to feel the magic required to start the process.

That was when it had all clicked into place. It was just a magical process, and I was a witch. I could do this. I just had to know how. And now I did.

After that, the shift felt almost natural. Even running in my wolf form with the others had been exhilarating. I could see why the shifters gathered in packs if this was how it felt. I'd never had any similar feeling from being in a coven. If anything, that had felt more like oppression, whereas running through the trees in my wolf form had been the freest I'd ever felt.

Colt and his pack were waiting at the bottom of the packhouse steps when we arrived. They were all on edge. Not just because we'd told them there was an attack, but they'd known it had to be Stone. They were undoubtedly terrified they were about to be dragged back to one of his facilities.

The other three rescued shifters had slipped into the house as we'd left, trembling with terror. No one had the heart to tell them to stand and fight. They weren't ready. Neither were the witches who'd all but barricaded themselves into the library.

Grey was right that we needed to move to the bigger pack. It would be safer there, even if it wasn't what we wanted.

I'd come to see this place as a home without realising it. It was the first time I'd ever felt this way about a place. Maybe it was the people here that gave it that feeling. Not only did I have Calli, but I was growing closer to the others in her mate bond, especially Tanner. There was nothing closer than doing what we'd done together.

A part of me wondered if I should feel ashamed about what we'd done, but there was no way I could see being with our mate as something to be ashamed of. We were all becoming so intricately bonded together that you could almost see the tethers between us with your eyes. There was only one way to break these types of bonds, and none of us would be willingly rushing toward death any time soon.

As we reached the steps, I saw the others bristle and felt the lingering touch of Calli's magic in the air. It was the only way I could tell that the wards had been breached around the pack because I hadn't received the rune to link me into the spell yet. There hadn't been time, and I supposed now that we were leaving, it wasn't really necessary. For now, at least.

When we heard the crunch of tires on the gravel, we all turned in surprise to see an old truck making its way down the driveway. None of us had even considered that we had visitors, especially considering what was no doubt happening at the house we'd just left. It would have been nice to see inside Calli's old home before it had been destroyed by what fate was throwing at us.

Grey and Davion appeared at the treeline as the truck slowed to a stop a respectful distance from the house.

I could see River and Maverick moving in front of Calli and Tanner, and I found myself mirroring their movements. We couldn't be too careful after one attack. It would be foolish to believe that Stone was done already.

When the door to the truck cracked open and a dark-haired man slowly stepped outside, it was only Calli's laugh of joy that broke the tension in the air. He had a Latin look about him with the tan of his skin and the dark brown eyes that shone with amusement. If I had to guess, I'd say Greek or something similar. He was clearly a shifter, and the plain white shirt he had on teased at the stereotypical shifter beneath.

The smirk on his face spoke of his confidence as he pulled off his sunglasses and clipped them to the neckline of his shirt. It only widened when Calli ran to him and threw her arms around his neck.

Who the fuck was this guy?

Calli stepped away from the man she was embracing, and

he playfully ruffled her hair in a way that only someone who had been familiar with her for years could have done.

If this was one of her ex-boyfriends, there was no way he would walk out of here alive, not if the look Grey was giving him was anything to go by.

"Everyone, this is Felix," Calli announced, looking at us with a wide grin on her face.

It was a far cry from the sad frown she'd had on her walk back to the house. Part of me hated that it wasn't me that had put it on her face, and given the expressions on the rest of her mates' faces, I wasn't the only one thinking that way.

"Wow, tough crowd," Felix murmured.

He seemed like a nice enough guy, and he was obviously friends with Calli. I could see that we were being unfair to him. It wasn't his fault they had a history together.

Taking pity on the guy, I stepped forward and held out my hand, "Hey, I'm Lachlan," I said, introducing myself as he shook my hand. "Calli mentioned you were coming by to help out."

"Judging by the smoke, I'm guessing I'm a bit late."

Sean, Marie and Wells walked out of the packhouse, and all of them came to greet Felix like the old friend he was. It wasn't helping the tension running through the others.

"The house?" Sean asked Calli.

"Gone, there's no way it can be salvaged," Calli said, her voice cracking as she explained.

I went to reach out for her, but Felix beat me to it as he wrapped an arm around her shoulders in comfort.

"I'm going to go and meet the fire crew," Grey barked out, turning around and striding away. "It will look less suspicious if one of us turns up saying we saw the smoke."

"I'll come with you," Tanner sulked, walking away without another word.

Calli sighed and looked at me with her sad eyes. The smile on her face was long gone as she watched her mates walking away. The poor woman had just watched her house be set on fire, and now her mates were acting like spoiled children because she'd dared to have a friend that was a boy. The horror!

"Why don't we move this inside?" River suggested turning away from where he'd been watching Grey and Tanner walk away.

I caught Felix's words to Calli as we moved toward the house, "I'm sorry if I didn't handle that in the best way."

"It's not your fault," Calli soothed. "It's just been an emotional few months."

"Felix! It's good to see you again," Ethan said, stepping forward and embracing the man. "I didn't realise you were on this side of the globe."

"Eh, you know how it is! I just go where I'm told and do what's needed," Felix said warmly with a shrug. He was clearly an important part of the underground if he was trusted to do certain jobs for Sean, and I was surprised we hadn't heard more about him.

"And here I was thinking you'd come running to my aid," Calli said sarcastically.

"Yeah, about that. I'm more here to see Sean."

Calli looked across at Felix, her eyes squinting in annoyance. "I suppose this is one of those secret conversations everyone feels like keeping to themselves."

"Hey, whoa, there." Felix laughed, holding up his hands as we walked through the kitchen. "I'm just under the boss man's orders. So you point that snark in his direction, hey?"

"You're just as bad," Calli grumbled, sidling closer to me as she glared at Felix, who only laughed at the move.

I wouldn't complain when it meant she was coming to my side.

"We should catch up later," Ethan told him, backing away toward a certain witch who looked to be heading back to her cabin. "I want to introduce you to some people."

Felix smirked as he watched Ethan turn and sprint after Cassia. "Hmmm, people," he muttered.

Making our way inside, it was almost laughable seeing Sean looking nervous about incurring Calli's wrath again. The poor guy was literally a toe out of her bad books and already about to get shoved back inside.

"I'll make the tea," Sean shouted, bustling around the kitchen, clearly wanting to stay out of the way of Calli's annoyance.

She humphed and then, looking around the room, realised that not everyone had followed us inside.

"River? Maverick?"

"We're just dealing with Colt and the others. Aidan and Hunter are going to take them to keep working on the cabins, but they're fairly suspicious about what's going on. Are you okay without us for a bit?" River answered through the link.

He sounded fine, and I doubted River was one to storm off just because his mate had hugged another man. But, Maverick, I wasn't so sure about.

"Yeah, we'll be fine," Calli responded before turning back to the others in the room.

Sean was looking at her strangely. We hadn't told them about the way the bond was developing so far, but I had a feeling he suspected what was happening, especially if he'd been talking with Wells, who'd been here when it all started to change.

If Sean was as old as people were assuming, he must have

been around when animages were in the world before. How much did he know about what would happen with our bond?

Wells sat on one of the stools at the kitchen counter, swinging his legs as he watched the awkward encounter like it was his favourite show. This seemed to be his go-to attitude about anything serious that happened around him, and I couldn't figure out how he'd gotten a seat on the Shifter Council. To be honest, his upbeat outlook was wearing a bit thin. My mate was hurting. This wasn't entertainment for him. She didn't deserve to become some kind of sideshow for his amusement.

As Sean reluctantly emerged out of the kitchen, he held out a cup of tea to Calli before she could say anything else. I could see it as the peace offering it was meant to be. She stared at it like this foreign thing she couldn't quite work out. Her anxiety and sadness were radiating down the bond and slamming into me.

Calli had completely lost control of her shielding, and I felt like an utter bastard for being grateful for that. She'd just watched the home her parents had made for her burn. Usually, Calli would have stood firm and carried on, crumbling on the inside without ever telling anyone about her pain. But now that the bond had changed and linked us closer than ever before, I finally had a way of seeing the part she tried to keep away from us. She didn't do it on purpose. Calli was just one of those people that worried about everyone else before herself. I was starting to think she'd done it for so long that she didn't even know how to put herself first for once.

"I need to start packing up the books if we're moving again," Calli suddenly blurted out before quickly turning around and fleeing the room.

"I'll erm probably go and…deal with that," I said awkwardly, backing out after her.

Calli was standing in front of the bookcases when I made it to the library. Even though I had only been seconds behind her, it still felt like she'd been standing alone for an age.

Staring at the bookcase, she had her arms wrapped around her, and a single tear tracked down her cheek. It was impossible to stay away, and three strides across the room had me pulling her into my arms.

"I don't want to go to Wells' pack," she said, her eyes never straying from the books. "I don't want to let them take this home from me as well."

My arms tightened around her, and I clung to her, desperate to make the pain she was feeling go away. There was nothing I could do to make this better. Wells' pack was possibly the only safe refuge we had at this point. Stone would come again, and he'd send more men next time. We simply didn't have the manpower to protect these lands and keep everyone safe, even if the remaining rescued shifters decided to stay with us.

"I know things feel like they're at their darkest right now, and it feels like such a cliché to say that you still have us, but we will get through this together. We move to the pack, and while we have somewhere safe to get our heads together, we put together our own plan. What your parents achieved in getting us all this far was nothing short of a miracle, but that doesn't mean we have to go along with everything they're telling us to do. We have our own path to forge, and fuck anyone that wants to keep us from it. You are powerful, Calli, but together we're unstoppable. We can do this. I know we can. And when it's all said and done, we can come home to this house and live the life we want."

Calli sighed and sagged against me. At first, I thought she would argue, but then she looked up at me with her watery eyes and a soft smile spread across her lips.

"You're pretty zen about this whole thing, you know. Aren't you a little pissed that you got dragged out of your home and thrown into all this craziness?"

"How could I be? This craziness gave me you, and this is the first time in my entire life I've ever felt like a place *could* be a home. I will fight just as hard for this as you, my love, because it's everything I've ever wanted too."

Calli gently took my glasses off my face before she carefully folded the arms and placed them on the desk beside me. Before I could even ask what she was doing, she pushed me backward, and I fell into one of the armchairs. Straddling my lap, she cupped my face in her hands and dipped her head to softly kiss me on the lips before she peppered kisses along my jaw.

"Make love to me, Lachlan. Let's make a happy memory so that it isn't all death and sadness when we look back on this day."

I couldn't deny her. The soft press of her lips against mine already had my cock standing to attention and begging for her touch.

Wrapping my hands under her, I stood from the chair, holding Calli tight against me as I moved us to the soft rug in front of the fireplace. She was right. I needed this just as much as she did. The soft touches and tender caresses to chase away the nightmares that haunted us.

I wouldn't regret what we'd done at Calli's house. We'd only been defending ourselves. But it was hard not to feel like there were eyes constantly on you when we were always waiting for the next blow to come.

I didn't want my life to be all about the fight. And as I

laid Calli down in front of me, I pulled her pants down her long slim legs as she hastily pulled off her top. Softly tickling my fingers up her legs, I watched as she squirmed at the sensation. The ghost of a smile started to play on her lips as she watched me.

I realised precisely what life meant for me now. It was her. It would always be Calli. I held her so close to my heart that I didn't think it would beat without her. I wasn't even sure if I'd want it to.

My breath caught in my throat as I stared down at her spread out on the rug in front of me, her golden hair fanned out around her. From the soft smile on her lips, I knew I was taking too long in my appreciation, but I couldn't help it. Whenever Calli smiled at me, I felt like a teenager in love. My heart set off at a gallop, and it was like I lost all control of my brain as it stalled to a halt.

Unable to hold back any longer, I ripped off my shirt and made quick work of losing the rest of my clothes.

"Please, Lachlan," Calli whimpered. "I need to feel you inside me."

I'd never be able to deny her.

As Calli's arms came up to pull me closer, I wrapped her in my embrace. My hard cock nudged against her wet core as Calli wrapped one leg over my hip, drawing me inside her.

My cock sheathed inside her in one fluid thrust, and we both groaned with satisfaction at the feeling of me bottoming out inside her. Her tight pussy gripped me harder than ever before, and I felt like one tiny movement would make me lose it straight away.

Calli's hand cradled my cheek as she drew me down for a kiss. As my lips sealed to hers, it was impossible not to rock into her. Calli's distracting kisses were just what I needed to start the slow worship of her, as I took my time, slowly dragging my cock out of her heat before pushing back inside.

Wrapping my hand under her luscious ass, I pulled her closer, grinding my hips on every thrust, so I could move across her clit. We might have rushed straight to the main course, but there was no way this was ending before I'd heard Calli screaming out my name.

Calli's hips canted forward, and I mirrored her movements, keeping up with the long, languid strokes of my cock inside her pussy. The feeling of her moving with me was pure ecstasy.

As our bodies moved as one, my hand roamed across Calli's soft skin, skimming from her thigh up to her creamy pale breasts. I circled my thumb around her nipple before drawing it into my mouth and gently raking my teeth across the hardened peak.

The way she moaned my name in response had me filing the move away in my brain so I'd remember to explore it in more depth later. For now, though, neither one of us wanted to stop. This was about seeking solace in the arms of the person we loved.

"I love you, Calli," I told her, meaning it with every piece of my heart.

Her eyes shone with happy tears as one of her hands came up to my cheek. Leaning my forehead against hers, I started to pick up the pace of my thrusts inside her.

"I love you, Lachlan," she whispered just before her voice broke, and she cried out as the wave of her orgasm crested over her.

I watched every expression move across her face as I slowly rode her through her release, cherishing how she clung to me until I couldn't hold back anymore. The way her pussy trembled and clenched at my cock had me roaring out as I emptied myself inside of her.

We both knew we couldn't hide in the library forever, but as I collapsed on the rug beside her, I drew Calli close to my chest, wrapping her in my arms. She came without complaint as she nuzzled against me. We might not have all day to lay in each other's arms, but we had a few more moments at least.

"I promise you, Calli, that I will bring you back home again. I won't let them take this place or the happiness we're building here away from us."

She nodded slowly, and I thought I'd said the wrong thing for a moment. That I'd ruined the moment by reminding her of all the reasons why she'd been sad before. But when Calli lifted her head to meet my eyes, I saw the fierceness had returned to hers.

"This is our home and our family. It's time we showed them what happens to those who try to destroy the ones we love."

She was like a vengeful goddess, and I was right there with her. I could feel the bond inside us radiating with the fierce passion of the others linked to us. They all felt the same way as they prepared to leave these lands. This wasn't a time to be sad. This was a time to make those who tried to stand against us realise just how big of a mistake they'd made.

20
RIVER

We just couldn't catch a break around here. The wards had triggered again, and I once more found myself standing in front of the house to see who the hell was coming to bother us now. I supposed that as Calli's house was currently in flames, it could just be someone from the emergency services coming to speak with us. Although, come to think of it, it was fairly surprising that we'd heard the sirens back at her house as soon as we had. We certainly hadn't called them, which begged the question of who had been close enough to realise the fire had broken out.

When Calli and Lachlan came out of the house, holding hands and grinning at each other, I could have kicked myself for not following her inside.

There was never enough time in the day to get everything done, and the sacrifice I seemed to be making was time with my mate.

Seeing the look on my face, Calli walked to my side and held my hand in her free one. It should have been weird holding her hand while she was holding another man's hand at the same time. It wasn't, though. There was nothing about Calli or our situation that made me uncomfortable. This was the best version of my life that I'd ever had, and I'd never complain about a second of it.

"You don't look happy," Calli pointed out.

"More frustrated that I wasn't the one to put that smile on your face," I admitted.

"Well, I think I'm going to be super sad tonight. Perhaps I could book you in advance," she joked.

The SUV coming down the driveway slowly turned to face the way it had come and then came to a stop.

"Might I suggest an afternoon nap then because I can already tell you're going to need hours of attention tonight?" It was so unlike me, and I almost wanted to cringe at how cheesy it potentially sounded, but from the flash of arousal that blazed through Calli's eyes, I didn't think I had much to worry about.

While we were distracted awkwardly flirting with each other, a woman in a pantsuit and aviator glasses stepped out of the SUV and started to walk toward us.

"Do you think they have wardrobe lessons at cop school, or do they get a free tote bag on enrolment that comes with aviator glasses and a flippy badge wallet?" Maverick joked as he came over to join us.

"Actually, my flippy badge wallet is custom-made," the woman snarked as she pulled it out of her jacket pocket to show us her badge.

"I'm Special Agent Veronica Milner. I was out this way a few days ago and talked to a couple of your friends. They about now?"

"I believe you're referring to Grey and Tanner, and I'm afraid they're otherwise engaged at the moment. You see, someone set a fire at one of our properties. They've gone over there to assist the authorities in whatever capacity they can," Calli smoothly interjected. Her English accent came out strong as she refused to back down from the woman in front of us.

The Fed wasn't intimidated as she slowly looked Calli up and down and then politely smiled in a way that screamed, 'if I could punch you, I would'.

"Not from around here, are you?"

"Actually, my house is just through those trees," Calli told her with her own passive-aggressive smile, intentionally missing her point.

"Let's not dance around the dog house here, shall we. You're making too much noise, and my bosses don't like it when you start to draw attention to yourselves. I know you know more about the missing persons than you've told me, and I know you've been told not to trust my kind. So I suggest you lay it all out on the line now while you have the chance, and I'll make sure that it all gets cleared up before anyone gets in any unnecessary trouble," the fed grated out.

It was impressive that Calli had managed to ruffle her feathers with such few words.

Calli reluctantly turned to me for input, but I could tell that she wanted to tell this woman to fuck the fuck off. I was kind of there with her. This was clearly one of the law enforcement officers aware of our existence, but the fact that she wasn't just politely asking for our help was grating on my nerves. If anything, her attitude smacked of someone who didn't like our kind.

Perhaps it was time that we showed her where her rudeness would get her.

I let my wolf push to the surface, and I knew my eyes flashed with his presence while she was looking at me. I could tell just from the revolted look of surprise that crossed her face.

"I'm not sure what people have been telling you, but I can assure you we don't have a dog, let alone a dog house." I smiled pleasantly at the Fed before hearing Maverick try to unsuccessfully cover his laugh with a cough.

Agent Milner took a deep breath, looking up to the sky as if begging someone for an ounce of patience. It probably wasn't fair of us to antagonise her so much, but in our defence, we'd had a terrible day. Anyway, it was really for Grey to decide how much we would say in this situation.

"Grey, we have the fed at the house again. What do you want me to do?" I asked through the link.

I swear I heard his sigh even though he wasn't here.

"We're on our way back; we'll be with you in a few minutes. Just keep her there. They've nearly put down the fire at the house, but they didn't want us hanging around. No one seems to be raising any eyebrows at it. They're all mumbling about kids being too bored and small towns not having enough resources."

The Fed was looking at me curiously, and I realised that while I'd been listening to Grey, my wolf had pushed through to the surface again. I could feel the same glimmer of magic running through me that I'd felt in the fight earlier. It was like now that I'd scratched its surface, it didn't want to be contained again.

"You're not what I thought you were," she said, watching me closely.

"Special Agent, I'm Luke Wells. I'm assuming you know the name," Wells said from behind, moving around us, seemingly prepared to take over the situation.

It was the most official and normal I'd ever seen the man

be, and I swear I saw the prickly fed batter her eyelashes at the boyish grin he gave her.

"Of course, of course. It's nice to meet you, Councillor."

"Now, you were raising some concern about the actions of my personal friends here. Can I ask what they've done to be causing you problems?"

"Well, erm, well, it's not their actions, so to speak—just a series of suspicious disappearances all around this area. And then there's the fire I heard reported over the radio," she spluttered.

"And these suspicious disappearances have been linked to the people who live here?"

Wells was being so overly polite, it was almost difficult to see the corner he was leading the now backtracking fed into.

"Well, no, there's no evidence linking them to any of the people who have gone missing apart from their acquaintance with one of the victims."

"Victims? Oh my, are you implying that something untoward could have happened to these poor souls. I could have sworn I heard you say they were being dealt with as disappearances." Wells all but gasped and swooned in what could only be described as an imitation of a fictional old Southern lady.

"Well, there's no evidence of any foul play yet. But when people disappear in these numbers, we have to consider all possible avenues of investigation, you understand?"

"Of course, of course. You wouldn't be doing your job if you weren't asking such questions. I'm assuming you've been asking these questions all over town. Have you followed up on the reports of every single crime in the area to make sure it's not linked to your disappearances? I'd hate to think you were harassing these fine people just because of some misconception you may have. Tell me, Special Agent, what position do you hold in the unit again?" Wells' features hardened the further he got into his speech, and for the first time, I got a flash of how this man had worked his way onto the Council.

He might not be the most serious person all the time, but he used that as a weapon to allow people to underestimate him until they'd said too much. Then he struck, holding their own words and actions in front of them and confronting them with flawless logic. It was even more impressive because we'd all fallen for the trap of underestimating him, up until now at least.

"I…well, this is my first case with the unit," the fed spluttered, and we all immediately saw her for what she was.

She was a green as grass newbie trying to make a splash on her first case by pulling some kind of conspiracy out of a bag.

She actually had stumbled upon a conspiracy, so maybe she wasn't all that bad at her job. It was a shame she'd never be allowed to find out the truth of just how right she was.

"Well, I think it's about time you finished asking whatever pertinent questions brought you here and report back to your supervising agent. I'll make sure he's fully apprised of the situation before you get back there to save you some time," Wells told her as a cold grin stretched across his face.

Yeah, this was one Fed we didn't have to worry about. No doubt she'd be behind a desk and banned from ever speaking with us by the time Wells was done.

"I have your boss on my speed dial, would you believe," Wells laughed, back to his happy-go-lucky exterior as he gently steered the Special Agent back to her car.

She didn't argue. If anything, she was doing everything she could to try and smooth the situation over.

This was what the Council should have been doing for

our people. Wells was the one person on the Council who we wanted to be there, and it was kind of ironic that if we followed his plan, he'd be the one we killed.

We couldn't afford for people like him to be taken out of the picture. He had a far more important future to follow, and it couldn't stop now.

Once Stone was out of the picture and the Council was exposed for what it had allowed to take place, Wells needed to be there to pick up the pieces. We needed someone on the inside we could trust to make sure this didn't get swept under the carpet, someone to make sure whoever took Stone's place wasn't just as bad as he was.

We lived in a world where Wells was the one reasonable voice we could trust, and I wasn't sure whether I should be comforted or terrified by that idea.

Grey and Tanner emerged from the treeline just as Special Agent Milner was driving away.

"I said I would deal with her," Grey growled, a flash of anger crossing his eyes. He still hadn't come down from the fight and his annoyance at seeing Felix's familiarity with our mate. He needed to run it off before he said something he'd regret.

In Grey's defence, it was beyond rude for Felix to have come onto our packlands and still not have addressed Grey as the ruling alpha. Felix might not have been a wolf, but he was a shifter and would have known the proper etiquette for entering a pack's territory.

"You may be a Council member, Wells, but you're not the ruling alpha here." Grey's voice dropped low, and I could almost make out the dark shimmer around him as his alpha power started to react to his anger.

Grey's eyes cut to Felix, and it was apparent who his dire was really aimed at.

"I owe you an apology," Felix rushed out, moving to the front of our group, so he could address Grey directly. "I have entered your lands without introducing myself, and I should have sought your permission to be here before entering your home. Forgive me, alpha. Sometimes it is hard to remember your manners when you've been on the road alone for so long."

Grey glared at Felix, and I think we all held our breath for a moment to see if he was going to explode or if he'd graciously accept the apology. He'd never been this quick to anger before, but he also didn't have an ominous black cloud of alpha power hanging around him either.

Bonding with Calli had made us all more powerful, and I could see from the worry in Calli's eyes exactly where her mind was about to go.

"You don't have to worry about the changes Grey is going through, Calli. We all need this if we're going to survive. All you've done is give us a chance at life," I said softly through our link, hoping like hell I'd held it back from the others.

We were all pretty new at this, and whilst using the link was pretty intuitive, I was also fairly certain I'd felt what Tanner was doing in the shower this morning, making breakfast very awkward.

Calli turned to me and nodded. She didn't look upset. If anything, she had a resigned acceptance on her face.

We'd get through this. Then we'd come home and find out what life would be like with these new powers she'd given us. I refused to see it as a bad thing. We were becoming what we were always meant to be. We were merely reclaiming our heritage, rediscovering what had been taken from us and hidden away.

"Thank you for acknowledging your error," Grey said slowly. It was difficult not to miss that he didn't say Felix was forgiven. "I know you've come to speak with Sean about what's happening around here, and I won't keep you from whatever discussion you need to have."

Grey turned to look at Calli and me and must have seen the look of surprise on my face. That was not what I'd been expecting him to say. If anything, he'd be entirely within his rights to demand they include him in their conversation. Hell, I was pretty sure we all would be.

"We have people on our lands who need to speak with us," Grey said slowly, looking over my shoulder.

Turning around, I saw the remaining rescued shifters slowly emerging from the house with the three male witches at their side. It had to be the first time that either group had happily occupied the same space without turning their ire on each other. The collective look of distrust they had for us right now was enough to unite them.

Well, at least they'd found some common ground.

"We need to know what is happening around here," Colt said when they all came to a stop in front of us. "It's obvious that the pack is in trouble. You've admitted as much yourself before now, but you still haven't given us the details. We've spent too long being shoved in a box and denied a voice. Don't keep doing that to us now."

It wasn't an unreasonable request, and Grey nodded in acknowledgement before looking at Wells.

"I should probably go with them," he said awkwardly, backing away from the conversation that was about to happen.

It wasn't like there was about to be a confrontation, but Wells was part of the problem these people had right now, and it wouldn't exactly help to have him with us.

"Very well," Grey sighed.

The rest of us stayed.

Maverick, Lachlan and I stayed grouped around Calli. If there were a spy amongst these people, we wouldn't trust them with such easy access to our mate.

Tanner stayed at Grey's side, ever the supportive beta that he was.

Nash and Aidan drifted back toward the house, and the others were nowhere to be seen. At least these people didn't have to feel like they were asking their questions in front of an audience. They looked nervous enough as it was, and they were only asking for answers.

"You know from your time at the facility that Stone is up to something. We believe he is conducting research to try and find out more about our physiology as shifters and how he can improve that to how we used to be. How Calli is and what the rest of us are changing into. From what we've learned so far, we know that shifters once used to be called animages. We were part of the witch community, but we were cast out when it was believed we were growing too powerful. Over the years, we have lost our power because we lost access to our mates, to those who could become Pack Queens and imbue an entire pack with gifts we have yet to discover. We believe Stone wants that power for himself, but we don't yet know how Neressa or the witches' own Council are involved or what they stand to gain from it," Grey explained.

The whole crowd looked surprised, but they weren't doubting what Grey was telling them, probably because of what they'd seen at the facility.

"The women you rescued, they were Pack Queens?" Colt asked with a glimmer of interest in his eye.

"No, they were human women who were turned into shifters against their will," Calli added. "A Pack Queen needs to have both animage and witch blood. They don't have that."

"So why was he changing all those women, why was

he…" another of the men stuttered out, his eyes wild as he no doubt relived the things they'd seen.

"We don't know. We don't have enough information at this stage, but we're working toward it. From what one of the women told me, I believe he was trying to breed a Queen. We went to the facility that night to take down Neressa because she was coming after us. It was her or us, and we were fed up of standing around and waiting to die. Stone retaliated today, and he will no doubt retaliate again. We can't protect ourselves here. It's too open, too easy to access. So we're moving to Wells' pack. He's spent the last, I don't know how long, building an army at his pack to move against Stone and stop whatever he's doing. He wants us to lead that army for him when we fully come into whatever power is developing inside of us."

It was the first time any of us had said it out loud, and when you explained it the way Grey was, it did make sense. What had sounded like an insane plan put together by Wells and Sean seemed slightly reasonable. Apart from the whole killing Wells and taking over his pack bit, that part was always going to be insane.

"How do you know you can trust him? How do you know he isn't working with Stone, and this is all some kind of trap to get you into a cage?" he asked again.

It was at that point that I knew they were leaving. There was nothing we'd be able to say that would change their mind. And that was okay. We couldn't even imagine what these people had been through, and even if their bodies were healing, it would take a long time to work through it mentally. We shouldn't be expecting them to fight at our side. These were the people we were supposed to be protecting. Asking them to fight would have been the same as sacrificing them to the cause, and none of us would have been okay with that.

"We don't," Grey admitted. "But we have to do something, and this is the only thing we can do now. I know you wanted to leave today, and none of us will stop you. Aidan already sorted out the truck, and we've put together supplies to help get you to wherever you want to go. There's a man inside who runs an underground, and if you want, we can give you his number if you ever need it. You know where we are if you ever want to come back here too, we won't turn you away."

The three of them looked at each other, and with slow resigned nods, they started to move back to the house. This was the right decision for them, and we shouldn't have even considered trying to get them to stay.

It was equally unsurprising when Brendan stepped forward. "We'll be leaving today too."

Calli's eyes cut to Elliot, and we could all see how upset he was about the decision.

"I found a book on healing that I want to give you," Calli told him. "Jessa has told me a way around the blood spell that prevents you from looking at the books. It will help you learn more about healing magic, and if you ever have any questions, I'm only a phone call away."

Elliot looked slightly happier at the offer, even though he still didn't seem to want to leave. But this was the decision of his coven, and he didn't seem the type to split from them. The three of them had been through so much that I doubted they'd ever stray far from each other again.

There was something about shared trauma that linked people together, even if it was in the most unhealthy way.

"We can make the same arrangements for you that we did for the others," Grey confirmed. "Do you have anywhere to go?"

"We'll figure it out," Brendan told us evasively.

None of us would take it personally, and the three of them slowly moved away from the group, heading back toward the house to gather their things.

Grey turned to Colt, who'd been watching the whole thing unfold in silence. Before, he'd said he would relinquish his place as alpha and join the pack. He'd known more about the circumstances of what was happening here than any of the others. I supposed it paid to be known as an alpha, even in a more progressive pack like ours.

"Tell me what the Fed wanted," he finally demanded.

It was like he was convinced we were keeping something from him, even though Grey was being open with the facts. He had cause to, though. We were keeping facts from him, but only because we didn't know if we could trust him either.

"She's looking into the disappearances in the area. It's caught the eye of the humans. Between Stone shopping for torture victims and the wraiths deciding to start calling in their shadow-touched chips, a lot of people have gone missing."

I could see the confusion on the faces of his pack members. We'd only briefly touched on the whole wraith thing with them. I think it was just too weird to seem true, even to those of us who'd lived through it. Thankfully, none of them asked any questions. I doubted they'd believe us anyway.

"I meant what I said. I think you're a good alpha, and we will stand with you. But we won't be coming with you to Wells' pack. At least not straight away. We've discussed it, and we want to head down to our old packlands and make sure there's no sign of any other survivors. After a few days scouting the area, we'll head back up to you."

"You could be walking right into a trap," Tanner warned Colt.

"Yeah, we know." Colt shrugged as if it didn't matter. "But we need to know, and going on with life as normal without at least looking would drive us all crazy."

"I can understand that," Grey said with a nod. "I'd feel the same way. You don't have to rush back to us if you don't want to. Wait out whatever fight is coming and find us after."

"Nah, if there's a fight on the horizon, we have a few punches we'd like to throw." Colt's mouth pulled into a vicious smile as he spoke. "It's blood for blood, and we're owed it by the bucketful."

Grey nodded thoughtfully for a second, and I could see the gears turning in his mind. "We're going to need more vehicles."

That was an understatement, to say the least. We had Calli's truck and ours. Blake owned one, and we'd bought one for the three shifters who were leaving. We were going to need at least three more if we were going to move everyone, four if we were going to do it comfortably.

"I'll call the dealership in the next town over and make sure we can pick them up first thing in the morning. I'm sure they'll work overtime to get it all ready with the amount of money this will cost." Tanner laughed as he walked away to the house to do what needed to be done.

We might have become slightly spoiled by the injection of cash Calli had been able to give the pack. I looked off to the side of the house to the wood that had just been delivered for the cabins. The stuff we'd paid extra for to get an expedited delivery and were now just going to leave untouched for however long it took for us to get back to this place.

We'd put so much into this house and these lands. We'd renovated the house room by room ourselves, pouring our blood, sweat and abundance of curse words into it. We couldn't leave all this behind. This had always been our dream, and I couldn't stomach the thought of losing it.

"We'll set out in the morning," Grey said, addressing the few of us that remained. "Calli, can you and Maverick get the kids ready to move. We need to make this as easy as possible for them."

"Of course. I looked through the library earlier at what I think we should take with us. I'm kind of anxious about leaving the rest behind if I'm honest, but there's just too much to travel with." I could hear the anxiety in her voice about leaving behind the books, and it was well justified. The information we held in that library was priceless, and we couldn't afford it to fall into the hands of just anyone.

"We should relocate the remaining books to somewhere safer," I decided. "If Stone came back here and started another fire, we could weather losing the house, but the loss of all that information would be devastating. We wouldn't have made it through most of what's come our way without it. We can't leave it behind unprotected."

"I suppose I could maybe look at some kind of protection spell for the library," Calli nervously suggested. She still hadn't gained a lot of confidence in her magic, even though she'd come on leaps and bounds in the last few months.

"No, it would be easier to move it to a secondary location," Grey decided. "I'll speak with Davion to see if he knows anywhere safe we can temporarily store them. The easiest way to deal with all this is to split up. Some of us take the kids to the packlands where they'll be safe, and the rest of us relocate the library and anything else we want to store safely."

Everyone nodded. It made sense, after all. The chances of us coming back and finding this place undisturbed were low. Even if it wasn't Stone, we'd caught the interest of the overzealous young Fed, and I wouldn't put it past her to have a look around if she came back and found the house empty.

"Okay, let's get to it. Calli and Maverick, you're with the kids. The rest of us can start to box up the books and anything else we want to be stored. Lachlan, do you know which books Calli is taking?"

"Yeah, we pulled them out onto the desk already," he said, a blush staining his cheeks.

We all knew what else they'd been doing in the library, but none of us was upset about it. Jealous? Maybe a bit. But only because we all wanted to be the ones to find some time alone with our beautiful mate.

I was definitely looking forward to tonight. Oh, the plans I had.

21
CALLI

Today was exhausting. The kids were excited about seeing what the other pack was like. I hadn't had the heart to tell them they'd be heading back to school when they got there. Their days of being allowed to eat junk food and play on the switch all day were over. Maybe it would be good for us to spend time where there was more of a routine for them. Jacob had actually asked me if cookies could be counted as a vegetable, and I practically felt the look of disapproval my mother was giving me from beyond the grave.

The guys had worked all day packing up the library and a few bits and pieces they wanted to keep safe. Most were things of River and Grey's mother that they'd saved. They'd never spoken of her before, but I got the impression it wasn't a happy story from the way they mentioned it.

By the time we'd ordered the dreaded pizza for dinner because no one had the energy to cook, everyone looked tired.

Sean, Wells and Jessa had made their excuses after dinner and set out for Wells' pack, so they could make the necessary preparations for our arrival. Apart from changing sheets, I had no idea what that could mean, but I didn't want to look stupid by asking the question. Felix had followed them back, saying his business with Sean hadn't finished yet, even if his eyes were full of regret as he left.

The witches and the three shifters had left as well, choosing to get on the road early rather than wait for the morning. Only Colt and his pack remained.

It left us with the question as to whether the spy had gone to report to Stone about our movements, together with the involvement of Wells, or if they were still here watching and reporting back without us knowing.

It added an air of unease to the last night we'd have at the packhouse, and everyone felt it if the sombre atmosphere was anything to go by. It was kind of fitting, though. None of us wanted to celebrate that we were being pushed out of this place. This wasn't a happy time for any of us.

"Are you sure that the others will be safe taking the books to Davion's storage place? Wouldn't it be safer if we all travelled together? At least then we'd have the advantage of numbers." I'd asked the same question in various forms since the plan had been decided, but I couldn't help but feel anxious about the idea of splitting up.

Everyone knew you never split up the party.

"It's safer to get the pups to the pack rather than have them out in the open. Would you want us to walk into a fight having to worry about their safety?" Grey sighed.

I knew he was tired, and I knew he was struggling to hold back the raging bitch face that was his alpha side now, but that was still uncalled for.

"You know I don't," I snapped. I tried not to let the fact that he was pissing me off enter my voice, but apparently, I didn't do a very good job.

"Okay, I think we're all tired, and it's been a long and stressful day. Let's get some rest, so we're ready for the morning," River reasoned, standing from his chair at the table.

The kids had already gone to bed, having had their fill of pizza. I'd hardly touched mine. The only slice I'd picked up still sat on my plate with just a few bites taken out of it. Just looking at it was turning my stomach. They needed to get some more take out places here. Pizza couldn't be the only lazy option for the rest of my life.

I supposed there was the diner too, but we seemed to be avoiding the place at the minute for some reason.

With a sigh, I pushed up from my chair. I was hungry, but the anxiety gnawing at my stomach made me want to throw up too. It was an odd combination to have.

River held out his hand to me, and I took it without question.

"Let's get some sleep, sweetheart," he murmured, pulling me close and gently kissing me while his other arm wrapped around my waist.

I sighed at the promise that brief kiss held and sagged against him.

"We're going to stay up for a bit longer and help Nash get the office squared away," Tanner told us, the cheeky grin on his face implying he knew exactly what River's intention was. It's not like it was a secret. Whenever I was pulled away by one of them, it was fairly obvious where we were heading.

After mumbled words of goodnight from the others, River and I headed upstairs, stepping into his room instead of Tanner's for a change.

"I thought one of the others was staying in here?" I asked

as River took hold of both of my hands and started to walk backwards toward the bed.

"We had a shuffle around now that fewer people are in the house. Plus, call me weird, but if I was going to spend the whole night making you moan my name, I wanted to do it in my bed." The lopsided grin he gave me as he spoke didn't have any edge of tension to it like you would have thought it would. We were all so up in the air that it was easy to understand the need for a moment of normalcy.

"The whole night, hey?" I purred as I moved closer, laying my hands on River's chest. "That's a big promise you're making there."

River laughed as he wrapped his arms around me and then fell back onto the bed, pulling me down with him. It was hard not to giggle at the move as we bounced softly on the mattress.

"How about I show you what I've got, and then you can mark me out of ten in the morning," he joked.

"I might need a pen and paper or something," I joked, pretending to go and get up from the bed.

River laughed at my antics, rolling me beneath him, so he could pin me to the mattress.

"I'll keep a running tally in my head for you," he murmured as he trailed kisses across my jaw and down my neck.

As he moved, River slowly started to undo the buttons on my shirt, gently pulling the material to the side, so he could lay a kiss on every inch of skin that he revealed.

"How did you get to be this perfect?" he murmured when he finally had the shirt open and stared down at me lying beneath him.

I didn't need to answer him. The voice in my head that

every woman had, screamed that I wasn't and started to list my many faults. But the look that River gave me at that moment pushed that voice to the side for once. There was nothing but love in his eyes, and he meant every single thing he said. He was just as perfect in my eyes too. I didn't know what I'd done to deserve the gift of so many mates, but I'd go through countless trials if that were what it took to keep them by my side.

Reaching up, I pulled River's shirt up and over his head, needing to see more of him. Needing to run my fingers across his skin to reassure myself that all of this was real.

River slowly lowered himself down to kiss me and then gathered me up in his arms as he languished me with kisses. Stroking his tongue against mine, River kissed me with wild abandon. What had started out slow and sweet seemed to suddenly catch fire, and we couldn't shed the rest of our clothes fast enough.

"River!" I gasped as he trailed one finger through my wet folds, playing with the evidence of my arousal before he finally lightly grazed against my clit.

I'd only been with Lachlan this morning, but I still felt like I would explode. I couldn't get enough of these men. I needed them with a fierceness I couldn't explain.

"So fucking beautiful," River murmured as he pulled his hand away, bringing his fingers to his lips and licking my juices from them.

It was so fucking hot, and I couldn't stop myself from slamming my lips against his in response.

Hooking one leg over his hip, I flipped us over, so I hovered above him.

"I want you in my mouth, River," I murmured against his lips between kisses. "I want to feel you moving your cock between my lips as I swallow you down."

A touch of heat came to my cheeks as the words I'd

spoken registered with my brain. I wasn't one to indulge in talking dirty with my mates, but something felt different, desperate almost. I knew what I wanted, and I felt like I would explode if I didn't get it.

"Fuck, yes," River gasped as I started to trail my lips down his body, laying kisses over every dip and swell of his muscles as I went.

River was always quiet. Always standing in the background, there if we needed him, but never taking charge of a moment. I supposed it came from having a brother as an alpha; you got used to living in the shadows. But I didn't want River to feel like that with me. I wanted him to know that I desired him just as much as any of my other mates. I craved the feel of his touch, just as I did theirs.

By the time I reached his glorious cock, my mouth was practically watering, knowing I was about to get what I wanted.

The tip glistened with precome, and I delicately ran my tongue over his slit, greedily, not wanting to waste a drop.

River's breath hitched at the touch. He watched my every move as he leaned up on his elbows, so he had a clearer view down his body to where I now lay between his legs.

Locking eyes with him, I ran my tongue from root to tip, slowly circling the head of his cock with my tongue before flicking the tip of my tongue across his sensitive tip.

River's mouth fell open as he watched me lick him like my favourite lollipop, his breath coming in pants as his pupils blew wide in desire.

I waited until his breathing started to slow before I swallowed him down without warning. Taking as much of him into the back of my throat as I could without any warm-up.

"Fuck!" he shouted as his hand came to the back of my

head, his fingers tangling in my hair. "Oh fuck, yes, Calli," he groaned as I forced him deeper still.

My thighs clenched at the sound of his cries, and I felt a burning need between my legs to have him inside me. I could feel my arousal slickening my skin as I slowly pulled his cock from my mouth, flicking my tongue over the slit before quickly swallowing him down again.

I only managed to repeat the slow withdrawal and sudden sucking motion down two more times before River panted out, "Calli, turn around. I want you to sit that beautiful pussy on my face. I need to hear you come with my cock deep in your throat like that."

I groaned at the idea, and I knew from that angle I'd be able to swallow him deeper still.

Silencing the nagging, self-conscious voice in the back of my mind, I quickly moved to do just as he asked. I wasn't exactly graceful about it. In fact, as I found myself kneeling over his face, I started to second guess myself until River grew impatient and grabbed my hips, pulling me down to his eager face.

River attacked my clit like he was a starved man. Sucking it between his lips as he lashed it with his tongue. All concerns I'd previously held about this position flew from my mind at the sensation of having him eating away at my core.

Quickly falling forward, I brought my mouth back to his cock. It was hard to concentrate at first, with River pulling so many delicious sensations from my body, but I soon found a rhythm.

I was right about the angle too. As I swallowed him down, River's cock easily pushed deeper into my throat, giving me the burn I'd been craving as he gently pulsed his hips, moving himself deeper still.

I groaned in delight at the sensation, which quickly turned

into muffled cries of joy as his fingers dipped into my core, fucking me slowly in time with each thrust deeper into my throat.

My hips moved on their own, grinding myself down on River's face as he teased my clit, driving me to the point of release.

River picked up the pace, driving his fingers into me as he wrapped an arm around me, pulling me down onto his face.

It was all too much, and I couldn't hold back as the wave of orgasm crashed over me.

Thrashing in his grip, I found myself pinned in place as River's grip tightened around me. My screams of ecstasy came out as muffled cries as I tried to keep working River's cock with my mouth.

As River worked me through my orgasm, I quickly reached the point where every touch was too sensitive. As I was about to cry out for him to stop, River withdrew his fingers from my pussy and gripped my hips, picking me up and moving me down his body.

A cry of surprise left my lips as I found myself suddenly being pulled away from him and moved. That cry soon turned into laughter because how could it not when I suddenly found myself airborne and bouncing back onto the mattress.

"What are you doing?" I laughed.

"This," River growled, sheathing himself in me in one swift move.

"Oh, fuck," I groaned, my head tipping back as I revelled in the feeling of finally having him inside me.

"You don't have to ask twice," River said with a smirk on his face.

Hooking his hands under my knees, River lifted up on his knees, taking me with him as he started to fuck me hard and fast.

It was exactly what I needed. I could feel every thought that had plagued me through the day falling away as I surrendered to River, giving him my body and my pleasure.

"I'm not going to last," River groaned in disappointment as his head tipped back in defeat.

I could already feel that knot of pleasure forming low in my stomach again, and I knew at the pace he was slamming into me, it wouldn't be long before I came again.

"Touch yourself, Calli. I want to feel you make yourself come all over my cock," he groaned, tipping his back down as he speared me with his gaze.

My hand drifted to my core without River having to ask again. I wanted to come just as much as he wanted to watch me. Perhaps Grey wasn't the only one finding a dominant side.

Slipping my fingers between my folds, I could feel River's cock pounding inside of me, and I took the opportunity to move two fingers to either side of him.

"Fuck!" he swore before I moved to concentrate on my clit, flicking across the bud in time to the pistoning of River's hip.

"Oh, yes! River, I'm so close," I mewled as I started to work myself back up into a frenzy.

River's eyes locked with mine, and I watched as his mouth fell open as he panted in exertion, trying to hold back his orgasm until I came first. I could feel myself balancing on the edge already, so close to that release I was craving again.

For some reason, watching this strong shifter hanging on by a thread was the last push I needed. I felt the muscles in my pussy clamp down as my back arched, and I came with a scream, soaring into the release and letting my mind slip away into the clouds of euphoria.

I watched as River's hips stuttered and the muscles in his

neck pulled taut. He looked beautiful when he came. It was like the pleasure drew him to a place of rapture, and I immediately reached out for him.

River collapsed down into my arms without needing any further encouragement. We ended up in a tangle of limbs on the bed, panting heavily, with a light sheen of sweat coating our bodies. River was still inside me, softly moving his hips, almost like he couldn't quite bear to stop.

"I love you, River," I whispered, stroking a lock of his brown hair out of his eyes.

"I love you too, Calli." He looked unsure of himself for a moment, and then he added, "I'm sorry if I've been a bit distant lately."

"I don't think you have," I reassured him.

If anything, we'd all been tied up with the events happening around here.

"I just feel like it's been forever since the two of us, well, did this. I miss you," he admitted.

"Oh, River. I know, and I'm sorry, I need to make sure that I'm splitting my time better with all of you," I said, immediately feeling guilty.

River leant up on one elbow, so he could look at me clearly before he spoke. "That's not what I'm saying, and I don't want you to think I'm complaining, Calli. I don't think you're favouring any of us, and it's just as much on us as it is on you to make sure we have time together. I don't know; I feel like we're all being pulled in so many directions with everything going on around here. Sometimes it's hard to take a moment and remember to stand still."

"You're right. Maverick was trying to persuade me to take a step back and not see everything as my responsibility. Maybe we all need to do that. I just want this whole thing to be over so we can have a normal life again. Not that I'm even sure what that will look like."

River settled back down beside me and gathered me up in his arms. "What do you want it to look like?" he asked.

For a moment, I genuinely didn't know. I even thought back to before all this happened, when it was just Jacob and me in our own house, building a life here. I didn't want to go back to that, though. Even then, we'd had our own set of difficulties that we were dealing with. I didn't think there'd ever been a time when I wasn't dealing with something.

"You were thinking about going to school, doing your degree," River pointed out. "You could still do that."

"It all just seems so...pointless now," I admitted. "I don't feel like I'm that person anymore."

"It's not pointless if it's something you want to do."

"What about you? What do you want to do when all of this is behind us?"

It felt strange talking about it. Almost like we were asking for something else to go wrong. But also, if we weren't working towards the future we wanted, what were we even fighting for?

"I was talking with Lachlan about this last night," River told me, which immediately had me intrigued. Was I the only one out of all of us that wasn't planning for the future? "We both want to set up a school here. Not just for our pups, but for other shifter kids to come and learn what it means to be a shifter without the pressures of the pack and position."

I nodded, taking in what he was saying and already seeing an image of it in my mind.

"You'd also be giving the kids an opportunity to meet people from other packs."

"Yeah, and we could have kids coming in from the covens too," River explained, getting excited. "If we're going to come out of this uniting both sides, we need the next generation to see that the old prejudices aren't true."

I couldn't help the smile on my face as I watched the enthusiasm setting in. I didn't think I'd ever seen River like this before. I'd known he loved his last job at the school, but when I met him, he didn't seem to have this level of excitement about it anymore.

"It would be nice to help restore our people to how they were. To help the women turn in a safe environment, without the risks they used to face," I admitted.

Okay, so maybe I had been thinking about this a little bit. Especially with Jean wanting to be turned. Why couldn't we help people be with the person they loved? Help shifters find their mates. There was no reason why our pups had to be the only ones out there. We could spread the joy back into the packs if we showed them that there was a different way.

"Do you think anyone would listen to us, though?" I asked, seeing the immediate flaw in our plan. "Whatever fight happens is most likely going to happen in the shadows. If the Council brushes it all under the rug, we could end up back where we started."

"Then we don't let them. Shifters need to open their eyes to what's happening in our world. This could be the only time we have to make a change, and I want to do it. Our people could flourish if we just had the chance to show them how."

I started to sit up, already seeing a plan forming in my mind. "Maybe if we..."

"Woah there," River laughed, pulling me back down to his chest. "Where do you think you're going?"

"We should talk to..."

"No, we definitely shouldn't," River murmured, instead moving in to pepper kisses down my neck. "I seem to remember I was promised all night, and there's nothing that needs doing that can't wait until the morning."

"All night, hey?" I said with a grin as River's kisses started to slowly move down my chest.

My breath caught in my throat at the feeling and the gentle fire starting up inside of me already.

"Mmmhmm. Now, rollover. I want to try something."

I went without question. There was nothing I didn't want to try with these men of mine. And River was imaginative enough to keep us trying things for hours to come.

Sex coma was a thing, people, and I highly, highly recommended you try it out.

22
CALLI

As we approached the coordinates we'd been given, the sense of weariness coming through our bond was nearly overwhelming. Everyone was exhausted. Not just physically, but mentally too.

Was this place really going to be the salvation we all thought it would be? It all seemed too good to be true at this point.

I'd tried not to think about what Sean had told me about my parents, but how could I not? The more I tried to push the thoughts down, the more they bubbled to the surface, mocking my attempts at ignorance.

The nightmares were getting worse. It was hard to accept the image of my mother in my memories with what I knew she'd done.

She'd taken my father from me. I couldn't get past that. I knew she did it to keep me on the right path, but I couldn't accept that there was no other way. There had to be. We shouldn't be required to sacrifice the people we loved so others could survive. How had the world become this twisted version we now lived in?

Tanner brought the SUV to a stop in front of a massive pair of gates. In each direction, as far as the eye could see, was a wall standing at least thirty feet high, topped with razor-sharp wire.

So this was it. This was the army they'd been building in secret—the answer to how we would survive this.

"Are we supposed to knock or something?" Tanner asked, leaning forward to peer out of the windshield up toward the top of the gate. "They knew we were coming, right?"

At his words, the gate began to rumble and slowly creak open.

"Does anyone else get the feeling that we're walking into a shit storm of epic proportions?" Maverick grumbled from beside me.

"I'm not sure we were ever out of the shit storm," Grey mumbled, "It seems to follow us around like a shadow."

I could feel Grey's anxiety resonating through the bond. However, I could also feel his attempt to block it from us.

No one would blame him for feeling this way. He was about to walk his pack into unknown territory. It wasn't exactly making me feel warm inside, either. Maverick was right, something about this felt like the worst decision we'd ever made, and we hadn't exactly been making fantastic life choices recently.

Looking over the seat at the backbench, I took in the four sleeping forms of the kids. We should have found somewhere else for them. We should have checked this place first before blindly bringing them here. The attacks on the pack meant it wasn't safe there anymore. Where else were we supposed to go? We had nowhere and basically nothing.

Maverick reached over and gripped my hand, drawing my attention to where he was sitting at my side.

"Nothing will happen to them," he told me confidently. "We won't let it."

I nodded in agreement, even though I wasn't wholly convinced.

"We can turn around," Tanner told me, spinning around in the driver's seat to look at me. "We don't have to go in there. We can run. We'll find a way on our own."

I looked between him and Grey, where they sat in the front, looking at me expectantly.

"No. We all know running would be a death sentence. We can't take the kids on the run and expect to stay ahead of everyone. The only chance we have is to make a stand," I said firmly.

I was trying to convince myself as much as I was everyone else.

Grey's eyes moved to the back window as he looked down the line of the convoy behind us. Those vehicles contained everyone we'd come to care about. Hell, two of my mates were back there. Being separated from them was killing me. It felt wrong. But we couldn't all fit in one vehicle, and we didn't want the kids to travel without us.

"Let's do this then," Grey said, his eyes glinting with determination as he met my eyes. "We may only be a small pack, but we're strong. We can do this."

I felt the fierceness of his determination flare through our bond, eradicating every ounce of anxiety there. His eyes glimmered as his wolf pushed to the surface, and that smoky energy of his alpha power pushed out to skim the surface of his skin.

My alpha mate had never looked sexier than he did now. This was the wolf he was always meant to be—powerful, fierce and all mine.

Tanner started to slowly move the vehicle forward, and

we all seemed to hold our breath as we passed through the gateway. I didn't know what we'd been expecting, the gates didn't snap shut, and there was no army of wraiths waiting on the other side. Instead, there was what looked like a small gatehouse, which a lone shifter stepped out of as he approached our vehicle.

Tanner brought the SUV to a stop again, and his window slid down.

"They're expecting you up at the packhouse. Just follow the road through town, and it will be straight in front of you. You can't miss it." Stepping away from the vehicle, he banged on the side in the universal sign to keep moving.

I hated it when people said that. "You can't miss it." It was almost like a challenge for you not to be stupid enough to get lost.

"I guess we just wander through town then," Tanner said with a frown as his window slid back up, and we set off slowly down the winding road.

"Just how big is this pack?" Maverick asked, looking out his window as we crested a small hill, and the buildings started to come into view.

"I have no idea," Grey murmured. "No one knows much about Wells, and if he's been taking in people from the underground to build this army, there would be no way to tell anyway."

"There's one thing I don't get," Tanner said as he slowly made his way toward the small town coming into view. "How does the Council not know about all of this? They must come here, right? They can't be that oblivious to all of this going on under their noses."

"The Council members don't visit each other's packs. In fact, from the brief interactions we've had with them, they don't even seem to like each other. It's not surprising they haven't come here," Grey theorised.

All conversation stopped as we reached the first few buildings and moved through the town. It was an actual town. I didn't know what I'd been expecting, but it hadn't been this. There was a small store, a coffee shop and even what looked like a bar. Shifters were walking along the streets with their families and their shopping bags. I'd never seen anything like it before. Wolfs walked down the street in broad daylight, winding between the shifters. I'd never been to a place where shifters could just be shifters without fear of reprisals or the need to hide.

It was pretty amazing.

The town wasn't big, and it didn't take long for us to move through it. I could see other cabins and buildings dotted amongst the trees outside town. It looked like most of the shifters lived on the outskirts rather than in the town itself.

As we'd made our way through, people stopped what they were doing and stared at our small procession. It was probably pretty unusual to see so many new faces all at once.

I didn't miss the few raised lips and squinted eyes of aggression as they took note of us. This might be a liberated town where shifters could be themselves, but, as far as we knew, they still followed some of the old pack laws—namely position and dominance. The majority of the pack might live their lives as they wished, but those in the upper ranks had to be strong enough to hold their positions and stand against any dominance challenges that came their way.

It wouldn't take long before we'd face our first challenges. We'd need to up our training again once everyone had gotten over the journey here. There wouldn't be a second to spare. At least the kids would be free from it all. Dominance challenges were usually banned until you reached sixteen.

Anyway, most shifters their age wouldn't have come into their wolves yet.

As we pulled out of town, I realised we were picking up extra people in our procession. Trucks and cars were pulling out of town and following us up to the packhouse. So much for time to get settled.

Grey growled in annoyance. "We're going to be arriving with an audience," he told us, staring into the side mirror on his side.

Leaning over the back seat, I started to wake the kids. The sleepy grumbles I got back were quickly replaced by excitement as they shuffled about to stare out the windows when they realised we'd arrived.

The four of them had squeezed onto the backbench. It wasn't exactly very safe, but there was no way they would be separated, and they hadn't even wanted one of them to sit between Maverick and me. The bond they had between the four of them was so tightly wound that I was slightly worried about how they would take stepping into this new environment.

"Kids, we're almost there, and we have the pack's attention. So I want you guys to stick close to us, okay. Don't wander off. We don't know who we can trust here just yet, and I don't want to lose anyone," I warned them.

"But Uncle Sean said it was safe here," Jacob told me, rolling his eyes. He was so much like I was when I was his age. It was funny at times, but not right now.

"I know what Uncle Sean said, but for now, we stick together okay, as a family, a pack."

Abby cocked her head to one side. I was starting to recognise the far off look in her eyes when she saw something the rest of us couldn't. When she smiled at me, I felt my heart surge in relief.

"We'll be good," she said, with an earnest look on her face only little kids could achieve. For some reason, it didn't make me feel better, and I could already feel the dread forming inside me.

I turned back around to see the amused look on Maverick's face. "Yeah, why don't we believe that?" he muttered, making Tanner snort.

"You don't believe me, Daddy Mav!" Abby gasped in outrage, which just made Tanner snort even louder.

"Yeah, Daddy Mav," Tanner mocked. "How could you not believe my little cherry bomb?"

Maverick swivelled around in his seat and tickled Abby's tummy, making her giggle. "Because you four are constantly up to no good," he pointed out, only to receive grins of confirmation from the boys.

Yep, this was going to go badly.

It was nice to see Maverick acting so carefree, though. He was nothing like the man who'd strolled into the Council chambers all that time ago. The one who was angry at the world and ready to set it all on fire.

Tanner brought the car to a stop just as I was turning around. The packhouse stood in front of us, large and imposing. It didn't have the homely feel that Grey's did. It was only then that it occurred to me, if Grey did take the alpha position as Sean and Wells intended, we'd never be going back to our home. This would be Grey's pack, and we'd have to stay here.

That thought had me looking around with fresh eyes. The shifters getting out of the cars that had followed us here didn't exactly look thrilled to see us. The town was impressive and everything, but we'd been carving out something special back at our pack, and I didn't know if I wanted to do that here.

"Well, it looks like the welcome party is all here," Tanner joked, peering out into the gathering pack.

"Calli, listen to me. This is important," Grey said, turning to stare at me. "You haven't been in a traditional pack before, and you don't know what it's like. So when you step out of this car, step out strong and confident. Don't give them an inch, or they'll think they can challenge you."

I nodded nervously. I could do this.

Tanner huffed out a breath and opened his door, stepping out. Maverick didn't exactly look pleased as he did the same, his old mask fell into place, and my heart broke at the loss of his happy self.

Grey moved out of the vehicle with one last look over his shoulder at me.

"Stay in the car until we tell you," I warned the kids quickly, and then I opened the door and stepped out into what I hoped wasn't going to be the shit storm Maverick had predicted.

23
GREY

Striding around the front of the SUV, I made my way to Calli's door. I could feel through our bond just how nervous she was about this whole thing. Who could blame her? Not only had she never been in a traditional pack before, but she was coming here with the label of 'other' firmly attached to her. The shifters here would know it as soon as they caught her scent.

The alpha power rolled out of me at the mere thought of a potential threat to my mate. The inky black smoke—that we all now associated with it—rolled out across the grass, spreading out away from me as wave after wave of power surged across to the gathering pack.

I wasn't holding back this time. If these people came to get a show thinking they could pick off the weaker members of my pack, they were about to see who it was they'd have to fight through.

A collective gasp rang out from the crowd as they all stepped back, moving away from the ominous smoke spreading from me.

I had to admit it probably looked sinister as fuck if you

weren't used to it. That was working in our favour right now, though.

Tanner was already standing facing the crowd, his feet planted shoulder-width apart, and his arms crossed over his chest as he stared them down. His wolf pushed to the surface, and the red glow of his emerging magic shone in his eyes.

Maverick moved to stand by his side, his whole form glowed with moonlight, and a couple of the females started to take more notice of him as he radiated with ethereal light.

Calli chose that moment to step out of the vehicle. Holding my hand out to her, she took it lightly in her grip as she stepped down. As the wind shifted, her scent flooded the area, carrying her floral magical scent to the crowd. I saw the subtle shift as they watched her closely.

Some of the women in the crowd sneered as I brought the palm of Calli's hand to my lips and laid a feather-light kiss on it. Her other hand came up to caress my cheek as she met my eyes and softly smiled.

Calli might not have been in a pack environment before, but she knew how to play the game, as she made it abundantly clear to the group that we were hers.

Moving away from me, she approached Tanner and Maverick. Wrapping Tanner's arm across her chest as she pulled him close to her back, Calli wrapped a hand around the back of Maverick's neck and pulled him in close as she kissed him deeply. Only when she was done did she tip her head back and give the same treatment to Tanner, who clung to her with a happy growl.

Lachlan and River made their way toward us from the car behind us, and, as I'd discussed with him earlier, Lachlan shifted into his wolf in full view of the crowd and trotted to Calli's side.

River pulled Calli away from Tanner, dipped her and

kissed her senseless before returning her back to her feet. She giggled happily like we weren't trying to make a point to the group of curious onlookers.

I could see the women in the crowd growing more and more annoyed by the display, but as soon as Calli shifted into her beautiful white wolf, that annoyance turned to shock as their mouths fell open in surprise.

Calli licked Lachlan's muzzle before nuzzling against his chest, clearly claiming him as her own as well.

The crowd didn't even try to hide their whispers as they speculated what we all were. It was only when Wells' delighted laughter flowed from the steps of the packhouse that a hushed silence fell across the crowd.

Walking slowly down the steps, Wells clapped, a grin stretched across his face. "Now that was quite the introduction," he said, his eyes sparkling with amusement before turning back to the gathered pack. "You don't normally turn out to greet our new arrivals. I'm assuming you must have realised how special these new guests are."

A hint of annoyance lined his voice as he stared the pack down. This was the first time I'd ever seen Wells act like the alpha he was, and it was like watching him sprout a second head and then continue talking like nothing had happened.

The pack shuffled uneasily, and it became apparent that there weren't any high ranking members in their ranks. These were the normal shifters who lived here.

"Who are they?" one brave woman said, pushing to the front of the group.

I immediately caught the scent of magic. It made sense that someone questioning the alpha wouldn't be one of the shifters. From the way they seemed to slowly shuffle away from this woman, creating space between them, they wouldn't dare question Wells.

"I am the alpha here. I didn't realise I was supposed to run all of my plans past you," Wells snapped. There was no hint of annoyance in his voice now; it was full-blown anger.

The woman inclined her head in a very small show of deference. "My apologies, alpha. But many of us here don't find it so easy to welcome newcomers when our lives are on the line. Bringing in a group this big is going to raise questions. People on the outside will notice an entire missing pack." Her lip lifted in a sneer as the word pack passed her lips.

It was curious. I would have thought any witches who'd chosen to come here for shelter would have grown used to the shifters by now. Perhaps all wasn't as well in Sean's army as he'd led us to believe.

"You're right. Their absence will be noted. But with the strength they add to our group, we don't have anything to worry about. The Council wouldn't dare wage an attack against me, and once the rest of our plan is in place, we will see an end to all of this madness."

Now that had the crowd's attention as they stared wide-eyed at their alpha. There was nothing but hope in that look. I just prayed we would be able to deliver what Wells was promising because, honestly, it was a big ask, and I had no idea how he expected us to achieve it.

Turning back to us, Wells grinned and winked before pointing out the sole man standing on the front steps. "Let me introduce you to Keelan. He's in charge of the guards, and the closest thing I have to a beta."

Keelan inclined his head to us, but made no move to speak. At first, it felt like a rebuff, but then I saw his eyes flick toward the crowd, and I understood what he was doing. This wasn't exactly the place to enter into a conversation when so many were standing and blatantly watching us.

"Shall we move inside to where there is less of a crowd?" Wells asked loudly, casting a disapproving look at the still lingering crowd.

Before I could open my mouth to answer him, three wolf pups and a tiger cub leapt out of the SUV and started to zoom around my legs.

Tipping my head back as I prayed for patience, I looked down at the manic pups speeding around my feet.

"I'm pretty sure we asked you guys to stay in the car and not make a scene," I chastised them.

It was hard to stay mad at them, though, when they looked up at me with their big puppy eyes, and they knew it.

I caught the look of surprise and awe on Wells' face as he looked down at the three younger ones. "I knew, but seeing it in front of me is something else."

Squatting down, Wells reached out a hand toward the pups. Jacob and Coby looked up at me in question, and my chest expanded ten times at the pride I had in them. They might still be pups who threw caution to the wind at times, but they still turned to me when they knew they should.

With a nod of approval, I watched in satisfaction as all of the kids launched themselves at Wells, knocking him to the ground as they pounced. A booming laugh burst out of him as he found himself pinned beneath three wolf pups and one proud looking tiger cub. Even the group of curious onlookers laughed at their antics as they took up a race around the laughing alpha, each of them darting in to tug on his clothes, trying to get him to join in.

Abby carefully peeled off from the group, and I watched as she stalked toward the watching Keelan. Of course, he saw her approach, but the way he pretended he didn't made me respect him, for now at least. With a wiggle of her bum in the air, Abby pounced with a kitten jowl, and Keelan fake fell to the ground as if she'd managed to knock him down.

Abby's triumphant kitten roar was nearly drowned out by the guffaws of laughter coming out of Keelan as the man beamed happily at the tiger sitting on his chest.

Calli shifted back to her human form, the same smile on her face that the pups gave us all.

"First one to pounce on Uncle Sean gets ice cream!" Calli cheered, and the kids took off at a sprint and sped toward the packhouse.

Wells picked himself up off the ground, laughing as he brushed dirt from his shirt. "I didn't realise what we were missing." He laughed, looking at Calli with fresh curiosity.

The alpha in me roared in disapproval, and before I could even stop myself, I'd hooked an arm around her waist and pulled her tightly to my side.

Calli went easily, even if she did give out a little 'ouff' of surprise as she collided with me.

Wells stepped back from us, raising his hands in surrender with a laugh before turning back to the packhouse and walking away, stepping over the still laughing Keelan, who was lying on the ground.

"We should probably go and rescue Sean since you just sicked the kids on him," Wells called out over his shoulder just as a crash sounded from further inside the house.

I hoped whatever it was hadn't been expensive. From the laughter that flowed out of Wells at the sound, he didn't care if it was.

He was right. The packs I'd seen, even our own before Calli and Jacob had arrived, had always felt cold and wrong. It was the lack of joy in our young. They watched their shifter parents lamenting the fact that they were missing out on a massive part of our lives. The way we trained them to be ready for shifting took all of the joy out of being a wolf. By the time they hit puberty and finally received their wolves, there was none of the pure carefree joy that Jacob and the others possessed. Instead, their lives became all about dominance and restraint. I hadn't realised until now just how much we took away from them with that attitude.

I watched as the pack started to disburse and move back to their vehicles. There was a carefree joy to them now at watching the pups' antics, even if there were still whispered questions and the odd lingering look in question.

This may be a pack that had been brought together to train as an army, but we needed to show them the joy that came from being a wolf. We all needed that. We couldn't lose ourselves in this war we'd found ourselves in. I wasn't willing to sacrifice the light I saw in my pack. They'd grown so much in the past few months, and I couldn't take that away from them. I wouldn't let anyone else steal it either.

24
TANNER

I hung back as the others made their way into the house, keeping an eye on the disbursing crowd. Something about this place didn't feel right, even if I couldn't quite put my finger on what it was.

It should feel safe. There was an enormous fucking wall around it, for Christ's sake.

But the lingering looks from the pack members and the whispered theories of what was going on were rubbing me the wrong way.

I'd seen the interested looks on the men's faces as they'd taken in Calli, even when she was basically claiming us in front of them all. When she'd shifted into her wolf, those looks turned hungry.

We'd worried about people challenging her for her position; we hadn't considered men trying to stake a claim on her to gain a position in a completely different way.

I hated so many things about this whole plan, and as I reluctantly turned my back on the few lingering pack members and made my way inside, I could feel a sense of trepidation building inside me.

The packhouse wasn't what you'd expect from a sitting Council member. Yes, it was massive, and from the outside, it did kind of seem a bit ostentatious. Inside was a completely different story, though. This place actually looked like a home. There weren't any displays of wealth, we weren't walking across a marble floor and whilst the light fixture hanging in the hallway looked fancy, it wasn't the chandelier I'd been expecting.

It was clean and tidy, but it was definitely lived in. I could hear the telltale sounds of people moving around the upper floor, and the delicious smell floating through the house spoke of at least someone making food.

The sudden clatter of dishes and loud booming laughter gave away that the pups must have found Sean, and sure enough, not a moment later, he appeared in the hallway with a wriggling pup clasped in his arms and two more trailing behind him.

My heart skipped a beat until Abby's tiger cub bounced out a moment later.

Of course, Sean wouldn't let anything happen to the kids, but the fact that the thought had been there, even if just for a second, meant something. I was learning to trust my instincts, and I started to take in our surroundings with a more careful eye.

"What's wrong?" Grey asked through the bond. "I can feel your unease."

"I don't know. Something just feels off." I wanted to elaborate more, but I had no idea what I was feeling right now.

"Everyone, stay alert," Grey projected out to those of us in the mate bond. "Tanner's right. Something about this whole setup doesn't feel right. It could just be our wolves being on edge about being in someone else's territory, but I'd rather not risk it."

"You made good time," Sean said, moving over to Calli and laying a hand on her shoulder.

It wasn't too long ago that they'd have both hugged at being reunited, and you could see the strain on both of their faces that they'd reached this point in their relationship.

Hopefully, I was wrong. Hopefully, this place was exactly what it was supposed to be, and they'd both get a chance to work on getting their relationship back to where it used to be. Calli deserved to have Sean in her life. She'd lost her parents already, she didn't need to lose anyone else. Calli had already been through too much.

"It was an easy enough drive," I said with a shrug, hoping to break some of the tension I could feel building in my shoulders. "The pups will be ready for some food, though, if that would be something we could arrange."

Maverick looked at me with a frown. In reality, the kids had done nothing but eat the entire way here. The easiest way to keep them entertained had been with movies and snacks. I was actually surprised none of them had thrown up.

But the excuse of feeding the kids was an excellent way to snoop further into the house, and getting our bearings around here might be enough to help settle the unease.

As I'd known they would, the kids shifted back to their human forms and started bouncing around at the mere mention of food. It was actually fairly impressive, the amount their little bodies could put away.

"It just so happens that I was making dinner when something distracted me. Now, what could that have been?" Sean said cheerfully, tapping one finger against his chin.

"Hopefully, that wasn't the crash we heard then." Calli laughed, and Sean seemed to relax a little at the sound.

"No, don't worry. That was just Wells' best dishes."

"Wait, what? You'd better be joking, Scales, because they were my mothers!" Wells protested, looking deadly serious.

It was the strangest interaction I'd ever witnessed.

"Does Sean live here?" I asked out into the bond. "Like, live live."

"What makes you think we know?" River pointed out, but I could see his eyes moving between the two men in question.

Sean was no stranger here, and I'd never picked up on anything between the two of them before. Although, come to think of it, I didn't think two strong alphas like them would be able to coexist in one place.

"What's going on?" Wells suddenly asked, looking suspiciously between us all.

"What do you mean?" Calli responded, and even though I knew we'd been talking through the bond about them, even I was convinced by the innocent look on her face.

The girl had mad skills. Or maybe it was just because I was madly in love with her?

"Something," Wells said with a frown as he gestured between all of us. "Something's different."

"Of course, there is," Sean told him. "They're still working through the stages of their bond. But why are we standing in the hallway talking about this? We should be eating!"

The kids cheered in agreement and then followed Sean back the way they'd all come as the big dragon led them away. It was a strange sight to see.

The kitchen in this place was massive. It had clearly been designed to cater for a large pack, unlike our own. A large farmhouse style table ran down the centre of the room, which could probably seat over twenty people.

We'd obviously been expected because the table had been set for us.

By the time I walked into the kitchen, the kids were already seated at the table, waiting eagerly to eat. Kai was trying to look above it all, but I caught him licking his lips hungrily as Sean started to pull lasagne dishes out of the catering sized oven.

Wells and Sean took the head of the table, and the rest of us sat any place we could find. Nobody spoke as the food was passed around and plates were loaded up. I was surprised to find myself ready to eat. I didn't think I'd have any appetite with my wolf on full alert, but then I hadn't eaten all day, spending far too much time making sure that everyone else was cared for.

"So," Grey started, finally breaking through the strange atmosphere that had gathered around the table, "tell us about your pack Wells. Why did you say that Keelan was the closest thing you had to a beta?"

"Where is Keelan?" Calli asked, looking around. "Did he not want to eat with us?"

A lesser man would have been jealous that his mate was asking after another male, but I could tell from the look in her eye that Calli was only looking for information. It helped that I was also tapped into her emotions, I supposed.

"Because I don't have one," Wells told us with a shrug as he shovelled food into his mouth. "Not really. If the Council ever had cause to turn up, Keelan would step into the position if needs be. But I run the pack differently. We had to when we started taking in shifters who weren't wolves, especially when the witches arrived. Pack hierarchy left too many people unrepresented, and it started to sow unease amongst our members, so we made some changes."

"Your beta at the time couldn't have been happy with that.

I imagine a lot of your pack wouldn't have been happy with the idea of stepping away from tradition," Grey said suspiciously.

Wells sighed and sat back in his chair, pushing his plate away from him slightly as he took hold of his wine glass instead.

"What exactly do you know about my pack?" he asked.

Grey mirrored his movements and gave up any pretence of eating. The food was insanely good, though, so I wasn't about to miss out on it. Instead, I quietly observed the two alphas face off while shoving as much food in my mouth as I could. This was, after all, the best entertainment we'd had in a long time.

"Not much," Grey admitted. "You were a guard the first time I met you. People say that you rose through the ranks of a pack and took a Council position by bribing your way in."

Wells full-on laughed at that.

"I'd heard the rumours, but no one has had the balls to say it to my face before. It's not, however, the truth. This pack was my father's, and yes, I was once a guard with the Council. I left that position after the entire pack was nearly wiped out. When Stone came to tell me the news, he told me it was the rogue witch clan."

Wells all but growled Stone's name, and I couldn't blame him. From what we knew now, there was no way what he'd said was true. Even if it was, it was more likely he'd either sent them there or had some hand in it. My mind cast back to that room of horrors filled with all those women, and I couldn't help but wonder how many of them had come from this pack.

"I left the Council grounds that night intending to burn this place to the ground and put the past behind me. When I got here, the things I saw," Wells' eyes cast to the kids as he stalled in his words. "Well, needless to say, it wasn't pleasant. But I did find a few survivors. There's a den further into the woods where the children used to play. One of the pack members had managed to hide some of the children there, and a few injured shifters had been left with them. They had a very different story to tell, one that involved shifters infiltrating the pack and attacking them in the middle of the night. No one had been prepared to fight back. We were a peaceful pack, and we didn't train fighters."

It sounded so familiar. It sounded exactly like how we'd been only months ago—a small pack with an idea and a naive view of the world.

"I buried a few shifters, but there were so many missing that I knew something else was going on. Instead of going back to the Council, I decided to stay. We started working on the wall that day. It took us six months to fully complete it. During that time, I made connections, friends, and allies who were also starting to ask questions. I found other packs that had just disappeared overnight. It didn't take long for Calli's mother and father to find me."

Wells cast a look over at Calli, and I felt the shock that rocked through her, even if her face remained completely blank. It hurt that she'd been through enough to be able to pull it off in the first place.

"They told me everything, and from that day on, I worked with them and Sean in building this pack to a size that was big enough to draw the attention of the Council. And then, well, the rumours are correct. Sean was able to dig up enough dirt on a couple of the Council members that we blackmailed our way into a seat. It was actually kind of impressive. It wouldn't have been possible without your mother, though, Calli. She was a force to be reckoned with."

Calli just nodded. The grief on her face was plain for

everyone to see. She didn't know how to feel about her mother anymore and who could blame her. My eyes moved to Jacob, who sat silently at the end of the table. She'd been his mother too, and there were times when we didn't treat him like she had been. Just because he was little didn't mean he didn't grieve as well. Or that he didn't understand the things people were saying in front of him.

Clearing my throat, I drew the attention of River, who was sitting next to Jacob. When his eyes met mine, I cast them to Jacob at his side, and he drew the little boy into him, wrapping an arm around him as Jacob pressed his face against his shirt.

These people might be building an army here; they might have been prepared to fight a war from the shadows, but had they grown so detached from everyday life that they couldn't see the grieving child in front of them?

I felt my anger flare and radiate down through the bond between us. Calli's attention was already squarely on her brother, and the sadness on her face spoke of just how keenly she felt his pain.

"I apologise, Jacob," Wells said softly when he realised all of our attention had been drawn to the child. "She was your mother too, and it was wrong of me to not say so."

Jacob's head nodded, but he didn't withdraw his face from where it was pressed against River. It had been a long day for the kids, and the journey had no doubt made them weary, even if they did have a nap in the car.

"I think I might take the kids up to get settled in their room," River said, scooping Jacob up from his seat as he stood.

The way he clung to him broke my heart, and all of the kids moved sadly out of their chairs, feeling the pain of one of their own.

"I can show you the way," Sean said softly, moving to River's side, where he leaned in to whisper something into Jacob's ear as he gently stroked his back.

I could tell that Calli wanted to go with the kids, and I could feel just how torn she was through the link.

"If you want to go with him, I can fill you in on what happens here," I told her through our link.

Calli's eyes met mine, and then with a nod, she stood and followed the others out of the room.

We fell into silence for a moment. It was clear that Wells regretted what he'd said, from the way his eyes stayed locked to the empty doorway everyone had left through.

"I am sorry," he murmured. "I'm not used to having children around, but I should have been more considerate of how I spoke."

Grey nodded in response to his apology, even if it was hard to accept.

"How have you managed to hide so many wanted people here, right under the Council's nose?" Grey asked, moving the attention away from the sad situation we seemed to have found ourselves in.

Ah, nothing like denial to keep the evening moving smoothly.

Wells shrugged as he took a sip of his wine. "The Council never pays that much attention to each other. They have so much going on with their own schemes that they never look at each other, just those that they see as beneath them. We try to intercept as many as we can before they end up in cells. Once they're in custody, it's virtually impossible to get them out. Not without someone blowing their cover to do it. I've watched too many good people disappear from those cells right into Stone's hands, and it will be the biggest regret of my life that I stood by and did nothing to save them."

"You did do something," I found myself saying. "You saved as many as you could, but at the end of the day, you're just one person. You can't do everything alone."

Wells nodded, but he didn't continue with his story. I supposed there wasn't all that more to tell.

We finished our food with some polite time passing conversation. "Let me show you to your rooms," Wells offered, standing from the table. "We have you all on the top floor of the packhouse. When the rest of your pack arrives tomorrow, we'll have a house ready for them and Davion's clan. Unfortunately, we don't have enough room to house you all in the packhouse, but if you'd prefer to be with them, we could ask Davion and his clan to move to another property."

"It's okay. We'll stay here at the packhouse," Grey decided as we followed him up the stairs.

We could protect the kids better here. Sean might not have been on the best ground with Calli right now, but there was no way he'd ever let anything happen to the kids.

"Will Jessa be coming to the pack?" I asked. "I know Calli wanted to discuss some things with her."

"She still has to maintain her cover with the Triquetra. She'll be here in a few days, though," Wells told me before he stopped at the top of the stairs. "I have some things to deal with for the pack. Why don't you take the night to settle, and then we can pick things up again in the morning?"

Grey didn't look impressed either with the blatant dismissal. It was for the best, though. Once we didn't have any eyes on us, we could discuss our next steps and what the fuck we thought was going on here.

As Wells backed away from us, we caught Sean slipping out of one of the bedrooms.

"Calli is reading the children a bedtime story," he told us, a lost-looking smile coming to his face. "I had forgotten what it was like to have a house filled with children. It will definitely make life more interesting around here."

"How's Jacob?" I asked, unable to keep the undertone of a growl out of my voice.

Sean gave me an understanding look, no doubt knowing how much seeing the kid hurting was upsetting us all.

"He's good. I was just telling him about a particular night when his father and I got lost in Edinburgh," Sean told us, laughing at the story the rest of us had no idea about. "Has Wells given you the tour?" Sean asked before he started to show us around.

An entire floor of the packhouse had indeed been cleared out for us. The kids were sharing two rooms between them, and I couldn't help but laugh at the idea of them remaining apart. They wouldn't even last an hour before they were all in the same room as usual.

"This suite was originally built for visiting alphas," Sean told us as he opened a set of double doors across from the kids' rooms. "We thought it would suit your needs, but it might be a bit of a squeeze. There's a small sitting room leading to the main bedroom and two smaller bedrooms on either side."

Sean blushed at the implication that we'd all be staying in the same room together. It must be hard for the old dragon to see the little girl he'd watch grow into a woman take five mates.

"I'll leave you to it, but, erm, could you ask Calli if I could have some time to speak with her tomorrow?" Sean looked scared as he asked, almost like any refusal from Calli would be more than he could bear. Perhaps that was why he left it to us to ask on his behalf.

Was it possible the dragon was actually a great big scaredy-cat?

He'd been put in a terrible position, and yeah, he'd dealt with it in a shit way, but maybe we were too hard on the guy. He'd been left holding the shattered pieces and expected to follow the plan without any say. And Sean had done that as well as he could. You couldn't deny that what they'd created here was almost unbelievable. Perhaps it hadn't been his decision to do what they did, but what choice did he have? If it was that or the entire world suffering instead, there wasn't much choice but to deal with the aftermath and pray you'd be forgiven. None of us had asked for this, and we were all just doing what we could to get ourselves and the people we loved through it.

25

MAVERICK

After Calli's shady uncle left us to get settled, Calli finally joined us when we checked in on the kids to find them already asleep and piled onto one bed together. Oh, to be young and not know what backache was yet!

We closed the door to our suite and took a moment to look around. It almost felt like we should be scanning the place for bugs, but I was pretty sure that was just leftover craziness from my time at my father's pack. Probably?

"Okay, so everyone else thinks this place is off too, right?" I finally asked as I started to peer into the top of one of the lamps by the side of the sofa, looking for a telltale listening device. Not that I had any idea what one would look like.

Tanner looked at me like I'd lost my mind before he turned to speak to everyone. "I don't know what it is. But I don't think Sean would do anything to hurt any of us." Calli scoffed at his declaration, and I had to admit, I was right there with her. But then, I wasn't so sure he could be trusted either. "Annnnd Wells seems to be on the same page as us. There does seem to be something off about the pack, though. The way they all trailed us up here. Something about it just doesn't sit right. They must have people turning up here all the time. It can't be unusual to see new people, and I find it hard to believe they turn up for every new arrival. So, I suppose the real question is, what do we think they're hiding from us?"

Everyone looked around at each other, and it was clear none of us had any clue.

"Maybe we're not looking at this the right way," I suggested. "Or rather, maybe we shouldn't expect someone to give us all the answers."

"What are you trying to suggest?" Grey asked. Strangely, he sounded pretty interested. It was slowly getting easier to interact with Grey without the suspicion and barely veiled hatred he'd had for me when I first turned up. I liked this version of him, though, and not just because we weren't plotting each other's demise.

"A couple of us slip out tonight. See what we can see," I told him with a shrug.

"You mean you want to spy on the pack," River said disapprovingly. "We've just fled our packlands after an attack, we have a powerful enemy gunning for us, and you want to possibly piss off the only people who can offer us shelter."

"Well, it sounds like a terrible idea when you put it that way," I admitted. "But I'm also going to point out that we aren't prisoners here. No one has told us that we can't have a walk around. In my experience, the quickest way to find out what you want to know is to get that information for yourself. No one offers up everything for free. Not when there's power and position on the line."

"You're forgetting that Sean and Wells invited us here

with the sole purpose of Grey taking over the pack. They don't have any power or position to fight for," River pointed out.

He did have a point. Flopping down into one of the chairs, I heaved out a sigh. Was I just being paranoid? I didn't think so. Perhaps it was my experience of living with an alpha that made this entire situation so hard to believe, even if that alpha had been an insane megalomaniac.

"He's not just going to walk away from this. He can't. There will be a fight regardless of what he wants. He's an alpha. Deep down, he won't want to give it all up. He can't," I settled on.

"Maverick's right," Grey said with a sigh as he slumped down on one of the couches opposite me. "Even if I knew you'd be better off without me, I'd find it almost impossible to walk away from the pack. It's hardwired into me to fight for you."

Biology blew when you thought about it. I had no idea now why I'd ever wanted to be an alpha. It was a terrible job. Yes, I could feel that my wolf had the potential to rise to the position, but there was no way I was selfless enough to be able to do that. Not that the majority of alphas out there fit the label of selfless. But I didn't want to be like them. It genuinely shocked me to the core when I realised I'd wanted to be like Grey. He was everything an alpha was supposed to be.

"Okay, so what you're suggesting is that we head into town and ask around?" Calli asked, looking like she wasn't entirely convinced it was a good idea.

"No, definitely not. I'm suggesting that River and I go into town and ask some questions while the rest of you stay here." They all started to object like I'd known they would, so I quickly explained. "Calli will be instantly recognised and a target for every horny shifter in the area. Grey, you hold too much power to not be noticed, even if they didn't already know you're the alpha. And if they know you're the alpha, then it's just as likely they'd know Tanner is your beta. Plus, we haven't exactly seen any witches yet, and until we do, it wouldn't be sensible to let Lachlan wander around unprotected. It makes more sense for all of you to lie low and let us do the asking."

"You forget that Calli claimed you in front of the entire crowd. Everyone knows your face, just as well as ours," Grey told him.

I hadn't forgotten it. It was the hottest fucking moment of my life, seeing that look in her eye and knowing she was ready to fight for me.

"Then think of it as us being the most likely to succeed. Everyone will just clam up around an alpha and a beta." I wasn't going to back down from this. Tanner was right, something here stank, and we needed information fast.

"I think I'd be the most likely to get answers," Calli argued as she sat down on the couch, crossing her legs. She held all of us completely enraptured with that one small movement. "They're more likely to tell me what I want to know in some kind of attempt to get into my pants."

The echo of growls that flowed around the room would have been funny if I hadn't joined in as well. Like hell I was going to let any shifter even think they had a chance of getting close to my mate.

The grin on Calli's face spoke volumes about how serious she was about the idea.

"Okay, okay. While part of me wants to argue that I'm a strong, independent woman who can do what I want, I'm also capable of considering other people's opinions. And I wouldn't want any of you to flirt your way into getting information, either. Which is my way of telling you that if I smell a female on either of you when you get back, I'm going hunting once you're all asleep."

She said it with a smile on her face, but I could see the deadly seriousness in her eyes. Why exactly was that so fucking hot?

26
RIVER

Walking out the front door with Maverick and heading into town, for some reason, felt wrong. It felt like *we* were doing something wrong. But Maverick was right, we weren't prisoners here, and there was no reason why we shouldn't be allowed to head to the bar and blow off some steam.

The fact that this pack even had a bar was insane! Wells' pack was what we'd dreamed of building. It was way ahead of our father's pack, and something I'd never thought would be achievable for us. This was more than just a pack. It was a community. A community of mixed species, and there was no reason why we couldn't aim to recreate something like this. Just without the weird vibe we'd all been feeling.

"What time are the others getting here tomorrow?" Maverick asked as the centre of town came into view.

"Blake texted Grey earlier to say they'd stored the books safely and were on the road already. They should be with us by about midday."

Maverick nodded slowly, his eyes moving rapidly around

like he was scanning for potential threats. I hadn't realised how on edge he felt until we'd moved out into the open.

"Hey, it's going to be okay, you know. I doubt there's anything here we need to worry about. Sean may not be in Calli's good graces at the minute, but he'd never do anything that put her in harm's way," I said, trying to ease his tension a bit.

Maverick sighed, his shoulders slumping slightly, almost like he was admitting defeat. "Yeah, I know. I don't even think there's anything here we need to worry about. I think we're all just feeling anxious, and with the new bond between us, all those feelings are bouncing around between us, making us all feel worse," he accepted.

I hadn't considered it that way, but when you thought about it, he could be right. Whenever I felt Calli's anxiety through the bond, it made my wolf antsy. Were we really all freaking each other out?

"You think Calli's nervousness about seeing Sean again is triggering something in us?" I asked, thinking back to how she'd been when we'd finally accepted this would happen.

"Well, I wouldn't word it quite like that to her, but yeah. It still makes sense to check out the town before the rest of the pack gets here. Even if it is just to lay a few boundaries where our mate is concerned," Maverick growled.

I chuckled at his obvious distaste at the idea of any of the shifters around here setting their sights on our mate.

"I couldn't agree with you more. Probably best not to start any bar fights tonight, though. Not until we've at least got the rest of the guys here as backup."

The wolfish grin Maverick gave me as we stepped into town reminded me of the man who'd first come to our pack. This was a man with a plan, and whilst I was discouraging him from starting something, I could admit that my wolf was practically howling at the idea of laying down the law to the first man who even looked at Calli the wrong way.

I nearly shook my head at the uncharacteristic thoughts and feelings flowing through me. Then, almost like an old movie, I relived Calli's comments as we'd left. Her threats to hunt down any females that came near us were so unlike her. It was, however, precisely what we'd all been thinking about when she'd mentioned using herself as a honey trap.

Yeah, the bond was definitely fucking with our heads a bit.

"Okay, now that I think about it, this is definitely the bond. We need to find some way to figure it out. Maybe we should head back to the others and fill them in on what we think?" I suggested.

As I spoke, I looked around and realised we were already strolling down the main street of town. The bar was only two stores away from us.

"We might as well head in now," Maverick murmured, eyeing two male shifters who'd stopped talking on the other side of the street just to watch what we were doing. "It's only going to raise suspicions if we turn back now."

He was right. This place was going to be home for us for at least a short while, and there was no point in alienating the people we were going to be living with. Hell, if Grey did as Sean and Wells wanted, these people would be part of our pack soon.

With a nod at Maverick, I pulled open the door to the bar and was hit with a wave of sound from inside. As we entered, it gradually filtered away to nothing, and no one even had the decency to pretend they weren't watching us.

The place was pretty busy, but there were a few open tables and some seats free at the bar. It was pretty nice in here. It had the standard bar vibe that most small towns had.

The main difference was that my shoes weren't sticking to the floor as we walked inside. Small wins.

Maverick headed to the bar, and I followed behind him. He moved with purpose, his head held high and his shoulders squared. He wasn't projecting that he was here for trouble, but he was filled with a confidence I wasn't so sure I could pull off myself.

The bartender gave us the universal greeting of a nod as he pulled a beer for another customer. At least no one had told us to leave. That had to be a positive, right?

Maverick slid onto one of the stools, and I took the one next to him. Leaning my elbows on the bar, I looked at the menu that was chalked on the wall behind it. I was surprised at the setup of this place. Not only did they offer the usual bottles of beers and different liqueurs, but they had two beers on draft and served the usual bar food.

When the bartender walked over to take our orders, Maverick asked him, "Kitchen open still?"

I had no idea how he could even think about food after the massive, awkward meal we'd just had, but it seemed he was.

"Yeah. The kitchen only closes an hour before closing," the bartender informed us. "What can I getcha?"

"I'll take a beer and some wings," Maverick said, nodding toward the draught pumps.

When the bartender looked at me, I added, "I'll take a beer as well, thanks."

He grunted in acknowledgement and tapped our order into a tablet. "Wings will be out in a minute," he told us before moving over to pull our drinks.

Maverick swivelled around his seat, leaning back against the bar as he rested his elbows on the top and surveyed the room. It was a ballsy move. We were still unfamiliar with the rules of this place, and his display could be misread as a challenge to anyone looking for a fight.

The conversation was slowly starting up, but there was no doubt that the whispered words we couldn't make out were about us.

Maybe we were judging these people too harshly? We had, after all, just pulled into their pack and taken residence in a whole floor of the packhouse. These people were here because they were running from something, and they had a right to know what was happening. Were we the ones in the wrong here? They'd come up to the packhouse looking for information, only to be turned away with nothing.

The sound of glasses being placed on the bar top pulled my attention back to the bartender. I could tell he was lingering because he wanted to ask something, yet he seemed unsure whether he should.

"I'm River," I said, taking pity on him and holding out a hand, which he shook.

"Mac. You guys rolled in with the newcomers this evening, right?" he asked.

The background noise slowly dropped as everyone listened to our conversation, and I realised this was an ideal way to sway some of their fears. There was no doubt that whatever was said here would slowly filter out through the pack.

"Yeah, that's right. The rest of our pack will be here tomorrow. We were hit by the Council, a warning because we made a move against Stone. We came here for shelter when Sean and Wells invited us to join the fight," I told him.

It was technically true, even if it did leave out a tonne of backstory.

"What did you do that got their attention like that?" he asked suspiciously.

Maverick gave me a side-eye, and his voice filtered into my head through our bond. "You might as well tell him the truth. It will be common knowledge soon enough anyway."

I nodded slightly and then responded to the bartender. "We took out a facility on Stone's packlands and freed the shifters he was holding inside."

His eyes widened in alarm. I suppose without our entire backstory, it did sound pretty insane.

"There was a lot of stuff leading up to it," I said with a shrug, trying to play it off as not a big deal. The snort of amusement that came from Maverick told me I wasn't entirely pulling it off.

"Were there any survivors?" the bartender asked quietly, a gleam of hope in his eyes.

"We pulled twenty-two shifters out and three witches. Five of the shifters will be coming in a few days, but the others ran. Sean has sent out some people to try and locate them and give them the option of coming here, but I don't know how successful they'll be at finding them."

I didn't mention the women who were being relocated somewhere else. They'd been human before that place anyway, but there was no way they'd ever come here, not with so many males around.

The bartender's shoulder slumped in disappointment, and it didn't take a genius to figure out that he was hoping to be reunited with someone. I imagined there would be a lot of people here feeling the same.

"We have a list of names of the survivors if there is someone, in particular, you were looking for," I added quietly, not wanting us to be inundated by everyone in the bar but wanting to help him in some way too.

"So many people here have lost people, entire packs

sometimes. And only twenty-two survived," Mac said in defeat.

"We don't know if it was the only facility," Maverick pointed out. "There could still be hope."

I wanted to wince at him putting that fact out there. Something about it didn't seem fair. We'd seen the tubes holding the failed experiments on the women. None of the ones I'd seen had held a male, so maybe there was somewhere else they were being held. It seemed more likely that when the men died from whatever Stone was doing to them, they'd just been disposed of in some way we probably didn't want to think about.

The bartender nodded, and a bell chimed somewhere in the background. Turning around, he grabbed a plate of wings from the window into the kitchen and placed them on the bar between our drinks.

"This is on me, guys," he told us before he went to turn away.

For some reason I couldn't explain, my hand shot out and grabbed his arm. "Who were you hoping to find?" I asked.

"My brother," he said quietly. "Stone's army hit our pack, and they swept through, killing everyone that stood against them. I was injured in the fighting and knocked out. Wells was there looking for survivors when I came too, and he brought us here. I looked for his body, and I couldn't find him. Wells told me afterward that some of the pack were taken, but we didn't know where. I was hoping…"

As he turned back to me, his eyes cast around the room, and I realised the whole place had fallen quiet again, everyone listening intently.

"Nearly everyone here is looking for someone. It's hard to give up hope even when we know there's no way they're still alive," he told us.

Could we have completely misread the situation when we arrived? These people hadn't come for information. They hadn't turned up looking for the next dominance challenge or trying to steal our mate from us. Instead, they were looking for the people they'd left behind—the loved ones who'd been torn from them.

Maverick slid off his stool and walked around the bar. Grabbing a towel from the side, he erased the menu from the large chalkboard on the wall. The bartender said nothing. He looked like the fight had drained out of him, and his mind was lost to his sorrow of losing his pack. If Wells hadn't found him and brought him here, he'd have lost his mind from the loss of his pack. Wells had saved him in more ways than one, but I'd bet there were dark nights when Mac wished he hadn't. Tonight looked like one of those nights.

Picking up the chalk beside the board, Maverick started to write, and I realised then what he was doing. Listing out the names of the five shifters we'd come to know, he added two more to the list before turning to me.

"I don't remember all the others. Do you have the list?" he asked.

I nodded and pulled my phone out of my pocket, opening up the app we'd been using at the pack before passing it across the bar to him. Everyone in the bar gave up any pretence of not listening in and started to gather around, watching every name that was written on the board. My heart broke for them as they silently watched the too short list being transcribed where everyone could see.

By the time Maverick was finished, we were sitting in a room full of disappointed people. The bartender, however, had never taken his eyes off the bar top and seemed to be refusing to turn around.

When he saw me watching, he shrugged, grabbed a glass

and poured himself a drink. "Sometimes, the hope is all we have to keep us going," he said before tossing back some whiskey.

Maverick moved back around the bar, and the gathered crowd parted to allow him back to his seat. There was no confident display of leaning against the bar this time as he grabbed his beer and chugged about half the glass in one go.

We'd come here to gather information on what we'd walked into. In some ways, we'd done just that. This wasn't a collection of people out for whatever advantage they could get to gain a better position in the pack. This was a tribe of people with one collective strand of hope, and we'd just taken that away from them.

27
GREY

Maverick and River disappeared an hour ago, and so far, I'd paced this room, checked on the kids, stared at my bag, considered if I should unpack, and then repeated everything on a loop. I could tell I was driving the others crazy, but they'd at least had the good graces not to call me out on it yet.

Calli was sitting in the middle of the bed, with her eyes closed, and the telltale glow around her of her magic. I had no idea what she was doing, but at least it was occupying her.

When my phone started to buzz in my pocket, I quickly answered it, trying not to disturb her.

"Yeah?" I really needed to stop answering this thing without seeing who it was. The problem was it so rarely rang these days; I answered it more out of shock than anything else.

"A wordsmith I wouldn't describe you as," Davion's amused voice sounded back to me.

I could imagine the smirk of amusement on his face without even seeing him.

"How far out are you?" I asked, instead of engaging in

what would have no doubt been his continued making fun of me.

"Yes, about that… there's something that needs my attention, I'm afraid." The change in his mood as Davion spoke was almost enough to give me whiplash, but then a heavy sense of dread settled in my stomach. Davion's fun going nature didn't break for much, and if whatever was happening was causing him to become this serious, I was almost afraid to ask.

"Is it what you were worried about before?"

"Yes. I'm afraid the situation has grown more severe than I'd been made to believe."

"And this situation would be?" I knew he wouldn't tell me, but that wouldn't stop me from asking.

"Now, now, alpha. Don't you have enough of your own problems without having to dip into mine?"

"You're pack, Davion. This whole situation can fuck itself. If you need us, we're there with you."

Davion fell silent at my words, and as I paced to stare out the bedroom window, I patiently waited for him to come to a decision.

"It means a lot to me that you'd even offer," Davion started. I could hear the rejection coming into his voice, but I could also hear the gratitude. "But this is something we have to deal with ourselves, and your situation isn't exactly one you can abandon."

"I beg to differ, but I can take your other point," I joked.

Davion's huff of amusement came through clear as a bell.

"Hopefully, that means you won't be too upset when I tell you Cassia and Hunter have stayed behind with us."

It was hardly surprising given the situation.

"Keep Cassia close by," I told Davion after having a second to think about it. "If the shit hits the fan, send her to come and get us, and we will drop everything to come help. It's the least we can do, Davion. Besides, now that I've found myself a vampire bestie, I don't feel like training up a different one."

"Bestie? I'm sorry, I think I just had a stroke because I could have sworn the big growly alpha I know just used the word bestie, and to describe me of all people." Davion laughed.

"Don't deny it. You love me!"

"Perhaps slightly," he admitted, but I could hear the truth.

"Can I speak with Hunter quickly?" I asked, instead of trying to cheer the vampire up any further.

I heard the shuffle as the phone was passed across to Hunter without a word. "Alpha?"

"How bad is it?" I asked without preamble.

"Erm, well... you're kinda putting me in an awkward position," Hunter said evasively.

"I'm not asking for details, Hunter. Can you deal with it without the pack?"

The silence on his end was nearly deafening, and it had my spine straightening in concern. I couldn't deal with our pack members being in danger and outside of my protection on top of everything else.

"We can handle it," Hunter eventually said. "But it's going to take some time."

"Okay, the slightest change in that, and I expect you to call me in. We have your back, Hunter. Always."

Hunter cleared his throat, and the sound made me smile. He might be a new member of our pack, but I still felt the same way about him as all of the others. I'd noticed Cassia and Hunter tended to keep to themselves. I'd chalked it up to two newly mated people doing what I wished I was doing for the better part of the day with Calli. But now, I realised that with everything going on, we perhaps hadn't made sure that the two of them were as settled in the pack as we should have.

"Does that mean you'll break it to Sean and Wells that we might have kept Felix and Ethan as well?"

"Ethan, I'd assumed as much, and Felix, you can keep," I joked. Well, only slightly. I might not still be over how he turned up at the pack. Shit, I really needed to apologise to Calli about how I'd handled that as well.

Hunter laughed in response, and it was good to hear at least some of the light-heartedness return to his voice.

"I'll speak with Sean," I confirmed. "Remember to keep me up to date."

"Same goes for you, alpha. If you need us, we'll find a way," Hunter told me.

Even though I agreed with him, I knew I didn't mean it. If things went truly downhill, Hunter and Cassia would be the only ones in the pack to survive. The Stoneridge Pack would live on through them, and I found some comfort in that. Obviously, that was assuming they didn't get themselves killed dealing with whatever it was Davion had dragged them into.

We said our goodbyes, and then I returned to pacing in front of the window as I ran the conversation through my mind again. Should we head out? Blake would know where Davion and the others were. If the situation was bad enough to have Davion concerned, then I was worried. He'd given a lot to help us, and his clan had suffered significant losses recently. Even with Cassia and the three shifters by her side, it didn't come close to making up the numbers.

"I will pull your legs off if you don't stand still for more than one minute!" Tanner finally burst out. "Are you going to tell us what Davion said?"

"Right!" I looked down at the phone in my hand, almost

like I'd forgotten it was still there. "Davion has been tied up with some kind of vampire business that needs his attention. Hunter and Cassia are staying behind to help out with Ethan and Felix."

"It sounded a lot worse than that when you were talking to Davion," Lachlan pointed out.

"Yeah, I think it is, but Davion was very hush-hush about it. Hunter and Davion have said they'll call us in if it gets out of hand."

"And you believe them?"

"I'm not sure, hence the pacing." And I resumed the path I'd previously been walking again.

"I'm one hundred percent serious about breaking your legs right now," Tanner snapped again.

Lachlan looked at him in alarm at the sudden un-Tanner like outburst and then busted out laughing.

"At least I know it wasn't just me it was annoying." He chuckled. "Calli, what are you doing, sweetheart? Because it's been bugging me that I can't figure it out."

Calli opened one eye to look at us, and then with a smile, she finally relaxed, and the glow around her faded away.

"I was tapping into the connection between us all and monitored Maverick and River," she admitted sheepishly.

"What?! We can do that?" I was kicking myself for not having thought of it before. Magic didn't come as naturally to me, though, so I supposed it wasn't something my mind immediately turned to for a solution.

"I can feel them, but I can't get any thoughts through to them. They're too far away, I think. It was hard to tap into, but I think it would become a lot easier with practice. They're both fine if that will help stop you pacing like a mad man," she told me with a grin.

"I suppose it does," I reluctantly admitted before dropping

down into one of the seats in the sitting area. "I don't like that they're out there without us. I'm their alpha. I should be watching their backs. I shouldn't be the liability that needs to be hidden away."

"No one thinks that," Calli told me as she slid off the bed and moved into the room with us. "And Davion can look after himself. He's been doing it for centuries. Trust me. You can't be that annoying and not know how to handle yourself in a fight." Calli laughed, but I could see the tightness around the eyes as she said it.

I could see her debating where she would sit, and I opened up my arms to invite her to be with me. I needed her close. I always needed her close by, but right now, I felt like it was the only thing that would keep me tethered to the here and now. The chaos in my brain was still calling to me, making me on edge.

"Why don't we talk about something else?" Calli suggested, "Try and take your mind off it."

"Hmmm, like how are we going to approach things tomorrow? We have the kids to think about. I don't want them wandering freely around the pack until we know who we can trust and have an idea of any potential problems. Even then, I'd feel better if one of the pack was with them at all times," Tanner said, his face scrunching up in thought.

Clearly, I hadn't been the only one spiralling through my thoughts for the past hour.

"Isn't that what Maverick and River are doing now?" Calli asked in confusion.

"Well, yeah, but I want to get a read on these people myself," Tanner admitted, shifting in his seat uneasily.

"Wells mentioned speaking with the pack tomorrow. If there is going to be a pack meeting, it might be a good chance to get eyes on everyone and see what we can feel out," I suggested.

"Are we maybe being a bit too suspicious?" Calli asked, looking around the group of us cautiously like she wasn't sure she should be asking. "I mean, yeah, maybe they followed us up here because they were suspicious, or maybe it was for completely different reasons. We have just rolled into their pack completely unannounced, and they're all frightened and hiding from something."

Why was it that when someone pointed out a reasonable suggestion, it made your mania want to spin higher? And even though I could feel myself wanting to spiral into another reason for why these people shouldn't be trusted, I paused and listened to what Calli was saying.

"You agreed that something didn't feel right earlier," Tanner pointed out.

Lachlan was watching the whole thing unfurl in interest, not adding any input, and I wondered if it was just us wolves who were feeling the change in our environment a bit too keenly.

"I did, but now that I've had time to relax and think, I wonder if maybe we were all getting ourselves worked up over nothing, well, not nothing. I'm not trying to say you're being unreasonable or that your concerns aren't warranted or anything. Definitely not crazy. Crazy wasn't a word I was trying to imply," Calli awkwardly rambled. "Fuck, I really need a cup of tea," she suddenly sighed.

I couldn't help but laugh, and from the adorable smile she gave me, she wasn't going to judge me for it. Squeezing a little tighter against me, I rubbed my face along the line of her neck with a sigh.

"I think you might be right," I admitted. "My wolf is spiralling from being here, and I got sucked into it. I think we're all getting sucked into it. That being said, I still think Tanner has a point, and at least for the first few days, I want someone from our pack to be with the pups. Even if it's just to stop me freaking out until I can get my wolf settled."

Lachlan nodded proudly, relaxing back in his seat without a word.

"You know, you're just as much pack as the rest of us," I told him, making him look at me in surprise. "If you see us doing something you don't think is right, you can tell us. We won't be offended or anything."

Lachlan shrugged, but then admitted. "I know, but sometimes it's hard making myself do it. I'm not used to being part of the decision-making process, but I will try harder to speak up." Lachlan adjusted his glasses on his face, which I was starting to realise he did when he was nervous. "Following on from that, I think we should talk about Calli's Queen status and why it doesn't seem to have been finalised."

Calli straightened in surprise at the mention of the word Queen. It was the subject we'd all been tiptoeing around because we knew she didn't want to talk about it. With everything going on with the attack on the pack and relocating here, she'd no doubt thought we were going to put it off again. And whilst I wanted to give her all of the space she needed to work through the whole thing in her head, she was just as bad as Lachlan was at not turning to the pack for support. Hell, we were her mates, and if she was struggling with something, she should know she could come to us with it.

"I don't…I just need time," Calli said evasively.

"We know you do, sweetheart, and we'd like nothing more than to give it to you, but at this point, we have no control over the timescale things are moving on, and I think we should at least talk it through," I suggested rubbing one hand reassuringly up and down her back.

"We don't have to talk about everything," Lachlan hastily added. "I think if you shared your thoughts on the Queen issue, we could maybe ease some of your worries and share the load."

Calli reluctantly nodded, but she didn't relax back against me. I wanted to reach up and pull her closer, back to where she had been, but I could see her mind spinning with what she was trying to say, and I didn't want to distract her from her thoughts. She needed this as much as we did.

Together as a pack, we were strong. But all of us were starting to hold things inside. If it wasn't Calli trying to shoulder the burden of what needed to be done, it was me with my need to protect everyone from every possible threat.

Tanner looked between the three of us. Of all of us in this room, he'd have the hardest time not pushing Calli to let him help her, and yet he was the one that seemed to be holding back. Whether that was because he didn't want to upset our mate or he disagreed with what we were asking her to do, I had no idea, but now we'd started, we might as well see if we could get Calli to open up to us.

"How about we don't talk about it, you just tell us what's on your mind, and we'll listen," I suggested, hoping she'd meet us halfway.

"I'm pretty sure that still counts as talking about it," she said before, with a sigh, she added, "fine."

Calli sank back against me, and my arms immediately wrapped around her to keep her there. It was more of a comforting gesture for me, and the fact that she was still thinking about my feelings while she was struggling with her own proved how perfect she was for us.

"I don't like it," she said slowly, almost like she was pulling each word from the back of her mind by force.

Tanner took that opportunity to laugh at the simplicity of her statement, and I found myself chuckling as well. Talk about stating the obvious.

"We'd pretty much gathered that on our own, believe it or not." He laughed. "What is it specifically that you don't like?"

Calli smiled at the gentle way he was making fun of her, but then her forehead scrunched up in thought as she waded through everything that had been troubling her for the last few weeks.

"It feels like I'm saying I'm better than everyone else," she finally admitted. "I ended up in Arbington because I was a frightened kid running from everything and trying to process the loss of my parents while becoming one myself. When I realised that I would be Jacob's sole carer, I was scared shitless. Knowing that you're responsible for another living person is absolutely terrifying, and I fucked that up so much when I met you guys. Now, people are throwing around the word Queen like that's not the most terrifying thing in the world. I'm shitting myself about this. I couldn't even look after one five-year-old on my own, and now? Now, I've got to become some kind of Queen?"

Her eyes were wild with worry as it all spilt out of her, and I felt like a complete prick for not seeing this before. Of course, Calli was scared about what taking the label of Pack Queen could mean. She hadn't been brought up knowing she would take on a role like this. She hadn't been trained in how to lead people. I'd barely had any kind of training, and I'd always known I would be an alpha.

We didn't live in a world where we were prepared to

shoulder the burden of leading people through a war, yet here we found ourselves.

"Calli, you're not in this alone. We will be right by your side. All of us will. But if this is something you truly don't want, then fuck it. Fuck them all! You just point in a direction, and we'll leave. You don't have to accept your place as a Pack Queen to always be my Queen. Who says this has to be our destiny? I think we make our own destiny, and as long as I get to do that by your side, then I don't care if the rest of the world burns in our wake," Tanner told her, sliding from his seat to drop to his knees in front of her.

Calli looked down at him, her eyes filling with tears as Tanner reached out and clasped her hands.

"He's right. We would follow you anywhere, and we would do it happily. Just because this is a version of the future your mother saw doesn't mean we have to accept it. Look at what Wells and Sean have achieved here. They've built an entire army if what they've said before is to be believed. We've done enough already. We've fought our fair share of battles. If you want to be done, then we're done. We'll pack the pups back into the cars and leave," I reassured her.

A single tear slid down Calli's cheek before she quickly swiped it away. Carefully looking at each of us, she weighed her options and then, with a shake of her head, said what I'd known she would.

"No. We can't run away. These people need us, and if it's in our power to help them, we should."

"Does that mean you're going to accept the role?" Lachlan asked. "Will you be our Queen, Calli?"

Something about the way he worded it struck a chord with my wolf. This was what we needed. Calli was always meant to be the Queen to my alpha. I could feel it deep inside me, in that place where the magic was starting to take root. We might have told her that we'd leave with her, and we would have, but we all knew this was where we needed to be right now. It was time to fight. We might not be entirely ready yet, but we were getting there.

Stone and his army were coming. But we'd be ready for them. Anyway, how bad could it really be? We did have a dragon on our side, after all.

28
CALLI

Will you be our Queen, Calli?

Fuck! Why did it sound so simple, and yet it threw my mind into absolute chaos every single fucking time?

How did you just decide to be a Queen? What kind of person did you need to be to think, 'yeah, sure, on your knees, I'm Queen now?' I'd never been that person. I didn't know how to be. I wasn't a natural leader. I cared for people, and I had a natural empathy that made me want to help them. But Queen? That just wasn't in my wheelhouse.

"You don't need to answer now," Grey reassured me, giving me a way to back down before I did something I'd regret.

Their offer of leaving had been so tempting. Packing up and slipping away sounded like an excellent plan. But then I wondered how I'd ever be able to face the kids again. They'd all lost someone they loved to this madness. How many other children were sitting alone because some fuckwit had ripped their parents away from them?

No, we couldn't walk away from this now. Someone

needed to make a stand, and if we could get a grasp of this new magic the pack was being filled with, we could end this before anyone else had to suffer through what we had.

It had to be us, and it had to be now.

"Tomorrow, when the rest of the pack gets here, we need to start training. We need to get you all to the point where you can access and use your magic like it's second nature. There won't be time in a fight to centre yourself," I said instead, a plan starting to form in my head.

Grey nodded thoughtfully. "We should add it into the training regimen. Probably in the morning, before everyone gets too tired to concentrate."

I could see the pride in Grey's eyes at my acceptance. I wasn't fully there yet, but I would work on it. Maybe helping the others learn to use their magic would help me bond with them more. Hopefully, that would go some way toward me being able to accept what they were asking of me.

Just the thought alone made me want to shudder.

"Have we heard anything back about the laptop?" Grey asked Lachlan.

Tanner shuffled at our feet before he turned to sit on the ground with his back braced against our chair. He kept one hand wrapped around my calf as he made himself comfortable and settled in for what was turning into a serious planning session.

"The guy I sent it out to thinks he'll be through the encryption in the next day or two. He was surprised at how heavy duty it was, but he's got a program he's been working on that he's confident can get through the firewall," Lachlan filled us in.

"Is that strange?" I asked. Something about this whole thing wasn't quite adding up, but I couldn't put my finger on what it was exactly.

"Yes, actually," Lachlan said with a nod. "A program like this isn't one you can buy off the shelf. It's been specifically designed for this purpose. So whoever installed it on this laptop either wrote it themselves or had it designed for them."

"Then it's not a government program?" I questioned. Of course, it wasn't, there was no way this was a conspiracy at that level, but for some reason, I needed someone to say it out loud. Maybe I was getting paranoid in my old age.

Lachlan shook his head, and I wasn't the only one in the room who seemed to relax. "No, if it had been a government program, it would have been easier for him to break through."

"Okay, that's not as comforting of a thought as I'd hoped it would be," Tanner said with a laugh, but it did nothing to diffuse the stress of the situation.

"Well, there's nothing we can do about the laptop's contents or the Stone situation until we have more information," Grey told us, running his fingers through my hair as he spoke. "The best we can do now is keep the pack protected and prepare for the worst. As strange as it might feel to be here, at least we have allies to stand with us if there's another attack. Stone would have to be pretty desperate to go after us here before whatever he's planning is finalised. Hopefully, taking out the facility will at least have slowed him down."

Grey looked deep in thought as he spoke. I hadn't thought that far ahead when I'd wanted to burn that place to the ground. My only thought had been to give those poor women the rest they deserved, but Grey had a point. Taking the facility out of play was tactically a good idea as well. And we needed to make sure we were thinking more logically from here on out.

Burning down the facility hadn't been an act of war on our part. It had been a declaration. It was the pack standing against Stone for what we believed to be right. We might have always been prepared to fight this war, but making that move meant our playing pieces were firmly on the board now, and there would be no backing down.

"He could still call us before the Council. We'd have no option but to go, and once we walk through that gate, no one will see us again," Tanner said quietly.

Reaching down, I threaded my fingers through Tanner's hair, scratching my nails across his scalp. With a sigh, he leaned his head against my leg, and I felt him squeeze me a fraction tighter. He was right, after all.

"If he makes that move, we don't go," Grey said with a shrug.

I might have been sitting on his lap, but my head still whipped around to look at him in surprise. It brought me nose to nose with him, and a flare of lust rocked through Grey's eyes.

"Do you really think Wells would risk everyone here just to give us shelter?" Tanner scoffed, obviously not believing he would.

"Yeah, I think he would. Think about it. This whole thing has one inevitable conclusion. Sooner or later, Wells will have to reveal what he's been doing here. Stone must have some kind of idea already. He and Sean clearly have a plan, and it would seem that we're an important part of that plan. They're not going to just hand us over to Stone and start again. They're too far into it now."

Tanner moved away from me, but only so he could turn around and look at Grey while he was talking to him. I still felt the loss of his touch all the same.

"We're in a strong bargaining position here, even if they might consider handing us over. They need us, and we need them," Grey told us with a shrug.

Just how much had he been thinking this through without us.

"What if Stone takes it to the Council? He could tell them that Wells is harbouring us, and then the whole Council would be after us," Tanner countered.

"He can't," I realised out loud. "If he makes a move against us, we can reveal what he's been doing to the Council. He can't afford to show his hand to them before he's ready, or he already would have."

This was good. This was the faintest glimmer of hope we all needed. We'd been sitting under the shadow of Stone, waiting to see what he would do next. But if we actually were somewhere relatively safe, we could finally make moves to strengthen our position rather than constantly looking over our shoulder.

"This is the safest we're going to be for a while," Lachlan told us. "We should use this time as effectively as we can. We have no way of knowing how long it will last."

Everyone was in agreement. I was just about to start discussing with Lachlan a program to strengthen the other's connection to their magic when Grey suddenly stood up, cradling me in his arms as he did.

"What the fucking fuck?!" I screeched, clinging to his neck as I found myself suddenly moving through the air. "What are you doing?" I gasped when it was apparent he would only laugh at my earlier statement.

"What Lachlan suggested," Grey growled with a smirk on his face as he started to stride toward the bedroom. "I'm going to make sure we're using this time effectively."

What…ooooohhhhh!

"If River and Maverick aren't back in two hours, find Sean or Wells and have them send someone in search of them. No one else leaves this house until they're back," Grey called over one shoulder as we moved through the bedroom doors.

"And if something else should happen while you're effectively managing your time?" Tanner called out with a laugh.

"Deal with it yourself," Grey said with a shrug before he kicked the door closed behind him.

Grey shifted me in his grip, and I automatically wrapped my arms around his neck and my legs around his waist. My body pushed flush against his. I could feel the promise of his hard cock grinding against my core as we walked, and I all but melted in his arms. It had been too long since my alpha had claimed me, and it was exactly what I needed to clear my mind right now—total surrender.

Grey held me tightly against him as he plundered my lips, then suddenly, he dropped me back down onto my feet, so I was standing at the end of the bed. Walking slowly backward, his eyes roamed over my body before he came to a stop, leaning back against the door, watching me closely.

"Take off your clothes, Calli," he growled low at me.

My hands moved to the hem of my shirt without a second thought. Ripping it over my head, I dropped it to the ground as my hands moved to the button on my jeans. I should probably be doing this in some sexy way, but I was too excited to slow down now. I could already feel my arousal slickening between my legs, and my hands shook as I pushed my jeans to the ground.

Standing in front of Grey in my underwear, I locked eyes with him again.

"All of them," he instructed, just as I'd known he would.

Trailing my hands up my body, I cupped my breasts before I unfastened the clasp at the front. There was something so sexy about front fastening bras, and from the way Grey licked his lips, he was in complete agreement.

Pushing the straps off my shoulders, I let the garment fall to the ground. I delicately brushed over my hardening nipples with my thumbs. Grey's eyes squinted in annoyance, and I knew he didn't like me teasing him. So rather than pushing him any further, I pulled my underwear over my hips and let them fall to the ground before stepping out.

Standing completely bare before Grey didn't make me feel small or weak. It made me feel strong. I knew how much he wanted me. I could see the evidence of it straining against his jeans. I also knew that even though Grey might be calling the shots, I was the one with the power in this situation. Nothing would happen that I didn't want to happen, and there was something so incredibly sexy about that.

"You like to tease, don't you," Grey growled. "Now, sit on the edge of the bed and spread your legs. I want to see you dip those fingers into your pussy and tease your clit. But don't you dare come, Calli. That orgasm is mine, and you have to earn it first."

My knees weakened at the growled instructions. I'd never done this with anyone else before. I'd never had any desire to try. But Grey was my alpha, and when he embraced this dominant side of his personality, it made me want to drop to my knees and beg for more.

There was nothing sexier than my alpha taking charge. And I'd do anything he asked me to.

Perching myself on the edge of the bed, I did exactly as instructed and opened my legs wide before trailing my hand up my thigh. Running my fingers through my folds, I coated them in my slick arousal and then dipped two straight inside me.

My breath caught at the feeling of finally having something inside me.

"Use your other hand to play with your clit, Calli. I want

to see you ride those fingers as you work yourself toward the edge."

Bringing my other hand to my needy bud, I drew the pad of a single finger across its surface. My hips surged forward, and I fell back on the bed with a breathy moan as I sank into the sensations I was teasing out of my body.

Doing exactly as instructed, even without having to think about it, my hips rolled as I rode my fingers, working my clit in time with my movements.

"How does it feel, Calli?" Grey asked, sounding closer than he had before.

"It feels incredible," I confessed. "But I want more. I need you, Grey." I wasn't above begging, and what I wanted more than anything right now was to feel Grey's cock in my mouth.

"I know you do, but you haven't finished what I asked yet," he said, sounding pretty confident in himself. "Now, take yourself to the edge, Calli. But don't you dare come," he warned.

The way he growled out his warning had me whimpering in need. As much as I wanted him, I also knew I wouldn't get what I wanted until I'd done as he asked. It wasn't exactly a hardship to do as he'd instructed, and the reward for being his good girl would be high.

Picking up the pace, I added another finger inside my needy pussy and started to imagine that it was Grey's tongue flicking against my clit instead of just my hand.

"Don't close your eyes," Grey told me.

Fluttering them open, I hadn't even realised I'd closed them. But the sight in front of me had me groaning in desire. Grey had lost all of his clothes and was standing naked at the side of the bed. His hard cock was in his hand as he lazily stroked its length up and down.

The sight was enough to bring me to the edge, and I whimpered again, knowing that I wasn't allowed to come yet.

"I'm so close," I whimpered, looking up at Grey.

"Don't stop, Calli. You can hold it back. I know you can."

As he spoke, Grey ran his thumb through the pre-come on the tip of his cock and bent over the bed to bring it to my lips. I greedily sucked his thumb into my mouth, savouring the taste of him on my tongue.

"That's my good girl," Grey purred. "It's going to be so good when you finally let go."

My breaths were coming out in pants as I edged closer and closer to the orgasm I was desperate to have. I could feel my body starting to quiver from the need building inside of me.

When I was at the point where I didn't think I could take it any more, Grey pulled my hand away from my clit and sucked my fingers into his mouth, cleaning them of my arousal. I pumped my fingers faster inside my pussy as I watched his tongue run around each finger.

"Get on your knees. Face to the bed and ass in the air," Grey instructed.

Reluctantly, pulling my fingers out of my core, I rolled to my front. The shaking in my legs screamed of the anticipation of finally having Grey touch me the way I wanted him to.

I felt the cool air of the room moving across the damp heat of my core as Grey came to kneel behind me. His hands ran up my spine, making his hard cock brush against my core as he moved.

As Grey's hands stroked back down my spine, they followed the curve of my ass as he reverently swept them across the skin of my bottom.

"Is there anything you want to take off the table?" Grey asked me, stroking his hand across my ass as he did.

I knew what he was asking. I knew what he wanted to do, and the clench of my core was indication enough that I wanted to try it out too.

"No," I whispered. "I want you to do whatever you want to me. I'm yours, alpha."

Grey groaned at the sound of the words slipping from my lips, and I barely had a second to prepare myself as his hand left my ass and then suddenly slapped back down.

Heat flared across my cheek, but the flash of pain was quickly soothed away as he stroked his palm across the skin.

It was a curious sensation, and I found that I didn't hate it. When his palm spanked back down on my ass again, I found that flash of pain flowed to my pussy instead, and I could feel my arousal starting to coat my thighs.

"Again," I whimpered when the next spank didn't come quick enough.

Grey groaned in delight as his hand slapped back down again. "You look so beautiful right now," he told me as his lips met my cheek and kissed the sting away.

Just feeling his lips against my skin had the need flaring even higher, and my hips moved, needing to feel something inside of me.

Grey trailed one hand up my thigh, and just as his fingers grazed across my clit, his other hand spanked down on my ass again. I cried out this time, not from the pain, but from the feeling of finally having Grey touch me where I wanted.

My hips rolled again, but it made Grey's hand pull away. He wasn't going to let me have what I needed unless it was on his terms, and for some reason, that made me even more desperate for the orgasm I was being denied.

"Are you ready, Calli?" Grey asked, spanking his hand

down on my ass again and then soothing away the sting. "Do you think I should let you come now?"

As he spoke, his cock grazed along my folds, moving my arousal up between my ass cheeks, and then he ran the tip back to my pussy again.

Again and again, he moved his cock against me, never giving me what I wanted.

I held as still as I could, knowing that moving would only prolong the torture of waiting. My thighs shook from the strain, and then it all happened at once.

Grey's hand slammed back down on my ass harder than the previous times, and he worked his fingers over my clit as he thrust his full length inside of me.

The orgasm burst through me, setting fire to all of my senses as I screamed through my release. I could hear Grey's words of praise as he slowly moved inside me, riding through wave after wave of pleasure as they slammed into me.

"Please, Grey, I need…" I had no idea what I needed. All I knew was that something was missing, and I was nearly desperate to have it.

"I know exactly what you need," Grey growled before his thrusts grew harder, and he started to fuck me just how I wanted.

It was impossible to hold still, and I rocked back against him, meeting every one of Grey's thrusts with my own. He ground his length inside me as he took complete possession of my body, and I revelled in it.

His thick length surging into my core was the only thing I could think about. It was like I couldn't possibly exist outside of this moment. There was nothing but Grey and me. The rest of the world and all of our problems fell away.

With one hand gripping firmly onto my hip, I felt Grey's other hand smooth over my ass again where he'd spanked me earlier. My pussy quivered at the sensation, and Grey gave a masculine chuckle of self-confidence as he no doubt felt it.

But instead of spanking me again like I was starting to want him to, he moved that hand to my rosette that was now slick from where his cock had spread my own juices.

"You have such a beautiful ass, Calli," Grey purred, but I could tell he was straining to hold back from his own release.

Grey's thumb pressed down against my asshole, and I gasped as he pushed inside me. Then, slowing down his thrusts, he started to gently fuck my ass in time with his cock.

"I want to take your ass so much," he groaned.

"Please," I begged, loving the feeling and knowing I wanted more.

I pushed back against him, and Grey groaned in approval.

"Do you want more?" he asked.

"Please…yes…god, Grey, I just…" I couldn't form a thought, let alone a complete sentence. All I knew was that I needed more than the gentle teasing he was giving my ass right now.

Grey pulled out of my pussy, and I whined in distress at the feeling. I'd never felt this needy before. I could feel my wolf surging to the surface, wanting more from our mate.

Grey's fingers speared into my core as he roughly fucked me with them, dragging them out and coating my asshole with my own come.

"You can't take my cock. We don't have any lube," he warned me, and I felt my stomach surge at the disappointment. "But I can give you more," he growled.

My hands fisted in the bedsheets as Grey slammed his cock back into my pussy and started to slowly keep up the momentum inside of me. This time when his hand came back to my ass, I knew exactly what to expect, and I was absolutely desperate for it.

Slowly, Grey pushed one finger inside of me, gently fucking me as he massaged the ring of muscles. It felt incredible. It was like he'd set an electric current racing through my body. Every movement pushed me closer and closer to the orgasm building inside of me.

When I felt the pressure of Grey pushing a second finger into me, I tensed.

"Relax, Calli. I'm not going to hurt you," Grey soothed, picking up the pace of his cock inside my pussy.

Tilting his hips, Grey surged over my g-spot, and I melted into the bed. It was all he needed to push that second finger into my ass, and as he started to move them inside of me, it finally tipped me over the edge.

The orgasm pounded into me without any warning, and I came with another scream. The top half of my body flew up from the bed as my pussy clamped down on Grey's cock. Pulling his fingers from my ass, Grey wrapped his arms around me, pulling me close to his chest as he came deep inside me, biting down into his mating mark as he did.

White lights flashed in front of my eyes as I fell straight into a third orgasm. Reaching back, I grabbed onto Grey's hair, holding him to my neck as he bit deeper, still moving inside of me. I could hear the howl of joy from our wolves echoing through my mind as I slowly started to float back down to reality.

My chest heaved as I panted, trying to suck in enough oxygen to recover some kind of sense in my body. I felt like my mind had flown away from my body on the waves of euphoria that surged from me.

Grey gently lowered me to the bed as he withdrew from me, cuddling me against him.

"That. Was. Incredible," I panted out, reaching up and lazily patting Grey on the chest in congratulations.

The huff of amusement from Grey spoke of how tired he was as well.

"I didn't hurt you, did I?" he asked shyly, pulling me closer.

"There was absolutely nothing you did to me that I didn't want and crave," I reassured him.

I knew it was hard for Grey to embrace this dominant side. It wasn't anything he'd had to deal with before. Neither of us had been virgins when we came into this relationship but being able to explore this new side of Grey made me feel like this was a part of him that was all mine.

Grey threaded his fingers through mine before he brought our joined hands up to his lips and placed a soft kiss over them.

"I love you, Calli," he whispered before laying a second kiss on my knuckles. "I can't wait to spend the rest of my life with you."

My heart warmed with love for my mate. He might be a big growly wolf at times, but I knew Grey would always be there for me. Besides, it was my fault that he had to deal with this new side of himself anyway.

"I'm sorry about how I reacted when Felix arrived," Grey started. "I shouldn't have walked away. It was hard seeing you with another man, and it felt like he knew you so much better than I did. I just…"

"Grey, you don't have to apologise," I reassured him, twisting, so I could lean on one elbow and see his face. "Felix is someone I've known for years, and yes, we have history. Not the sexy kind," I quickly added before I got myself into any more trouble. "But you never have to be worried about other men in my life. I have my mates, and you're all I need.

When I imagine my life in the future, it's with you and the others by my side. No one else. Geez, I'm only one woman, and I can barely keep up with you five," I joked.

Grey chuckled in amusement at my lame joke, his hand coming up to run along my cheek. "And what does this future look like?" he asked.

"You know, you're not the first person to ask me that."

Did everyone have all these future plans, and I was still stuck on the idea of just trying to survive this mess?

"Hmmm, really? I'm going to guess it was River. He was always anally organised even when we were kids."

"Be nice!" I laughed, playfully slapping him on the chest and not quite being able to admit it had been River.

"Do you, maybe, see a couple more pups in that future you definitely haven't been thinking about?" Grey asked, trying to sound casual about it.

"Do you?" I asked, leaning my chin on his chest to stare up into his now blushing face.

The half-smile on Grey's face was one that came from thinking of happier things rather than any kind of self-confidence. Maybe there *was* something to thinking about the happy ever after that would come after we'd dealt with this nightmare. You had to know what you were fighting for if you had any chance of surviving.

"Yeah. I think I'd like to fill that house with pups," Grey told me dreamily. "Even if they aren't all ours, they will always be pack, and we'll love them all the same. There must be a lot of pups out there that have lost their families in this fight."

I didn't want to burst his bubble by saying that I doubted Stone would have let the children go. But Grey did have a point. Where were the children? It was something we should raise with Sean and Wells later.

"That sounds like a good idea to me," I agreed, and was then hit by a yawn as exhaustion settled in around me.

Grey pulled me up onto the pillow and then slipped out of bed and headed into the bathroom. I could feel my eyelids slowly falling as I fought to stay awake. Talking about what we wanted to come next was suddenly the only thing on my mind. I wanted to daydream with Grey about the future we'd have when we returned to the packhouse.

Grey returned with a damp cloth and cleaned me up before settling back into the bed and pulling me into his arms.

"Sleep, Calli," he whispered, kissing the top of my head. "Dream about our family, our pack, and tomorrow, we'll start making it a reality."

My eyes fluttered closed as I gave up the fight to stay awake, Grey's words echoing through my mind as I drifted off to sleep. We'd find a way out of this and get back to the packhouse sitting amongst the trees. The pack we'd been building had been beautiful, and there was still so much more we wanted to do. I wouldn't let Stone take that away from us.

29
TANNER

I must have stared at that closed bedroom door for all of five minutes before I decided I needed some fresh air. With Grey putting us on lockdown, that wasn't going to happen. I could have snuck out and gone after the others, but he was right that we should stay close to the house until we at least knew what the others had uncovered.

"I think I'm in desperate need of finding a snack," Lachlan suddenly said, drawing my attention from the wooden door.

The old me would have walked through that door and made a joke about joining in to see if I could tempt Grey into letting me. Hell, the current me would too, because, apparently, I was a kinky fucker now.

It was more like I would have done it to the old Grey.

Grey had changed, but not in a bad way. He'd been a good alpha before. He'd been the type of alpha we needed. But when we met Calli, he started to go through some changes. He started to come into his powers more, and not just because of the boost Calli gave us. He was becoming the alpha we needed him to be now before we'd even known we needed it.

Grey had a lot riding on his shoulders right now, and the best thing I could do was be the type of beta he needed at his side.

Plus, he was a bit of a scary fucker now if you got on the wrong side of him, and I didn't have the energy to deal with a pissed off Grey.

"Food sounds like an awesome idea." It actually didn't. I was still stuffed from dinner, but I got what Lachlan was getting at, and the kitchen seemed as good a place to retreat to as anywhere.

We even made it out of there before Calli's delicious moans could start to fill the air. I didn't much fancy dealing with a rock hard cock for the rest of the night, either.

As we closed the bedroom door behind us, I gave in to the temptation of sneaking a look into the kids' room. Grey had been in and out of here all night, checking on them anxiously as we waited for the others. It was a good thing they all seemed capable of sleeping through pretty much anything.

As we'd all expected, the pups had piled into one bed again, seeking the comfort of the puppy pile in their sleep. I could remember the days when Grey, River and I would do the same things. The days when I'd been too lost in my grief to be able to do much of anything. If it hadn't been for Grey and River back then, I didn't think I would have made it through.

Lachlan moved silently down the hallway, and I gently closed the kids' bedroom door to follow him. He'd been taking this whole thing in his stride, but it was a massive difference from his previous life, living in the shadows at his coven as he tiptoed through life.

"How are you holding up?" I asked him as we made our

way down the stairs. "Everything's been pretty chaotic since you joined the pack."

"That's an understatement," he said with a laugh. It was good to hear his genuine amusement in his tone, and it settled my concerns. "If I hadn't found Calli and pretty much all of you, I don't think I'd have been able to cope. But I feel so connected to you all that it's hard not to find some peace in that." Lachlan shrugged at his explanation like it didn't make sense. I supposed it probably wouldn't to someone who hadn't been born a shifter.

"I get what you mean. It's the feeling of pack, but it's also more than that. I can feel the bonds between us tightening now that we're all mated to Calli. I was close with the others before, but it was nothing compared to now. I suppose that's to be expected when you suddenly find yourself being able to feel each other's emotions."

"Yeah, that's taking a bit more to get used to."

He wasn't wrong there. I hadn't stroked one out since I'd come in the shower the other morning, then had the terrifying thought that I could have accidentally transmitted something through the connection to the others.

"Do you think the others knew when we were having sex with Calli?" I suddenly asked.

It made sense with where my thoughts had been, but I must have seemed like a crazy person to Lachlan.

With a sudden burst of laughter, Lachlan turned on the spot to look at me as he walked backward toward the kitchen. "I suppose we'll find out soon."

I couldn't help the cringe that came across me at the thought. It wasn't that I was grossed out by Calli and Grey being together. Hell, I'd give anything to be able to watch, but it felt kind of creepy to feel it if they weren't aware.

"Surely someone would have mentioned it," I reasoned as Lachlan swung open the kitchen, and we strode inside.

We probably shouldn't have been, but for some reason, we were both surprised to see Wells and Sean sitting at the kitchen table with a bottle of whiskey between them. They didn't seem that surprised at seeing us. In fact, Sean seemed pretty happy about it.

"Mentioned what? Is there something you guys need a hand with?" Sean asked happily, looking keen to try and help and not quite understanding when Lachlan and I started to furiously shake our heads.

"Nope, nope, no, nothing, everything's fine," Lachlan rushed out, stumbling over his words.

"Definitely a sex thing," Wells declared with a laugh as he stood up and went to pull two glasses out of one of the cupboards.

Sean spluttered in distress before picking up his glass and downing the rest of his whiskey. Then, he grabbed the bottle and quickly poured himself another drink before filling the glasses Wells set down on the table.

"Maybe don't discuss your sex drama with me," Sean said with a cringe as he gripped his glass like his life depended on it. From the slightly glazed look in his eyes, I'd guess they'd been sitting here a while.

Wells was finding the situation highly amusing as he took his seat and indicated to us to join them both.

Sean had nothing to worry about. Even *I* wouldn't be able to joke about that with him, it was too weird.

"Now, I can think of literally nothing to say that doesn't have to do with…the other subject," Sean muttered, taking a massive drink from his very full glass. "Will you stop laughing," he snapped at Wells.

"Oh, calm down, smokey. It's all in good fun." Wells slapped Sean on the shoulder as he laughed, and the look he got back wasn't one that would make me want to tangle with the dragon.

"I could swallow you whole, you know," Sean taunted with a smirk that spoke of a long friendship.

"It's weird seeing you both like this," I commented as I picked up my glass for a drink.

They both looked at me and shrugged. This was, after all, the story we were all supposed to be in the dark about.

"You both must have known each other for a long time to be able to have put something like this together," Lachlan pointed out as he pulled the glass closer to him. "It can't have been easy keeping all this hidden."

"We had exceptional motivation," Sean deadpanned before picking up his glass and draining it again.

It was then that I looked at the half-empty bottle and the two others on the kitchen counter. It was impressive they'd gotten through so much and didn't seem to be feeling the effects at all.

"It doesn't affect him," Wells told me, seeing where my thoughts had taken him. "It's actually pretty annoying."

"It's the fire in my veins," Sean barked, prompting him to flex his arms. Maybe he was a bit drunker than I'd anticipated.

"It's your dragon's metabolism, you dick."

Watching the two bicker weirdly reminded me of Jean and Holly when they got together.

In a different world, these two would be sitting at this table with Wells' mate and Calli's parents, celebrating that Calli had found her mates. The world we lived in now had robbed them of that chance. Wells was separated from his mate because our world wouldn't accept them, and Calli's parents had lost their lives in an attempt to right the many wrongs we'd all blindly lived with up until now.

It seemed unfair that a small group of people had the fate of our entire species resting on their shoulders, sacrificing so much, while the rest of us went about our lives as normal. Yes, we were fighting with them now, but they'd spent years putting this together in the background while we'd been happily building a house and starting a fucking garage. Everything seemed so trivial when you put it in that light.

Picking up my glass, which had a Sean sized measure in it, I knocked back half in one mouthful. Gulping down the burn of the liquor, I felt the fire inside of me grow at the unfairness of the world.

I felt my wolf reaching for me. His own outrage at what our family had been through brushed against my anger. Because these people were our family now. We might not be sure if we wanted to join this pack officially, but the men at this table were linked to us through Calli, which meant something to us.

Sean looked at me more closely, his head cocking to the side as he searched my eyes.

"Your magic is growing," he murmured.

"Hmmm, it came out to play a bit yesterday, but we haven't really had a chance to do much else. We need to start training, learning how to access it without thinking about it."

Sean nodded, and I could see the gears turning in his head as he thought it all through.

"There's one thing that I don't understand," Lachlan said, looking sheepishly down at his whiskey glass like the mere thought of taking a sip made him want to throw up. "If this is the underground, where did you send the women who didn't want to be a part of this whole thing? And Blake's mate! Is she here?"

It perhaps went to just how preoccupied we were that we hadn't considered Jean and baby Tucker could have been here. But, wow, what a super good friend I was!

"Not everyone comes here. Not everyone wants to fight. We actually do have an underground to hide people in, you know. We haven't sat around with our thumbs up our asses all this time," Sean slurred as he downed another glass.

"Wow, who'd have thought the third bottle would be the charm? Apparently, you do have your limits." Wells laughed as we all watched the dragon start to sway a little.

Come to think of it, perhaps it wasn't the best idea to let a guy who could suddenly transform into a dragon get drunk.

"You're not going to do it, are you?" Sean asked, slumping back in his seat, abandoning his glass on the table and picking up the bottle to drink from instead.

"What do you mean?" It seemed like a better idea to pretend I didn't know what he was talking about.

"You're not going to follow the plan we've spent decades putting into motion. You're all too soft to put Wells down and take his place."

Okay, so apparently, the dragon got a little bitchy when he was drunk.

Tipping the bottle back, Sean drained the rest of it down in one go before slamming it down on the table.

"We need another bottle!" he declared.

"I'm going to have to disagree with you there, friend." Wells nervously chuckled as he took the empty bottle from Sean's hand. "You see, I can tell you must be drunk because you suddenly seem super eager to see me die. You're kind of hurting my feelings right now, smokey."

"I don't think you can call me smokey anymore, old friend. I'm like a…impotent dragon. I can't get my dragon on. I'm limp…laaaaaaame."

Darting a look at Lachlan, it was reassuring to see he was feeling just as awkward as I was about this whole situation now. I was desperately searching for a way out when the sound of the front door closing had me sighing in relief.

Please, for the love of God, let that be River and Maverick!

As the footsteps echoed through the hallway away from us, I started to panic that a rescue wasn't coming and Sean might want to tell us just how impotent his dragon was. He might have only been an honorary uncle to Calli, but that didn't mean I wanted to sit here and discuss his dick with him.

"We should, erm, probably go and make sure that's River and Maverick," I said, all but falling over my chair as I tried to stand quickly from the table.

"Yep, yes, definitely, Grey said…erm, check! Yep, he wanted us to check," Lachlan rambled quickly, getting ready to exit the room.

"That's right, leave me to deal with the drunken ten-tonne beast," Wells grumbled, standing himself as he tried to scoop Sean up from his seat, presumably to get him into bed.

From the way that Sean was batting his hands away and giggling, it wasn't a task I envied him for, and I was definitely grateful we had an excuse to leave, even if we had been awfully obvious in the way we'd delivered it.

"To be fair, you were the one that allowed him to get into this state in the first place," I pointed out.

"In my defence," Wells huffed as Sean let him take his full weight, "I was under the impression that Smokey couldn't get drunk."

"Well then, we've all learned a valuable lesson here today."

"Really? That's how you want to play it? How about you

help me get his fat ass in bed, and then I won't have to show you some other valuable lessons," Wells joked.

I couldn't help but laugh as Sean started to slur about how magnificent his ass was.

"That kind of sounded like a sex thing," Lachlan surprised us all by saying, mainly because he sounded deadly serious as he pointed it out.

Wells opened his mouth as if to protest but then, with a roll of his eyes instead, just said, "I think I can hear your friends calling you."

"Yep, definitely being called away." I backed out of the room, taking in the unusual picture of the two of them together. "In all seriousness, though, you got this?"

"Yeah, don't worry about it. I need to take pictures for bribery purposes later anyway. Can't let you have an excuse to steal my thunder."

"Wouldn't dream of it." Then, turning around, I followed Lachlan out the kitchen, shouting back over my shoulder. "Shout if you need any help."

The muttered curses followed by Wells' raucous laughter settled my concern, even if I was now feeling a bit guilty for leaving Sean at the mercy of Wells.

30
MAVERICK

By the time we filled Tanner and Lachlan in on what had happened at the bar, it was pretty obvious we wouldn't be seeing Grey and Calli for the rest of the evening, so we all headed to bed.

The next morning, I woke up to a small pair of cold feet jolting me out of peaceful sleep as a sleepy child snuggled into bed with me.

I'd never moved so fast in my life as when I leapt out of bed in surprise, staring down at the little girl who was snuggling into one of my pillows.

"Morning, Daddy Mav," she mumbled around a yawn and then started to fall asleep again.

A shuffling of feet had my eyes whipping to the doorway where the boys were nervously gathered.

"Erm, hey guys?" I knew I sounded awkward and freaked out, but I had no idea what to do in this situation.

"Why do your pants look like that?" Jacob asked innocently, and I quickly snatched a pillow off the bed to hold in front of my morning wood.

Frozen to the spot, my mind ran away screaming, refusing to tell me how to deal with this.

"Oh, look! Daddy Mav is awake," Tanner's voice laughed from behind the boys.

Realising he'd set me up, I was tempted to launch the pillow at him, but it was the only thing between me and committing a felony, so I clung on tight instead.

"We're heading down for breakfast," Calli called out from inside our suite, and the kids were suddenly running.

Honestly, the idea of food was the only thing that motivated them. They should be rolling out the door with the amount they put away. I supposed it helped that they moved everywhere at top speed. Walking was definitely not in these pups' vocabulary.

"Coming?" Tanner asked innocently, and now we were in a child-free zone, I gave in to the temptation to launch the pillow at him.

The bastard didn't even move, letting it slam into his face and then fall to the ground as he started to cackle away at his own joke.

"Oh, it's on, brother!" I warned with a laugh in my voice.

I'd missed out on so much by not having Tanner in my life, and it was weird, but nice, to have a glimpse of what everyday life would be like for us.

"It's always been on, and you're already behind." Tanner cackled again, as he sauntered away with his hands in his pockets and a self-confident smile on his face.

I should be annoyed. I should be planning my revenge. But instead, I was pretty sure I'd never been happier than I was at this moment.

I took my time in the shower, enjoying the quiet in the suite, before heading down to catch the tail end of breakfast. And, boy, was I glad when I turned up late.

Moving into the kitchen, I grabbed some food from the pans still sitting on the stove and then leaned back against the kitchen counter to watch it all unfold.

"Why do I have to go to school?" Jacob pouted, sitting with his arms crossed in his chair and a look on his face that would've had me telling him to stay home.

"Because you're a kid and kids go to school," Tanner pointed out.

"I'm not a kid. I'm a wolf!" And then, predictably, he shifted, and the whole thing turned into a race around the kitchen to try and catch the pup.

I was starting to see the logic for why we shouldn't shift until we were teenagers. At least we had some slight control at that stage or at least the fear of God in our parents.

In the end, it was Grey's shout of "Enough!" that had the pups skidding to a halt and then shifting back into their very repentful looking human forms.

"We need to know that you are safe, and this is the safest place for you right now. I know a certain step on the stairs at the packhouse sees a lot of use when we discuss the events that have been happening. So I also know you're all more than aware of what we've been facing. Just because we're here, doesn't mean that has gone away. For now, we need you to go to school while we get ready for the fight that is coming for us. It's the only way we can keep you safe."

I was expecting an argument. But, instead, the look on the boys' faces spoke of them being about to offer their services on the fighting front, and at that age, who didn't think themselves invincible?

"Papa Grey is right," Abby said quietly, looking each of the boys in the eyes to make sure they were listening. "We need to go to school today."

All three boys nodded. It seemed the little girls' word was

law in their little pack, and I couldn't wait to see what the future held for the four of them. We just had to make sure they got to have one first.

Abby turned to look at Calli and the rest of us. When her eyes locked with mine, I felt the food in my mouth turn to ash. There was something in her eyes that terrified me. We all knew she could see what was coming, and we equally knew she'd never tell us what it was. But the sorrow that lingered in her gaze had me gulping my food down. Whatever was coming wasn't going to be good.

I felt the magic inside me beginning to react to the mild panic starting to take hold. There was something comforting about the cold glow of the moonlight that still flowed through my veins.

I'd spent so much time in my moonlight form, that sometimes I wondered if life would be easier to let it take hold again. But then I'd think of Calli. Hell, I'd even think of Tanner and the others. If something was coming to hurt my family, there was no way I'd leave them to stand against it alone.

A throat clearing at the doorway to the kitchen had me breaking the locked on stare I seemed to be having with the child. Turning to glance in that direction, I found Sean looking slightly worse for wear. Tanner and Lachlan had filled us in on what had gone down last night, and I couldn't help but be disappointed I'd missed out on seeing the drunken dragon.

"I've had word that the rest of the pack have just entered the packlands," he told us, a wince of pain on his face betraying the fact that perhaps he wasn't entirely over the aftereffects of last night.

The kids raced out of the kitchen, heading for the front door, no doubt hoping that this would be the distraction that got them out of having to go to school. But, from the look of determination on Calli's face as she followed them out, there was no way that was going to happen.

We all headed out, waiting at the front of the house for the three trucks the others had left in to pull up. When only two appeared, Grey stepped forward, a resigned look of sadness crossed his face, and I knew his thoughts were on Davion and the others who'd stayed behind.

The trucks pulled to a halt, and Nash and Holly climbed out of the first one, followed by Blake and Aidan exiting the second.

"Davion contacted you?" Aidan asked.

Grey nodded grimly. "Do you think they have it handled?" Grey asked.

"I don't know. Whatever Davion found rattled him. But it's hard to get a read on him. We've got no idea what they're dealing with," Aidan said, squinting in concern. "Cassia and Hunter refused to leave, even when Davion tried to force them to go. We were worried about leaving, but with Cassia and the others staying behind, at least the clan has some backup."

When Tanner had filled us in last night on Grey's call with Davion, I'd been concerned. But seeing someone who'd been there explain it, made me realise it was a bigger problem than I'd first realised.

Glancing at Calli, she met my eye and gave her head a subtle shake. I guessed we were leaving it for now, then.

Holly took the opportunity to skip over to Calli and threw her arms around her, hugging her tightly.

"I'm so glad you all got here okay. Don't worry, I made sure the boys moved all the boxes in safely, and Cassia set up some of her mojo to keep it secure. So you should be good until you're ready to collect them again."

"Thank you, Holly. I really appreciate it. If I'm honest, I feel bad for making you do it for me," Calli admitted with a blush.

"It was nothing, boo. Now, tell me where Jean is. I need to squish on my little love bug and then get that bitch drunk."

Holly cackled like a madwoman, and I suddenly feared for Jean's safety.

"Jean's here?" Blake gasped, striding up to the group.

"Of course she is. This is the underground, silly. Where else did you send her?" Holly laughed before turning to look at Calli expectantly.

The soft clearing of a throat drew our attention to Sean again, leaning against the front door, looking slightly greener than he had before.

"I'm afraid Jean is not, in fact, here. We sent her to a different location, but I've sent word for someone to escort her here to the pack for you, Blake."

Blake's face dropped, and my heart broke at the crestfallen look on his face. The poor guy had spent so long without his wife and pup at his side. I had no idea how he was coping, but he seemed to be surviving in his own way.

"You, erm, you don't need to go to any trouble. It's probably safer for them to stay wherever they are," Blake mumbled, blushing for a second before his hand came up to rub the back of his neck as he ducked his face out of view.

From what I'd heard, Blake had always been the one to stand up and volunteer to help. After all, he'd sacrificed to stay with the pack to see this through. It wasn't a surprise that he wasn't the type of person to accept help when it was offered to him.

"It's no trouble at all. I'm just sorry I didn't think to have her brought here earlier," Sean apologised.

Blake seemed lost for words, and Grey put a hand on his

shoulder, squeezing him tight. "Accept this as a kindness, Blake. It's one you deserve. You don't need to worry about Jean's safety. I will make sure she's protected while she's here. I wouldn't have brought the pups here if I didn't believe a pack this size would be able to keep them safe," Grey reassured him.

Blake nodded without saying a word, but his eyes screamed how uncomfortable he was with the situation. Maybe we'd all been wrong about how hard it was for him to be apart from Jean and the pup. Perhaps they were on rocky ground and had looked for an opportunity to get some distance between them. They wouldn't be the first couple that had needed it.

"I'll help unload the trucks," Blake mumbled quietly before slowly walking back to the truck.

Looking around, I realised how comforting it was to have the others join us here. My wolf was overjoyed at the pack being together again. I'd never had this sense of companionship at my father's pack. Everything here was different. I'd fight for these people, whatever the cost. They were my family now.

"Aidan!" The kids suddenly cheered when they saw him grabbing a bag from one of the trucks. "Save us! Calli is trying to make us go to school," Jacob whined dramatically.

The funniest thing about the whole situation was how much it was winding Tanner up. He hated the thought of not being the kids' favourite. Aidan had the advantage of being the fun one because, at the end of the day, he was Jacob's brother, not a father figure. He could get them into all kinds of mischief, while Tanner would have to be the one to deal with the fallout.

"How about I come to school with you?" Aidan suggested.

From the 'pfft' of disgust that came from Jacob, I didn't think it was quite the solution he'd been hoping for.

"Will you sit with me?" Abby asked sweetly, and Aidan scooped her up onto his shoulders before he replied.

"Of course, I will!"

There was nothing that kid wouldn't get if she asked for it. We were all unable to resist her big doe eyes, apart from maybe Calli. At times, it felt like she was the only grown-up out of the whole bunch of us.

It took a surprising amount of time for us to organise where the others would be staying and then get the kids off to school. They were definitely going to be late, but Sean assured us that it wouldn't matter on their first day. Calli's face at the idea of them showing up late was priceless, and I wondered if our mate wasn't as selfless as she seemed and maybe just a massive control freak instead. As it was, we had no school supplies or anything to send them with, much to the kids' disgust. After Jacob tried to use it as another excuse to not go, Sean reassured him that everything they'd need would be at the schoolhouse.

The pack had set up a small building as a school for the kids. The basement below had been reinforced into a panic room of sorts which definitely made Calli, and if I had to admit it, me as well, feel better about leaving the kids there.

There weren't a massive amount of kids in the pack yet, only twelve now, including the four we were adding to the class. They all took lessons in the same room, and the three pack members who worked in the school moved between them, making sure they were all set up with the work they needed to do.

It was actually a pretty sweet set-up they had. There was a corner with toys and books for the younger kids. The old kids had proper desks set up with computers and books for their courses, and there was a small fenced-off playground at the back for when they had their breaks. The pack even catered lunch for them all.

Maybe I'd volunteer for a couple of school days if it meant hanging out here. I was pretty sure there was a nap corner set up as well.

Once the kids realised they would be staying together, all arguments about going to school fell away.

Kai still looked nervous about the prospect, but he didn't say anything. I hadn't considered how much school he'd been allowed to attend, and I made a mental note to speak with his teacher about it at the end of the day. I had a feeling he wouldn't have wanted it being drawn to the attention of the others.

Leaving the kids behind and heading back to the house without them definitely felt strange. Even the packhouse felt too quiet without them, which was crazy because we'd been here less than a day, and this place had been as silent as a mausoleum since we'd turned up.

"I've set up a meeting with Sean and Wells to discuss training and how we'll be moving forward," Grey told us as we made our way through to the front door. "They should be waiting for us in Wells' office."

Grey strode across the hallway and knocked on a door I hadn't investigated yet. In fact, I was pretty shocked Grey even knew what it was. When did he have the time to speak with Sean and Wells about this?

We heard mumbled words come from inside, so Grey swung open the door. We all headed inside, only for Tanner to screech, "Gah, my eyes!" and backed into me hard enough to send me flying back into the doorway.

"What the hell?!"

"Don't look, Maverick! You're too young for such indecency," Tanner cried melodramatically, all but throwing himself at me, his face cracking with a mischievous smile.

"I told you to wait, damn it," Wells grumbled.

Peeking around where Tanner was pretending to swoon and fanning himself, I found Jessa sitting on top of Wells' desk, her lips red and puffy. It didn't take a genius to figure out what we'd just walked in on.

"Jessa! Wow, this is weirdly awkward." Calli chuckled nervously. "I feel like I just caught my mum making out with a stranger."

I could feel her upset radiating through the link. Calli might be trying to make light of the whole situation, but at the end of the day, Jessa was her mother's twin, and we could all feel how much it hurt to see her.

"I'm sorry, sweetheart. I just arrived, and, well, yes, this is rather awkward." Jessa chuckled before scooting off the desk and smoothing down her clothes. "Perhaps the best way forward is to try and pretend it didn't happen."

Moving smoothly around the desk, Jessa plopped herself down in Wells' chair and kicked her feet up on his desk. The Councilman looked enamoured with the witch who made herself comfortable in his seat, but then I probably looked at my mate the exact same way.

"We can come back later if you want to, you know…" Grey circled his hands around awkwardly, making the whole situation worse when he seemed to be implying, we'd leave them alone to bone.

I must have projected that down the link because Tanner barked out a laugh and slapped me on the back.

The glare I got from Grey confirmed that I had indeed thought it loud enough for them all to hear.

Oh, well. He was basically saying that.

Sean striding into the office saved us all from the

awkward encounter, and we backed ourselves into the far end of the office, as far away from the couple we'd so rudely interrupted.

I had no idea why, but it did feel like walking in on your parents doing it.

"I've drawn up a plan for trai… what?" Sean asked, looking around, realising we were all acting weird.

"Just move past it like it's not happening, Sean," Jessa told him, beaming at him with a smile.

"Riiiiight. I've drawn up a timetable for you all to look at. It's pretty heavy going, but we have a lot to cover. We don't know how long we have to do it, so I thought the best option was to cram as much in as possible," Sean told us while he looked around the room with a confused look on his face. "I'm sorry, I can't help but feel like I'm missing something."

"You missed Wells and Jessa getting dirty on the desk," Tanner helpfully filled him in.

"Oh, for God's sake. We barely get any time together, and we're both grown adults. You may, on occasion, see us kissing. Now put away the pearls, ladies, and just get over it," Jessa snapped, her calm exterior giving way to the annoyance she'd clearly had simmering underneath.

Tanner sniggered again, and it was clear he was enjoying getting a rise out of everyone.

Sean started to pass out some sheets of paper to us all that had a printed timetable like we were back at school. The grin on his face gave away how amused he was finding the whole thing.

"I can have a copy of this circulated to the pack guard," Wells said, examining the sheet. "I'd like some of them to get in on the fighting practice with you. While they had the experience of training with each other, it would be good for them to go up against someone fresh. We don't know what

Stone will throw at us, and we need to be prepared for anything."

"You mean we need to be prepared if he's found a way to obtain animage powers for himself and his pack," Calli pointed out.

At least we were done beating around the bush.

"I don't think he has." Wells shrugged. "If he'd already succeeded, I doubt he would've held off making his move. He's not the 'sit back and wait' kind of guy. But it doesn't hurt to be prepared."

Grey nodded absentmindedly as he examined the paper he held. I'd barely glanced at mine, prepared to do what I was told, but something about it seemed to be bothering Grey. I could probably read through the whole thing to try and figure it out, but I found myself not wanting to look away from the alpha.

Keelan strode into the room while we were all looking over our new schedules and was immediately greeted by Sean as he reached for one of the papers.

"Good of you to join us all, Keelan. You'll no doubt remember Keelan from yesterday. He works with the guard and will be overseeing your training. He has the most experience out of all of us when it comes to combat training."

Keelan nodded at us all, his eyes landing on Calli as he paused for a second. "First session, I'm going to push your limits to get a read on where your levels currently are. After that, I'm going to bring in some of the guards to work with you as training partners to try and push you through the training quicker than normal."

Grey nodded in agreement, even if he did step closer to Calli while he did it. I wasn't the only one who'd noticed his interest in our mate then. Fucking hell, if every interaction with the pack was going to be like this, it would get exhausting.

Keelan smirked at Grey as he moved, and it was evident that he knew the reason behind it. Whether intentional or not, I supposed we'd just have to wait and see.

Sean chuckled at the masculine display and then stepped between the two shifters. Given that Grey already had his smokey alpha power starting to leak out of him and a subtle red glow starting in his eyes, he was a braver man than I was. Although, perhaps when you could shift into a massive dragon, you did take certain things for granted, like your safety.

At least, I assumed he was a massive dragon and not one of these little Spiro miniature things. Fuck, how hilarious would that be?

"I'll be working with you all every morning, but then I'll also do some one on one sessions with you in the afternoon, starting with Lachlan. Of course, it will mean missing some of your combat training, but all things considered, your emerging power will be your most dangerous weapon in the fight to come," Jessa explained, rolling her eyes at Keelan as she did.

"Why start with me?" Lachlan asked, looking genuinely worried about the whole thing.

"Well, we can't leave your magic bound forever." Jessa laughed.

Lachlan paled to the point I was interested to see if he was going to pass out or throw up.

"It's nothing to worry about, dear," Jessa reassured him.

Calli stepped closer to her only witch mate and tentatively took his hand. Apparently, I wasn't the only one who had noticed the worry on his face.

Lachlan nodded and then did what the rest of us probably

would have done in his shoes—pushed that feeling deep down and tried to ignore it.

"Well, seems as the day is already underway, I'd suggest we start with combat training this afternoon and give you folks a chance to settle in properly. That will give you the opportunity to catch up with the rest of the pack as well," Wells said, pushing away from where he'd been sitting on the desk and striding toward the door to open it again.

It was clear we were being dismissed, and it was only when Wells and Sean asked Grey to stay and discuss logistics that he looked like he wasn't about to explode.

Watching Grey had me thinking, I didn't feel like whatever changes I'd gone through were overwhelming me. I could feel the moonlight magic still simmering inside me and even the changes in my wolf. But it didn't feel out of control, or like something I needed to try and keep contained. Was it because Grey was an alpha that his power seemed so out of control? His dark smoke was the exact opposite to the soft light of my own power, so perhaps the two were complete opposites in every way. Whatever the case, I was glad I wasn't in Grey's shoes right now.

31
LACHLAN

I hated being put on the spot, but something about Jessa wanting to start with my magic was ringing alarm bells in my head. Not only was I terrified of what we were about to unleash, but I also had a feeling she knew more about the binding than she'd admitted; not that she'd said anything about it at all. In fact, she hadn't even been present when we'd discussed it before.

Jessa was the only person at the coven who'd ever been kind to me, apart from one of the cooks who made sure I was at least fed. I was so young when I was left there that I didn't understand what was happening, and Jessa had been the one to explain it all to me when I was older.

I didn't have any memories of my parents. It was probably for the best. They didn't care enough about me to keep me when they found out I wouldn't be powerful. Although thinking about it now, that wasn't the case. So either my magic had been bound without them knowing, or what Jessa had told me wasn't the truth. Either way, something about the whole situation didn't add up.

"I can feel your worry. Do you want to talk about it?"

Calli asked as she joined me in the bedroom, where I was unpacking the few things I'd brought.

Sitting down on the edge of the bed with a sigh, I wrapped my arms around Calli's waist as she came to stand between my legs. She softly ran her fingers through my hair, and it was like I could feel the tension draining out of me as I let my head fall forward and rest on her stomach.

"What if something happens?" I asked quietly, not quite brave enough to look her in the face while I said it aloud. "What if my magic was bound for a reason? Like, maybe there's something wrong with it?"

Calli didn't say anything straight away, and my stomach dropped, thinking she was working up the courage to agree with me.

"People think there's something wrong with Cassia's magic. They've treated her differently her whole life because they're afraid of it. I was hidden from the world because my parents told me I wouldn't be accepted because of what I was. I wasn't even allowed to practise my magic, apart from the bits of healing my mother taught me. When I was younger, I always thought it was because there was something wrong with it, something wrong with me. And I suppose, in a way, there is. Look at what I've done to all of you and the changes that have happened because I'm linked to you."

I went to protest, but she shushed me as she kept running her fingers steadily through my hair.

"I'm not saying that was right. I suppose I'm saying I understand how it's easy to be afraid of something being different. But just because it's different doesn't make it dangerous or bad. At the end of the day, it's your magic, and you're a good man, Lachlan. Even if your magic does have the potential to be dangerous, you'll be the one wielding it, and I know you'd never do anything to hurt any of us."

"But what if I do it by accident," I protested. "I might not be able to control it at first."

"We are linked as a coven, Lachlan. We'll help you. And if it turns out to be something terrible, or something you don't want, you always have the option of binding it again," she said with a shrug.

I hadn't thought about it like that before. The coven would be able to help me, and there were powerful witches in our bond. If anyone could do it, they could.

"Do you…" I leaned back and looked up at Calli, interested to see her response. "Do you think Jessa knows more about my binding than she's admitting?"

I knew Jessa was Calli's aunt. Even though they'd only just met, and she hadn't had the opportunity to get to know her yet, I was hoping Calli wouldn't be insulted by the question. Instead, she actually surprised me with the confidence in which she answered.

"Definitely." And then she laughed. "I can see how shocked you are by that. I know Jessa is family, but she doesn't quite feel like it yet, and the fact that she's my mother's twin is causing me all kinds of trauma I'm not ready to examine yet. But there's something about the whole binding issue that's bothering me."

"Like how she knows about it when we've never told her," I deadpanned, realising how ridiculous my suspicion was, given Jessa's abilities.

"I suppose there's an argument that she saw it in one of her visions. Or that she felt it on you at some point. I mean, you must have spent some time together at your old coven. But I think what's worrying me the most is why she wouldn't have taken it off you before now. Especially considering that you were ostracised at that place because of your apparent *lack* of power."

Calli sounded outraged when she finished speaking, and I realised it was because of her complete inability to understand why someone wouldn't help another person if it was within their power.

"Some people don't do things for free," I said with a shrug.

There truly was something wrong with how I'd been raised that I saw it as an acceptable excuse. But it was true. There were many things in our world that we could do or give to other people to help them, but the sad reality was that it was only through the exchange of goods and services for money that most societies worked the way they did.

"Wouldn't it be nice to be able to set up a pack as big as this that was self-sufficient enough so that wouldn't be an issue anymore? Then, we could all just do things for the greater good, not because of whatever gain we could achieve from it."

"I think people have tried before and got disbanded for becoming cults," I laughed.

I could see the dream she was looking at, but I could also see the harsh reality of how these things generally turned out. People were the problem. We were born with a selfish need to corrupt things for our own gain. It was inevitable in our world. And it was so sad that it was the world we lived in.

"Why don't we go and find Jessa and have a chat with her? If we want answers, then maybe we need to start asking some questions," Calli suggested.

Standing up, I kept my hands on Calli's hips, so she couldn't step back. It kept her directly in front of me so I could lightly press my lips to hers.

She was the most perfect woman in the world, and I'd never be able to do enough to prove that I deserved her.

"You're pretty incredible, you know?" I told her, laying another soft kiss on her lips.

"I'm not entirely sure what I just did to warrant that, but I shall try to keep doing it." Calli smiled before kissing me back. The urge to throw her on the bed and declare that I didn't need to know whatever it was Jessa was keeping from me was strong.

I groaned in disappointment when she laughed again and took my hand to lead me out of the bedroom.

"Come on, we need to do this now before you change your mind. I promise you we will come right back to that thought as soon as we have this sorted out," she swore.

She was right that we needed to do it now, but I'd never get enough of how she felt when she was in my arms.

Calli tugged harder on my arm as I started to drag my feet, considering how I could persuade her to put it off a little longer and stay in here with me instead.

"The quicker we do this, the sooner we get back," Calli pointed out, and that had me practically sprinting to the door.

I didn't know when I'd become this person, or even if I ultimately was. But when I was with Calli, it was like she cleared the clouds, and I could see the person I was supposed to be. The shy, reserved guy I'd always been was a product of being placed in a corner all my life. From listening to all the people telling me I wasn't good enough to be considered one of them. But then Calli came striding into my life and showed me that I would always be enough for her, no matter how strong I was. That it wasn't a competition. She showed me what life could be like to be part of a coven, part of a family.

The thought had a silly grin on my face, which only

broadened when Calli slipped an arm around my waist, and we headed downstairs together.

As we reached the front door, Blake came bustling inside, practically oozing stress. I hadn't had the chance to spend much time with the guy, but we could all see what he was going through being so far away from his family.

"Calli!" Blake's eyes shifted around the room as if he was looking for the others. It wasn't unreasonable. We did spend a lot of time together. "Where's Grey and the others?" he asked, echoing my thoughts.

"They're about. I think Grey is with Sean and Wells still, and Tanner and the others were heading to you guys to make sure you were settling in okay. They wanted to talk to you about training this afternoon."

"Right, right. Yeah, I wasn't with the rest of the pack. I decided to head to the school and make sure the kids were settling in okay. I know they were nervous about heading back."

"Yeah, they seemed happier when Aidan said he'd stay with them," Calli laughed, no doubt imagining what Aidan was going through having to sit through a school day.

"I think he must have had to slip out or something," Blake said with a shrug, surprising me. I couldn't believe Aidan would just leave the kids like that, and from the look on Calli's face, she wasn't happy about it. "Jacob's really upset about the whole thing. So I told him I'd come and see if you'd mind stopping by the school to see them all."

"Sure, I can do that. You don't mind if we do that first before seeing Jessa, do you?" Calli asked me.

"No, that's fine. I actually wouldn't mind having a chat with some of the teachers at the school to see what it would take to set something similar up at home."

From the misty-eyed look I got from Calli at that, I was

pretty sure I'd unintentionally won myself some brownie points.

"Ah, erm, would you actually mind running and telling Grey that I just got held up with something, and I'll be there soon? I'll head back to the school with Calli. No one should be wandering around alone until we get a lay of the land."

"Wouldn't it make more sense for you to go and see Grey if he's waiting for you, and I can take Calli?" I asked, confused.

"Probably." Blake laughed. "But I promised the kids I'd pop back in. They're good kids, and it must be hard trying to settle into a new place. Plus, I've totally got a soft spot for Abby. Don't tell the others, but she's totally my favourite."

I couldn't help but laugh. I'd never admit to having favourites, but the little girl was pretty damn cute, and I was sure she had all of us wrapped around her finger. God help us when she's a teenager.

"No worries, man. I'll find Grey and then catch up with you guys later."

Calli pecked me on the cheek, and before I knew it, she and Blake were heading out the door and disappearing off up the road. I stood and watched them walking away, not able to take my eyes off her.

I'd never asked Calli how she felt about suddenly becoming a kind of mother to all the kids. She took it all in her stride, without complaint. It might have been something she'd thought about for the future, but she was still young.

Selfishly, a part of me wondered if it would affect her wanting to have kids of her own. Not that the kids we had in the pack weren't part of our family. But, hell! I didn't know. The thought of a few little Calli's running around had me feeling things I didn't know if I was ready to feel. It wouldn't even matter if I wasn't technically their father, but

I wouldn't lie and say I wouldn't be over the moon if I was.

Shaking my head clear of all the daydreams, I turned back the way we'd come and headed to the office where I'd last seen Grey and the others. Finding it empty, I was about to start exploring the rest of the house in my search for him, when I could have kicked myself for forgetting about the link.

"Grey, where the hell are you? I can't find you, man." I laughed down the link to him.

"I'm round the back of the house. Can you head out here? I want to show you something."

"Sure, on my way."

Heading out the front door, I looped around to the back of the house and found Grey standing with Jessa and Wells, talking and pointing around what had probably at one point in time, been a backyard. The whole thing had been transformed into an obstacle course of sorts, and it had my inner nerd quivering in fear. I'd tried to take the whole combat training thing in my stride. I wasn't exactly a stranger to the gym. But there was a huge difference between running on the treadmill and having a full-grown shifted wolf leaping out at you to attack.

"I really hope you didn't ask me round here just so you could watch me run around this thing," I only partially joked.

Grey must have seen the look of horror on my face and laughed at my expense. "Don't worry, we'll all be doing it together tomorrow. Today, you're safe, though. We're only going to be running through what Hunter taught us at the pack to get Keelan and the other instructors up to speed on where we're up to."

"Oh goody," I deadpanned.

Was it too much to ask for more of an administrative role in the ongoing revolution?

Wells seemed to be finding the whole thing highly amusing, but Jessa patted me reassuringly on the shoulder. What had once been a move that would've comforted me, now felt strange. I didn't know where I stood with Jessa, and the fact that it was shadowing all of her past kindnesses to me made me feel like a bit of a dick.

"I actually wanted to get your opinion on the training Jessa had in mind. We worked together a lot when I was struggling with control, and you were an outstanding teacher, Lachlan. I wouldn't have been able to make it through that ritual if you hadn't been able to put up with my insanity and guide me through the process of controlling my power."

I nodded, taking the folder he was holding out to me. Teaching Grey had actually been pretty enjoyable. I hadn't had all that great an experience at school. The teachers saw teaching me as a waste of time.

It looked like a reasonably comprehensive syllabus on how to control strong magic. Not something I'd ever been taught, but something I'd witnessed. There were sections detailing lessons for every different type of magic. It must have taken years to accumulate this much information and set it all out into a short, intensive course.

"I can't believe how much time you must have put into this," I said as I continued to flip through the papers.

I found a section relating to lightning magic and started to read it in interest, given that it was an affinity I'd found myself leaning toward.

It was only when Grey's hand came into view as he slowly grasped the folder and pulled it out of my hands that I looked up and saw the amused looks on everyone's faces and realised I must have zoned out a bit.

"Ah, sorry about that." Pushing my glasses further up my nose, I shuffled awkwardly, not liking everyone's attention on me suddenly. "It's a very comprehensive course. I'm not sure I can really add anything to it, but I doubt that's why you were asking my opinion."

"No, Jessa and I discussed whether it would be better to work with us in groups rather than individually. I think it would be better to move through the material quickly, and I was saying that you would be able to help out with the basics while she dealt with the more complex issues. If that's something you'd be comfortable with," Grey explained.

"Yeah, I can do that. But if the contents of that folder are Jessa's knowledge on magic, my own is definitely very much basic fundamentals," I admitted.

"Ah now, I've seen you work, Lachlan, and I know you could achieve much if you put your mind to it," Jessa said, waving off my way of putting myself down. "We can still work together to help you with your own magic, but I have no doubt that it won't take you long to master. Come to think of it, Calli will probably be able to assist too. If any of you has even a basic affinity for healing, it would help to have more than just her able to heal in a fight."

"Where is Calli?" Grey asked, looking around as if she would pop up out of nowhere.

"Ah, crap, I was supposed to tell you. Blake came to say the kids were having some problems settling at the school, and he asked Calli to go back with him to see them. He asked me to come and tell you he was running late."

"Running late for what?"

"To do whatever you asked him to do," I explained, confused.

A glimmer of concern started in the back of my mind, but I refused to pay any attention to it.

"I never asked Blake to come and do something," Grey said slowly.

"Wait," Wells butted in. "What exactly did Blake say to you?"

"Just that he wanted me to tell Grey he got held up with something, and he was running late. That he'd be here soon."

I could feel the colour draining from my face, and by the deadset look of sad acceptance on Jessa's face, I knew that no matter how much I didn't want it to be, something was wrong.

"Calli!" I shouted through the link to her, only to hear Grey's voice doing the same thing.

Nothing came back.

Pulling on the magic through the coven bond, I reached out for her, but there was something wrong with the link, almost like it was blocked.

"I can't feel her," I gasped, panic clawing at my chest. "I can't feel Calli."

Turning to Grey for some kind of reassurance or answer, I stumbled back in shock at the sight before me. The black smoke that had become so familiar nearly completely obscured him from vision. Only the red glow of his eyes pierced through the gloom as he tipped back his head and unleashed an animalistic howl.

"That's it, Grey. Don't hold it back. Let it flow," Jessa encouraged.

When Grey snarled, his head snapping in her direction, Wells tried to pull his mate behind him, but she pushed him away.

"Embrace it all, alpha. It will lead you to her," Jessa directed.

Grey's legs seemed to give out beneath him, and he dropped to his knees. Panting breaths punctuated by growls flowed from him as he pushed through whatever was happening to him.

"What's happening?" Tanner rushed out through the link.

"Calli is missing, and something's happening to Grey."

"What do you mean Calli is missing?" Tanner roared, and I could hear River and Maverick both screaming the same question into my head.

"I…I don't know. I think, I think Blake took her."

It all went quiet on the link as everyone reeled from the shock of what I was saying.

"It can't be Blake," River said quietly. "Not after everything they went through. It just, it can't be Blake."

Even as they spoke, I found myself following the link to where Calli should be and slamming against the wall blocking me time and time again. This was my fault. I'd been right there. I should've known that something wasn't right. Looking back, Blake had been acting strangely. I should have realised something was wrong. I should have been better.

"It's not your fault, Lachlan," River reassured me through the link, and I realised I must have been screaming it out for them all to hear.

Thick tears fell down my cheeks, and I didn't care who saw them. It didn't matter. The only thing that mattered was finding Calli.

Trying again, even though I knew it was futile, I slammed back into that wall with my mind and almost felt the impact reverberate through my body.

I needed to get through this. If I could just break through, I could ask Calli where she was. If I was stronger…

"You have to break my binding," I shouted, spinning back to Jessa as I saw a solution to what was happening. "Break the binding now, so I can find her!"

Jessa opened her mouth to answer me, but whatever she

was saying was drowned out by a wave of power slamming out of Grey as he tipped back his head and howled. The sound echoed around us, and several other howls picked up across the packlands in answer to the alpha's rage.

"I found her," he growled, climbing back to his feet. "Everyone to me. We're going to take back our mate."

32

CALLI

"Why did you park the truck all the way over here?" I asked as the blue of the painted exterior came into view.

"There wasn't any space left next to the house, and I didn't want it to be in the way," Blake said with a shrug. "Thanks for coming with me to get my phone. I can't believe I left it in there again."

"No problem. Jacob and the kids will be fine at school. It's not like they're in any danger. Besides, I'm pretty sure Jean will kick your ass if she's trying to reach you and can't, so really, I'm doing this for your own protection." I laughed.

Not for nothing, if Jean came at me in a rage, I'd be pretty scared. She had the momma bear thing going about her now.

"You must be excited that she's on her way. Her and little Tucker. I'm sorry that you've been away from them for so long, Blake. If it wasn't for Jacob and Abby wandering off, you'd have still been with them."

It hurt seeing the look on Blake's face when he didn't realise anyone else was watching. His pain must have been what I felt echoing through the bond when I'd been overwhelmed by magic trying to heal Wells.

"Yeah. I didn't think they'd be coming here so soon," Blake mumbled, his steps seeming to slow slightly.

"You've been a massive help to all of us, Blake. None of us will forget how much you've sacrificed. I'm not sure we can ever repay you."

"You really believe that, don't you?"

"Yeah, of course. I know how much it hurt when I lost my parents. Leaving Jean and the baby behind must feel like you've lost a part of your pack. When Jacob and I first came here, it was hard to cope without having a part of my pack around anymore."

Blake sighed and slowed to a stop as he stared down at the ground.

"I don't deserve your thanks," he ground out, not looking up to meet my eye.

"Of course you do."

I wanted to wave him off, but there was something about the tone of his voice that worried me. He seemed so lost and just, well, sad.

"You did so much for my family, Calli. You saved Jean and even little Tucker when we thought he was lost. You sacrificed the only piece of safety you had to keep them with me. I should be binding myself to you, swearing to serve you in whatever way I can. But they're my family, Calli. I had to do it for my family."

"I know you did," I whispered back, already seeing what was happening before he admitted it.

It hadn't just been pain I'd felt through the bond when I'd been lost in the surge of magic. It had been shame too. And now it all made sense. I was feeling it now too. The shame.

How had we been so blind to his pain that he'd do something like this? In a way, we were the ones that had failed Blake.

"Just tell me the kids are safe, Blake. That's all I ask."

His head snapped up, and he finally looked me in the eye. "I would never…"

"They won't understand what you've done. Blake. You have to make sure they understand. Jean and Tucker need you. Go to River or Lachlan first. The others will lash out before they can listen." My mind was racing with how to get him through this.

"I never wanted to hurt you, Calli. But they were coming back for Tucker. Stone was going to take him, and he said this was the only way to keep him safe." Tears streamed down his face as he hiccuped his way through his confession.

Of course, they would target him. He was the only one with something to lose that was currently outside of the protection of our pack. Something so vulnerable that we'd all have done anything to keep him safe.

"It's okay, Blake," I reassured him.

"No. It's not…run, Calli," Blake suddenly rushed out, pushing me back in the direction we'd come. "Go, now. Quick. I'll hold them back as long as I can. Tell Grey what I've done. Tell him…tell him I'm sorry."

A sudden boom blasted through the trees, and my body recoiled automatically at the sound. As it echoed around me, I reluctantly straightened, not understanding what was happening.

The red bloom appeared slowly at first, but as the blood started to saturate Blake's shirt, it was like his body finally realised what had happened to him, and he sank to his knees. His mouth opened and closed as if he was trying to say something but kept changing his mind.

I tried the link, but before I could bring the thought to my mind, a magical barrier crashed into life around us, sealing us inside. The silence was almost deafening, especially where the link to my mates should have been.

Darting forward, I caught Blake before he could fall face forward and brought him closer. I didn't even have to call on my magic as it surged out of me and into him. Healing as much as I could as quickly as possible. I knew time was short, but if I could stop the bleeding, I might still be able to save his life. He was the only one who'd be able to tell the others where I was and what had happened.

Blake might have been the reason I was about to be taken, but he was also the only chance I had to be found.

"Don't," Blake whispered, trying to push my hands away. "Don't waste time trying to save me. Run, Calli. You still have a chance to get away. I'm sorry. I'm so sorry. I should have found another way. I should have told Grey what was happening, and we could have done something, anything."

"I'm not going to let you die, Blake," I told him adamantly, pushing more and more magic into his body. "You need to live through this and tell them what happened. But you have to let them think you're not going to make it," I whispered as I felt them drawing closer.

He nodded slightly against my arm, and I pulled on my best acting skills as I sobbed as loudly as I could, letting Blake slip to the ground as if there had been nothing I could do to save him. We were out of time, and there was nothing else I could do to help him heal. I just had to pray what I'd already done was enough.

Making sure that his face was hidden from view, I shuffled away from Blake's body. It wouldn't do to let them examine him so closely.

The fact that feminine laughter followed my move actually surprised me. I spun around to face whoever it was that approached, wondering why Stone wasn't the one standing on the other side of his barrier. My brain didn't seem able to register that he wouldn't have been able to construct the barrier on his own.

The woman standing on the other side was familiar, but I couldn't place her as panic seized my brain.

"Well, that was easier than I thought it would be. I thought you'd put up at least a bit of a fight, but I suppose the story is always better than real life," she sneered.

I was about to tell her where she could shove her expectations, but I felt my head start to spin, and the ground seemed to float up to meet me. Before I could do anything, blackness swallowed me, and the only place I had left to scream was in my head.

I came to with a gasp as I jolted awake. My body tried to sit up, but I was met with resistance and a tight pain flared across my chest instead.

"Ah, you're back with us, I see," the woman said.

As my eyes fluttered open, I realised I was somewhere different. Somewhere really fucking dirty and creepy too. Great, it was just my luck to pass out and wake up in some kind of murder shack in the woods.

Looking around, all I could see were old wooden walls and dusty cobwebs. I seemed to be tied down to some kind of tabletop. Leather straps ran across my chest and hips, holding my arms tight at my sides. The contraption was finished off with a final strap over my calves. They were all tight enough that I could barely move apart from rolling my arm over, so my palms were at least not pressed down onto the tabletop.

"What happened?" I croaked, my tongue feeling dry and swollen in my mouth.

I'd kill for a fucking glass of water right now. And it would be no chore to start with the bitch in front of me.

"I sucked all the air out of the bubble I placed you in until you passed out. I released the spell before you asphyxiated, though," she explained, almost like she was waiting for me to thank her.

"Who the fuck are you?" I blurted out instead.

I was done with niceties. These people were relentless, and it was starting to piss me off that I was always at the top of their 'to do fucked up shit to' list.

"Don't you recognise me, sister?" she smirked, swarming over the table as she brought her face close to mine.

She paused for a second while I had a moment to try and suppress the vomit that wanted to surge out of me.

Tipping her head back, she cackled in glee, and I nearly fucking laughed with her, hoping that she was actually joking.

"Well, I suppose, sister-in-law, but us girls should stick together, don't you think, Sis?"

"I never knew Stone had a daughter." I tried to shrug, but it was difficult being tied down and everything. "I guess he was ashamed of all of his children."

"While I don't argue with you there. But, no, I'm not Stone's daughter. I will soon be his wife, though. Huh, I guess that means I'll also be your Aunt, no mother-in-law? Wait, what?" she tipped her head to the side, and her finger trailed through the air as if she was trying to follow the lines on some kind of fucked up family tree.

Finally, she shrugged and moved over to a small table by the side of where I was strapped down. I made the massive mistake of following her with my eyes and seeing what lay on the top. I was so fucked.

"You really shouldn't give a man the job a woman could do, you know. I learned that when you just kept slipping away every time I tried to lure you in." She started to shuffle about out of view, and I panicked even more when I couldn't see what she was doing.

When she appeared with a water bottle at my side, I would have leapt out of my skin had I not been in my current predicament.

"Drink? You sound parched."

Well, the fact that she was certifiably crazy really did explain a lot.

"I think I'll pass."

"You're only punishing yourself," she pointed out before lifting the bottle to her lips and taking a long drink.

I found myself watching every single gulp she took and tracking one lone drop of water that escaped her lips and flowed down her neck. She was right, I was only punishing myself, but I wasn't going to admit that to her.

"So, are you just going to ramble away with random comments that don't make sense, or are you actually going to tell me how you could possibly be my sister-in-law?"

She turned back to me with a grin on her face, and I knew she was doing all of this just to play with me. I didn't care if she was, though. She'd piqued my interest, and the little bit of information I could get out of her now could help us in the fight to come. Because there was absolutely no doubt in my mind that I was going to make it out of this place.

"Well, you are mated to my brother. It might not be a traditional marriage as such, but, well, it's basically the same thing isn't it," she confessed like we were two friends gossiping in some café.

Grabbing a stool, she pulled it up to the side of the table and sat down, resting her elbows on my thigh as she dropped her chin into her hands.

"Mated, hey! That must be strange, with so many men wanting all of your time. How on earth do you cope with it? I fully intend to bring my own harem of men into my mating once I take the position of Pack Queen. Stoney might not know it yet, but, well, I will definitely be the one wearing the pants in our relationship," she told me with a wink.

This whole situation was blowing my mind. Who was this crazy-pants woman? There was no question that something inside her had definitely broken.

I could place her face now. She was the woman outside of the facility that we'd seen quarrelling with Stone before he'd driven away.

"I can see that," I said, deciding to play into whatever delusion was currently running through her head. "You were both having a hell of an argument the last time I saw you together. I suppose it will be easier once he realises who has the power in your relationship."

"Oh, you must be talking about the one at the lab. I thought I felt you there, you sneaky minx!" she laughed, shoving my arm playfully like I wasn't currently strapped to her torture table. "It was terribly rude of you to burn down my lab, you know. I suppose my research had nearly run its course, but still."

"I'll try and only set fire to less convenient things in future," I deadpanned.

"Oh, you!" She laughed, playfully shoving me again.

"So, who is your brother? You have to at least tell me that much." It was making me want to hurl talking to her like she was my friend, but if I could keep it up, I thought she might actually tell me what I wanted to know.

"I'll give you a clue, and you can try and guess," she suddenly said, clapping her hands together like it was the best idea in the world. "Okay, so there was a relative of mine in the lab, but she wasn't in a prison cell."

Something flashed across her eyes, but I couldn't tell what emotion it was. It was gone that quickly.

There was only one 'she' I could think of, but surely it couldn't have been Neressa.

I hesitated to answer, trying to follow through on what this could mean.

"Oh, don't worry, silly. I'm not angry that you killed her," she laughed, confirming my suspicions.

"You're related to Neressa?" I said slowly, trying to piece it together in my mind. "You're... Lachlan's sister?"

"Yeah, not that he knows about me. We never actually met. That kind of happens when you get kidnapped at birth. But dear old great-great-great-great grandmother, or whatever she was, didn't need him really. Not when she had me. I was the one who would make it all happen. She couldn't risk working the procedure on herself, not when there was a possibility it could go wrong. So that's where I came in. A handy little blood-related guinea pig. The silly old bitch actually thought I'd let her experiment on me. Talk about drinking your own Kool-aid." She cackled again like it was the best joke ever.

"So, whatever you were trying to find out at the lab, it was to change Neressa?"

"Oh, you haven't figured it out yet?" She looked down at me with the first serious look on her face since we'd started the whole strange conversation. "Hmmm, I thought you were supposed to be clever. Now, I don't know if I want to bind your DNA to mine. Oh well, it's not like I can pop down to the store and pick up another Queen." With a shrug, she reached behind her and produced what looked like a corkscrew from the tray I'd glimpsed earlier.

So it was time for this part then.

There was no way I was getting out of these straps without at least some time to work on them, and the only way that was going to happen was if I was alone.

Fuck, I could already tell this was going to really fucking hurt.

"Now, be a dear and hold still. I'd like to say you're only going to feel a small pinch, but that would be a huge lie." She laughed and then, raising the corkscrew up into the air, she rammed it into my hip.

My scream ripped through the air as it felt like she'd just pinned me to the table, and I was suddenly grateful to have the straps holding me down as my body seemed to take on a life of its own.

"Hoooo wee, that sounded like it hurt." She grinned down at me, and then she started to turn the corkscrew.

I tried not to scream. I tried to grit my teeth and refuse to let the sound, she seemed to so enjoy, out. But it was impossible. I could feel the metal tearing into my bone, and it flowed through my body, lighting my nerves on fire as it consumed my mind.

I really tried not to scream.

But I did.

I screamed until the pain started to pull at the edges of my mind, and then I wrapped it around me, begging it to pull me into the darkness again, but for some reason, it refused.

It refused to save me, and I had no option but to endure it.

I didn't even notice when she started to turn the corkscrew the other way. It all felt the same anyway. Even when she pulled the thing out and held the bloody implement up into the air, it still felt like it was turning and turning, burrowing into my bone even though it was no longer there.

"Still with me?" she asked, leaning over the table to look into my eyes. "Huh! I was sure you'd pass out at some point. Good lord, girl. You've got my ears ringing with all that screaming. You're just being a baby, you know. It's barely a scratch, and you're hardly bleeding." Glancing down at the table, she winced and then looked back up. "Well, maybe a little bit."

With a shrug, she turned back around, and I heard the clang of metal as she dropped the corkscrew down onto the metal tray I'd seen earlier.

You know how sometimes you watch a movie and see someone in a torture room, and they're all stoic, and like 'fuck you, I can take this'? Well, I could not fucking take this. Pain was pain, and there was no way anyone could just lay back and take it.

When she turned back around, whistling a happy tune and fiddling with a massive fucking needle, I pulled what little sense I had left and tried to take note of what she was doing. Maybe if I could draw her back into a conversation, she'd get distracted enough that I could buy some more time. It could be enough for the others to come and save me. All thoughts of possibly saving myself had been thoroughly put in their place.

"You… haven't told me your name…sis," I panted out, feeling sick to my stomach at calling her that.

She didn't deserve the title of sister. Not when there were other women in my life far more deserving. Women who would kick her fucking ass when they got here.

"Oh, didn't I?" she paused as if to think, and then she rammed the needle into my hip with her full strength. It was only when I stopped screaming that she said, "It's Zoe."

Zoe? It didn't seem to suit her. It just wasn't evil enough.

"What? You don't like it?" she asked, pausing what she was doing to pay attention to me again.

"It…I don't know. You don't seem like a Zoe to me," I gasped, trying to fight through the pain and desperately keep her attention on the conversation rather than what she was doing to me.

"I know, right! It's like they had my brother, gave him frankly an awesome name, and then they got to me and were like, eh, Zoe will do. It's not very Queenly, is it? I'm thinking of changing it, but I can't decide what I like."

And then she went right back to what she was doing. It wasn't so much that it hurt now. The pain throbbing down my leg from the already embedded needle was probably helping with that. The sensation was strange, though, and when she wrenched the needle free of my hip, I was pretty sure she was going to rip the bone out with it.

"Huh, will you look at that! It didn't break or anything." She held the needle up in the air, showing it off, and my eyes were drawn to the blood-like liquid inside. "I'd like to say you did good, but geesh, did you need to scream so much?"

I very nearly apologised. It was like my inner British floated to the surface, and it was going to automatically fall from my mouth without consent. But I shoved that bitch back down because fuck that, I would not apologise for screaming while she fucking tortured me or whatever this was.

Putting the needle down on the table, Zoe dusted her hands off and picked up the water bottle for another drink, unknowingly taunting me with it.

"Right," she said, turning back to me. "I'm going to mix your marrow with the tincture I've made and take it. I'll keep you alive for now, in case I'm going to need a second dose. So I guess you can just hang out here for a bit."

"What's the tincture for?" I gritted out, hating that I was even engaging with her.

"To make me like you, obviously. That was the whole point of this whole thing. How to home grow your very own Queen." She must have seen the look on my face and laughed. "I know you think it's impossible, but we've spent a long time tinkering with the process, so it will work on turned female shifters. Of course, it hasn't so far, but I know this is the missing piece. Your blood wasn't saturated enough with magic, but your bone marrow? That's the juicy stuff. It's either that or we just chop off a leg and blend that fucker up!" She laughed like it was the most hilarious thing anyone had ever said.

I looked at her a bit closer, trying to piece together what she said to me. If she was Lachlan's sister and Neressa was some relative, then it was safe to say she was definitely a witch. But her scent was so strange. I suppose there was a hint of magic there, but it was unlike anything I'd ever scented before.

"Still trying to work out what makes me so different, aren't you?" She laughed. "I already gave you the answer. You just aren't concentrating enough. I suppose that's my fault," she said, looking down at the ruin that was my hip. I was glad I couldn't see what state it was in right now. From how much it hurt, I was sure she'd made a mess, and I just had to hope that my shifter healing would kick in to heal it enough for when it came time for me to run.

"You're working with turned females," I realised.

"Ding, ding, ding. Of course, I'd already gone through the process before you rudely ruined my lab, but it's still inconvenient to not have any test subjects to work with in this final step. Do you know how many women we went through to get just a handful to work with?" She sighed like the whole thing had been a massive inconvenience for her.

I did know how many she'd gone through. I'd walked through her chamber of horrors and seen them lined up. That was why she'd kept them. To refine the process, to learn from her mistakes. They were her failed experiments that she'd retained as test specimens. It made me want to throw up, but I swallowed it down rather than spew the meagre contents of my stomach all over myself. I'd been through enough already, and the fact I hadn't either passed out or thrown up already was a minor miracle in itself.

"So, you were going to be the final step in the testing before Neressa allowed the process to be done to her," I realised out loud. "It's pretty good for you that she's dead then. I doubt she would have let you live once you'd outlived your usefulness."

"You're right. Of course, I'd have killed her once I successfully went through the process anyway. It's not like I would go through all this and then just give away the prize at the end. No, I will have my harem and my pack, and then I'll take the Councils. The humans can keep their side of the world, and we'll stick to ours. I'm not totally insane."

"But what does Stone stand to gain from all this?"

"Power, obviously. He thinks I'll be his little puppet Queen and sit at his feet while he benefits from all the power I syphon his way. Now, that one's delusional! I suppose I'll have to kill him too. He's not exactly harem material. Now yours, on the other hand, phew girl, you lucked out with them." She fanned herself in appreciation, and I felt my wolf rise to the surface at the mention of her mates.

A growl flowed from my lips before I could stop it. Thankfully, she just found the whole thing hilarious, not seeing me as a threat at all. A glimmer flickered across her eyes in response, and I found myself suddenly fascinated.

"Have you been able to shift?" I asked. "I didn't know a witch could be turned."

"They couldn't be," she shrugged, but I could see the need to brag lighting up inside of her. "It has taken years to perfect the process, but the only real breakthrough came through my work and my genes."

She looked expectantly at me, as if waiting for me to gush with praise. Even if her motives had been pure, I wasn't sure I'd be able to. The whole thing was way over my head.

With a sigh, she turned back to the table and started to empty the contents of the syringe into another vial.

"Well, you stay there. I'll be back in a few hours to either kill you or maybe take a leg next time." And with that, she walked out the door, slamming it closed behind her.

It was the way she could say something like that without it sounding like a threat, but more of a casual observance, that made my blood run cold. It didn't take long to let the dread settle into me at the thought of what was to come. There was one shining ray of hope, though, because there was one thing I hadn't heard when the door slammed, and that was the lock. She hadn't locked it behind her.

That didn't mean there wasn't an entire army waiting on the other side of the door for me, but I would take this for the win it currently was.

Flexing my wrist, I tried to see if there was a way I could slip my arm out from under the strap. While I had some slight movement, I definitely wasn't getting out that way. Resigning myself to doing this the hard way, I shifted a single claw on one of my fingers and got to work cutting through the strap from this awkward angle.

It didn't escape me that this wasn't the first time I'd

resorted to this since I'd come to the US. I somehow doubted this situation would end as happily as the last one did, although hopefully, I'd end up back in my mates' arms at the end of this.

The leather itself was a lot tougher to work through, and it didn't help that I had to nearly bend my wrist all the way forward. It seemed impossible at first, but with each scrape across the material, I became more and more determined that this was going to work.

The strap gradually loosened as I made my way through it, making it easier to reach the furthest side away from me without feeling like I would snap all the tendons in my wrist. As it was, I had a cramp running through my finger, right up my arm, but there was no way I was stopping. I wasn't losing a leg to this woman's batshit crazy experiment to become the next Queen.

Was it even possible? Before, I'd have said no, but she'd managed to find a way to turn herself. I'd noticed she never answered if she could shift or not. Instead, she opted to brag about how her breakthrough made the process possible, and I had a suspicion she couldn't. At least not yet. Who knew what she would turn herself into when she finished whatever she was doing right now?

As if my thoughts had prompted it, a feminine scream ripped through the house where I was being held. Rather than stopping in fear like my body was telling me to, I renewed my efforts at the strap, scraping quicker across the surface.

It hadn't been a scream of rage. It was one filled with pain, and whilst it gave me a sick satisfaction that the process was at least hurting her, it also meant it had started, and I had no idea how much time I had left.

When the strap was finally nearly cut through, I took a deep breath and wrenched my arm up. The feeling of it snapping was better than anything I'd ever experienced. I just maybe wouldn't admit that to any of my mates.

Working through the other two straps was far quicker now that I could at least move my arms more. I quickly cut through the one banded across my chest, and then once I could sit up, I got my legs free.

Sitting up made my hip feel like it was filled with fire, and leaning down to reach the last strap was even worse. I couldn't bring myself to look at what she'd done yet. I'd get free and then deal with that problem when I had to.

As the last strap came free, I gingerly spun on the table so I could dangle my legs off the side. My first thought was to get off and check the door to see if I could hear anything outside, but I was worried putting weight on my leg was going to make the agony I was currently experiencing much, much worse.

Deciding to be brave, I instead lifted my shirt and pulled down the side of my leggings I'd had on to check underneath. At least she'd decided to pierce straight through my clothing rather than stripping me naked to do what she needed. There was a small mercy in that, I supposed.

I couldn't help but stare at the puncture wound on my hip. It was actually kind of disappointing. It wasn't exactly tiny, but it also wasn't the gaping hole it felt like it should be. It hurt like a motherfucker because she'd gone into the bone.

It at least gave me some confidence that I'd be able to stand, and I slowly slipped off the table to test some weight on my leg.

Blazing heat radiated from my hip, but I was able to hold steady. Running was going to be hard, but I was pretty sure I'd be able to make it through if I shifted. I didn't really have any other choice. It was that or stay here, which definitely wasn't an option.

Taking a deep breath to fortify myself, I limped over to the door and listened, pressing my face against the surface.

I couldn't hear much of anything from the other side apart from the grunts and screeches of pain that punctuated the air.

Turning back around, I leaned back against the door to think. There were no windows in this room, so I wasn't going to be slipping out quickly that way. In fact, there was pretty much nothing in here apart from the table I'd been strapped down to and the smaller table with her tray sitting on top.

The water bottle was still there, and I licked my lips in thirst. The need to go over there and finish the small amount left in the bottom of the bottle was strong, but the stubborn part of me refused to drink her leftovers. It was stupid, and I'd regret it eventually, but I would let my pride rule this decision.

The only way out was through the door, and I knew it would be better to go while she was distracted by whatever she was going through than to wait for her to recover.

As a last-ditch effort, I reached out for all of my bonds. The silence resonating through them sliced at my heart, and I hoped whatever it was that was interfering with them was temporary.

Tipping my head back, I looked at the connections I had inside. My magic wasn't as strong as it would have been if I hadn't stopped to heal Blake, but it was still there deep inside of me. It seemed to rise at feeling me turn inwards to inspect it, and I took a second to let the feeling of it wash over me.

In turn, my wolf rose, eager to assist. She wanted to tear into Zoe and show her what a Queen was capable of, even though we had yet to earn that title. I felt the rustle of her fur at my thoughts that we weren't ready yet, and smiled at her huff of annoyance.

We would be ready.

We weren't going to lie down and take whatever this bitch had in mind for us.

With a final moment of assessing my capabilities, I gritted my teeth and turned to face the door.

The cold door handle reminded me that this wasn't really the weather to be running around outside without a coat on, but I had no idea where mine had gone. It didn't matter anyway, I'd shift as soon as I was outside, and then there would be no stopping until I was safely back with my mates.

Turning the handle slowly, I held my breath and prayed that it wouldn't make a noise. In the end, a long scream ripped through the air, and I took the opportunity to open the door far enough for me to slip through.

Outside of the room, everything fell quiet, and I assessed the situation as quickly as possible. I seemed to be inside a simple cabin. There were two other doors on this corridor, and at the very end was the door that led to outside.

The view of the trees through the frosted door window was almost taunting. It was a glimpse of where I wanted to be, even though I had no idea if I'd ever be able to reach it.

I refused to acknowledge the pain radiating from my hip. If I thought about it, I wouldn't be able to stop, and I still had what would be a long run in front of me.

There were just two doors between me and the outside, and I slowly started to creep down the corridor. There was no point in lingering here waiting to see if they'd open. Walking down the corridor wasn't going to urge anyone out here if I could do it silently. But staying in one place was a sure-fire way to get caught.

Drawing level with the first door, I skittered to the other side of the corridor as another scream flowed out into the corridor from inside the room. So that was where she'd gone. At least I knew where crazy pants was. The problem was not knowing if anyone else was in here, or outside for that matter.

It seemed unlikely that she would have risked coming onto Wells' land alone, but surely she wouldn't have been stupid enough to come with an army either. No, it would make more sense to bring a few trusted fighters. A smaller force had less chance of being spotted, but at least she'd have some protection. That meant there were either other people inside the cabin or they were waiting for me outside.

Taking a few steps closer to the front door, I made a decision I really fucking hoped I wasn't about to regret. Bracing myself for what was going to be a painfully unpleasant experience, I shifted into my wolf. Rather than acknowledge how much it hurt, I set off at as fast a pace as I could manage.

I had my target in mind, and once this was done, there would be no mistaking that I'd escaped. I had to hit the ground running and not look back. Speed was everything right now. I didn't have time to warily peek through the door and then shift once I'd made it outside. I needed to be fast, and this was the fastest route I could think of.

Leaping for the frosted pane of glass, I closed my eyes and braced for the pain of breaking through. This had to work. I refused to die in this place.

33
GREY

Running to find my mate with my pack at my back had a sense of rightness flowing through me. This was what we were made to do. We were made to hunt, and hunting was what we were doing because when I found the person who'd taken my mate from me, there was no doubt in my mind that they were prey.

Blake.

I couldn't wrap my mind around the fact that he would betray me this way. He'd been with the pack since the beginning. We'd grown up together. He'd pledged himself to the pack and started his own family there.

In the back of my mind, I knew there'd be a reason for this, but I didn't know if I cared enough to listen. The black smoke of my magic was overwhelming. It didn't just swarm out of me; it flowed through me, saturating every part of my body.

It wasn't that it was a malicious power. It was strong and powerful. This was a magic that was meant to protect, and now that I'd let it loose, it knew what it needed to be satisfied.

The steady thump of paws hitting the ground at speed filled my mind as more wolves joined our run to find my mate. Behind me, Tanner and Wells ran shoulder to shoulder, protecting my back. The presence of the other alpha was calling to his own pack, and before I'd even realised it, we were an army charging toward a fight.

I'd rejected the idea of taking the pack before. It wasn't mine, and it didn't feel like it was supposed to be. But running with them now, heading our charge, I could feel the call of this growing power inside of me calling out to add them to our side.

I couldn't listen to it right now. I didn't have room in my mind to concentrate on anything that wasn't Calli and getting her back.

I couldn't explain how I knew where she was. The bonds between us were blocked, and no matter how much I tried, I couldn't force my way through. The sad fact was, I had no idea how to wield my magic that way or if it was even possible. Once again, Stone had caught us unaware and unprepared. We might have been planning how to learn to use the new power we were gaining, but we hadn't gotten far enough for it to be of any use.

How was he always one step ahead of us? It was like we were playing a chess game, but he was three moves ahead of us, already knowing exactly what we were going to do next. Either we were predictable as fuck, or he had some other way of knowing. It couldn't be information Blake fed to him because we didn't even know it yet ourselves. No, something else had to be going on here.

Suddenly, the scent of Calli's magic filled my head, and I altered my course to aim straight for it. Underlying it was the tint of blood, and I couldn't entertain the thought that we might be too late. No, deep down inside, I knew I'd be able to tell if my mate was already lost to me.

"I have her scent," Tanner confirmed through the bond, and the rest of the pack echoed his sentiment.

I could feel the hope coming from him and her other mates.

"Grey, I've moved the kids into the school's basement, and the teachers have said they will stay with them. Do you want me to come to you?" Aidan asked, hope lining his voice.

I knew he wanted to come to the aid of his sister. He'd only just found her, and he deserved to have the family that had been long denied him. But the pups were more important, and Calli would have our hides if something happened to them while we were out trying to save her.

"I know you need to be here with us right now, Aidan, but Calli needs you to make sure the kids are protected first. As soon as we have her, I will let you know. I promise you. But please, fuck, I need to know that the pups are with someone I can trust right now."

I'd thought I could trust Blake, and look at how wrong I'd been there. Even Wallace. I'd given him a chance, and he repaid me by trying to kill Calli. Was I so blind to the members of my pack that I couldn't see when they were about to stab me in the back? What kind of alpha was I that was so out of touch with my pack members?

Shaking my head, I snarled. I couldn't give in to doubt right now. I didn't have room for self-doubt and mistakes.

"I won't leave their sides," Aidan promised. "Grey...I need her."

"I know. We all do."

Gritting my teeth, I pushed on, keeping the pace fast, but found the pack had no issue keeping up with me.

We weren't far from the packhouse when a crumpled form on the ground came into view. How had they made it this far into the packlands without anyone knowing? We were supposed to be safe here.

"They've infiltrated the packlands, Aidan. Stay on alert," I shouted down the link before shutting it down as soon as I had his acknowledgement. I couldn't afford to be distracted now. Not when we had prey to play with.

I slowed to a stop a few paces away from Blake. He'd lost a lot of blood, but he was breathing and conscious as he tried to stand when he heard us approach.

"Alpha, I…"

"Don't speak unless you are directly answering my questions," I roared as I shifted back into my human form.

I cast an eye over him. From the look of the blood on the front and back of his chest, I'd say he'd been shot. The fact that he was still alive could only be because Calli had healed him. The bullet holes were positioned too close to his heart for him to have survived any other way.

"Did you tell her you'd betrayed her before letting her save your life?" I shouted, even though it was wasting precious time. But the thought of him lying there and letting her heal him when he was the one that had done this to her grated at my nerves, setting them on fire.

Blake dropped his head to look at the ground, unable to meet my gaze. "They told me they would take Tucker. They told me this was the only way they'd stop. I know I don't deserve to live for what I've done. I…I tried to get her to run." A sob burst out of him as he worked up the courage to finally meet my eye. "You have to save her."

Dammit!

I wanted to hurt him. I wanted to kill him, if I was being completely honest.

"You should have come to me, Blake. I'm your alpha, and you didn't trust me enough to ensure that your family was safe."

"I know. I know that now. I don't even know why I didn't. I think I panicked."

"As touching as this whole thing could turn out to be, might I remind you that we have a very small window of opportunity here," Wells interrupted.

Spinning around, the smoke whipped out of me in his direction. I'd never seen it work with such precision before, and I didn't even voluntarily do it. I only just managed to grasp control of the tendril and rip it back toward me when it was inches away from his chest.

"I am very much aware of the situation Calli is in. But don't you think it is pertinent for me to calm down enough to not kill the man in front of us before he can tell us where they've taken her?"

Wells nodded and raised his hands as he backed away.

"I deserve to die," Blake said resolutely as I turned back to him.

"Yes, you do." I wasn't going to disagree with him.

"She was taken by the woman that Stone is working with. She made it this far into the packlands with four guards. I don't know how they made it through, but I believe they have a man in your guard. I was told to bring Calli to this spot and that they would take her from here. The deal was that it would be the end of my involvement."

I heard Wells growl and storm away before he started barking orders at some of his pack. At least we weren't the only ones with a traitor in our midst.

Tanner broke his silence and stepped forward, shouting, "And then what? Did you plan to stay in the pack, pretending to be our brother, when you were the one that sold our mate to Stone?"

"It wasn't like that," Blake protested, but then he wilted on the spot. "It wasn't like that," he muttered quietly.

Maverick stepped to his brother's side, pulling him back and speaking softly, trying to calm him down. "You know what our father is capable of. You shouldn't judge him when we would have done the exact same thing in his position. There is nothing I wouldn't do to protect our pups."

I couldn't help but be surprised by his statement, and I hated the part of me that agreed with him. I would have done the same thing if it had protected the children. Not to our mate, never our mate; I'd have died trying to protect them all. But someone else? I wasn't entirely sure what lengths I'd go to.

"She has my blood on her," Blake said, drawing my attention back to him. "You can follow the scent of my blood."

"If we're too late…" I warned.

"Either way, alpha. My life is yours, and I will accept whatever judgement you have when we have her back with us."

Nodding, I turned away from my old friend. At least he seemed at peace that his end was drawing near. It would need to be done properly, in front of the pack. It was skating too close to the old ways, to the traditions we'd turned our backs on. But Blake had turned his back on us when he'd accepted Stone's offer, and I didn't know if it could ever be forgiven.

Shifting back into my wolf, I reached for that faint trace of the connection I held with Calli. It was like the smoke formed in my mind and mapped out a path to her. I didn't need to follow Blake's scent to find her, but it wouldn't hurt to have something to reassure us we were on the right track.

I set off at a fast pace again, trusting the others would

follow. To be honest, I didn't care if they did or didn't. My pack was by my side, and there was nothing we wouldn't do to get Calli back with us. We didn't need the rest of Wells' pack to back us up. We had everything we needed. We had the gifts Calli had given to us growing inside, and now that we were on our way to her, nothing would keep us apart.

34
CALLI

The glass shattered around me as I broke through, and the sliver of doubt in my mind broke with it.

I could do this. I *would* do this.

Landing on the ground, the jolt to my hip had pain blazing through my senses, and my steps stumbled, but I didn't let it slow me down as I headed straight for the trees.

Lifting my nose to the air, I scented my surroundings. A faint trace of hope started to light inside me until it was smothered by the sight in front of me.

I wasn't alone out here. Three wolves were already sprinting toward me, having heard the sound of me breaking through the glass. I probably could have outrun them if everything had gone to plan. I was small and fast. Even with my hip begging me to stop, I knew I'd be able to push through. But the magical barrier surrounding the house was something I should have foreseen. It was how she'd trapped me in the first place, and it was the reason I'd lost my connection to the others.

One of the guards shifted back to his human form as the other two moved around my other side to circle me. My lip raised in a growl as I tracked their movements carefully. I wasn't going back inside that place without a fight, and without Zoe and her magic to subdue me, I actually had a shot at getting through this.

Because I had something they didn't.

I had my magic.

Shifting back to my human form, I braced for a fight, knowing I'd be able to control my power more easily on two feet rather than four.

"We have orders to keep you alive, but not in one piece. If you come back inside with us now, this doesn't have to get bloody," the man in front of me sneered.

I couldn't help it. I laughed. And I kept laughing as they started to close in around me.

"I would have let you live," I whispered as the magic rose inside of me.

It was a magic I hadn't used as much, but it came to me when I called, along with something I'd felt when I'd been overwhelmed before. A tremor of worry ran through me when I felt it. I couldn't afford to be overwhelmed right now. But then a sense of resolve set in. This was my magic, and I would use it to protect myself. I shouldn't be the one that was afraid right now.

As they leapt, jaws wide, ready to take me down, vines ripped from the ground, wrapping around them. My mother would have shown mercy; she would have told me that they were only doing what their alpha had ordered them to. But at that moment, I didn't care. Why should I show them mercy when they had none for me?

I paid little attention to the pitiful yelps and whimpers of the wolves behind me. They'd decided their path when they'd decided to follow Stone's word.

The man in front of me watched with wide eyes of horror

as his packmates died terribly behind me. He didn't even flinch when the veins wrapped around him, and I started to slowly walk in his direction.

"Did you ever, for one second, think what you were doing could possibly be wrong?" I asked.

I felt like a piece of my soul was stripped away as the screams died out behind me.

"I…I…" he stuttered as if only just realising the situation he was in. "Please, please, don't."

"Don't?" It was like my mind was working through a fog as I struggled to understand what he could possibly be begging for. "Do you actually believe you deserve to live? Mere seconds ago, you were threatening to hurt me."

A voice was shouting in the back of my mind, but I couldn't quite hear the words. All I could concentrate on was the man in front of me and the magic that wanted to make him pay. He was a threat to our bond. They were *all* a threat to my bond.

The vines wrapped around his neck and torso, and I watched as they slowly tightened their grip, squeezing the life from him.

His mouth gaped as he fought for the air he needed to live. It was fascinating. The magic inside me purred at the sight, and I couldn't take my eyes away from him as I watched the life draining away.

I saw the moment he realised that struggling was futile, the moment he accepted all was lost, and this was his end. Then, as the light started to dim in his eyes, another scream tore from the house, and the barrier around us flickered for a second as it weakened.

At that moment, when the barrier dimmed, I heard them.

I heard them all calling out for me, and it cleared the clouds.

Recoiling back in horror from what I was doing, the vines withdrew, and the guard fell to the ground. I watched for a terrifying second until I saw the faint rise of his chest accompanied by his rattling breath.

I couldn't believe what I'd been about to do, what the power inside of me had tried to urge me to do.

This wasn't me. This wasn't who I wanted to be.

I couldn't bring it in me to turn around and see what I'd done to the others. Instead, I turned to the barrier and assessed how the hell I was going to get out of here. When it flickered again, I sent a wave of love to my mates. I knew they'd feel it. I'd felt them reaching out after all.

The barrier flickered again, but the screaming seemed to be lessening not in frequency but in amount. I had a terrible feeling that whatever it was she was doing to herself, it was nearly over, and if there was one thing I knew for sure, I didn't want to be here when she was done.

I didn't have the knowledge to be able to break whatever spell was holding the barrier in place around the cabin. I was toying with the idea of trying to force my way through in one of the moments when it flickered with weakness. But then my eyes caught on the way the trees around me swayed in the breeze. How the branches seemed to be able to move even though the barrier should have been holding them in place.

With a theory forming in my mind, I scuffed my shoe across the dirt until I came across what I needed. Picking up the rock, I tossed it in my hand as I imagined the inevitability of this thing bouncing off the barrier and smacking me right in the face. So with a grimace and an embarrassingly bad throw, I sent it at the barrier—and that fucker sailed straight through.

Moving closer, I held up my hand, but when I met with the barrier, it was like pressing up against cold stone.

So it would seem like this barrier either kept people, or more specifically me, inside.

That meant I needed to find another way out of here.

I had the crazy idea of seeing if I could just drive a car through it, however, there wasn't one here. But on the back of that, I started to think of something else. What if I could just dig my way out? Would the barrier extend down past the ground? I had no idea how strong Zoe was, but given that the barrier was still flickering, she had to be weakening.

I was about to shift into my wolf form and go through the embarrassing task of digging myself out when my magic rolled back to the surface instead.

I wanted to push it away, afraid of what would happen. I'd never been so afraid of my magic as I was right now. I'd never experienced a loss of control, except it was more than that. It wasn't that I'd lost control of the magic. It was that it had taken over me. And for some reason, that felt infinitely worse.

Deciding that I didn't have the time to wimp out of this, I let the magic pool to the surface again, except this time, I made sure not to allow it free rein. I felt it reaching for the ground and the root systems that ran beneath my feet. In my mind's eye, I watched as they moved, rearranging themselves to move the earth away and construct a tunnel insulated by the roots themselves.

It didn't take long for the dirt on the surface to fall away, revealing a hole large enough for my wolf to be able to walk through. Quickly shifting, I entered the tunnel without hesitation. The cabin behind me was quiet, and the screams seemed to have stopped. I couldn't afford to delay now in order to work up the courage to step into a damn hole.

I ran through, trying not to think about being buried alive, and with my eyes closed for every step of the way. It was a straight shot through; it wasn't like I would get lost.

I only opened my eyes when I felt the tunnel floor starting to rise back to the surface, and when I did, I was granted the blessed sight of the sky above me. I'd never realised I was a tad claustrophobic, but then I'd never run through a hastily constructed tunnel held up by nothing but tree roots.

A shudder ran through my body as I reached the surface and used my magic to quickly seal the tunnel behind me.

I didn't turn back or hesitate for a second as I ran for the trees as fast as my paws could carry me. The bond blazed back into life, and I could hear all of my mates sigh in relief.

"I'm coming to you. Please tell me that you didn't hurt Blake."

35
TANNER

Hearing her voice in my head again had me nearly falling over my own paws. Thank fuck, she was safe, and we were so close to having her back.

None of us slowed our pace, not wanting to stop until we had the reassurance of her back in our arms. The poor woman wasn't going to get a moment's peace after this. I doubted we'd ever let her leave our sight again.

"She's alive, and we're nearly with her," I sent down the link to Aidan, who I knew would be anxiously waiting for word of what was happening.

He wasn't her mate, so he didn't have the same overwhelming need to find her, but I was still impressed he'd managed to stay with the pups rather than running out to join us in our hunt.

Grey's howl had echoed across the packlands, and even members of Wells' pack had transformed at the sound. It was the call of an alpha, and they were powerless but to answer it.

A shiver ran down my spine as I remembered the pain in that sound. I knew straight away that something terrible had happened. I'd never heard him sound that way before, and I hoped I'd never have to again.

Calli. She'd become our entire world overnight, and I didn't know how I'd survive without her. Perhaps the insanity that followed from losing a mate was actually a blessing. Why would anyone want to continue on without them?

Stone had to die. There was no other end to this whole mess. The fact that he was my father should have made it a difficult conclusion to come to, but he'd long ago lost the right to claim the title. I hadn't thought of him as my father in years. In fact, I'd tried not to think of him at all.

I should have hated him for what he'd done to me when I was a child, but I'd dealt with that long ago and written him off as not worth it. Then, meeting Maverick and learning how deep his deception ran made me change my mind. I wanted to see him suffer. I wanted to stand over him and see the look in his eyes when he realised his life was about to end. He was the ghost in my past I'd never exorcised, and it was time for Stone to be eradicated.

It was impossible to miss the white flash of fur darting through the trees toward us, and everyone picked up the pace to reach her.

We clashed in a tumble of wolves as everyone tried to reach her at the same time. It was only her yip of pain that had us all backing away.

"What's wrong? Are you hurt?" Grey asked, circling Calli in his wolf form as he scented her for any injuries.

"She did something to my hip. She took some of my bone marrow. It hurts, but I can make it back," Calli reassured him, nuzzling against Grey's wolf to stop his pacing. "Grey, please tell me that you haven't hurt Blake."

With a growl, he stepped away, shaking his head. "He

will pay for what he's done, Calli, but he's alive for now. He's betrayed the pack. There have to be consequences."

In a move I never would have thought him possible of, Grey turned away from our mate to face the way we'd come. We hadn't travelled too far out of the packlands. To be honest, I was surprised Wells would have allowed there to be a location so close to his lands where his enemies could take shelter. We were out in the middle of nowhere here. It was actually pretty shocking there even was anywhere for miles around.

"Let's return to the pack. I want Calli back behind the walls as soon as possible," Grey ordered.

Lachlan and River both moved to Calli's side, pressing close to her in reassurance. Calli's head fell to the side, and I saw her eyes flutter closed as she sought the comfort of the touch of her mates.

Maverick watched them closely, and a flicker of his indecision filtered through the bond to me. I knew exactly how he felt.

We might not consider Stone to be a father to us anymore, but he was still our blood. How could Calli ever trust us when it was our family who kept trying to tear her away from us?

It was only when her mates pulled away from her that Holly bounced over to Calli in concern. Rubbing against her side like a cat until Nash barged her out of the way. Nash dipped his head to Calli respectfully and then darted to the side to avoid the ire of his mate who was now snapping at his tail.

The run back to the pack was at a slow pace. Grey headed our pack, and I found myself falling beside Maverick as we took the rear. River and Lachlan stayed at her side, and we kept her protected in the centre.

Calli was favouring one of her back legs, and I was glad

to see that Grey had at least slowed the pace to account for her injury, despite his annoyance.

I could tell something was bothering Maverick, but he had a firm wall around himself, projecting nothing into the bond. He'd gotten far better at it than I had.

"He needs to die," Maverick finally said to me through the bond. "We have to promise each other that he doesn't get to sit in a prison cell when we get to the end of this. I don't want to risk that he has any chance of freedom."

"I couldn't agree with you more, Brother."

My wolf snarled, and I did nothing to suppress it. I caught River's glance of question in my direction, but shut down the bond as much as I could. He wouldn't understand. He'd want Stone to stand trial, to admit the things he'd done in front of our people and be held accountable for them. There was only one way he could pay for his crimes, with his own life.

When the gate to the packlands came into view, it was accompanied by the sight of Wells standing there with a group of his guards, waiting for us. He looked more stressed than I'd ever seen him before. I supposed it was expected when you were waiting for one of the most powerful alphas you'd ever met to return after a traitor in your pack had caused the loss of his mate.

As Grey picked up the pace, I knew he was going to do something stupid. Even though the beta side of my brain was urging me to intercept him and encourage him to think this through, the other part of me was enraged that my mate had been put in danger.

The black cloud of Grey's alpha power flowed around him, making it look like he was running on a storm cloud of his own rage. The guards all stepped back, looking worriedly at Wells for reassurance.

We hadn't trained with them yet, and they wouldn't have

seen the evidence of our power. I doubted they'd ever known before now that we were different from them, unless Wells had been considerate enough to give them a heads-up about what was returning to the pack.

It didn't take long for the rest of us to show evidence of our own power. We weren't as strong as Grey, and we didn't have as much practice with it, but it was like the cloud of his power around us called to mine. I felt the warm rush of magic crackle over my fur, and I saw the answering glow in the others who ran beside me. Only Calli seemed to retain control of her power, but having had it all her life, she must have had better control than us.

Grey shifted as we neared and strode forward to our greeting party without even breaking his step.

"We have Blake contained in the cells in the packhouse basement," Wells said as a greeting.

It was smart. To redirect Grey's rage at another target rather than face it head-on alone. Wells would have made a good beta if he hadn't taken an alpha role.

Calli shifted and stepped out of our circle, addressing Wells directly before Grey could even open his mouth. "Keep him in the cells tonight, and we will speak with him tomorrow. No one is to be allowed anywhere near him. If he requires further healing, I will deal with it myself. In the meantime, I need to speak with Grey and my mates about the information I have obtained. Perhaps you and Sean would like to join us?"

My mouth would have dropped open in surprise if I'd been in human form. Thankfully, my wolf was panting and at least hiding the shock that would have been on my face otherwise.

This was the first time Calli had stepped up and looked every inch the Queen she was supposed to be. No one questioned her. Grey might have bristled at first at her speaking before him, but I knew him well enough to see the pride shining in his eyes.

For whatever reason, Calli was avoiding the whole Queen issue. None of us had pressed her on it, apart from mentioning it the first night we were here. I couldn't work out what her issue was. Something was holding her back, and it wasn't fear of not being enough for the role. There was something specific, and the fact that I couldn't put my finger on it was driving my beta need to fix everything mad.

"Sean is waiting for us back at the house with Jessa," Wells said before turning to the guard. "I want one of you in every guard pairing for the rest of the night. No one moves without your knowledge. In the morning, I want a thorough report on every single move everyone made today. Someone let those people into our pack, and I want a name by the morning."

The guards nodded in agreement and slowly filtered away, casting a curious look back in our direction. It was impressive that they'd done as he asked without question, but I couldn't help but consider if it was a good way to manage these people. If he was giving them this job, they were his most trusted inner circle. Still, by not telling them everything, he was essentially admitting he didn't trust them completely.

Perhaps we couldn't afford to give our trust so freely, not when there seemed to be traitors around every corner. Maybe we'd gotten ourselves into this position because we trusted too easily and didn't ask enough questions.

Turning back to us, Wells addressed Grey directly. "If you are happy to take this back to the packhouse, I think there is a lot we need to discuss."

Grey nodded. "I'll have Aidan stay with the children while we break down what's happened. We need to discuss how we're going to address this whole situation with them. I don't want to leave the pups unprotected all the time, but I'm finding it hard to know who we can trust with them. We can't afford to have one of my pack guarding them all the time when they're one of the few animage fighters we have."

Wells nodded in agreement and quietly led the way back to the packhouse. I could see that he was struggling with what had just happened, and his mind was trying to figure out who could have betrayed him.

I found myself wondering how Wells coped without a beta at his side. I knew he'd explained that they ran the pack differently, but leadership wasn't the only reason to have a beta. Alphas needed someone beside them who could keep a calm head when their alpha need to protect was pushing them to do something rash. I supposed Sean did that to some extent, but he couldn't be here all the time.

Wells led us through to the kitchen, where the table had been laid out with food. For some reason, the sight made me pause. It seemed strange to think about something like eating at a time like this.

"Eat," Jessa urged, appearing next to the table with an enormous platter of cold meats. "You've all expended a lot of energy for one of the first times. If you don't feed yourselves now, you will crash later."

After placing the platter down on the table, she walked around to Calli and pulled her into her arms.

"It is good to have you back, niece," she said earnestly.

We all saw Calli stiffen at the touch, and there was no way that Jessa wouldn't have felt it, but she chose not to address it. It would take time for Calli to be able to form any kind of close relationship with Jessa, and she was nothing but understanding about it.

Sean appeared next with a tray of tea, and I swear I saw

the glimmer of a tear in Calli's eye. There were even those weird oat cookies that Grey had basically stolen from me when I'd discovered her stash.

Almost as if he could read my thoughts, Sean slid the tray further away from me and nearer to Calli. The dragon could try all he wanted, but one of those cookies was mine!

The weird internal monologue I had going on was actually helping me feel more like my old self again. I broke the bizarre stand-off we all seemed to have entered into by grabbing a plate and starting to load it up. I had a plan that if I casually made my way around the table, I could end up by the cookies and make my move then.

Calli sat down at the table with a pained look, and Grey knelt at her side, tenderly taking her hand in his. It baffled me how he'd turned into this grumpy hard-ass overnight, but when it came to Calli, he could never hold out for long.

"Let me see," he all but ordered her.

Calli carefully lifted her shirt and let Grey pull the leggings she was wearing down enough to bare her hip. The bruising had already taken hold, and the entire area was a deep purple, almost black. At the centre was a small ragged hole that had thankfully stopped bleeding, but the scent of her blood still filled the air.

Maverick slammed his plate down and had to take a step back as he turned around, fists clenched at his side. I still got absolutely nothing through the bond from him, but I could tell he was barely containing his rage at the sight of Calli being hurt.

Grey carefully examined the wound before turning to Sean, "Do you have any antiseptic? Her wolf should be enough to heal it as long as there is nothing inside the wound, but I don't want to risk an infection setting in."

Sean nodded and moved over to the sink, rummaging

through the kitchen cabinet below before he pulled out a kit that looked similar to our own. I took it from him and moved around to help with Calli's injury.

Up close, it didn't look any better, but it didn't look any worse either. I could tell it was deep as I gently cleaned it and applied the antiseptic. Calli bravely held still as I worked, but there was no way this wasn't hurting her.

"I don't think it needs a dressing. The bleeding has already stopped, and the hole will probably have healed over by tonight anyway," I told her, looking up only to find Calli smiling down at me and holding a cookie out in her hand.

"I think I'm supposed to give *you* one for being so brave," I joked, but I took it from her anyway. I wasn't going to pass up what could be my only chance. These things were well protected normally.

Did it say something about me that I was as motivated as the kids were if cookies were involved?

Her soft smile brightened into a full-blown grin, and I nearly swooned at the sight. She'd been through a traumatic experience, she looked tired and like she really didn't want to be going through the whole thing with everyone, but she was still the most beautiful woman I'd ever seen.

"We can do this later if you want," I reassured her.

I didn't care if anyone disagreed with me. If she needed a break, I'd make sure she had it. Hell, I'd even take on the dragon for her.

"No. It's okay. We need to get this done, so we can work out what we're going to do next." Looking around, she found Lachlan off to the side, and a flicker of sadness crossed her face. "You're going to want to sit down for this," she told him grimly.

Lachlan looked more confused than anything, but he took the opportunity to sit on Calli's other side and take her hand in his. If anyone looked worried, it was Jessa. Although, that perhaps wasn't quite right. She looked more sad than anything else.

Calli looked over at her aunt, and they took a moment to regard each other. I had no idea what was going on, but it was only when Jessa nodded sadly at Calli that she turned to Lachlan and started to talk.

"The woman we saw standing outside of Stone's facility. The one he was arguing with. She was the one who took me. She was the one that was running the experiments at the facility. She's your sister, Lachlan," Calli explained.

No one spoke as we all waited to see what he would say. In the end, he just nodded, and Calli went on.

"Stone is using her to find out how to make his own Queen. Ultimately, the experiment was then going to be performed on her. If it was successful, Neressa would have undergone the procedure."

"So, she has a shifter and a witch parent?" River asked, "That wouldn't explain why we couldn't place her scent, though?"

"No, both her parents are witches. They've already found a way to turn witches," Calli told us.

"I don't understand why she would risk undergoing the procedure herself. If it was unsuccessful, they would have lost the one doing the research. Surely it would have made sense to use any other witch from Neressa's coven," Wells interjected. "There's no guarantee that just because it works on one witch, it would work on another."

"From what I can gather, they were working on a genetic basis. They believed if it worked on Zoe, the process would transfer to Neressa because she was one of the last remaining blood relatives she had."

Everyone in the room looked shocked by this information,

and it took a moment for my brain to put together what Calli was saying. At first, I didn't see the importance of this woman being related to Neressa. It was fairly ordinary that she'd have relatives out there somewhere, even if they were distant. But then it clicked, and my head whipped to look at Lachlan to see how he was taking it.

Lachlan was slowly nodding his head. It was like you could see the cogs turning in his mind.

After a moment, he said, "It doesn't change anything. She's dead now, and we don't have to deal with her ever again."

Calli looked nervous, and it was clear she knew something else and wasn't relishing the thought of having to be the one to tell him.

Jessa stepped forward as if to speak, but Lachlan raised his hand. "I would rather hear it from my mate." Lachlan cradled Calli's hand against his chest as he looked at her like she was the only other person in the room. "I can deal with anything if it's from you," he said quietly.

Calli gripped his hand tighter, and I moved around her to stand at Lachlan's back. I was his beta, and I would always have his back, even if he didn't understand what that meant yet.

"Zoe, your sister, she said you were stolen away from them. I believe your magic being bound was done to hide you, so they wouldn't be able to find you."

Lachlan nodded, and then he shrugged like it was no big deal. Turning to look at Jessa, he simply said, "It was you, wasn't it?"

Jessa nodded as Wells came to her side, wrapping his arm around her waist. "It's time to tell them the whole truth."

She looked up at him before placing her head against his

chest. "They will never forgive me. I only just got them. I never had a chance to show them how sorry I was."

"It's time, Jessa. Lachlan deserves the truth, and you deserve to be free of the burden of keeping this a secret. You will always have me. We'll always have each other."

No one pointed out the flaw in his logic. Even if Grey had no intention of following through and making the challenge, as far as Wells was concerned, he'd be taking the pack and, most likely, his life along with it.

Jessa didn't turn back to look at any of us. Instead, she kept her forehead leaning against Wells' chest, like she couldn't bear to see the look on any of our faces as she spoke.

"I was young when they first approached me. I barely had any freedom in the coven. They watched me so closely. I was never allowed to go anywhere alone, to have a moment's peace. They were so worried that they'd lose their seer. I knew my sister was on the outside, putting together the plan to stop the terrible future we'd seen when we'd last been together. And I started to hate her for it. I started to resent the fact that she was the one who got to be free, and I was trapped in that coven, with those despicable people every day." She spat the words as she spoke, and it was easy to see just how much she meant them.

"Then, one day, a man approached me. He paid attention to me because of who I was, not what I was. He seemed to understand how I felt, what I was going through as being seen as nothing but a tool to be used. Looking back now, he was grooming me, but he became my entire world back then. The only person I could talk to who truly understood me. And then he told me about a different kind of coven. Of course, I knew which one he meant, but my resentment had grown so thick I couldn't see clearly. I lost sight of…everything."

Calli stiffened in her seat, and I watched the knuckles of the hand she held onto Lachlan with turn white.

"At first, I fed them information on what the Triquetra was doing. Every move they planned against Neressa, I told her. I wanted her to bring them down. I wanted to stand over them at the end and see the look on their faces when they realised their little tool had been working against them the whole time. Then one day, I'd been taken to Neressa's coven through a portal, and everyone was running around panicking. They'd hit a bigger pack to gather more crystals for the resurrection process, and the pack had managed to fight back, to injure some of the coven members. Because they hadn't been able to go through the extraction process, they'd captured as many shifters as possible and put them into cells. They were…children. So many children."

Jessa had moved away from Wells' chest as she told us her story, and the tears were streaming down her cheeks. She had a faraway look on her face, as if she was living through the whole thing again.

"The things they did to them. I realised I'd made a mistake. I saw what they really were and what I'd become, and I knew I needed to do something to try and make amends, to try and make a difference. The crystal magic was taking too long, and they were starting to grow desperate. Someone started to look at other ways to boost Neressa's power, to resurrect her. They started to look into other sacrificial magic. You were born so strong, Lachlan. A bright light in a dimming line of witches. Some believed that with Neressa remaining in stasis, her magic couldn't return to the well. That she was withholding magic from her line. But then there you were, a miracle child, stronger than any that came before you."

Lachlan rocked back in shock at the words. Nothing so far

had surprised him more than her talking about his power as if it was this fabled thing.

"I couldn't let them take another child. One night you were just there, alone in your room, and there was no one around to stop me. I saw it as a sign from fate, and I took you. I stole you away and hid you at the coven, binding your magic and placing an enchantment on you that would turn the hearts of others away from you. It was the only thing I could think of to keep you safe. To make you unseen, just one face in an ocean of witches."

"But how did you stop Neressa's coven from drawing you back in? They couldn't have been happy to lose you?" Grey asked, his eyes shifting from Jessa to Lachlan in concern.

"I continued to visit the coven as normal for a while, feeding them information that the Triquetra was starting to become suspicious. Eventually, I told the maiden I'd had a vision that someone would break into the coven house and make an attempt on her life. Security in the coven was tripled overnight, and there was no moving without being seen then."

"You made my entire life miserable," Lachlan said quietly, his eyes cast to the floor as his forehead scrunched in pain.

"It was the only way to keep them away from you," Jessa rushed out. "It was the only way I could hide you. They would have had you sacrificed. As soon as I saw you, I knew who you were. I knew how important you'd be. I couldn't let them take you away from Calli. Losing you would have ruined everything."

Lachlan reared back like she'd slapped him. "Ruined everything?" he scoffed as he quickly stood from his chair, rocking it back to crash against the kitchen floor. "I am a *person*!"

I could see he wanted to say more. He wanted to rage and

lash out. The house trembled as his rage began to build, and all the time, his eyes were locked on Jessa.

She didn't cower. She didn't try to hide away and escape his wrath. She stood strong, and the tears fell down her cheeks, but she was prepared to face his punishment for what she'd done to him.

In the end, Lachlan turned and stormed out of the room, slamming the door closed behind him.

"The binding is nearly broken," Jessa said quietly. "He will be free soon, even if we don't break it ourselves."

"That won't take away what you did to him," Calli said quietly. It would seem that she was the only one of us capable of speaking. The rest of the room was still reeling from the show of power Lachlan had put on and the fact that it wasn't even completely free yet.

"I know."

"I need to know one thing," Calli added, standing from her chair as she went to follow Lachlan. She paused by the door, holding onto the handle with what looked like a death grip. "Did you have anything to do with my parent's death?"

Jessa gasped in horror at the implication of what Calli was asking. I couldn't see how she was surprised. She'd basically confessed to working against the underground for years. It wasn't a far leap into assuming she could still have been feeding them information at that time.

"No," Jessa said sadly. "I would never have betrayed my sister like that."

"That lie may help you sleep better at night, but you know you betrayed her every day you worked with those monsters," Calli spoke softly, and for some reason, it was harsher than if she'd have screamed it at Jessa.

"Calli, I…"

"Don't. I can't look at you right now. Not when Lachlan

is hurting. He needs me, and I won't let you keep anyone else away from him."

I wanted to go with Calli when she left, but Grey's hand on my shoulder stopped me from going. Looking up at him in confusion, he shook his head, and I knew what he was saying. To let them be alone. But I didn't want to. I didn't want to leave Lachlan to work through this, even if he did have Calli by his side.

"We need to decide what we're going to do about the Blake situation," Grey said gravely, and I reluctantly turned back to the room.

Wells had Jessa in his arms, trying to comfort her as best he could. He didn't look like he wanted to talk about traitors right now. Sean was the only one sitting at the table now. The frown he had on his face betrayed just how troubled he still was about what Jessa had done, and this couldn't have been the first he knew of it.

When you sacrificed years of your life trying to build a movement and save a species, it must be pretty hard to listen to how someone you thought you could trust had been working against you. But, even if it wasn't exactly new information, betrayal would still cut just as deep as the first time you found out about it.

With a sigh, I sat down in the chair Calli had left. Even the plate of the coveted cookies in front of me wasn't going to improve my mood now.

"None of us would have done any different if it had been the price to keep one of our pups safe," I said, looking at Maverick. Since he'd said the same thing, I couldn't get the thought out of my mind.

"You would never have put Calli in that…" Grey started.

"No," I interrupted. "But someone else, someone who

wasn't my mate. If I was desperate enough. If I felt alone enough that it seemed like my only chance…"

"The coven are experts at finding your weaknesses and exploiting them. They are masters at manipulating your emotions. Neressa would have told Stone exactly what to do. If things had turned out differently, I would be just as upset as you are. But we have Calli back safely," Jessa pointed out.

I didn't envy Grey for having to be the one to make this decision. Hell, it was one of the reasons why I'd never wanted to be an alpha. It wasn't that I didn't care about the pack. It was that I couldn't handle the responsibility. I could be the hard-ass if I absolutely had to be, but I preferred being the lovable goofball everyone came to with their problems.

"She was hurt," Grey gritted out. "We still don't know what they did to her or how it will affect the coming events."

"How about we take the day?" Wells suggested. "Nothing needs to be decided now. Spend time with your mate, rest and think it through. Then, we can come back to the Blake situation in the morning with fresh heads and calm minds."

It was so unlike the councillor to be the sensible voice of reason that everyone was giving him the side-eye. It would be just our luck to find out he'd been replaced with an evil witch and was the traitor all along. Fucking hell, could they actually do that?

Grey almost deflated on the spot as he dragged his hands down his face.

"What about Jean?" River asked. "Isn't she on her way?"

"Yes, she'll be here in the morning," Sean confirmed sadly.

It didn't help that it wasn't too long since we'd been through a similar situation with Wallace, and that had turned out all kinds of fucked up. Blake was someone who deserved our sympathy and understanding, but Grey was burned from the Wallace situation, and I doubted he'd have it in him to risk it all again. No, he was merely biding his time to accept that he had to come to the worst possible conclusion, and it was going to be my job to persuade him not to.

What was I saying about responsibility earlier? Nothing like a life or death situation to keep you on your toes.

36

CALLI

I hadn't found Lachlan last night. I'd made it as far as the front door, which was standing wide open, when his voice came through the link to me.

"I just need to blow off some steam, sweetheart. I promise I'm okay. I'm going to shift and run. Now seems like as good a time as any to give it a go on my own."

"Do you want me to come with you?"

"No, I need to try and do this myself. I'll come and find you when I get back, okay?"

I didn't want to agree. I didn't want him to be alone. He'd been alone all his life, and he didn't have to be anymore. But I could understand the need to think things through without having to deal with anyone else's emotions.

"Be safe," I told him, knowing I needed to let him go.

Lachlan didn't return until well into the early hours of the morning. I knew because he still hadn't returned when I'd fallen asleep around 3am.

The following day, I woke up in an empty bed, and my stomach just about leapt out of my throat in a panic as I assumed he'd never made it back. However, when I'd leapt out of bed and went running through the suite to Grey, I'd found Lachlan slumped in one of the armchairs in the sitting room asleep with a bottle of whisky still cradled in his lap.

I had a moment where I didn't know what to do. Was I supposed to wake him, or just leave him to sleep it off? He looked so uncomfortable where he was.

"How long have you been standing here staring at him?" River whispered in my ear as he came up behind me and pulled me to lean against his chest.

"I only just found him. I didn't know what to do."

"I'd suggest letting him sleep it off. He's going to be feeling that bottle this morning if he drank all of it. Yesterday was tough on him. Come on, the rest of us are waiting for you in the other bedroom," River said, threading his fingers through mine and gently tugging me away.

River led me through to one of the other bedrooms that was off the suite, and I found the rest of my mates inside.

"He still asleep?" Tanner asked, nodding toward the bedroom door.

River nodded quietly, closing the door behind him, and I had a moment where this felt a bit like a trap.

"Come and sit down, sweetheart," Grey murmured, opening his arms for me to go to him.

There wasn't even a doubt in my mind as I walked straight to him and allowed Grey to pull me onto his lap. This was Grey, and no matter what we went through, he would always be my mate, my alpha.

There was a twinge of pain in my hip as I snuggled against him, but it was nothing compared to yesterday. My wolf had healed me as much as it could through the night. By tomorrow, I doubted there'd even be a wound. It might hurt like a son of a bitch, but in actuality, the wound itself was pretty minor.

"It's time to tell us everything, Calli," Grey told me once I was settled in a comfortable position. "What happened?"

"I woke up in what looked like an old cabin. She'd strapped me down to a table, and was preparing to take my bone marrow. She explained everything I told you last night about who she was and who…who Lachlan was to her. Her name is Zoe. She knew Neressa intended to kill her once she knew the procedure was successful, but I suppose we sorted that out for her. She intends to take the position of Pack Queen and kill Stone. He thinks she will be his puppet Queen, and she'll give him the powers of an animage. She had absolutely no intention of letting that happen, though."

"I can't say my father deserves better. It's quite fitting that after all of his scheming and the things he's done to try and get this power he craves so much, in the end, it's going to be the thing that gets him killed. Maybe we should just let her do it," Tanner mused as he leaned back on the bed. It wasn't like him to sound so cold-blooded.

"She intends to take over the shifters and the witches," I told him, shocked by how accepting he was of his father's death. I knew he hated him, but there had to be a part of him that remembered Stone when he was happy, when his mother was alive.

Looking at Maverick, I could see the same determination on his face.

"This could be the thing that draws the humans' attention. None of the packs or covens will go quietly into being led by this woman. The Triquetra and the Shifter Council won't just step aside for it. There would be war, and this would be the thing that brings about the end."

Grey sighed. It was a lot of responsibility to place on our shoulders, the fate of not just our race but also the witches. No one had mentioned them before, but it seemed inevitable that if one of us would fall, so would the other. It was kind of ironic when you thought about it. All this time spent hating each other so much—the lies, the betrayal. And in the end, we'd all die side by side in the same mud, in a war we brought upon ourselves. A war our rulers allowed to happen by fostering hate and greed for their own purposes. Perhaps this was what we deserved.

"She has to be stopped," Grey agreed. "Even if we don't want to do it for the others, we have to do it for ourselves. If she wants to rule absolutely, then she can't afford to let any other Queens live. She'll come for Calli. She's too much of a threat."

The others looked panicked just from the mention of her coming. It was too soon after they'd lost me, even if it had only been for a few hours.

"What happened after she took your bone marrow?" Maverick asked, taking us back to what we'd been discussing.

"She added it to another mixture, and then she took it somehow. Whatever she was going through, it was painful. She was screaming as I…escaped."

"I still can't believe they found a way to turn a witch," Tanner muttered, shaking his head. "This will change so much in our world when it gets out."

"I got the impression that she can't shift yet, though," I added. "When I asked her, she avoided the question, and she was more than happy to tell me everything else I wanted to know. She almost acted like we were friends. It was creepy as fuck."

"Maybe she's not fully turned then," Grey said in interest. "If she isn't, maybe the Queen procedure won't work on her. That could be why it was so painful."

"I don't know about you, but I don't think we're lucky

enough for that to be the case." Tanner laughed. "With how things have been going recently, it's pretty safe for us to go with a worst-case scenario situation in everything we have to plan."

He did have a point.

"There's something you're not telling us," Grey eventually said, his arms banding slightly tighter around me, as if he thought I'd try to flee to avoid the question. "Something else happened."

"Oh, you know me that well, do you?"

"Yes, I do. So, stop avoiding the question."

Pffft, stupid man and his stupid paying attention to me and all my needs.

"When I escaped, I found myself inside a barrier with three guards. I lost control of my magic again," I admitted reluctantly. "I lost myself to what the magic wanted me to do, and I couldn't pull myself back from it. It was worse than last time."

"You haven't put your amethyst back on," Lachlan said from the doorway.

When I peered around River, I found him leaning against the door frame, looking like he could barely stand up, and he definitely looked like he was about two seconds away from throwing up.

Even though the amethyst wasn't there, my hand immediately went to my chest. It hadn't been since I'd given it to Jean. For some reason, when she'd given it back to me, I didn't want to put it back on. Even though it had become akin to a safety blanket for me. It felt like putting the amethyst back on was saying that I wanted to hide away again. And I didn't. I'd found so much when I came to Arbington. I'd not only found my mates, but I'd found myself. I'd finally been free enough to step outside as my true self, and my mates had shown me what it meant to not be afraid of that.

Jacob was still protected and always would be. At least he would be until we found some way to remove the spell from him. That would be his decision for the future now.

I couldn't bear the thought of going back to a life where I was afraid of the very thing I was. I shouldn't have to be. I cherished both sides of myself, and I refused to shut a part of myself away ever again.

"Jessa said it was the only way to regulate your power. It must be a way to help you control it," Lachlan explained before he staggered further into the room and sank down onto the bed.

I thought he was going to explain more, but he just sank onto his side with a groan instead.

Tanner laughed at the sight before poking him in the face. "Regretting your life choices?"

"No. They were all very well-thought-out, sensible decisions," Lachlan deadpanned before rolling to lie face down. "But I may die very, very soon. Remember me as a sober and less intoxicated person," he groaned.

I couldn't help but laugh at his dramatics. You'd have thought he'd never been hungover before. For a moment, I nearly reached out to try and heal his headache and settle his stomach, but then a cold sense of dread settled over me. What if I lost control again? What if I hurt him?

"Jean will be here soon. We need to decide what we're going to do about the Blake situation," River pointed out.

I could tell by the look on his face that he was buying me some time, and I appreciated it more than I could ever express.

Avoidance was definitely one of my worst qualities, but I found that when it came to things about myself, I needed to examine it in my mind from every possible angle before making a decision. It was definitely a character flaw I needed to work on.

"I've already decided," Grey told us before he lifted me off his lap and rose to his feet. "We should go and eat before she gets here. I'm going to ask the rest of the pack to come to hear my judgement, but I think you and Holly should be there for Jean, Calli. She's going to need your support."

"I won't let you kill him," I snapped out, facing down the alpha. "Blake did what he thought he had to, and none of us would have made a different choice. He tried to warn me and make me leave before I could be taken, but I wouldn't leave him there to die. You know Blake. You've known him all your life, and you know his true heart. He made a mistake but look at everything he's done for the pack."

"I am his alpha, and he betrayed me and his pack," Grey said, striding for the door.

"I know you think you're doing the right thing, Grey. But you will never forgive yourself if you take his life."

"I showed mercy once, and you nearly died, Calli. I'm not going to make the same mistake again." Grey paused in the doorway, his hands braced on each side. I could see how much this whole situation was hurting him, but if he took Blake's life, he would hurt so much more, I knew he would.

"Don't let Wallace take your integrity away from you, Grey. He's taken too much already."

"I need to speak with Wells. I'll meet you all downstairs," Grey told us grimly before walking out the door.

We all watched the doorway, hoping he'd come back, that he'd offer us some kind of reassurance that everything was going to be okay. I knew Grey was struggling with the amount of pressure he was under at the moment. If he'd let me, I'd help him shoulder the burden. Isn't that what we were supposed to do? He was my alpha, and I was supposed to be his Queen. A Queen terrified of her own magic who didn't feel deserving enough to slap that label on herself. He probably would have been better off if I hadn't walked into his life. At least his pack wouldn't have been drawn into this mess then.

They would all have been saved from so much if they'd never met me.

"I don't know what you're thinking right now, but stop," Tanner warned me, and I cast my eyes in his direction to where he was gently rubbing Lachlan's back, who looked to have fallen asleep again. "You're getting good at putting that block up, Calli, but I can still feel your pain and doubt."

I squinted in annoyance at him for calling out my self-doubt. There were definite pros and cons to this link, but I supposed in the long run, even some of those cons were actually pros when you looked at them. I didn't like being called out on my shit, but I could admit that it might be something I needed.

"We should go downstairs and wait for Jean to arrive," River pointed out, and I wasn't the only one that flinched at the idea.

I turned to look at Lachlan, who was now snoring softly on the bed. "Leave him for now. He definitely needs to sleep it off," Tanner snickered. He might be making fun now, but it didn't escape me that he'd been helping Lachlan fall asleep in the first place.

Tanner was a good man, no matter how much he tried to hide it behind jokes and laughter.

We had word that the cars were approaching the packhouse as we finished eating breakfast. The kids were excited to get back to school, and Maverick had promised to go with them today. I didn't know whether I should be insulted or glad they hadn't asked me to go. Why couldn't we go back to the simplicity of this morning?

"Calli, can we have a proper dinner tonight?" Jacob asked, looking at me with the big eyes he used when he wanted to get his own way.

Little did he know I was craving the exact same thing, and if I could get what I needed, I was definitely on board with the idea.

"Yes! Proper dinner!" Sean cheered. "Don't panic. I'll make sure you have exactly what you need," he declared.

"I guess that's a yes, then." I laughed as Jacob fist-pumped the air.

Predictably, the mere mention of food had Tanner's attention.

"What's a proper dinner?" he asked, looking at Jacob, who was now bouncing on the spot. "Oh my god, is it?"

Sometimes it was like I was surrounded by children as Tanner started to bounce up and down in tandem with him.

"Yorkshire puddings!" They both cheered, and I rolled my eyes even though I was laughing along with them.

Maverick and Lachlan, who had managed to make his way downstairs despite us trying to persuade him to go back to sleep, both looked confused. Either we hadn't had them for a while, or I was totally out of touch with how fast time was going by.

"You can't have any!" Tanner suddenly snapped,

waving his finger between the both of them. "You won't like them anyway. They're not that good," he said, trying to play it off.

"I'll make plenty for everyone."

"I would offer to help," Lachlan started, and then I was pretty sure I saw him visibly gag at the mere thought of food.

"Don't worry about it."

Standing on the front doorstep now, all I could think about was how I wanted to go back to the kitchen and randomly talk about Yorkshire puddings like they were the most important thing in the world.

I didn't want to be waiting for a woman I'd come to think of as a friend, to tell her that her husband had betrayed us all and was currently sitting in a cell in the basement.

"This is all kinds of fucked up," Holly grumbled, standing at my side. "Ten minutes ago, I was warm and cosy lying in my bed, worrying about this exact thing. Now you've dragged me out into the cold to experience what is possibly the worst thing in my life."

I nodded, even though I wasn't sure what she was trying to get at. We were all dreading what was about to happen, but I had a feeling she had a point coming up.

"I'm glad you agree. You can make it up to me by taking point on this."

"Yeah, I'm not sure it works like that," I murmured as the vehicles started to pull up in front of us.

"I'm seriously shitting myself right now," Holly said, her voice cracked with emotion, and my fists clenched at my sides.

Fuck Stone for putting us through this. Fuck him for taking one more thing away from us.

As Jean got out of the car and then fussed with the straps of the car seat to get little baby Tucker out, my mind raced with how we were going to do this. She turned to us with a beaming smile on her face. This should have been a happy time. It had been too long since we'd been together, and I could already see that Tucker had grown so much.

"It's okay, I'll do it," I told Holly quietly, and I saw her relax a fraction at my side before she reached out and took hold of my hand in solidarity.

Grey was my mate, and I was supposed to be the Pack Queen. Even if I didn't think I was up for the role, the least I could do would be to prove to the rest of the pack that I'd at least work hard for it.

Our feelings must have been showing on our faces because as Jean stepped forward, her face dropped, and her voice quaked in fear. "What's wrong? Where's Blake?"

Words completely failed me, and even though I opened my mouth to speak, nothing came out. My brain flatlined and hid, refusing to give me anything to say that would soften the blow of what we had to tell her.

"I'm right here, sweetheart," Blake said from behind us, moving through the crowd toward his wife.

Taking the baby carrier from her hand, he fussed over baby Tucker before pulling Jean into his arms.

"I missed you so much, Jean," Blake murmured into her hair as he held onto her tightly.

Grey came to stand beside me, and even though I should have been happy about what he'd done, I was also pissed that he'd left us out of the loop, assuming the worst.

"That was kind of a dick move, you know," I told him through the link, making sure the others could hear as well.

"It was only just decided. There's no point stressing her further by trying to keep her from him. Blake can tell Jean what's happened, and we can all talk about this like grown-ups."

"That's a massive change of attitude since, I don't know, five minutes ago," I snarked.

It probably wasn't wise to poke the previously annoyed alpha, but he needed to learn to share more. We were linked together, for Christ's sake, he didn't even need to come and find us.

I could feel amusement coming through the link, which I was pretty sure was coming from Tanner. Trust him to find something funny about this whole thing.

"You're right. I'm sorry," Grey told us, shocking no doubt a few of us. "Wells is surprisingly level-headed when you need him to be, and he made me realise that no matter what we decide to do now, Blake poses no threat to the pack. And with Jean and Tucker here, I doubt he'll be going anywhere."

"That was nice and yet still had an undertone of menace. It's weird reconciling this new uber-alpha version of you with the annoying brother I grew up with," River joked, but even through the link, I could make out the tension in his voice.

I hadn't thought about how difficult it must be for the others to watch the changes happening in their friends.

"Imagine how I feel," Grey grumbled before all of our attention was drawn back to Jean and Blake.

"So why do they all look like that? What happened?" Jean insisted.

I could see she was digging her heels in, and Blake wouldn't get away with not telling her anything. She was a strong woman in her own right, and she wouldn't stand for being kept in the dark.

"Let's head inside, and we can talk it through together," Blake suggested, looking nervously at Grey.

"If someone doesn't tell me, right now, what's happened,

I'm taking this baby, and I'm going back to where I came from!"

Blake locked eyes with his wife, and the rest of us all but held our breath to see what would happen. I wanted to hide inside. I didn't want Jean to think this was my fault because, to be completely honest, I was a little bit scared of the feisty woman.

"You're breaking my hand," Holly hissed, and I realised I was holding her tightly as we waited.

Jean's eyes darted to us at the sound, and for a second, I thought Holly was going to leap behind me.

"I am a traitor to the pack, and I'm waiting for judgement from my alpha," Blake told her calmly.

Well, talk about ripping the band-aid off.

Jean reared back like he'd slapped her, her eyes wide in disbelief.

"What do you mean? This has to be a mistake. You would never do anything to hurt the pack."

"It's not a mistake, Jean. I did something terrible, and Grey is within his rights to take my life for it."

It was strange to hear Blake say something like that so calmly. What was it with the men around here and being so weirdly accepting of death?

Jean turned to look at me. Rather than tears or upset in her eyes, she seemed calm and level-headed. It took a particular type of person to be able to step up when they heard that from someone they loved, and Jean was never going to be the type of woman that broke down.

"Explain it to me, please," she asked.

I had no idea why she needed to hear it from me, and I hoped like hell that if Blake saw his way through this, his relationship with her wouldn't be permanently damaged.

"Jean, I…" Blake started, only to be shushed by her.

"Not you. I need to hear it from Calli. She delivered my baby. She's going to turn me into a shifter. I know I can trust her with anything. I know she'll tell me the absolute truth."

Blake wilted on the spot, but he seemed to accept that he'd just lost some respect in his wife's eyes.

"Stone has been blackmailing Blake on the basis that he would hurt you and Tucker if he didn't work with him to hand me over. Yesterday, he led me to a place in the woods where I was taken by a witch who wanted to take my bone marrow and then kill me. Blake was shot in the process because, at the last moment, he tried to get me to leave. I was able to escape from where I was being held and make it back to the pack, but they were already on their way to save me," I told her frankly. It spewed out of me like word vomit. As soon as I started, it all poured out like I was delivering a report to a superior officer. For some reason, it felt important that she understood the pack would have come. That even though I was in danger, I would have been saved if I hadn't saved myself.

Jean nodded thoughtfully, her forehead scrunched in thought, before turning back to Blake. "You did this because you thought you were keeping our family safe?"

Blake nodded sadly before he added. "It was stupid. I should have gone to Grey as soon as I was approached. I should have trusted the pack to keep you safe, but at the time, the shadow demons had just attacked, and Holly was hurt. I didn't think you'd be safe at the pack. I'm so sorry, Jean."

"It isn't me you should be apologising to!" she screeched. "Calli brought our son safely into this world. Every time something has threatened the pack, she has put everything on the line to save us. She sacrificed so much to help me when the witches attacked. How could you doubt her?"

This was the entirely wrong time to be proud of the fact

that she saw his betrayal to me personally so much worse than the pack he'd been a member of for basically his entire life. Jean saw me and the things I was doing. I might not think it, but she saw me as worthy of her loyalty, and I understood how precious something like that could be.

Blake turned to me, tears in his eyes as he dropped to his knees in front of me. Hanging his head in shame, he admitted. "You could have got away if you left me to die, but you stayed to save me even though you knew it would mean being taken. I know I've committed the worst kind of crime against you, of all people, Calli. I wouldn't have Jean or Tucker if it weren't for you. I know an apology will never be enough, but I will give it to you anyway. I am so sorry I betrayed you. I swore my life to your protection, and I broke that oath. There is no possible excuse that could make that okay."

Grey stepped forward from my mates to stand next to me as Holly moved away to Jean's side. She looked broken at that moment. Like she'd already accepted the inevitable, and while she understood, it broke her heart anyway.

"We have had a member of our pack work against us before, and I was lenient with him to the detriment of the pack. I couldn't see the threat that he posed to us, and the pack, my mate, was hurt because of my short-sightedness, because I didn't have the stomach to do what was necessary. Under the laws of our people, you have two options available to you, Blake. You can accept death at my hands or walk into exile and accept your fate as a rogue."

Like hell I was going to let either of those things happen. Wallace had been an evil son of a bitch, and the day we'd burned him alive should be marked on a calendar as a national holiday. But Blake was just trying to protect his family, and Grey should understand how it felt to protect those who needed you.

"But, before my mate jumps in and verbally tries to castrate me, I know your heart, Blake, and I would never send you to either of those fates. The old ways, hell, even some of the new ways, don't work. We've always known that, and it's why we've tried to be different in our pack. It's why we live as a family of equals and not in a constant challenge for dominance. This cannot go unpunished, though, so I have spoken with Wells, and he has agreed to accept you into his pack. You have two options, you can take your family and go back to where Jean was taking shelter. Live out your life there in peace and put all of this behind you. Or, you can stay here. Show us that you are worthy of coming back to our pack and fight at our side."

Part of me wanted to fight. It didn't seem right that Blake had to leave the pack, but I could understand Grey's position. At least this way, he'd left a window open to give Blake the opportunity to come back if he wanted to.

"We'll stay," Jean declared, standing at her husband's side. "We'll both prove that we deserve a place in this pack. Because, after all, once Calli changes me, you're going to need to take me in too."

Grey chuckled at the smirk on her face. "And God help me, having you and Holly to contend with.

"Hey! I take offence to that! I'm a fucking delight, I'll have you know!" Holly protested, but the smile on her face showed just how relieved she was right now.

She wasn't the only one. It was only 8:30am, and I felt like I'd just lived through an entire week of stress and nightmares in the last two minutes.

"You scared the crap out of me, you know?" I laughed through the link, ready to move past this whole thing already.

"You should never have doubted me, sweetheart. I might be quick to anger right now, but when I've got the opportunity to think it through, I am capable of coming up with a reasonable solution."

"Hmmm, let's not get ahead of ourselves. This was just one occasion."

Tanner burst out laughing while the others started to move to the car to help with the enormous amount of baby things Jean seemed to have.

"They still doing that weird mind talking thing that we're pretending we don't know about?" Jean asked Holly, linking her arm with her friends.

"Yeah, it's exhausting keeping up the pretence that we don't know." Holly laughed before she pointed down at where Blake still knelt on the ground in shock. "I think you dropped something."

Jean looked down at Blake with a smile on her face. It was a smile you had when you looked at someone you truly cared for. The love practically radiated from her. "He can get himself up." She laughed. "Now show me where this bar is that you sneaked out to. Blake can handle the baby. Lord knows he's banked up about six years of babysitting duty."

"You've been gone for like two months," Blake protested, only to be drowned out by Nash asking. "When the hell did you sneak out to a bar?"

"Oh, I don't know. Maybe it was one of the million times you all went off to do pack stuff and forgot all about me," Holly snarked as she and Jean marched past him.

Ah, it was nice to have the ladies back.

"Maybe we could persuade Wells to take them both," Tanner whispered to Grey, only to be heard by them, judging by the look he got.

As Holly and Jean disappeared inside, whispering conspiratorially, Grey turned his attention back to Blake.

"I won't let you down," Blake insisted. "I will prove that I can be a valuable member of the pack."

"I know you will." Grey placed a hand on his old friend's shoulder and squeezed it gently. "And you need to start by coming to talk with Wells and me about how Stone contacted you and anything else you can think of that might help us."

Blake nodded determinedly and scooped up the baby carrier before following Grey inside. Maybe this was a good thing. Maybe Blake had some information that could help us. There had to be a reason why they wanted him out of the way.

Looking down at the ground, I realised I was surrounded by all the baby paraphernalia the other guys had gotten out of the car.

"You realise they're not staying here, right, and all of this needs to be at their house on the other side of town?" I pointed out.

They all looked at each other and then, with a sigh, turned around and started to try and get it all back in the car again. Why did babies need so much stuff?

37
RIVER

Sweat poured down my back as I ducked under Maverick's swing and darted up again, throwing a punch aimed at his kidneys, only for him to dart away with a laugh.

"This isn't supposed to be fun," Keelan barked out. "This could be the difference between life and death, so take it seriously."

Keelan was a massive hard-ass when it came to training. If he was like this with the guard, then Wells must have a very capable army ready to go here.

We were nearly a week in, and it was already becoming apparent that where we lacked the skill, we more than made up for it in enthusiasm. Not that enthusiasm would save our asses on the battlefield, but at least it had us showing up for training every day.

For some reason, I was actually really enjoying the training sessions. It was nice to feel like I was using my body for a change. I didn't realise how much I'd missed it when I'd been stuck behind a desk at work all day.

The magic lessons we took in the afternoon were just as

much fun, probably because Jessa was always so excited to see what we could do. She'd made it through most of us now, and it was Lachlan's turn this afternoon. I knew he was worried about having his magic unbound, but I think the thought of having to be alone with Jessa was bothering him the most. He'd avoided her completely since the revelations of his past and her role in his childhood.

Getting distracted as I watched Calli flip Aidan, I took a punch to the jaw from Maverick and fell on my ass. Rubbing my jaw, I looked up at the grinning wolf as he held out his hand to help me up.

"Get your attention on what you're doing and not staring at your pretty mate's ass!" Keelan barked.

A whip of Grey's alpha power lashed out toward him, grazing across Keelan's forearm before he managed to pull it back out of the way. Grey grimaced at the uncontrolled burst of magic, but Keelan waved him off.

It was the same problem we all had. Power wasn't a problem. It was controlling it that we struggled with. Jessa thought it was because Calli was so strong. Whatever it was, the power running through me was incredible, and I think we were all getting a bit too full of ourselves because of it.

The cackle that came from Holly only proved that I wasn't the only one watching what the others were doing.

Holly had taken to training like a machine. But we were definitely creating a monster. She was fast, like faster than most of us guys. As soon as Keelan showed her how to use her smaller size to her advantage, none of us stood a chance against her.

Because Holly, Nash, Aidan and Blake didn't have the same strength in their magic as the rest of us, they'd separated into their own group for training. And Holly was dominating that group to the extent that the other three seemed genuinely terrified when it was their turn to partner with her.

Holly was, of course, finding the whole thing hilarious.

Maverick tried to take advantage of my continued distraction by aiming a kick for my midsection. Grabbing his leg like I'd been taught, I dropped backward, pulling him down with me. Then as I flipped him, I shifted and made sure my jaws were at his throat by the time his back hit the ground.

"Nicely done, River," Keelan shouted across to us. "In the unlikely event that you're drawn into a fight before you've shifted, your best tactic is to shift at a time that offers you an advantage. You can all shift without pause, catching any attacker off guard is your best chance, especially if you're in a situation where you're outnumbered."

"I'd think my best advantage would be to take them down with the power I have available to me," Tanner joked.

"You can't grow to rely on it too heavily. You all struggle with control. If you end up in a high-pressure situation and lose the ability to call on it, you'd be lost to the cause immediately."

"Yeah, the cause. Because that's the most important thing here," Tanner grumbled, not liking being called out.

He'd always been like that, our sensitive joker.

"The cause is the only thing that matters," Keelan stated, his chest puffing up as he got ready to launch into his rhetoric.

It was one thing we'd all noticed over the last few days as we'd slowly started to integrate with more people in the pack. They were so fixated on the cause, the end goal of taking down Stone and whoever he was working with, it was almost like they'd forgotten they had the right to have a life.

Some of them seemed to almost worship Sean and Wells for what they'd done. On the one hand, I could see why they would. These people had been at their lowest when one of them swooped in and essentially saved their lives. Some of the stories we'd heard from the people here were harrowing, to say the least.

But then, knowing how they felt about their leaders, I had no idea why Wells thought Grey taking over this pack was even remotely a good idea.

Most of the pack had welcomed us with open arms. This was the first mixed pack of its kind. They were used to magic, and yet we were still viewed by some of them with distrust because of how different we were.

Grey had spoken with Sean and Wells and expressed our concerns about the pack's lack of knowledge of what we were. They needed at least some information if there was a chance they'd be going through the same changes as us in the future. Not that Grey had any intention of ever going through with it.

I backed away and let Maverick up, letting him shift as we started to circle each other. It was harder to train in this form without injuring one another, and Calli hated it when we did. So far, it hadn't been anything our shifter healing couldn't handle, but it was only a matter of time before one of us got carried away and made a mistake.

Maverick lowered himself down to his haunches, and his top lip raised in a snarling warning as he looked for his opening. It was a typical example of how training always went once we shifted.

My wolf responded in the only way it could, my ears laid back, and a growl rumbled through my chest. We might not want to hurt Maverick, but my wolf was having fun showing him that we were stronger.

I was always underestimated in our pack. I was the reserved one. The one who worked at the school. The little brother of the alpha who never amounted to anything. I knew that wasn't what they really thought of me, but it was how I thought of myself, in the dark moments at least.

But when we shifted, with all of this new power thrumming through my veins, it was hard not to revel in my newfound strength.

A crackle of soft light flowed across Maverick's fur, and I knew he was getting ready to use his magic. It was all of our tells, and even Jessa couldn't figure out how to mask the outward sign that we were about to make our move.

My own magic crackled across my fur in response, and the world fell into shades of blue as I stared out through a field of magic. Ever since I'd tapped into the power, it had started to grow, or perhaps it was just that it came more easily now. Either way, I knew my eyes would have lit up with the blue glow that signalled my magic was at the surface.

Keelan stepped further away from us, having grown used to the chaos when we started to fight, and magic came into the mix.

Maverick darted forward, his jaws snapping as he lunged for my foreleg. I felt the touch of his magic graze my paws as it tried to hold me in place, but I jumped to the side before he could grasp a hold of me.

Instead, I ran my claws down his flank. The sizzling sound of magic rubbing against magic filled the air, and blue and white sparks showered around us as our two powers clashed together.

Maverick growled in pain, throwing himself to the side as he tried to lessen the damage my claws were causing. Before he could draw another magical attack, I chose to shift directions. Using my magic, I locked my paws to the ground so I could turn quicker than ever before. Before Maverick had the time to move any further away from me, I latched my jaws around his rear leg.

The effort it took not to close my teeth around his bones brought sweat to my forehead.

It was a fight-ending move, and Keelan quickly called the fight before it could get out of hand.

"Disabling blow by River," he shouted. "Now, pull it back. You fools are not supposed to engage your magic in these sessions."

I darted backward, putting space between Maverick and me. It wasn't that I didn't trust him to not stop once the fight was called. It was more that I could feel the tinge of blood lust running through my wolf. It reminded me of the days when I'd struggled to control him, and I didn't like the reminder of how I'd come so close to failure on so many occasions.

Maverick shook his fur and then shifted back to his human form. There were no hard feelings. In fact, the grin on his face showed just how happy he was for me at gaining the upper hand on this occasion.

"That was incredible! I've never seen you move so fast before," Maverick said, walking over and slapping me on the back in congratulations. "How did you know how to do that?"

"I didn't. It just kind of happened. I knew I needed to turn quickly, and it was like the magic responded without me even thinking about it."

"Impressive," Keelan said, approaching the two of us. "You're starting to move instinctively and couple your magic with your physical movements. It's not something I can teach you, but I didn't think it would come to you this fast."

I glanced around at the others. Tanner was busy playfully tickling Calli, who had him trapped on the ground, and Nash was limping away from Holly, rubbing his ass for some reason, while Aidan took great pleasure at his distress.

Blake, as usual, was nowhere to be seen. The last few days, he'd asked Keelan to train him separately in the afternoon. It was easy to see that he was starting to slowly withdraw from the pack, and it hurt us all to watch. None of us wanted to lose him. At first, he'd been so adamant that he would prove himself, but then he started to pull away from us, and none of us knew what to do to encourage him back.

Grey and Lachlan had already started talking, no doubt discussing the basis of how to channel their magic for Grey to be able to mimic a similar mood.

Since he'd finally embraced his nature, Grey had a thirst for knowing everything he could about his changing wolf. He needed to as well. It was kind of terrifying how much power had come to Grey and the physical changes his wolf had gone through. Whereas the rest of us had to call on our magic, it seemed to always be there for Grey, moving across the fur of his wolf, like a dark cloud. Coupled with the red glow in his eyes, he cast a menacing picture. I definitely wouldn't want to face him in a fight.

Rumours had already started in the pack that Grey was possessed or some kind of hellhound. It wasn't causing us any problems at this point. In fact, we were all finding it fairly amusing, but someone would have to deal with it sooner or later.

"Let's call it for today," Keelan shouted, dismissing us.

We'd only been training for two hours, but Keelan's keen eyes had noted Maverick's slight limp, and as he assessed him, he seemed to decide we were done for the day.

I felt terrible that I'd hurt him when we were only supposed to be training, but Keelan was right. We were going up against wolves who'd had countless years to train. We couldn't afford to go easy now to spare anyone from getting hurt. It could be the difference between coming back from this fight and lying dead on a battlefield.

When had our lives turned into something that involved battlefield decisions? It only seemed like yesterday I was stressing out about unpacking my office and where I was going to hang my calendar on the wall.

38
LACHLAN

Training this morning had finished earlier than usual, which meant we'd broken for lunch earlier. That, in turn, meant I got to start my magic training earlier than usual.

Yey for me!

"Do you want me to come with you today?" Calli asked as she finished the last bit of the sub Tanner had made for her.

When it came to simple man food, Tanner was an excellent cook. Stick him in front of a grill, and the steaks that came off it were out of this world. It was actually surprising they all seemed to basically live and breathe pizza when he had the skills of a grill-master at heart.

"Actually, yeah. Do you mind?" I asked sheepishly.

It would be good to have Calli there as a buffer between Jessa and me. It wasn't that I didn't trust her. Yeah, she'd basically set me up for an entire life of torment and neglect, but she'd done it in an attempt to save my life. It was hard to be mad at someone when that was the reason behind their actions.

The problem was that I couldn't get past the betrayal. I'd thought for so long that she was the only person at that godforsaken coven I could trust. She was the only person I spoke to and the only one who was anything like a friend to me. And now I found out that she was the reason for it.

I just didn't know how to measure the person she was against the person I always thought she was.

The amethyst around Calli's neck caught the light, and as always since she'd put it on, my fingers itched to reach out and touch it. The pendant was such an unusual design. The big faceted stone wrapped in copper was unlike anything I'd seen before. It was beautiful, though, and it suited her.

Calli's fingers grazed against the pendant when she saw me looking. I'd noticed more and more that she did it without even thinking. Looking back, it was a move she always made even when she hadn't worn it. I supposed if it had been there all her life, it was probably more out of habit than anything else.

"Of course, I don't mind," she told me with a smile. "I wouldn't have offered otherwise. Besides, how else are you going to be able to avoid her when you're in the same room, and she's trying to teach you, if you don't have me as a buffer?"

"Wow, it's been that obvious, has it?"

"Yeah, you're about as subtle as a brick to the face." Tanner laughed.

"It might have been the way you always walk out of the room whenever she takes a breath to say something that gave it away," Maverick said, joining Tanner with his laughter.

It was nice seeing the two of them getting on. It had to be hard discovering a new sibling. Something I was keenly aware of myself. But at least for the two of them, it was like they'd always had the other at their side. We were probably going to hate it soon, but for now, it was still nice to see that they had each other.

"Well, I have no excuse other than I felt like it," I told them with a shrug.

At this stage, I didn't feel like I needed to explain myself. If anything, I felt completely justified in how I'd been acting over the last couple of days. But hand in hand with that, I could also accept that maybe it was time to get over myself.

We had a mission now. I had a mate I needed to keep safe. I didn't have time to pout over hurt feelings. It was time to step up and become what the pack needed me to be. It was time to unbind my magic and unleash everything I had on those who thought they could hurt us.

Calli held out her hand to me, and the gleam in her eyes spoke of the unwavering support I knew she had in her. I'd never need for anything when I had her at my side. She was everything. Calli was the reason we were all here and why we were fighting so hard to stay. I'd never let her go, and I sure as fuck would never let anyone take her from us again.

"Let's do this," I said, feeling a sense of determination come over me.

"We can all come with you if you need the support," Grey offered.

The others watched me carefully, almost as if they were waiting to see who they needed to fight for me. It was nice to finally have this family around me who would walk through hell if I needed them.

"I think I'm going to be okay."

Grey nodded in support, and I knew his unspoken words. I knew I only needed to reach for them through the bond, and they would be there.

Calli's hand squeezed mine, and we left the kitchen, heading to the small glade amongst the trees that Jessa had adopted as her training ground. It was one of those places that, even though it sat in the middle of a busy pack, it was silent, almost like you were completely alone in the world.

Jessa was waiting for us when we got there. She'd set out some blankets on the ground and sat in the middle with her eyes closed. Her face looked completely at peace, and I was actually jealous of her for a moment. She shouldn't be able to find a place of such serenity when my mind was spinning, knowing the truth of our past now.

Calli walked us over to the blankets, and I could admit that she might have had to tug on my hand a little as my feet started to drag.

Shit, maybe this wasn't such a good idea.

Settling down on the blankets, I suddenly found myself sitting in front of Jessa, who was now looking at me with a curious look on her face.

"Maybe this isn't such a good idea," I said as the panic started to set in. "Maybe we should move further out, away from the pack and anyone we could hurt."

"What exactly do you think will happen when I unbind the spell holding back your magic?" Jessa asked.

It was strange to enter into a conversation with her so normally. But, avoiding the truth of the awkwardness between us seemed like the only way we'd make it through this.

"I...I suppose I'm expecting some kind of backlash." I shrugged as I said it, realising how ridiculous it probably was. It's not like the binding was holding back a wall of magic. Was it?

"You may feel a surge, but I doubt it will hurt anyone in this clearing, let alone outside of it," Jessa replied calmly.

Unfortunately, her words had the complete opposite effect on me.

"Maybe you should go back to the house," I said, spinning to Calli in panic.

Was bringing her here a stupid idea? She would be right next to me, the first target my magic would have.

"Calli being here or at the house won't make any difference," Jessa told me. "I unbound your magic as you entered the circle. Now, close your eyes and concentrate on the well inside of you. Take note of the power that rests at your core and take your time to become familiar with it."

"What…what?" I stuttered.

At first, anger surged inside of me. How dare she? How dare she work magic on me without my consent again?

Except, she did have my consent, sort of. I'd come here with the intention of her doing just this. Was this the magical equivalent of ripping off the band-aid?

Making myself comfortable, I closed my eyes and sank down into that well of magic inside me, my rage still running in the undercurrent of my emotions.

It was like diving headfirst off a waterfall. The torrent of magic thundered around me before I was completely sucked in. It was unlike anything I'd ever felt before, and the turbulent stream of magic felt like it pushed and pulled at the very fabric of my being.

I wanted to gasp for breath, but I reminded myself that my body wasn't lost inside this raging magic. It was still sitting in the clearing with my mate and an old friend at my side. I was safe, even though I felt like I was about to be dragged down to my death.

Just acknowledging that this raging power couldn't hurt me had the torrent calm, and I found myself floating in what felt like a vast ocean of power.

Was this really *my* magic? Is this what I'd missed out on all my life?

A sense of loneliness welled inside of me as I thought about all the nights I huddled cold and unloved on the kitchen floor with no one to tell me that it was going to be alright. As if it sensed the sadness inside me, the magic around me warmed, enveloping me in a warm embrace.

It had always been there. Throughout every hardship, it had been there, quietly waiting inside of me. And now, when I was about to fight my hardest battle, it was ready to lift me up.

I felt a tear of gratitude fall down my cheek as I reached out into the well of power I'd sunk into, hoping it could feel how much I loved and wanted it. This felt like finally finding my place in the world. It was the part of myself I'd always been missing, and now that it was there, I could feel the part of me that had been a gaping hole before and was now filled with warm, comforting love.

Opening my eyes, I found Jessa's smiling face in front of me.

"You will achieve such amazing things, Lachlan. You were meant for so much more than Neressa's guinea pig. Your magic is beautiful, and I hope that one day, you'll be able to forgive me for holding it back from you for so long."

I looked down at my hands and watched as the strands of magic wrapped themselves around me like lightning, embracing the storm rather than striking out from it. The warm crackle of the magic was soothing. It made me feel strong. It gave me a sense of hope I hadn't even realised I was looking for before.

Turning to Calli, I saw the tears coursing down her face as she watched. "I can feel it," she gasped. "I can feel its happiness for being reunited with you."

It felt exactly like that. My forehead crinkled in thought. I'd always been taught that magic was a tool. Nothing different from a fork you held in your hand to eat with. But right now, I could feel my magic's joy. I could feel the way it rolled and surged with happiness. Was this how it felt for everyone? And if so, how could they not see it for the living thing it was?

Turning to Jessa in question, I found her holding out a deep purple gem. As the light from my magic hit it, it reflected in purple rays across my skin, and I recognised it as a large piece of amethyst.

I looked at her in confusion, not understanding why she would be giving it to me.

"This is a piece of amethyst that is the twin to Calli's. It was hewn from the same piece and crafted into this bracelet for you when her pendant was made."

Taking the gem from her, I felt it heat in my hand.

"Why are you giving this to me?"

"For the same reason I told Calli to wear her amethyst again. The power that you hold inside of you is vast, Lachlan. When you call upon it, it will come with a force no one has ever experienced before. The amethyst will help you to focus that power on what you need. But it will also provide a filter for your coven bond. The two amethysts will work in tandem to make sure you both don't overwhelm the others in your bond."

It hadn't even occurred to me what the others in our bond might experience when my power was unbound, and I blushed in embarrassment that my own hurt feelings had clouded the concern I should have felt for the children. I was pretty sure Cassia could handle anything if she put her mind to it.

"The children?"

"Are powerful enough in their own right," Jessa said, patting my knee in comfort. "They will have felt the flow of the coven bond rush faster, but not enough for it to cause them any discomfort or much of any notice. We really should discuss putting them into some form of magic classes soon. I'm already dreading the chaos they're going to cause once they get a grasp of it."

Jessa laughed at the thought as she turned to Calli, who nodded in agreement.

"Cassia was going to start teaching them, but then, with everything that happened at the pack, we were never able to set up a classroom. And of course, now she's had to go and help Davion out of whatever mess he's gotten himself into."

Calli sounded annoyed as she spoke, but I could feel the fondness for the vampire radiating through our bond.

Over the last few days, we'd all started to use our shielding less and less, becoming accustomed to sensing each other. It felt less like an embarrassing inconvenience now and was more of a comfort. Especially after Calli had been taken. If we hadn't been holding our shields so firmly in place at the time, we might have felt that something was wrong much sooner.

"So now, the hard work begins," Jessa said, clapping her hands together as she stood. "I want you to aim a bolt of lightning at that tree without hitting the two bottles I've placed in front of it."

My eyes followed where she was pointing on the other side of the clearing and then widened in alarm.

"That's got to be only a foot gap!"

"Yep. We can move them closer together the more you practise," Jessa said with a nod, completely missing the reason for my shock.

Calli laughed and settled back to watch.

"No need for you to get comfortable, dear. It's time you started working on the aim of your vines."

"What? No, it's okay. I don't want to intrude on Lachlan's time. I should probably go anyway. I have to make an enormous roast dinner tonight because apparently there weren't enough Yorkshire puddings last time," Calli said, rolling her eyes.

It was true that after we'd all realised the true glory of a Yorkshire pudding, there had been some bickering at the table along with a lot of pouting when Jacob had gifted Abby the last one. Yes, we were grown men, but Maverick and I hadn't had them before, and Tanner had like eight before we even had a chance to try one.

"You can't avoid it forever, dear," Jessa told Calli softly.

Calli stepped backward slowly as she started to retreat from the clearing. "I'll be in the kitchen if anyone needs me," she said instead of addressing the statement, and practically sprinted out of the clearing.

As I turned to Jessa in question, she raised an eyebrow at me. "Surely you can't tell me that you haven't noticed Calli has avoided her magic since the night she was taken."

I shrugged because, in all honesty, I hadn't noticed, but Calli wasn't like most witches I knew. She didn't use her magic all the time like some of them did. In fact, she barely used it at all most days. I'd chalked it up to the fact that she wasn't used to pulling on it for every little thing.

With a sigh, Jessa explained. "I suspect she's avoiding using it since she admitted being overwhelmed again."

"How do you know that? You weren't there when we talked about it," I realised, squinting at her in suspicion.

"Haven't you realised yet that I don't need to be somewhere to know things? Really Lachlan, of all people, you should understand how this works. Now, stop avoiding your training. I want one perfect strike on that tree."

Shaking my head, I tried to wrap my brain around what

she was talking about and not the fact that she just seemed to know things at times. Jessa was right, and I should be used to it by now. Was Calli really avoiding using her magic?

I thought back over the last few days and couldn't think of a single occasion when I'd seen Calli reach for her magic.

No, that couldn't be the case. I was sure Calli had healed some of us during training the other day. But then, when I really thought about it, I remembered how she'd rushed over, and Tanner had stopped her, not wanting her to drain any energy when we didn't know when an attack could begin.

In fact, we'd all just assumed she was going to heal him. She'd never actually said she was going to. It could have just been concern over the fact that her mate was bleeding.

"Jessa, if what you're saying is right, this could be a massive problem. Calli is the biggest gun we have in this fight at the moment. Not to mention that her magic will protect her if Stone or that Zoe woman tries anything again."

"You can call her your sister, you know. No one will judge you for it."

"She isn't my sister. I've never met the woman. The only bond between us is a few shared genes. She's nothing but a stranger to me, and a dangerous one at that."

It should have been harsh. Perhaps I should have wanted to get to know her, given that she was the only blood relative I had left. But there wasn't a single part of me that wanted to. I'd already found my true family at the pack, and I didn't need the evil bitch complicating things.

"Hmmm, I suppose you're right. Don't worry about Calli. If push came to shove, she'd do what needed to be done. But that doesn't mean she doesn't need to practise in the meantime."

"I'll speak with the others later, and we'll talk to her," I promised Jessa.

"I imagine that will go amazingly well for you." She laughed in response.

She was right. Calli was going to be pissed. I'd have to risk incurring her wrath, though. Calli not being comfortable using her magic was putting her in danger, and there was nothing about that I was okay with.

39

MAVERICK

The schoolhouse was practically pulsating from the shrieks and laughter of the children inside. I actually hesitated at the door, second-guessing my sanity at even thinking about returning. Sitting through the chaos of school yesterday would haunt my nightmares for weeks to come!

The pups we had were pretty awesome, but that didn't mean I wanted to socialise with other people's kids. I mean, what if they tried to talk to me or something? Was I supposed to try and be friends with them, or could I just ignore them? How were you supposed to talk to kids anyway?

Panic started to claw in at the edges of my mind, but by the time I realised this was a terrible idea, I was already standing in the big open room they used for a classroom, and everyone was staring at me.

Fuck!

"I've come to pick up Kai," I told his teacher.

That was something you could do, right? Just come and collect a kid when you needed one? Shit! That sounded bad. Oh fuck, why was she looking at me like that? She hadn't been here yesterday, and she was already looking at me like I was some kind of child snatcher.

"Kai is in the middle of his math lesson at the moment," she told me, eyeing me suspiciously. "And just who might you be?"

"Daddy Mav!" Abby cheered from the corner as the little redhead launched herself at me.

Catching her mid-air, I swung her around into my arms, a smile pulling at my mouth from her giggles despite the panic I'd just been about to give into.

"Hey, firecracker, you being good today?"

Abby grinned at me, and I immediately knew they were up to something. Looking around, I noticed Jacob was missing, and I had no doubt I was being used as a diversion.

"What mischief are you both up to?" I whispered, actually pretty proud of the kid.

"Nuh-thing," she sang, smiling sweetly at me.

This kid was dangerous. She knew exactly how to get anyone to do what she wanted. Luckily for us, she didn't seem to have a bad bone in her body. Maybe just a few trouble-making ones.

Jacob sidled back into the room, and I didn't miss the cookies he was quickly shoving in his pocket, the little thief.

Feeling weirdly proud of the two of them, I let Abby skip back to her co-conspirator before turning back to the teacher who'd looked like she was about to shank me before. Now, she was practically swooning at the sight of me with Abby, and it was probably more terrifying than the murderous look she'd had before.

"Erm, yeah, right, so I'm here to pick up Kai," I repeated, feeling really uncomfortable as she came over and put her hand on my arm.

"Oh, I'm sure we can spare him for the afternoon. You are

so good with your daughter. It must have been hard bringing her up yourself."

My head cocked to the side, but not because she assumed I'd brought the kid up alone. Hell knows where she'd gotten that idea. But it was the first time anyone had called Abby my daughter. She called me Daddy, and there was nothing I wouldn't do for the pup. I supposed she was my daughter—that was pretty cool.

The woman currently stroking my arm completely misread my smile and tried to step closer. Before she could, Kai moved in front of her, almost shoving her back away from me.

"He has a mate," he all but growled. "And you know full well he does because I've heard you talking about Calli."

Now, this was interesting.

The woman spluttered in embarrassment at being called out by one of her kids. "Of course, yes, Calli, right? I, erm…I suppose we can excuse Kai for the rest of the day if you need him."

She stepped away from us. Her cheeks blazed bright red before she turned away and started to fuss over one of the other kids.

"Come on," Kai grumbled. "Let's get out of this place."

He stormed ahead of me, and I found myself trailing in his wake. I hadn't had much time to spend with Kai since we'd gotten here, and that was part of the reason why I was here now. But I also had another reason for wanting to pull him out of school for the rest of the afternoon.

As I exited the building, I was surprised to see how far he'd managed to get and jogged to catch up. "Hey, Kai, wait up! What's going on at the school?"

"It's stupid. I don't need to go to school. I should be

learning to fight with you and the others. I'm a man now, not a stupid kid."

"Hey, hold up." Reaching out, I grabbed his arm and pulled him to a stop, turning him to face me. I could see the anger on his face, but I had no idea what was causing him to blow up. "What's going on, man?"

Kai scuffed his feet in the dead leaves on the ground as he glared at the dirt like it had offended him. "It's nothing," he mumbled.

"Clearly, it's not nothing."

Giving him a nudge, I started to walk back to the packhouse with Kai at my side.

"I heard them talking about Calli and how she has too many mates. They called her names," he admitted.

Even though anger raged inside me at the bitch singling out Calli where the kids could hear her, I managed to hold it back from the surface, not wanting to stress Kai out any further.

"Most people here are fairly accepting of us, but we're still different from them. Some people can't handle looking past the surface of a situation. It makes them feel small and inadequate. Calli is such a glaring ray of light. It's inevitable that some small people will feel intimidated by that. The trick is to leave them to their pettiness. It doesn't bother Calli, and you shouldn't let it bother you."

"How do you know it doesn't bother Calli?" Kai asked, unconvinced.

"Because she's not the sort of person that would let other people's opinions about stuff like that bother her," I told him with a shrug.

We'd known coming here that people would think our situation was strange, but we decided we didn't care. We were happy with each other, and that was all that mattered.

"Calli doesn't deserve people saying mean things about her," Kai sulked.

"You're not wrong there, kid." Wrapping an arm around his shoulders, I pulled him in closer. "So I thought we could spend a couple of hours training. How do you feel about that?"

Kai immediately brightened up, like I'd known he would. "Really?"

"Yeah, but this doesn't mean you're coming into any fight with us, okay? I want to get that straight before we even start."

"Then why are you training me?" Kai asked, sounding almost disappointed.

"Because I need you to do something even more important for me." Kai looked at me, confused, and I continued. "You spend all your time with the other kids, and when the fight finally comes, you will be the one at their sides. I need you to make sure you all get to someplace safe, and I need you to look after the younger ones."

Kai nodded seriously, and I could see a sense of resolve set into him. "I can do that."

"Grey and I have been checking around the pack for places where you can take them if you aren't at the school. We have a map to go over with you later. When everything is over, one of us will come to you. Before then, it's going to be up to you to keep them safe."

It was an important job, one we'd worried could be too much to give to an eleven-year-old kid. But the reality of the situation was that the pack was small, which meant there weren't many of us with the animage power. We needed every wolf we had on the battlefield when the time came, and we all had a reason to be in this fight. None of us would be able to hold back, and we couldn't ask anyone else to do it either. Besides, at this point, the kids were practically experts at slipping away, and it seemed inevitable that they'd be without one of us when the whole thing went down.

"I promise I'll keep them all safe," Kai reassured me, his fists clenched in determination.

I didn't doubt him. This kid had been through shit before we took him away from that pack. He was more than capable of looking after himself.

"I'm going to run through some drills with you now. Later we want to teach the others some basic self-defence, but I want you more comfortable and working through some moves by the end of the day."

"Are you going to teach Jacob and Abby how to fight with their magic?"

"I doubt it. We're only just touching the surface of what we can do ourselves. I don't think we'll have enough of a grasp on it to be able to teach them anything in time. Why do you ask?"

"No reason," Kai said evasively.

Obviously, I knew he was being suspicious as fuck, and equally, that it meant the kids were no doubt up to no good, but I didn't have it in me to stop them. Maybe Tanner was right about wanting to be the favourite. Or maybe I was just too chicken to be the one in charge. Whatever it was, I was leaving this subject well alone for now.

We moved over to the training yard Wells had set up.

"Time to warm up on the obstacle course," I gloated.

This fucking thing was the bane of my existence. Tanner and River were actually starting to look like they enjoyed it, but there was nothing about being run through the mud that would be enjoyable to me.

I was starting to get on board with the combat training

and even the magic side of things, but running this thing was my idea of a nightmare.

Kai took off like he was running for his life, and his laugh of joy as he cleared the first obstacle had my stomach bottoming out.

Shit, he was definitely going to beat my time. Tanner was never going to let me hear the end of this.

40
TANNER

We'd trained hard all week, and it was starting to show. Those of us who were mated to Calli could pull on the magic when we needed it, quicker and quicker. It wasn't quite at an instinctual level, but I had a feeling it was as good as it was going to get in such a short amount of time.

It was actually pretty impressive that we were working at the level we were. It should have taken a lot longer than it was. It probably helped that we didn't have to cast spells. The magic we seemed to wield was different to what the witches had. It was different to what even Calli and Lachlan seemed to have. Whereas they could produce something, ours acted more like whips of light, or smoke in Grey's case.

We only had to be able to direct the magic to where we wanted it and concentrate long enough to keep it in a solid form. Even so, it came pretty easily. It was like recovering a missing part of ourselves, but one that had always been there; you just hadn't realised it.

The problem, however, was with the rest of the pack. They had a glimmer of the same magic, but it was nothing like ours. They could manage one, possibly two moves if they didn't try and push the magic too far, but then they were tapped out.

Wells strode out into the training area, watching closely as I circled Keelan. My magic snaked out across the ground, and even though Keelan tried to dance away from it, the whips moved faster than you could track with your eyes as it caught him around one front leg. Once it had a hold of him, it was impossible for Keelan to break free and more and more lines of magic joined the first, wrapping around him and pulling him to the ground.

Poor Keelan had been our guinea pig for long enough now that he knew escape was impossible, so with a huff, he laid his head on the ground and waited to be released.

This was what we were supposed to be doing, and he should be happy we were starting to get it, but I think it was a point of pride with Keelan now that he needed to win just one time. I, for one, wasn't going to go easy on him. We had our pride too.

Aidan, Blake, Holly, and Nash were all missing today, having gone for extra magic lessons. It was nice having time alone for our mate group, even if that meant Keelan was the third wheel for today. We didn't have much downtime now. Between training, the kids, and trying to keep in contact with Colt's pack and Hunter and Cassia, our days generally ended with everyone passing out from exhaustion.

Blake had become more than a little reluctant to train with the others. We rarely saw him now. He seemed to spend his time between his family and taking up a post on the guard. Jean had spoken to Calli about how worried she was for her husband. He seemed almost obsessive in his pursuit to make the pack as secure as possible.

Calli too was starting to look like the stress was getting to her, and even though we were tip-toeing around the subject, she needed to step up and face her fears. Lachlan had told us Jessa's theory that Calli was actively avoiding her magic. Since then, we'd been keeping an eye on her.

She hadn't accessed it once since we'd started to observe her, and now we were reaching the point where we were avoiding having to confront her about it.

We all knew why the rest of the pack struggled to access and control their magic.

Calli needed to take her place as our Pack Queen.

I understood she was frightened. She'd told us so already. But this was moving beyond that. Unfortunately, we didn't have time for her to doubt herself. We were moving on a timetable we'd never had the opportunity to see. Every day, we were constantly looking over our shoulders, waiting for the next attack to come.

Wells had been at the Council headquarters for the past two days trying to find out anything he could about Stone, who was suspiciously absent now. Even the other Council members were starting to ask questions, and Wells had opted to stay at the headquarters for a few days to begin to sway them to our side.

I didn't rate his chances of success. They might not be actively part of the problem right now, but I had no doubt they'd sit by and let it happen once they were aware. As long as they had Stone's word, it wouldn't impact their own packs. They'd sit back and view it as a wolf problem. It was short-sighted naivety if they actually thought he wouldn't be coming for them next.

"Tanner!" Keelan barked, pulling me from my thoughts.

Looking down, I realised I still had him wrapped up in ropes of magic and lying on the floor. From the look on his face, he didn't appreciate it.

"Sorry," I laughed. "I forgot you were down there."

It was the truth, but I got the impression Keelan wasn't my biggest fan right now.

As I withdrew my magic, pulling it back into myself, a rush of shivers flashed through my body at the unnatural feeling of the move. It didn't want to be contained. It wanted to be unleashed.

Keelan dramatically got up off the ground and brushed himself down like I'd inconvenienced him for doing his job. He had pretty much drawn the short straw by becoming our training dummy, I supposed.

"I've arranged for some of the other guards to join us this morning. I want to work on group manoeuvres where you'll have more than one attacker. More importantly, this will be the first time you face someone who's unaware of what you can do. I want to see how quickly you can incapacitate them when outnumbered. This will mean that some of you will have to be able to split your attention to take on more than one attacker at the time," Keelan explained.

It made sense. In real life, your enemies didn't wait politely on the sidelines for you to finish fighting before they made their move. There were no orderly lines on the battlefield.

"Take a break. Drink some water but keep moving around so your muscles stay warm," Keelan instructed before walking off to the side to talk with Sean.

Whatever they were discussing, Keelan wasn't impressed with Sean. I wanted to listen in because I had a feeling it had something to do with us, but I'd be polite for now and give them the opportunity to come clean.

I could see Grey bristling with annoyance as he gulped down some water, keeping his eye on the pair of them. He was doing surprisingly well because we essentially lived with two other alphas. I'd expected to be constantly on edge trying to keep him calm, but Grey seemed to be actively managing his magic and alpha rage a lot better than he had been able to in the past.

"What do you think that's about?" I asked. It wasn't the most sensible approach to poke at Grey when he was clearly already annoyed by the situation, but it was concerning me enough that I wanted to discuss it with him.

"I think Keelan is concerned by Wells' continued absence from the pack," Grey explained, crushing the now empty water bottle in his hand and tossing it into the recycling bin. "He wants him back with the pack because he's expecting an attack any day now."

"Makes sense. It's his job to ensure Wells is protected, and he can't exactly do that when he isn't here."

"I'm sure Wells wouldn't stay away if he didn't think it was completely necessary," River interjected, ever the voice of reason. "Besides, if we can at least soften the other Council members, when it all goes down, they might hear us out instead of deciding to kill us straight away."

"I'd like to see them try," Grey growled.

It was a good point. In the past, every pack had been terrified of the Council's hit squad of guards, but now that we had some power behind us, and we were learning how to use it, maybe it was time for them to be afraid of us.

"How many guards do you think he will send to take on the six of us?" I asked Grey out of interest.

"Ten, maybe," Grey said with a shrug. "Keelan said he wanted us outnumbered."

My eyes moved to where Calli was grabbing a drink out of her bag, and I quietly asked the others. "Do you think Calli is ready for this?"

She'd hate that we were talking about her, but I was genuinely worried.

"She has the combat skills, but she still hasn't reached for her magic yet," Lachlan said, his brow furrowing in concern.

Grey sighed, his eyes following Calli closely as she stood to take a drink. "No, I don't think she's ready, and I have no idea how to help her get there. But this is just a training exercise, and she isn't going to get hurt. Keep an eye on her, and if she doesn't look like she's softening about using her magic, we're going to need to talk to her again."

This had been the topic of conversation between us most recently. I still didn't think pushing Calli was going to work. She was scared, but she was also working through it. I'd seen her reading her mother's book more and more, and I knew it was her way of dealing with her emotions. Calli was one of those people who needed all the information before she made her decision. The problem was, we didn't exactly know if we had the time for her to work through this. Maybe we should talk to her, then perhaps she'd let us help her find the information she needed.

"Okay, tonight after dinner?" I suggested.

We paused in our conversation at the sound of voices approaching, even though they were not who we'd expected. As Aidan, Holly, Nash and Blake went to talk with Keelan, it became apparent that they'd been sent back to join us.

Blake stood awkwardly at the back, trying not to interject too much. It was upsetting to see him hanging out at the rear, trying not to draw too much attention. I knew he wanted to prove himself, and he needed to. He'd fucked up. But it was hard looking at the shell of the man he used to be.

Grey hadn't severed his pack link with us, so he still had access to the small amount of animage power the others seemed to have inherited. To be honest, I doubted Grey would ever sever that link. He wanted Blake to be able to find his place back with us. Grey might have told him that he'd be joining Wells' pack, but they'd made no moves to actually do it. We couldn't afford to risk losing a wolf with access to the animage powers. Not when there were so few of us, and some didn't seem to have full access to them either. But hanging in limbo like this didn't do Blake any good.

They moved over to speak with us, leaving a stern-looking Keelan watching them walk away.

"We're with you for the rest of the morning, apparently," Aidan filled us in without needing to be asked. "So, we're all about to be attacked then?"

"That's the plan. We should try and put together some sort of game plan. If we rush into this without any idea of what the others are going to do, it won't take long for them to outmanoeuvre us."

It was almost as if my words had summoned them, as twenty wolves rushed into the training clearing. Twenty against ten, were they terrible odds?

Grey immediately shifted and ran to intercept the two wolves, who were slightly faster than the rest and were heading up the front of the pack. The rest of us followed the example of our alpha and shifted, running to engage with our attackers.

After that, the whole thing was a shit show of epic proportions.

Aidan, Holly, Nash, and Blake didn't have enough control over their powers to be able to fight effectively with them, but because the rest of us had drawn our power to the surface, it was almost like it pushed theirs out as well.

Grey's smoke lashed out, wrapping around two wolves as he faced the other front-runner, darting forward with a snap of his jaws. Grey was a giant wolf, being an alpha, and I had no doubt he could defend himself wolf on wolf fairly easily. It wouldn't be the first time he'd had to do it.

I drew my attention away from Grey and turned toward the pack running at us. Two of them had already set their sights on me, and when I moved to intercept them, I felt a force wrap around my back leg and unexpectedly pull me backward.

"Fucking, shit, I'm sorry," Aidan rushed out through the pack link as I quickly rolled in time to miss a snap of jaws that came straight at my head.

These guys weren't pulling any punches. If he'd made contact, I was sure I'd have been missing a chunk of my ear.

The second wolf came in hot on his heels, and I was able to send a tendril of my power out in a snapping lash like a whip, striking him across the left flank and making him fall to the ground with a yelp.

"Can you let go of my fucking leg?" I barked out at Aidan through the link as I tried to dodge another snap of jaws.

"I… I'm trying," Aidan panicked, and then I saw a wolf leap and pin him to the ground.

Aidan's yelp filled the air as the wolf ran his claws down his side, opening a large wound from his shoulder to his flank. With a whimper, he tried to get back on his paws, but then Aidan collapsed back to the ground in a heap.

Luckily, as his eyes started to flutter in pain, his power withdrew, and I was freed in time to jump out of the way as two more wolves came straight toward me.

Our problem was that we were completely uncoordinated, and these wolves we were facing had fought together for a long time. They paired off, switching out when needed and backing up the others if they seemed to be struggling or facing someone who put up more of a fight.

They didn't even have a pack link to communicate like

we did. This was nothing short of hours and hours of experience.

It would seem that Keelan had decided he needed to make a point today.

"Don't get separated," Grey barked through the link, seeing the confusion with the rest of us at the same time as I did. "Keep someone at your back and work together. If you don't have adequate control over your power yet, stick with one of us who does."

His words came too late as four wolves swarmed over Lachlan. A bolt of lightning crackled over his fur as he gave out a warning shot, scorching the earth right at the paws of one of his attackers.

The problem was, they didn't slow down, and before he could regroup, they were already on him. They were fighting for real, and most of our group was still in the mindset that they didn't want to hurt them.

Holly stumbled and crashed down to the ground. The power around her stuttered, and then she passed out. Blake and Nash stood protectively over her, and I could already see Nash starting to spiral with worry for his mate. It didn't take long for Blake and Nash to be taken down in a similar way that Aidan had been.

River and Maverick were trying to reach each other across the field, but the chaos between them was more than they could take.

That was when I saw Calli backing up slowly as a large wolf came head-on, snapping his jaw at her and preparing to attack.

"Calli, you have to defend yourself with your magic," I all but screamed through the link. "He isn't going to go gentle on you. He's going to hurt you. You need to put him down…"

I didn't have time to finish what I was saying as a wolf

barrelled into my side at the same time as one dived in front of me, locking his jaws around my throat.

I felt the pinch of my airway as his jaws tightened, and I knew in a real battle, I'd be dead right now. Hell, I was starting to wonder if I was about to die anyway because this guy wasn't fucking letting up.

"Calli!" River screamed.

I couldn't move between the weight of the two of them, and my wolf panicked at the sound of River screaming out for our mate. I thrashed, and my magic snapped out in my defence to try and free me, as my wolf was determined to reach our mate.

It was a stupid move, but it wasn't done consciously. It was a knee-jerk reaction, and I felt terrible for the guy who would be beating himself up about this later.

As my wolf thrashed, I felt the teeth at my throat tear into my flesh. It was too late to stop it. Even as the pressure of his hold released when he realised what was happening, the damage was already done.

A hot wave of blood flowed down my neck, and I felt the air stutter out of my lungs. Yet, strangely, I didn't feel the pain. I knew it would be excruciating, but all I could think of was getting to Calli.

The wolf who had me pinned yipped in pain, as his weight was suddenly removed from me. I didn't have time to see what had happened to him. The content thrum of my magic let me know that he wouldn't be a problem for now.

My wolf was so overwhelmed with worry for Calli that all I could think about was her safety. The fact that this was only a training exercise flowed from my mind, and in its place was pure need.

I stumbled to my feet, my paws slipping on the blood-soaked ground. The large wolf was still advancing on Calli, and he was so close. She cowered back away from him, fear in her eyes. She was a shadow of the strong warrior she'd always been in times like this. It was too soon. We'd pushed her too hard when she wasn't ready, and we should have seen this coming.

Without even thinking, I leapt for him, my magic lashed out, and I zeroed in on my target. As the whipping cords of power reached for his neck, I felt a surge of satisfaction in knowing that in his complete focus on Calli, he'd left it too late to defend himself from my attack.

Just as my magic started to wrap around his neck, I felt a force latch on to me and haul me backward.

"Tanner!" Grey barked through the link.

But I was too lost to the rage inside of me to listen.

Keelan's wolf barrelled into the wolf advancing on Calli, pushing him out of the way of my attack, even if he had been seconds too late. Calli's attacker whipped around in my direction. His eyes were wide as he looked back at me, stepping away from my mate. But I still wanted to hurt him. I *needed* to hurt him.

My movements became sluggish, and I could feel a weariness trying to set in, but I thrashed my way through it. Fighting whatever I needed to, so I could get to my prey.

A weight settled on top of me, trying to hold me steady, but I wouldn't go down that easy. Throwing my body to one side, so I could get enough space between us to get my claws to their side, and I racked them down as deeply as I could.

"Fucking hell, Tanner!" Maverick's voice shouted in the back of my mind. "Calm the fuck down. You're hurt, brother."

For the first time in my life, I felt like I was separate from my wolf, trapped in my mind. Maverick's panicked words registered, and I knew I needed to stop. I was safe. Calli was safe. This was just a training exercise. But my wolf was too far gone. I felt almost rabid, like something had snapped inside of me seeing Calli so defenceless and alone, facing down that wolf that wanted nothing more than to hurt her.

I could feel the lethargy in my muscles, and I knew this was starting to get bad. I shouldn't be this tired from the work we'd done, and I realised that I was probably more hurt than I could feel.

At first, I thought my eyesight was starting to fade, that I was sinking down into that dark, quiet place where I could finally rest. But then a calmness flowed through me that reminded me so much of Grey that I knew it was him helping me through the madness.

Shaking my head, I focused on the smoke surrounding me and the comforting waves of alpha power that came with the touch of smoke.

I tried not to think of Calli's frightened face and instead pushed my wolf toward the reassuring presence of Grey. He had always been my calm in the storm when I needed him to be. I brought the image of the tattoo on my chest to mind, the compass where Grey was my north. He'd saved me as a child, and I knew he'd always be there for me. He was my alpha, and I would always be his beta.

The calm settled around me, and I felt my wolf pulling back from the madness. The tiredness settling in now was probably due more to blood loss. I was trying not to think about the wet sticky sensation on my fur that hinted at how bad my injuries were.

"Get out of my way," Calli shouted, and I watched as she shoved a wolf out of the way. She must have shifted back into her human form while Grey tried to calm me down.

"Maverick," she gasped, moving to his side.

Struggling to get up, I realised Maverick was lying,

panting at my side. He'd been the one to try and restrain me, and I'd rewarded him by injuring my own brother. As if I didn't feel bad enough about losing control right now, I got to watch my brother lying in pain.

Maverick shifted back to his human form, a pained grimace on his face. "Tanner first," he told Calli, pushing her gently to my side.

My wolf panted shallowly. I couldn't feel much of anything, which wasn't a good sign.

"Oh my god, Tanner," Calli burst out as she dropped to her knees at my side.

Calli's hand immediately moved to me, and without hesitation, her healing magic started to flow into me.

After a few moments, I felt my muscles relax from the pained strain they were under, and I felt confident enough to shift. I probably should have saved my strength, but I wanted Calli to see my face while I spoke to her.

Tears poured down her face, and she hiccuped with a sob as he concentrated on pouring as much healing into me as she could.

Pushing through the shift, I took a moment to catch my breath before I reached up and held onto one of her hands.

"This is all my fault," she cried, gripping my hand tightly. "I saw you. You were only trying to get to me."

"It's not your fault, sweetheart. You weren't ready for this. We knew you weren't, and we should have just talked to you about it rather than waiting to see if you could come to it on your own."

I caught a glimpse of Keelan standing behind us as his group of wolves moved over to talk to him. The large wolf that had been threatening Calli shifted into a bear of a man and spoke softly to Keelan, who nodded, a proud smile on his face.

They'd planned this, the bastards. They knew if one of us got hurt, Calli wouldn't be able to stop herself from healing us. This was their way of making sure she went back to using her magic without question.

I squinted in annoyance at Keelan, and he lifted one shoulder in a shrug when he noticed. As far as he was concerned, this was a calculated risk that paid off. But the fact that he'd put Calli in danger to do it was unforgivable. I could feel my wolf starting to rise again, even though Calli hadn't finished healing the damage to my neck yet.

"Calm down, Tanner," Grey spoke softly at my side, his calming alpha energy still pulsing through my veins. "You were too close to rabid. I didn't think I would be able to pull you back for a second there."

"They did this on purpose," I gritted out, feeling the anger rising as I said it aloud.

"I know they did. But it's done now, and there's nothing we can do about it. For now, we need to concentrate on getting everyone healed, and then we need to figure out how to fight better as a team. We don't have time for hurt feelings at the moment."

My eyes whipped in the direction of my usually steadfast friend. I couldn't believe he was so willing to push this under the rug for now. It was so unlike him. Usually, the alpha in him would have been the first to fly into anger and punish the wolf who would have hurt our mate.

But then I saw it. I saw that demonic red glow in his eyes, and I could see that his words didn't match his demeanour. He might be trying to act relaxed for my sake, but there was no way Grey would let this go.

For some reason, that thought was what it took to calm me. Grey wouldn't let this go, and neither would I.

41
GREY

Calli was wiped out after healing Tanner and Maverick and had already gone to bed for the night. The others had agreed to watch over her, given our concerns about her safety in the pack now. Not only had she been taken right out from under our noses, but our so-called trainer essentially arranged a hit on her.

Yes, it was a training exercise, and I had a suspicion that Sean was involved in what went down. But it would have been an awfully convenient excuse to quietly remove her from the picture.

Wells never did find his traitor, and maybe it was just my anger speaking, but my attention was solely on Keelan now.

Wells had returned to the pack a few hours ago, and waiting to speak with him was like torture. I wouldn't be the one to march down there and confront him as soon as he appeared. No, he knew I was coming, and I wanted to leave him waiting for the time being.

By the time I made it downstairs, Wells had retreated to his study, and from his bark of annoyance as I knocked on the door, I knew he was feeling the tension.

Storming in, I strode over to the now-familiar armchair by the fireplace and dropped down into it, leaning back confidently as I crossed my legs.

Locking eyes with Wells, I waited for him to speak first. It was about time I established that I was the stronger alpha here.

"It's time then," Wells said, sitting back with a smirk as he braced his elbows on the chairs of his arms and steepled his fingers in front of his face. "I was starting to think you'd never make your move."

"Oh, you've got this all wrong. I don't want to take over your ragtag pack of misfits. Not when you still haven't been able to find your traitor."

"Those are strong words for an alpha who recently lost his mate to one of his own traitors," Wells taunted.

"I know what you did. I know you set up that exercise to make sure one of us was injured. You wanted to force me to attack you out of rage."

"It was a bonus that it pushed the lovely Calli to embrace her magic again. You seem strangely calm for someone who just figured out I tried to have one of your mate bond killed."

"Hmmm, well, it occurred to me that the best way to piss you off was not giving you what you wanted. Besides, you're not the one I need to kill. I'll find the one who dared to touch my mate," I threatened.

"He was just following his alpha's orders." Wells shrugged, but I could see the panic in his eyes.

"He should know his alpha is a dumbass and learn to think for himself." I shrugged in response to his own. Even though the wolf inside me was raging, I was learning to play it cool. We'd not only fallen into a fight for our lives, but smack bang into a game of politics as well.

"If you don't step up and do what is necessary, all of this

will have been for nothing," Wells suddenly snapped. "Do you know how long we've planned for this? The sacrifices we've had to make? And you just come along and decide you know better. This is what you were made for, you snot-nosed upstart. Now, do your duty and take the pack. We need the power that only Calli can give us if we have a chance of living through this."

"You can't have it."

"WHAT?! You dare to sit there and tell me I can't, that after everything we've done it's been for nothing. Who do you think you are, you little shit?"

"I think I'm the man with all the cards, and you're the ageing alpha, out of options and out of fucking luck."

"So, what's the plan, alpha? You realise this fight isn't going away just because you've decided not to play, right?"

It was a good question. What was the fucking plan?

"Equipping a pack this size with the animage powers is not how we're going to stay under the radar. If the whole point of this is to save our race before a war starts, throwing a nuke at our enemy is a really fucking stupid idea."

"Stone is the immediate threat. So we deal with him first, and then whatever fallout comes, we can deal with later."

"That's a stupid fucking idea," I pointed out again. "It's about time you filled me in on the entire plan. We're not going along with anything else until we know exactly what you're planning."

"All the cards on the table, hey? I'll make you a deal. I'll lay it all out there, and you swear not to take the animage powers off the table for good."

"You realise they're not my powers to trade. Calli is the one you should be bargaining with."

"You're the alpha. If you decide to take the pack, the power comes with you. Calli has no say in the matter."

"Calli has yet to accept the position of Queen, and I suspect that is the reason why the others haven't obtained true access to their powers. It would do you no good if I took the pack at this stage."

"She'll come around eventually." Wells shrugged off my concern, and I couldn't believe how much he was underestimating Calli. She might not be feeling herself at the moment, but once she was back, she'd be stepping into the line of fire without a second thought.

"You clearly don't know her very well." I laughed at him.

"Hmmm, just like her aunt then."

We locked eyes across the room, and I could tell he was weighing me up. Trying to decide just how much he was going to tell me. Of course, I wasn't going to accept anything less than everything. He needed my pack more than we needed theirs. Yes, they had the numbers, but now that we knew Stone was on his way to acquiring the same power for his entire pack, we were about to be outnumbered and outpowered.

"Stone has become too powerful, and we don't stand a chance against him as we currently stand. At this stage, even if Calli were to step up and distribute the power amongst this pack, we'd still be outnumbered even if we were on even power levels. Jessa has a theory, though, that the strength of the Queen would determine the strength of the pack. We don't know enough about Zoe to determine if she's an even match to Calli, but given the level of your own power, it's pretty safe to assume that Calli stands in the upper levels of animage Queens."

"This isn't just a numbers game then."

"No. If she's a factory-made Queen, then there's a chance her power won't be anywhere near Calli's. We need to find out more about her. We need to send a spy into Stone's pack."

"Or we need to draw her out and onto the battlefield in a controlled set of circumstances to assess her power level," I suggested.

"That would work," Wells agreed. "If she's a weak Queen, we can stick with the original plan. If she holds a power that rivals Calli's, we're going to need to make a definitive move."

"And what move is it you're thinking of making?"

I could already tell by the look of excitement on his face that whatever it was, it was going to be a bad fucking idea.

"Then we're back to a numbers game, and we need to vastly increase our own numbers to put Stone back in his place, or preferably the ground."

"And how exactly do you intend to do that?"

Fucking hell, I'd have more luck beating the information out of him. This man was exhausting.

"We have to take the Council and consolidate our species," Wells said, a look of satisfaction spreading across his face. "We do away with the idea of packs and bring everyone together under one ruler."

"Oh right, and here I was worried you might have gone insane. I suppose the person fit for the job will be you?"

Sometimes I felt like I was stuck in a daycare, and this was all some kind of weird fever dream I was having.

"Of course not." Wells laughed, surprising me for the first time. "After all this, I deserve a day off. I'm retiring and moving to a beach somewhere away from all you stressful fuckers."

"Then who?"

"Personally, I think Sean should take the throne. He's the oldest of our kind, and you cannot even imagine the sacrifices he's made for us to reach this point. But I suppose the easiest way to decide is to let the people vote once all of the dust has settled. Jessa thinks the role should go to a Queen. But Sean has an idea to make the role temporary and have a vote for the best candidate every few years. Make our leaders work for their jobs for once."

"That's... that's actually an excellent idea."

"But taking the Council doesn't sound like something we should be taking on at the same time as dealing with Stone. We can't fight a battle on every side and expect to come out alive at the end."

It was bad enough that Calli was in danger from one enemy. But did I really want to add three more packs to the list? No, of course, I fucking didn't.

"So, first things first. How do we lure out a wannabe Queen?"

"Oh, I doubt we have anything to worry about there. She'll be coming right to us," Wells said with a shrug. "She wants to take out Stone and become some kind of glorified Queen of everything, right? She'll be coming to us sooner rather than later. She can't go through with her plans and let Calli live, and there's no better time than now to take her out when she's weak and barely able to access her magic. Or at least that will be the story their spy should be reporting back to them just about now."

"Wait. Then today..."

"Was more than just a show to give Calli a push in the right direction. If I'm honest, that was just a happy by-product. No, it was a demonstration for our little spy on how weak and pathetic our biggest weapon was. He scuttled off to tell his masters all about it roughly an hour ago."

"Then you knew Keelan was the spy all along?"

"Keelan?" Wells barked out a laugh at the mere suggestion. "Keelan would lie down and die on the spot if he thought it would help. He's that loyal. No, Denna is our spy.

He struggled to fit in when he got here and found himself outside of a hierarchical system. He's the big bad wolf that was going to attack Calli for us. It was pretty hard to make sure he didn't follow through, but Sean made sure to keep a short leash on him for the entire exercise, I can assure you."

"I've never even seen him before," I mused aloud.

"Wouldn't be much of a spy if you knew who he was. The whole point is to wait in the shadows and gather as much information as possible without alerting your mark. Have you never watched a movie?" Wells laughed.

I shook my head at the implication. I was a small-town mechanic and so far out of my league with these people. As soon as I thought I had the upper hand, I realised they were already twelve steps ahead of me.

"Then the disagreement between Sean and Keelan before the exercise started?"

"Keelan was concerned that we were putting Calli in too much danger. He didn't think it was right to go ahead with the exercise without at least telling some of you so you could protect her if needed."

"He was right. You should have."

"Perhaps," Wells said with a shrug. "The important thing is that Calli is fine, and everything went to plan."

"I nearly lost my beta!"

"That was hardly something any of us could have foreseen. Even if he had known what was happening, it would have gone exactly the same way, possibly worse, because he would have realised just how big of a threat Denna truly was."

Fucking hell, I hated it when he sounded all reasonable, and I started to wonder if he was right.

Getting up out of the chair, I strode toward the door, done with the conversation and done with him. The man had my head spinning in circles, and I realised exactly how much I wasn't cut out for this job.

"You're still going to have to take the pack, you know?" Wells called out after me.

I let the door slam closed without answering. I didn't care how thought out this plan was, or even if it did make fucking sense. I wasn't going to take this pack from him. I didn't want it. All I wanted was to go back to my own packlands and live a quiet life with my pack brothers and my mate. All of these politics and bullshit were one of the reasons we left a bigger pack in the first place.

As I strode through the packhouse, my head spun with everything I'd learned. It didn't escape me that the next step in the plan was to put Calli in danger yet again. Only this time, we were waiting for an insane Queen to come along and take a shot.

If we were going to walk out of this alive, we needed to get our act together. We had some reasonable fighting skills, even if this morning's exercise had been a complete cluster fuck. But if we couldn't learn to work together, we were as good as useless.

It was easy to feel like a failure right now, but I started to concentrate on how far we'd come since we set out on this journey. Those of us who were mated to Calli had reasonably good control of our magic. Even if it was difficult to control it and our wolves at the same time if today had been anything to go by.

Control would come with training, though, and that would be our lives from now until the inevitable attack took place.

I needed Hunter. He'd learned about tactics back in his time as a guard. He'd have been able to brief me better on how to direct the others during a fight. The link we had between us was a skill others didn't have, and it should give us the ability to turn into a cohesive fighting unit. That would only happen if I was a strong enough leader to guide them through it, though.

The suite was quiet when I reached it, and I moved through to the main bedroom, where I'd left Tanner and Calli to rest. Maverick's wounds hadn't been as bad as they looked, but he'd still opted to sleep alone so no one could graze his side. He was putting a brave face on because he didn't want Calli to try and heal him, but I knew he was in a fair deal of pain right now.

I'd expected them to be asleep when I walked into the bedroom, or I'd maybe have knocked or something. But finding Tanner with his face buried between Calli's legs was a definite sign that my beta was feeling better.

Calli locked eyes with me from the bed as her mouth opened in a soft gasp. I could see Tanner paying special attention to her clit with his tongue as he slowly pushed three fingers inside her.

"Are you just going to stand there, or are you going to help me show our mate what it means to belong to the Stoneridge Pack?" Tanner cheekily asked.

A soft growl flowed out of me at the challenge, even if it had just been a playful one. If anyone was going to be giving orders in this bedroom, it would be me.

"You'll have to learn to do what you're told, beta," I warned him.

To my surprise, the look on Tanner's face was one of lust and acceptance. I'd heard about his experience with Calli and Lachlan, so of course, I knew he wasn't opposed to sharing. I just hadn't realised he was quite so excited about the idea.

My cock twitched in anticipation, even if my mind stalled for a second on whether we should do this.

"Did you know that this is a fantasy of our mate?" Tanner

asked me before he gently nuzzled his face against the inside of Calli's thigh. "And I may have thought about it once or twice myself," he admitted.

Yep. We were definitely doing this.

Grabbing the chair from the corner of the room, I dragged it closer to the bed before sitting down. Tanner had leant up on his elbows, watching me curiously as I did.

"I only have one rule," I stated as I sat back and made myself comfortable. "I'm in charge."

Calli licked her lips as she looked between Tanner and me. She knew how I liked to play the game. The question was whether Tanner could get on board with that.

Tanner's eyes moved back and forth between mine like he was trying to figure something out, and then a slow smile stretched across his face. "Yes, alpha." I could hear the lust in his voice, and the twitch of his hard cock only reinforced how turned on he was by this turn of events.

"Good. Now, I want to see you make Calli come. Don't stop until she's screaming your name."

Tanner didn't need any other encouragement as he practically fell on Calli, devouring her pussy with his mouth.

Calli fell back against the bed, her back bowing in pleasure as she gasped at the sudden onslaught.

She was so fucking beautiful when she let go like this. Her perfect breasts bounced with every hitch of her breath, and her hands slid up her body to cradle them before her fingers sought out her nipples.

Tanner pumped his fingers inside, his mouth fastened to her clit as he eagerly followed the instructions I'd given him.

I watched, completely enraptured by the sight in front of me. It didn't take me long to push down my own jeans and stroke my aching cock. I needed to be inside of her. I needed to feel her pussy clamping down around me as she cried out her release.

Part of the reason why I loved being the one in charge was that I was starting to relish holding off on what I wanted. Denying myself that perfect moment of plunging myself into her heat made it feel all the better when I finally gave in.

But mostly, it was the look in Calli's eyes as she submitted to me. The pure lust that dripped in her gaze when she completely let go was addictive.

"Don't forget about her beautiful ass, Tanner. I need you to get her ready for me," I told him.

Calli whimpered at the sound, and I knew she'd be dripping at the idea of it. She was so open to the idea of ass play that it was a miracle any of us had held off this long.

Tanner's finger circled her asshole as his hips ground against the bed's surface. He was probably desperate for someone to touch him, but he wouldn't get what he wanted until I decided he was allowed.

The thought alone had the precome dripping from my cock as I stroked it quickly, spreading that bead of lubricant over the head as I did.

I wanted Calli's mouth so bad right now, but I also knew if I let myself indulge, I'd come far quicker than I wanted to, and I had a specific plan for what I wanted to happen tonight.

"Please…can I come?" Calli gasped, and that one little question had me groaning in delight.

"My perfect mate. You know what your alpha likes," I purred.

I purposefully didn't answer her question. Waiting a second, so I could watch how she writhed and bit down on her bottom lip as she tried to hold back her orgasm. Tanner didn't give her any relief as he continued to lash his tongue against her clit, pumping his fingers in her pussy and ass.

"Come for me, Calli," I finally told her.

Calli's back bowed as her breath hitched, and with a cry, I watched as she screamed out Tanner's name, her hips twitching as she rode his fingers.

Panting, Calli sagged onto the bed. Tanner finally lifted his face with a satisfied smile.

"Tanner, lie back on the bed, head on the pillow," I instructed as I stood up and slowly removed my clothes.

Calli peered up at me with hungry eyes as I slowly revealed my body, and she licked her lips hungrily.

"Yes, alpha," Tanner murmured, reaching down to touch himself.

"Don't," I snapped. "You wait for Calli."

Tanner looked at me with a squint, and I could see he was considering ignoring my instructions.

Striding forward, I gripped his chin in my fingers, his naked body mere inches from my own.

"I gave you an instruction, beta," I growled at him, staring down into his eyes.

Tanner's tongue darted out to lick his bottom lips as he stared up at me with a look I'd never seen on his face before.

I trailed my hand down his neck until it came to rest on the compass tattooed on his chest. Our childhood had pulled Tanner and me into an unbreakable bond. In truth, I didn't think I would ever have had the balls to step away from my father's pack and form my own if it wasn't for Tanner.

Tanner always said that I was his north, but I didn't think he understood what a pillar of strength he was to me too. How much we all relied on him.

"Yes, alpha," he breathed, reluctantly moving away from me before climbing onto the bed.

Calli moved to the side as Tanner slid into position, and my cock twitched at the thought of my beta submitting to me.

Calli dipped her head down, kissing Tanner deeply on the lips as a reward for doing as he was told. He'd soon learn that giving over control came with rich rewards.

"Calli, straddle Tanner. I want to see you take his cock into your perfect pussy."

She didn't even hesitate as she followed my instructions. Swinging one leg over Tanner's hip, she raised herself up on her knees.

I watched as Tanner helped hold himself in position, and Calli slowly lowered herself down over his aching cock. As his length slowly sank inside her, Tanner's groan proved just how much he'd wanted it. Who could blame him? I'd spend days inside her if I could.

Walking over to the bedside table, I pulled out the things I'd had the forethought to order. The pack had a PO Box set up in the nearest town and distributed any deliveries once a day. After my last time with Calli, I'd made arrangements, and Keelan had explained how to have it delivered to the pack. There was no way I was going to ask Wells, even if I had no intention of telling him what I'd wanted to order.

"Tanner, grab the rail on the headboard. Calli, I want your hands next to his. It goes without saying that I don't want to see you riding that cock yet, sweetheart."

They both moved without question, grabbing hold of the rail that seemed to have been made for this purpose. I could see the glimmer in Tanner's eyes as he no doubt wondered what I was up to, but then he seemed to realise that the position I'd put them in had Calli's perfect breasts right in front of his face, and I saw as he parted his lips but on a second thought, stopped himself from sucking her nipple into his mouth.

"Good boy, Tanner," I purred, and then Calli groaned as Tanner's cock no doubt twitched inside her.

It seemed my beta liked to be rewarded by his alpha.

Not wanting to waste any more time, I quickly put the velvet restraints around their wrists and secured them both to the headboard. In reality, they could both easily pull themselves free. It was more of a reminder to stay exactly where I wanted them.

Moving behind them, I ran my hands over Calli's perfect ass, and she sighed, her head falling forward at the sensation of finally receiving my touch.

My fingers trailed down her asscrack and dipped inside her pussy, stretching her tight as I slipped in beside Tanner's cock.

Calli's breath hitched at the sensation, and I heard Tanner groan as I pumped a finger inside our mate, stroking against his length.

I'd never touched another man before. I doubted I'd ever want to spend a night alone with Tanner, but here and now, between just the three of us? I wanted him to enjoy this experience just as much as Calli would.

Settling in behind them, I ran my tongue up the crack of Calli's ass, circling that tight ring of muscles with the tip.

"Fuck! Oh, fuck!" Tanner gasped. "Whatever you're doing, she very much enjoys it."

I already knew just how much Calli liked it when you paid attention to her ass, and I had no doubt that her pussy had a stranglehold on Tanner's cock right now.

"Tell me, Tanner, is her pussy working your cock without her even having to move?"

"She's so fucking tight right now," he groaned out.

"I think you should reward our mate for how well she's staying still. Those nipples look like they're begging for your attention, Tanner."

Part of me was disappointed that I didn't have a view of

what he was doing to her, but from the groans that started to come out of Calli, I knew she was enjoying it.

I pushed the tip of my tongue into her ass, relaxing her to get her ready for what was to come. Tanner had already played with her ass a little, but she was getting more than just a finger this time.

It was time I finally indulged myself in the one thing I'd been dreaming about.

Reaching down, I gently cupped Tanner's balls as I used my other hand to push a thumb into Calli's ass.

Tanner's breath hitched at the contact, but he didn't say anything to stop me.

"It only takes one word if you want anything to stop," I told them both, knowing that we were moving into unknown territory for both of them, and whilst I was firmly in charge, I wasn't going to cross any boundaries unless they wanted me to.

"Please don't stop," Calli breathed out.

"Tanner?" I needed to know that he was okay with this.

"I…I don't want to stop, but…." he trailed off, almost like he wasn't sure what to say next.

"Don't worry. I'm not going to fuck you, Tanner. There's only one ass here that I've got my sights on."

Tanner chuckled at my response, and I gave his balls a light tug as a reward.

"Fuck," he gasped. "I'm having some very confusing thoughts right now."

"Don't think, just feel."

Moving my hands to Calli's hips, I raised her up Tanner's length before slamming her back down on top of him.

"Argh, shit! I'm definitely going to come if you keep doing that," Tanner warned.

"Hmmm, we should probably stop delaying then," I said

thoughtfully, reaching for the bottle of lube that I'd dropped on the bed beside me.

Spreading a generous amount along my length, I squirted the liquid onto Calli's ass.

"Ah, cold." She laughed, squirming in response, which had Tanner swearing in frustration again.

I couldn't help but chuckle at the pair of them. This couldn't have been more perfect if I'd choreographed it ahead of time. Come to think of it, if I had, I definitely wouldn't have thought of half the things we were doing right now.

I used my thumb to spread the cold liquid over Calli's ass, gently fucking her to make sure there was nothing about this that would hurt her. I wanted her to enjoy herself just as much as the rest of us.

Calli mewled at the sensation, and I could feel the quiver in her hips as she desperately wanted to move.

"Grey…please," she groaned.

"Don't worry, sweetheart. I've got you."

I replaced my thumb with the head of my cock, grasping Calli's hips as I worked her up and down Tanner's cock one more time. He hissed out at the sensation, and I could tell he was close, the teasing touches becoming too much for him.

Slowly, I started to push into Calli's ass, pausing to make sure she was okay when the tip of my cock had pushed inside.

"Oh fuck, I can feel you," Tanner gasped out.

Running my hands over Calli's ass and up her spine, I made sure she was relaxed and happy with what was happening. From the way she gently pushed back against me, I guessed she was.

"More, Grey. Please," she panted.

"I've got you, sweetheart," I moaned as I pushed deeper inside her.

She was so fucking tight. I could feel Tanner's cock through her thin walls, and he groaned at the sensation.

"I need you to move," Calli gasped. "I feel so full, I, I need…"

"I know. I've got you," I reassured as I grasped her hips and gave in to the temptation to shallowly thrust inside of her.

Every time I bottomed out on a thrust, it pushed Calli down onto Tanner's cock, and I lifted her back up from him as I slowly started to withdraw.

I could feel them both trembling beneath me as they let me take control. Fucking Calli down on Tanner as I took her ass just like I'd dreamed.

Even though it still felt like her ass was trying to strangle my cock, I felt the moment she completely relaxed, and I knew she was ready.

Moving swiftly, I took her the way I wanted, pumping into her with abandon as I felt myself pushing closer to the edge of climax.

"Yes, fuck, yes. Don't stop. Both of you, don't stop."

Looking down, I could see that Tanner was working at one of Calli's breasts with his mouth. Sucking her nipple and as much of her breast into his mouth as he could, he bit down harshly, and Calli's hips kicked beneath me.

I felt her clamp down on my cock at the sensation. I already knew Calli liked a touch of pain from how much she loved to be spanked.

Lifting one hand, I slapped it down on her ass, partly as a warning for moving, but also to reward her for being such a good girl in how she was taking both our cocks.

"Oh fuck," Tanner groaned. "Shit, she likes that." He chuckled.

"Yeah, she does," I crooned proudly as I stroked the sting away.

Moving Calli over Tanner's cock, I took her deeply, savouring the feeling of all of our bodies coming together.

"I'm going to come," Tanner groaned.

"You'll come when I say you can, beta, and not a moment sooner," I warned.

The growl of my wolf lined my voice, and I could feel him panting in delight as I embraced the need to dominate. His own pleasure rubbed against mine, banking my need to come, higher and higher. I wasn't going to last long myself. Everything about this experience had my balls pulling up tighter, and I knew I would explode at any moment.

Reaching around Calli, I worked my hand between her and Tanner until I found her clit. She whimpered as my fingers flicked over the bud, and I knew she was growing closer and closer to release as well.

"You're both doing so well," I crooned as I strummed away at Calli. "I'm going to let you both move, take what you want, and you can come when I let you."

Tanner swore, but his hips surged up into Calli nonetheless, as he desperately slammed his length inside of her.

Even Calli was rolling her hips as she completely surrendered to chasing the pleasure she was craving.

"Five."

I worked my fingers faster over Calli's clit wanting her hanging onto that edge in desperation, knowing she wasn't allowed a release.

"Four."

Tanner's strokes were getting wilder as he tried to hold himself back but couldn't stop himself from fucking our mate.

"Three."

I picked up my pace, slamming into Calli's ass as hard as I could, knowing it would end soon and wishing it wouldn't.

"Two."

My voice broke on the word as it became me trying to hold back, me clinging to that edge, desperately hoping that I wouldn't fall over before the others.

"One."

Our screams echoed around the room as waves of pleasure crashed over us. Calli tensed between us, her ass clamped down on my cock so fucking hard. I surged inside her, nonetheless, as I spilt my load. I could feel the come draining out of me, almost like Calli's ass was wringing me dry. I could even feel Tanner's cock twitching against my own as he came deep inside her pussy.

It felt like an orgasm that went on forever. I could feel the waves of ecstasy raking my spine as my hands gripped tightly onto Calli's hips. I could hear a chorus of howls in the back of my mind, and I knew it was all of our wolves rejoicing as the bond closed tighter around us.

I reluctantly slipped out of Calli's ass. As she gently lifted her hips, almost chasing my cock, Tanner slipped free of her pussy. I could hear the pout in the whimper she gave at the loss.

Chuckling at my insatiable mate, I gently ran my hands over her back. I'd never be able to stop myself from touching her. Calli's skin was like pure silk, and I loved how she always arched into my touch, craving more.

Leaning over her, I released their bindings. Tanner's arms swept around Calli, cradling her against his chest as she collapsed down against him in exhaustion.

I took a moment to slip into the bathroom to clean myself up and brought out two wash cloths for Tanner and Calli. Part of me didn't want to clean the evidence of what we'd done away from Calli. A primal part of me loved that she was marked with our scent now. Practicality won out over the insanity of my wolf as I gently wiped the cloth over Calli, making sure that she was cared for as she lay completely blissed out in Tanner's arms.

Tanner passed her across to me, and I snuggled onto the bed with my mate as he cleaned himself and then disappeared into the bathroom to dispose of the cloths. He almost looked shy as he reappeared in the doorway and looked at us both, still lying naked on the bed.

"I think after what we just did, you don't need to worry about whether you're welcome in this bed," I told him.

"It's not so much that I don't know if I'm welcome, and more that I'm wondering just how welcome I am."

Now I was confused. I was pretty sure there was some kind of hidden message in what he was saying, but my post-sex brain wasn't putting two and two together.

As the silence dragged on and Tanner stood watching me expectantly, Calli finally took pity on me and added, "He's wondering if you're harbouring some kind of newfound love for his dick."

I couldn't stop the bark of laughter that burst out of me at her frank evaluation of the situation.

Tanner was finding the whole thing just as amusing, but thankfully it was enough to break the ice for him to feel comfortable enough to slip into the bed on Calli's other side.

"Tanner, I could not do half the things I needed to do without you at my side. That, however, doesn't mean that I now find myself in love with you and wanting your cock in my mouth."

"I was wondering more about my ass, if I'm honest."

Calli's giggles were infectious, and it took more than a

few minutes for us to get to a place where we could calm down enough to talk again.

"No, I don't want to do anything to your ass," I gasped out between laughter. "Look, if we both ended up in the bedroom with Calli, I'm happy to make sure you're both having a good time. But I'm not interested in doing anything more hands-on with you. I'm sorry if that's disappointing or something," I quickly added, realising that might not be what he wanted to hear.

"Oh, thank fuck," Tanner sighed, putting my fears to rest. "I love you, dude, but this hole is staying a virgin."

"So you wouldn't let me do anything?" Calli asked, leaning up on one elbow to look at Tanner.

The look on his face had the laughter bursting out of me again. It was best described as a cross between horror and constipation. I had no idea if Calli was being serious, but if there was one thing we'd all learned tonight, Tanner was definitely not going to be letting his guard down around her for a while.

42

CALLI

As we sat around the breakfast table, I could see the sideways glances coming from River and Maverick, as if they were desperate to ask something. Every time they looked my way, I was pretty sure my face was getting redder and redder. Yes, I'd spent the night with Tanner and Grey. It wasn't exactly the first time I'd been with two of my mates at the same time, and it shouldn't be a big deal.

"We had a threesome, okay! It's not a big deal," I suddenly burst out just as Tanner was putting some toast in his mouth and started to choke on it.

Grey cocked his head to the side and then burst out laughing.

If I'd thought I was red before, that was nothing compared to now.

"Right. Erm, that's nice?" Maverick said, squinting in confusion.

"I think Calli thought you were being weird because of… last night's activities," Grey pointed out as he slapped Tanner on the back, who was trying not to die from bread inhalation.

"Oh, I was wondering when we were going to talk about the fact that you finally used your magic," Maverick sheepishly added.

Wow, someone was feeling blunt this morning. Just going to get straight into that one then.

"Jeez, you take a short paranoia-fuelled break from doing magic, which was totally justified by the way, and suddenly everyone wants to be all up your arse about it," I sniffed, feeling quite indignant about the whole thing.

"I love the way she says arse," Tanner whispered to Grey, who gave him a playful shove back even if he was nodding in agreement.

"I can say arse!" I scoffed, getting the wrong end of the stick entirely.

"Can I say arse?" Jacob cheered as the kids charged into the kitchen for breakfast.

Thank god they hadn't been within listening distance when I'd blurted out the word threesome. I probably should be more careful about what I said when they were around.

"Absolutely not," I said when I heard Tanner telling him, "As long as no one hears you."

Peering around Grey, I gave Tanner a glare and got nothing but a cheeky grin in return.

"You have five minutes to eat, and then your butts need to be through the door, so you're not late for school," I warned the kids as they descended on the food.

The speed with which they could inhale food was fairly impressive. It was like a plague of locusts had descended on the table as every scrap of food was demolished.

Sitting back, I took a moment to soak in the normality of the whole thing. Tanner was trying to tame Abby's mad hair into something that didn't look like an explosion, while River was talking through some homework with Kai, who was nodding away and chewing like a mad man.

This is what we were fighting for, the everyday moments like these. Times when we got to be a family. My mind fast-forward a couple of years in the future. I could see Grey bouncing a baby on his knee as he tried to get them to eat. The kids would still be the tight-knit group they were and driving us mad as the boys probably started to realise Abby was a girl.

With that thought came the sudden realisation of what I wanted to be doing myself. I had all this power, and I wanted to be able to help people with it. I needed to learn how to control my magic to get back to what I loved most—healing.

I wanted to help women shift, help our species become what it was always meant to be, what had been stolen from us. And I wanted to make a safe place for people to be able to do that.

These kids should be able to live in a world where they could be themselves without the fear that someone would kill them for having the audacity to even be alive.

We all deserved that.

And it was time to make sure it happened.

I couldn't sit back and expect everyone to solve all of our problems for me.

I nearly lost Tanner yesterday because I'd been too chicken shit to grab hold of my magic and teach that guy a lesson about coming for me. He'd singled me out from the rest of the pack because he thought I was weak. Well, I was done being weak. I was done being afraid.

For the first time since I'd been kidnapped, I let myself look inward toward that well of magic that dwelled inside of me. It was still a burning ocean, raging to be free, but I stood my ground this time, rather than being afraid of it.

This was my power, and it was time it learnt I was the one in control.

I felt the amethyst warm against my skin as I shoved myself into that well of power. I heard a gasp of amazement from one of the kids, but didn't let myself linger on it for now.

The coven bond was there, underneath all the chaos that was my power. I could feel the others and the steady stream that flowed through us all. It was calming to know that they were there, so close if I needed them to be.

My power twisted and turned, almost like it coated the bond. Not quite joining, but allowing small amounts of itself to be syphoned inside. The rest of the magic that couldn't access the flow seemed to surge up, trying to find an escape route.

I saw it for what it was now. It was a living entity that needed to be free, not caged away inside of me, looking at those bonds like a taunting window to the outside world.

Suppressing this force out of fear was the worst thing I could do. It needed to be free, and I knew exactly where it needed to go.

I had this power because I was supposed to be the Pack Queen. I realised now that it didn't mean I was supposed to rule over them all, but instead gift them the power I contained inside of me. It raged and stormed because it was supposed to be uniting with the others and finding a home with them.

When I realised what I'd done, a wave of sadness rolled over me. It was no wonder this force was fighting against me. I'd shoved it inside a box when it was made to run free through the forest at the side of the pack. It was a wild, untenable force, and I'd tried to put it on a leash.

I reached out for the pack bond, that twisted braided rope of many souls that linked me to the others. I could almost see the strands that didn't shine strong enough as they lay dark and weak against the shining light of my mates. But I realised even those weren't as they should be. They might shine now, but they should radiate like the sun.

Turning back to the magic inside of me, I saw how it had calmed, almost like it was watching and waiting to see what I was going to do.

I was ultimately making this up as I went along, and I had no idea if I was about to do the right thing or essentially electrocute the entire pack with a surge of magic. But as I reached a hand out to that well of power and grasped onto the pack link with my other, a sense of rightness flowed over me.

The magic made no attempt to stall. Instead, it slammed into me, racing toward what it had always wanted. I felt it surge through my body as it used me as a conduit to reach the others.

I flinched, expecting it to burn, expecting some form of punishment to come for having tried to hold it back in the first place. But there was nothing like that. I felt the magic's joy at going where it was needed, where it wanted to be. It was like the power was being reunited with the people it should have been with all along. I'd just been holding onto it for them until they were ready.

The pack bond flared to life, glowing with unrestrained power as it filtered out to every member. I could feel their surprise and happiness as they started to realise what was happening. I could feel every single one of them becoming who they were meant to be.

When it was finally over, I opened my eyes and took in the room around me. The kitchen was filled with the entire pack. Sean, Wells and Jessa stood at the back and tears of happiness coursed down Jessa's face.

"You did it," she murmured, more out of happiness than anything else.

I could feel the tears on my own cheeks, but they were tears of joy. As I looked around at the other pack members, I could almost see the newly gifted power shining just beneath their skin.

Holly looked at me in awe, her mouth hanging open in surprise.

"What just happened?" she asked. "We were outside getting ready for training, and then I knew I needed to be here and find you."

"She's accepted us," Aidan said proudly. "Calli accepted her place as our Queen."

The title still made me feel uncomfortable, but I knew he was right in my heart. It wasn't just a point of realising what I needed to do. It had also taken accepting that it needed to happen. This was a massive responsibility. We were all linked together now, more closely than ever, more than any pack had been for a long time.

"Just don't call me that, okay." I laughed, trying to play the whole thing off as a joke as I started to feel uncomfortable being the subject of everyone's attention.

Grey moved to my side, dropping to his knees as he leaned his forehead against my stomach.

"You will always be my Queen," he told me as his hands came to rest on my hips. "You've gifted us with so much, Calli. You turned our pack into a family, and you helped me be the alpha I needed to be to make my family safe. We'd do anything for you if you would only let us."

Grabbing his hands, I gently moved them away from my hips, dropping to my knees, so we were level with each other.

"I don't need you to do it all for me. I want to stand at

your side, Grey, not have you at my feet. We are a family, and everyone here is important to me. It's time we showed Stone what it means when he threatens the people we love."

The feral grin on Grey's face should have been scary. There was a subtle layer of his smokey power gathering across his body, and I felt the way it trailed across our clasped hands.

"I couldn't agree more with you."

"It's time for you to take my pack," Wells said confidently as he moved through the rest of our pack and approached us. "Now that Calli has accepted her place as your Queen, you need to take the pack and spread the power to the others before Stone can make a move against us."

"I'm not so sure it's as easy as that," I realised aloud, seeing the flaw in the plan that no one else had thought of. "I'm not a never-ending battery, you know. The power that was inside me has flowed out to where it was supposed to be. There is very little left. I probably have enough to pass it to a handful more, but there's no way it will be enough for everyone you have here."

Wells looked like I'd just torn the floor out from under him as he stalled in his steps toward us. His eyes were wide in shock, and I could see a glimmer of terror moving through him for possibly the first time ever.

"No! No, that can't be right." He spun to look at Jessa and Sean. "It has to happen this way. We've been working so hard. This…this can't be the end."

"What do you mean the end?" I asked in confusion.

"There have always been two possible outcomes to this scenario," Jessa said sadly. "The pack is gifted with the power to move against our enemies, and we succeed in what we've been working toward all this time."

"Or?" Tanner asked nervously.

"Or we don't," Jessa said simply, her eyes darting to the kids in the room as she purposefully held back the information they should never have to hear.

Or we all die.

That's what it boiled down to in the end.

"If I may," Lachlan interrupted. "I think there may be an option we've all overlooked."

"Overlooked?" Wells scoffed. "We've been at this for decades. We've looked at every possible solution there is. Calli is the only Queen of age in existence. If she can't give the animage power to the pack, then we've lost before we even had a chance to fight."

The fear inside of Wells was starting to bank toward rage, and I realised for the first time why he was so keen to put his life on the line and hand the pack over to Grey. He was doing this for Jessa. We'd spent so long wondering how he could bear to think about leaving her, when we hadn't considered how he'd feel knowing she would die. This was his way of saving her, and if he had to sacrifice himself to do it, he would.

"That's exactly my point, though. Calli isn't the only Queen in existence because Stone made himself one. So, why don't we make another one? Cassia can already shift into a wolf. It's not exactly the same thing, but we know we can do that much, at least. Calli already turned Holly, and we have Zoe's research notes on the laptop. How much harder can it be?" Lachlan said excitedly.

The whole room fell quiet. I could see the kids had lost interest, and even though they weren't bored, they also didn't want to leave in case they missed something. The adults, though, saw the glimmer of a possibility taking form.

"It has to be me," Jessa suddenly said, rushing to Wells' side and clasping his hand. "If I became a Queen, the power would filter through to the pack. We would still get to be together, Wells. You wouldn't have to risk yourself."

"No!" Wells shouted, stepping back. "I'm not going to risk you to some kind of science experiment."

"I'll do it," Holly bravely declared, even though she looked like she was about to shit herself. "You already turned me. You just need to finish off the last bit."

"I don't think that would work," Lachlan explained with a frown. "From what we know about the process Zoe was researching, the human women were unable to go through the transformation. She was the first successful subject as far as we're aware, which would indicate that it would need to be performed on a witch."

That left Cassia or Jessa, and I wasn't about to volunteer Cassia to be experimented on when she wasn't here to decide for herself. If she wanted to go through the process later, I would gladly do it.

I turned back to Jessa, and I could see the determination set in on her face as she started to think through the plan.

"I'm willing to get you the marrow you'd need if you're sure about this. We need to get into the laptop to find out what Zoe mixed it with; otherwise, all of this means nothing."

Jessa nodded, and a sense of resigned dread seemed to be setting in around Wells.

"I don't like this," Wells grumbled.

"Oh, hush. Anyone would think you were looking forward to getting rid of me," Jessa laughed. "It's my turn to do something for us. This could work, Wells. This could actually work."

"The obvious flaw in this plan is the amount of power you would gain," Sean pointed out, finally giving his opinion rather than lurking quietly by the wall. "If Calli only had enough for a relatively small pack, I don't see how we can expect Jessa to be able to produce enough to cover a pack of this size. It has to be, what? Fifty times the size of Grey's?"

He did have a point there.

"Maybe we should deal with that when we get to it," Jessa reasoned. "We don't even know if it's possible yet. The first hurdle is that someone needs to turn me."

"I think I'm going to be sick," Wells mumbled, stepping further away from her.

It was a reasonable reaction. Up until recently, turning a female had been nearly impossible. For all we knew, what had happened with Holly had been a fluke, and I'd had Cassia help me that time. We had no idea where she was now, and I didn't know if this was something I could do alone. Zoe had been through what looked like hundreds of women and only managed to turn two, and they'd been human.

"Perhaps the research notes will help us determine a way to safely turn Jessa," Lachlan pointed out. "Stone had to be the one to turn Zoe, and I doubt they would have risked her if it wasn't a sure thing."

"I don't know. It seemed like she was barely a step above guinea pig at that place. You have to remember that she was just the final test subject before they were going to do the process on Neressa."

"Yes, but she was also their main researcher. They wouldn't have been able to afford to lose her, or the entire project would have died with her," Lachlan argued.

He also had a point.

"So we're back to trying to get into the laptop," Grey nodded as his face crinkled in thought. "Have we made any progress on that?"

"My guy said any day now," Lachlan supplied confidently.

"How did you turn Cassia?" Sean asked.

"I have no idea. It wasn't on purpose, if that's what you're asking. I'm not even certain she has been turned. She still smells like a witch to me, and Zoe has such an unusual scent. I think she's just a witch that can shift now, if that makes sense."

"Not really," Tanner laughed.

I could see Abby shuffling on the sidelines, and I knew there was something she wanted to add to the conversation.

"What's wrong, cherry bomb?" Tanner asked, scooping up the little girl when he saw her move.

Leaning forward, she whispered into his ear, and Tanner nodded in response before he put her on the ground. Abby quickly skipped out of the room, and the boys trailed after her, just like they always did.

We all fell quiet as we waited for Tanner to tell us what she'd told him. He was so busy watching her skip away with a smile on his face that he didn't notice the rest of us getting restless.

"What did she say?" Wells finally snapped.

"What?" Turning around, Tanner realised we were all waiting for him to tell us. "Oh, they're late for school," Tanner told us, hitching a thumb over his shoulder in the direction of the front door, which the kids had just left through.

It was easy to forget that everyday life was still happening around us while we were getting sucked further and further into the craziness.

43
MAVERICK

Training this morning had been insane. When Calli had funnelled the animage power out to the pack, I'd felt it pass through me, but some had stayed. Now, I was impossibly stronger, faster, more than I had been before.

Everything came so much easier. I didn't even have to think about the magic now. It was there, always on the surface. It knew what to do before I'd even consciously had time to think about it.

It was like when a glass fell from a table, and your hand automatically reached out and caught it.

My wolf was so in tune with me that it didn't feel like we were two separate beings anymore. I'd always been the wolf, but now it wasn't like I had two sets of thoughts or emotions running through my mind. It had all flowed together into one power-filled stream.

The others were doing just as well as I was. Grey's smokey power was like a constant cloak around him. Sometimes you had to squint to see it, but it was always there.

River and Tanner had a subtle shine in their eyes, one

blue and the other red. They both moved seamlessly through fighting moves, their magic whipping out like another set of arms that they used to restrain their opponents or drag them down to the ground.

The most amazing of all, though, was Lachlan. I swore I could see lightning flashing in his eyes now.

After a few moments of practice with Keelan, he was determined to be too dangerous to spar with the rest of us. When your strike was a lightning bolt to your opponent, there were very few volunteers to spar with anyway.

His lightning was incredible. Not only did it fire out from him now, but it writhed across the ground like a living snake, striking out at any who tried to stand against him.

It was easy to see the difference in him since his magic had been unbound. The boost from Calli wasn't needed, but I suspected he'd had one anyway.

The matching amethyst he had with Calli was strapped around his wrist. The subtle glow warned anyone stupid enough to think he was the weak link in our pack.

I could feel the moonlight flowing through me even keener now. It was a cold rush that almost felt like a hum beneath my skin. I had a feeling that I might be stronger now, but in the darker hours, when the moon was at its strongest, I wanted to try out just how much I was capable of.

The biggest change, though, and the one we were all probably the happiest about, was to the rest of the pack. Holly, Nash, Aidan, and Blake had finally strengthened their connections to the animage power. Not only were they stronger and with more control, but they could use the magic as consistently as we could without it seeming to run out like before. Everyone was relieved that it was finally working for them, but we were trying not to show it because we could all feel Calli's guilt over the whole thing.

"We should go for a pack run tonight," I suggested as we started to leave the training field, leaving behind an exhausted-looking Keelan and a few of his trusted guards. "I want to see what we can do when we shift."

This was the first time I'd been excited about being a wolf. I'd moved from chaining my wolf up in my mind, to almost giddy at the thought of going for a run.

"It might be a sensible idea to take the kids," Tanner said as we moved toward the house. "We need to see if any of this has sparked any changes in them. It would probably be best to do that away from anyone who could get hurt in the crossfire."

"I don't know," Grey mumbled, shutting the door behind us, so we were alone in the packhouse. "I don't like the idea of being outside with the pups until we have more of an idea of what Stone is up to. I don't like sitting by and waiting for him to strike."

"You want to make a move?" I realised and saw the reason why he'd guided us into the house to somewhere quiet.

"I think it would be sensible to scout out around the edges of the packlands and see if we can find any signs of other wolves nearby. It would make sense for Stone to have some nearby to keep an eye on the pack and strike quickly if an opportunity should present itself."

"And you want to present them with an opportunity?" I could practically feel the lust for a fight humming inside me as I asked.

"Hmmm. Just us, out for a run in the middle of the night. We'd present a tempting target. Especially after Stone's spy has told him that we're basically inept at using our powers."

"You don't think we're getting ahead of ourselves?" Calli asked nervously. "We've only had a few hours to get used to the new power you've got now. Could this just be overconfidence from a good training session clouding your mind?"

She made a good point, and whilst she was right to some degree, that didn't mean Grey's plan wasn't worth a shot.

"Probably," I agreed with a shrug. "But Grey has a point. If Stone has a small contingent of wolves on the border, it would be better to face them now when they have little idea of what we can do, than when they know more about our abilities and have the chance to call in further reinforcements."

The others nodded in agreement, and I could see their need for a fight starting to take hold.

"Striking out against Stone could also be the push he needs to attack," River reasoned. "We don't want to prompt him to move against us before we're ready. We should wait until Jessa has had the opportunity to start the process."

Even as he spoke, I could see the disappointment starting to form in him. River might be the voice of reason right now, but that didn't mean he wasn't on board with the plan. After all, they'd made the last move, and it had resulted in Calli being taken and hurt. My father needed to learn he didn't hold all the cards, and we weren't going to sit helplessly by waiting to die.

"I think we should do it tonight," I decided. "If we wait, we could lose the opportunity of going against a smaller force. If we can capture some of Stone's wolves, we might be able to get some information on his timeline."

That seemed to be the deciding factor for everyone. I wasn't the only one fed up with sitting and waiting for the axe to fall. Even Wells' pack, which should have been used to the waiting by now, we're starting to grow restless. We were shifters and witches, forces of nature. We weren't meant to be contained like this.

We'd determined the best time to go for our run would be early evening. Most of the pack would be quiet as they settled down for the night. Plus, the guards were changing over for night watch and wouldn't be an intimidating presence for those we were trying to lure in.

Waiting for the time to leave had been torturous for all of us. A rabid kind of anxiety was running through the pack. All of us were itching for a fight. Even Calli had a gleam of excitement in her eye.

We'd decided to ask Jessa to watch the kids so they didn't try to follow us. Wells and Sean were standing by, ready to bring reinforcements if we needed them. They hadn't been entirely on board with the idea at first, but even they couldn't argue with its logic when we laid it out.

Yes, it would have been better if Jessa had already been through the process, but once we started, we couldn't afford for word to get back to Stone of what we were doing. We didn't know if he had anyone else in the pack. This could be our only opportunity to make a move when he still assumed we were weak.

"Of course, I'm coming," Holly snapped at Nash, who'd been trying to convince her to stay behind and watch over the pups. "I'm just as strong as the rest of you. I can shift, and I have the same amount of power as you do. This is my fight too, and I'm fed up of being asked to sit out of it."

Nash looked to the rest of us in exasperation for backup, but I managed to find a really fascinating painting on the wall to stare at to avoid the uncomfortableness of the whole situation. With Tanner at my side, we must have looked ridiculous, but at least we weren't Lachlan, who'd been tying the same shoe for about five minutes now.

"I don't want you to get hurt, Hols," Nash sighed, looking at his mate, imploring her to see his point of view.

I knew how he felt. If I could tie Calli to the bed and leave her there for the night, I would. I was sure I'd be able to find a way to make her forgive me when I got back. In fact…

Turning to Calli, I was about to open my mouth when the glare she sent my way had me backing down and turning back to the wall.

"You didn't actually think that would work, did you?" Tanner asked, a smirk on his face.

"As if you haven't thought about it as well."

"That's not the point. At least I knew she'd cut off my balls before agreeing to something like that." Tanner laughed, nudging me with his shoulder as he did. "Calli is strong. Probably stronger than any of us. She can look after herself, and she'll have all of us at her side to make sure she's okay."

"Yeah, I know. But I'm starting to regret suggesting this. Now that we're about to set out, I'm starting to second guess myself."

Nash and Holly continued to bicker in the background, adding some entertainment to the nervous waiting period we were all going through as we hung around waiting for Wells' signal that the gate was quiet. It was strange having the alpha telling us when we could sneak out of his pack, but when one of your guards was reporting back to the enemy, you had to make sure you had everyone where you needed them.

"This is the best move forward. We would have all slowly gone as insane as Nash if we hadn't done something soon. This is our best shot at getting some information."

"I know, but…maybe it would be safer for me to go alone. I think I could pull on my moonlight form. No one would be able to catch me, and I could scout the area, see how many we're up against."

"None of us are going to agree to you taking that form again," Tanner sighed as he wrapped an arm around my shoulders. "I only just found you, little brother. Don't ask me to risk losing you again so soon."

He said it quietly so only I could hear, and I felt a tug in my chest at his words. I'd never had people who worried about me before. People who would be torn apart inside if I didn't return. It was a nice feeling, knowing that you were wanted.

"Do you want to have kids?" I suddenly burst out.

"Well, I don't know how much school you had, but generally, that takes a boy and a girl, and it would be a bit gross with you being my brother and all." Tanner laughed.

I gave him a shove at how he'd purposefully misinterpreted my words.

"I just thought it might be nice after all this is over, you know. Having a whole load of kids around. To give them a place where they know they're wanted and loved."

"Yeah, I know what you mean," Tanner said softly, a dreamy smile floating across his face. "The pack was fine in the beginning, but I don't think we realised what we were missing. When Calli came along, and then all the kids slowly started to move into the packhouse, it was like life came back to the house. Wallace kept Coby so far away from us that we didn't realise what was going on right under our noses. But I think we also didn't appreciate how much we needed him with us. How much the pack would grow through the injection of new life into it. He was right there all along, and we completely failed him. After everything, I can't believe I let a kid slip through the cracks like that. I, out of all of us, should have known better."

"I know you all feel like you failed Coby, but looking at him now, I don't think he agrees with you. The kid's happy. He's found his people, and he looks up to you guys. All we can do now is make sure that going forward, he has everything in his life to know he's safe, and we know what we need to do for that."

Tanner nodded and turned to face the door, waiting for word that it was time to go.

We were all ready. We were beyond ready. This was a fight that had been a long time coming.

Blake shuffled nervously off to the side. All of us had tried to draw him into some kind of conversation, well, everyone but Grey. I had a feeling the alpha was still holding a slight grudge against him. I was following Calli's lead, though. If she wasn't going to hold it against Blake for what he'd done, I wouldn't either. It helped that we all felt like, in his position, we might have done the same thing too.

No matter what we tried, Blake wouldn't engage with us for long. In some respects, there wasn't any need to punish Blake for his actions. He was doing a good enough job on his own.

"We'll keep an eye on him," Tanner told me through the link when he saw me watching Blake in concern.

"I'm worried that he'll lose himself if he keeps pushing the pack away. It would be the same as if he'd decided to go rogue."

"We won't let that happen. Let's see if he can work through this himself, and if he can't, we'll intercede," Tanner reasoned.

"You've mellowed since your initial reaction," I pointed out.

I couldn't help but think that Blake was pushing us away

because, deep down, he thought we all hated him, even if we weren't admitting it to his face.

"Anything that puts Calli at risk will push me to the edge of insanity, and I doubt you could say any different. But I keep coming back to the fact that I feel more like I failed him first. He should have known we had his back. He should never have thought the pack wasn't a safe place for his family, and that's on us. Throughout this whole thing, we keep losing sight of what's important. It's my job to make sure that the pack is happy, and I didn't do that."

"This isn't your fault." I couldn't believe that Tanner would even think that way.

"I think, deep down, it isn't really anyone's fault. They saw Blake as our weak link and exploited it. None of this stops until Daddy dearest is dead."

I looked at Tanner, and the deadly serious look on his face spoke to my own ferocious need to see him in the ground as well. There was something so right about it being us to end him once and for all.

The next few minutes seemed to drag by as we anxiously waited. When Wells finally appeared, I think we were at the point of leaving whether he thought it was a good idea or not.

"If you're doing this, you need to do it now," he told us, striding through the door.

"We're doing it," Grey said firmly.

Following our alpha down the steps of the packhouse, we shifted, and the pack started to pick up the pace toward the front gate. We didn't go through the centre of the town, which would have been the quickest route. We chose to skirt the border and stick close to the trees. We didn't want to draw attention from the pack and have any of them try to join us.

They didn't have the same level of protection as we did yet, and part of me felt like this was our fight anyway.

They'd come for our mate, and it was time for us to send a message back.

We emerged from the trees right by the gate. The guards on duty were barely paying any attention. They were so absorbed in watching the outside they paid us no mind until Grey shifted to his human form and approached them.

"We're coming through," he told one of the guards, his smokey power billowing around him.

The guard looked up in surprise and almost seemed to back away until he realised what he was doing.

"I…I haven't had word from the alpha that anyone would be leaving tonight," he stuttered nervously, his eyes casting around the pack of wolves standing at Grey's back.

It was pretty impressive that this guy was even thinking of standing against Grey. He was obviously a powerful alpha, and the two of them stood no chance against the number of us here.

"We aren't prisoners here. I'm taking my pack for a run. Now open the gate. We've been caged in here for too long, and they need to blow off some steam."

As if to demonstrate what Grey meant, Tanner and River started to snap and growl at each other before Tanner leapt at River. I could hear the pair of them laughing through the link, so it was fairly obvious that the whole thing was for show, but it seemed more than real to the two guards.

"Just open the gate," the second guard sighed. "He's right, he's not a prisoner, and if he wants to be stupid enough to run out into the night, it's not our place to stop him."

The fact that Grey managed to hold back from that comment was a testament to his control now, even if his top lip quivered with a subtle sneer. This guy didn't know how lucky he was that Grey already had his sights set on a different target. He was probably one of those who'd been at the training event when they'd wiped the floor with us. I imagine we'd lost a lot of respect amongst the guards that day.

The guard shrugged as if he wasn't bothered and unlatched the gate. Then, shoving his shoulder into the door, he swung it open.

Grey immediately shifted into his black wolf, and with a howl, he set off at a sprint, urging the pack to follow him.

There was something about having the others running at my side, the damp forest floor beneath my paws, and knowing I could just run forever if I wanted, that stirred something inside me.

The steady thump of wolf paws hitting the ground was almost cathartic, even if I was keeping an eye on Holly. She had taken to nipping at your tail when you were least expecting it.

I could feel the pull of the moon overhead, and my heart leapt for joy. The power inside me stirred, reaching up and out, finding the moonlight and joining with it, finally free of any constraints.

This was the first time I'd run at night and felt this freedom. I'd been right earlier. I could change into the moonlight form if I wanted to, but Tanner was right to be worried. With the joy of unrestrained freedom singing to me, I didn't know if I'd be able to change back, and it was only the fear of losing myself that made me stop.

As my power stretched and flowed into the night, I realised that I could sense something off in the distance.

"I think I can feel them," I said in awe through the link. I'd never had these kinds of senses before, but it was almost like I could feel the entire forest around me.

"Where?" Grey asked without question.

"Over to the East, about a ten-minute run out from our current position. I can't believe they'd get this close without worrying they'd be discovered. My father is definitely feeling overconfident right now."

"If he's even still in charge," Calli pointed out.

Something about that pulled a smile across my lips. It was about time he had something to worry about. I wondered if he even suspected Zoe was about to make a move against him. Probably not. He was conceited enough to think she'd go along with whatever he planned.

"Can you tell how many there are?" Grey asked as he turned the pack to intercept the group I could sense.

"I think there's about seven," I realised. "One of them is a lot stronger than the others."

"Could it be Zoe?" Calli asked. I could feel her need for revenge itching beneath the surface.

"I don't know," I admitted. "I can just tell one of them is brighter than the others."

We ran at full speed toward our target. It wouldn't matter when it came to the fight. I felt like I could keep up this speed for hours now. Especially now that we were running freely through the forest, something about this place sang to me.

"Split into two groups," Grey ordered as we approached. "We take them from all sides and pin them in the middle. We outnumber them enough that this should be an easy fight, but be on guard. If the stronger wolf Maverick can feel is Zoe, we can't rule out that they all have the animage power now."

We split into two groups of five and veered apart so we could trap Zoe and her wolves between us. Grey and Tanner naturally split to head up each group, and I found myself following my brother.

I had a second of distrust as I saw Blake head up the back

of Grey's group with Calli running in front of him, and then I felt bad about it. He'd made a mistake, but I think we were all on board with knowing he regretted it. Blake seemed to be working hard to show the pack they could trust him. I wasn't sure he'd dare face the wrath of his wife if he fucked up again.

Tanner slowed our group to a walk as we approached. All of us hunkered down instinctively, on the prowl and ready for the inevitable explosive ending of our hunt. My mouth felt like it was watering in anticipation of what was to come.

The group of wolves we'd tracked down were moving slowly, but it was clear they were heading closer to the pack. Whether they'd only just arrived or had been here for some time was unclear, but I could at least tell there were no more in the vicinity to surprise us later.

"We move in on my word," Grey ordered through the link, and a bristle of anticipation ran through my fur.

Suddenly, the wolves we were hunting came to a stop, and one in the middle lifted its head, scenting the air. That was when I finally got a good look at the one I could sense the most power coming from, and I really wished I hadn't.

It was a muddy brown wolf with patches of missing fur and open rotting sores in the patches. Now that we were closer, I could smell the wrongness of it all. It wasn't like a festering wound. It was more like the sour smell of corrupted magic. It was almost like it was fighting back against her for having taken something that didn't belong to her. This had to be her.

Unfortunately, Zoe seemed to be moving fine, the wounds not slowing her down at all. The power levels simmering inside of her were insane as well. She'd definitely shared what she had with the wolves around her, but she still had so much more to give. That couldn't be a good sign.

"Go, now," Grey barked just as the wolves we were surrounding seemed to break apart.

They turned quickly, facing outward as they tried to keep Zoe protectively inside their circle. The six of them stood no chance, though.

I felt a rumble beneath my paws and darted to the side just in time to miss a lash of what looked like barbed magic coming straight at me. Of course, they'd have some twisted version of what we did.

Striking out with my own magic, I was able to wrap one of the wolves in ropes of power and drag him down to the ground. I wasted no time sinking my teeth into his neck and tearing out his throat as I held him down. It probably wasn't a fair fight, but I couldn't risk his barbed power anywhere near Calli; that shit was made to maim.

I could hear the sounds of growls in the background when my eyes locked with Zoe. She didn't look panicked at all. If anything, she had a smile on her wolfie face before she shifted into her more vulnerable human form. It wasn't a smart move when everyone else was fighting in wolf form, not unless you had something else up your sleeve.

"Calli, dear, you brought your mates right out to me. I know I told you I wanted them, but you didn't have to deliver them yourself. I was more than happy to come and retrieve them on my own."

Whips of Calli's vines shot from the ground, lashing out at Zoe, and even though she danced back out of the way, cackling in glee, one still managed to open a gash on her cheek.

"Are you here too, brother? Don't you want to meet your sister?" she goaded.

Lachlan shifted into his human form, and the look of satisfaction on her face matched the annoyance I could feel running through the bond from Grey. Lachlan should know better than to allow himself any vulnerability in a fight.

Tanner dove in front of him, taking a lash of magic to the side to protect our bond, brother. It didn't seem to do too much damage, but it was enough to slow him down.

The wolf who'd struck out didn't last too long, though. He'd taken his eye off Holly to make his move when he thought he saw a weakness, and it gave her the window she needed.

Cords of pale green light wrapped around the wolf, and even though he struggled to free himself, there was no escape. The unmistakable sound of snapping bones echoed through the trees, followed by his howl of pain as Holly added more and more cords of power to his bindings. In the end, she didn't need to make the killing blow. As the cords grew in number, growing tighter and tighter, he soon stopped struggling and then it was only a moment before the wolf dropped to the ground dead.

"Impressive," Zoe murmured. "It would seem the rumours of your ineptitude have been greatly exaggerated."

"Give up and turn yourself in," Lachlan said, staring her down. "Come back to the pack and give us the information we want, and they may yet allow you to live."

It was strange seeing him taking the lead, and even stranger still that Grey was letting him. But as Grey started to circle around the clearing we'd ended up in, his intention was clear. While Lachlan drew her attention, Grey intended to take the threat down.

"Oh brother, there's no need to make threats. I'm more than happy to tell you what you need to know."

Now *that* I hadn't been expecting. Calli had mentioned she was chatty as fuck as she was carving her up, but I didn't expect her to agree to just roll over and give up.

"Where's Stone?" Lachlan asked, getting straight to the point.

Time was running short. From the look on Grey's face, this woman had very little time left to live.

"Oh, he's around here somewhere." Zoe laughed.

"She's lying. There's no one around for miles," I told everyone through the link.

"When does he intend to attack the pack?" Lachlan asked her. It was clear she wasn't going to give us what we needed. But if all we got today was to take out a threat against us, we could chalk it up as a win all round.

"Any day now, I expect. He doesn't exactly keep me in the loop. He's moving the pack as we speak, though."

Grey was in position at her back and ready to take her down.

"Do it now," Tanner shouted through the link. "She's not giving us anything we don't already know. She's just buying time for something."

Grey leapt at his words, and his power snapped out of him, aiming straight for Zoe's vulnerable throat. As he did, a burst of laughter came out of her, and I knew we'd made a mistake.

Before Grey could make contact with her, blinding power lashed out at Grey and wrapped around him at the same time that a barrier came crashing down around them. Calli roared in rage, her vines whipping out and slamming into the barrier. It was no use, though, they just bounced off, and a shimmer of magic reverberated across the dome as it held strong.

Lachlan cocked his head to the side as he regarded the scene in front of him.

"Grey! Grey!" Calli cried out through the bond, but there was no response from him.

He was conscious, but it didn't seem like Grey could hear

us through the barrier. Our link had been severed, just like it had when Calli was taken from us.

Lachlan took a step closer, squinting his eyes as he examined the woman in front of him.

"I don't really see the family resemblance," he said, almost like he couldn't see our alpha struggling against the cords of power currently wrapped around him.

Zoe shrugged in response. "Perhaps we have different fathers. Either way, you do descend from the same bloodline as me. I can feel it in the power you hold."

"Hmmm, yes, power. I can feel yours too," Lachlan said slowly. "You've not been playing nicely with it. It shows in your wolf form."

"Yes, that was unexpected," Zoe shrugged. "It will right itself when I absorb some of your Queen's, I suppose."

"I doubt that's the solution to your problem. In fact, I'm pretty sure that's the cause of it."

"Whatever it is, I need her to become stronger, and I will have her power to add to mine. Calli, dear, if you've stopped having your tantrum, I need you to come here. I'll even trade you for this man you seem to care so much about."

Zoe had us right where she wanted us. She'd come ahead of the others for a reason: to get hold of Calli.

As she stepped forward, I knew Calli wouldn't even think twice about trading herself for Grey. That was the type of person she was. She'd sacrifice anything to keep those she loved safe.

"No," Lachlan interrupted. "I don't think we need to be doing that."

Zoe looked at him in confusion. She wasn't the only one. We could all see Grey's thrashing was starting to slow, and no matter how much we tried, no one's magic was a match for Zoe's. She was a lot stronger than we'd bargained for.

"You would prefer to see this man die?" Zoe goaded, tightening her grip around Grey as she spoke.

"No. I'd prefer it if you just died already," Lachlan sneered.

I saw the moment his amethyst flared with blinding light, and then Lachlan unleashed the full extent of his power on Zoe. Strike after strike of lightning slammed into the barrier, and with each one, it flickered a bit more.

"Now, Tanner!" Lachlan shouted through the link, the strain in his voice showing as he continued the barrage.

Tanner's power whipped forward, but instead of reaching for Zoe, it wrapped around Grey and wrenched him free of her hold. I hadn't seen him moving slowly toward the back of the bubble, but now that my eyes were growing used to the blinding light coming from Lachlan's attack, I could see the point of the whole thing.

Lachlan was strong, stronger than any of us. It was the reason why his magic had been bound in the first place. To stand against it, Zoe had moved the majority of her power to the front of the bubble to hold it in place and shield herself from his lightning. Every time the bubble flickered under a lightning strike, the rear of it thinned away. It would have been easy for Tanner to break through when her attention was split like it was.

Tanner pulled Grey to safety, and the alpha shook himself in annoyance once he was free. The red gleam in his eyes glared brighter before he added his own power to the barrage against the bubble.

Zoe had picked the wrong wolf to mess with, and as the smoky power grew thicker, she must have realised she was on the losing end of this fight.

With a screech, she threw out a wave of power as the barrier around her finally gave way. The force of it breaking sent a wave of magic out from her, and we were all blown backward off our feet.

It was only a second, if that, before I was back on my feet, but by the time I was, Zoe was gone.

"Where is she?" Grey roared through the link to the rest of us.

I sent my power out around us and, sensing nothing, pushed it as far as it would go. Impossibly, there was nothing out there.

"She's gone," I gasped through the link, not believing it myself.

"So what? She's just teleported herself away?" Tanner asked in confusion. "Can we do that?"

"I doubt it," Calli told us, shifting into her human form as she moved across the clearing to Tanner and started to heal his side. "It's more likely she was able to move quickly enough to get enough distance between us before her power finally drained. Without it, Maverick won't be able to sense her."

She was right. It was the magic I'd been able to sense, and if she had none, she might as well have been invisible to me.

Lachlan wilted on the spot now that the whole thing was over. "Fuck me! I do not want to be the one to draw attention next time," he sighed, blanching pale as he looked like he was about to throw up. "How did you even know I could do that?" he asked, looking at Tanner.

I realised that the rest of us had obviously missed a conversation between the two of them, but it was hard to be annoyed when it had gotten us out of the situation we were in.

"Had absolutely no idea," Tanner admitted, then winced in pain as Calli poked his side in annoyance.

"Next time, can you let us all in on the plan?" Calli snapped, but it was clear from her face that she was more relieved than annoyed.

Grey wrapped an arm around our mate and kissed her deeply.

"Did we win?" River asked in confusion. "This doesn't feel like a win."

"Well, we didn't lose," Tanner said with a shrug.

I looked around the clearing at everyone, counting heads as I went. The six wolves that had been with Zoe were down, five of them were dead, and one only had a glimmer of power left in him. We might not know where Zoe had gone, or if anything she'd said was true, but we'd at least taken out the wolves she'd chosen to have at her side. That had to be something.

As I looked around, I realised not everyone had shifted back to their human forms.

"Where's Blake?" I asked. Surely we couldn't have been so wrong about him that he'd have left with Zoe.

Everyone looked around, but I could see they were all more concerned than angry. Not one of them suspected him. It was interesting that even though Grey had deemed him out of our pack, he still retained his link with us. He'd received the boost of power just like everyone else had, and he'd still been trusted enough to come with us today. It seemed like the alpha wanted to give Blake every opportunity to stay at our sides.

Calli saw him first and took off at a sprint. "Blake!"

My eyes zeroed in on his still form, where he lay beside one of the trees. I couldn't determine if he was breathing or not, and for a sudden moment, I thought we'd lost him. The sense of loss that swept over me was unexpected. This is what it felt like to lose one of your pack. The wrenching pain of losing a piece of yourself.

"Stay with me," Calli gasped as she dropped to her knees at her side. The glow of her magic quickly flared into existence as she started to heal him, and I almost sagged to the ground in relief.

"What the hell happened?" Grey raged as he rushed to Blake's side.

Staring down at his fallen friend, I could see the truth on Grey's face. He didn't want to lose this man. None of them did. I hadn't had as much chance to get to know him as the rest of them, but even I didn't hold any ill will toward him. He was a father, a husband, and a man who had desperately tried to keep his family safe. It was hard to criticise him for that.

We all moved to Calli's side, trying not to crowd her while she worked, but also wanting to make sure that he was okay. The ragged gash across his side could only have been caused by one thing.

"I saw one of the wolves using barbed cords of magic," I explained. "This must have been caused by something similar."

The wound seemed to wrap completely around Blake's torso. There was so much blood around him that it seemed impossible for him to survive. It was almost like they'd tried to cut him in two.

"Is anyone else injured?" Calli gritted out. "I don't know how much I'll have left after this, so I need to know now."

"We're fine," Grey said softly. "Blake is all that matters now."

I felt a tug on my magic, and I realised it was coming from the bond, or rather it was my magic trying to push into the bond.

"I think I can help," I said slowly, not entirely understanding what I was feeling. "I think I can add to your magic through the bond."

"I feel it too," Tanner said with a frown.

There was nothing else left to say as we all pushed whatever we had left toward the bond, hoping that it would be enough to help our mate save the man dying on the ground.

It shouldn't take someone's looming death for you to realise you weren't ready to let them go.

44
GREY

It had been a long and exhausting night, and we were all too restless to be able to sleep. When Nash came stumbling back into the room holding the laptop at his side, my brain was too exhausted to put it all together.

"We're in," he said, holding out the laptop. "Lachlan's guy just contacted us to say he's broken through the code."

I looked down at the machine in confusion. We were in?

Fuck! We were in!

I nearly reached out for it, but then I realised it was pointless. "There's no point giving it to me. I won't have any idea what I'm reading. Who's going to be the best out of all of us to interpret the data?" I asked.

"No idea. None of us, probably. This seems like something Wells and Sean will have to sort out," Nash admitted with a shrug.

"Right."

I looked at him expectantly, still not understanding why he held the blasted thing out to me. It was kind of making me feel dumb now.

"You're going to need to give it to them," Nash said slowly, almost like he wasn't sure if that was the case now.

"Right!" I gasped again, finally taking the laptop from his hand. Fuck, I was more tired than I thought.

"How is he?" Nash asked, his eyes moving to the closed door behind me.

"Feeling pretty stupid." I smiled happily as I said it, more out of relief than anything. "Jean has been tearing him a new one for about half an hour, and it's actually been quite comforting to listen to. Apparently, he took his eye off the fight to try and back Calli up, and one of them got the drop on him."

"He knows better than that," Nash said with a frown.

He was right, I'd been confused at first about why Blake would make such a stupid mistake, and when he'd admitted his reason, I felt pretty guilty about it.

"He didn't want her to get hurt. He said he owes the pack, and he was going to repay us by making sure that Calli was safe."

Nash looked about as sad as I did when I'd first heard him say it. Blake had been ready to sacrifice himself to prove that he was loyal to the pack. We weren't the type of people to expect someone to do that for us. We were supposed to be different from the other packs.

"Do you think he's up to talking?" Nash asked, his eyes moving back to the closed door.

"I'd say he'd be relieved for the interruption, but you're a braver man than I if you intend to step between him and Jean right now."

"Good point." Nash laughed, and then his eyes darted back from the way he'd come. "If Holly got in on it, I'd be downright terrified."

The terrified look on his face had me laughing along with

him. Yeah, Holly was definitely a force to be reckoned with, and I wouldn't want her and Jean ganging up on me either.

Looking at the laptop in my hand, I realised we were getting so close to achieving our goal. It was actually starting to feel like there was an end in sight to all of this.

"I'm looking forward to going home," I told Nash. "Now that we have the cabins, you and Holly should take one."

"Trying to kick me out of the house already?" Nash laughed.

It wasn't that I didn't want him there. It was just that now there was Calli and the pups in the house, it felt like it was becoming more like a home and less like a place me and the guys hung out at night.

I found my mind turning to that small bedroom on the top floor that had been on the plans for the renovation and Tanner's idea to turn it into a nursery.

"You're always welcome, Nash. But don't you want your own space away from us. I don't want you to think I'm kicking you out of your home, but you and Holly must want some alone time too."

As always happened when you mentioned Holly in a conversation, Nash got a dreamy look on his face at the thought of his mate. It made his pale complexion light up like a headlight. He'd never been able to hide his emotions well.

"I'm going to ask her to marry me when all of this is over," he suddenly said, like it was paining him to keep it inside.

"That's fantastic." I slapped him on the back in congratulations.

"I...erm, I might have slipped away to pick up the ring that day you couldn't find me. I'm sorry I lied to you, alpha," he said, looking more embarrassed than anything else.

"Don't worry about it. No harm, no foul." I laughed. I

couldn't believe he'd managed to keep it a secret for this long.

There was no doubt in my mind that Holly would say yes. She was his mate. They'd always be together.

"When are you going to pop a certain question to your beautiful mate?" he asked, waggling his eyebrows at me.

"Huh, it's not exactly that easy for us," I realised. "If we can't all marry her, then it wouldn't be fair for just one of us to take the honour."

I hadn't thought about it before now, but our situation wasn't exactly one that would be endorsed legally. There was a part of me that was sad about that. Would Calli always be looked at like she was doing something wrong by being with us all? Human society didn't exactly embrace differences, and we were definitely different by any standard. Hell, even shifter society still looked at five mates as being a bit strange.

"Who says it has to be legal?" Nash shrugged. "It's the words that matter, not the piece of paper you hold at the end."

"Shit, Nash, did you just get all philosophical on me there?"

It was easy to crack a joke about it now, but he actually had a point.

"Come on, let's go give this to Sean and Wells and see what's going to happen next." I shoved his shoulder playfully, and we moved through the house together, talking about the pack and what we wanted to do when we got home. If we had a home to go back to. I hadn't forgotten the burned-out ruins of Calli's house. It would be just like Stone to go back and set fire to the packhouse too. He was that much of a dick.

We could hear the raised voices coming from Wells' office before making it down the stairs. It probably would have been polite to wait for them to finish, but I strolled through the door anyway. We were past the point of polite manners now, and this argument had to do with what we were holding now anyway.

"You can't forbid me from doing this," Jessa screeched as we walked through the door.

Shit! Maybe we should have waited outside.

Jessa's head whipped in our direction, and for a second, I had the urge to cringe back away from her. I could tell she was in for an argument and wasn't about to back down. I was actually on her side, though, and not just because it took some of the light off Calli. If she wanted to do this, she should be allowed to. It was no different to Wells risking his life through a dominance challenge to keep her safe.

"What?" Wells shouted in our direction, slamming his fists on his desk as he surged out of his chair. "Can't you see we're busy screaming in here?"

That at least had Jessa softening a bit as she fought the urge to smile at how ridiculous her mate was.

"The laptop is unlocked. We have the data we need. We just need someone who can read it." I held the machine out in front of me, and Jessa took it from my hand, just like I'd known she would.

"That would be my job," she preened, taking the machine and walking out of the office.

Turning back to Wells, I could see his struggle to control himself. A part of me wanted to reach out with my alpha power to help him calm down and contain his wolf, but I knew he'd find the move insulting as an alpha himself. It would be akin to me saying he could not control his wolf himself.

After a moment, he dropped down into his chair with a huff. "The woman can be infuriating," he sighed.

I moved over to one of the chairs in the office, ready to

settle in and discuss what happened next. When I looked back, I saw Nash frozen by the door looking between Wells and me like he was waiting to be devoured. I supposed we did make a pretty intimidating picture.

"Well, sit down then," Wells snapped at Nash, still not fully in control yet.

Nash shot across the office and slammed his ass into the closest chair as I did my best to control my laughter at his discomfort.

"This isn't funny, you know," Nash whined through the link. "You two could squash me with the amount of alpha power leaking out in this room."

It was only then that I realised my control had slipped a bit, and the black smoke had already seeped out and covered the majority of the floor in the office.

"Apologies," I grumbled, pulling back on the power until it just cloaked me with its comforting warmth.

Wells lifted an eyebrow in question, and I answered with half a shrug. It was what it was. I was learning to just live with it now.

"So now that you've given my mate all the information she needs to experiment on herself, we need to discuss what happens next," Wells pointed out, a hint of annoyance still remaining in his voice.

"We need to move forward as quickly as possible. Zoe implied that Stone was already on his way. Even if he isn't, it would be prudent to move quickly, so your pack has time to get to grips with the animage powers."

"It didn't take you long to control them," Wells pointed out.

"Actually, it did. Calli's mates, me more than the rest, got the powers quickly. I struggled the most because it enhanced my alpha energy exponentially. You're a strong alpha, Wells.

Just like I am. You're going to need time to learn how to control it."

"Time, the one thing we never seem to have enough of," Wells mused.

"If I may?" Nash all but squeaked out to get our attention. "Jessa will presumably be granting the entire pack with power a lot quicker than Calli did. Mainly because she has the benefit of knowledge which Calli was never given. She's got to spread it out to a lot of people. It may be that you don't all get the same injection of power as we did."

I hadn't thought of that.

"You think because it's going to more, everyone will get less," I thought aloud.

"That could be a problem," Wells realised. "If it spreads too thin, it could become all but useless."

"There's only one way to find out."

Wells nodded uneasily. "I hate everything about this."

"I know. I've been in your position for what has felt like an age. But Jessa is strong. The women of that family are a force to be reckoned with, and you'll have us at your side in support."

Wells nodded, but I could tell my words had done little to calm him.

"I'll go and talk with Jessa. Make sure she has everything she needs. We should try and move ahead with this tonight."

Wells left the room without any further discussion, and it was like the tension left with him. I hated that he was going through this. We weren't exactly friends, I didn't think. But I'd grown to respect him over the last couple of weeks.

"Have we had any word from Davion?" I asked Nash, who was the one that always seemed to be in control of what happened in the background. "Or Hunter? Cassia?"

He shook his head. "I sent them an update to the secure

email we set up for them, but there hasn't been a response. From what I can see at our end, I believe the message has been read, but whatever is happening, they haven't had the time to respond."

"I suspect it's more that they don't want to involve us when we already have our hands full."

"You're worried about them?" Nash said, pointing out the obvious.

"Of course, Hunter and Cassia are pack, and so is Davion and his clan to a certain extent. I don't like having them out of contact and knowing we aren't going to be able to help if they get into trouble. Even though I'm more than sure Davion is capable of handling himself. Shit, we need him here probably more than he needs us. The clan would have been useful to have around when the fighting starts."

"Yeah, they are pretty useful when there's blood that needs to be spilt."

"Hmmm, this time last year, if you'd have said this was what life would be like, I would have slapped you silly."

"I don't know what's more unbelievable, the fact that we're sitting in the middle of a war that's about to explode around us or that we both somehow ended up with mates."

Nash laughed light-heartedly, and I realised how much I'd missed this.

"I wonder if Wells has a grill. We should throw something on tonight. Take a night off from the chaos."

"You mean after we turn Wells' witch mate into a shifter and then draw lots to see who's going to harvest Calli's bone marrow," Nash joked.

Shit, I'd forgotten about that part.

Why was it that our life never got any easier?

45
CALLI

For the life of me, I couldn't remember why I'd agreed to go through this again.

Holly and Aidan stood on either side of the clinic table I was currently lying on, holding one of my hands. It had been comforting at first, but now it felt suspiciously like they were preparing to hold me down.

Sean had ended up being the one who was "volunteered" to do the procedure, and I didn't know if I trusted him enough, to be honest. I wasn't sure I trusted anyone without a medical degree to do it. In the end, it came down to the fact that no one else could stomach the thought of drilling into me, and Wells had stupidly allowed Ethan and Felix to go off and join whatever chaos Davion was currently causing.

Goddammit! This was fucking torture!

I tried to grit my teeth and pretend that the fact someone was burrowing into my hip bone again didn't feel like my bones were about to rip through my skin. Unfortunately, Sean had a look on his face like if I dared to even moan in pain, he would throw up. I was pretty sure he'd pass out if I screamed.

Aidan wasn't looking much better. In fact, he'd had his eyes fixed on one spot on the wall and refused to look away since Sean had first broken through my skin.

Holly gripped my hand tighter as I held onto her so hard it must have been hurting.

"You've got this. You're nearly done, and then it's all over."

"Thank you, I needed that," Sean said, sounding like he was about to cry.

"Yeah, because I was talking to you," Holly snapped. "You should have let me do this," she pointed out.

So, not everyone hadn't been able to stomach the idea. The problem was that Holly seemed genuinely intrigued by the idea, which made me even more nervous.

"It could be worse," Sean pointed out. "You could be Jessa right now."

"Hey, I went through the change, and it wasn't that bad," Holly told him. She actually seemed to puff up in pride.

"Because you were unconscious and nearly dead at the time. Cassia and I were funnelling all of the pain away from you, and I can tell you now it was excruciating," I added, slightly annoyed that I wasn't getting any of the credit for it.

Holly patted me on the head, and I had the urge to throttle her.

"Done!" Sean suddenly exclaimed, and I realised that I'd been so distracted by thoughts of violence to Holly that I'd completely missed him inserting the needle and extracting the marrow.

"You're welcome," Holly preened, knowing precisely what she'd done.

The feeling of not being pulled apart slowly started to lessen, and then I was just left with pain radiating through my hip and leg bones. Never thought I'd see that as a positive. A part of me wanted to volunteer to help Jessa through the process. I'd at least be able to filter some of the pain away from her. But I also really didn't want to. I'd been through a shit tonne of it already, and no one had been there to help with my part. There was also the logistical problem that they were out in the woods, and I didn't have the same adrenaline as last time running through me.

Yeah, there was no way I was getting up for a while.

"Thank god that's over," Aidan murmured, sagging on the spot. "I love ya, sis, but I need to… you know… throw up," he suddenly blurted out and ran from the room.

"Erm…yeah. You know what you need?" Holly suddenly said. "Margaritas. They're going to be gone for a while. The kids are asleep. We should get Jean and get smashed on Margaritas."

"As tempting as that sounds," Sean started, again thinking she was talking to him, "they won't be that long, and then we've got to complete the last steps of the process. Transferring the animage power will go better if Calli is there to aid her."

"Why do you always think I'm talking to you?" Holly snapped.

Sean shrugged and moved away to mix the bone marrow with the potion Jessa had prepared earlier. We were putting a lot of faith in the notes we'd retrieved. It had already occurred to us that Zoe could have purposefully left something out of her notes to safeguard the process, but at this point, we were out of options.

"I wish Cassia was here," I groaned, missing the grumpy witch.

"Rude! And here I was thinking we were having a bonding moment," Holly accused. "I was all holding your hand and being like 'you got this', and the whole time you were thinking about another woman!"

"It's not like that, you weirdo. I mean, because then it wouldn't all be sitting on me, and she'd be able to do that shadow thing and spy on them so we'd know what was going on. I hate that they did the first stage without me."

It was still smarting that they'd left me out of the first part of the ritual. I was supposed to be the one to turn Jean after all this was over. Out of everyone, I was the one who needed to see how it went this time around. Besides, I'd turned Holly, so I was also the only one with any experience in this whole thing. It was understandable that Jessa would want her mate to be the one that turned her, but still, that didn't mean I couldn't pout about it.

"You don't want to be there, trust me," Lachlan said, walking through the door and nearly staggering to my side. "It's fucking awful."

He was white as a sheet, but with that same almost green tinge Sean had about five minutes ago.

"It's not going well then?" Sean asked in concern.

"Apparently, it's all going according to plan. But it's still pretty brutal. Not to mention the fact that Wells is losing his shit. It's taking Grey, Tanner and Keelan to restrain him."

With a sigh, I struggled to sit up, breathing through the pain flashing down my leg.

"Someone's going to have to carry me. I don't think I can walk out there by myself," I told them, resigned to the fact that what was about to come would be brutal enough.

"The fact that you can't walk there on your own should be enough to tell you that you need to lie the fuck back down," Holly snapped.

I could tell she was ready to push me down if she had to,

but the fact that Lachlan disagreed with her right now spoke volumes.

"Does she need my help?" I asked Lachlan, seriously making Holly huff in annoyance at being ignored.

Lachlan winced. He knew the truth, even if he didn't want to be the one to have to say it out loud. In the end, he sighed and nodded. "I don't think she can do it alone."

As he went to help me off the table, Holly stepped in front of him. I could tell she was pissed that this was about to happen, and even though she was angry with me, it was nice to know that someone cared that much about me.

"On one condition," she gritted out. "You let me do what Cassia did last time. You bring me in, and I will help shoulder the burden. I know you can do it because you brought Grey into my head."

I was pretty sure I could do it too, but the question was more about whether I should do it.

"And don't try to lie to me. I can tell by the look on your face that you already know you can," Holly snapped out.

"This is going to hurt like fuck you know," I pointed out, wanting to give her an opportunity to back out if she wanted to.

"I know. But you did this for me, and I want to help you do it for her. It shouldn't all be on you all the time, Cals."

I nodded slowly, but before I could agree, Lachlan and Sean both chimed in too.

"Then I will assist as well."

"You know me and your other mates want in too."

Maybe this would work. How many could I link to pass the pain through? There had to be a limit. But maybe it wasn't about people and more about bonds.

"We'd better get there fast, then," I told them, reaching

for Lachlan, who had already stepped around Holly to pick me up from the table.

As he scooped me up into his arms, I had a swoon-worthy moment. Why was it when a man picked you up like you weighed nothing that it made your stomach dip in happiness?

"I'm bringing Calli out. She has a plan to help Jessa through," Lachlan said through the link to the others.

"You'd better be quick about it. She doesn't look like she can take much more, and Wells has already taken a chunk out of Keelan," Grey gritted out, and it was apparent just from the tone of his voice how much trouble they were having holding Wells back from his mate.

This process shouldn't be as brutal as it was. There had to be a reason why it was so painful and some way to make it easier on the women. It just felt so wrong that they went through all this.

"Tell Wells that I have a way to help her, but I need him to calm down enough to help me. That might buy you some time," I suggested, not really thinking it would. He must be way past the point of being reasoned with now.

Lachlan ran as fast as he could while carrying me in his arms. Every step jolted pain through my hip and down into my leg. Then, just as I was getting to the point where I was about to beg him to stop, we broke through the trees and into the clearing where the ritual was taking place.

I flashed back to the night we had to help Cassia deal with her shadow magic overload. That night stayed in my nightmares for weeks after. I'd been so convinced I'd killed her.

Looking at the scene in front of me now, I could see Lachlan was right. Jessa looked like she had hardly anything left to give. She was barely conscious, panting in pain and coated in sweat. She only seemed to flare to life when pain ripped through her body, and she'd bow her back from the ground, screaming as loud as she could. Her voice was cracking and gravelly, and it was obvious she'd been screaming for a long time.

Grey and Tanner both had Wells restrained on the ground. His arms were twisted painfully behind him as they tried to stop him from entering the magic circle that was supposed to help Jessa through the transformation process. It looked like he'd already dislocated one shoulder, and from the blood running down his chin, I'd guess he'd done some damage to Keelan.

Looking around the clearing, I found Keelan slumped against a tree with River and Maverick at his side. Maverick was topless as he pressed his shirt against a wound on his side.

"Do you need my help?" I called over to them in concern.

Keelan looked like he was hurting, but his eyes were still fixed on Jessa in concern.

"I'm fine," he gritted out. "Help her first."

"It's not a case of first. I don't know how much it will take out of me. I might not be able to help you afterward. If you need help, you need to tell me now."

"I've had worse. I can heal this myself. Just help her, please."

I tapped Lachlan on the chest, and he gently put me on the ground. We didn't have much time to do this if we wanted Jessa to make it out alive.

"I don't have time to explain, but this will really fucking hurt," I warned them as I stepped up to the circle.

I could feel the hum of Jessa's magic as it crackled through the air where the circle had been cast. Laying my hand on the magic, I asked for admittance. I felt the rush of air as the magic parted, and, grabbing Holly's hand, I quickly rushed us through before it closed.

Inside the circle, it seemed so much worse. I could see the paleness of her face and the way her eyes were rolling in her head. Jessa's head flopped to the side as she saw me approach, and I quickly dropped to my knees and pulled her onto my knee.

"I'm…so…sorry," she stuttered out. "I…"

"Don't try to talk. I'm going to help, Jessa. Just hold on." I looked up and found Holly kneeling on Jessa's other side. "Last chance to back out," I told her as I held out a hand.

She didn't answer. She just grabbed hold of me and braced for what was to come. Having been through it once before, I knew this would be bad, and I was proud of Holly for being so ready to help when she could see evidence of what it was doing to Jessa.

Without even hesitating, I dropped down into the well of magic inside me, pulling Holly along for the ride. I took a moment to centre myself and find the bond I held with my mates. Then, once I had it fixed in my mind, I let the magic flow through to Jessa.

It was strange moving along with the flow of the magic and pulling the bond with me. I had a moment where the almost hysterical thought of hurting her more than she already was flashed through my mind, but there was no other choice if we were going to help her. She shouldn't feel a thing anyway, except for the relief as we filtered the pain away from her.

I found the core of Jessa's magic, and I could see the darkness swirling around her as it tried to force its way through to her core. It was so like when I'd changed Holly, and yet completely different at the same time. Where the energy had been trying to push through to Holly's soul, this time, Jessa's magic was actively trying to fight back against the changes. Both forces were trading blows, and every so often, it looked like a piece of Jessa's magic was torn away in the fray. That must be what was causing the majority of the pain for her. I couldn't even imagine what it would feel like to have those pieces torn apart inside her.

"What do I do?" Holly asked, reminding me that she was still here with me.

"Keep hold of my hand. Whatever you do, do not let go."

That seemed like better advice than admitting I had no fucking idea.

I sent a tendril of my own magic out to Jessa's. It was so busy fighting the force attacking it that it barely paid me any mind. Wrapping myself around the glowing core, I used my magic to create a protective barrier around Jessa's soul to ensure it stayed intact.

When I was confident that I'd reinforced the core as much as possible, I reached for the wild energy trying to unite with her. I could almost smell the damp earth and the scent of the forest at night as I tried to soothe the wild force of nature.

It rebelled and lashed out at my touch, and I felt a sting of the pain that Jessa must be going through. If this was going to work, we needed to try and calm them both, so I could guide them through the transition and help them unite. Jessa didn't have much fight left in her.

Jessa's soul quivered beneath the net of my magic, and I could feel a glimmer of the pain she was going through. Latching on to it with my mind, I pulled the bond forward and offered it a different path. Almost like Jessa's magic knew she was reaching her limit, it grabbed hold of the bond, and a wave of pain surged through it, away from Jessa.

Holly screamed, and for a moment, I panicked, trying to pull the wave back.

"Don't you dare try and back down now," Holly gritted out. "Ignore how we feel and do what you need to do."

I wasn't going to argue with her. She was right. The quicker we got her through this process, the quicker we'd be able to recover.

Turning back to the task at hand, I blocked out Holly and tried not to think about what my mates were going through.

I could feel the pain clawing at the back of my mind as it taunted me into giving up. Trying to concentrate while filtering this much through me felt impossible, but I forged on anyway. I couldn't afford to give up now. I might not be close with Jessa, but I wasn't going to lose another member of my family if there was any way to stop it.

The wild shifter energy seemed to have stopped trying to force its way through to Jessa's soul. It was almost like it was watching me in interest, gauging what I was trying to do.

Soothing Jessa's soul, I started to create a path. I'd seen this happen before, and I knew where we needed to get to. The wild energy needed to find a way into Jessa's core so that it could unite and become one with her soul. The difficulty was, the added layer of magic that seemed to be trying to protect her. Almost like her magic didn't want to give her up and clung to her possessively. I just needed to make it realise that it wasn't going to lose Jessa. It was going to gain a shifter side that would make it stronger and help it forge connections to spread the power wider, giving it more freedom.

It was almost like the magic could hear what I was thinking, or it could feel my intention through the magic I'd reinforced it with. I felt the moment it seemed to soften. When it relaxed and stopped trying to fight back against me.

Working diligently, I started the process of making a way for the energy to find a path to the core of Jessa's soul. The shifter energy felt like it started to work with me as I showed it the way. Whenever the magic started to fight back, we withdrew, taking the time to soothe that radiant energy that made Jessa who she was before moving on again. It was a slow process, but we were making progress at least.

Once the path was complete, there was only one thing left to do. Sit back and funnel as much of the pain away from Jessa as the two forces merged together.

That meant finally acknowledging the pain clawing away at the back of my mind.

It was a strange thing allowing yourself to feel pain, especially in an environment like this where you weren't actually inside your body and were nothing really apart from consciousness.

If you put your hand on something hot, your automatic reaction was to pull your hand away to stop the thing that was hurting you.

We couldn't do that now.

There would be no pulling away. To pull away meant to leave Jessa to her fate and hope she could pull through the other side.

It went entirely against your instincts to lean into the pain of something. But as I finally acknowledged the agony that wanted to course through me, I also felt the bond that pulled as much of it away from me as possible. I could feel Holly's hand in mine as she held on tightly, never once slackening her grip to try and move away.

Turning to the woman who had instantly become my friend, I saw the strength on her face as she gritted her teeth and bore the pain of someone she barely knew. She wasn't doing this for Jessa, though, I realised. She was doing it for me.

Holly was sitting here going through this terrible experience because she didn't want me to have to do it alone. Because Cassia and I had sat in her place and done it once for her.

Was this the key to getting the women through the process of being turned into shifters?

Was it the bonds we made and the support of the people who loved us?

Barely anyone had made it through this process alone because it was something we were never supposed to face alone. This should have been the beginning of someone being brought into the loving bond of a pack, and it needed to be done with the entire pack easing the burden of what they were going through.

Had we become so lost from what we once were that shifters had completely forgotten about even these fundamental things about how we survived?

I was so lost in my thoughts that I didn't notice at first that the pain was starting to recede. But when my attention returned to the glowing core we were trying to protect, I could see the two energies intertwining as they learned how to exist in harmony.

A new light had started to bloom between those two forces, and I recognised it as the beginning of the animage power. It was the unity of the two forces that created it. Jessa was a strong witch, and she was turned by a strong alpha. Hopefully, with the introduction of my magic to the mix, we'd be able to turn that new blooming light into a force that would spread through the entire pack.

Our lives depended on this working. The lives of our entire species depended on this working.

No pressure, then.

Withdrawing from Jessa's mind, I pulled Holly back through the connection with me, and we both fell back into our bodies. There was no other way of describing it. It was like when you fell asleep too quickly and felt like you were falling before you jolted awake. It was disconcerting, to say the least, but it was always followed by the relief that you'd made it back into yourself and I hadn't accidentally body swapped myself with someone else.

"The next time I offer to help you, I need you to remind me about this," Holly groaned from where she was now lying on the ground. "I think my head fell off. That hurt so much. I must be missing a limb or something now, right?"

"I'm pretty sure you're completely fine." I tried to laugh, but it came out as a groan instead.

"Oh god, what if you gave me a tail or something," Holly panicked.

"You already have a tail."

Where was the trust?! Jeez!

"Right! Good point…do you think we can have margaritas now?" Holly asked, sounding more like herself again.

"If you do, I want one," Jessa groaned out. "No…I want six," she decided.

My head flopped to the side, and I looked Jessa over to make sure she was still intact. Holly was right. That amount of pain really did feel like you should have lost a limb or something. The flash of agony from my hip reminded me that I was already injured myself. There was something so unfair about the fact that after all of that, I still had to bear this.

We'd flopped to the ground, all lying in a row, with Jessa in the middle.

I saw Holly's head flop to the side like mine had as she looked over Jessa, then she screeched, "NASH!"

"Oh fuck, did it not work? Holly! Holly! I can't get through the circle to you!"

She was such a dick. Poor Nash sounded beside himself.

"Will you make us margaritas?" Holly whined in response. "Jessa needs six, and I need at least five, and we should probably let Calli have at least one for saving the day again. Oh, and Jean might want one too."

"Babe!" Nash ground out. "You know you'll pay for that later, right?"

"Oh, I hope so." She laughed before sitting up with a groan. "Jessa, you might need to drop your circle thingy. Wells is looking a bit scary."

Jessa waved a hand tiredly through the air, and I felt the snap of magic as the circle receded. Seconds later, the men sprinted to us. Jessa was pulled into Wells' arms as he buried his face in her neck, unable to speak as sobs raked through his body.

Holly and Nash were reunited with minimal bickering, and it wasn't hard to see the love between them.

I found myself being pulled into the arms of Grey, and Tanner wrapped himself around the two of us.

"I can't believe you went through that alone last time," Grey murmured, dropping kisses on my head as he did.

"I didn't. I was with Cassia," I reminded him. I didn't dare point out that it had been much worse with only the two of us in the link. "Wait! How's Keelan?" I asked, remembering he'd been hurt.

Grey spun us around, and I saw that Maverick and River had stayed by his side. Keelan didn't look like he was doing too well, and I was starting to doubt his reassurances that he'd be able to heal the wound by himself.

Maverick looked over at us and subtly shook his head.

I was about to tell Grey to take me over there when he started to walk anyway.

"Have you got enough left?" he asked me quietly, as if it would make any difference.

"Yeah, I'm fine. Sharing the load made the whole process a lot easier for me."

It was true too. I barely felt like I'd used up any of my own magic. Worst case scenario, I could have drawn on Lachlan as well. In fact, while I was thinking about it, we really needed to see if Lachlan was able to heal now that he'd had his magic unbound. It would make life a lot easier if everyone wasn't so reliant on me for healing. Not to mention the fact that there would finally be someone around that would be able to heal me. I was starting to feel pretty salty that I was always there for everyone else, but I had to suffer through the wait of healing myself.

Grey set me down on the ground next to Keelan, and I could see that Maverick's shirt was soaked through with his blood.

"You were supposed to be healing this yourself, remember?" I joked, trying to make light of the situation that this man was potentially dying.

"I started, but then you didn't seem like you had enough to do, so I thought I'd save it for you," Keelan responded, but when he went to laugh, he winced in pain instead. "Can you heal this before Wells sees it? He won't be able to forgive himself when he realises what he did," Keelan told me quietly.

Gently putting my hands on his arm, I reached out with my healing magic. However, he'd managed it, Wells had torn open Keelan's stomach, and he'd managed to damage some of his organs in the process. This was a mortal wound, even for a shifter. There was no way he would have been able to heal this himself.

"I've got it," I reassured him as I started to push the magic into his body.

It would take some time, but I was reasonably confident I

could fix it. He'd lost a lot of blood, though. He wouldn't have lasted much longer on his own.

Healing Keelan was surprisingly easy after what we'd just done with Jessa. It almost felt strange to be alone while working my magic. It was nice having the others linked with me when I was going through the motions, but doing it now was like sinking into one of your favourite armchairs. There was something peaceful about the quiet. Working through the familiar motions of moving through his body, healing and stitching together his wound was almost hypnotic.

By the time I was done, there was no hiding the fact from Wells that he'd done his friend some significant damage. Keelan had passed out somewhere along the way, and it had taken longer to stitch together the damage without leaving too much scar tissue behind that wouldn't hinder him in the future.

I felt the drain by the time the work was done, but I was satisfied it had at least been done properly.

When I opened my eyes again, it was to find Wells kneeling at Keelan's other side, facing me. The sorrow on his face spoke of the guilt Keelan had known he'd feel when Wells realised what he'd done.

"Is he going to be okay?" he asked gravely.

"Of course he is. What type of healer do you take me for?" I said with a smile, feeling fairly proud of what I'd done here.

I noticed we were missing a few in the clearing now. It must have taken me longer than I'd realised to get the whole thing done.

"Where's Jessa?" I asked, wanting to see how she felt after what she'd just been through.

"Holly and Nash have taken her up to the house to rest. She's insisting that she finish the process tonight, but she looks exhausted. I think she should at least rest until the morning, but thankfully she's not up to arguing about it right now, so she agreed to at least wait until I knew Keelan was going to be okay. I can't believe I did this. I don't even remember…"

"It's not your fault," Grey reassured him. "You weren't yourself, and he knew that. He doesn't blame you. It's just one of those things that happens."

"Generally, 'one of those things' isn't something that can kill your friends," Wells responded grimly, not taking his eyes off Keelan.

"Well, you can repay him by carrying his heavy ass back to the packhouse," River joked, offering me a hand to help me stand while he did. "I don't know about everyone else, but I'm starving."

The rumble from my stomach was all the agreement I needed to give him. Hell, it had probably been going strong for a while with how hungry I was feeling right now.

"Let's all grab some food, and then we can at least talk to Jessa about the best next steps," I suggested.

I was actually in agreement with Wells. She wasn't up to doing this again tonight. I'd heard Zoe going through the process when I was getting out of that place, and there was no way Jessa would make it through round two of what she'd just been through.

46
GREY

Last night had turned into a night of eating and arguing. It was nearly as tiring as going through the process of whatever it was that had happened when Jessa was turned.

We all watched her carefully as we ate. Someone had at least had the forethought to ask one of the pack members to set out food for us, and we returned to roast chickens, salad and fresh bread. It was a lot healthier than what we'd have had before we met Calli, and a part of me was in complete agreement with her about the whole pizza thing.

There was something different about Jessa which I supposed made sense. She had a presence about her that hadn't been there before. It was like she was more aware of her surroundings. She didn't sit back and let things happen around her anymore. There was the hint of an ever-watchful predator to her now.

After a few hours of arguing, Wells convinced her to at least take the night before going through the next part of the process. Calli was exhausted too, so whatever would happen, she would have had to do it alone, and I think that had been the deciding factor in the end.

I couldn't quite decide how I felt about Jessa. Her assumption that Calli would be there to share the load pissed me off. But it wasn't like her usual self to act that way. Perhaps it was because she was dealing with another side of herself that she hadn't had before.

"Are we sure we haven't just created another problem by doing this?" Maverick asked as we all moved around the suite, getting ready for the day. "I mean, how do we know that after all this is said and done, Wells won't make a move to take over the other packs and Jessa won't try and take out Calli if she sees her as a threat. We could have made this entire situation so much worse."

He had a point, but did we really have any other choice?

"We aren't strong enough to stand against Stone on our own, and this is the only option we have," River reminded him.

"Aren't we, though? That Zoe chick looked pretty sick when we saw her. What if she isn't able to transfer the power to the pack. She was coming to get Calli because the process didn't work fully, and she needed her to finish the whole thing off. If we're only up against a handful of wolves like us and the rest and just the normal pack, we have more than enough power to take them on," Maverick argued.

"The problem is that's a lot of what-ifs, and we don't have the luxury of taking a time out halfway through a fight if we realise we're outmatched."

The fact that he was right annoyed me more than him making the suggestion. The fact that I hadn't thought of this myself was downright pissing me off.

"We need more information," Calli said in that quiet way she did when she was thinking about something.

"What are you planning?" I asked, knowing her well enough that I could tell when she had an idea brewing.

Calli shrugged and continued pulling on her jeans. Christ, the way they cupped her ass had me wanting to sink my teeth into it and from the look on her face as she caught me watching, she knew exactly what I was thinking about.

"Isn't it about time that we pulled the spy in and found out what he knows?" she asked. "If we're as close to the fight as we think we are, then we have nothing else left to gain by letting him feed information to Stone. Plus, we can't afford for him to get wind of the fact that we're in the process of creating a second Queen. Not until Jessa has gone through the change."

A knock at the suite door had us all pausing. It was so strange that no one moved at first. We weren't used to anyone coming up to this end of the house that wasn't the kids, and they just charged in like their asses were on fire, which was generally the speed they travelled anywhere.

River was the first to move, and he cracked open the door wide enough to see who was inside without giving them a glimpse of the room. I appreciated his forethought more than I'd have thought I would when I felt the simmering annoyance of someone having approached our den.

The alpha in me had calmed a lot over the last few days, but I was still prone to a flare-up every now and then. If anything, the injection of power Calli had given us actually helped with my control. It was like the last part of the process clicked into place, and I wasn't dealing with the rampaging struggle anymore.

"We'll be down in a minute," River confirmed to whoever was on the other side before closing the door again.

Turning back to us, I could see the surprise on his face.

"Jessa is about to start the change. Wells wants us to try and talk her out of it," he said, sounding exhausted.

"Aww, what? I don't want to get between the two of them again," Tanner whined. "Listening to them argue is exhausting."

He wasn't wrong.

"Why does he want us to stop it? I thought the plan was to go ahead with it all today?" Calli asked in confusion.

It was pretty fucking annoying that when we were expected to go through all the changes, everyone had been adamant it needed to be done straight away. But now that it involved his mate, Wells was slamming on the brakes and wanting a time-out.

His priorities were showing, and I was starting to think that Maverick might have a point.

"Do we know where the mixture that Sean prepared last night is?" I asked, suddenly worrying that we were making a huge mistake.

"No idea. Given what River just said, I'd guess Jessa must have it by now," Calli answered with a corresponding shrug. "Why?"

"I think Maverick has a point. We need to get that mixture back and really think this through. For now, that means we need to go along with Wells and get Jessa to back off for a day or two."

"You do realise the likelihood that we have a day or two before Stone turns up is about zero," Tanner deadpanned.

"Fuck!" This whole situation felt like we were stuck between a rock and a hard place. But the reality was, we couldn't afford for Wells to turn into the next Stone and then have two giant packs to face down. If that happened, we were done for. There was no way we'd come out the other side of that fight.

"Well, whatever we do, we need to at least buy ourselves some time to think."

The others nodded in agreement. It felt like we were rushing into a disaster at this point. I'd give anything to have Davion here to talk to now. He was always the reasoned voice when I needed to talk something through. Yeah, I'd had that with Sean and Wells, but now, looking back, it felt more like they were guiding me toward the outcome they wanted, whereas Davion had nothing to gain from this whole situation.

"We'd best move quickly then," Tanner sighed in resignation.

Yeah, listening to Wells and Jessa getting into it again was not something I was looking forward to.

Calli was the first one out of the door, and while everything inside me wanted to move her to where she was safer, I was starting to appreciate the fact that my mate was better to lead in some situations. And this situation was definitely one of them.

They might be estranged, but Jessa was Calli's family. If anyone had it in them to talk her down, it would be Calli.

It wasn't difficult trying to find them. Mainly because we'd already planned to do this in the dining room when we'd discussed it last night. Out in the clearing felt too out in the open, and the dining room was the biggest indoor space we had. Wells had arranged to have the furniture moved out overnight, and when we walked in, it made a surprising difference.

This place was massive.

I still preferred our packhouse, and again my mind started to wander. I hated the thought of not knowing what we'd be returning to when we went home. Because we would be going home. All of us. I wasn't going to lose a single person to this mess, including Blake. I'd come to realise that if I sent him to join Wells' pack, I'd only be letting Stone take one more thing away from us, and I was done letting that fucker win.

"This is not your decision to make, Wells. I will be the Queen here. Me. This pack will respond to my power."

Yep, we were definitely making a terrible decision here.

"Jessa, you don't even sound like yourself anymore. This isn't you," Wells said, trying to reason with the woman.

He was right. There was a wildness in her eyes that I'd never seen before. If she'd been a shifter all her life, I would have thought she was on the verge of turning rabid and losing control of her wolf. But could that really be the case here? She'd never shifted. We didn't even know if she could. There shouldn't be a reason for the wolf inside to be turning rabid.

"Jessa…" Calli started, but stopped when her Aunt whipped around to face her with a snarl.

Wells looked as shocked as the rest of us at the sight. Jessa had worked so hard to try and make amends with Calli. It had seemed to physically hurt her whenever she had to tell her something she knew would only push her further away. This definitely wasn't her acting like herself.

"Has she shifted yet?" I asked Wells. It perhaps wasn't the best idea talking around Jessa like she wasn't in the room, but it at least had the effect of drawing her attention away from Calli as her sights became firmly set on me.

"No, not yet. She was so exhausted last night that she basically passed out. When she woke up this morning, she was like this."

"Do not talk about me like I'm not here!" Jessa roared.

Her eyes moved between Wells and me, and it was only a matter of time before she lashed out. Being used to alpha fits,

Tanner could see it coming as clearly as I could, and he slowly pulled Calli behind him and out of the line of fire.

Something wasn't right about this whole situation.

"You're right, Jessa. I'm sorry." Raising my hands in front of me, I approached her as cautiously as I could. I needed to get in close enough to restrain her, but the added difficulty of her magic would make this nearly impossible. "Jessa, I need you to listen to me. I think you need to work through a shift before we do anything else. Your wolf is trying to get out, and it's messing with your emotions. Trust me, we've all been through it. If you could let us help you through the first shift, I promise you'll feel more in control."

It was complete bullshit. I had no idea if it was going to help at all. The only thing we ever did in these situations was put the shifter in a cell and wait for them to cool down. With her magic, who knew if a cell would even contain her.

"You can't tell me what to do," Jessa seethed as her eyes squinted in annoyance.

I could see her calculating her next move. She was assessing the room for a weak point, where to strike and how to make her escape. She was wild, and the glint of the wolf in her eyes showed she wasn't in control.

Wells approached her from the other side as slowly as I was. His eyes darted to me, and I could tell he understood what I was trying to do. As an alpha, it probably wasn't the first time he'd had to do this, but he'd probably never thought he'd have to do this with his mate.

Shit, Calli would never forgive me if I put her in the cage. Even if it was for her own good. If we thought their arguing was bad before, I hated to think the levels it would rise to now.

Just as I took another slow step forward, I saw Jessa's muscles bunch and realised we were too late. She leapt toward me with a snarl, and deadly claws burst out the tips of her fingers.

I could feel the shift starting to react inside me and my own magic coiling inside, ready to strike, when a bolt of lightning flew across the room and hit Jessa square in the chest. She was immediately thrown off course, the force of the blow slamming her into the wall instead.

The roar that came from Wells had me worrying that everything was about to get violent, but instead of tearing into Lachlan like most would have, Wells rushed to his mate's side.

"She's out," he sighed, checking her pulse before his eyes slowly moved to Lachlan. "You and I will be having a conversation later," he threatened.

Stepping between them, I made sure Wells knew that he wasn't getting to Lachlan without going through me first.

"We need to get her into one of the cells before she wakes up," I told him, drawing his attention to the unconscious woman in his arms. "Will the cells hold her?"

"I have no idea," Wells sighed as he scooped her up in his arms. "At this stage, what other choice do we have? I've never seen her like this before. This isn't her."

"It's the wolf," I told him, reassuring him. "She needs to learn how to deal with the wolf before she can move any further."

Wells looked at Calli, who was staring at the whole scene in shock. "Calli, can you restrain her magic?"

"What?" Calli squeaked. "I don't know how to do something like that."

"Call Marie and ask her how to bind Jessa's magic. It's the only hope we have of keeping her contained."

Calli nodded, pulling out her phone to do as he was asking.

"Where is the transfer potion?" I asked, "We need to get it somewhere she can't find it, in case she manages to get free."

Wells nodded to the fireplace, and there sitting on the top was a bottle with a grey looking fluid inside.

"Is that all of it?" I nodded to Maverick to go and get it as I opened the dining-room door to help Wells through.

Maverick quickly rushed to the bottle and shoved it in his pocket. The relieved look on his face was probably a mirror of my own.

"Yes, that's the only one. Hide it well. I will get her secured, and then we need to talk about our next move. This is going to set back our timeline significantly."

I nodded in acknowledgement as he moved past me, heading toward the basement with Tanner at his back to help how he could. The rest of us held back while Calli talked quietly with Marie on the phone, pacing back and forth in front of one of the windows.

After a few minutes, she ended the call and looked up at us with a tired determination. "I think I can do it," she said, not sounding terribly convinced. "How do we deal with her wolf, though?"

"The only way we know how is to wait it out." It wasn't the best option, but it was the only way we'd ever been able to deal with it before. Once the wolf took over, there was no reasoning with the person. The only thing to do was wait to see if the two of them could work out some kind of compromise to live in harmony.

"So, what do we do now?" River asked.

"Calli, go and bind Jessa's magic, so we know she will at least be safe where she is for now. Maverick, you need to destroy that bottle and the contents."

"What?!" Calli gasped. "Do you know what I went through for them to make that?"

I winced at her words. I did know, and it was killing me that we might have to ask her to go through it again.

"We can't afford for Jessa to get her hands on it in her current frame of mind. Even when she comes back to herself, we need to decide if it's something we should be handing over so easily in the first place."

Calli huffed in annoyance, but then she nodded. "You're right. Something about this doesn't feel right. We rushed into this because we were scared about what might happen. We need to think through what it would mean to create another Queen. You saw what Zoe looked like. Even if it was the best decision all around, I'm not sure we should be so ready to do that to Jessa."

We separated as Calli went to deal with Jessa, taking Lachlan for some support, while the rest of us went outside to destroy the mixture. Deciding the easiest way to do it was to burn it, we started up the fire pit. Once the flames took hold, we opened the bottle and poured the liquid into it, tossing the bottle in afterward for good measure.

"I'm not so sure that was a good idea," Sean's voice came from behind us.

Turning around, I saw him leaning against the wall of the house, where he'd obviously stood and watched what we were doing. The fact that he hadn't tried to stop us was curious.

"Wells is locking Jessa up in one of the cells. She's lost control. We can't afford for her to have this kind of power if she can't regain control of herself," I told him.

It sounded better than telling him we didn't know if we could trust them.

Sean nodded but said nothing. The old dragon saw and knew more than he ever let on, and he could probably guess the rest of our concerns.

"We need to send out scouts," he said finally. "See if we can determine how far out Stone is and how much longer we have."

"Do you have anyone in mind?"

Sean sighed and pushed away from the wall, moving over to join us at the side of the fire pit. "I don't even know who we can trust anymore," he said sadly, staring into the flames. "This all feels like it's spiralling out of control."

"The information you had about the need for the pack to have the animage powers. Did that come from Calli's mother?" Maverick asked. The way that he was trying to make it sound like an innocent question did nothing but make him sound more guilty.

"No, it was one of Jessa's more recent visions," Sean admitted. "And I know what you're trying to imply. I'm not so sure I disagree with you."

We all stood there and stared into the flames, assessing the implications of what this could mean. Had we just been played? Or were we so used to betrayal and constantly looking over our shoulders that we were seeing enemies where there weren't any?

"This is really fucked up," River suddenly moaned, making the rest of us chuckle in amusement.

Standing here feeling sorry for ourselves wasn't going to accomplish anything. Sean was right. We needed information about what was happening and where Stone was. Only then could we decide on our next move.

"Sir!" Keelan called out as he ran into the backyard. "We have injured people coming in through the front gate."

"What the hell! Are they attacking now?" Sean shouted, moving quickly across the grass to the vehicles parked out the front of the house.

The rest of us ran after him, eager to see how bad the situation was.

"Calli. We've got injured coming in through the front gate," I called out through our link.

"I need another minute," she gritted out. "She's resisting even though she's unconscious, but we're nearly through. Go ahead, and Lachlan and I will follow you."

"Okay. Be careful, sweetheart. If there is too much fighting by the gate, I want you to go to the schoolhouse and wait for us there."

"Yeah, sure, I'll totally do that," she snarked.

Beautiful, stubborn mate.

"Promise me you'll be careful," I demanded as I climbed into the truck's passenger side as Tanner got in behind the wheel.

"Only if you do the same."

"Tell us when you're on your way, and we'll update you," I settled for instead.

"Okay, now stop distracting me."

I didn't respond because she probably had a point. Calli was doing magic she'd never done before. I was proud of how she'd jumped back into learning what she could. I'd caught her at night, sitting in the moonlight at the window as she read through the book her mother had left her. Part of me wanted to know what it said, but it felt too intrusive to ask. This was her last connection to her mother. Despite Calli's turbulent emotions about whether she was responsible for her father's death or not, I knew deep down there was still an unbreakable love there for her mother.

Turning my attention back to the men in the truck, I tried to concentrate on what we could be going into. "Everyone stays together," I instructed. "We assess the situation when we get there, and if the fight has breached the gate, shift as soon as you can. We stay in constant communication through the bond. I don't want to risk anyone getting separated or cornered. We push them back through the gate, then we work with whoever else is there in securing the pack again. No one follows them out into the trees. Understood?"

"Yes, alpha," they all replied at once.

It was almost strange to hear them responding that way, but it made my wolf hum in satisfaction. We were entering an unknown situation where there could be people out for our blood. But I knew I could count on these men's unwavering support. We might be a small pack, we might be inexperienced, but when we were together, we'd fight with everything we had to protect those we loved.

As Tanner brought the truck to a stop at the gate, it became apparent that we weren't walking into the battle we'd thought we were.

Guards had the gate secured, and there was no one there that shouldn't be. Chaos erupted as someone tried to organise a contingent of guards to move out of the gate. When Sean got out of Keelan's truck ahead of us and started barking orders, everyone seemed to calm down.

As guards moved to the roles Sean assigned, I saw the five injured men lying on the ground that some guards were trying to treat.

"Is that Colt?" I suddenly realised as my eyes ran over the small pack in front of us.

"Shit!" Tanner swore, flinging open his door as he leapt from the truck.

We were all out of the truck and running, heading straight past Sean, who was organising the guard into finding out what had happened. I didn't give a shit about that right now. Colt and his pack might not have officially become part of our pack yet, but that didn't mean they were any less a part of us.

"Colt!" I shouted as we approached.

They were all laying too still, and it wasn't until we skidded to a stop at his side that I even saw the other alpha move.

With a groan, Colt turned his head to me. The tears in his eyes told me all I needed to know about the conditions of the others. He opened his mouth to speak, but a rattling cough came from his chest instead.

There was so much fucking blood. He had several bite wounds on his arms, and a set of claw marks ripped through his abdomen. The worst was a deep gash to the top of his thigh, which was bleeding heavily.

"Don't try and talk," I told him, gripping his hand tightly. "Calli will be here soon. You just need to hold on until she gets here."

"Calli!" I screamed through the link. I didn't care if Jessa was bound or not, these were our men, and they were more important than Jessa.

"I'm almost with you. That is, if Lachlan doesn't kill us with his driving. River told us it was Colt and his pack. What are we coming into?"

Looking up, I saw the guards covering the bodies of two of Colt's pack members as they looked up and grimly shook their heads at me. The others were still working on Bast and Danny.

"We've got two dead. Colt is badly injured. I don't know how long he can hold on, Calli. Bast and Danny are being worked on by the others. I don't know their condition."

How had this happened?

"Okay, make sure I have access to all of them at once. I'm

going to need you to move them so Lachlan and I can bring all three of them into one link."

"What are you planning?"

"Something I really hope works, but we don't have time to explain. I can see you. We're coming right to you," Calli told me.

Looking up, I could see the truck speeding toward us.

"Move Danny closer. Calli and Lachlan will need to link to them all at the same time," I instructed the others.

Tanner grabbed Danny and hauled him closer while one of the guards continued to work on him. The grunt of pain from Danny at least let us know he was still alive.

"Hold on, Colt. We've got you," I told him, looking back down only to find that he'd already passed out.

Looking up in desperation, I was relieved to see Calli already running from the truck to our side with Lachlan right behind her.

"I don't have time to explain," she rushed out, grabbing hold of Lachlan's hand as they both dropped to the ground. "Grab hold of Colt and push your knee up against Danny. I've got Bast. Don't break the connection because we're doing all three at once."

"What…" I started to ask, confused how she'd even figured out how to do this. But I didn't have time to finish my question as Calli closed her eyes, and her usual glow turned into a blinding light.

Everyone shied back away from her. The light almost felt like it was burning my eyes at first. The guards looked like they were about to piss themselves, and I even saw one reaching for a gun strapped to his waist.

"You even think about pulling that out, and I'll rip out your intestines through your mouth," I growled.

Sean spun in the direction I was glaring, and if the guard

wasn't terrified enough of me, he gulped and shrunk back at the look from the dragon.

Keelan squinted up at the guard and then, without hesitation, pointed to one of the other guards. "Arrest him and put him in the cells. He's not to be freed until I've had the chance to question him and determine he's not a spy."

The man's eyes widened in alarm, but he didn't have time for much else before two of his fellow guards had him restrained and dragged away to wherever the holding cells were on this side of the pack.

"Do you think that was necessary?" Sean asked, sounding pretty impressed by Keelan's forethought.

"Better safe than sorry. We don't know if the enemy still wants Calli or if they just want her out of the way. Until we can determine that I'm not taking any risks."

A growl rumbled across our gathering from Tanner, and I almost wanted to brag about the fact it hadn't come from me. Finally, I wasn't the one always on the brink of losing control.

"Settle down. I don't have any interest in your mate," Keelan laughed before quietly adding. "She's lacking the parts I find myself most interested in."

River looked confused for a second, but then a look of understanding flared on his face. I hadn't known Keelan was gay either. It made me feel better about having him around Calli, though.

Now that the guard had been dragged out of sight, I returned my attention to my mate. The intense glow around her seemed to have settled down. In fact, it seemed to be flowing into the three men she was trying to save.

I felt a tug on the packbond and having felt it once before, I knew what she was about to do.

"That's it, sweetheart," I encouraged, hoping she could

hear me. "Bring them into the bond, and we can all help them."

It was moments later that I felt the reverberation of the pack bond clicking into place. Just like it had when she'd accidentally done it with Coby, the realisation of pack struck through me. At the same time, I felt Calli starting to draw from the pack bond. This time I closed my eyes and breathed slowly, trying to calm myself the way that Lachlan had once taught me to.

I couldn't see my magic the way that Calli described it, but I could feel the warm cloak of smoke that seemed to settle around me. I'd always been able to feel the pack bond, and since Calli had joined it, it was like a shining beacon inside of me. It was easy to direct that smokey power of mine toward the bond. Once it realised what I was trying to do, it moved with little prompting, allowing Calli to syphon from my power to help heal the new members of our pack.

By the time I felt the tug lessening, and I opened my eyes, the sun was high in the sky. We must have been doing this for a couple of hours, and it had barely seemed like any time had passed at all.

I could feel the effects of the drain on my power as weariness clung around me, and now that Calli was starting to pull back from the healing, I could see her swaying on the spot.

"That was incredible," Keelan gasped as Calli moved her hand away from Bast.

Looking at the three men now, it was only obvious they'd been hurt because of the amount of blood lying on the ground around them. They were completely free of injuries now, and Colt was starting to wake, confusion marking his face.

He looked up at me in surprise. "I'm alive?"

"Yeah, but we came close to losing you," I told him. "I'm sorry it happened this way, Colt. I know you said you wanted to join the pack, but we didn't have time to find out if you'd changed your mind."

Colt's hand drifted to his stomach where the claw marks had once been. The skin was clear of any marks, and he seemed fascinated for a second as he drew his fingers across the surface.

"I don't…" and then his eyes drifted to where his two former pack members lay.

Colt's breath hitched as he sat up, his eyes fixed on his former friends.

"We went out to our old packlands. There wasn't anyone there, but we needed to see it. We needed to say goodbye, I think. We waited for a few days, and then we decided to come back. We knew you'd need our help. We should have come sooner. We shouldn't have wasted time there. We were ambushed when we got about five miles out of the pack. There's a huge mass of wolves gathering outside your borders. We fought our way through as best as we could, but there were just so many of them."

He stopped speaking as his eyes fixed on his friends. Bast and Danny had moved to their friends' sides, moving the covers away from their faces so they could say goodbye. They didn't need to say anything else. It was obvious what had happened.

Stone had taken one more thing from us.

"There were four wolves who helped us escape," Colt said quietly. "Some left the fight when it was obvious that we were done for, and the four of them turned on the others that remained. If they hadn't…"

I knew who he was talking about. It seemed that the men we'd let go had made it back to Stone's pack, and they'd persuaded at least a few of their friends to see the light.

"Who is he talking about?" Sean asked, looking at me almost accusingly.

"I'll fill you in later." We still didn't know who we could trust here, and I wasn't about to betray them.

Sean nodded, turning to look at the gate that some of the guards were securing. "The attack will be any day then," he said grimly.

"That doesn't matter right now," Calli told him wearily, reaching out and taking hold of Colt's hand. "Tonight, we bury our fallen friends. Tomorrow we plan for our war."

"Calli, we might not have the luxury of that much time," Sean told her wearily.

"It doesn't matter. Anyway, you've been planning this for years. You really want us to believe that you don't already have a hundred plans in your head. This is what we need to do for our pack. If they attack tonight, so be it. If they don't, then we prepare in the morning."

"How about a compromise, and we briefly go over a plan before calling it a night," I suggested. I could already see that Calli was dead on her feet. She needed to rest if she was going to recover enough magic to fight at all. But both of them were right. We needed to do this for our pack, and yet we couldn't afford to wake up in the middle of the night under attack and with no idea what we were supposed to do.

They both reluctantly nodded, and Colt turned to look at me. A fire burned in his eyes. I knew exactly how he felt.

"I want in on this talk too. I'm not sitting this out."

I clasped his shoulder and helped him up to his feet. "We will make them pay for everything they've done," I told him.

Colt turned back to his friends, a grim determination on his face. I could feel his rage glittering in the background of our bond.

"We should move them up to the house," Sean said sadly

as he looked down at the fallen wolves. "We already have an area cleared for a pyre if you want a traditional shifter funeral."

Colt nodded in agreement. I wasn't completely sure he even knew what he agreed to. He was so consumed by rage, I was sure all he could see were his dead friends and the vengeance that burned inside of him.

47
CALLI

The funeral had been one of the saddest things I'd experienced since I'd come to the US. Even when I'd found out that my own parents were lost, we never did this step. The fear and the determination outweighed the sadness at first. Yes, I was grieving, but I rarely had the time to stop and feel.

Watching Colt, Danny and Bast standing beside the pyre as they said goodbye to two of their friends was one of the hardest things I'd ever done. If only I'd been quicker. If only I'd been able to push past Jessa's magic. If I'd…

"Stop it," Lachlan said gently as he moved to my side and wrapped me in his arms. "I know you're blaming yourself, but you are the last person in the world to blame for this. You did everything you could, which was far more than most. You wouldn't have been able to save them, even if they had still been alive when we'd gotten there. Not without sacrificing at least one of the others in their place."

He was right. Spreading the link through the three men was one of the hardest things I'd ever done. Healing the most life-threatening injuries and coaxing the packbond into life had felt nearly impossible. If Lachlan hadn't been there with me, it would have been. As it was, even with the massive amount of power he'd added into the mix, it had barely been enough.

Lachlan was quiet for a moment, but then he added, "The way you heal is truly incredible, Calli. Do you think you could teach me once this is all over?"

"I don't see why not. You're powerful, Lachlan. Most people can only heal if they have an affinity for it, but with the amount of power you have, I suspect you could accomplish most things you tried, at least to some degree."

He didn't respond. I knew he was still uncomfortable talking about his magic. It was hard for him to look at it when it had been the thing he was most ashamed of for most of his life.

Jessa had a lot of explaining to do when she was back to herself. I know she'd done what she did to hide Lachlan and keep him safe, but that was no excuse for not telling him. Once he was old enough to understand, she had no reason to keep it from him. Perhaps if he'd known the truth, he wouldn't have felt so broken and alone.

Grey had pulled me to one side earlier and explained their suspicions. No one had dared raise it with Wells yet, but someone would have to soon. She was his mate. He was bound to her, whether she was about to try and incite some kind of coup or not. I couldn't even fathom how he would feel if it turned out to be true. It seemed to track from the briefest glimpse of what she'd been saying when we walked into the dining room, but we shouldn't judge her based on a couple of overheard sentences.

Either way, there was no way we could rely on Jessa in this fight now. Which meant we wouldn't have any way of gifting the animage power to Wells' wolves.

Colt, Danny, and Bast were in our bond now, and they'd start to feel the changes soon. If the attack was coming as soon as we thought, I doubted it would happen quick enough to make a difference. That meant it would all come down to the rest of our pack. Only ten of us against what we were starting to think was an entire army.

Many of Wells' pack had come out to stand in vigil at the funeral. Seeing everyone come together for such a sad event gave me some hope for our people working past this. They stood in the cold night air and watched as people they didn't know made their final journey. But none of them complained. I'd even seen tears on a few of their faces.

Wells' pack could sympathise with these men. They'd stood in their place, and they'd also been denied the opportunity to do this for a lot of their loved ones. It was almost like this became a way to say goodbye to everyone Stone had taken from us, and the list was too fucking long.

By the time the pyre burned down, most of the pack had started to leave. There would be some kind of event at the bar for people to talk about those they'd lost. It was a nice idea, but it was one none of our pack would be able to be involved with.

We had other plans.

We gathered in Wells' office. It wasn't really big enough, but none of us wanted to go into the dining room, and the kitchen looked over the side of the house where the funeral had been held. We all needed the separation for now.

Wells rolled out a set of plans across his desk, and we all moved closer to see.

"We approached on this road," Colt pointed out, running his finger along the same road we'd travelled to the pack. "We saw the first signs around here, and we were ambushed here. This was where we saw most of the wolves when they pulled us from the truck."

The area he was pointing to was only a few miles out from the pack.

"How did we not know they were there?" I asked in disbelief.

Wells frowned, and I could see how much it was troubling him too. "The last scout that went out was the guard Keelan had arrested at the gate. But the one before him was one I trust absolutely. They can't have been there for more than half a day."

"Still, moving that amount of people. We should have noticed something."

I had no idea what we were supposed to have noticed, but the fact that they were just sitting out there waiting was freaking me out.

"We can't count on the fact that this is the only group out there. If I was Stone, I'd be moving groups to surround the pack and simultaneously attack at various points along your wall. It would make you have to pull your fighters to multiple locations and thin out your forces if you wanted to hold the wall," Grey said, surprising us all.

When no one responded, he looked up and flushed in embarrassment. "I may have been reading a few books," he admitted.

"Well, whatever you've been reading, you're right. If he does that, we have little chance. The pack is big, but not everyone here will be able to fight."

"How many can we count on outside of us?" Grey asked.

"Maybe three hundred."

Looking at the map, I could see the problem already. It was such a big area that to cover it all would be impossible.

"We should split into groups, hold the wall as best we

can, but take the majority of our fighting force to where Stone and Zoe are. If we take them down, the rest of the pack will pull back. They'll be without an alpha, and the loss of an alpha should be enough to send them into a panic," I pointed out.

Wells nodded, and I could see the proud look on Grey and Sean's faces as they weighed up my suggestion. Grey wasn't the only one who'd been reading. A section in the book my mother had left me detailed a battle at an old fort my ancestors had tried to protect. It was a fascinating section from a strategy point of view.

"So the question is which direction will Stone attack from?" River asked.

"The front," Tanner and Maverick both said at the same time. It was actually kind of cute.

"He won't want to be at the back. He'll want to be in full view to take all the credit," Maverick added. "He'll be front and centre, far enough back that he won't have to do anything, but close enough that you'll be able to see him when he takes you down."

Wells nodded. "He'll be where he thinks I'll be. I'm going to make my presence known at the front gate tonight. If we can draw Stone to me, he will bring a bulk of his force to hide behind. We'll need enough fighters at the gate to hold them back. But then we can split the rest into groups of thirty, and we should have enough to cover the wall, but keep them close enough to back each other up if they need to."

It was all we could do.

"It's kind of a shame that you haven't spent the last few years laying an elaborate series of booby-traps around the walls," Tanner joked, even if there was a point underlaying the whole thing.

"Can you imagine the heat we'd have gotten from the humans if we'd have taken someone out with a landmine?"

"Can we count on you in this fight?" Grey asked Sean directly, voicing the one thing we all probably wanted to know.

"Me? Yes. My dragon? No." No one pushed Sean for his reasoning; we all knew it, and having to admit it out loud wouldn't have been fair on him. Sean no longer had control over his dragon, and letting him loose could do more damage than good.

Colt's eyes widened in surprise to a frankly hilarious degree at the mention of the word dragon.

"We'll answer any of your questions later," Grey reassured him, and Colt just nodded as he stared at Sean in awe.

"There's not really anything else we can do for tonight," Wells sighed, looking at the map in resignation. "We may as well…"

And then the phone rang.

"What the fuck now?" he barked down the phone by way of a greeting.

After a few seconds, he slammed it down and looked at the ceiling like he was begging someone for a break. With a sigh, he finally looked at the rest of us.

"We have vehicles approaching the gate," he said grimly. "Time to put your best game faces on."

Everyone moved to the vehicles outside. No one bothered to tell anyone to stay behind. We were all in this now, and we wanted to know who it was and what they wanted. There was no way Stone would have let anyone through who was going to support us, and that only meant one thing, whoever this was, they were bad news.

By the time we pulled up at the gate, the guards were already surrounding whoever was driving and calmly explaining that Wells was on his way. They hadn't let the vehicles through, and there were some kind of metal spikes sticking out of the ground where the gates would typically be, to prevent any vehicles from being able to drive inside.

Wells calmly climbed out of his car, and it was like looking at the annoying Councillor who kept turning up at the pack a couple of months ago, and not the man we'd all come to know.

It probably would have been more sensible to wait inside the car, but I knew this would affect us, and to hell with waiting behind.

Grey and my other mates all exited the vehicles at the same time as I did. Only Colt seemed to stay inside, and I wouldn't be surprised if it was because the others had been worried about him being able to stay calm enough to face down the enemy.

I was actually surprised when Stone stepped out of his vehicle. I didn't expect him to have the balls to turn up here himself. With what I could feel through the link, I wasn't the only one surprised to see him either.

Eight other wolves got out of the other cars and stood at his back. The smarmy look on Stone's face screamed that he thought he had the upper hand here.

"Oh good, you've brought her out for me," he said as he walked toward our group. "I've come to take custody of the witch. She's to be held for crimes against our people."

Grey growled low, stepping in front of me to try and keep me out of Stone's view. I was surprised that this was going to be Stone's tactic. It screamed of desperation.

"What evidence do you have of these crimes?" Lachlan asked calmly.

"I'm a Councillor. I don't need to present my evidence to

the likes of you, witch. You will hand her over, and I will be taking Calliope into my personal custody."

"You do, however, need to present that evidence to me though, Councillor," Wells told him, stepping forward confidently.

"Wells," Stone sneered. "It's best that you just hand her over. I'd hate for anything to happen to this strange little pack you seem to have gathered around you. Such strange stories are coming out about this place."

"I wonder if they're anything like the stories we've heard about you, Councillor," I chimed in, unable to stop myself. "I had such an interesting chat with an acquaintance of yours a few days ago. She seemed to have some bold claims to make. Which reminds me, congratulations on taking such an interesting mate, Councillor."

Stone's lip lifted in a sneer at the mention of Zoe, and I wasn't the only one who found it interesting. "I'm not here to discuss whatever lies you've heard about my personal life. Now surrender yourself, or we will be forced to take action."

Three of the men behind him shifted into wolves. It was probably meant to be a show of aggression, but knowing that we could kill them without even moving made it look a bit ridiculous now.

"Calli will be staying with me," Wells said, stepping between Stone and me. "I have a written order from the Council signed by four of its members that she is to remain in my protective custody."

Wells pulled a piece of paper from his jacket and passed it over to Stone, who snatched it out of his grasp before reading it carefully.

"This is clearly a fake," he snapped, waving the paper at Wells. "They would never…"

"Wouldn't they? I was at the Council Headquarters only

days ago when this paper was prepared. When was the last time you were there? If you wish to call the validity of the paper into question, you will need to call a meeting of the Council. Any move against my pack until that is done will be seen as an act of war, and I will respond appropriately."

The rest of the men at Stone's back shifted, but so did the guards who'd followed us out of the gate, and we outnumbered them significantly.

Stone's eyes moved around the group before they fixed on me, and he sneered. I couldn't believe he actually thought this was going to work. Maybe he wasn't desperate. Maybe he was just stupid.

"You're making a huge mistake," Stone seethed. "All of these people here, it would be a shame to see them all wiped out for the sake of one little girl."

"We both know that's not what this is about, Stone. At least have the decency to not treat me like I'm stupid," Wells responded. He was back to his usual laid back self, and I could see now why he was like this in his professional role at the Council.

People doubted him. They didn't view him as a threat, and all the time, he was there in the background manipulating the scene and gathering what information he needed. They wrote him off as inconsequential when he was the one getting ready to stab them in the back.

Stone rumbled with a growl, and I watched as his eyes moved around the scene in front of him, looking for a weakness he could exploit. He wouldn't find one. We were united, and we knew what we needed to do.

"Don't say I didn't warn you," he said in his last trading blow as he turned his back on us and strolled back to his car.

We all watched as he climbed into the vehicle, and they started to drive away.

"Why didn't we just kill him now?" I asked, realising we could have just missed our best chance to take him out.

"Because he knew that paper was a forgery, and I have a feeling that means we aren't aware of all the players in this game just yet," Wells added, obviously working through the possibilities.

"You bargained for my life with a forged document!" I didn't know if I should be insulted or impressed. Mental note, never play poker with Wells.

"Oh please, it's not like we would have let them walk away with you even if he had realised it." Wells turned around and started to walk back toward the gate as he called over his shoulder. "We might still need you yet."

Okay, yeah, insulted, it was definitely insulted.

"So where does that leave us now," River asked as we all started to trail our way behind Wells to head back up to the house.

"Get as much rest as you can," Wells shouted across to us as he climbed back into his vehicle. "The attack is coming at any moment. You'll need to be ready because you're the only chance we have at surviving this."

We all stumbled to a stop at his words as reality crashed in around us. Everyone here was counting on us. The small town pack and an English girl who'd stumbled across them. Maybe we should have let Jessa absorb all the power she wanted. At least then, we'd have someone else on our side for now.

48
MAVERICK

I hadn't managed to get any sleep. I'd spent the last few hours listening to Calli's breathing as I stared out the window at the moon hanging in the sky. It called to me, and I wanted to respond so badly, but I couldn't leave this place, not now that I had her. I could never leave her.

We'd all ended up piled together in one room again. Wells' ominous words about the fight hanging over us had us wanting the comfort of each other, and no one wanted to sleep alone. I was done finding the whole thing weird now.

It wasn't even surprising when the bedroom door flew out, and the little firecracker jumped on the bed with a cry. I could see the tears streaming down her little cheeks as she scrambled across the covers to Calli, kneeing Tanner in the balls as she went.

"What's wrong, little one?" Calli asked, scooping the little girl into her arms and cuddling her tight as she wept.

"They're coming," Abby whispered through her tears.

Everyone moved at once as we started the mad rush to pull on clothes. We didn't need an explanation of who she was talking about. We'd all been waiting for word to come down from the front gate. We were just fortunate enough to have an early warning system in the form of Abby.

The kid saw far too much, and it couldn't be good for her to have all these images of death and violence in her head.

We had to end this tonight, even if it was just for her sake. That kid needed us to protect her, and if it took taking out my father and smashing through whatever kind of army he'd gathered at his side, we'd do it in a heartbeat.

Calli sat in the middle of the bed, holding the little girl as she calmed her tears, gently wiping them from her face.

"Do you know what you need to do now?" Calli asked her gently.

Abby nodded with a sniffle, pushing the mess of red curls out of her eyes as she hiccuped. "Get the boys and hide at the school," she told Calli.

"And what if you hear scary noises?"

"Stay quiet and stay where we are until you come to find us," Abby repeated.

We'd been drilling the kids on the plan since we'd come up with it to ensure they didn't stray anywhere near the fighting.

"And if someone bad gets into the school, and it's not safe there anymore?"

"Shift and run, run until we can't run anymore. Then find somewhere safe to hide and stay there."

"And why are you going to stay there?" Calli asked softly.

Abby looked up at Calli with her big sad eyes, and I watched as awe set into her. Reaching up with her little hands, she placed them on Calli's cheeks, and a flicker of a smile came to her lips. "Because you will always find us."

Calli nodded and pulled the little girl close as she

wrapped her tightly in her arms. "We're family now, Abby. All of us. And we always protect our family."

Once he was dressed, Tanner moved over to the bed and reached for Abby, who happily jumped into his arms now that she'd calmed down.

"Time to go and make sure the boys are ready," Tanner told her, carrying her out of the room.

The plan was that Tanner would take the kids to the school with River, and they'd make sure everyone was there before they left to join us by the front gate. It wasn't just our kids that were supposed to be taking shelter there, and amidst all the chaos that was no doubt about to start, we wanted to make sure they all made it into the shelter.

Grey darted out of our room, and I could hear him striding through the house, banging on doors as he went. There weren't many people in the house, and, like us, I'd guess most would still be awake. But getting a head start on this could save lives, and we needed to get everyone into position before Stone made his first move.

Calli quickly pulled her clothes on, and I dropped to my knees to check her boots were correctly fastened. I wouldn't risk her falling. I couldn't risk her at all.

"Maybe you should..."

"Don't even," she sighed. "Even if I wanted to, you know you need me in this fight if we want any chance of all of you walking away from it."

"We're strong now. We could…"

"As if I would let you," she told me softly, pulling me back up to my feet.

I knew I wasn't the only one thinking it. I could feel a kind of sadness coming from Lachlan, who was still in the room with us. None of us wanted to take her into this fight. We didn't care what we were walking into. I knew I spoke for all of us when I said it felt wrong to put Calli in danger like this.

"Besides, that bitch owes me, and I'm looking forward to seeing how she likes to feel the pain for a change."

The vicious look on Calli's face was so unlike her, I was a little surprised, but I could understand her need for vengeance. I felt the same way about my father. I couldn't believe this whole thing started off because of him. I was hoping like hell we'd see him out there. Even if I had to fight through his entire pack to get to him—I would. He needed to pay, and I desperately wanted to be the one that put him in the ground.

"It's time," Grey said, sticking his head back through the door.

His eyes moved over Calli before he finally nodded and started to head for the vehicles. I had no idea how the alpha stayed so calm about Calli doing this. If I was freaking out, there was no way he wasn't. But there was nothing but a calming strength coming from the alpha through the bond right now. He had his game face on, and he was ready.

As we were loading up into the truck, I noted that the one Tanner and River were taking the kids in was gone. At least that side of things was going smoothly. My brother was another factor I was worried about more than I probably should be.

Wells and Sean were loading into their own vehicle. It hadn't seemed necessary to have Wells on the gate all night. Stone had shown his hand, and we all agreed he'd head straight to the gate, thinking it was the quickest way inside and to Calli. I couldn't understand why he was so fixated on her now that he'd made his own Queen. Unless she wasn't living up to expectations, which I doubted she was given her insane nature.

The drive to the front gate was filled with tension as we all sank into whatever headspace we needed to get through this. I'd never walked into a fight before. I suppose we did when we went to raid the facility at my father's pack, but something about that felt different to this.

This was two sides walking onto a battlefield with the intention of only one leaving. At least before, they hadn't known we were coming, and we had the naive expectation that we'd be in and out without any trouble.

When the truck stopped, we all had a moment where we just sat there. None of us went to get out, and none of us said a word. This could be the last time we were all together. It felt like I should be making some kind of declaration to Calli to make sure she remembered me if I was about to die.

I turned to look at her across the backseat to find she was already looking at me. Words weren't enough. I'd never be able to express just how much she meant to me. Instead, I hauled her toward me and slammed my lips on her. She wilted against me, humming in contentment as her mouth opened and the tip of her tongue grazed across my lips.

My mouth opened, and I stroked my tongue against her, mapping every second of the experience to memory.

When we broke apart, Calli's chest heaved as she gasped for air. The fire in her eyes had nothing to do with the fight we were about to walk into.

"Fuck," Lachlan mumbled from the front seat. "I'm starting to see why Tanner finds that so hot now."

"You know he's my brother, right?" I pointed out, slightly freaked out that my brother thought it was hot to see me kissing our mate.

"I don't mean you," Lachlan sighed, opening his door and getting out of the vehicle.

Striding around to Calli's side of the truck, he opened her

door before leaning in and unbuckling her seat belt. Then, scooping her up in his arms, he pulled her out of the truck and pressed her against the side before thoroughly kissing her.

I watched as Calli's legs wrapped around his waist, and she clung to Lachlan like she never wanted to let him go. His tongue darted into her mouth, and the sweet whimpers she made had my cock growing harder.

Okay, yeah, I was getting his point now.

Grey's chuckle from the driver's seat had me turning to him, even though I was far more interested in the show that Lachlan and Calli were currently putting on. I found him smirking over his shoulder at me.

"Tanner has a weird logic sometimes, but there are some things he's never wrong about."

It was so weird to be thinking of my brother right now.

Grey slipped out of the truck as Lachlan let Calli slip down his body, kissing her on the tip of her nose before he backed away.

The way that Grey strode toward Calli was all alpha. Her tongue darted out as she licked her lips, watching him prowl toward her with that smokey magic of his trailing across the ground as he went.

He'd bulked up since we'd been training, and with that cloak of smoke constantly surrounding him, he was an imposing guy now. Not that Calli seemed to agree.

Grey wrapped one hand around her throat as she tipped her head back to look up at him. Hooking the fingers of his other hand into her waistband, he slowly pulled her to press against his body.

I wasn't even involved in this, but the way he slowly dipped his head to hers was almost excruciating. I could see how Calli writhed at the anticipation of his touch. He dominated the kiss between them, and now I was having some confusing as hell feelings about Grey as well.

When he pulled away, Grey looked straight at me. The smirk on his face said he knew exactly what I was thinking, and I made sure to slam that barrier around me as tight as I could.

I didn't have the time to unpack those feelings right now, so denial was the best way to go.

Scrambling out of the car, I spotted Wells and Sean waiting for us over by the gate, trying their best not to look in our direction. From the playful jostling going on between the two of them, I'd guess that Wells was getting great amusement from Sean's discomfort about the whole thing.

Grey didn't waste any time taking Calli by the hand and walking over to meet them. There was a small raised platform at the top of the wall by the side of the gate, which the guards used to watch over the road while they were on duty, and we used that to try and get a read on the area.

Tanner and River jogged over to us just as we reached the top.

"The kids?" Calli asked.

"All tucked up with the others in the basement of the school. We made sure that the two teachers staying with them secured the doors before we left," Tanner told her calmly, even if I could see a look of panic in his eyes.

It went against everything we believed to leave the pups unprotected while we headed into the fight. They might have two of the teachers with them, but they weren't part of our pack, which meant we'd never fully trust them.

"I'm telling you, there hasn't been any reported movement along the wall," Keelan said as we all made it up to the top.

The cold breeze whistling through the trees felt freezing

up here, but it could have just been the dread that was starting to form inside me about what was coming that had me chilled to the bone.

Keelan was right. There wasn't any sign of anyone. But it was also pitch black, and I couldn't see a fucking thing.

"Probably should've gotten some lights out between the trees," Grey unhelpfully pointed out.

From the look on Wells' face, it wasn't appreciated either.

"I...might be able to help," I realised.

I could always feel the moonlight, even in the middle of the day, albeit muted then. But now, standing under the moon, I could feel an almost hum across my skin. My power reacted to it, reaching out for it and entwining with the moonbeams.

Taking a calming breath, I concentrated on that light, then held out my hands and slowly released my breath. A ghost of moonlight filtered out from me, the cloud of breath highlighted by the beams of light projecting out in the treeline in front of us.

I'd had no idea if I could actually do this, and now that I was, I was pretty impressed with myself.

Either way, I became a beacon as I sent out the light in front of us, lighting up the darkness our enemies used to hide their approach.

At first, I didn't see anything, but then a slight shift of movement at the very edge of the light I'd been able to produce pulled my eye in that direction. Once I'd seen one of them, it was impossible not to see the rest, sitting out there, just at the edge of the light. Sitting and waiting.

"There are hundreds of them," Keelan gasped.

It was impossible to count the number of glowing wolf eyes sitting amongst the trees. It was at least comforting to note that the mass of them didn't span the entire length of the wall. They all seemed to be sitting along the main road that led toward the front gate.

"We can't guarantee there aren't any further along the wall," Sean said grimly, turning around and striding down the steps back to the ground. "How many fighters do we have coming to the gate?"

We all followed him down. Now wasn't the time to be scared. Now was the time to get ready. This was where we'd be making our stand, and we couldn't afford to fall. This was like a one-shot revolution. We stood up now, and we refused to back down, no matter what was coming at us.

"There are fifteen guards stationed at the wall now. We have a hundred more fighters on route to back up and then the twelve of you," Keelan reported with a grim look on his face.

"And three more," Colt said, striding up to the gate with Danny and Bast at his side.

"Are you sure you're recovered enough for this?" Sean asked, casting an assessing gaze over the three of them.

"Thanks to Calli, I've never felt better," Colt lied.

We could all see it on his face. The grey shadows under his eyes proved how exhausted he was, but he had a reason to be in this fight, and none of us would tell him that he couldn't be.

"If you get into trouble out there, there will be no one to help you," Wells told him sternly.

"You don't have to worry about us," Colt told him, turning to Grey. "Tell us what you need us to do, alpha."

It was the first time that Colt had really spoken about Grey being his alpha. He must be feeling sore that the position had been taken from him without his consent, even if he had agreed to it weeks ago. But looking at the determination on his face now, there was no resentment there. He was fully with the pack, which meant he was part of our family now.

Wells might not think anyone would have their backs out there, but he was wrong.

Another truck pulled up at the gate, and Aidan, Blake, Nash and Holly piled out of it, heading in our direction.

Grey looked at Wells before stating, "I'll brief my pack and leave you to organise the others unless you need me."

Wells shook his head, already moving over to where a group of guards were nervously waiting. Sean looked over Grey and nodded his approval at what he saw before he followed his friend to organise what would be the second wave of fighters coming out of the gate. We were heading out first because we had the hardest job of the lot.

Turning back to us, Grey addressed the pack. "This is going to be a hard fight, and I'd like to say everyone will come out of it alive, but we need to face the reality that people will be hurt, and we could lose a member of the pack to this. I don't want that to happen. No one strays into the fight alone. You are to stay in groups of at least three. Always have a member of our pack at your back. Do not allow yourself to be drawn off alone."

We were all listening intently. This was a case of staying alive. We couldn't afford to be distracted right now.

"Colt, if you're in agreement, I want to split you guys up. We don't know if you've received any of the animage powers yet, and if you have, you don't have any control over them," Grey told him.

I could see from Colt's face that he wanted to say no, but he nodded in agreement anyway.

"Holly and Nash, you're with Colt. Aidan and Blake, you're with Bast. Maverick and Tanner, you're with Danny."

We all welcomed them into our group as we moved into position. Part of me hated not being with Calli, but I couldn't deny that I made a good team with Tanner.

"That leaves me with Calli, River and Lachlan."

Grey looked around the pack, and it was the first time I saw the shadow of worry in him. We'd all trained together and were more than capable, but still, this wasn't something we'd worked our entire lives toward. We'd had a handful of months, and most of those hadn't been as productive as the last few weeks had been.

"Wells' pack will concentrate on dealing with as many of the wolves as they can. We have the job of weeding out anyone we see with evidence of the animage powers. The other pack have no defences against them, and it's our job to keep them safe. While we're out there, our targets are Stone and Zoe. Wells and Sean are also going to try and get to Stone. Only Calli and Lachlan are to face down Zoe. If anyone else spots her, you tell us through the link, and we will make our way to back you up. It is vitally important that we take the two of them down as quickly as possible. If we want to end this fight without wiping out a significant portion of our species, we need to stop the other pack where it stands. If we take down their alpha, they will retreat."

I had no idea why everyone was so confident about that. Yes, it was our nature to follow our alpha, but how did they know that losing an alpha wouldn't just make the pack try to wipe us out for revenge?

"Any questions?" Grey asked.

No one spoke. What was there left to ask? We were walking out the gate and killing as many as we could. It wasn't difficult. The hard part was going to be staying alive.

"Stay in contact with each other through the link," Grey reminded everyone, finally starting to show his nerves.

This had to be killing him. His alpha side would be rebelling at the idea of leading his entire pack out into danger like this, even if he did need us by his side to get through this fight.

But maybe it was time for Grey to realise that it didn't need to just be him standing against our enemies alone. We were his pack, and he was our alpha. We would stand beside him no matter what.

Grey led us over to the gate. Wells was done briefing the guards, and they waited nervously by. The small group of fighters that had come from the pack looked far too few. A hundred people weren't as many as you thought, especially when they were your only backup to keep you alive.

As the gate rumbled open, I felt the link starting to open up between the pack. Everyone started to drop their barriers, and even though the nervousness between us all ramped up as a consequence, so did the determination.

I could feel the underlying need for blood. I wasn't the only one who had been wronged by my father. We all had a reason for wanting revenge.

My adrenaline started to pick up at the thought of the fight ahead. I could feel the others preparing themselves as we moved toward the open gate.

Whispers started between the guards as we moved past them. Grey's smokey aura was out in full, gliding along the ground around him. The crackles of Lachlan's lightning highlighted the black cloud, giving it an almost storm-like quality.

We were all drawing our magic to the surface, and it showed in a display of colours gleaming from our eyes.

Coming to a stop outside the gate, we waited, standing tall and strong. Our pack would hold this gate, and we would succeed. I might have started my life somewhere else, but I was Stoneridge now, and nothing would stand in our way.

49
CALLI

I stood at the front of the pack with Grey at my side and Lachlan and River at our backs. This was our display of strength.

The wolves of Stone's pack hadn't approached yet. They were no doubt assessing the show we were putting on for them. Even though I was hoping some of them would see and turn tail to run, I knew it was unlikely they would. Stone would no doubt inspire more fear in them than we did.

I reached out with my power, sending it through the ground like the vines I now controlled. I could feel those hiding amongst the trees, waiting for whatever signal they needed to move into the fight. But I wasn't doing this to assess their numbers. We already knew we were outnumbered, knowing just how badly didn't seem like something I really wanted to know.

"I feel four sets of animage energy," I told the others. "Zoe's with them."

"She hasn't spread it to the entire pack then?" Grey sounded relieved as he spoke, and I was right there with him.

An entire pack, the size of Stone's, wielding the same powers as we had, would mean certain death, and even though we hadn't admitted it to Wells and the others, we did have a plan if that was the case.

I wasn't even ashamed to admit that it was to fight our way to the kids and leave. Leave the other pack behind to fight whatever was coming for them alone. There would be no victory for us against hundreds of animages, and Wells and Sean knew it. Wells insisted that he would stay with the pack, and we didn't expect anything less of the alpha, but there were key fighters who were given instructions to withdraw and regroup away from the fighting. To leave their friends behind. If we were facing hundreds of my kind, the only chance we had for survival would be to change tactics and make targeted attacks to take out key players.

Too many would have died if that was the case. And to say I was relieved that we weren't adopting the turn tail and run plan was an understatement, to say the least.

Even as we'd talked it through, I could see the looks on my mates faces. Most of them wouldn't have been able to do it anyway. It just wasn't the type of people we were.

"Can you find Stone?" Grey asked hopefully.

"No. I can only tell which one is Zoe because of her power level. I have no way of identifying anyone."

It wasn't the most useful skill, but at least we knew what we were facing now.

"Why are they just sitting out there?" Holly asked nervously from behind us.

I could see Grey assessing the scene before him, trying to think what could be holding up the attack. Did they want us to make the first move? It would give Stone the necessary means of showing the Council that he hadn't started the fight? But he'd brought his entire pack to sit on Wells' border? There was no way you could explain that away.

No, we had to be missing something.

Why would they be waiting? What would make you stall an attack before it even started?

If everyone wasn't in position yet.

"They must be waiting for their fighters to get into position," I told the others through the pack link.

"Then we should send them a message to show them we aren't willing to hang around waiting on them," Grey answered, and I could hear the growl of his wolf in his voice. "Lachlan, how far out can you make a strike?"

"No idea," Lachlan responded cheerfully. "How about we find out?"

I felt his magic before I saw it. I felt the change in the atmosphere as it charged the air around us. The hairs on the back of my neck stood on end as the heavy load of magic filled the air. Lachlan's power was incredible, but what was possibly more impressive was how he could use it as if he had been doing this all his life.

The amethyst on his wrist glowed as Lachlan drew his power to the surface. Then throwing out a hand, he sent it to his target.

His range wasn't as far as we would have liked. The lightning shot out from him, bending around the trees in its way before it split into what looked like a hundred bolts, raining down on the outskirts of the pack waiting to attack.

It was deadly magic, but there was a beauty to the display that I couldn't deny.

It didn't reach Zoe or the others holding the animage power, but the lightning struck out at the wolves standing on the edge of their ranks.

Chaos erupted from across the battlefield as cries of pain filled the air, quickly followed by growls of anger. Some of the wolves split from their ranks, charging toward us, their teeth bared in anger at our audacity for striking against them.

There were shouts to hold, but none of them stopped their charge as at least twenty shifted wolves barrelled toward us. I could see past them to the line of wolves lying dead on the ground, and my heart wept for the loss of lives here today. It was going to get far worse before it got better. How had we got so caught up in the machinations of one man that it would come to this?

"Now it's our turn," Sean yelled as he ran past us, a pack of wolves keeping pace at his side.

Sean might not have been able to shift into his dragon, but the menacing aura surrounding him should have been enough to have the other side doubting their actions. When he drew a broadsword from his back, a few of them actually did slow their charge.

Sean's group met the charging wolves head-on. It was an almost choreographed show as the wolves working with Sean incapacitated the enemy, or merely pushed them into Sean's path as he cut a path through them.

Could we actually do this? Yes, they far outnumbered us, but if we could face them down in small groups like this, there was a glimmer of hope. We'd get tired of facing wave after wave eventually, but perhaps we'd be able to make it through. Surely, Stone would have to turn back if we cut down the majority of his pack.

It didn't matter in the end because before the thought had even finished forming in my mind, an explosion rocked the ground from the other side of the packlands. That was apparently the signal they'd been waiting for as what looked like hundreds of shifters all shifted at once and charged toward us.

Now that we'd pissed them off, they only seemed to have one target in mind.

50
GREY

This was it then. This was what it had all boiled down to.

As the army of shifters charged toward us, I started to draw more and more of my magic to the surface. I'd never tried to control such a large amount of power before, but now seemed as good a time as any to strike out a deadly blow.

My eyes ran across the mass of shifters charging toward us, and it wasn't until I was just about to release the power that I realised what my eyes were seeing.

These weren't just wolves. There were bears and tigers, lions and a few coyotes that I could see just in the group in front of me.

At the end of the day, it didn't matter. They'd chosen their side, and it wasn't ours. It was kill or be killed, and I didn't intend to lose anyone else I loved.

Releasing the mass of energy inside me felt almost like a sigh of relief. Pulling the swarming cloud to the surface, but trying to keep it contained, had felt unnatural. But freeing it?

Sending it out to wreak havoc on our enemies? It was almost orgasmic.

It needed no direction. The cloud moved like it was a separate living being. It knew what needed to be done, and it set out on a path of destruction through the shifters heading straight for us.

Moving from shifter to shifter, it enveloped them. Screams of pain could be heard from inside the storm of magic as it swallowed its victims, leaving nothing behind but dead wolves in its wake.

But with each life it took, the cloud lost some of its mass. It slowly shrank as it consumed more and more until it was nothing but thin wisps of smoke in the air.

The wolves in the other pack looked terrified as we started to make our way toward them. Some of them even diverted their path, choosing to go after what they saw as weaker targets rather than face me.

Fools! They'd soon learn that none of my pack were weak.

Through the trees, I could make out a collection of people standing by, watching the bloodshed before them. I didn't need to try and make out who they were. It was obvious by the collection of shifters that ran toward us, following their alphas' orders to kill and maim.

The whole Council was out there, standing with Zoe in their centre. Curiously, Stone was cowering on the ground and even from here, I could see his beaten and broken body. So the man we'd held up as the big bad in this whole thing was nothing but the errand boy, and his masters were disappointed at his lack of results, no doubt.

I shifted into my wolf, knowing that the only way to end this fight was to take down those that stood at the head of the opposing army. I hadn't considered before now that it would

HIDDEN MOON

mean facing down the Council, but this shouldn't change our plans. We knew we'd be facing the animages that Zoe had created. Yes, it would be more difficult with them being the strong alphas they were, but hopefully, if Calli could take down Zoe while we distracted them, it would sever them from whatever power they'd gained.

"It would appear that the animages Calli felt are the rest of the Council members. We need to push our way through to them and bring this to an end," I called out to my pack through the link.

I didn't get a response from them, but I felt their determination to move forward. They were busy fighting for their lives, and I wasn't about to chastise them for not entering into a conversation. They needed to keep their heads clear.

"Calli, stick behind Lachlan and I while we clear a path. As soon as you see your chance, take her out," I instructed, hating every part of me that sent my mate into danger. "Tanner, Maverick, Colt. I need you guys to make your way to us. We have four alphas to face down, and it will take all of us."

"It would be a pleasure. I just have one request," Tanner replied through the link.

"Stone is yours," I confirmed.

Tanner and Maverick deserved the chance to take down their father. He might not have been the mastermind behind this whole thing like we thought, but he had been the tormentor through the majority of their lives. Just because Tanner had escaped when he'd been abandoned, didn't mean Stone wasn't still the nightmare that haunted his sleep.

A group of four wolves broke away from those charging forward and came straight for me. It was almost impressive that they had the balls to think only the four of them could face us down.

As they drew closer, a rush of magic passed me by. Blue

cords of power wrapped around the wolf at the head of the four, dragging him to the ground as River leapt past me, setting his fangs at his jaw, and tearing out the wolf's throat.

Bolts of lightning took down the two on the left, and Calli's vines snapped out of the trees, dragging the final wolf away. The yelps of pain cut out suddenly, and a thud followed the sound of his body dropping to the ground.

We didn't even break our step as we pressed on. The Council members were firmly in our sights now, yet they didn't seem to be paying us any attention. Only Zoe had her eyes fixed on our group, but I knew it was only Calli she could see. For some reason, she was obsessed with her, and even all the killing happening around her couldn't seem to draw her out of that obsession.

The Council members looked like they were having a chat. Completely unphased by the fact that members of their packs were being slaughtered in front of them. They didn't even look like they cared. Yes, our side was taking losses, too, but we were holding our own so far.

Two bears and a lion stepped into my view, leaping toward our group. Lightning hit them in midair, moving them out of our path as they were thrown back against the trees. The sound of snapping bones followed before they crashed back to the ground.

"How long can everyone keep this up?" I asked, feeling a sense of fatigue coming from some of them through the bond.

"I'm starting to slow down on my magic side, but I'm still good to fight," Aidan replied.

Nash, Holly, and Blake all agreed with him.

Calli's guilt was quick to reach me when she heard their update. The others weren't as strong because they hadn't had time to train and develop their powers. It wasn't her fault. We never should have had to do this on a timescale. This should have been a joyous event that the pack went through when we were ready.

This was what our lives had been up until this moment. *Take, take, take.* The Council were nothing but a group of greedy bastards, stealing what they wanted from our people and giving nothing back.

They never protected us from the witches. They didn't stand up for our people when they started to disappear because they were the ones who were taking them. Experimenting on them. And for what? Just so they could take something else that didn't belong to them. Because they'd learned of a power that even the witches couldn't rival, and they wanted it for themselves.

A roar of anger came out of my mouth, and finally, the Council members seemed to start paying attention to us. Looking around, it was like they'd only realised a fight was going on around them. They even seemed surprised to see how many of their side were falling.

Gates erupted into his bear, his eyes firmly fixed on us as we made our way to them. Crane and Carson shifted as well, moving out to the sides, no doubt with the intention of flanking us. That left Zoe standing alone in front of us with Stone cowering at her feet. She kicked out one foot, connecting with Stone's jaw and sending him sprawling as she lifted her hand and innocently waved at Calli with a grin on her face.

"Calli?"

"I've got this. Go kill me a bear, sweetheart."

Fucking hell, she was even beautiful when she was thinking about killing people.

51
RIVER

Grey separated from our group, stalking toward the massive bear alpha. His sight was so firmly set on him that he didn't see the panther approaching from his side. Or at least I didn't think he did, but then his smoke snapped out and speared the cat straight through the chest.

I kept my attention on Calli. I wouldn't let her walk into this fight alone.

Tanner and Maverick moved quickly, with Colt shielding their backs. Carson didn't even see them as they approached from his rear. He was so engrossed in watching Calli, Lachlan and I, thinking that he was pinning us between the Council members, that it wasn't until Tanner pounced on his back that he realised he was even there.

Foregoing his magic, Tanner took him down quickly. Dragging the Council member to the ground as Maverick and Colt rushed in from the side. They became a growling, swarming mass as they ripped into Carson's smaller fox beneath them. He hadn't even had a chance to use his magic against them.

Tanner led the other two to our side, and Calli stepped to the front. Her eyes were locked on Zoe, who remained in her human form, looking down on us like we were nothing to be concerned about.

"Stay away from her," Calli warned through the link. "She's strong, and it will take everything I have to take her down. I need you to watch my back and make sure no one else tries to take a bite while I'm not looking."

I hated this plan, but we couldn't argue with it. As we approached, I could feel the magic in the air emanating from Zoe, and it was more than I'd ever felt before. Possibly even more than I thought Calli might possess.

"We have your back," Tanner confirmed.

I could see his eyes were fixed on his father, and Stone's eyes widened in alarm as he saw both his sons prowling toward him. Then he did the only thing we should have expected him to do. He shifted, turned, and ran.

Tanner darted forward a step before he made himself stop with a growl, shaking his head in annoyance.

"Go after him," I instructed. "We can't afford to let him get away. Colt and I can watch Calli's back."

As long as Tanner and Maverick stuck together, they'd be fine. It wouldn't take the two of them to bring Stone down, but they'd at least be able to watch each other's back. Like the coward he was, Stone was running away from the fighting, but we couldn't rule this out as being part of a trap.

Tanner and Maverick didn't take any more convincing as they sprinted after their father, the need for revenge pushing them on.

Colt came to my side as we watched Calli slowly approaching Zoe. I wanted to scream at her when she shifted into her human form, but there was no way I could afford to distract her now.

"Is this what you wanted?" Calli asked, moving closer to Zoe.

"Well, I would have preferred to have a few of my subjects left alive when this whole thing was over, but I think once I've killed you and then your mates, the rest will fall into line fairly quickly."

"And that's all this is about. You fancy yourself the Queen of everything, and you'll do anything to get your way?"

"What else is there?" Zoe asked with a laugh. "Did you expect me to live as some kind of pet experiment for that bitch Neressa? All the poking and prodding. The bleeding and screaming. It's enough to drive a woman insane, you know?" she screamed.

As the two women faced each other, wolves appeared all around us, moving closer and closing in on us. Wells' pack was busy facing the main force trying to push through the gate, and it was taking all they had to hold their ground. Grey, Lachlan and the others were busy with the other two alphas, and Sean and his group were far across the battlefield dealing with what they could.

We'd been outmanoeuvred. We'd allowed ourselves to be drawn too far across the field, and now we had about twenty wolves between us and the others. Even if Grey and Lachlan took down the alphas straight away, four against twenty weren't the best odds.

I could feel my magic starting to cool inside of me. I'd burned through a lot fighting our way here. We might have trained to see what we could do, but we didn't have the endurance to keep it up inevitably.

This was bad.

Colt pressed against my side, no doubt because he could feel the anxiety starting to set into me.

"We've got this," he said, and I saw the glimmer of the power inside of him, even though he didn't know what to do with it. "These are the wolves that killed my friends. I won't let them hurt anyone else."

He was right. We needed to be strong. All we had to do was follow the plan and keep them busy while the others were dealt with. If the alphas fell, the attack would fall apart. It had to.

Scuffing my paws on the ground, I got ready to make my stand. Digging deep, I pulled the reserves of power I had left inside of me to the surface and got ready to strike. If I could wait until they were close, I could take down more of them. After that, I'd have to trust Colt to deal with anyone I missed.

Before I could even think about unleashing the last of my reserves, I felt the gentle wave of power brush over my fur that was unmistakably Calli.

"You didn't think trying to ambush us was actually going to work, did you?" Calli scoffed at Zoe.

The spider web of light spreading through the ground didn't just draw my attention. Even the wolves who had been running at us and were now starting to back away were watching what was about to happen.

The ground rumbled and creaked, and just as the wolves decided it was better to turn and run, the whole network of tree roots beneath our feet shot out of the ground, wrapping around not only the wolves that had been advancing on us, but every shifter who wasn't in our pack for a twenty-metre radius.

"Shit!" Colt swore in awe as we watched the tangle of tree roots ensnaring all the shifters who had come here to try and harm the pack who were hiding behind Wells' walls.

They tried to struggle against the roots, some of them

clawing and biting at the wood, but it was pointless. Calli had them firmly captured in her magic.

Then, just as suddenly as they appeared, they withdrew, dragging the shifters underground.

Colt and I stood and stared in shock. The fighting around us had paused as everyone turned to look at the two women facing each other down. We thought we had enough to walk into the fight at her side, but Calli was on an entirely different level to us. Now that she'd finally accepted who she was, it seemed she'd also realised there was no limit on what she could achieve.

If I hadn't been so in love with her, I might have been afraid.

52

CALLI

Holy fucking shit, that actually worked!

Zoe cocked her head to the side as she regarded me. It was almost like she was trying to tell if I was full of bullshit, and I was really hoping she wasn't about to figure out that I was.

Wow!

Talk about making shit up as you go along.

I think I was about two seconds away from peeing my pants in panic.

A sly smile spread across Zoe's face as she looked at me, and then slowly, as if she wanted to make sure I was watching closely, she pulled a knife from behind her back.

I recognised it in an instant. It was the same one we'd seen when the coven had invaded my old house, the one that Neressa had plunged into my stomach when she thought I'd been forming the last of my bonds as we faced her down.

As if my body remembered the injury, a phantom pain flared to life in my stomach.

Yes, I remembered the blade, and I remembered exactly

what it had felt like when it had been pushed into my abdomen.

"Ah, I see you recognise the midnight blade," Zoe said, casually turning the dark blade in the light like she was examining it for flaws. "It's beautiful, isn't it?"

I could feel the same wrongness radiating from the knife that I'd felt before. Something about it had fucked with my magic before, and I didn't want to go through that again.

"Inherited something else from Neressa apart from your batshit crazy attitude, I see." I tried to sound casual, to make it a passing barbed remark, but even I could hear the crack of fear in my voice.

"Hmmm, no. This blade is the twin to Neressa's. I got it from darling Stone. Did you know he was the one to actually recover them from some tomb? I doubt he even realised what he had. He gave it to Neressa as a gift, and she knew exactly what to do with it."

"I can tell you're practically dying to tell me what it does," I said, rolling my eyes as I did.

I couldn't work out how to take this woman. She really was halfway out of her mind. I wouldn't be surprised if she suddenly stripped off her clothes and ran naked around the battlefield just to feel the breeze on her nips.

"I am!" she cried excitedly, throwing her head back as she laughed in glee, practically dancing on the spot.

I let her have her gleeful moment as I tried to assess what to do next. I could hear the sounds of Grey and Lachlan still fighting behind me. It seemed the alphas had managed to avoid the roots I'd sent their way. The rest of the battlefield had fallen into silence which I was going to take as a good sign. I didn't dare take my eyes off Zoe to check, though.

I needed to take her down quickly and stop dragging this out. I could feel the power radiating from her. She was stronger than before, and she had that annoying barrier magic. All I had was an innate knowledge of healing and some control over nature.

The root trick wasn't going to work again. I probably should have used it on her, but I panicked when I heard all those wolves approaching, knowing that River and Colt would end up having to face them alone.

No, I needed to find a way to use what I had at my disposal.

"Are you even listening to me?" Zoe snapped, and I realised I actually hadn't been.

"Sorry, my bad. I've got quite a bit on my mind at the moment," I told her with a shrug.

"Oh, don't worry. I understand. It must be hard knowing you're about to lose everything. Annnnyway, as I was saying, the blade is special because it absorbs... oh, do you know what? Fuck it. You ruined it now," she said with a pout.

It absorbed magic. Yeah, I knew that from the last time someone shoved it in my stomach. Well, at least I knew what she was planning now.

Zoe took a step closer, and I held my ground, my mind spinning on what I could possibly do to bring this to an end. I started to pull on my magic, sending it out into the earth. If I could bring her to the ground, perhaps I could restrain her. I was reasonably confident in the skills I'd learned during training. Still, now that I was facing a knife fight, I didn't mind admitting I was slightly nervous about the whole thing.

Why couldn't I have learnt something useful like fireballs? It's not like I could just heal her mouth closed and hope for the best.

But then I remembered what Ethan had once said to me, and I knew immediately what I needed to do. And now that I could see the end, the way I was going to bring her down, it actually made me feel sad.

This was a woman who'd been used all her life for someone to reach some kind of maniacal goal. She'd been seen as disposable, and this version in front of her was her fighting back against this whole thing.

It was hard to hate her when you realised she was just as much of a victim in this whole scheme as the rest of us. How had everyone gotten so caught up in this quest for power that it resulted in this madness?

Holding out my hand to Zoe, I tried to give her a chance to step back. To actually look at what was happening around us and choose a different path. I knew it was futile, but I felt like, for once in her life, Zoe deserved someone to offer her a choice.

"You don't have to do this, Zoe. I know you didn't start this whole thing off. You got dragged into it like the rest of us. No one can judge you for trying to survive. But this whole thing has gotten so out of hand that somehow you've lost yourself along the way. Let me help you. Stone is gone. The others will be taken down. Let me help you set this right and go on with your life."

When she reached out and took my hand, I could tell from the look on her face that she thought I was the insane one. Maybe I was. But I also wouldn't be the person I was if I didn't at least try.

It all seemed to go in slow motion from that moment. I felt the tug on my hand as Zoe pulled me closer. I saw her arm start the arc of the strike she was aiming for. She was going to plunge that thing into my chest. I didn't know if that would be better than taking it to the gut. It didn't matter, though.

Less than a second was all it took.

I'd already pulled my magic to the surface, and as soon as she'd taken my hand, it had started to travel through her body.

I'd known I was going to have to do it all along. Even if I wanted to give her a choice, I knew her response was inevitable. She'd gone too far. She was too lost to be able to turn back and find herself now.

At least I could do this much for her.

Sending a jolt through my magic, I worked my healing magic inside her. But, instead of healing a wound, I used it to open one. I broke through one tiny blood vessel in her brain, and that was all it took.

Zoe dropped to the floor almost instantaneously. Her arm kept swinging under its own motion, but the knife had already fallen from her now limp grip.

She was like a puppet with its strings cut as she collapsed into my arms, nothing but an empty shell.

At least I was able to end it quickly. She might have been one of the reasons why so many people had been hurt, but I was starting to think it wasn't really her fault. She'd been manipulated and twisted by so many people, she hardly seemed to be in her right mind anymore. After living through a painful, brutal life, it only seemed fair that she should get to experience a painless end.

Staring down at her body, I realised that the sounds of fighting had stopped around me. Glancing over my shoulder, I could see that Lachlan had taken down Crane, and Grey had the last remaining alpha restrained on the ground.

It all felt so anticlimactic as the shifters who had seconds ago been intent on tearing into each other, looked around the battlefield, at all the dead, and didn't know what to do next.

How had we all ended up in this place? Playing along with the insanity of a few men?

53
TANNER

It wasn't hard to catch up with our father. Beaten and bruised as he was, he didn't have much energy left, but he'd never been that much of a wolf to begin with.

As Maverick and I closed in on our father, he looked back over his shoulder to see where we were, making the same mistake so many did.

His paws tripped on something on the forest floor, or maybe his strength finally failed him. Whatever the case, he crashed to the ground, skidding forward a few feet under his own momentum.

Shifting back to his human form, he started to scramble backward away from us.

He was a shadow of the man I remembered. But even beaten as he was, he still had the same sneer on his face as he looked at his sons.

Needing to hear some kind of reason, I shifted back into my human form, even if it was just to scream at him before I killed him.

Maverick followed my lead before coming to stand at my

side, both of us staring down at the man who had taken so much from us.

He should have been afraid. He must have known this ended only one way for him, but he was a dick right up until the very end.

"This is what it comes down to then," he sneered. "Death at the hands of the useless sons that bitch bore me."

Maverick growled low, but I felt his pain through our bond. He'd never had the opportunity to know our mother. Even though I'd had too few years with her, and I could barely recall her face now that I was an adult, at least I had some memories of her smile; of the fact that she'd been far too good for the man at our feet.

"You're not even going to try and beg for a way to live then?" I asked.

"Maybe I should have kept you and tossed the other one in the trash. At least you have some balls about you," he spat.

The pain I felt from Maverick was what had me stepping back. Not because I didn't want him dead. Not because I hadn't spent years dreaming of the day I finally wrapped my hands around his neck and watched the light fade from his eyes.

No.

My brother needed this more than I did.

I'd moved past my father's cruelty a long time ago. I had Grey and the pack to help me see that I was more than what he saw me as. To show me that I was worth it.

But when Maverick looked at our father, he still saw the pain, the malice. He still heard the taunting, barbed remarks and believed they were true.

No, Councillor Stone had stopped being my demon long ago, but Maverick still needed to conquer his.

"Perhaps you don't quite have the balls I thought you did," he actually had the nerve to say.

He could say what he wanted; it didn't matter anymore.

A growl flowed from Maverick's lips as he slowly advanced toward our father. He had the nerve to sneer at him in dismissal, but then he started to look worried. As he started to back away again, I almost thought he would start begging for his life. But Maverick had his piece to say first.

"Don't you dare speak to him," he spat. "Tanner is more of a man than you could ever dream to be. He's shown me how twisted and wrong you are. He's my family, but you? You're nothing."

Our father actually rolled his eyes at that. Apparently, when he was staring death in the face, he lost all common sense, or maybe he just didn't think that Maverick had it in him.

"Don't be ridiculous, boy," he snapped. "Do you think rolling around the woods with the halfwits will turn you into the man you should be? You would have been at my side as I ruled. I would have built you a kingdom that would have been yours one day. But you just couldn't follow instructions. You had to go and try and have a thought of your own. Well, look at where that got you! Living in the gutter with that whore of a mate…"

Stone's words turned into a garbled scream as Maverick leapt at him, shifting in midair before tearing into our father's throat.

He didn't die then, though. The stubborn bastard never was one to let go.

His screams filled the air as Maverick let loose every piece of hatred he held for our father, tearing into him with claws and fangs until the screaming finally stopped.

As Maverick backed away from the ruin of a corpse, I had

a moment of worry when I thought Maverick might break down when confronted with the reality of what he'd done.

It had been bloody, and it had been brutal, but I was proud of my brother for standing up for our family, for our mate.

Maverick shifted into his human form, wiping his face on his sleeve.

"We should head back," Maverick said, his eyes firmly fixed on the body on the ground. "They might still need our help."

His voice sounded hollow, not quite like himself.

Closing the distance between us, I gently put my hand on my brother's shoulder and turned him to face me. The pale colour of his face told me everything I needed to know, and I pulled him close, holding him tightly.

We both cried, standing there alone in the forest with our father's corpse at our feet. We cried for everything we'd lost, for the time we'd missed having each other in our lives, for the abuse and torment he'd put us through, but most of all, we cried because it was finally over.

54
CALLI

Sean and Wells stood side by side, watching as their pack members extracted the shifters from the ground I'd trapped in the caverns beneath our feet.

"I actually thought you'd killed them," Wells said again in surprise.

I didn't know if it was a good thing or not that they all thought I was capable of doing something like that.

"What will you do with them?" I asked, ignoring the statement once again. Truth be told, it was starting to get a bit insulting.

"There's too many of them to place in the holding cells, and I don't fancy adding mass murderer to my resume. They'll be given the option of swearing allegiance to an alpha of my choosing or leaving to live the life of a rogue."

"Don't you think that will create more problems than it solves?" I asked in surprise, imagining a mass of rogue shifters moving across the continent.

"No!" Wells laughed. "No one in their right mind would choose the life of a rogue. Besides, can it be any worse living under a new alpha than what they've just been through? We'll threaten to send you after them to keep them in line if they get any ideas."

Okay, yeah, now I was definitely starting to get pissed.

Wells laughed as he wandered off to deal with the fallout of the fight we'd just had.

Sean moved to my side, slinging an arm around my shoulders as we watched the last of the terrified shifters climb out of the hole.

"You did good, kid," he told me.

My eyes travelled back to the figure under the sheet that I'd been looking at for the past hour while we'd been standing here. I didn't know why I felt so sorry for Zoe, but I'd wanted to save her for some reason. It didn't feel right that this was the end for her.

"She was too far gone, Calli. There was no saving her," Sean told me, knowing me better than I thought he did.

"That could have been me," I realised. "If my parents hadn't hidden me away and the witches had gotten their hands on me, I could have just as easily become her."

"Yeah, but we weren't going to let that happen."

"Because you knew I'd be the one to end all the madness?" There was a part of me that still felt a bit bitter about having my whole life manipulated to bring me to this point.

"No," Sean said, hugging me closer to his side. "Because we love you, kid."

I let my head fall to his shoulder as a tear rolled down my cheek. They had loved me. They gave me a happy childhood, protecting me from as much as possible. And when they knew they couldn't stand by my side for the whole of my journey, they'd made sure I met the men who would.

I watched Grey and the others as they moved between the members of Wells' pack, making sure that everyone was okay after seeing what just went down. Quite a few of them were looking at us with fear in their eyes, but a few seemed more curious than anything else.

"What's going to happen to Jessa?" I asked, finally getting to the question I hadn't dared voice.

"She'll stay in the cage until she gets her wolf under control," Sean said with a shrug.

"And if she can't control it?"

"Then Wells has got a hard decision to make."

I knew what the implication was, but I didn't want to think about it right now. Maybe there was a way I could help her. I'd helped Holly through the transformation when she was lost inside herself. Perhaps I could do the same thing for Jessa.

"You won't let him make a decision without telling me, right? Once we're back at the pack, I'll start researching to see if I can find a way to help her."

"We won't do anything without talking to you first," Sean reassured me.

There was something so strange about standing here in the aftermath. I almost didn't know what to do with myself.

"It's actually over," Sean said quietly, almost to himself.

It had to be more shocking to him than it was to me. He'd been living this for a lot longer than we had.

"What are you going to do next?" I asked.

"Help Wells get everything settled, and the elections set up. Then? I don't know. I might travel a bit. I'm feeling the itch to not be in one place all the time," he said slowly, his eyes turning to where the sun was starting to rise.

"Calli!" the voices of children cheered from behind me.

I didn't even have time to turn around when I suddenly found myself on the ground under a pile of little bodies.

"Did you see the explosion?" Jacob cried in excitement.

"I didn't. I hope you didn't either."

"No," he sighed, sounding disappointed. "Kai wouldn't let us go outside. But then a big man came into the school, and Kai took him down like a ninja warrior!" That at least had him perking up.

"What?!" Looking around in surprise, almost like I thought another attack was about to sprint up in their wake, I couldn't believe what I was hearing.

"It wasn't all that exciting." Sean laughed, plucking up Jacob and sitting on the ground with him on his knee. "I've already had a full report. Stone's pack placed a small charge on the wall at the rear of the pack, and a small group made it through. They were quickly caught and brought down, but one of them got as far as the school. Kai was able to disable him before my man had a chance." Sean looked at Kai proudly, and the kid blushed, squirming on the spot.

"I just did what Mav taught me," he mumbled.

"They went after the kids," I realised, dread forming inside me even though it was all over.

"Yes. It would seem the backup plan was, whilst we were all distracted at the front, they'd take the kids as insurance to make sure you complied with their demands."

I was definitely going to throw up. We thought we'd been keeping them safe by securing them in the shelter, but we'd just left them alone to be taken from behind our backs.

"Calli, stop freaking out. It didn't succeed, and the threat was neutralised. It's over," Sean said, nudging my shoulder playfully.

"We've got two vehicles approaching," one of the guards called out from the top of the wall.

"Uncle Sean jinxed us," Jacob said as he and Coby broke into sniggers.

Looking around at the chaos around us, I realised this was

definitely the worst timing anyone could have. This was either someone else coming to try their luck, or we were about to have a very awkward conversation with someone as we tried to explain the bodies lying all around us.

In fact, maybe this wasn't the best place to be sitting around chatting with the kids. What the hell was wrong with me?!

As two dark SUVs pulled up in front of the gate, we all moved to see what the hell was about to happen next.

"Come on, guys, let's go check out what snacks we can find in the car," Colt said, ushering the kids away. "I hear Tanner has a secret candy stash somewhere that he thinks no one knows about."

Ah, candy, the way to manipulate the children of the world—and apparently Tanner.

As the doors to the first SUV opened, I was relieved to know the kids were at least out of the line of fire. I felt inside me at the dwindling reserves of my magic and pulled what little I had left to the surface. Whoever this was, we weren't going down without a fight.

"Always so vicious," Grey whispered, coming up behind me and wrapping me in his arms. "You can back down, little warrior. It's going to be okay."

I was pretty surprised when the Fed from before climbed out of the driver's side of the SUV, and an older guy I'd never seen before exited on the opposite side.

"Director! We must be lucky to receive a visit from you." Wells laughed as he stepped over an actual dead body and walked toward the humans with his hand held out.

The director shook his hand briefly and then looked around at the chaos we were surrounded by.

"Yes, well, when the shifters go to war, it requires some special attention."

He had one of those voices that sounded like he was seconds away from erupting into a coughing fit. His skinny frame was only accentuated by how his suit literally hung off his body, and his gaunt complexion was highlighted by his thinning hair. This was not a healthy man at all.

"War! That seems like a bit of an overstatement, don't you think? It was more of an internal disagreement in the Council, but as you can see now, it's all been dealt with." Wells swept his arm around at the corpses, and the collection of shifters tied up by the gate like this was the best solution we could have presented.

The director sighed, and I could see the Special Agent we'd had run-ins with before starting to look smug in the background.

"Wells, I don't have time to be dealing with shit like this. Time is short, and the vampires are kicking up a mess all up and down the Country. I would like your assurances that this is over with, and I want a full report on my desk by the morning."

"Of course," Wells said, stepping forward in full politician mode as he turned the director back to his car.

"Director! You can't just walk away from this!" Special Agent Milner gasped. "This is a gross breach of the accords. This group has been connected with the spate of missing humans, and someone has to be held accountable."

Her finger pointed squarely at me, and the vindication glaring in her eyes spoke of a woman with prejudices in entirely the wrong job.

The director turned to me, following her gaze, but I could see the tiredness on his face as he did. This wasn't a man that wanted to deal with a situation. He was squarely on board with sweeping it under the rug if this bitch would just let her hatred of shifters go.

"Do you wish to make any response to this accusation?" he asked, looking me up and down and realising he didn't know who I was. "Miss?"

"Fairchild," I told him with a beaming smile and pulling out my best English accent as I swept toward him as gracefully as I could. "Calliope Fairchild. I am aware of your colleague's accusations as she has tried to lay them at my pack's door before. But I can assure you we have not harmed any of the humans she is speaking of."

I held out my hand to the director, and he reluctantly shook it. As he did, I sent a small tendril of my magic into his body. I could feel the old wound to his abdomen, which had wreaked havoc on his liver. One of his kidneys was failing because it wasn't receiving an adequate blood flow due to the scar tissue. This was a man with very little time left to live if he didn't have an organ transplant soon.

Without even having to direct it, my magic went to work fixing the issue, knitting the blood vessels back together and dissolving the scar tissue away.

The director cocked his head to the side and squinted at me suspiciously.

"What did you just do?" he asked, looking at me closer.

"Someone who is a friend to shifters should be looked after, don't you think? We wouldn't want to see them becoming ill over something that could be easily fixed. Especially if you had access to the right kind of...means."

His eyes widened slightly, and a smile crossed his face. His colour was already beginning to brighten, and I realised this was what I should be doing with my life.

"I don't…"

"I'm sure the Special Agent here can let you know where to find me. We'll be returning home soon. I'd be interested in talking with you about how we might be able to work together in the future."

He nodded thoughtfully before letting go of my hand and stepped away, his steps lighter already. "I'll have my people set something up."

With that, he turned around and ushered the Special Agent back to their vehicle.

We all stood there and watched them drive away, lost in thoughts of going home soon.

But what the hell was Davion mixed up in, and why hadn't he come to us if he needed help?

Looking around at the blood and the bodies, it was pretty obvious why he hadn't. Well, at least he had Cassia and Hunter with him, who hopefully would have received a timely boost of magic through the bond they had with us.

"Someone should reach out to Davion and let him know it's all over," I said to no one in particular.

"It's already done," Grey reassured me, pulling me back into his arms.

Abby skipped over to us, now that the coast was clear of people she didn't know. Reaching up, she grabbed hold of Sean's sleeve and tugged on him until he knelt down to eye level with her.

Cocking her head to the side, she looked firmly into his eyes before saying, "It's time to go and find her again."

Sean looked taken aback by the little girl's words. Even as she turned and skipped away to join the boys, he didn't move from where he was kneeling on the ground.

It looked like Davion wasn't the only one about to get himself in some kind of trouble then.

EPILOGUE
CALLI

SIX MONTHS LATER

Leaning against the porch railing, I sipped at the mug of tea cradled in my hands. This was one of my favourite things to do in the morning. Take a moment of quiet to look out over our pack and clear my mind of everything that needed to be done.

When we'd first come back to the pack, every quiet moment had been filled with flashbacks of the fighting and second-guessing every move I'd made in the lead-up. I obsessed over what I could have done differently to save more. In the end, all I was doing was torturing myself over something that couldn't be changed.

Killing Zoe still haunted me. She'd deserved a chance to have a life. It wasn't her fault that she'd been twisted and broken by the people around her who used Zoe for nothing more than their own gain.

I knew I wouldn't be stewing in my regrets alone for long, and I felt him through our link before I even heard him. He always found me out here. The pressure of being the alpha that saved the day weighed heavily on Grey. We'd wanted to return to our packlands and have life return to normal. But we'd soon learnt that normal was something we'd never get to have.

Grey grasped the railing, one hand on either side of my body, as he leant into me. His smokey power slowly trailed up my body as he dipped his head and ran his teeth over the skin on my neck.

"Good morning," he purred.

Leaning back against him, I felt a part of me calm just from being in his presence. "Good morning," I murmured back.

"Nervous about today?"

"No. Or at least, I don't think I am."

When we'd returned to the packlands, we finished the two cabins that Tanner and Colt had started. Colt, Danny and Bast had taken one, and Nash and Holly had moved into the other. The third kit, which had been lying untouched, was put together further away from the houses and had become my clinic. It was the first official day that we'd be open, and I already had appointments booked for nearly four months in advance.

That wasn't the only project we'd been putting together. Lachlan and River had both jumped at the chance to build our own school for the pack and put in place a transfer program for kids from other packs to come and learn with us. It hadn't been an easy deal to broker. Most of the shifters, especially those at the attack, were afraid of us. But once word of the clinic began to spread, it seemed to ease most of their fears. It also helped that there were a lot of inquiries about how we could help the packs turn their mates and help with their pups shifting.

Life was definitely about to get a lot busier for us around here.

As with nearly every other morning, my second frequent visitor also appeared.

"Calli, babe, we need to talk," Holly yelled as she waddled across the grass toward the steps, cradling her growing belly in her hands. "When can you get this pup out of meeeee?"

I laughed at her antics, knowing she didn't mean it. Holly loved being pregnant because Nash saw to her every need, completely in awe of her. It was nice seeing the two of them so happy. They were the happiest ending to this fiasco that we could have hoped for.

Nash had asked Holly to marry him as soon as we'd gotten back home, and she'd enthusiastically said yes. However, plans for the wedding were on hold until after the baby was born because, to quote Holly, she wanted her banging body back first.

Holly huffed her way up the steps, pushing her hands into the small of her back as she did. "You do realise that Jean has been sitting outside the clinic for two hours already, right?"

"What? Her appointment isn't for another hour!" I had one of those moments when you mentally ran back over every conversation you could recall just in case you were wrong, but I knew I wasn't.

The clinic was due to open in half an hour, and Jean would be the first appointment at 9:30 am.

"She's really been there since 7:30?" I asked, feeling bad for not checking in with her.

"What time is it?" Holly asked, pulling my arm toward her and checking her watch. "Ah, right. No, she's been sitting there since 7:00 am."

"I should go and get ready," I said, shaking my head.

I should have realised that Jean would be early. She'd been so excited about today for weeks. Today was officially the day she was going to become a wolf. I was nervous, but I was also pretty confident that now we'd figured out how to bring the whole pack into sharing the burden, it should go off without a hitch.

If anything, I was more nervous about how Blake would react. Grey had wanted to lock him in one of the cells until the whole thing was over. He saw containing his wolf as the safest option. But Jean wanted him to be there, and she should be able to have her husband at her side while she went through something like this.

We'd agreed to use a circle, similar to how Jessa had when she'd gone through her own turning. It would allow Blake to be in the room, but keep everyone inside the circle safe if he lost control of his wolf.

Jessa still sat in a cell in the basement of Wells' packhouse. She'd transformed into her wolf a few days after the attack, and no one had been able to get through to her since. Even if Wells wasn't at a point where he could admit it yet, she was rabid. Her human side seemed lost entirely, but I wasn't giving up hope yet. There had to be a way to reach her, and I wouldn't stop looking for answers for them both.

Cassia and Hunter still hadn't returned to the pack. We'd had word from them that they were safe at least. Grey had even managed to speak with Davion briefly, and even though he'd made him promise to call us if he needed help, the call had never come.

Every so often, I'd get a flash of something through the bond from Cassia, but no matter how much I tried, I was never able to connect with her properly. I had a feeling she'd found a way to block me out, not wanting to draw the pack into a second fight so soon after the last one.

The Director of the Containment Unit had been in contact with Wells three days after the attack wanting to speak with us. It had been a tough time wading through the politics of the humans knowing about me. I never thought I'd say this, but thank god for Wells being on our side because he made sure they didn't overstep their boundaries.

The first request had been that we were put on call to help when high ranking officials fell ill. I'd turned that down straight away. I wouldn't put politicians' needs above anyone else. The wealthy already had access to far more than most people in this country. Wells hadn't even come to us with most of their requests, turning them down on the spot. I'd heard him discussing with Grey about the military requests, and it scared the crap out of me enough that I didn't want to even know what they were.

We'd come to an agreement in the end. I would be available for the Containment Unit if any of their agents were hurt trying to keep our secret. I'd also agreed to deal with three requests a year that the Director deemed urgent. We had the right to refuse when they were presented to us, but if it was the case of saving someone's life, I knew I'd probably say yes. It had been the deal that had ensured our safety, so it wasn't really something I'd been able to turn down anyway.

After all of that had been dealt with, we came back to the house and started to try and live our lives the way we'd been dreaming about.

Besides, Wells didn't need us hanging around. His dream of retirement was a long way off. Now that Sean had disappeared, he'd been left to shoulder the fallout of the Council attack alone. The packs had questions. Most of them were about Councilman Gates and when he would stand trial. And by trial, I, of course, meant they wanted to know when he would be executed. The memo about the old ways needing to end wasn't quite getting through to the other alphas. But then, with the number of deaths on his hands, I wasn't sure we could argue for a different fate for the now ex-Councilman. It was no longer our problem. We'd done enough, and we needed to recover our sense of self after everything we'd been through.

Wells probably needed a break, too, but when Grey had, albeit half-heartedly, offered, he'd adamantly refused any help.

Maybe we should have pressed the issue harder, but we'd been through so much. We'd had so many pieces chipped away from us in this journey that I didn't know if we could take much more.

It was strange, though, because now that we were back at the pack, I could feel a sense of calm slowly starting to take hold of us. We didn't physically have anything more than before all of this had started. Yet, I'd never felt freer than I did right now.

Maybe after having so much pressure on our shoulders for so long, it was inevitable that we'd feel lighter when it was finally lifted.

We'd survived the fight, and we'd come out the other side of it stronger and with more friends at our sides. We were lucky. There was no other way to describe it. We'd made mistakes, and they could have ended so much worse than they did.

But we'd had people looking over us. My parents, Sean, Jessa and Wells, had always been there in the background, doing what they could to ensure we were safe. My parents had sacrificed everything to make sure of it.

I still wasn't entirely sure how I felt about what they'd done, but it was easier to deal with when I looked at it as a sacrifice.

Sean had disappeared the day Abby had spoken with him, and none of us had seen or heard from him since. I'd tried asking Abby about what she'd seen, but she refused to tell us. At least the slight smile on her face had me hoping it had been a happy vision. The fact that it had revolved around a woman had me hoping for the best on Sean's behalf. He deserved to find some happiness at the end of this whole mess.

Rushing upstairs, I finished getting ready. When I came downstairs, the kids were finishing up breakfast, and Jacob rushed to give me a hug.

"Can I come with you today?" he asked, looking up at me with pleading eyes.

"Not today. Besides, you have school to get to."

The pout he gave me at that, indicated just what he thought about the idea of school.

"You need to help Lachlan and River get the classroom ready for the new students coming next week," I reminded him, which at least had him perking up a little.

"Are we going shopping tomorrow?" Abby asked, bouncing up and down in excitement.

Now that the top floor of the house was done, we'd moved most of the bedroom furnishings up there. That opened up enough rooms on the main floor for us to put together some bedrooms for the shifter kids who were coming as part of the transfer program. We would have to get them to double up for now, but we were still trying to figure out another plan.

That, of course, meant we had a lot of rooms to furnish, and Abby, who had become an expert at it by now, was jumping up and down in excitement at the thought.

Kai drained the last of his drink before he jumped up from the table. "Can we train tonight, Mav?" he asked, rushing to put his dishes in the dishwasher so he wouldn't be late for school.

It would take some time to get Kai caught up on all the school he'd missed while at Stone's pack, but he was taking it all in his stride. Especially when Maverick had promised to keep up with his training.

"Once you have all your schoolwork finished," Maverick yelled out the door after him as all the kids charged to school, not waiting for his answer. "I don't know why I even bother speaking sometimes," he mumbled, but the smile on his face showed just how much he loved having the kids around.

Kai had decided that he wanted to stay with our pack. None of us were surprised. I doubted he could have left the other kids, even if he'd wanted to. He and Maverick were the closest, but he was slowly starting to let the rest of us in as well.

He was a good kid, and he deserved the chance to just be a kid for a while. Not a guard or a soldier, as Stone would have had him be.

"Apart from the bedrooms, are we ready for the kids coming next week?" I asked.

"Absolutely not." Tanner laughed, spinning me into his arms and kissing me lightly on the lips. "Good morning," he whispered, nuzzling against my neck.

"Hmmm, morning."

"We should talk about how we're going to supervise the kids while they're here and brainstorm some activities for the evenings," River decided, grabbing the rest of the dishes from the kitchen table and carrying them over to the dishwasher. "The more we can keep them busy, the less trouble they'll be able to cause."

"I think that's wishful thinking." Lachlan laughed as he came over to give me his own good morning kiss.

Life was definitely busy for the Stoneridge Pack now, but at least it was for happy things and not in a constant fight for our lives.

Strolling down to the clinic, I saw Jean sitting on the front step, bouncing Tucker on her knee as she showered him with kisses.

"Do you know how long I've been waiting here?" she huffed when she saw me approaching.

"You weren't supposed to get here until 9:00am," I told her with a sigh.

"And I told you that wouldn't give you enough time to pull this off without them realising what you were doing."

Holly came rushing over at the fastest pace she could manage. I could see she was practically vibrating with excitement. "They really don't have a single clue," she gushed, clapping her hands together in glee.

Opening up the clinic, I rushed them both inside before they could give the game away. Checking that the coast was clear, I quickly closed the door behind me.

"Oh god, I think I'm going to throw up," I complained, pulling open the cupboard and pulling out the five ring boxes I'd hidden before a wall of tampons.

The easiest way to hide something from a guy—tampons.

"You don't have anything to be nervous about," Holly told me, playfully shoving my shoulder. "I don't even know why you're doing this. You do realise they're planning on asking you in some kind of elaborate thing tomorrow night, right?"

I did actually already know that, but I wanted to be the one to ask them for some reason. I loved all of my mates more than I even knew was possible. Now that we had this chance of a life together, I wanted to live it with them knowing that I chose every single one of them, and there was nothing I would have done differently even if I'd had the chance to. Besides, if I asked them today, we would all be free to enjoy the celebration tomorrow. Or at least that's what I was telling myself.

"Okay, so run through the plan with us one more time," Jean said in an attempt to settle my nerves.

"We light all the candles. You slip out the back and make sure all the guys are heading to the clinic together. I wait here, shitting myself, until you all arrive. They walk in, I pop the question, and then try not to throw up on the floor at the same time."

"That's a lot of shit and puke for a proposal." Holly laughed. "I've never heard of something so romantic in my life." Then she attempted to bounce on the spot, clapping her hands in glee but gave up with a groan as she started rubbing her back.

The next five minutes were spent with the three of us rushing around the clinic and lighting as many candles as we possibly could, and then Jean ushered Holly out the back door as they headed out to intercept the guys.

I could feel a light sweat starting to form on my brow. Checking that my shields were firmly in place, I pulled them even tighter around me. It would be just my luck that Grey would catch a glimmer of what I was feeling and barge in here thinking I was in trouble.

Shit, I'd never been this nervous in my life. I didn't even know why I was. It's not like there was any risk they would say… oh shit, what if they said no?

Shaking my head, I tried to stop freaking myself out and decided the best way to do that was to occupy myself with something to try and take my mind off things. Clearly, now was the perfect time to take stock of the first aid supplies, so I opened the cupboard, starting to count the rolls of bandages.

We'd had some disagreements about the need for these when setting up the clinic. Holly was still yet to understand the need when there was not only me but also Lachlan, who had the skill to heal. Lachlan was still only learning, and it would be some time before he could do anything major on his own. In the meantime, there was only one of me, and if multiple emergencies came through at once, well, it never hurt to be prepared.

"Why are there so many candles in here?" Tanner said from behind me. "Did the power go out? Maverick, did you fuck up the power?"

"Firstly, I wasn't responsible for anything to do with the power…"

Slamming my head on the cupboard in surprise, I quickly whipped around to find my five mates standing before me and a giggling Holly and Jean behind them.

Shit, I'd gotten too distracted.

Looking at them, my mouth ran dry. They were so beautiful.

"You've got a little bit of drool…" Tanner started before River elbowed him in the ribs.

I opened my mouth to start to speak, and then realised I'd completely forgotten what I was going to say.

Panic started to set in, and I was pretty sure a waterfall of sweat was starting to fall from my pits.

Grey stepped forward and pulled me into his arms as he sealed his lips against mine. All sense of panic left me as he did, and I sagged against him. I had no idea how he managed to get this reaction out of me every time, but I was there for it.

Stepping back, he dipped down to one knee.

"Calli, I've faced down demons, witches and shifters, and none of that compared to how lucky we were the day you walked into our lives. Even after River called us, begging us to put in a good word for him. As soon as I laid eyes on you, I knew you were supposed to be mine. You are the fiercest, smartest, most magnificent woman I've ever met, and I would be honoured if you would be my wife," Grey said.

Tanner moved up beside Grey next, dropping down to one knee before he began, "I know I can be a fool at times. I like to be able to see people smile, but nothing compares to how I feel when you smile at me. Life before was sad and lonely, and we didn't even realise until you showed us how beautiful life could be. You saved us when you walked into our lives that day, and we can never repay you for everything you've given to us. But if you would agree to be my wife, I'll spend the rest of my life showing you just how grateful I am that you chose me."

The tears were starting to flow now, and I had my fingers pressed over my lips as I watched River take his place on one knee beside Tanner. The radiant smile on his face showed how happy he was. "I feel like I should point out that I did see you first, so if you say no to these bums, I hope you'll say yes to me." The others laughed, and Tanner nudged him in protest. "You gave us a family, sweetheart. You showed us what it meant to be a pack, and, for some inexplicable reason, you decided to love us. We all became better men by having you in our lives. I will love you for the rest of my life, whether you say yes to me or not. But I hope you will agree to be my wife."

Maverick took his place next, dropping down on one knee as they all formed a line at my feet. "I wasn't a good man when I came here. I was brought up in a place devoid of love, and I don't think I even knew what the word meant. Until I saw you. Until you showed me what it meant to care about someone. You always had this unwavering faith in me, in all of us, and it was impossible not to try and live up to that. I gave up everything for you once. I would have happily walked into death if it meant that you were safe. But you refused to let me go. You reached into the abyss, and you pulled me back. I love you, Calli. I will love you forever, and nothing will ever tear me from your side again. Not because I wouldn't sacrifice myself for you, but because there is nothing we couldn't fight together. Please, marry me and make this worthless man just a little bit better."

I could see how much Maverick meant what he said. His voice cracked at the end as the emotion became too much, and I wanted to reach out and hold him. But then Lachlan stepped forward and took his place with the rest of my mates.

"I was so lost when I came here. I didn't know my purpose in life, and I was starting to believe that maybe I was the worthless wretch everyone told me I was. Even before we knew that I had more power inside me, you never looked at me as lacking. You never saw me as less than you or any of the others. You opened up your heart to me even though I don't think I've done anything to deserve it. Everything I have is yours, Calli. Everything I am is nothing if I don't have you in my life. If you agree to be my wife, I'll spend the rest of my life proving that I deserve you."

The tears were running down my face now. I hadn't seen the pack sneak in through the door behind the guys, we might as well have been the only people in the world. I only had eyes for the five men on their knees in front of me. How could any of them think that they didn't deserve me? Didn't they know?

"I was supposed to be the one to ask you," I finally said, once I was able to get my tears under control. "How could you ever think that I would say no to you? I was so lost before I came here. I was broken and scared. I didn't know how I was going to be enough for anyone, let alone for the little boy I was trying to care for. But then I found you, and you showed me that it was okay to be a little bit broken. You filled me with so much love. You helped me become whole again. You supported me when I was given an impossible task, and even when I didn't feel like I was worthy, you proved to me every day that I could be. I love you all so much that it hurts sometimes. I couldn't imagine a life without any of you there by my side. I will be your wife if you all agree to be my husbands."

The room fell quiet as we all took a moment to stare in wonder at each other. Then Grey pulled a small box out of his pocket. Opening it, he finally got to his feet as he pulled out the most beautiful ring I'd ever seen. Slipping it onto my finger, he said, "You never needed to ask us, Calli. Nothing in this world could tear us from your side."

"Is that a yes then?!" Holly suddenly cried, drawing our attention to the rest of the pack.

They all had tears pouring down their faces, and Jean and Holly were holding onto each other, looking at us expectantly.

"Of course, it's a yes," I cried happily.

All of my mates leapt to their feet, surrounding me as they held onto me and each other. I could feel the love they had for me radiating through the link we shared, and I'd never been more grateful for it.

This is how life was supposed to be. Forever connected. A pack, standing for each other and making this a home filled with love. I came to Arbington having lost nearly everything, and in turn, I'd found my heart and the five men that each held a piece of it.

"This is so fucking amazing," Jean said through her tears. "But can we get back to me now? I want to be a cool black wolf, like Grey. Wait, no. Maybe white? Whatever, just make me prettier than Holly."

"Bitch!" Holly yelled, clearly taking offence.

"Well, yeah. That's the hope."

And then they both fell into each other's arms, cackling like they always did. Lord help us when Holly had her baby, and the two of them were able to drink alcohol together again.

The End
Read on for a sneak peek inside.

COMING SOON
PREORDER YOUR COPY HERE

THE
ARCANE
PART I

CJ COOKE

COMING SOON

PreOrder Your Copy Here.

THE ARCANE PROLOGUE

Looking back now, I never would have guessed that the day I'd truly start to live would be the day I died. I didn't even see death coming. When you were younger, and you still believed in fairy tales, you always believed that if your youthful immortality were to end, it would be in a heroic final stand. You would be fighting for something truly worth dying for, and in the end, you'd die and finally rest amongst the stars.

What a load of shit!

I was minding my own business, walking home from lectures, when death came for me. It was confusing at first. I didn't realise what was happening. The pain of the knife slipping into my back and severing my hepatic artery was quick and blinding. I stumbled to my knees and cried out in pain. It wasn't until I was lying on the pavement and saw the growing puddle of blood surrounding me that I knew I wouldn't be walking away from this. There was so much of it, and it was growing so fast. The last thing I remembered thinking before I slipped into darkness was… I really wish I'd put better underwear on this morning.

Even right to the end, I was such a fucking idiot.

※

I'd been floating in the darkness for what felt like an eternity. Who knew death would be so boring? Wasn't I supposed to be going somewhere or something? Maybe I was supposed to be using this time to reflect on the life I'd had or the mistakes I'd made? Argh, trust death to make me feel like I'd just wasted the twenty-four years I'd had!

Twenty-four mediocre years. That was all I got. God sucked! If there was a God, he fucking sucked! *That's right, God, I'm calling you out on this one.* If you were only going to give me twenty-four years, you could have at least had the decency to make them interesting. Maybe with a hot Italian boyfriend named Giovanni. Ooo, or maybe you could have given me an exciting job like a fashion designer or a photo-journalist. I should have done more things, seen more places, and definitely got laid a hell of a lot more.

Maybe calling out God wasn't a good idea in my circumstances. Maybe that was why I was still here in the dark. I'd probably pissed him off.

Or her.

Yeah seemed like a vindictive God would more likely be a woman. Women did get shit done, after all. Creating a world seemed like something only a woman would have stuck at.

※

Pffftt… I was crap at doing nothing.

※

How long had I even been here?

※

 Maybe I wasn't dead. Maybe this was one of the Matrix type situations. Give me the blue pill! Wait, was that even the right one? This was why you should pay more attention to pop culture references, for when you have to entertain yourself in the black void of death.

※

An unimaginable pain seared through me, and I realised this was a be-careful-what-you-wished-for type of situation.

I didn't know what was worse, the boredom of the void or this—the blinding light and searing pain. I was pretty sure I was going to Hell. That was what happened, right? You were tortured for an eternity. I'd scream in outrage at the thought, but I didn't think I had a voice anymore.

"She's coming back," I heard a serious voice say.

Wait, back? Have I died before? I'd have thought that would be something I wouldn't have forgotten.

"I can't wait to see what she becomes," another voice said.

Well, that was just fucking weird. Unless it was some other Hell thing. Argh, man! Was I going to turn into a slug or something? Was this some weird torture thing?

"Move out of the way. She doesn't want your ugly face to be the first thing she sees," another voice snapped.

Well, that was just rude! Even if you were a demon or something. The other guy was just excited to see me turn into a slug. This could be the best part of his day.

Suddenly, I realised I could feel my face again and the rest of my body, but for some reason, my face seemed more important to me right now. I opened my eyes, rapidly blinking against the bright light.

"Dim the lights. They're too bright," the first voice said. It had a growly sexiness to it that I was definitely appreciating right now.

The lights dimmed, and it wasn't as harsh on my eyes anymore. Squinting, I tried to focus on my surroundings while I struggled to sit up. Pressure in the centre of my chest pushed me back down, and when I looked, I saw a male hand gently pressing on me. I tracked my gaze up the arm attached to that hand and located the blurry form of a man standing over me. He had the bluest eyes. I couldn't quite focus my eyes on the rest of him, no matter how much I blinked, and the pain flaring over my body was making me want to move to seek out some form of relief.

"Stay still. Your body needs time to adjust to the rebirth," he told me.

Rebirth? Maybe I wasn't dead.

Another blurry form appeared next to him and the excited voice from earlier butted in. "Stop dragging it out! What is she?"

The hand on my chest ran up my body and gently cradled my cheek. For some reason, I leaned into it. It was warm and soothing, and it chased the pain away. I tried to keep my eyes open. I tried to flutter my eyelids until my vision would clear, but the pain was pulling me back under. Just before I slipped back into the darkness, I heard him stutter.

"I… I don't know."

Preorder it here

NOTE FROM THE AUTHOR

It has been my incredible honour to write the Stoneridge Pack series, and I cannot thank all of you enough for taking a chance and reading the books.

I know a few things haven't been closed off (please don't hate me). But as I got towards the end of the series, I realised that there were so many other characters people loved who needed to have their stories told too. So I am very happy to announce that there are currently three spin-off books on my schedule from the Stoneridge Pack world. I'm not going to say who they are—although I think it's pretty obvious that Sean gets one—or when they're coming out yet, mainly because I haven't yet decided.

There are so many people that I need to thank who made these books possible and who helped me on this crazy journey to become a writer in the first place.

Ross, you are always there for me. Through the ups and downs and the crazy moments. You will always be my rock, the shoulder I cry on and the man who makes an awesome cup of tea. I love you. There's nothing more I can say which beats that.

NOTE FROM THE AUTHOR

Kris and Em. You ladies are the best friends and team anyone could ask for. You don't judge me for my insane questions, and you generally put up with more than I think any other person could.

Jillian, Shawna and Sandy. Thank you so much for the time you put into beta reading through, not just this book, but all of them.

Finally, I want to send out a special thanks to the team at MiblArt who did the artwork for the covers. I love the covers so much, and they are such an amazing company to work with.

If you want to stay up to date with what's coming out next and get a sneak peek at upcoming covers and books, you can sign up for my newsletter at www.authorcjcooke.com.

If you enjoyed the book, I'd be eternally grateful if you could leave an honest review.

Printed in Great Britain
by Amazon